~ Sororate ~

By
K.R. Smith

~ Acknowledgments ~

I'd like to start with a shout out to Maryann, Ally, Darianne, Karen and Paul. In either moral, emotional or written support, you were there. Thanks for the purchases, reviews, emails, text messages, or what you said in our catch-ups. Most of all, thank you for your friendship.

Cheers Mum and Dad, for explaining what a shilling and a thrippence was. Also, thanks for putting up with my questions about old age ;-) And 'gracias' to my cousin Bianca, for letting me interview you about the year you lived in Peru.

I'd like to convey my gratitude to Nina Ackerman and Isabel de Sequera; Neen for letting me use another one of your photos of our favourite state in the U.S.A. and the awesome artist Izzy, for the glorious graphics. Your combined generosity is not only invaluable, but it's wonderful.

Thank you very much Hazel Yates for being my Beta Reader. It's been a learning experience for the both of us, but thanks for coming along for the ride. Your encouragement, corrections and prodding made me try harder.

~ **Contents** ~

~~~~~~~~

"Blood. Pain. Sacrifice. Anguish, and death."
-- "Sounds like marriage alright."

(Worf and Bashir Star Trek: Deep Space Nine)

~~~~~~~~

~1~

2nd August 2226

We strolled hand-in-hand in a comfortable silence as we stared out at the picturesque views. Declan and I were enjoying the walk and I must admit, I was starting to really like this part of our holiday in China. We were into the second day of our hike along the Great Wall and right now, our trek took us through a mountainous part of the country.

The Wall curved around before it sloped downwards and then upwards again as it followed the peaks. The sky was blue, the air was clean and the breeze was cool, which kept us from overheating. However, when my husband first told me that we would be hiking for three days, I must admit I wasn't what you might call, 'excited' by the idea.

"Are you frickin' nuts?!" I barked.

"Relax B." He customarily rolled his eyes. "We won't be camping but we'll be hiking. Each night we'll have a hotel booked so you can still get your creature comforts of hot showers and a soft mattress to sleep on."

"But hiking all day, for three days straight?" I complained.

"Look, we won't even be walking the whole thing! It's less than half that we'll be doing as they're still restoring it."

"I don't care if it's only a quarter of the way! This is three days that we'll be hiking the thing?!" I said indignantly.

"B, sometimes we run up to 200 km's in one night, during a hunt." He gave a funny look.

"Yeah, but that's one or two nights a month and I have the bloodlust fuelling me along." I frowned.

We were of course talking about the fact that my husband and I were Werewolves.

Declan was a 163 year old European Werewolf with the appearance of a man in his mid-thirties in human form. My blue eyed and blonde haired husband was finally growing out his crew cut he had for 140 years, so now his scruffy hair sat just below his ears. However when he was in European Werewolf form, he looked completely different.

His height of 190 cm's almost doubled as his muscular build practically tripled in width. His hands and feet turned into dangerous claws. He was hairless but his head changed into more of a wolf's as he had a short snout over jaws of razor sharp teeth. His eyes glowed green with his round pupils turning into thin, black slits. As a European Werewolf, he would run on all-fours in speeds up to 300 km/h and he was so strong he could lift up a car on each arm.

Me on the other hand, I was a 160 year old Lokoti Werewolf with the human appearance of a half Native Alaskan in my late twenties. I had dark blue eyes and recently, my hair was restyled. Now I have a fringe and my former long, black hair was cut just past my shoulders.

Lokoti Werewolves have a more humanoid appearance in our supernatural form. Although my 170 cm height remained the same, my body bulked up like a weightlifter's with extra muscle. My eyes glowed bright turquoise as my black pupils vanished. My teeth became elongated and sharp and the nails on my hands and feet grew longer, like claws. Lokoti Werewolves can run up to speeds of 200 km/h in our upright form, but because I was also a Circulator I could move in the speed of light.

The Lokoti call Circulators the 'Light People,' because we can phase through time by our biological bodies dissolving into beings of light. The same way light passes through glass, a Circulator could pass through time. Only a few Circulators could also instantaneously phase which looked like a person disappearing in a bright burst of light, but instead of just moving locations you would also move to a different time.

When I instantaneously phase from Earth to the Circulate HQ on Taurus Six, I'd disappear in a flash and then reappear in another. This could produce electromagnetic interference where the temperature dropped or even make your hair stand on end. The existence of Circulators was clouded in secrecy and occasionally if we had a witness, we were mistaken for a ghost. Because of this, I hardly aged and I could move like light. Time travel was a handy gift to have when one had a doctorate in Ancient History and Mythology... heh heh!

I'm called the first female Lokoti Werewolf because supernatural genetics dictated that only the males in the tribe could be 'activated' to join the ranks. However on the full moon before my 18th Birthday, I turned to replace the fallen. It was a surprise to everyone least of all me and curiously, I remained the only female. I was also the only member in the pack who was both Circulator and Werewolf.

The second bedroom in our house had never been converted to a nursery due to another difference between me and the other Werewolves; I was barren. Aside from being stronger, faster and living for longer, my kind was also known for their virility. I guess any being who could turn part animal could behave like one with all-consuming urges to feed and procreate. Most of the pack had two kids or more and their bodies could shut down reproduction. However, I didn't even have a choice as I've never been able to breed.

What I saw as a curse, my husband saw as a blessing. Over the years he's been vocal about his dissatisfaction of children. He was sceptical of how they would affect our marriage, or the fact that he would be creating more European Werewolves; *Declan sniffed me and then he said seriously, "you're not pregnant, I can't get you pregnant and that works out fine with me. I have a hard enough time controlling my own bloodlust that I don't think I'd cope if I created offspring which had it too."*

Once, we had an argument when he was tired of hearing me moan; *"You only mention them after a tribal gathering, because you feel left out. When there isn't a tribal gathering, you're quite happy to write your essays and lecture just as I'm happy with the Garage. I like having you whenever I want, where ever I want without worrying about if kids are asleep or not! We don't want kids!"*

My husband's obsessive love for his wife was well known, although not many were game to tease him about it. Declan may not be a man-eater, but his growl or when his eyes would glow green could still scare people. His height and muscular build was also off-putting. But I must admit, everything that I just described here turned me on and our short tempers certainly kept the chemistry ignited.

Declan became the honorary sixteenth member of the pack after he was attacked by the European Werewolf whose bite turned him. The incident also claimed his father's life, after which the three year old and his pregnant mother were taken in. The Lokoti Werewolves helped raise the only toddler in the tribe to have the bloodlust and trained him to hunt animal instead of human. Thanks to his years of loyalty, honour and fighting to protect his family and tribe, my mate was made Second in the pack.

However, the European Werewolf would rant and rave if his wife was away more than twelve hours for a guest lecture. He would snarl at anyone or anything that showed interest in either my Lokoti Werewolf pheromones or my aura as a Circulator. Quite often I'd be sitting at the dining table typing out an essay or organizing a presentation, when Declan would decide to do the paperwork from the Garage so he could sit beside me. When we read books or listened to music or even watched movies, we always sat on the same couch tangled in the other's arms or legs. Werewolves love to eat, so unsurprisingly his other passion was cooking. He liked watching me devour what he had procured so in exchange, I did the housework.

Although the commercial recovery after the Third World War meant food was no longer a luxury item; we still grew many of our own vegetables and herbs in our greenhouse. Together, we would work to loud rock music as we planted and tended to our crops. In a way, this became our 'child' from the amount of time we spent cultivating.

Last year, Declan started to grow orchids amongst our vegetables as a hobby. They needed constant care but they became his pride and joy, especially since they were 'our flower'. Before we were formally acknowledged as mates, he used to give me orchids which were grown by other members of the tribe.

"OK Brandon." He looked warily on our great, great, great, great grandnephew, Brandon Sabre. He handed the 14 year old, a list of things to do in the greenhouse while we were on our tour of Asia. "I know these lands and I know where you live. With my sense of smell, I can track you no matter where you go on this planet. If I come back to a dead garden, your ass is grass and I doubt your parents will miss you THAT much."

The poor boy's eyes widened as he visibly gulped whilst looking on his tall, muscular Great x4 Granduncle standing before him, glaring menacingly.

"Declan, don't traumatize the kid!" I rolled my eyes.

My husband handed over the list to Brandon whilst he stared long and hard to instil his threat.

"Er, no sweat Uncle." The boy nervously licked his lips.

I walked over to his side to pat him on the back reassuringly, "Don't worry Brandon, the job's pretty easy and the list of instructions is straightforward."

For some reason, his eyes widened further as he looked in my direction. I even overheard him inhale deeply, which Declan caught as well. My mate rolled his eyes in a weary manner.

"Frickin' hell woman..." he complained, "...I can't take you or your pheromones anywhere!"

My husband suddenly pulled me into his arms which were away from the teenaged boy, whose face fell as soon as my scent was removed.

"Dude, she's your Great x4 Grandaunt and she's also a married woman." He growled. "Now scat!"

I watched Brandon quickly turn around and leave the greenhouse before he broke into a run and disappeared from our property.

Then my mate shook his head, "I hope your scent isn't going to get us into trouble again on this latest holiday."

"What do you mean 'again'?" I looked on unimpressed. "When have MY pheromones gotten us into trouble?"

"Gee, let's see now..." he pretended to think, "...how about in Russia when the European Vampires tried to feed on you?"

"That wasn't just because of my Lokoti Werewolf pheromones, it was also because of my aura as a Circulator." I refuted.

"And that other European Werewolf Marcus, who tried to claim you?"

"That was because there aren't many female Werewolves left in the world."

Out of the blue, Declan picked me up in his strong arms as he laughed evilly, "I know and you're mine! MINE I say!"

I squealed with laughter as I squirmed out of his grip and then I too ran out of the greenhouse and back into the house to finish my packing...

...

... now here we were, hiking the Great Wall of China with our large backpacks strapped on. The Wall was busy with other tourists and we passed a couple of other people also with backpacks, who had the same idea as us. However as the afternoon grew late, Declan pulled us aside to check the GPS on his mobile phone.

"Right." He looked on his watch and then back at the GPS. "It's 7 PM and it's still 5 km's to the town where our hotel is."

"So what if we have to walk in the night?" I shrugged. "We're 'different' Declan, we shouldn't be afraid of the dark."

My mate gave a peculiar look as he put his phone back into the front pocket of his backpack. "You think I'm afraid of the dark?"

"We are creatures of the night, aren't we?" I smirked. "With your big build even in human form, you're still intimidating. I doubt we'll get mugged."

"That's not what I'm worried about." His scowl deepened as he looked around at the surrounding countryside, whilst sniffing the air. "We're on somebody else's territory."

"Huh?" I gave a funny look. "Well, yes we are. It's called China, Declan. Chinese people claim ownership of this country."

Rather than laugh, my husband looked indignant. "B, sometimes I wonder whether you're more 'Light Person' than you are like me." He hinted at my being a Circulator as well as a Werewolf.

"What's that supposed to mean?" I asked offended.

"Smell the air!" He barked.

I closed my eyes to help me concentrate as I breathed in deeply through my nose... I smelled vegetation, I smelled moist earth, I smelled the warm humans walking past, I smelled the distant aroma of somebody cooking somewhere and then I smelled something else... This something was like a pungent animal smell, so strong that it left behind the realm of the natural and entered the supernatural.

My eyes snapped open to look on in surprise before I managed out quietly so no passersby could hear, "Is - is - is that Asian Werewolf?"

The European Werewolf nodded as he looked down the side of the Wall at the valley below.

"They've marked this as their territory, as a kind of invisible fence warning off other supernatural beings. We should be safe in the hotel, but I don't want to be out here when it's dark. They could mistake us as hunting on their territory."

I looked on impressed at how he knew this, or sensed this with his intuition. I guess being a Circulator could interfere with my Lokoti Werewolf instincts, but my husband was attuned to his. He immediately knew things about the European Vampires or the European Werewolves we encountered without ever reading the SSIT Reports.

After a moment, Declan noticed how I was still looking on him, or smiling rather.

"What?" He gave a funny look.

"You're hot when you go all authoritarian about this kind of thing."

To which he smirked back, "I'll remember you said that later on in our hotel room."

Declan retook hold of my hand and hurried us along. We picked up our steps until we were power walking as the sun sank lower in the sky. We were walking so quickly, we attracted some peculiar looks from the other tourists we passed.

We managed to walk another three kilometres before the red sun touched the dusky horizon. The view from the Wall showed the upcoming town where our hotel was situated but it was still two kilometres away.

"Come on, let's leg it." He ordered as the sun started to disappear.

My husband ran in front, practically pulling me along, because I felt tired from walking all day. We ran in a speed which would have been considered fast for humans, but it was slow for our kind. It was too risky to show off our supernatural speed in public, nor could I just instantaneously phase us there.

He led the way down the exit steps from the Great Wall and onto a road. Then we bolted the rest of the way into town, with Declan still pulling me along. With the force he was squeezing my hand, there was no way he was letting me slip from his grasp. He didn't let go until we entered the safety of settlement. I stopped to catch my breath as I against the side of a building.

"Come on B, you're a 'growly thing' as well as a 'Light Person', that was just a slow jog for us!" He taunted.

"I've also been walking two days straight!" I snapped amidst my puffing. "My feet are sore and my legs are tired!"

"Moan moan moan." He rolled his eyes then he looked around warily.

"What is it?" I watched him.

"When we ran into town, I smelled more markings. This town is somebody's territory so being outside after dark isn't safe here either. Let's just hurry up and get to the hotel."

Declan grabbed hold of my hand again and pulled me after him, down the road. We walked down several streets before we stopped under a street light so he could check our itinerary. He input the address of the hotel into the GPS then we followed the device's directions.

We passed through a bustling commercial section where many people were either walking around or sitting at different outdoor tables and chairs. Out of curiosity, I glanced through shop windows or a few of the front windows of restaurants. It was the eating establishments which had the outdoor seating where families sat down eating. I also noticed at a couple of these tables elderly people played Mah-jong.

"Oh look, Mah-jong." I paused to watch until Declan pulled me along again.

An old Chinese man with a long, thin, white beard who was smoking a long, thin pipe looked up from his game as we passed. To my surprise, his brown eyes abruptly turned white, with just his tiny black pupils remaining. Frickin' hell, he's an Asian Werewolf! The old man showed me his eyes to let me know that he also knew what Declan and I are.

"OK, let's go." I walked out in front and next, I was the one pulling him along.

I wished I'd brought my Katana along with me, the silver-coated Japanese sword. I would have felt a whole lot safer with that insurance policy in my backpack. Declan spotted our hotel's brightly lit sign and he escorted me off the street and into the small foyer where the check-in counter was located.

"We have a reservation for Sabre." He handed over our itinerary with the barcode for the hotel clerk to scan.

"Welcome to the Jade Hotel." The Chinese man smiled politely. "I believe your reservation has you in the Lotus Suite. Our room service will bring up your complimentary bottle of champagne for your stay."

"We don't drink alcohol." He returned.

Well we can't, if we got drunk and lost our control of the bloodlust being Werewolves? No, it was too hideous to consider…

"Very good Mr. Sabre," the clerk didn't miss a beat. "Then we can arrange another beverage to be served instead. We have a selection of de-alcoholised wines or soft drink or juice or iced tea -"

"The de-alcoholised wine would be fine," my husband interrupted.

I could tell he didn't mean to be rude, as he looked over his shoulder at the door of the hotel. Declan just wanted us to hole up protectively in our room.

"The hotel has a gym as well as a sauna and a pool." The clerk went on. "In the gym you can purchase massages and we even have an acupuncturist -"

"No thanks, we won't be leaving our room." He said shortly and then he read his name tag. "Sorry, Hsu? My wife is really tired and we'd just like to get checked-in."

"Of course Mr. Sabre," the clerk continued politely.

However, he mispronounced our surname, to my husband's chagrin. Instead of saying *Sar-bra*, it sounded like the clerk said *Say-ber*. The European Werewolf hated it when outsiders would incorrectly spell or mispronounce his Italian surname. However he didn't correct the stranger this time, all he wanted to do was get out of sight.

The clerk requested, "If I could please get your credit card as well as sight your passport for identification purposes?"

Declan handed the items over to him and he scanned them into his computer before giving them back. Next, the clerk passed him our hotel room's electronic key.

"Inside your room, you will find a menu for Room Service and your complimentary de-alcoholised wine will be served shortly." The clerk finished.

"Thanks." My mate retook hold of my hand to lead me away.

Then I don't know why, but I think it was because I sensed something? I looked back over my shoulder at the hotel clerk who was watching us leave, when I caught him sniff. He wasn't sniffing because he had a cold, but he was sniffing us.

Frickin' hell, he's another Asian Werewolf! They're everywhere! This town really is their territory.

Just then I surprised my husband when I stopped, turned around and marched back over to the counter. The small lobby of the hotel was quiet with no other people around and the clerk was standing by himself.

"Look," I began, "we know this is your territory. We'll keep to our room and then in the morning we'll leave. We don't want any trouble. If you guys are good trackers as I've heard you are; you'll smell that we don't eat human."

Declan's eyes widened when he realized who it was that I was talking to. Whereas, the hotel clerk's face remained perfectly calm. He even smiled politely again.

"We are aware of that particular quality about you as our guests, thank you Mrs. *Sar-bra.*" The clerk said, now mysteriously pronouncing our surname correctly. "If the hotel had any objection, we would not have proceeded with check-in. But thank you for sharing your dietary requirements with us, we will be sure to notify the kitchen."

My mate came to stand protectively beside as he looked suspiciously on the hotel clerk – slash – Asian Werewolf.

"We hope that you enjoy your stay at the Jade Hotel. Please feel free to enjoy our features such as the pool, spa or sauna which is included in the cost of your room." The hotel clerk ended with a slight bow.

I sensed that he meant it and he didn't see us as a threat, so we were allowed.

"Come on, B." My husband gently pulled me away.

We walked down a plush hallway until we spotted our hotel room door. As soon as Declan let us into our suite, I emitted a loud sigh of relief to be able to take off my heavy backpack, which was the first thing I did. I dropped it onto the suitcase stand by the wall and when I turned back around, I found Declan standing by the closed door. I think he wanted to make sure we weren't being followed, as he listened closely and he even sniffed.

"It's cool, Dec." I walked over to collapse wearily onto the King-sized bed. "They're allowing us to stay tonight."

However my mate didn't move away from the door immediately, he continued to listen. When he did move, he walked over to the window and parted the curtains to look outside. I heard his growl as he dropped his backpack, as if preparing for battle. What now?

Tiredly, I stood up and crossed over to see what he was glaring at. I saw two Chinese men who appeared to be in their twenties, wearing black clothes complete with black sunglasses, which made them look like gangsters. They were standing across the street whilst looking up at our window.

"More Asian Werewolves?" I guessed.

"They don't trust us, so they're letting us know we're being watched." Declan said with dissatisfaction.

"But they're trusting us enough to let us stay." I turned away from the window to walk back over to the bed.

As soon as I sat back down, I took off my hiking boots before I laid back. I stretched out on top of the bed as I felt my muscles begin to loosen. Ah finally, I could unwind.

Just then there was a sharp knock on the door that made the both of us jump!

My husband made a move towards it and looked through the peep hole before he opened the door. Next, a male hotel employee wearing a black uniform, carried in a tray with a bottle of de-alcoholised wine in a cooler and two wine glasses.

"Would you like this on the table?" The staff member queried.

"Yeah whatever." He answered as he looked on the man warily.

The man in the uniform carefully put the tray down and then he turned to leave. But before he departed he said lastly, "In appreciation of you showing consideration towards the safety of others; if you should order dessert with your meals this evening, it will be free of charge."

After that, he swiftly left with Declan locking our door behind him. Then my mate tiredly walked over to the bed I was sitting on, to flop down beside. I lay back down onto the mattress so we were lying side by side.

"I wish when I planned our trip, I had a map of all the areas marked by other Werewolves or locations of Vampire covens, so we knew where to avoid." He complained.

"But then we'd never leave tribal lands because like humans, supernatural creatures are everywhere." I pointed out.

"Yeah, I guess so. Hell, I was bitten by a European Werewolf in Alaska of all places."

Next, Declan rolled onto his side so he was facing me. He turned quiet for a minute or two, as he rested his head on his hand to look down.

"What?" I wondered.

"You're fearless, you know that?" He smiled softly.

"Fearless?" I gave a peculiar look.

"The way you walked up to the hotel clerk and laid it all out like that? I thought he smelled funny, but you saw through him immediately."

"Only because I caught him sniff us." I confessed.

"My wife the sleuth," he chuckled as he placed a kiss on my forehead.

He moved in closer as he wrapped his arm around my waist. His mouth brushed my cheek before his lips smothered my own. I felt his ardour but all I felt was tired.

"Not yet!" I giggled as I moved my head away. "I need to unwind first."

"Hey, you're the one who said I'm hot when I go all authoritarian." He reminded before he began to gently 'maul' my neck with his open mouth.

"You are hot when you go all authoritarian, but I'm also tired." I grabbed hold of his hair to lift up his head.

"Is this the real reason why you asked me to grow out the crew cut, so you've got more hair to pull?" Declan shook my hand off.

"Definitely." I tittered.

"You don't see me pulling your hair, do you?" He lightly scolded.

"You wouldn't dare."

"You're right." He smirked which expanded into an evil grin. "Besides, I'd rather pull the hair elsewhere on your body."

"Eew!" I cried out which turned into a squeal of laughter, when he ducked his head to take several playful bites.

*****

I didn't sleep well that night and neither did my husband. Every time I rolled over and opened my eyes, I found him lying awake. He lay with his arms about his wife as he constantly watched the door or the large window of our room. I came to realize he was on guard by the way he kept his hold.

"Get some sleep." I murmured sleepily. "We're safe here, Dec. If we weren't, I would have one of my warning feelings as a Circulator."

"Shhh." He stroked the skin on my back. "You're more tired than I am, B. You need the sleep more than I do."

"Declan, please go to sleep. If I sensed we were in danger I would have instantaneously phased us back to Alaska."

"Close your eyes and be quiet," he growled softly.

I rolled over so I could rest my cheek on his hot, strong chest. That was the good thing about having a European Werewolf for a mate, their bodies consistently ran at high temperatures. Although hot weather could leave him disgruntled, I never needed an electric blanket in the midst of a hard Alaskan winter.

My mate appeared to appreciate our contact, as his arms tightened and he planted several kisses on my forehead.

We were quiet for a couple of minutes as I settled back down again. I guess Declan must have thought I had fallen back asleep. He thought now would be a good time to say, "I love you B, always and forever."

I surprised him when I mumbled back, "Love you too Dec."

Pause... then after a moment he said, "Oh you weren't supposed to hear that."

"Whatever."

You were making your sleeping noises so I thought you were asleep."

"Whatever."

"No seriously, you were breathing deeply and you were making those little sighing noises."

"Whatever."

"Were you faking it, knowing I was going to say that?"

"Declan, frickin' shut up and let me sleep!"

*****

The next time I opened my eyes again, it was morning and it was by my husband shaking me awake.

"Come on, let's get out of this place." He greeted with a kiss on the nose then he leapt out of bed as if he had been the one who had slept.

Half conscious, I raised my head and marvelled at how quickly he dressed.

Declan started to chuckle as he looked over at my dazed expression. "Man, I've been married to you for 136 years and your bed hair still cracks me up!"

Grouchily, I threw his pillow at him as he continued to laugh, before I rolled over and tried to hide under mine.

*****

An hour later when we were dressed, breakfasted and our teeth brushed, we checked out of our hotel. The same hotel clerk was behind the desk, when we handed in our electronic key.

"Altogether 488 credits will be charged to your credit card Mr. Sabre, for your accommodation, your entrée and main as well as the additional de-alcoholised wine you ordered. However your dessert will not be charged as it came compliments of the hotel." The clerk read off his computer screen.

My mate handed over his credit card to pay while he still looked on the clerk warily. A moment's silence passed as the clerk swiped his credit card and then he raised the EFTPOS device for Declan to punch in his PIN.

"The food was delicious, thanks." I suddenly said.

My husband gave a funny look but the clerk smiled politely, "I will pass your compliments on to the chef."

He handed Declan's card back to him however when we turned to leave, we were stopped.

"Will you both be walking in a westerly direction along the Great Wall today?" The clerk asked out of the blue.

We both turned back around to look on in surprise.

"Maybe and maybe not." Declan said vaguely.

We were, but he didn't want the Asian Werewolves to know of our movements.

"I ask because when I saw your itinerary last night, it has your accommodation tonight at the Bamboo Inn in Wuwei, which is in a westerly direction. Wuwei is in the Gans province and I feel I must advise you that the area is the territory of the Hsin family." The clerk said simply.

"The who?" He asked.

"The Hsin family is not as enlightened as we are, and they have not seen or smelled a female of your kind in a very long time." The clerk stopped smiling. "Mrs. Sabre may not be safe there."

My heart almost stopped as my mate's eyes widened and I felt one of my tell-tale ominous feelings from Hsu's warning.

"But we start a new tour tomorrow morning and we're getting picked up by bus from the Bamboo Inn in Wuwei." Declan sounded annoyed. "What are we supposed to do? Boycott the tour as well as the town?!"

The clerk looked on unimpressed before he spoke in a low voice, "My apologies, I did not realize how different we are with our separate cultures. I was speaking as a friend. My family is very protective over our wives, mothers, sisters and daughters. We have not allowed our women anywhere near the borders of Gans province, since one of our females were kidnapped by the Hsin family 50 years ago."

My husband's eyes almost popped out of his head when he heard this and my heart began to race.

Declan threw innuendoes to the wind as he looked on the clerk suspiciously. "I was told there was only one female Asian Werewolf left."

"Then whoever told you that was not truthful or accurate." The clerk said simply.

"Figures." He rolled his eyes.

"Didn't either Leo or Marcus tell you that?" I remembered.

Declan gave a short nod, "It makes you wonder what else they lied about, doesn't it?"

"Our people know of the Lokoti Werewolves." The clerk spoke plainly as there was no-one else around. "They are respected by my family. It is because we know that you are not man-eaters you were allowed to stay last night. It is a sign of respect that I warn you now, avoid Gans province."

"Maybe we should just go back to Alaska?" My husband complained.

However a plan started to formulate in my mind, "Show me the itinerary."

"What? Why?" He gave a funny look.

"Please?" I held out my hand.

He pulled out the itinerary from the front pocket on his backpack to hand over. I looked on the tour details we were meant to be embarking on tomorrow as well as the nightly stopovers before I turned back to the clerk.

"OK, so if we boycott Wuwei today, what if we head south instead until we come to Yushu? It's where we're supposed to stay for the first night of the tour." I spoke to both the clerk and my husband.

"Yushu is not in anybodies territory and you should be safe." The clerk gave a single nod.

"What about for the rest of our holiday?" I held out the itinerary to the clerk who took the document out of my hands to look on it again.

"In Cambodia you may meet the Truong clan who live in the northern region. But if you do not go out at night and remain in your hotel room, they should leave you alone." The clerk handed the itinerary back.

"So after this place and if we avoid Wuwei, the other Asian Werewolves we'll come across are in Cambodia?" Declan wanted to double check.

"The route your proposed holiday takes you on will be avoiding the territories of the other clans." The clerk answered.

"Right," Declan returned the itinerary to his backpack before he looked my way, "now to find our way to Yushu."

"If you head down the main street to the south side of town, you will find a reputable car rental company." The clerk offered.

"Thanks." I smiled at his helpfulness.

"I wish you a safe journey on your travels." The clerk smiled at me but then it disappeared when he looked on my mate, "And I must ask you Mr. Sabre that you do not come into our territory again."

What the...? I didn't see that coming! Declan and I exchanged a surprised look which we turned towards the clerk.

He spoke as he looked upon my husband, "You were protected last night because of my family's respect for the Lokoti Werewolves. However my family has not had the best experience with your breed before. I cannot vouch for your safety should you return to our territory again, with or without the company of your wife."

The clerk was referring to Declan being a European Werewolf. The clerk didn't seem so nice now and I saw that by suggesting the car rental company it was because he wasn't trying to help us, he was trying to get rid of us. I recalled the sight of the two Asian Werewolves standing outside of our hotel window, watching. Now I saw it wasn't because they didn't trust me, it was because they didn't trust my mate.

I was going to protest Declan's innocence when he stopped me.

"Come on B." He gently pulled me backwards.

My mate walked me to the door of the hotel and held it open. Then as he followed me out, he threw the clerk a parting glare.

*****

Declan was quiet for the remainder of the morning. We walked to the car rental company where he took charge of organizing the vehicle. I made a call to my PA at Hodge Endeavor to arrange for us instead of starting the tour in Wuwei, we would join it in Yushu.

Once we were zooming down the highway in our plasma-engine car, I noticed Declan's moody expression as he glared over the wheel.

I placed a comforting hand on his lap. "Look, it wasn't anything against you personally. They, like us, have had a bad experience with European Werewolves before."

He spat out, "In the beginning the Lokoti Werewolves didn't trust me, so they married you to Grant. Then my own kind tried to leave me for dead and steal you. My breed must be the most hated of all the Werewolves out there!"

I squeezed his leg supportively, "But you solved that problem; you became the last of your kind when you killed Marcus and Michelle then Gran and Grandfather took out Leo."

However, this didn't make Declan feel better which I saw when his frown deepened.

"Yeah well, according to that clerk back there, I'm one too many."

My chest hurt as I felt his embarrassment and pain of rejection. I didn't know what else I could say to make him feel better, so I stared out the windscreen.

"I love you Declan, always and forever." I breathed.

My husband overheard and next he raised my hand to kiss it several times before passing me a wink.

*****

Driving to Yushu took a lot longer than we expected. We ended up driving all day and as the sun set, Declan was still behind the wheel. We had stopped though for morning tea, lunch and afternoon tea but according to the road signs, we were still 53 km's away.

"Get out the map would ya, B?" He said impatiently. "See if there's a short cut or somethin'."

I turned on the GPS in the centre of the dash board and began to fiddle around with it.

"From our current position, which is the fastest route to Yushu?" I issued the verbal command.

The female voice of the car's computer replied, "The current highway you are on is the main route to Yushu."

Declan growled impatiently, "But is there a short cut?"

I didn't know if he was asking me or the computer then, however the computer answered. "There is another route which will reduce the journey by 13 km's but it is not the main road."

"Who cares!" My mate barked. "Where is this other route?"

The GPS began to issue the directions and Declan turned off the highway and onto several smaller streets. I felt nervous about the idea of leaving the main route because we at least had the safety of other vehicles and the bright street lights. But this small road in the country was dark and poorly kept with many potholes and I didn't see any other cars.

"Declan," I began, "maybe we should turn back onto the highway?"

"Why?" He gave a funny look. I glanced away troubled as I huddled on the seat. He looked on in concern, "Are you OK?"

"I'm just cold." I came up as my excuse. My mate switched on the heater and aimed all of the air vents my way. "Thanks," I said flatly.

We drove onwards through the inky darkness with the only light coming from our headlights or the computerized features on the dash board.

"Turn right after fifty meters," the GPS directed.

My husband obeyed and we turned down an even smaller road which was only one lane wide and constructed of dirt. We're driving down a dirt road in the middle of nowhere in a foreign country at night? It's the frickin' 23rd Century! All roads were meant to be sealed now, even the roads about our tribal lands were and they were in the middle of nowhere.

"Declan," I began, "I don't like this."

He looked away from the road in my direction for a moment or two.

"Why, are you getting one of your warning feelings, B?"

But before I could answer, suddenly we were jolted forwards as if we ran over something and our tyres blew out!

BAM! BANG!

"What the hell?!" Declan slammed on the breaks as our car skidded to a halt. Then he quickly put his hand on my leg, "Are you alright?"

I blinked and although the shock had almost petrified me into a statue, I managed back a nod.

My mate was the first to undo his seat belt and hop out to survey the damage. I watched him walk around the car to the rear then I heard him growl out expletives as he kicked at something on the road. I undid my seat belt to climb out and see what he was looking at.

In the red glow of our tail lights, I saw what looked to be a fence post lying in the middle of the road with several large nails sticking out of it.

Declan walked back over to the driver's seat and I watched him lean towards the GPS and press the green 'assist' button. The screen started to flash a green colour, indicating that a signal had been sent to the satellite relay system so a repair vehicle would be dispatched to our location. If he had hit the red 'emergency' button, we would have the Police come and find us instead.

"OK, a repair truck should be on its way." He sighed in annoyance as he looked about. "But being in the middle of nowhere, it could be a while."

I scowled as I looked away in frustration. I knew we should have stayed on the highway! I shivered again as the cold night air stung my bare legs since I was wearing shorts. Declan saw this, so he came back over to lend his greater body heat by holding me close.

"We'll wait inside the car and keep the heater on." My husband offered.

He started to walk me around to the passenger's door when he abruptly stopped. I watched him look in a particular direction and he even started to sniff, which was a worry. Oh oh, don't tell me we have company?

"Not more Asian Werewolves?" I guessed.

"Uh huh." His blue eyes turned glowing green so he could use his Werewolf sight to see better in the dark. "There's a bunch of them coming this way."

Just then the dread which had been growing in the pit of my stomach became worse, as something else occurred to me. "The fence post with the nails sticking out of it was deliberately left on the road. The Asian Werewolves who live nearby, use it to stop travellers so they can eat them."

"Great!" My mate growled as he began to take off his clothes. "It's just what we need; man-eaters!"

I stood back to give him room. He quickly stripped so when he expanded into his European Werewolf form, his clothes wouldn't be torn to shreds. I too started to undress, as I took off my jacket as well as my shoes and socks but I left on my t-shirt and shorts. My shorts would be safe as it was primarily my upper-body that bulked up, and my t-shirt was made of a stretchy material.

My mate was completely undressed within seconds and he tossed his clothes and shoes onto the passenger's seat along with mine. Then he stood back from his wife and the vehicle, to shape shift from his human body into his supernatural form.

Declan's height almost doubled as his width tripled, while his skin turned into a tough hide over his muscle bulk. The nails on his hands and feet grew longer, sharper and pointier. I heard the soft cracking noises his bones made as his human skull morphed into a canine's head with a short, stubby snout over razor sharp jaws. In his European Werewolf body he could stand and walk upright but when he ran, it was on all-fours.

I underwent a change of my own, as I felt my muscles bulk up and my nails grow longer and sharper on my hands and feet. I felt my teeth turn elongated and sharp, which jutted past my lips. The surrounding night lit up as if it were day, thanks to my Werewolf eyes, as my dark blue colour turned glowing turquoise.

Although we were fairly sure the Asian Werewolves wouldn't try to eat us, we didn't trust man-eaters as they were dangerous. With my night vision, I saw them come out from between the dark trees and bushes.

At first they looked like ordinary wolves, except all of their eyes were glowing white with tiny black pupils in the centre. They all appeared alike; thin builds with silvery grey fur. My acute hearing picked up the sniffing noises they made as they tracked our scent. I counted ten of them appear from the night as they fanned out to surround us.

The European Werewolf emitted a dangerously, low growl to warn them off. He soon sniffed out who the leader was, as he stood on his hind legs to tower over his foe. He moved to stand in front of me with his larger size to show the head Asian Werewolf that I was his mate and therefore under his protection. The snarling in return from his henchmen or hench-wolves I should say, didn't seem to appreciate this.

Oh oh, don't tell me they're attracted to my Lokoti Werewolf pheromones too? Frickin' hell, Declan was right; he really CAN'T take me anywhere! My husband roared loudly at the Asian Werewolves to back off, but instead of moving away they began to circle.

Just then one of the Asian Werewolves tried to snap at my arm but Declan, in lightning fast speed, swatted the creature and sent him flying through the air!

The Asian Werewolf landed over twenty meters away thanks to my mate's greater strength. It whined in pain when it hit the ground however it was quick to return to all-fours and rejoin its pack. They kept circling whilst snarling or sniffing, as if they were trying to smell a weakness in our defences.

The European Werewolf remained upright on his hind legs as he gently pushed me against the car with himself in front, to act as my shield.

"Maybe we should instantaneously phase out of here?" I asked in my deep, rumbling Werewolf voice.

But my husband shook his large canine head to say 'no' whilst his glowing green eyes never left his foe.

The Circulator in me wanted to phase the both of us to Alaska, but my Lokoti Werewolf instincts stayed this thought. They warned that the Asian Werewolves wanted to kill my mate and kidnap me, to try to force me to become their concubine or some nonsense. I sensed if we did take flight the Asian Werewolves would pursue, thinking that they were the dominant because we ran away.

I remember reading in the SSIT Report that Asian Werewolves were the best trackers of all the breeds. If they pursued, we would have to relocate to a different time period to throw them off our scent! If we did instantaneously phase back to Alaska and they came after us, it could put the humans of the tribe at stake. And that was something my Lokoti Werewolf protective instinct was not prepared to do. It was best to fight it out, here and now, to declare our dominance.

Besides, looking on my mate's huge, hulking, hairless European Werewolf body, actually made me think that we were dealing with a stupid bunch of males anyway. No matter how much they wanted to use me to try to breed, they were going to go up against Declan looking like that...?

My mate may have been bigger and stronger but unfortunately Asian Werewolves were faster. They started to run around in a circle, speeding up so much that they began to look like a silvery blur! As they ran, I noticed that they were beginning to move closer. Declan growled fiercely and swung out his strong claw, but he missed... and then it was on!

Three Asian Werewolves leapt on the European Werewolf in lightning fast speed and the one in the middle went right for his throat! Before I could come to his aid, another two leapt on top of the car and grabbed me from behind. They thought by separating us, it would weaken us.

My mate swatted off two of his attackers with his greater strength. Then he lifted up the Asian Werewolf that was trying to rip out his throat and he looked like he was about to snap the creature's back! But before he could, another five leapt upon him!

"Declan!" I roared at the sight of the five Asian Werewolves all biting into and clawing at him!

Using my light speed reflexes, I managed to whip myself out of the two Werewolves jaws. Next, I turned around and used my Lokoti Werewolf strength to belt them both so hard, they flew ten meters away! Then I grabbed onto two of the Asian Werewolves who were on my husband's large back. I pried apart their jaws with my greater strength, to force them to release him. Lastly, I too belted these two away.

They rolled away on the ground, but were quick to leap back to their feet. By trying to use their faster reflexes to leap on top, they still hadn't cottoned on that I was a Circulator too. Moving in the speed of light with my self-defence moves, I ducked from one then I caught and flipped the other to the ground.

I continued to fight this way and the more I threw to the ground, or aside, or belted away; the weakened they became. I was fighting four Asian Werewolves and Declan was fighting off six. Two of his enemies went flying into a tree from one of his wallops! They collapsed to the ground, bleeding profusely thanks to his larger claws. My mate and I fought side by side, as our foes began to falter.

When I whipped one foe across the snout with my claw-like nails, cracking open its jaw, it yelped in pain. Three down and seven to go... As one tried to go for my throat, Declan caught it in mid-air as he roared in fury! He lifted up my attacker into the air above and this time he did snap its' back! The Asian Werewolf dropped to the ground like a sack and didn't get up again. Four down and six to go...

Next, I pulled off one of the Werewolves which were trying to bite into the back of my mate's bulky neck. I delivered several punches into its rib cage with my supernatural strength, before I flung it into the air and it landed fifteen meters away. It too didn't get up again. Five down and five to go...or so I thought.

As soon as the Asian Werewolves discovered half of their pack had fallen in battle, they began to back off.

They released their sharp jaws from the European Werewolf's hardened hide, to slowly back away. Declan continued to growl threateningly, as he stood tall on his hind legs with his front claws ready. His glowing green eyes with the black slits for pupils, didn't leave our retreating enemy.

We watched the five remaining members of the pack, pick up their wounded and sling them across their backs. After throwing us a parting growl, they slunk off defeated into the night. But Declan and I didn't move, not for the first couple of minutes anyway.

We stood with our sharp claws and teeth ready, as we listened to the Asian Werewolves paw-steps fade away into the darkness. Their scent gradually grew fainter the further away they went. After five minutes of sniffing the air continuously and watching the surrounding landscape in case they made a reappearance; I deemed it safe and looked away.

I gazed upon my enlarged mate, standing tall on his hind legs. I saw the multiple bite marks in his hide were bleeding. They weren't deep thanks to his bulky muscle, but still I hated to see him hurt.

My Lokoti Werewolf instinct guided me on what to do. I placed my mouth over one of his wounds and ran my tongue over it, to use my saliva to speed up his regeneration process. Declan whined softly in affection as he remained still and allowed me to treat several of the worst bite marks on his upper body. When I stood back, I saw that he was no longer bleeding and new skin was there instead.

Next, my husband growled quietly and I think he was ordering me to stand still. He put his heavy front claws on my shoulders before he too ducked his head. I closed my eyes and accidentally giggled because his large, hot tongue tickled. The sensation became so distracting, it accidentally made me revert back to human which was too soon. There was still a long claw mark going down my back.

"Oow! Frickin' hell!" I swore in pain, my injuries felt a lot worse in my weaker body.

Declan rolled his glowing green eyes and shook his head as if to say, 'well that was a smart thing to do, change while you're still wounded'. Then he turned me around to begin to lick at the deep scratches in my back. His saliva thankfully turned the stinging wound numb, as it began to heal.

After the husband had seen to his wife's injuries, he began to shrink as he too reverted to his human form. As soon as the reversal was complete, we hugged and kissed each other in relief.

"Are you OK?" We asked each other at the same time.

"I'm OK." I nodded.

He held me closely as he warily looked into the night, "That was too easy."

I said incredulous, "What do you mean THAT was too easy?"

"They backed off too soon." He frowned. "I don't think that was all of them, I think they've gone for reinforcements."

My eyes widened in alarm. I was betting he was right, since he's been proven correct before about other supernatural beings. He was right about the European Vampires, just as he was right about the European Werewolves. I guess being a predator, he recognized dangerous behaviour in others like us.

"I'm going home to get my sword." I announced.

"No, wait!" He grabbed hold again before I instantaneously phased away. Then he surprised me by what he next said, "I want you to go to Alaska but I want you to stay there until I call you."

"Huh?" I asked puzzled.

"I want you to go back to Alaska and stay there." He repeated. "I'll be fine, I have to do this alone."

"What the...?!" I looked on as if he had lost his marbles.

"B, this isn't up for debate!" He barked out. "I need to fight them alone, do you understand me?"

"No!"

Declan took a deep breath as he tried to put it another way, "The Asian Werewolves who attacked us, I think they're the Hsin clan we were warned about. Somehow they got wind of us and they've come for you."

"But why me? I can't frickin' breed for them!" I cried indignantly.

"You know that and I know that, but because of your pheromones THEY don't know that. They think you're fertile because of how you smell."

I tried to pull away as my objection, but he held me firmly by the shoulders as he looked on demandingly.

"Now listen to me, B..." he said seriously, "...I have to declare my dominance. I have to fight them for you because if I don't, they're liable to track us back to Alaska and that would put the tribe at risk."

"I know that Dec which is why I'm gonna fight with you -" I tried but he interrupted.

"No you can't! What Leo and Marcus told me about the Asian Werewolves? It was mostly a lie but a small part of it's true. Sure, there's more than one female left but they are small in number. The Hsin clan doesn't appear to have any which is why they're so interested in you. Females of any breed of Werewolf including the Asian kind, are becoming rare in this world. Think about it B, why were Hsu's family afraid of letting their women near the Hsin clan?"

I pushed his hands off, "How the hell do you know THAT much?!"

"Because I can smell it!" He snapped. "I can't explain it, but I can smell it just as I can sense it. My instincts are telling me since the Third World War, not many female Werewolves are created which is why they're so rare. The other breed's females are dying out from old age with hardly any new ones created. I don't know why exactly, maybe it's because of the underlying effects of the fallout? Humans may have been able to cure the radiation sickness in the natural world, but what about the supernatural world?"

"But -" I tried to interject but he interrupted again.

"You're unique, B." My mate cupped my face in his larger hands. "You're the first and only female in the pack of Lokoti Werewolves. With your pheromones, you're like a winning lottery ticket blowing down a street in the Depression era."

I believed him but my stubborn Lokoti Werewolf protective instinct refused to abandon my mate in a time of danger. "Then I'll fight with you."

"No." He released his hold.

"No? What do you mean, no?"

"I'd fight better without you by my side." He said to my surprise.

"What?!" I cried out, offended.

"B, when I fought those Asian Werewolves just then, I was holding myself back."

"You were holding yourself back?"

"Yeah."

"What do you mean you were holding yourself back?" I put my hands on my hips demandingly.

My husband said guilty, "I've always been holding myself back around you and the other Lokoti Werewolves, B. I've been doing it ever since I was 5 years old and I first realized I was a different to the rest of the pack."

My eyes widened as this new truth began to dawn on me, "You mean even on a hunt you hold yourself back?"

"Of course I hold myself back!" He said incredulous. "You think that by hunting one or two animals a month placates my bloodlust?"

"Well..." I faltered.

"Remember when Derik died?" He brought up the memory of his little brother passing away from old age. "Do you remember when I came back from a spontaneous hunt and you smelled the blood of at least ten different animals on me? I almost lost control over the bloodlust. But that's what it's like for me, B. Always. I'm insatiable! I want to hunt human and since I can't eat them, then I eat animal. My bloodlust would happily eat something supernatural instead, like these Asian Werewolves... which is why I was told never to return because Hsu's clan can smell it."

My heart raced with anxiety as I almost felt afraid of him. I swallowed hard, "Does that mean that – that you want to – to eat me too?"

"NO!" He was quick to pull me closely against him. Declan gently banged his forehead into mine as he inhaled deeply. "You're part of every fibre of my being and my bloodlust knows this. You're more part of me than Derik's progeny is. As I said once, if anything ever happened to you? Then I'd be the first European Werewolf to die of a broken heart than to have it pierced by silver."

I turned quiet as his words reassured and so did his body language. We both momentarily closed our eyes as we enjoyed the feel of our hot, strong bodies pressed together. I felt his fingers dig into my waist possessively.

"Which is why I'm asking this of you now," his eyes met mine again. "Return to Alaska and I'll fight the Asian Werewolves and I won't hold back. And I'll win because of this."

The picture of my husband going on an insane, murdering rampage as he indulged his supernatural hunger for one night to embark on a vengeful feeding frenzy; ran through my mind. It was like, 'sniff at my wife like that and you'll pay.' The bloodlust in his breed was far more primitive than I gave it credit for.

Just then his head snapped around as his human blue eyes turned glowing green again. I heard it too, the approach of more predators heading in our direction.

"Please B," he looked on pleadingly. "Not only do I want you out of harms way, but I don't want you to see what I do tonight."

My heart pounded as I was touched by my husband's honesty. But the Lokoti Werewolf inside blindly refused to leave my mate in a time of danger.

"I have a confession too..." I laughed weakly, "...I've been holding out on you as well. With my speed and strength – albeit it's not as great as yours – there's nothing that I can't fight. This is why I'm coming back for you after I've done this."

Then I surprised him when abruptly I disappeared in a bright flash of light! I instantaneously phased from the middle of the Chinese countryside, into my bedroom inside of my house in Alaska.

I rushed over to my wardrobe and threw open the doors. I went straight for my Katana, which was hidden behind a long, black, woollen overcoat. I pulled the polished, silver sword from its sheath before I instantaneously phased back to China.

By the time I re-appeared beside Declan in another bright flash of light, he had expanded back into his huge, hulking, hairless form. It was just in time too, as twenty Asian Werewolves closed in on our position.

I changed into my stronger Lokoti Werewolf body before I growled to my mate, "I won't hold back if you don't. Stay out of my way and I'll stay out of yours."

I think I caught him smirk with his canine jaws, before he turned towards our attackers. But this time Declan didn't wait for the larger group of Asian Werewolves to make their first move... he made his.

On all-fours, the European Werewolf barrelled his way into the circle of smaller and weaker creatures! His hungry roars almost deafened. I didn't have time to stand back and feel horrified by the view of my mate not just fighting, but EATING his way through our enemy. Ten of our attackers engaged him as I fought off the other ten.

An Asian Werewolf tried to use its supernatural speed to leap onto my arm which was holding the sword. But using my time manipulation as a Circulator, I saw him come towards me in slow motion. This enabled me to move my arm away as I next spun around. Then using my greater strength, I didn't just slice my sword through the Asian Werewolf...I cut him in half.

Two bloodied halves which once belonged to a whole, landed in the dirt. The remaining nine paused in their attack, long enough to see a member of their pack fall to the ground in pieces.

At that moment, my attackers and I were momentarily distracted from the blood-curdling whines, yelps and squealing. It was coming from the faltering seven who were fighting my mate. I saw three Asian Werewolves already dead on the ground with either their heads, throats or their chests eaten out, thanks to his larger jaws.

The Asian Werewolves may have been faster than the European Werewolf, but their speed was showing no effect with his greater strength and size. Watching Declan let loose his bloodlust, was like watching a Great White Shark be unleashed into an Olympic sized pool during a swimming event. The victims saw their attacker coming but other than trying to escape, there was little they could do. However, they didn't try to run, instead they fought on to claim dominance over the strangers on their territory.

The remaining nine I was dealing with, returned their attention my way, which made me hold up my sword higher.

One tried to leap onto my right side as another attempted to jump my left. Moving in the speed of light, I was able to duck backwards. I continued to fight as such, which made my movements look like a series of bright flashes with me suddenly changing positions.

Whilst moving around, I swung my sword with my supernatural strength. Another two Asian Werewolves fell to the ground, either missing a head or the bottom half of their body. Their flesh which had come into contact with the silver, looked singed with small wisps of red smoke, snaking into the air.

After I polished off my fourth attacker, I slowed down to real time when I realized the other six were now absent. I looked over at Declan who was mangling his seventh enemy – slash – meal, where I saw my six were battling alongside his remaining three.

My mate almost paused with his mouthful when I appeared beside him in another bright flash of light. I swung around my sword and chopped the head off one of his opponents! He dropped his half-eaten meal and together we faced off the remaining eight.

It was here we saw the Asian Werewolves begin to back away. For a second time this evening, the enemy retreated due to the loss of numbers. But this time I didn't buy it. Who's to say that they're not going to come back AGAIN?

When one of the pack stopped to pick up its dead, it yelped in fright when Declan charged at it! The supernatural creature bolted away and only just escaped by its' greater speed. Once more, we were left standing alone on the road, with our broken down car, panting with our bloodlust ignited.

Asian Werewolf blood dripped from my sword as the same blood covered the European Werewolf's jaws.

I sensed Declan was battling to retain his control on the bloodlust, which made me stand a safe distance. I wasn't afraid of him turning on me, but I was wary of being knocked aside as soon as our enemy resurfaced. After five minutes of standing there panting, I realized he wasn't trying to calm himself, he was waiting for them to come back. I even caught his stomach rumble.

Frickin' hell, was this fight going to go on ALL night? How many Asian Werewolves were there in this part of China anyways?! I just had to ask that, because I soon got my answer...

Through the darkness, I saw with my glowing turquoise eyes the arrival of thirty more male Asian Werewolves.

What is this, tit-for-tat? At first we beat off ten, then we fought twenty and now they're coming back with thirty...? Where the hell are they all coming from?!

Then my sense of smell detected some slight differences about these new Asian Werewolves - that they didn't all smell alike. I realized we were dealing with more than one clan here. But they didn't smell like Hsu's clan, which was one small relief. If they had, then we'd have thought that this whole thing had been a set up.

Declan roared threateningly at the new arrivals, who looked on with their glowing white eyes and tiny black pupils. Next, they started to spread out to encircle us again. Maybe that's their plan, to keep fighting with their greater speed and numbers until they've exhausted us?

This made me remember something in the SSIT Report on our foe; *There are stories of human victims being unable to escape a vendetta placed against them by an Asian Werewolf, even if the human moved to the other side of the world.*

Has my status as one of the few remaining female Werewolves left, become the males' vendetta? Not to kill but to capture?

Yes little wolf I heard the familiar deep, rumbling inside my being. This voice often seemed to pop up when I was fighting for my life. *There is a reason why you as the first female Lokoti Werewolf are unable to breed*

Unable to breed...unable to conceive...unable to bear children...that's it!

Next, I whipped out my mobile phone from my pocket with my claw-like hand. I opened it and quickly spoke to the small computer; "Access translation program. Translate from English to Mandarin the words: I am barren. If you're good trackers then track this, can't you smell my womb has never been used? Don't you wonder why?"

"Processing your request." My computerized phone responded and within a second the words appeared on the lit-up screen.

Declan overheard what I was doing which made him snarl unhappily. He was angry about what I was about to do and he roared furiously at the Asian Werewolves for making me do it.

In my thunderous voice I called out the message in Mandarin. I hope I got the pronunciation right and I wasn't telling them instead I wanted to become pregnant? But whatever I said was met with silence...

The Asian Werewolves stood still as they looked on, with their glowing white eyes. Standing here in the dark countryside which had turned so quiet, I held my breath in fear I might miss something. The only thing that was audible in the night air was the sound of the Asian Werewolves sniffing; they were sniffing me.

Declan flexed his two front claws, waiting for them to come closer. However, one of the Asian Werewolves whom looked slightly bigger than the others, turned away. Casually, it trotted away into the night and next the others turned to follow the one who must have been the leader.

They all slipped quietly into the darkness as their glowing white eyes and silvery-grey fur disappeared from sight. This time my all-knowing feelings as a Circulator, said that it was for the last. After a minute, I reverted to my human body whilst lowering my sword.

"That's it." I said. "They're not coming back."

I walked over to our rental car and opened the boot to put my sword inside. While I was there, I opened up my backpack and took out a towel and a bottle of water. Next, I opened the passenger's side door and sat down on the seat to put my shoes and socks on again. Lastly, I pulled on my zip-up sweater over my torn t-shirt.

When I stood up again, I noticed that Declan hadn't moved. He was still standing in front of the car and his huge, hulking, hairless form looked intimidating in the headlights. He was growling hungrily at the night, like he was hoping that the Asian Werewolves would return. This disturbed me, as I didn't want my mate to be known in the supernatural world as a cannibal.

I approached him with the towel which I began to dampen with my bottle of water.

I held out the wet material, "Here." My husband turned his beastly head my way, as his glowing green eyes narrowed. I said casually to hide my knotting stomach, "To wash the blood off."

Declan shrunk back into his naked human body, to use his hands to take the towel and wipe himself clean.

As I walked a little away, I looked about at the sliced open or half-eaten bodies of the Asian Werewolves, which were lying around.

To my surprise, they simply looked like a bunch of dead wolves on the ground. They didn't revert to their human bodies when they died, like the other breeds did. Oh well, at least we wouldn't have to explain the carcasses of dead humans to the mechanic, when they show up in their repair vehicle.

My mate walked past as he went over to the car for his clothes. He didn't look my way nor did he speak, as he dressed. Then he moved to sit inside the vehicle to use the rear-view mirror to check his mouth and face and make sure that he had removed all traces of blood.

I sensed he was angry about something, actually he was infuriated about it! So much so, it kept his bloodlust burning inside. What was he angry about? Was he pissed off that he didn't get to eat the other thirty Asian Werewolves? I watched him through the windscreen, as he wiped off the last of the blood on his hands and especially around his nails. I sensed he was deliberately not looking in my direction.

Oh, was he angry with me? Why? What did I do? I just removed a vendetta against us by a breed of Werewolf which was known to never give up!

Next, he shut the car door as he sat back into the driver's seat. He switched off the internal light and I watched him close his eyes and take several deep breaths to calm himself. Warily, I walked over to the passenger's door to climb in. Once I was seated, I shut the door again to keep out the cold night air.

The silence in the car was palpable as Declan opened his eyes to stare angrily out the windscreen. The road before us was littered with our fallen enemy, whose silvery-grey coats almost shined in the car's headlights. I caught him growl again under his breath, as he looked on the carcasses. After two minutes, I couldn't stand it anymore.

"OK Declan, what is it?" I looked on demandingly.

Silence... He kept his lips pursed together whilst sitting in a tense manner as he refused to look my way.

"What's wrong?" I asked, annoyed. "Are you angry that I interrupted your feeding frenzy? Well guess what, I don't know how many of them there were, but we were fighting more than one clan tonight. If we had beaten that thirty then they would have come back with forty, then fifty and maybe even sixty as they pulled in the other clans. We were becoming a vendetta to these people and they DON'T give up!"

"Don't you think that I KNOW all of this, B?!" He shouted, which made me look on in surprise. "Don't you frickin' get it? I was fighting for YOU tonight! I was fighting for my mate! I was fighting for your honour!"

My stomach sank as I stared at my husband in shock. He was truly upset that I had put a stop to his 'defending'. I thought his primitive bloodlust was so behind the times, it didn't appreciate that his female stopped their attackers rather than him.

Then I caught him glance my way in disgust before he vehemently bit out, "If a male yelled out what you said about yourself tonight, I would have shoved my claw down his throat and ripped out his still-beating heart! You shouted out to your possible rapists, that they shouldn't want you because you're barren like you were some common -"

But he stopped himself here as he looked away whilst blinking hard.

Like I was a common what...? A common prostitute? Hang on, prostitutes aren't barren, or not that I'd heard anyways. Why, was it a common trait for women who couldn't have children, to become prostitutes? Maybe I've been hidden away in my nice, little, safe world on tribal lands for too long...

"Like a common prostitute?" I bit out. "You think I yelled out that I was barren like I was a common prostitute or something? Why do you think prostitutes are barren?"

Before I gave him the chance to answer, I swung open my door and hopped out. I slammed it shut and walked around to the back of the car. I popped open the boot so I could pull out my backpack and sword. Then I slammed the boot closed, slung the backpack over my shoulder and carried the sword in my left hand.

"Where the hell do you think you're going?!" Declan was quick to jump out.

"Excuse me, I think there's a barren prostitute's convention in Las Vegas that I'm due to make an appearance at." I said coolly.

I had to blink fast to try to hide my watering eyes, coupled with the sensation of my heart splitting into two.

"Don't be stupid B -"

But I didn't give him the chance to finish his sentence, when I instantaneously phased home to Alaska.

Abruptly, I disappeared in a flash of light before I reappeared in another, inside my bedroom for a second time that night.

I dropped my backpack onto our Queen-sized bed then I carried my sword over to its sheath which was lying on the floor. Once it was encased, I returned the two together to my wardrobe. The master bedroom was dark, but the familiar smells were welcoming.

Our two-bedroom home was a small, two-story, dark brown painted, wooden house with a stone chimney and a front veranda. We had a European style garden with a gravel driveway and a separate garage. Inside the house, our furniture was predominantly constructed of pine in country style, except for our sleigh bed or the red, over-stuffed, suede couches in the living room.

I was so angry that I noticed my hands were shaking. But to get my mind off things, I turned on my bedside lamp and then the Internet Radio feature in Declan's digital clock. I blasted my ears with loud music whilst I unpacked.

Alanis Morissette played, as I separated my clothes into the clean and dirty. I put away the clean clothes but the dirty clothes I dropped into my laundry basket. Lastly, I picked up the basket to take down to the laundry, when my mobile phone started to ring.

Whilst carrying the basket on one arm, I fished my phone out of my pocket with my other. Declan's name appeared on my screen and in a temper, I switched it off and slammed it down on top of the tallboy! It almost broke but I continued on with what was doing.

He can go to hell... or remain in China alone for all I care. I didn't even mind that we'd be apart for longer than twelve hours. It's not like I was leaving him in danger. I had seen to his safety, which was what really pissed me off about his behaviour tonight.

Declan's always shaking his head and telling me that I behave too much like a 'Light Person'. When I thought I heard the voice of the Lokoti Wolf, my people's spirit guide, talk through me again tonight? I thought that was what I did do, behave like a Lokoti Werewolf to ensure my mate's safety. I didn't care if a foreign breed now knew that I couldn't have kids! It certainly wasn't a secret around here.

I saw the quiet pity in my tribe's eyes whenever they looked my way. But that was nothing to what I heard instead. Once with my acute hearing, I picked up whilst shopping in the supermarket in Alma, two women whisper behind my back. They weren't Lokoti but they were used to seeing me around.

"She's definitely had work done, how else does she stay looking like that?" Bitch One hissed.

"She may be pretty but I heard from Shana that she can't have kids. I guess looks aren't everything after all." Bitch Two gloated.

Afterwards, I refused to go grocery shopping off tribal lands for twelve months, although I didn't tell Declan why. Usually I enjoyed the experience of visiting the supermarket in Alma. The huge shelves and the wide range of choice they offered, seemed like a special treat to one who has memories of when food was a precious commodity after the War. My husband knew this, which is why he couldn't understand when I either refused to shop with him or I started ordering our groceries online, to be delivered instead.

I sensed that the Asian Werewolves who were low on females, wouldn't want one who couldn't breed for them. So what was sharing this fact with a bunch of sniffing strangers, for the safety of my mate and tribe? And Declan has the gall to act like HE was the one who was insulted tonight...? Screw that for a joke!

*****

~2~

I stayed up until dawn because I knew if I went to bed, I wouldn't be able to get any sleep. So I busied myself by doing laundry and cleaning out my backpack, before storing it away in the attic.

For comfort food, I cracked open a jar of Nutella. I curled up on the couch, spooning out the delicious chocolate hazelnut spread as I ate it straight. Heart-aching moments like these made it a bitch not being able to drink alcohol, so over the years I found replacements; like eating or hot scented bubble baths or loud music. Tonight called for all three.

After I ate the whole jar of Nutella, I turned the music up then I headed upstairs for the hot scented bubble bath.

By 4 AM as the sun came up, I finally felt tired enough to go to bed. Sleeping in daylight has never bothered me since hunting the night of a full moon, it was the custom for the tribe's Werewolves to sleep in late. When my eyes opened again, Declan's digital clock read as 11.34 AM.

I didn't bother to brush my hair, after putting on some old 'around the house' clothes. Instead, I traipsed downstairs and into the kitchen to make some scrambled eggs on toast. Once the dirty dishes were stowed inside the dishwasher, I set up shop at the coffee table in the lounge room. I turned on my laptop as I began to organize my next presentation on the topic of, 'Female Deities in Ancient Mythology: Early Expectations On Women'.

At 4 PM as I was writing up the section on 'Goddesses of Fertility', suddenly my front door swung open with the appearance of my husband.

I was sitting calmly on a cushion on the floor with my un-brushed hair, doing work. Declan stormed into the lounge area and glared my way in fury. I could tell he was expecting an apology or something with his demanding eyes, but I ignored him by returning to work.

He dropped his backpack loudly onto the wooden floor as he stood over my position. Still I ignored him, as I picked up my glass of root beer and drank from it. Then casually, I continued typing up comparisons between Demeter, Isis and the Virgin Mary.

"Hi Declan, you're home early from your six week holiday aren't you?" He cried out sarcastically, as he began to have a two-way conversation with himself. "Yeah, I was left stranded in China. Oh really, why was that? My wife instantaneously phased home and left me by a broken down car in the middle of nowhere. Declan, that's terrible! Tell me about it! I had to wait an hour by myself until the mechanic in his repair vehicle appeared and then I had to help him replace ALL of the frickin' tyres when his motorized jack broke! Then I had to drive to Leshan instead of to Yushu which was another long drive so I could catch the first available flight to Juneau. From Juneau, I flew to Fairbanks, where I had to get another frickin' rental car. I RUSHED here so I wouldn't be away from my mate for 24 hours, who ABANDONED me in a frickin' foreign country!"

I didn't look up nor did I pause with my typing. The enraged European Werewolf turned around to stalk upstairs. I listened to him go into our bedroom when I overheard further furious snarling. Then he stomped back down the staircase whilst holding up my mobile phone which was still switched off.

"B, I would like to introduce you to the 23rd Century mobile phone. It was advertised when we bought it, 'that the self-recharging battery in this model of phone means that you never run out of power and with our world-wide coverage, you're never out of range'." He continued sarcastically. "Now let's just get this clear so we're both on the same page here; you're supposed to leave your phone switched on let alone on you at all times, so you don't give your husband a frickin' heart attack when he tries to call you over thirty times after you ABANDONED him in a frickin' foreign country!"

I closed my eyes as I inhaled and exhaled loudly, whilst trying to keep my cool.

He continued to rant, "And it's nice to see you sulking with your bed-hair showing that you at least got some sleep in the last twelve hours as for me, it's been two days since I slept a wink! If I'm not staying up all night in our hotel keeping watch in case we're attacked by Asian Werewolves; it's me being ABANDONED in a frickin' foreign country!"

Wearily, I rubbed my face as my husband wouldn't shut up. The deep breathing wasn't working and I could feel my previous anger begin to boil again.

"Thanks for your concern, B. Thanks for just leaving me like that. Thanks for not asking me how I got home, or if I was OK or if the Asian Werewolves came back to have another go -"

But I cut him off, "I knew you weren't in any danger."

"Oh right, because you had one of your all-knowing feelings as a Circulator? Well how about acting loyal like a Lokoti Werewolf for a change!"

I shouted back well and truly enraged now, "I yelled out the dirty little secret that the wife of Declan Sabre can't conceive to a bunch of Asian Werewolves; to break off their pursuit for the safety of my mate and tribe! Then I get called a frickin' prostitute for doing it?!"

Declan tossed my mobile phone down onto the couch as he seethed, "I did NOT call you that word! I would NEVER use that word in relation to my wife! What I nearly said was, 'you shouted out to your possible rapists that they shouldn't want you because you were barren like you were some broken test tube, which they couldn't use to grow their frickin' spawn'!"

This angered me further as I looked away... I think I preferred it when I thought I was being called a prostitute.

My mate looked on in disbelief, "You honestly thought I would use the word 'prostitute' when referring to you?!"

"Next time frickin' finish your sentences so stupid misunderstandings won't be created!" I fumed.

"Then I frickin' WILL!" He snapped back. "And if you EVER put yourself down again because you think you're protecting me? I will sling you over my shoulder and drop you into the frickin' river!"

"You've already done that, now how about a new threat?!"

"Fine." Suddenly he picked up my laptop and started to walk towards the front door. "Instead I'll throw your laptop, with all of your precious diary entries, essays and presentations, into the river."

"DON'T YOU DARE DECLAN SABRE!" I leapt to my feet. Then moving in light speed, I stood in front of the door. I looked on murderously whilst holding out my hand, "The laptop or your life, because I won't just drop you into the river; I'll frickin' drop you into the middle of the Pacific Ocean!"

"Go for it." He trained his steely-cold gaze my way. "I'll survive and what's worse is I'll take your precious laptop with me, before I let go of it. It'd sink to the bottom of the sea."

Next, I tried to snatch it out of his hands, but he whipped it away. I shouted in frustration at his dominating behaviour, "Give it back!"

"No."

"GIVE...IT...BACK!" I roared out in my thunderous Werewolf voice as my eyes flashed glowing turquoise.

"Not...until...you...promise." He growled back as his eyes flashed glowing green.

"Promise what?!"

"That you will NEVER again do what you did in China! That you will NEVER put yourself down like that just to make a sub-standard male not want you! I mean come off it B, if you heard of another woman telling a possible rapist that he didn't want her because there was something wrong with her? You'd hit the roof!"

I whirled around and stormed back over to the coffee table to begin to pack up my work. "Whatever! Keep the frickin' laptop! I have back-ups of my work and diaries stored in the Circulate Mainframe on Taurus Six anyways."

I was so angry, my hands were shaking again as my nose started to run. I wasn't crying, but I didn't want it to look like I was either. I struggled to pack up my research coherently that I didn't notice Declan walk up behind to hold out my laptop.

Annoyed, I snatched it back and carried it and the rest of my work over to one of my shelves where I kept the majority of my academic work. Considering I'd been doing this for over a century, I had several bookshelves which took up the whole wall. The shelves which held my husband's novels and large music collection, sat on the other side of the room.

As I started to put my books away in alphabetical order, Declan came up behind to try to wrap his arms about my shoulders.

"No!" I shrugged him off and after a moment I said sulkily, "You haven't paid my pimp the hourly rate yet."

"Oh yeah and what's that?"

"A million credits."

This made him snicker back, "You must be better than Julia Roberts in 'Pretty Woman' then."

"Maybe if she was a barren prostitute, she would have earned that much. We have a pretty good union you know."

"I guess so," he humorously went along, "do you also have medical insurance?"

"My pimp manages that."

"OK, who is this guy so I know who to kill by ripping out their hearts via their throats?"

"Why do you presume it's a guy?"

"So you have a 'madam' then and not a pimp?" I paused in my shelving to give a funny look, wondering how the hell would he know the correct terminology? He said coolly, "You're not the only one who can read a book you know."

"Yes, I do have a 'madam' and she's very cross with you for offending her worker." I turned away again.

"Then would your 'madam' mind if I offered not only my apology, but also reparations for this gross offence?"

A smile escaped when he said that, but I said breezily, "You would have to pay the million credits first."

I watched him pull out his wallet from his back pocket then his credit card appeared before my face.

Indignantly, I snatched it from him as I said, "You don't have a million credits!"

"After slaving away at the Garage for over a century, I'm a quarter of the way there. I was saving the money for another holiday for my wife, just don't tell her that."

"Oh." I tried not to show his words affected me as I handed back his card. "I heard your wife has some money of her own."

"My wife is one of the smartest people I know and she's well-regarded in her field." He said proudly. "Which is why it makes me angry when people act in a demeaning way towards her, or she demeans herself to strangers."

"So you're here soliciting hookers instead of lying with your wife?" I asked curtly.

He watched me walk into the kitchen to check the pantry to see if there was another jar of Nutella. "I was actually hoping to solicit your services as a surprise for my wife."

"It doesn't sound like a nice surprise."

"Yeah well, she's difficult to please." He followed me into the other room. "She's feisty as hell and more inflexible than a plank of wood."

"So why do you want me for your wife, to buy a three-way or something?" I asked crassly.

He frowned at the idea, "Look lady you seem attractive and all, but my wife and I don't swing that way. Besides, I don't think you'd live through a night with my wife AND me."

I tried not to snicker before I closed the pantry door, with my search unsuccessful in finding any more Nutella. It was then Declan walked over to the medicine cupboard above the fridge and opened it up. He reached behind the vitamins and painkillers to pull out a hidden jar.

My eyes widened in surprise, "How long have you been hiding THAT for?"

"Two months." He shrugged. "It's my emergency supply for when my wife experiences her famous mood swings thanks to PMS. I need something to placate her between hunting on a full moon. Her tantrums can even bring a European Werewolf to heal."

I threw him a withering glare as I tried to take the jar off him but he held it away.

"Nah ah!" He shook his head. "This is a business transaction, is it not?"

"Why? What do you want?" I folded my arms defiantly.

"I'll give you my emergency stash of Nutella instead of the credits, if you'll do something to my wife for me." He said firmly.

"Hit her over the head with a shovel and bury her in your back yard?" I asked dryly.

"Not quite." He pretended to look tempted by the offer. "I will pay you to walk up to my wife and say something to her. You see, I'm hoping that if this comes from a complete stranger she might start to believe it. She certainly doesn't listen to her husband."

I looked on impatiently as my foot began to tap the floor.

He continued, "I will pay you in Nutella if you will walk up to my wife and say just five words to her. You'll have to put your hands on her shoulders like this..." he demonstrated by making me face him, "...and you look her right in the eye," next he did this too, "and you say to Bianca Sabre, 'you're more than worth it'."

I said unimpressed, "What kind of hokey, shampoo-commercial, message is that?"

"Alright you can say this instead, 'I would fight every single Asian Werewolf in existence because you're worth it'."

My broken heart started to superglue itself back together, but I battled myself not to smile. "That's longer than five words."

He chuckled, "Yeah I know, but she's generally not pedantic with numbers so it should be fine."

Now I did laugh and Declan pulled me closer so he could gently rub his nose against mine. Then he looked from me to the jar of Nutella he was still holding in his hand, which was sitting on my shoulder.

"Screw it, I will pay for your services tonight." He sniffed me and then he sniffed the jar. "I want the pleasure of licking chocolate hazelnut spread from your body then you to do the same to me."

I giggled again, "We may need more than one jar of Nutella if you want to be like that." He gave a mischievous grin before he knelt down to open up the cupboard where our pots and pans were kept. From behind a large saucepan, I watched him pull out another hidden jar! Next, I looked about my kitchen in wonder. "No way! How many jars have you hidden in here?"

"Sorry, if I told you, I'd have to kill you and I'm not allowed to eat humans." He joked whilst pulling out his Hodge Endeavor credit card I'd given him, so he had access to company funds in times of an emergency. He slapped it into my hand, "Consider your services duly paid for."

Then I squealed with laughter when he bent over and slung me over his shoulder! Whilst carrying his wife and her Nutella, my husband proceeded upstairs to our bedroom.

"What about me not surviving an experience with you AND your wife?" I laughingly reminded. "What about you not swinging that way?"

"I'd better marry and change you then." He chuckled as he kicked shut the bedroom door behind.

*****

Two hours and one and a half empty jars of Nutella later, the two Werewolves in the Queen-sized bed were showing no sign of winding down.

The female moved steadily over the male, who laid back and looked up at her athletic form. Their crotches which were grinding away against the other, slowed. Her arms were stretched out over him, whilst leaning over she hung onto the bed head to achieve the perfect angle of his entrance. His large, hot hands held onto her waist, pulling her hips closer to his, each time he pushed.

When she slowed down, her breasts hovered over his face which gave him another opportunity. He momentarily let go of her waist to pick up the half empty jar. Using his fingers, he scooped out some more and covered her left nipple with it. She heard the satisfied growl he emitted when he licked it off with his wet, hot tongue before gently chewing on her flesh.

She felt his teeth sharpen in arousal, which enabled him to tenderly break the skin to taste her blood. Whilst licking off the last of the chocolate hazelnut spread intermixed with her life-giving liquid, his crotch increased in speed. They both groaned in delight as he pushed harder and then pushed some more.

"Man, why didn't I think of this before?" He grunted out. "In 136 years of marriage, we could have done this sooner."

I giggled back, "You've eaten tiramisu off my naked body."

"True," he chuckled back.

Then he grabbed hold of my arms to make me let go of the bed frame so he could flip me over and roll on top instead.

"You know..." he began to talk as he moved, "...officially we still have three weeks of our holiday left. We could hole up in our bedroom for three weeks uninterrupted pleasure and do this all day, every day, if we want."

"Hmm, we could too...," I tittered, "...do you think you're up to it, trying to placate the lust of a Circulator and a Lokoti Werewolf?"

"Am *I* up to it?" He raised his eyebrows. "Baby, do you remember that little speech I gave you in the Chinese countryside, about me holding back?"

Then I squealed with laughter when he emitted a loud roar and drove his face into my right breast. His mouth opened wide to completely take in the whole of the rounded flesh as his movements sped up. A layer of sweat appeared on the surface of our skin as our body odour was intermixed with the smell of Nutella.

"Mmm," I inhaled his maple syrup scent coming off his skin, "man you smell good."

"...right back at ya, B..." he mumbled back with a mouth full of breast.

The mattress jarred with each of his strong thrusts and now it was my hands holding onto his wide waist. Whilst his head was ducked, I looked over his shoulder to admire his muscled back ripple with each of his movements. I felt his finger tips dig into my buttocks as he held my crotch firmly to his, to take the brunt of his constant hunger.

When I felt another orgasm build up from our marital misbehaviour, so did Declan when I dug my nails into his skin. This was always my indication his actions were working, by me suddenly biting or clawing him as I lost control from ecstasy. His sign was pushing harder and faster which was usually followed by one last, large thrust. After the final push, half the time he might slowly wind down and the other half, he would fall limp over his wife.

We both knew the other was coming, by my nails embedded in his epidermis and his pushing was speeding up. We both gasped, held our breaths as we tried to hold onto the escalating pleasure, then we gasped again. I felt my internal muscles ripple upwards which was moving my ecstasy higher in my torso...

...when all of a sudden, my mobile phone which was on the floor with my discarded clothing, began to ring.

"No! No! No!" Declan cried out when he saw my head turn towards it. He pushed faster as he spluttered out with a red face, "We'll frickin' call 'em back!"

However, my oncoming orgasm had quickly dissipated from the interruption and instead a feeling of dread had replaced it. Oh oh...I was experiencing an all-knowing feeling. Something was wrong which was why somebody was calling.

I shoved my husband off and rolled to the side of the bed, to pick up the communications device from the floor. I saw Chiron's name on the screen and I answered it before it rang out. Declan futilely tried to stop me to recommence satisfying himself, but I was too fast.

"Hallo Chiron." I greeted.

He was our great grandnephew and First in our pack, to whom Declan was Second. As soon as he heard it was our 'supervisor', my husband lay back defeated on the mattress. We couldn't very well hang up on our relation let alone 'boss'.

"Aunt B," our First said gravely, "I'm sorry to interrupt your holiday but I thought you should know."

"Yes?"

"My father died an hour ago." He said simply and I heard in his voice he was trying to be strong. "The funeral will be in three days, so if you could come it would be appreciated."

Declan who overheard with his sensitive hearing, his eyes widened as we exchanged looks of horror. Chiron's father had been my first cousin, Phoenix Riverclaw. It looks like time had caught up to the elderly 156 year old Lokoti Werewolf.

"We're coming over." I sat upright.

"No, you don't have to right now." Chiron said guiltily. "But if you wouldn't mind instantaneously phasing home for the funeral, then you can go back to your holiday."

"We are home." I declared. "Look, it's a long story. We'll see you in a couple of minutes."

"Thanks Aunt B," my grandnephew exhaled emotionally, "I look forward to it."

We hung up and I put my phone on my bedside table before I stood up. My mate shook his head as he looked away unhappily.

"This is typical timing of your cousin to meet his demise when we're supposed to be on holiday." Declan joked ruefully. "If he wasn't already dead, I'd kill him."

Then he too got out of bed to dress beside me.

*****

Although the old Riverclaw home was just down the hill from ours, we still drove in Declan's metallic black, plasma-powered, pick up truck.

The Lokoti Tribe lived in the World Heritage Listed, Lokoti National Park. We were situated in the Alaska Range approximately 4.5 hours north of Anchorage and 1.5 hours south of Fairbanks. The tribal lands looked like a small village of wooden houses along tiny streets. We were surrounded by forest, snow-tipped mountains and interconnected river ways. Every full moon I hunted with my mate and pack inside the vast wilderness, to feed on large prey such as bear, caribou, moose or else.

My husband drove the short way and pulled up in the driveway of the large, two-story, log cabin which had been in the Riverclaw family for several generations. The 19 year old Forrest Riverclaw, come out onto the front veranda to greet us.

"Grandfather says you're already back from your trip?" He shook Declan's hand before kissing my cheek.

"We ran into some trouble with some Asian Werewolves." My mate said shortly. "But we'll explain later. Where's your grandfather?"

Forrest opened the front door for us and we followed him inside. As soon as I came into the house, I halted in surprise as I experienced the strongest sense of déjà vu. Last year Declan and I came with the death of my Uncle Julian, whom was Chiron's grandfather. Then we saw the younger generations of Riverclaws mill sadly around the living room and today they were doing it again.

"Aunt B and Uncle Declan." Sharon nodded in acknowledgement.

She was Stone's middle-aged, human wife. Then the youthful appearance of her husband who was Chiron's son, jogged down the stairs. He shook my mate's hand and placed another kiss on my cheek.

"Thanks for coming so fast." Stone said gratefully. "Dad is upstairs with my grandfather."

Forrest sat next to his mother on the couch, as his little sister sat on the other. He was the pack's youngest Werewolf, as he turned after Uncle Julian's death and he tried to be strong for his family. We watched him put a comforting arm about his mother's shoulders and pass a smile his sister's way. Declan and I noted this, before we headed up the stairs with Stone leading us into one of the bedrooms.

We found the middle-aged Chiron, sitting on the side of the bed that the elderly Phoenix was lying on top of. My younger cousin whom looked much older; was fully dressed, showing he must have passed away in his sleep during an afternoon nap. His son put down the deceased's hand to stand up and face the arrivals.

"Aunt B and Uncle Dec." He nodded tearfully.

I rushed forwards and engulfed him in hug, as my mate gave an understanding nod.

"Dad wasn't the same after his father died." Chiron sighed sadly when he released me. "The last twelve months, seemed like he was just waiting to rejoin his family and mate in the Holy Hunting Grounds."

As Declan and I approached the bed to say our goodbyes, Stone came to stand beside his father and place a supportive hand on his shoulder.

My eyes stung as I stared down into the elderly man's peaceful face which was framed by his long, white hair.

"Hi Phoenix, its bitch-features." I tearfully joked to my late relation. "Say hi to Mum and Dad, Uncle Jules and Aunt Danika, Phoebe and Vincent for me."

My usually obnoxious cousin of course didn't reply, and seeing him like this was upsetting.

You would think being Werewolves, we were the predators however our supernatural abilities were no match for Time itself. My husband could live for 300 years because of his breed and I could live for over 1,000 years as a Circulator. However Declan's human mother and little brother passed away long ago, which affected him deeply. With my family's passing, it happened a little differently although philosophically you could argue it was the same thing.

My grandmother and mother had too been Circulators. They turned my Lokoti Werewolf grandfather and father into Circulators as well, to evolve with them to the space time continuum. My youthful grandmother and mother did this by putting their elderly husbands' bio-electromagnetic fields, into temporal flux.

Humans in a sense 'evolve' when they die, by leaving behind their biological existences as their spirits move on. Some people including myself, conjectured the space time continuum could be called the afterlife. Our Tribal Elders called the space time continuum 'the Holy Hunting Grounds', where spirits visit before returning to the timeline to live again, as in reincarnation.

I had asked Declan at my grandparents' Remembrance Ceremony if he would come with me to the space time continuum as a Circulator one day. Although he agreed, we weren't in a rush to evolve just yet. Our human, Werewolf or Circulator predecessors may have left us, but their progeny remained. Frequently, my mate and I were invited to family gatherings or received babysitting requests. Our second bedroom functioned as a guest bedroom, with a line of great, great, great grandnephews and nieces occasionally staying over.

The tribe was used to Declan's and my extended youth because the fourteen other members of the pack could live up to 200 years. Lokoti Werewolves aged slower than their human wives or members of the tribe. Our people held the Werewolves in high esteem because of their history of protection. In return, the tribe guarded the identities of the pack which included us.

I turned away from the bed to pass my mate a haunted look, "Phoenix was my first cousin and he was the last family member from my childhood. You and I are the only two left from our era!"

His eyes watered, "I know B, I know."

Then I threw my arms about my mate's neck as I clung onto him and cried into his shoulder.

"I still remember fighting with Phoenix when we were little." I sobbed. "I remember when he used to call me bitch-features, how I would punch him for it. I remember when he used to pull my hair, or once he kicked a soccer ball at my head but it accidentally hit Uncle Jules and the trouble he got into."

My husband pulled away so his tearful eyes could meet mine. "Then tell him all of this."

He gently turned me around and sat me on the side of the bed, before standing closely behind to rest his hands protectively on my shoulders. Gingerly, I picked up Phoenix's cold hand and held it between my warm ones. I looked on his aged face once more to reminisce.

"I remember the Christmas you ate all of the brandy butter before the plum pudding was served and it made you sick." I recanted. "I remember when Phoebe used to read your mind and tell on you when you did something wrong. I remember playing Monopoly with you and how you cheated by sneaking money and hiding it under the board. That was until Phoebe told on you and you punched her on the arm. I remember I punched you back and you tackled me for it and then we both got into trouble..."

Just then Declan chuckled, "Yeah I remember that night, it was when my family was having dinner with your family at Easter. I was seventeen and B was fourteen so Phoenix would have been ten."

Stone exchanged looks of amusement with his father at our unusual reminiscing. Usually when somebody close died, people recalled the best things about the deceased. However since my cousin and I fought like brother and sister, our best times were spent fighting. I wanted to remember my cousin like that, in affectionate enmity.

Then I lightly punched the dead guy on the arm, "And that's for all the times you called me bitch-features and ran away before I could hit you."

*****

The time was approaching 10 PM when we left the Riverclaw's and went home. Declan powered down his vehicle in the garage before turning my way. He opened his mouth to say something, but he hesitated to look on concerned.

"What?" I wondered.

"Your aura is faded." He remarked unhappily. "How about I make us some fettuccine carbonara with garlic bread?"

I knew he was trying to cheer me up, but I felt tired and emotionally wrung out.

"Nah, it sounds like too much of a hassle to cook up something complicated this late." I frowned. "How about just something on toast?"

"What about bacon, eggs, grilled tomato, fried mushrooms, hash browns and toast?"

"Now we're talking." I couldn't help but to smile. "I'll see if the crop of tomatoes in the greenhouse are ready and check on the rest of the plants."

We both hopped out of his pick up truck at the same time and whereas he went into the house via the front door; I walked around the small building to the smaller one behind, which was constructed of glass.

Our greenhouse wasn't that large but it had numerous shelves which held planters full of different vegetables and herbs. The planters on the floor had the taller plants, like tomatoes, cucumber, capsicum, celery, zucchini and squash. The shelves above had lettuce, radish, carrots, broccoli and cauliflower. Then the small pots in between grew parsley, chives, oregano, thyme, rosemary, lemongrass, coriander and garlic and we even had a small chilli bush.

As our food producing plants took the most room, the back right corner had Declan's orchids on display on a triangular set of metallic shelves. He had pink, purple, white, orange and yellow varieties, which he paid close attention to. Upon inspection, the flowers were thriving just as the other plants were which means our Great x4 Grandnephew would live. I giggled at my mate's temper, which could still scare people and in particular, our human relatives.

Just as I moved away to gather some tomatoes, something caught my eye. I stopped and turned around to lean in closer, at the pot which was sitting on the floor in front of the orchids.

The plant was withered and the flower which used to peak out from the top, was long gone. The soil in the pot was a combination of red and brown dirt. The red soil was from Mars coupled with the brown from Alaska. The plant was the Martian Dandelion that my father gave to me, the day that the Circulate HQ on Mars was destroyed and my parents left for the space time continuum.

"Oh no..." I sunk to my knees to get a better look. I picked up the drooping stalk with the dead flower bud, to see that the leaves were shrivelling too. "Oh no..." my eyes refilled with tears as my heart sank. I knew there was nothing I could do as the plant too was on its way into the afterlife. "Declan!"

Within a minute, my mate came out the back door and headed down the small garden path towards the greenhouse.

"Yeah?" He poked his head through the open doorway. He looked around at the healthy plants as if he were making sure we weren't returning to ruined produce. "What's up?"

"Declan..." I pointed at the dying dandelion, "...look."

He came into the greenhouse and knelt beside on the cement floor. "Oh," he frowned as he looked on our last piece of Mars which was fading fast. His large hand moved towards it and he gently examined the shrivelled leaves with his fingertips before he sighed out, "I don't think there's anything we can do."

"Frickin' hell!" I cursed. "First the Martian Circulate HQ gets blown up, then my parents and my Calculator evolves to the space time continuum and now the Martian flower also bites the dust?!"

"And your cousin died today." He put in. "Talk about, 'when it rains it pours'."

"Oooh!" I fumed. "We did everything right! We watered it and talked to it and we were careful about fertilizers and whatever else."

"Well B, it is from another planet." My husband shrugged. "Maybe it needs Martian conditions?"

"But the vegetation on Mars died out!"

"So there you go, it was doomed from the start." He rested his hand on my back and gave it a sympathetic rub.

"Oh...!" I whined as I deflated almost as much as the flower did.

"C'mon baby," he stood up and then pulled me to my feet. "Let's get some dinner into you and I'm sure there's another stash of Nutella in the kitchen somewhere."

"No." I sighed wearily. "I don't want anymore Nutella today."

"Shit." My mate suddenly went still and looked on in shock. "I think hell just froze over."

Playfully, I whacked him on the arm and turned to depart from the greenhouse.

~~~~~~

6th August, 2226

Three days later, the family as well as the tribe, attended my cousin's funeral on the Holy Grounds before the Sacred Totems. I clung to Declan's arm through the service and it was like my mate literally held me up. The Tribal Elders sang the funeral chant as the pyre burned the body wrapped in the woven funeral shroud, as Phoenix's progeny looked on.

After the service, the tribe split up to go their separate ways as did most of the Elders, to leave the body to burn overnight. Declan and I left with Chiron and his family for the wake at the old Riverclaw house. The fourteen other members of the pack and their wives – the ones that hadn't passed away from old age – came to share food and drink with their First whilst reminiscing about their fallen.

Everyone brought a dish or bottle of soda to share and Declan had made three large plates of goodies. On one serving plate sat an antipasto mix complete with salami, marinated mushrooms and smoked oysters; on another sat Capsicum and Potato Frittata as well as on the third, Bacon and Olive Cakes. The antipasto plate he had put together today but the other dishes he cooked up the night before.

When he made them, I sat up on the bench in the kitchen to watch. It became the custom in our marriage for most of our discussions to happen over food and this way, I also got to sample what he was cooking. Declan often interrupted me in the middle of conversation to allow me a taste of what he was preparing. Last night, this reoccurred and I relished the deliciousness of the samples. From seeing how quickly the plates of food emptied, it became evident everyone else thought so too.

In the beginning of the Wake, I was sitting next to Sharon who was busily gossiping to another two wives. However I started to tune out during discussions of school fees or the best nappy rash treatment. My eyes wandered over to my husband who was nursing a small plate of nibblies, whilst telling Chiron, Stone and Forrest Riverclaw, as well as Meadow Shallow Water and lastly, Jake Wisetail about our altercation in China.

"Excuse me," I stood up to the women's surprise when my departure interrupted their conversation. "Er, it's pack business."

I used this excuse often, which the women never minded since I was a member. They watched me cross over to Declan's side and rest my arm about his waist. He angled his plate of nibblies my way to share and I stole a marinated mushroom. Then he moved the plate to his right hand to hold, as his left arm was slung over my shoulders.

"So the Asian Werewolves broke off their attack?" Chiron double checked.

"Uh huh." His Second confirmed. "I don't think they'll be tracking us back here."

"Are you a hundred percent certain of this?" Meadow spoke as the concerned Medicine Man.

"Yup." Declan straightened. "They stopped their pursuit."

Chiron's eyes momentarily flashed in my direction before he spoke to my husband. "Perhaps for the next couple of weeks, we should have a Werewolf run the borders of our land, just to make sure we don't have any surprises."

But this got my back up and I said curtly, "But they're not coming. I don't have any warning feelings as a Circulator. I don't foresee any further trouble from that clan or breed."

Our First looked in my direction but for longer this time, before he said, "Let's call it peace of mind."

Just as I was about to argue this further, Declan spoke up, "It wouldn't hurt."

Then Forrest also sided with our First by volunteering, "I don't mind doing a run tonight."

"Then I'll do a run tomorrow night." Stone agreed.

"I'll go the night after." Meadow shrugged.

"Night four works for me." Jake Wisetail nodded amiably.

He was my cousin five times removed, from my father's side of the family, who inherited Mum and Dad's house with their evolution. He also inherited Dad's place in the pack by his Lokoti Werewolf DNA activating on the following full moon. The same time Jake received my childhood home as a Housewarming present for he and his new wife, another adjustment had to be made when he had to take time off work, to learn to control the bloodlust.

"Fine." I said coolly. "I'll do a run on the fifth night."

However, my husband and the rest of the male members of the pack didn't look happy to hear that, and neither did our First.

"No Aunt B." He said seriously. "Just as you weren't permitted to patrol during the years of lawlessness after the War, nor can you do so now."

"What?" I objected. "Why not?"

Declan rolled his eyes, "Don't start this again."

But it was Meadow who spoke patiently, "There are humans in Alma who still whisper stories of male Lokoti Werewolves who helped the townspeople rid themselves of a bad element after the War. However no-one talks of a female Lokoti Werewolf because to outsiders, there's no such thing."

"Except to a bunch of horny Asian Werewolves," my husband said unhappily before he turned back to Chiron. "I think I should go back to China and finish what I started. I'll eat the other thirty who know about B."

"Declan!" I elbowed him sharply. "Yeah, what a good idea in helping the concept of living quietly; by embarking on a murderous rampage and placing a new vendetta on your head!"

Our First looked on his overprotective Second in the pack. "No Uncle, there'll be no further Asian Werewolf blood spilt. Unless of course they come onto our territory then you can unleash your wrath. But according to Aunt B, it's unlikely."

"Then if it's unlikely, it should be OK if I go for a run around our borders." I tried again.

"Yeah, what a good idea of helping the concept of no such thing as a female Lokoti Werewolf; until a townsperson catches sight of you." Declan repeated sarcastically.

"Oh shut up!" I rolled my eyes, as I stepped out from under his arm.

When the male Werewolves began to think up a roster over the next month, I lost the last of my already short patience and broke away. To look like I wasn't sulking, I returned to the seat beside Sharon as if I were returning to a previous conversation. The women smiled and recommenced their discussion about the escalating cost of childcare centres, for those who juggled part time work and young children.

Frickin' hell, I wasn't enjoying this Wake. I had either male chauvinism or baby talk to bounce between. Not that I blamed the women, for those that were mated to a male Lokoti Werewolf; children were an inevitable part of that marriage. I just felt left out, since I was the only woman in the room let alone the tribe, whose union to a virile supernatural species didn't produce 'rug rats'.

In the past, my Calculator Vincent who had been a doctor, examined me for 'non-specific ovarian failure'. He ran multiple tests to ascertain I didn't have tubal disease or endometriosis nor did I have ovulation disorder. But for some reason things just didn't add up, my eggs refused to be fertilized nor could they embed themselves in my uterus. Vincent diagnosed that my differences as a Circulator had unusually affected my biology and it was as if my reproductive system was also in temporal flux. That day I learned my status as the Last Circulator was responsible for truly making me the last on the line.

"Excuse me," I stood up a second time, "I just have to check on something outside."

The women were starting to look a little disgruntled at my comings and goings and truly, I didn't mean to be rude. My head ducked shyly as I slipped out of the room via the front door when I found refuge on the veranda steps. There I sat, looking up into the changing sky.

It was nearing 10 PM and the sun was only starting to set, thanks to Alaska's extended daylight during summer. But in the dusk, I caught one or two stars peak through. The darker it turned with the onset of evening, the more stars emerged.

"Hallo Mum and Dad. Man, I miss you guys." I sighed sadly at the celestial objects, as if they were my loved ones. I felt my eyes sting and I continued talking under my breath. "Mum, I miss how you fought for equal rights for women with the pack. Dad, I miss how you would talk quietly with Grandfather on your verdict but you'd always hear us out if someone had a different point of view. I also miss not talking about academic work with you guys or Circulate stuff. There's no-one to laugh over time travel stories anymore."

Then I turned quiet as I looked out at the garden in the twilight. The Riverclaw as well as the Wisetail families copied off Declan and I, by doing up their gardens after we did up ours. They used different plants though and made them unique in their own way. I loved looking on the gardens in summer, at how the flowers bloomed for an extended time or the smell of freshly cut grass. I closed my eyes and breathed in deeply through my nose and out of my mouth, as I inhaled the change of smell produced as it went from day to night.

At that moment, I was disturbed by the sound of the front door opening and closing, as Declan came to sit beside. He was carrying two glasses of orange flavoured Fanta and he passed me one. Then he too looked up into the sky.

"Are you missing your parents and grandparents?" He guessed.

I nodded whilst staring at the neatly kept lawn, "And my Calculator."

"Who, Vincent?" My husband screwed up his face in distaste. "I don't know how you or anyone would miss that guy. He had a permanent chip on his shoulder and especially a grudge about our kind."

This made me smile, "He thought Werewolves were sexist, archaic, primitive beasts."

"And because we still won't let you patrol, it reminded you of that?" He raised his eyebrows unimpressed. "Oh yeah, we're real bastards for trying to keep the existence of a female Lokoti Werewolf, a secret. We're real Neanderthals for trying to protect our female, when there are male Werewolves out there who've tried to kidnap and claim her for their own purposes."

"It's not just that." I sighed out. "There's no-one to talk to about Circulate business anymore."

"Hang on, I thought Vincent programmed the Circulate Mainframe to act as your Calculator in his stead?"

"Yes he did and it does a very good job. It sends me via email, notifications I should be aware of within Hodge Endeavor or even in the timeline. But..." I faltered as my eyes briefly met his before they skipped away again, "...I don't have anyone to talk to about time travel anymore."

"What am I, a Neanderthal bastard who's so stupid that you can't even communicate with anymore?" He riled up. "You can frickin' talk to me!"

"Oh OK." I sarcastically put on a cheerful tone. "Declan, I'm thinking of visiting Ancient Egypt and taking some photos of the statues of Isis in the temples in Thebes and Memphis. Now which season do you recommend I should visit in to avoid mosquitoes; or in which Kingdom should I go, New or Middle?"

"Say what?" He blinked dumbfounded. "I thought you had a frickin' smart computer to think of these things for you!"

"I do have a computer for a Calculator to answer my questions but it can't say to me, 'oh B, I was in the New Kingdom last week. It was the time of year when the flooded Nile had receded and I saw this temple with amazing statues which you would absolutely love!'"

"What do you mean, the Nile was flooded? B, I don't think it's a smart idea to visit flooded destinations."

"The Nile is supposed to flood, Declan! The floodwaters leave silt which helps crops grow!"

"Well if you already know all of this, why do you need to go there to look at frickin' statues?"

"Because it helps with my academic work!" I rolled my eyes. "My papers generate interest, because my work isn't just guessing what life used to be like; I provide proof of what it really was like because I've seen it with my own two eyes!"

My papers ensured casual employment of guest lectures in the academic field where I was known as Dr. Bianca Riverclaw, which was my mother's maiden name. I'd been Dr. Bianca Sabre for forty years and then Dr. Bianca Wisetail for another forty. I had to start all over again because my other two identities are supposed to have either retired or 'carked it' by now.

Since Declan's always worked at the Garage on Lokoti Tribal Lands he didn't have to worry about assumed identities. In fact, if a person ever suggested to him to pretend to be somebody else, he would figuratively bite your head off! My husband had a low tolerance for anything superficial and calls it as it is, much to my amusement and our tribe's. The only time he humours subterfuge, is hiding his European Werewolf nature from outsiders.

"So do you sign at the bottom of your work, 'written by the Last Circulator, the woman who's actually been there'?" He rolled his eyes back. "If you do, I think we should be more worried of people finding out you're a Circulator let alone a Werewolf."

Exasperated, I started to bang my head against the wooden veranda railing. Declan growled under his breath and instead of putting out his arm to merely stop me, I found myself in a headlock!

"Hey, let go!" I complained.

"Nah, I don't think so." He said coolly. "You stuffy, snobby, time traveller for a cheat, University Professor."

So I bit into his side, which made him cry out and loosen his hold. We were both half laughing and half snarling, as Declan tried to grab onto his wife and I kept swatting his hands away. Our drinks sat half drunk and forgotten about.

"Right that's it!" He growled and his eyes momentarily glowed green when he bent over and lifted me up, onto his shoulder.

"Hey! Declan, put me down!" I squealed louder in laughter.

"Nope, I'm dragging you back to my cave Mrs. Neanderthal!" He stood up and walked away from the steps.

I grabbed hold of his hair and pulled hard, which tipped his head backwards and made him lose his balance. Together, we tumbled onto the front lawn, with me landing on top. But then we paused, as our senses told us we weren't alone.

We looked up to see Stone with his wife and son, as well as Jake and his wife and baby, standing on the veranda in their dignified black clothes; staring at their immature elders who were wrestling in theirs.

"Let me guess, 'pack business'?" Sharon raised her eyebrows.

*****

Declan and I were still chuckling about what happened tonight, as I lay over him in bed. Our bare flesh was pressed against the others as our panting subsided from another session of wrestling, only it had been the naked kind. I enjoyed the feel of his sharp nails, running lightly up and down my back, which he often did to show his satisfaction afterwards.

"Do you think people still have sex in the space time continuum?" I wondered aloud.

"I dunno." I felt him shrug as my head rested on his chest. "If it's supposed to be the afterlife, maybe they're too dead to? On the other hand, if it's supposed to be heaven, they'd probably be 'doing it' for all of eternity."

I perched my head in my hand so I could look down into his sweaty face, "Maybe they don't have bodies to use to 'do it' anymore? You saw how Mum, Dad and Vincent's bodies turned into clouds of energy and light when they evolved."

"Screw that!" The European Werewolf emitted a dissatisfied growl. "What's the point of volunteering to go to the afterlife if you have to leave behind one of life's greatest pleasures?"

"But then again..." I continued to ponder as my finger started to trace the ripples his muscles caused to his torso, "...when I visited the space time continuum, I went there as a bodiless mass but once inside, I had a body again. But it wasn't my Werewolf body, I was human just like everyone else was too."

"You mean I'd have to give up being a European Werewolf when you turn me into a Circulator?"

"Only inside the continuum." I shrugged.

Declan looked away troubled, "I don't know if I like the sound of that. I mean, sure my supernatural strength gets annoying sometimes as I keep accidentally breaking things. But I don't remember anymore what it was like being human, before I was turned."

I smiled on my mate, "You were human in the space time continuum, when you greeted me. You showed yourself as your previous incarnation, Captain Greyson."

"So you keep saying." He said gruffly as he stretched out before resting his hands behind his head. "But I have no recollection of being that guy."

"Have you ever thought about being hypnotized and undergo past life regression?"

"Now there's an idea," he said sarcastically, "get hypnotized and momentarily lose my control of the bloodlust. When I wake up, I'd find the hypnotist in pieces and the walls and floors of their office all covered in a sticky, red colour."

"Well," I conceded, "at least you have past lives. Since I'm a Circulator, I've never lived before and I'll never be reborn. I just keep goin' and goin' and goin' like a supernatural 'Duracell Bunny'."

"Heh heh! You're my cute little bunny." Declan happily wrapped his arms about my waist once more. "Maybe we should buy you a set of fluffy bunny ears. Hey yeah, you could even wear them in the bedroom! I'll buy you a Playboy Bunny costume!"

"Oh shut up!" I laughingly slapped him on the chest.

"And you said you can't talk about Circulate matters with me?" He mockingly rolled his eyes. "What do you call this?"

"Maybe the next time I phase through time to Ancient Egypt, I should go dressed as a Playboy Bunny?"

"Hey!" My possessive mate's eyes glowed green in a bad-temper and he rolled us over so he was lying on top. "Nobody gets to see my wife in her bunny outfit but me! The Egyptians bitched and moaned about the ten plagues? I'd do worse if an Egyptian saw my wife in a costume that's meant for her husband only!"

I tittered like a little girl before I cupped his face to hold his eyes with my own. "Thanks Dec."

"Thanks for what?"

"For this and for never changing." I sighed in resignation. "Lokoti Werewolves die earlier than you, my Circulator and Calculator relations evolve, not even our Martian plants can hold their own. But my European Werewolf mate soldiers on and his stubbornness and bad-temper, remain as my rocks to hold onto."

Declan started to smile, "So if I did get a Playboy Bunny outfit, you'd wear it?"

Then he laughed out loud when I knocked him off, sat on top of him instead and tried to smother his face with my pillow.

~~~~~~

~ 3 ~

It was approaching six o'clock and I knew Declan wouldn't be home for another hour. He's had a lot of work at the Garage lately, so I didn't wait for him to cook dinner. Mind you, my food preparation was nowhere near his gourmet skills, so I resorted to heating up leftovers coupled with a supermarket bought salad.

Maia and Brandon were staying with us this week, whilst their parents were away. They were attending a conference for Tribal Elders of indigenous people, to discuss environmental issues. Their parents went along as assistants to the Lokoti Tribal Elders. It was a hoopla of an event, with the President of the United States and the Prime Minister of Canada, attending. They were joined by several UN Environmentalists, as well as a couple of Hodge Endeavor representatives.

I was invited to attend, thanks to my role as the Head Chairwoman on the Board of Directors, but I didn't feel inclined. Besides, I like playing the role of the mysterious owner of one of the world's most powerful companies, where only the Board knew what I looked like. I had given the Circulate Mainframe the go-ahead to send the company's best lawyers and scientists to assist the Lokoti Tribal Elders. There had been a couple of pollution problems without the proper protocols followed, which I knew would be brought up. I gave the Hodge Endeavor Legal Department, the 'green light' to nail our competition over their failings.

Since Declan and I were seen as the 'old but not elderly' couple with no young of our own; our relatives had no qualms about 'dumping' their kids on us. However Maia and Brandon Sabre were now 17 and 15 years old, and although they were old enough to take care of themselves for one night, they weren't mature enough to be left alone for five days. This meant that the sister and brother, were sleeping in our spare bedroom. We had twin beds which were perpetually on standby, in our role as our families' backup babysitters.

In the beginning, we helped Declan's human brother Derik and wife Rachel, mind their kids for a night here and there. Next, we helped their children by babysitting their offspring now and again. As time passed and our grandnieces and nephews had kids of their own; our spare bedroom and services continued to be used. We didn't mind, we saw it as a change to our rather solitary lifestyle. We managed to keep our hands (or claws) to ourselves, for a night here and there in the company of little folk.

As our relatives died of old age - with the humans faster than the Werewolf ones - and new generations were born; my mate and I were simply called 'Uncle Declan' and 'Aunt B'. It would be too much of a headache to call us by the correct titles, 'Great, Great, Great, Great Granduncle Declan' or 'Great, Great, Great, Great Grandaunt B'. We appreciated the fact that our human relations looked up to us and appreciated our advice. Our elderly relatives whom we had babysat in earlier years, deferred to us on many family matters.

Into the third night of our babysitting adventure; I was in the kitchen tossing the home-made dressing through the pre-made salad whilst the lasagne was heating up in the microwave. Maia was supposed to be helping, but she was too busy complaining about her on again/ off again relationship with a non-Lokoti boy she was dating from Alma High School. I tried to stifle my growl, this girl has been boy-crazy since she turned 13 years old.

"I don't get it Aunt B," she whined, "Hiro keeps running hot and cold! One minute he buys me flowers and the next he ignores me!"

Brandon, whom was playing with an interactive, electronic, comic book on the couch; he too was getting tired of hearing about his older sister's love life.

"Yeah well, Maia? I'm trying to ignore you too. So whoever said 'ignore them and they'll go away,' was lying." He grumbled.

She rolled her eyes before she continued, "I mean, Hiro bought me flowers last weekend when he took me out for hamburgers and a movie. But today when I walked past with my friends and he was standing by his locker talking to his; he didn't even look at me when I said 'hi' to him!"

"I would have gone one step further, by putting a paper bag over your head." Her brother muttered.

I had to turn away and pretend to check on the lasagne, so I could stifle my snicker.

"When we were watching the movie, he tried to... you know, make out with me? But I pushed him off because I don't want to do that in public." She leaned back against the kitchen bench. I had asked her to set the table, but she'd forgotten about it. "Aunt B, I don't mind holding his hand and giving him a quick kiss when other people are around, but I don't want to be groped like that!"

My overprotective instincts as a Lokoti Werewolf, didn't want her to be groped like that - period.

"Maia..." I tried to tell her that she shouldn't feel coerced into doing anything she wasn't comfortable with, but I didn't get the chance.

"What do you think, Aunt B? I can always talk to you about this stuff instead of Mom or Dad, because they'd hit the roof. Do you think he's pissed off that I didn't make out with him, and that's why he ignored me?" She fretted.

"No, it's because you left the house today without wearing a paper bag over your head!" Brandon taunted.

"Shut up you little runt!" She shouted back.

"I'd talk to me a lot nicer if I were you." He threatened. "If I mention one word to Mom and Dad what Hiro tried to do with you in the cinema, you won't be allowed to date him!"

That was it... she stormed out of the kitchen to take him on, leaving me to both set the table AND make dinner.

Next, I heard a loud SLAP!

"Oow!" Brandon yelped. "That's it! I AM going to tell Mom and Dad!"

"You wouldn't dare, if you don't want me telling them about your secret stash of porn!" She threatened. "You dirty little pervert!"

"That stuff isn't mine! I'm stashing it for some friends!" He tried to lie.

Then I heard further scuffling as the two went at it; scratching, hitting and probably pulling the other's hair, as I had seen them do before.

"I'll just set the table then, shall I?" I talked to myself.

I left the lasagne warming in the microwave, as I grabbed the table cloth and cutlery out of the drawers. Then I walked over to the dining table, whilst partially listening to the fight, to ensure they didn't kill the other.

"Oow, Brandon! That HURT!" She squealed.

"You hit me first!" He retorted.

Just as I returned to the kitchen, I heard this strange hissing noise. Oh no! Quickly, I darted forward and stopped the microwave. Damn it! I overheated the lasagne again, making the pasta turn hard.

I could hear Declan's words now, "I hate it when you re-heat it in the microwave! How many times do I have to tell you, to slowly warm lasagne in the oven? Next time, wait for me to come home. I'm supposed to be the cook, anyways."

"Don't maul the messenger." I sighed under my breath. I used a tea-towel to take the hot dish out of the appliance. "Or the person who was just trying to do something nice while you're slaving away at the Garage."

Suddenly, I heard a deafening SMASH!

"That was Brandon's fault!" She quickly called out.

"But Maia pushed me into it!" He was quick to refute.

What the hell was that?! Hastily, I walked into the lounge room where Maia and Brandon were standing awkwardly. On the floor between them, lay the pieces of my Venetian vase, which I had bought during our European holiday.

My cherished, hand-blown piece of Venice, I had bought during the first time Declan and I ever went away together; was now in tiny pieces over a five meter radius. The vase had completely smashed and there were shards scattered everywhere!

"W - w - what the hell happened...?!" I exhorted in both anger and shock.

"Maia pushed me into it!" He repeated as he pointed her way.

"Brandon said I was so ugly that he was surprised that Hiro would touch me at all, let alone with a six foot pole!" She pointed back.

The two were standing there with only their socks on, so I had to deal with the issue of safety first...then I'll kill them!

"Stay right there and don't move." I glared their way.

Fuming, I went to retrieve the 'wet & dry' vacuum cleaner from the linen closet. I returned with the machine and switched it on. I made the two stand there for a full ten minutes, whilst I vacuumed the whole room. I had to make sure there weren't any errant pieces which could find a way into their soft, human feet.

"Don't move!" I growled at Brandon, when I saw he was about to take a step. When I finished, I looked at the pair unhappily, "Fine, it's safe now."

Lastly, I carried the vacuum to the bin out the back of the house, so I could empty it. As I tipped out the waste compartment, I saw the sharp, sparkling pieces from the hand-crafted artwork, be laid to rest. Frickin' hell, I really liked that vase too.

When I carried the vacuum back into the house, I found the two fighting again. This time it was Maia, whom was knocked backwards into Declan's shelves! His prized, antique music collection, rocked precariously.

"HEY!" I roared at the two. They did a double-take when they saw my human blue eyes flash my Werewolf glowing turquoise. "Knock anything else over and I will pick the both of you up, run you down the hill, and throw you into the river!"

"But Aunt B - " Brandon started.

"I don't care who started it, but right now I'm ending it!" I snarled.

Both brother and sister exchanged wary glances at aggravating their supernatural Aunt. Next, I spun around and stalked into the kitchen to serve up. I was going to wait until Declan came home, but I think these two were playing up because they were tired and hungry. The sooner I feed them, the sooner I can put them to bed. Here's hoping...

I served up the lasagne and the salad in the kitchen, before I carried their food-laden plates over to the table.

"OK monsters, go and wash your hands then come and eat." I ordered.

Within two minutes, we three were sitting down and starting on our meals. When I cut into my slice of lasagne, I felt the pasta truly had hardened from being overcooked... double damn! I could hear Declan's dissatisfied growl, now.

Maia and Brandon were still throwing hateful looks at one another, but she ended it when she tried to talk to me again.

"Aunt B, you're a Werewolf so that makes you a strong, old woman..." she began, and I almost choked on my mouthful at how she made me sound like an old hag! "...so that means you're wise, right? What would you do about Hiro?"

I would tell the loser to go jump - particularly into the river in the middle of winter. I wanted to tell her that she shouldn't be ignored by her boyfriend, especially after she told him to stop groping her. I didn't like the lack of respect he treated her with.

Just as I opened my mouth to tell her this, I stopped myself. Once upon a time Declan used to run hot and cold. It was when he was fighting his feelings for me, in respect of his little brother who also had designs in that area.

So I tried a different tact, "I think that you should open the door to communication. Talk to Hiro and hear his side before you make a decision. Ask him why he was ignoring you in school? Tell him how that made you feel. If he doesn't have a good reason then you can tell him to go jump."

"Yeah and if you do, make sure you do it in front of his friends like Steve and Jason!" Brandon's eyes widened, in excitement.

"Who are Steve and Jason?" I turned his way.

"Two of the school's biggest losers!" He rolled his eyes. "Just because they're on the football team and Jason's parents are away a lot, so he can hold lots of parties; they think they're so cool!"

"They're not like that!" She snapped.

"You're just saying that because you're dating Hiro, so you're invited now." Brandon sneered.

"Yeah right! I was invited to their Halloween party last year before Hiro asked me out!" Maia tried to defend herself.

"You were only asked, because Hiro, Steve and Jason had a bet that they were going to 'score' that night with either you, or the other girls that they'd invited." He quipped.

Maia's face fell and I was starting to really dislike this Hiro, Jason and Steve. I felt a growl start to crawl up my throat, as my nails grew a little longer. I looked down and saw this, whilst they were drumming on top of the table.

"Maybe I should have a 'talk' with these boys." I said coldly.

"No Aunt B, don't!" She cried out worriedly.

Brandon cracked up laughing at the idea of his Great x4 Grandaunt who as a Lokoti Werewolf, put the three non-Lokoti boys, in their place.

"Go on Aunt B! Do it!" He guffawed. "Take Uncle Declan with you! If those three losers saw the two of you angry, they'd definitely treat Maia and I, with more respect!"

"Shut up, Brandon!" Maia's face turned bright red.

"I'd love to see their faces, if they heard Uncle Declan growl and saw his eyes glow!" He went on.

"Stop it!" She kicked her brother under the table.

Just then the front door opened and the subject of conversation, came inside. The kids had been so loud, I didn't notice the sound of his pick up truck, pull up outside. His denim work clothes were dirty and he looked tired.

"Who am I supposed to be scaring?" Declan greeted, showing he had overheard.

"Maia's soon-to-be ex-boyfriend and his two loser friends." Brandon eagerly filled him in.

I noticed my mate was looking on the fact that we had started without him, in mild offence.

"Sorry we didn't wait, but these two are tired and hungry." I sighed as he walked past into the kitchen, to grab his plate.

"Aw, B!" He immediately complained. "You heated up the lasagne in the microwave again, didn't you?"

"Then chuck it out and cook up a whole new lasagne for yourself!" I flared.

Declan ignored me as he came and sat down at the table with his meal. However overcooked lasagne or not, he was soon cutting up his food and scoffing it down, hungrily.

"Thank god that there's another male in the house!" Brandon declared. "I've been hearing Maia whine all afternoon, about her boyfriend troubles!"

"Is this the kid that I'm meant to scare the crap out of?" My mate asked in amusement.

"She's going out with this idiot on the football team, who's only nice to her when he wants some." The 15 year old, summed up.

"Shut up Brandon, or so help me I'll kill you and then I'll dump your body in the river!" She shrieked in embarrassment.

My husband's eyes narrowed as he looked from Maia to Brandon, before he enquired, "So what does this idiot look like and where does he live?"

The 17 year old girl waved her knife at her brother, "Not one word!"

But he ignored her, "Hiro Yakasake has a Japanese appearance. He's not that tall but he is strong. He says his grandfather was a Sumo Wrestler."

I think he was enjoying the idea of setting up the jock for the scare of his life.

"Sorry Declan, I've already marked this one as my quarry." I said coolly.

"No Aunt B, let Uncle Declan have him!" The boy whined. "He's bigger than you."

I looked on unimpressed, "Our nephew thinks you're more dangerous than I am."

"I am more dangerous than you." My mate said matter-of-factly.

"Oh, so the fact that I'm also a Circulator, is no never mind? Or my Gran who was another Circulator, was the one who took down the European Werewolf who changed you?" I asked sarcastically.

He pretended to think, "Nope! I'm still more dangerous than you."

Brandon began to laugh again, as he liked it when his Werewolf Aunt and Uncle argued about their supernatural differences.

"You are not!" I rebuked. "Trust me, I think this Hiro is going to be a darn sight more worried about what I can do with my sword!"

"But I think Uncle as a European Werewolf looks a lot more scarier, Aunt." The teenaged boy disagreed.

"Nobody is going to harm my boyfriend!" The love-sick girl said adamantly.

"Maia sweetie..." my mate looked on his great x4 grandniece, "...I'm not going to harm him, well not right away. I'm going to have a talk with him, man to man."

"Will claws be used in this 'talk'?" The boy asked hopeful.

In a huff, she stood up and carried her half-eaten plate into the kitchen. We heard her drop it into the sink before she stormed past and upstairs to her room. Next, we heard a loud BANG! when Maia slammed her bedroom door behind.

Unperturbed, my mate carried on, "So what kind of car does this idiot drive?"

"A red Jeep Cherokee." He answered.

My fingers drumming on top of the table turned louder, as I could tell he was planning something.

"Declan, didn't you hear me when I said that *I* would handle this?" I asked in annoyance.

"Yeah I heard you," he said coolly before he turned back at Brandon. "So again I ask, where does this kid live?"

"Brandon, not one word." I ordered.

The boy looked torn as he glanced from his Aunt to his Uncle, as he was worried about angering one of us.

"B, this is a guy thing." My husband said simply.

"No it's not."

"Yes it is."

"No it's not! Maia came to me first, which makes it a girl thing!"

"Trust me B, a teenaged male all juiced up on testosterone, is NOT going to be afraid of a verbal warning by a hot woman that smells as good as you. This one's for me."

"He will be when I deliver the warning as a territorial Werewolf, looking after her young!"

"He's NOT going to see you in your supernatural form!" Declan barked back. "No humans in Alma can know that my wife is a Werewolf! It's going to stay that way and that's that!"

I crossed my arms as I sat back and glared at him. "What is this? You think just because we're married you can boss me about?"

"No, it's an order from your Second in the pack." He seethed.

Screw this, I thought as I too lost my appetite.

The sexist males were left sitting alone at the table, when I also stood up and carried my unfinished plate into the kitchen.

The next morning, Declan's digital alarm clock woke us up at 7 AM. Normally, we would rise at 7.30 however with the kids staying, we'd set it earlier to get them off to school on time. The mornings we slept in, were either on a weekend or after a hunt during a full moon.

My mate beat me downstairs as usual and when I eventually came down, I found him in the kitchen. He was not only making himself a packed lunch, but Maia and Brandon as well. I brushed past, to turn on the kettle and make my morning coffee, whilst watching him in the corner of my eye.

He was smearing some slices of wholegrain bread with pesto, before layering some cold meat and salad in between.

"You want a sandwich too?" He offered. "I can put it in the fridge and you can take it out at lunch time."

"No thanks." I answered. "I'm going to Circulate HQ today, so I'll use one of the meal synthesizers in the Mess Hall."

He passed me a long look, before he completed the lunches.

"What are you going to do there?" He wondered aloud.

"Research for my next trip back in time." I replied.

I tipped the milk and then the artificial sweetener, into my beverage. Then I picked up the hot mug and held it in both hands to enjoy the warmth, before taking a sip. Mmm... nothing beats your first cup of coffee for the day.

Declan turned quiet for a moment as he wrapped up the sandwiches and then put them into three paper bags, along with a banana each.

Eventually he asked, "Whereabouts is Taurus Six anyways?"

"On the far side of the Milky Way Galaxy." I educated. "It's inside of an unstable, gaseous, green coloured nebula."

"An *unstable* nebula?" He echoed unhappily. "That doesn't sound very safe."

"It's only unsafe for space ships who try to enter." I shrugged it off. "But Taurus Six is a Terran-Class planet, with vegetation and a breathable atmosphere. Since I instantaneously phase to the surface, I don't have to go through the nebula, do I?"

"B," my mate began, as he put the ingredients back into the fridge. "Maybe you should wait until I come home from work? You haven't taken me to this second headquarters yet and I should see it for myself, if it's safe or not."

"Declan," I put down my coffee to object, "what's with the, 'I'm the boss' attitude lately? I've been to the back-up headquarters PLENTY of times, and you've never complained. Besides, I don't think the Circulate's best minds would be stupid enough to set up a base camp, inside a keg of dynamite."

He opened his mouth to argue further, when we were interrupted by another arguing pair in the shapes of brother and sister.

"You're such a bathroom hog! I almost peed myself, waiting for you to finish!" The boy grouched.

The immaculately groomed 17 year old, retorted, "When don't you pee yourself, Brandon?"

"Ha ha!" He sung sarcastically. "Just admit it Maia, you take so long in the bathroom to try and make yourself look pretty, because you really are a hog."

"Alright you two, knock it off," their Uncle growled. "Here are your lunches and I'll give you both a ride to school today."

"No!" Maia looked horrified at the idea of being seen with a parental figure. "I want to catch the bus."

"I don't mind a lift." Her brother said amiably.

"That's because you have no social status in school, so you don't care who you're seen with!" She snapped. "I'll catch the bus with Lucy and Nina."

With that, she snatched up her lunch and her school bag, before flouncing out the front door.

Their Uncle rolled his eyes at his niece's behaviour and then he turned to plant a kiss on their Aunt's cheek.

"I'm gonna be home late again." He said as his farewell. "But text message me when you're back from Taurus Six."

"Yes sir." I mockingly gave a salute. But before the males could disappear, I sung out knowingly, "You driving Brandon to school today, wouldn't be related in anyway to you trying to see what this Hiro looks like, would it?"

Both Brandon and Declan stopped in the front doorway to look back. Whereas the boy appeared surprised, the older man was trying not to smirk. Lastly, he threw me a wink then he shut the door behind.

*****

As soon as my teeth and hair were brushed, I locked up the house whilst I was still inside. Then in a bright flash of light, I disappeared from our living room in Alaska, to reappear in another bright brilliance, inside of the Viewing Room on Taurus Six. The electromagnetic interference by this mode of travel caused the screens to momentarily show static, before returning to normal.

"Welcome to Circulate Headquarters, Bianca." The female voice of the Circulate Mainframe, greeted.

"Hey CM," I said back, as I took one of the three seats in the room. "How are you today?"

"All systems are operating within normal parameters." She reported. "How may I assist you?"

Instead of typing my instructions into the crystallized control panel in front, I sat back into the chair and gave voice commands instead.

"I'd like to see how the conference is going, as well as do some research for my next circulation through time."

The computer responded, "Would you like me to show you day four of the congregation?"

"Yes please."

The huge, upside down, three-sided, crystal pyramid which was slowly turning around in the centre of the room; instantly changed it's images.

In one side, it had shown a scene of Ancient Egypt in 2,000 BC, in the second triangle it had the Roman Forum in 200 AD and the last scene, it had showed my house in Alaska from the date I had just left, 2227 AD. All of these were now replaced by the view of the United Nations Headquarters, in New York City.

I was looking at an amphitheatre, which had a crowded seating area around a podium where somebody was speaking.

The delegates whom were sitting down, were listening with their assistants taking notes on iPad's or laptops. I spotted Julius and Therese Sabre, sitting behind three Lokoti Tribal Elders, whom were paying attention to the speaker. Therese was typing away in her laptop, as Julius leaned in to show one of our Elder's some information, on his iPad. The Elder took the iPad from him and then passed it to the woman in the expensive suit, who must have been one of Hodge Endeavor's legal team.

"Would you like me to activate the sound so you can hear what the speaker is saying?" The computer offered.

"Please."

Instantly, the Viewing Room was filled by a male voice, speaking in an authoritative manner.

"...as you can see, the plutonium-eating microbes, are combating the radiation spill in the National Park." The speaker pointed at the large screen behind him, which showed scenes of Kakadu, in Australia. "We are developing more microbes, to apply to the other damaged areas to ensure the contamination doesn't spread."

It was here the Hodge Endeavor lawyer, passed on the iPad to an Australian Aboriginal Tribal Elder who next put up their hand.

"But how long is it going to take the microbes to eat all of the radiation?" The dark-skinned woman, interrupted. "According to this data, the Hodge Endeavor Environmental Department say it's going to be at least 24 months! The flora and fauna are already dying by your mining disaster. Kakadu doesn't have 24 months!"

"Hutchins Earth & Minerals, are doing all they can to minimize the damage." The suited speaker said guiltily.

"No, Hutchins Earth & Minerals are doing all they can to try not to be sued!" The woman rebuked. "But you're too late. The Hodge Endeavor Legal

Department says not only can we sue, but we can prevent you doing any further damage by breaking your contract."

This made the speaker go on the defensive, "But our contract is with the Australian Government, not with the Gagudju People."

"That means we can sue you both!" The woman fired back. "And when the Government sees the size of the damages we can claim, do you really think that they'll continue to ally themselves with you?"

I could see the speaker, whom must have been a lawyer for the corporation in the wrong; was rallying to the debate. He too was holding an iPad, which controlled the images on the large screen behind the podium. He changed the image of Kakudu, to show his corporation's contract. But before I could hear the company's excuses, I cut him off.

"Computer, cease audio."

The Circulate Mainframe instantly returned silence to the Viewing Room, so I was simply looking on the conference instead of listening to it.

"What can Hodge Endeavor do, to help the contamination of Kakudu National Park?" I ordered.

The Mainframe went quiet for a few seconds, as it computed. Then it offered, "Hodge Endeavor has a medical lab close by, outside of Jakarta in Indonesia. The pharmaceutical facility could be converted to a bio-chemical lab to produce more plutonium-eating microbes."

"Do it." I stood up from the chair and began to pace around the glass-top, circular desk, on which the three crystallized control panels were placed. "Don't charge the Gagudju People for this service, but charge the Australian Government. They're partially to blame for what's happened, so let them pick up the tab."

"Acknowledged." The computer chirped. "The cost would be 3.3 billion credits."

"Say what?" I paused in surprise. "Can the Australian Government afford it?"

"The Australian Government would not be able to pay the 3.3 billion credits for the microbes, as well as the 6.7 billion credits in damages that the lawsuit will ensue, without raising taxes."

"Then contact the Hodge Endeavor Legal Department as well as the Gagudju People. Wrangle a deal that nobody sues anybody, if the Australian Government will pay for the microbes, to get this disaster fixed faster." I thought on my feet.

"Acknowledged," the computer complied and I noticed the crystallized control panels glow, as it acted on my commands.

My Calculator Vincent once explained to me that the Circulate Mainframe could send messages to me as well as Hodge Endeavor, on beams of light travelling through space and time. The light beams were of a high frequency on the light spectrum that the eye couldn't see, and were partially related to the way a Circulator could phase through time. The same frequency of light which could escape Black Holes or others which could pass through solid matter, was similar to a Circulator's light frequency.

Although the Circulate Mainframe could send emails and text messages through time to either myself or other Circulators, Calculators or even Hodge Endeavor; we couldn't reply the same way. The technology for that hadn't been invented yet, which was why the Mainframe operated smoothly and efficiently with its futuristic, 25th Century systems. The smart computer which acted as Calculator to the last Circulator in human history, consistently watched over my well-being via the Viewing Room; as its sentient programming could also maintain itself with self-diagnostics.

I liked the Mainframe, we had always gotten along well. Its core directives were to keep its charge safe from harm, and to make sure I didn't irreparably damage humanity's timeline. I liked the idea of the computer acting as my Calculator, because in my opinion, it seemed to be doing exactly what Vincent had done anyways. He was a Calculator and although he could see through time; he couldn't phase through time like a Circulator could. Whereas the human Calculator saw through time via visions, the computerized Calculator saw through time by specialized beams of light.

"Bianca," my computer – slash – Calculator, spoke again. "You should know that Hutchins Earth & Mining has also applied to the Alaskan Government to drill in the Arctic Ocean."

This stopped me in my tracks, "No way in hell!"

"I would recommend that we send instructions to Hodge Endeavor's Legal Department to obstruct the application." The Mainframe plotted. "The Elders of several Native Alaskan Tribes including Lokoti, would support this decision."

"Right." I stood still as I thought aloud. "Send this information to Julius and Therese Sabre's email account. Let's give the Lokoti and the other Native Alaskan Tribal Elders, a heads-up with this information. Maybe while they're combating Hutchins Earth & Mining over this debacle, it will put off the corporation from making another."

"Agreed." The computer chirped once more.

Then I saw the effects of the computer's work, when the images showed the Sabre's faces as they received our message. Julius passed another iPad to the Elder to show them, which the Elder read before passing it to the Hodge Endeavor Lawyer. Now the Caucasian woman in the expensive suit stood up, to interrupt the Hutchins Earth & Mining speaker, in his haute couture clothing.

I didn't have to hear what she said, when I and the rest of the conference, saw the man turn pale.

*****

I was feeling pretty proud of our little feat when I phased home at the end of the day.

Once I had reformed into my solid shape, I went over to the bookshelves to retrieve my laptop. I plugged the crystallized computer chip, into the USB port and switched the technology on. Then I downloaded the historical information onto my hard drive that the Circulate Mainframe had retrieved for me. Lastly, I sat down at the dining table to start on my academic work.

I returned to my paper on, 'Female Deities in Ancient Mythology: Early Expectations On Women'; and incorporated the images I had saved from the Viewing Room. The Circulate Mainframe had helped me search for pictures of one of the sub-themes; the roles of wives in the ruling houses of the ancient cultures. As my formal paper was on the computer, I used a pen and paper to jot down some personal notes. I was thinking of circulating through time, to visit an Ancient Egyptian wedding during the Middle Kingdom.

Whereas a normal person may make a 'what to pack' list for an upcoming holiday; I wrote down my ideas of what to wear, how to have my hair, and how I could smuggle my digital camera back in time.

With the heat of Egypt, even the upper classes could dress as scantily as the lower classes did. It wasn't just the men walking around topless but sometimes the women as well. I knew my husband would hit the roof, if my breasts were bared. I decided to wear a large, flat, gold necklace, which could cover that area of my body and it would look appropriate amongst the rich.

Suddenly, I was interrupted by a very loud, BAM!

Startled, I turned to see a furious Maia standing in the front doorway. She had flung open the door so hard, it banged against the wall. She stood there seething, wearing a mask of indignation whilst her hands rested on her hips.

"Hiro broke up with me today!" She proclaimed. "And when he did it, he kept apologizing for what happened in the cinema! He was so nervous, he wouldn't look me in the eye! What the hell did Uncle Declan do to him?!"

"Say what?" I shook my head in confusion. "Why do you think your Uncle has something to do with it?"

"I hate him!" The 17 year old cried out overdramatically. "It's all his fault!"

With that, she stormed through the living room and upstairs to the guest bedroom where I heard another loud BANG!

Frickin' hell, I'm not going to get any work done with this melodrama going on. Wearily, I rose from the table and followed after my grandniece. Tentatively, I knocked on the bedroom door she had slammed shut, before making my way inside.

"OK," I took a deep breath, "let's start from the beginning. Tell me exactly what happened today."

Maia was lying face-down on top of one of the single beds, sobbing her heart out.

"C'mon sweetie, tell me all your problems." I sat down beside to rub her back sympathetically. "You never know, I might be able to help somehow."

"My social status in school is over!" She sniffed. "No boy will ever date me again!"

"I'm sure that's not true." I pulled her upright so I could see her face. "You're a very pretty girl and just because one horny toad treated you disrespectfully -"

"You're just as bad as HIM!" Maia pushed my hands away.

"I'm as bad as who?"

"The interfering Uncle Declan!" She re-collapsed into her pillow.

"Then tell me what you think he did, to make Hiro break up with you!" I cried out, exasperated.

She wiped her cheeks as she sat up to face her Aunt. "I don't know exactly, but all I know is when I got off the school bus, I saw Uncle Declan was in the student car park from dropping off Brandon. He was walking back to his truck, away from Hiro who was standing by his jeep. When I started to walk towards him to say 'hi', Hiro went white as a sheet and ran off in the opposite direction! Then at recess, he dumped me!"

Just then I snorted, which made her look on betrayed. I tried not to laugh, but it didn't work. I couldn't stop myself from roaring with laughter!

"This ISN'T funny!" The girl stood up in indignation. "I'm never going to be invited to the cool parties, ever again!"

"Sweetheart, from what I hear what girls have to do, to be invited to these so-called, 'parties'? Maybe that's a good thing." I tried to point out.

"You don't understand!" She wailed. "The snobby girls were just starting to talk to me. All the boys noticed me. Now I'm down at the bottom of the food chain and no boy will ever ask me out again!"

With that, she swept from the room to go and sulk in another part of the house.

*****

That evening, my husband came home from work earlier than expected. However the sound which came from his truck, were two doors shutting instead of one. When the front door opened, in human form a European Werewolf and a Lokoti Werewolf, crossed the threshold.

"Hi honey, I'm home!" Declan's voice rang out.

I came out from the kitchen, where I had been contemplating on what to make for dinner.

"Forrest?" I looked in surprise at our unexpected guest. "What are you doing here?"

"Hi Aunt B," my Riverclaw relation gave a wave. "Uncle Dec asked me to come to dinner."

"Yeah, I wanted to say thanks for his help at the Garage today." My mate said appreciatively. "Bruce called in sick and I still had three vehicles to fix."

"You worked at the Garage today?" I looked on the younger Werewolf.

"Um, yeah I helped out Uncle Dec, Gracie and Phil, with the repairs." Forrest's face flushed with modesty.

From what I understood, since completing High School the Lokoti Werewolf paid his way by doing odd-jobs around the tribe. One day, he was cleaning gutters, another fixing a roof and then the next, repairing somebody's plumbing. So it didn't surprise me he also knew his way around a plasma-powered engine.

"So, what's for dinner?" I looked on my mate expectantly, as I didn't feel like cooking.

"I think we've still got some mince and pasta sheets left over, so I was thinking cannelloni." He breezed past, through the kitchen entryway.

I stood back and watched my husband wash his hands first, before picking out the ingredients from either the fridge or pantry.

Forrest stood politely yet awkwardly, by the dining table.

"Oh I'm sorry, would you like a glass of water, or juice or root beer?" I offered.

"The root beers sounds good." He gave a nod.

"Yeah, me too." Declan included himself.

I took three glasses out of the cupboard to serve the beverages. As soon as they were poured, Forrest took a glass and my mate helped himself to another. The males gulped them down, whilst I returned the bottle of soda to the fridge. By the time I picked up my glass, they were putting their empty ones down.

"So, what did the Circulate computer say today?" My husband enquired as he began to cook.

"Oh, nothing much..." I drawled as I nursed my drink, "...the timeline is behaving itself, and I'm planning my next circulation in time to a wedding during the Middle Kingdom of Egypt. Oh yeah, it's also helping me sue the multinational corporation, Hutchins Earth & Mining for causing a disaster in Kakadu National Park."

"Where's that?" Forrest asked interestedly.

"The Northern Territory, in Australia." I informed.

"Oh yeah, you have some distant relations in Australia, don't you Aunt B?" He remembered.

"So do you." Declan chuckled. "Except in your case, they're very distant now."

"Yeah..." he nodded along, "...we're something like ten times removed now, aren't we?"

"Probably." My mate shrugged, as he began to roll up the mince inside the raw pasta sheets. "B hardly talks to the Baker family now, as they barely remember us."

At that moment, we were interrupted by Brandon coming home. He was puffing as if he had run, whilst carrying his schoolbag on his back and a soccer ball under one arm. He often played sport in the community centre on tribal lands, after school.

"Forrest!" The 15 year old's eyes lit up.

"Hiya Brandon, how are ya?" The 20 year old greeted amiably.

Then the teenager dropped what he was carrying, and rammed the much bigger and stronger, Lokoti Werewolf! The younger and older males engaged in a play fight, with the older easily fending off the younger. It got to the stage where Forrest was fighting Brandon with just one arm, which made Declan and I laugh.

The members of the pack were treated a little like celebrities by the humans of the tribe. People could still stare at Declan and I, when we left our house on top of the hill and shopped in the general store, or ran errands about tribal lands. Where the townspeople in Alma lived in ignorance of what went on, the Lokoti bonded over the supernatural secret.

"Stop cheating!" Brandon taunted his stronger opponent.

"You wish!" Forrest guffawed.

Then to the Aunt and Uncle's amusement, we watched the young man easily pick up the boy, sling him over his shoulder and begin to spin him around!

"I'm gonna be sick! I'm gonna be sick!" The teenager threatened. "I'm gonna throw up, all down your back!"

"If you do, I'll hunt you instead of moose on the next full moon!" The Werewolf returned.

However, the fun and mayhem was interrupted by the unhappy voice coming from the top of the stairs. "What's all this racket? I can't concentrate on my trigonometry homework!"

Immediately, the young man halted as I watched him raise his head. Then he completely froze and by doing so, he accidentally dropped his load! Brandon landed head first on the floor with an audible, "Oomph!"

"Oow, that's gotta hurt." Declan flinched in sympathy.

I put aside my drink to help him up. "Are you OK?"

"Forrest!" The teenaged male whacked the older one on the arm, but it was barely acknowledged.

We watched the young man slowly move towards the staircase as his eyes never left what they beheld.

"Hi Maia, how are you?" He asked in a tight voice.

The 17 year old gave the 20 year old a funny look at first, and then we saw her face turn pink.

"Um, I'm OK thanks Forrest. How are you?" She managed back, shyly.

I whispered to my mate, who was standing nearby, "Oh now it's OK, when earlier this afternoon, her world had ended."

Declan emitted a snicker, as he proceeded to place the rolled up, raw cannelloni into a baking tray.

"I've been invited to dinner." The Lokoti Werewolf told her. "Will we have the pleasure of your company tonight?"

The Lokoti girl almost giggled back, "I was going to meet up with Lucy, Nina and Tash tonight, but I suppose I could stick around."

"Really?" Forrest's eyes lit up. "So you didn't have a date with that Japanese boy, I occasionally see you with?"

"Who, Hiro?" She scoffed. "Hell no, he's long gone!"

"So the 'talk' worked then?" Brandon asked his Uncle, in amusement.

He nudged his nephew to shut up, especially when his wife shot a wary look his way.

"Here, make yourself useful." Declan shoved the table cloth into the teenager's arms.

I stood back to let the boy set the table for dinner, whilst subtly watching his sister talk to her next romantic suitor.

Just then I felt a kick to the leg as my husband hissed, "Would you quit staring?"

Reluctantly, I moved from the entryway to sit up on the kitchen bench. Our cook had placed the tray of cannelloni, smothered in sauce, into the oven and was now slicing up the ingredients for a salad. Whenever Brandon was out of earshot by putting the next items onto the table, I interrogated my husband.

"So, how was Brandon's ride to school this morning?" I began.

"As much as you'd expect; we hopped in the truck, I turned on the ignition and the truck moved." He gave his glib reply.

"Did you get out of the said truck, at any stage?"

"Nope, I sat in it all day and from behind the wheel, I instructed my mechanics on what to do."

Now it was my turn to kick him, to turn off the sarcasm. He chuckled once more as he sliced the capsicum, before scattering it over the lettuce.

"So you didn't walk away from a red Jeep Cherokee, back to your truck which was in the student car park?" I continued.

"I may have walked away from a particular red Jeep Cherokee."

"And away from a certain Japanese-background student?"

"There may have been a student of that description, standing beside the said Jeep."

"Well, what did you say to him?"

"I asked him if he's ever seen the 20th Century movie called 'Uncle Buck'."

"You asked him if he's seen a movie which was made 200 years ago?"

He recanted, "When he said no, I told him it had one of my favourite actors in it, called John Candy. When he didn't have a clue of what I was talking about, I started to tell him about the story, of an Uncle looking after his nephews and nieces, while the parents are away. I told him that there was this particularly funny part, where the Uncle scares off the sleazy and therefore, undesirable boyfriend. I started to laugh about the scene where the Uncle opens up the boot and the said boyfriend is inside, after being kidnapped from a party where under-aged drinking and sexual activities were taking place."

It was here our nephew interjected, "And then the meat-head for a jock, finally got a clue. And can you believe it, he tried to scare off Uncle Declan by saying he knows Sumo Wrestling!"

"Thanks Brandon, but you can go and put out the bread and butter plates." His Uncle ordered him away. As soon as he had walked off with the crockery, my husband continued. "So I happened to have been touching the said, red Jeep Cherokee when the vehicle starts to lean on a peculiar angle."

My mouth fell open in horror, "You didn't lift up the truck to show off your supernatural strength, which finally frightened off the kid?"

"You could say that the right side of the said Jeep, wasn't exactly touching the ground at that stage."

"Declan!" My hand whipped out to deliver a slap to his arm. "You're always lecturing me about not giving myself away and then you go and do THIS?!"

"B, my eyes weren't glowing and I kept my teeth and claws to myself." He promised, as he scattered sliced cucumber around the salad bowl next.

"He did, Aunt B." The 15 year old stuck up for his 164 year old Uncle. "There's no way that Hiro would know Uncle Dec's a Werewolf. The jock is so stupid, I don't think he'd even know what a Werewolf was!"

"You - upstairs and doing homework - now!" I shooed him away.

"Aw, can't I do it after dinner?" The boy whined. "I haven't got much to do anyway."

"Alright then Brandon, you can help me instead." My husband relented. "I'm gonna teach you how to make home-made garlic bread."

Next, my mobile phone beeped to alert me to a message. I took it out of my pocket to see it was from the Circulate Mainframe. It was sending me a status report of converting the pharmaceutical company, into a bio-chemical lab. It advised that the Indonesian staff had already begun preparations to produce the plutonium-eating microbes, as well as ways of transporting it the short distance to the Northern Territory.

"Who's that?" Declan leaned in to see the screen.

"The Circulate Mainframe." I announced. "Preparations are underway and we could have the plutonium-eating microbes, being shipped to Kakadu by the end of next week."

"Oh is this about that mining accident in the National Park?" Brandon looked impressed. "Mom mentioned something about that on the phone last night. In school, we're doing a debate on it, for Legal Studies."

"That's my B." My mate said proudly, as he slathered the French rolls with garlic butter. "Your Uncle slaves away in the Garage or kitchen, whilst your Aunt secretly controls world affairs."

This made the teenager pass a pleading look my way. "Hey Aunt B, could you help me with my homework tonight? I'm supposed to be on the 'against team' to sue Hutchins Earth & Mining."

I almost laughed at the boy's about turn, from hero-worshipping the male Werewolves to now seeing his Circulator for an Aunt, in a new light.

"Yeah, I suppose I could." I smiled back. "But I'm not going to write it for you and you'll still have to do the research yourself. I'm just going to point you in the right direction."

"Really?" He looked grateful at this. "Thanks Aunt B, you're the best!"

Then he took off out of the kitchen and ran past Maia and Forrest who were talking amongst themselves, to get his textbooks.

*****

During dinner, the 20 year old's attentiveness towards the 17 year old, ran at record levels. She didn't have to reach for the salad bowl or slices of garlic bread, all she had to do was look at something and he would immediately pass it to her. When Brandon looked like he was about to take the last piece of bread, Forrest snatched it up and put it on her plate instead.

"I asked Maia if she would like to go on a picnic with me this weekend." The Lokoti Werewolf spoke politely to the European Werewolf, "With your permission of course, Uncle."

"I don't mind." My mate shrugged. "I know where you live."

"Uncle Dec, stop it!" Her face reddened in embarrassment.

"Ignore him, Forrest." I shook my head. "Maia and Brandon's parents will be home from the conference, so they'll be back under their 'jurisdiction'."

"But still, Uncle Dec is her elder and he's my Second in the pack." His eyes dropped respectfully. "It's protocol that I ask him too."

"Don't encourage him!" I moaned as I stood up from the table. "His ego is big enough as it is."

"That's my wife for you," he sung sarcastically, "can't you feel the love, honour and obey vibe, just radiating out of her?"

Forrest chuckled quietly, as I rolled my eyes at Declan's behaviour.

"OK Maia, since your brother set the table, it's your turn to clear it tonight." I ordered.

"I'll help clean up." Her suitor was quick to jump to his feet and began to collect everyone's plates.

"Forrest," my mate said dryly, "I've paid you and now I've fed you, for your work at the Garage today. Go home. The kids have homework to do."

Obediently, the young man gave a smile to his amore, a respectful nod to his Aunt and his Second, and lastly a wave to the boy. "G'night all."

"See ya tomorrow." My mate watched him leave before he turned to his niece. "Weren't you in the middle of trigonometry or something, before you turned all goo-goo eyed?"

"Uncle!" She blushed again and with a crimson face, she cleared the table.

*****

My husband was tired from repairing vehicles all day and I was tired from instantaneously phasing all over the place. So we were quite happy to lie on the couch with our feet up, and watch a new horror movie on the Internet TV. The blood and guts of the story, hardly batted an eyelid from the Werewolf couple and I even caught his eyes begin to droop.

However, what kept us up was not the fighting on screen, but the kind which was going on upstairs.

"Brandon, turn that music off!" His sister yelled.

"No."

"You know I hate that song!"

"Yeah, I know." He chuckled as he turned the music up.

When he did, we could hear it as clear as a bell downstairs. We heard the 'Nine Inch Nails' song called 'Closer,' blast out. With the particularly graphic lyrics, I must admit that it wasn't my favourite song either. He had played it loudly yesterday too, to annoy her when my mate had been at work.

"Not this song again." I moaned.

Declan hit the 'pause' button on the remote to yell at Brandon to turn it down, when his eyes widened in alarm at the words in the chorus.

"What the hell...?!" He sat upright in shock.

I had to remain seated or be bowled over, when my mate jumped to his feet and stormed upstairs. I listened to what took place in the guest bedroom, when the music abruptly ended. I imagined Declan had ripped the speaker chord out of the boy's iPod.

"Uncle Declan..." the teenager objected, "...if it's too loud I CAN turn it down!"

"Brandon, if you ever play this song again, I will break your frickin' iPod! Do you understand me?" He snarled.

Maia cracked up laughing and I heard her applaud him.

"What's wrong with it?" The boy whined.

"What's frickin' right with it more like, and there's nothin' right!" His elder snapped.

"But it's just a song..." The boy back-pedalled.

"Tomorrow, you and I are going to go for a walk and have a long conversation about what's wrong with that song." His Uncle declared.

"Ha ha, sucked in!" Maia laughed at her little brother, for getting on their Uncle's bad side.

I had to admit, I found it impressive that Declan did that. I admired his attack-dog-like determination, to do what he thought was right. Either scaring off sleazy males, or teaching others to respect women; he would charge through a brick wall if he thought it had wronged a female family member.

Lastly, I heard his heavy footfall as he returned and I tried to hide my grin. As he fell back onto the couch, he replaced his arm about his wife and used his other to pick up the remote and resume the program. I ended up resting my right hand over my mouth, to try to hide the smile that kept escaping.

After a moment, he noticed what I was doing. He paused the program once more to ask in annoyance, "What are you laughing about?"

"I'm not laughing." I smilingly shook my head.

"Then what are you grinning about?"

"You."

"Me?"

"Yes, you."

"What about me?"

"Declan Domitian Sabre, patron saint to women. You're the defender of teenaged girls and the hero against sexually explicit songs, which are derogatory towards women." I pronounced.

"Saint, did you just call me a saint?" He looked incredulous. "I'm anything BUT a saint B, you should know that. I have the bloodlust burning me up inside and out and I know a little too well, what it's like to constantly fight for self-control. Human males don't have the bloodlust and it pisses me off when I hear the words, 'I couldn't control myself'. They CAN control themselves but they still try to shirk the blame."

"I know, Declan." I sighed, as I started at the TV screen. "I feel you battle your dangerous desires, everyday."

"You do?" He asked in surprise. "You know B, we've never really talked about this."

"Talked about what?"

"Male Lokoti Werewolves are empathically attuned to their female mates. Since you're a Lokoti Werewolf, I wonder if you feel my emotions?"

"Sometimes." I admitted.

"Heh heh! I have my very own female Lokoti Werewolf, who can wane when she's away from me." He chortled.

Grouchily, I took the remote out of his hand to hit the 'play' button.

"Hey!" He snatched it back. "Nobody has the remote control but me!"

"Hog."

"Yeah but you like it when I take control, admit it." He chuckled again.

"You wish!"

Laughingly, he placed a sloppy kiss on my cheek, before holding me closer as we resumed our movie.

~~~~~~

~ 4 ~

"B...!" My husband bellowed from downstairs. "It's10.45 AM, this thing starts in fifteen minutes!"

As usual, Declan was dressed and ready and waiting downstairs; whereas I rushed about our bedroom half dressed and undecided on what shoes or even a coat to wear, with my formal outfit.

"At this rate, the Bride will get there before us!" I heard him complain.

I tossed aside my black, high-heeled boots then my black, strappy, high-heeled sandals and even my black, high-heeled 'Mary-Jane' style shoes. None of these were right! Nothing would go with my red silk, cocktail dress I was wearing. Oh why oh why, do I only have black shoes in my wardrobe?

"Don't make me come up there and get you." He threatened.

Knowing my domineering, European Werewolf for a mate, he would. I started to panic as I went through my shoe collection. From past experience, Declan would grab me whether I was ready or not. Next, I heard his heavy jog up the stairs... oh oh.

He walked into the bedroom to catch me bent over in my short dress and black stockings, as I was rifling through my wardrobe. His eyes widened as he looked me over, appreciative of the way my legs were on display. I thought he looked good in his black suit and light blue, pressed shirt, which brought out his bright blue eyes.

However, when his mouth opened to berate, I beat him to the punch.

"I can't find the right shoes to wear with this dress!" I snapped. "So don't start!"

Coolly, Declan walked over and picked up my black, strappy high-heels from the floor which I had discarded earlier. Then he pulled me over to the side of our bed and sat me down, before sitting beside. When he proceeded to put the shoes on my feet, I objected.

"Not THESE ones!"

"Yep these ones."

"But they're sandals so they don't go with stockings!"

"They're strappy so they'll go with the cocktail dress." He put down my left foot and picked up my right to put the second on.

"I don't think so..." I started to argue, "...I want to change out of this dress."

"Don't even think about it!"

"But a dress isn't practical, especially not a cocktail dress. Maybe I should wear my black, pin-striped pants suit?"

Declan ignored my fretting and as soon as he finished, he grabbed my black, woollen overcoat, which was lying beside the others. He raised me to my feet as he simultaneously placed the warm garment about my shoulders. The next thing I knew, I found myself being traipsed down the stairs by my bossy husband.

"But – but – but what about my purse?" I halted half way down.

"I've got it." He held it up in the air.

"But – but – but I didn't put on any perfume!" I tried to pull back.

"You don't need any!" Declan snapped back. "Besides, with your pheromones I don't need anymore trouble."

"I HAVE to wear perfume if I'm all dressed and made up!"

When I attempted to turn around and go back, Declan bent over picked me up over his left shoulder!

"NOT AGAIN!" I complained. "Put me down! Put me down right now!"

He ignored my shouting as he carried me out the front door.

Casually, he closed and locked it behind, before he carried his wife down the porch steps to his pick up truck. He pointed his remote key at the vehicle to release the central locking and didn't put me down again until he lowered me onto the passenger's seat. Angrily, I shot him a glare which he also ignored, whilst he walked around the vehicle and opened the door for the driver's side.

He saw I was still seething as he sat down and did up his seatbelt. When he pressed in the ignition code to start the engine, he barked out, "You're one of the prettiest girls in the tribe, so stop acting so insecure every frickin' time you have to dress up to go out!"

"Bite me!"

"I wish." He muttered, as he reversed out of the driveway.

We drove down the hill and turned left at the first intersection. Instead of driving into the community centre, he turned towards the Holy Grounds which were situated in the quiet, glassy glade beside the river which flowed through tribal lands. He pulled up into the first available car space he saw, before he turned off the engine.

My husband was quick to jump out, walk around the truck and open my door to pull me out. I was reluctant to be seen with how self-conscious I felt. Walking hand-in-hand, he used his other which was holding the remote to reset the central locking. We joined the crowd as everyone had come today to witness Maia and Forrest's Joining Ceremony.

We were a little late, the bridal couple was already at the front of the gathering, along with their families. Declan half pushed and half excused our way through the throng of people, until we were standing with the Sabres and the Riverclaws. They stood before the Tribal Elders, who were behind a campfire which was burning in front of the Sacred Totems.

I halted as soon as I saw the bridal couple in the traditional 'skins' of our ancestral costume. Made from either caribou or moose hide, Forrest wore suede pants, shirt and a jacket, which was decorated with tassels and beads. Maia wore something similar, but instead of suede pants it was a long, suede skirt with moccasins on her feet.

I was hit by the strongest sense of déjà vu... I swear I was looking on Grant and I, standing before the Tribal Elders when it was our Joining Ceremony.

Both Forrest and Maia had their long, black hair either tied back or plaited in the traditional way. Their faces were painted with the 'claw mark' of the Lokoti Wolf, as were our Tribal Elders whom were also wearing the Lokoti clothes of old. In the background, we could hear the traditional drum beat which was played at many of our tribe's ceremonies.

The 24 year old groom led the 21 year old bride by the hand, to stand before the Tribal Elders. The council moved to sit in a half circle around the fire, which prompted the couple to lower themselves to the ground and then so did the rest of the tribe. Declan sat down first before he helped me because I felt awkward in my high-heels and cocktail dress. Once I was seated, I repositioned my woollen coat over my legs so not to give anything away.

"You have the council of Tribal Elders convened here for you today. What do you ask of us?" Chiron as one of the Elders, asked the couple.

Forrest spoke clearly for all to hear, "I have come to ask for the blessing of the Tribal Elders, as the Guides of the way of the Lokoti Wolf, to take this woman as my mate."

Declan squeezed my hand as we watched what took place.

"And do you have the permission of your family for this union?" Meadow as another one of the Elders, enquired.

"He does." Stone Riverclaw answered.

"And do you have the permission of the woman's family for this union?" Hazel Elm asked, another Elder.

Suddenly my mate spoke up, "He does."

Oh that's right, sometimes I forgot that Declan was the head of the Sabre family. He had been the older brother of Derik whose progeny lived on, which meant that my mate was the longest living member of the Sabre clan.

"He does." Julius Sabre said after him, who was Maia's father.

As the ceremony proceeded, I noticed in the corner of my eye Declan's solemn expression as he watched the ritual. I sensed inside of him, a touch of envy when he observed Forrest and Maia drink from the sacred Lokoti Tribal Cup, which looked like a small, wooden, painted bowl. As we observed the ceremony play out with reverence by our people, I felt his fingers fidget with my wedding ring. I sensed that in a way, he was wishing this could have been us.

I recalled long ago, something he said on the day he moved in, *"But don't you think that I would have liked a Joining Ceremony? Wouldn't it be nice if the whole tribe threw us a Housewarming too? But instead, we have our one-person celebration squad, of only my Mom supporting our relationship."*

In a small way, Declan and I did get a Housewarming, but he never got his Joining Ceremony.

This made me wonder, does he still wish that we had one? It was such an antiquated notion to me, these days many Lokoti preferred to have just the Housewarming. I was surprised when Forrest and Maia declared that they wanted a Joining Ceremony as well.

As I snuck many a glance towards my mate, I began to see that he saw differently. Declan was such an old fashioned romantic, more so than anyone ever suspected; including myself. The more I thought about this, I could see many similarities between his romanticism when compared to his faith.

Before World War Three, his parents had followed Catholicism. Afterwards, Declan was brought here to be raised on tribal lands in much the Lokoti way. However, his family did celebrate Christmases and Easters with mine, who also followed Christianity. Maybe there was a Catholic part of him that desired ritual and ceremony and pomp? There were many aspects about his life which were Catholic, aside from the gold crucifix he wore around his neck, which used to be his human mother's.

For one, he's only ever had one partner in the bedroom – me – now that was traditionally Catholic. When I was married to Grant, he did wait. Sometimes I wondered what he would have done if my first husband hadn't died early? Would he have given up waiting and left in search of another female Werewolf? When I thought about his bloodlust empowered lust, it was hard to imagine him waiting five years let alone a hundred.

The bloodlust demanded we partook in fresh flesh with regularity. The full moon heightened our cravings as its lunar cycle affected our brain chemistry. The taking of life kept up our supernatural strength and longevity. The same bloodlust which controlled our need to hunt, also goaded our sexual desires.

We had a daily routine of addressing our lust however, I had the distinct impression that his needs were greater than my own. Sometimes he would act like he was powerless to his hunger, as the act could either strengthen or weaken him. He could still wear this helpless look on his face, before and during sex especially if it came after a fight. I would lie on my side of the bed sulking, when the European Werewolf would either roll me onto my back or sidle up behind before removing my garments. No matter how angry he was, he still made the first move.

It's hard to imagine what it'd be like to still be married to my first husband. My second mate permeated through almost every aspect of my life. We hunted together, we fought each other, we fought together... Declan had managed to ingratiate himself into every facet of my being. It was like, not only was I the centre of his universe, but he also demanded the same. Even if I sat at the dining table, doing my academic work whilst he was in the kitchen cooking dinner; he would be firing off constant questions about what I was working on.

"So Heracles was Hercules?" He would ask.

"Yep."

"Then why is the name different?"

"It's a culture thing. Heracles was Greek whereas Hercules was more Roman." I shrugged.

He would cook and then growl at me if I didn't eat all of my dinner. I would do his laundry and growl at him if he left things in his pockets. We fought over the remote for the Internet TV whilst we argued about which program to watch. Yet our long years of marriage made us so alike, we ended up liking what the other put on.

Gratefully, I rested my head on his shoulder and he planted an appreciative kiss on my forehead.

Just then all of the Tribal Elders stood up, which prompted the bridal couple to stand too, as did everyone else.

"You have the blessing of the Lokoti Wolf over your union. You may leave us to start your new lives together. Go with the blessing of your Tribal Elders." Chiron announced.

Declan held me close, as we stood back and waited for everyone to finish congratulating the 'newlyweds' before we could. I caught an expression of longing on his face, as we watched from afar the dressed-up couple greet the tribe together. I started to wonder if it wasn't just that he missed out on having a Joining Ceremony, but maybe it's because he still felt like an outsider sometimes?

My mate stuck out with his blonde hair and blue eyes against the majority of the Lokoti, with their black hair and brown eyes. There were a couple of members of the tribe who had black hair but whose eyes weren't brown because they weren't full Lokoti; like I wasn't either.

I inherited my dark blue eyes from my maternal grandparents. My English grandmother had wavy, chestnut brown hair and bright blue eyes. My grandfather was three-quarter Lokoti, as his grandmother had also been Caucasian; so he had the strong Lokoti Werewolf build and black hair, but he too had blue eyes. Although there was a multi-cultural element to our tribe, Declan's blonde hair still stood out.

Smilingly, I turned to my tall, strong, blonde-haired mate. "You look very handsome by the way, in your suit."

"Really?" He looked on, pleasantly surprised.

"Yup." I grinned. "A fancy black suit, suits you."

"Yeah well, too bad my wife won't let me wear a tie with it." He jested.

He was referring to the fact that every time he tried to put on this fashion accessory, I was quick to remove it. With his thick neck thanks to his muscle bulk, it didn't look right. I also told him to keep his top button undone because if he didn't, he could look like he had no neck in a collared shirt.

"You didn't need a tie baby," I leaned in to say in a sultry voice. "You're all man, so much so that the tie is jealous of you."

A snicker escaped before he growled playfully, "Keep talking like that and you may find you won't need clothes anymore, either."

"Ah here we are, Uncle Declan and Aunt Bianca." A male voice interrupted.

The middle-aged but strong appearance of Wade Elm, came to stand before us. He was a Lokoti Werewolf like his late grandfather, Stuart Elm had been. I was close to the Elm family, not just because I was once married to one. But because Grant's older brother Ian, had been best friends with my father.

He complained, "Look at you two; your relatives are born, marry and die of old age and you continue to look like you belong in a fitness commercial."

"Wade." My mate greeted curtly, as he didn't appreciate the Elm family humour. "Why aren't you dead yet?"

Hastily, I moved along, "How's it going, Wade?"

"Oh you know..." he sighed tiredly, "...my wife is elderly and my kids are having kids of their own and turning me into a grandparent. Just as I think I've got one set of childrearing done, my kids hit me up with looking after their own."

"It's a hard life." I joked along.

"Tell me about it!" He rolled his eyes. "Meanwhile, look at the two of you. You're both still strong as the youthful couple everybody envies, as Mr. European Werewolf and Mrs. Circulator."

"I'm aging." Declan said simply. "My wife isn't."

"Yes and isn't it convenient that she just happens to be YOUR wife, Uncle Declan?" He ribbed. "When we're on the hunt you don't like to share your kill. And it just so happens you've also claimed the forever young female of the tribe."

"Who said he picked me?" I joked back. "Maybe I picked him?"

"Hmm, let's see..." Wade pretended to think about it, "...Aunt B has her pick of anything natural or supernatural in the world, let alone the tribe, and who does she choose? The meanest Werewolf both has to offer. Admit it Aunt B, he clubbed you over the head and dragged you back to his cave."

"I'll frickin' club you, in a minute." My mate snarled, bad-temperedly.

Wade laughed in good humour as he came to stand beside as he too, watched Maia and Forrest thank their well-wishers.

He spoke again, "Tell me, what's it like seeing that 21 year old girl whom you helped raise with your endless babysitting duties, now embark on one of adulthood's greatest trials such as marriage? Do you look on and think that in nine months, she could be enlisting your services to help her raise her kids?"

I watched the 19 year old Brandon, shake Forrest's hand before he kissed his older sister on the cheek. He behaved so maturely, it felt surreal to see. Mind you, with his girlfriend standing nearby, I wondered if it would be his turn next?

"They grow up so fast." I sighed sadly.

Declan agreed, "It seems like only yesterday we cooked for them, cleaned up after them and broke up their fights."

"Maybe that's where you went wrong?" The aging Werewolf mocked. "If you had just stepped back and let them kill each other; you wouldn't have to worry about them reaching the age of procreation."

Right at that moment, Wade's grandkids Stioux and Maxine, ran in front of us and ceremoniously pushed the other onto the grassy ground.

"You see?" He shrugged. "I could break them up or I could save myself the grief. By letting 'em kill each other before it's too late, they'll never grow up and produce litters of their own."

Next, we saw a tired Julie walk over and pull up her kids by the scruff of their necks.

"Dad, a little bit of help, please?" She glared, before she chastised her children, "Look at the two of you! You're getting dirt all over your good clothes!"

Wade let out a sigh as if this was asking a lot, before he looked our way. "Thank fate that you don't have any kids...really."

With that, the grandfather tiredly walked after. He took hold of his grandson, as Julie dragged his granddaughter and all four rejoined the Elm clan.

Declan and I exchanged raised eyebrows as we both thought the same thing.

"OK..." we shifted uncomfortably.

*****

An hour later, everybody left the Holy Grounds to reconvene at Maia and Forrest's new home for the Housewarming.

The majority of the festivities took place outside, whilst many of the women helped themselves to exploring inside, to see how their presents were put to use.

Customarily of Lokoti shindigs, people sat around in fold-up chairs they had brought, since there was no way our tribe could fit into one house. We were seated out the front of the couple's abode and the crowd spilled out onto the small street, with several fold-up tables which were covered in food people had brought, as well as bottles of soda. Hardly anybody drank alcohol as a sign of respect to the tribe's Werewolves, who always had to remain sober.

The air hummed with happy chatter as the adults were engrossed in different conversations. This went along with the laughter of children, who were chasing each other around. The blue sky had turned grey and an icy wind had picked up, but luckily the rain was staying away.

I sat beside Declan with my half-eaten plate of food in my lap, whilst nursing a bio-degradable cup filled with soda, in one hand. We were sitting in a small circle of people whom appeared older than us, when in fact we were a century older than them.

The bride's parents Therese and Julius Sabre sat on Declan's left, with the groom's parents Sharon and Stone Riverclaw, next to them. On my right, were Claire and Peter Wisetail, whom were Jake's parents.

Since my mate and I were revered as 'Great Granduncle Declan' or 'Great Grandaunt B' by the middle-aged parents or grandparents in our company, we felt quite at home with the, 'do you remember when?' anecdotes. However my participation in the feasting and conversation was half-hearted, as I was too engrossed in my own thoughts as I stared at Forrest and Maia.

The newlyweds had changed out of the 'skins,' and washed the paint from their faces. Now, Maia was wearing a flowery yellow dress, similar to the plain yellow one I wore for my Housewarming. Spookily, Forrest was wearing a black shirt although his was patterned, whereas Grant wore a plain black one.

The couple were milling around the seated families, as they thanked everyone for their presents. I kept giving myself a scare, because every time I saw Maia and Forrest in the corner of my eye? My mind played tricks and I saw Grant and I together, on the day of our Housewarming.

"... hey, B?"

What was that? I turned to Declan whom had spoken, "Hmm?"

Stone chuckled at my expense, "You're a million miles away, Aunt."

"Just smile and nod." Peter joked.

I acquiesced, before I looked back over to where Forrest was standing with his arm about Maia.

"Are you reminiscing about your Housewarming?" Therese guessed.

"Huh?" I looked back, startled.

Why she would bring up my first husband in front of my second?

"B and I didn't have a Housewarming like this." My mate scowled.

"Oh." She appeared surprised.

Phew! Therese wasn't talking about Grant, but Declan instead.

"Our Housewarming wasn't a tribal affair." He said sombrely. "It was just our families in the Sabres, Riverclaws, Wisetails and Elms."

"A family-only occasion?" Julius asked, intrigued. "I like that idea."

"You do?" His wife gave him a funny look.

"Well, yeah. Instead of hardly spending any time with your family, you have to schmooze with the whole tribe and make sure you thank EVERYBODY for giving something. Heaven forbid, should you forget anyone and accidentally insult someone!" He rolled his eyes.

We cracked up laughing as we could guess what he was talking about. When Julius and Therese had their Housewarming, a dispute eventuated because old Mrs. Huntington had been offended that she hadn't been thanked by the couple on the day.

"Don't worry," Stone guffawed. "I heard that before old Mrs. Huntington passed away, she said to the Medicine Man; 'tell that ungrateful Julius Sabre that I forgive him and I hope his kids and his grandkids, get good use out of those crochet blankets, I spent months making'."

We laughed harder as we could very well imagine the old and grumpy Mrs. Huntington saying that.

I looked at my European Werewolf mate. "It's weird calling her 'Old Mrs. Huntington' considering she was born years after and yet died before us."

"Tell me about it." He frowned. "I think it's weirder that no matter what era we live in, there's always an Old Mrs. Huntington. We had one growing up and now our great x4 grandnieces and nephews had one."

"Just how old exactly are you two, anyways?" Claire wondered.

My husband glanced her way as he chewed on some chicken and potato salad, before he looked at the rest of the group.

"I'm three years older than B and I'm 168 years old."

"And you don't look a day over 39." Sharon eyed him, enviously.

"I wish we could all be European Werewolves." Claire joked and she started to laugh, but then she noticed that Declan, Stone or Peter weren't.

"No you don't." My mate said curtly, as he looked away.

Peter, Stone and I sensed Declan's constant battle with his bloodlust. Right now, the humans sitting around him would have been appealing as that juicy, cooked chicken on his plate. It took his whole childhood, to train his hunting pattern, to prey on animal instead.

"How about becoming Circulators instead?" I moved the conversation on. "Not only will you become youthful for much longer because you can travel through time; but you get a Headquarters on another planet too."

"Sign me up!" Claire cried out excitedly, making us all laugh when her hand shot up into the air.

Therese looked from her husband and then to me, "I've always wanted to meet Napoleon, and see if he really was as short as the history books made him out to be."

"Short dead dude." My husband and I said at the same time, as we remembered the movie, 'Bill & Ted's Excellent Adventure'.

"Say Uncle Dec..." Julius began, "...do you ever go back in time with Aunt B, when she visits Ancient Greece or wherever else?"

"Nope," he said simply.

This made our group of relatives do a double-take in disbelief, so he thought he should explain.

"From what she's told me, she does a lot of preparation before her trips. She researches what time period she wants to go to, as well as the culture. She learns the language and she dresses up into clothes of the era. B even has money to take with her, which is provided at this Circulate Headquarters on Taurus Six, wherever that is..." he rolled his eyes, "...it sounds like too much of a hassle, to me."

"But it also sounds like an adventure." Claire smiled upon the idea.

"It is fun." I grinned back. "But I tell you what, my skills in self-defence has come in handy. That, as well as my ability to instantaneously phase is my safety net, when one needs a fast getaway."

"Why?" Stone's smile faded.

"Are you gonna eat that?" Declan hungrily looked on my leftovers, as he put down his empty plate.

I handed him my half-eaten meal, much to our families' amusement to see his perpetual hunger. Then I answered, "I've nearly been sold into slavery twice."

I snickered as I said it, but it was soon made clear that my overprotective Lokoti Werewolf relations didn't find it funny. Even their wives' mouths hung open in surprise.

Hastily, I moved on with my story, "The first time I visited Ancient Greece with my mother and grandmother, some slave traders tried to abduct us in the market place. The third time I visited Ancient Rome by myself, something similar happened when I was followed down a dark alleyway. In Greece, I fought them off and in Rome, I gave them the slip when I instantaneously phased home."

Both Stone and Peter emitted low, dangerous growls upon hearing this, as their wives looked just as angry.

"You're kidding!" Therese cried out in a shrill voice. "They tried to just kidnap you off the street like that?!"

Even Julius eyed my husband demandingly, for allowing his wife get into these kind of situations. Declan paused in his eating when he picked up their glares.

"Hey, don't look at me! When I found out, I demanded that she take me back in time and let me loose on those guys...but she wouldn't."

I said moodily, "There's no point in exacting revenge on humans who have died thousands of years ago."

My mate said with his mouthful, "That's exactly what she said when I told her to take me to the kidnappers."

"Declan broke the front door after I told him what happened." I crankily crossed my arms. "He stormed out of the house in one of his temper tantrums, because I wouldn't take him to find the males who tried to abduct his wife."

It was here Peter exchanged a wry look with Stone, "That would be the time you called me to deliver the new door I had just built?"

To which Stone smilingly replied, "Yep and why I got you to help me to install it. It explains how the old door had the wood split directly in the middle; from a furious European Werewolf and his supernatural temper."

Now my mate smirked at the two, "You did a good job with the new door. It's even stronger than the last one."

"Why, because you haven't broken it yet?" Peter chuckled.

"Yup." He finished off my plate and put it aside, on top of his.

"Aunt B." Stone cleared his throat. "I don't think it's a good idea that you visit these sorts of places where things like that happen."

"That's what I said." My husband rolled his eyes.

"Well in that case Stone, I would never get any time travelling done." I said coolly. "No matter where you go in human history, humans will always be doing the wrong thing."

"That's what she said to me too." Declan said in annoyance.

Peter tried to reason, "Maybe you shouldn't travel to these sorts of places alone."

"But I am alone, I'm the last Circulator. Once upon a time there used to be more. For my first circulation, my mother and grandmother took me to Ancient Greece. Gran even bought me this bracelet to commemorate the event." I held up my arm with the gold jewellery to illustrate. "But now that they're gone, I travel by myself."

When I caught Julius start to look Declan's way again, I was angered over what I perceived as sexism.

I snapped at my great x3 grandnephew, "And don't look at my husband as if he should be keeping me on a leash! He's not a Circulator, so he isn't interested in travelling through time. I'm fortunate to be able to visit the places I write about in my academic work. The ancient times aren't Declan's scene and I respect that. He's offered to come with me as my bodyguard after the last kidnapping attempt, but I said no. You have to enjoy time travel so you can embrace learning another language and a new culture. I don't want somebody to accompany me who sees it as a chore. What's the point in that?"

Then I stood up, picked up our disposable plates and I walked off to dump them in the bin. But I didn't return to my seat, instead I kept walking.

I went inside the house to make it appear that I too wanted to see the new home, instead of walking off in a tantrum. However as soon as I walked into the newly-furnished abode, I wondered if this was a good idea? Although the house was in a different lay out; I had another flashback of seeing my house on the day of my Housewarming.

As I walked through the living room, it reminded me of seeing my newly-furnished lounge and dining areas when I came back from my Joining Ceremony. I even helped myself by going upstairs but when I walked into the main bedroom, I halted in the doorway... the furnishings were almost identical to what I had with my first husband.

Long ago, our bedroom suite was changed after Declan moved in. It was done at the behest of my second mate, as he had difficulty with the idea of sleeping in the bed that Grant used to share. Over the years, we also replaced our lounge room furnishings by buying new couches, but our pine coffee table and dining table set, were still the originals.

I walked over to take a closer look at the home-made curtains, which hung over the windows which somebody in the tribe had made for the couple.

Following Lokoti tradition, Forrest had purchased the house as a wedding gift for Maia. However, Declan was one of the family members whom helped move the gifts of furniture and household goods into their first home. Yesterday, he as well as several older males of the Riverclaw, Sabre, Elm and Wisetail families; helped the groom assemble any furniture which came in boxes. It was a male-bonding moment, as the husbands could trade jokes and 'war stories' about matrimony.

This was my first time seeing the house even if it wasn't Declan's. I looked about myself, as I sighed with nostalgia. I swear it only felt like yesterday, I moved into my first home with Grant.

Just then my second mate walked through the bedroom doorway and paused when he saw me standing by the window.

"I know what you're thinking, B."

I arched my eyebrows, "You do?"

He came further inside of the room to stand on the other side of the bed. "Yeah, I do."

"Then what am I thinking?"

"Aw, c'mon!" He rolled his eyes. "It's pretty obvious."

"What's obvious?"

"I could tell from the first moment we arrived at the Holy Grounds, and by how you've been watching Forrest and Maia all day." He folded his arms as he shot off a glare. I folded my arms too as I waited for my husband to come to his point. He declared, "You're thinking of your wedding day with Grant."

Oh... I didn't know my thoughts were that transparent.

Guiltily, I sat down on the bed so my back was to him, as I stared out the window.

"I must admit," he walked around to lean on the windowsill, "that the similarities are uncanny."

"Hmm?" I stared blankly.

"Maia looked identical to you, dressed in Lokoti costume with her hair like that and her face painted so. Now with her wearing a yellow dress, it's like what you wore for your Housewarming. It's freaked you out, hasn't it?" He asked knowingly.

My head turned sharply, "How would YOU know what I looked like at my Joining Ceremony? How would YOU know what I wore at the Housewarming? You and your family boycotted the events, as I recall."

He shrugged as he looked out the window, "I was watching from a distance."

"You were?"

"Yup," he spoke casually, which belied his pain. "I watched your Joining Ceremony as I imagined killing Grant and taking his place beside you. I imagined drinking from the Tribal Cup with you. I imagined putting my finger in my mouth and sucking on it, with the Tribal Elders saying that we would always have each other's scent..."

My eyes widened in shock, as Declan recalled in detail my Joining Ceremony.

He went on, "...I watched from the woods, yours and Grant's Housewarming. I imagined it was me sitting beside you, holding your hand, regaling our families with stories of how I fell in love with you, when we were growing up. You looked so young and beautiful in that yellow dress. When Grant was the one who got to fetch your coat when you felt cold; I had to watch from afar and control my bloodlust, not to rip his throat out."

I managed to utter out my shock, "How long did you watch us?"

"I wasn't watching *him*," he said icily, "I was watching *you*."

"Then how long were you watching me?"

His voice sounded faraway, "I saw you leave the house all dressed and painted up and get into your father's truck with your parents. I ran through the woods beside the road, as I followed you guys to the Holy Grounds. I watched Grant who was also painted up, greet you and then your parents handed you over to him. I was imagining it was me whom your parents trusted enough to give their daughter and only child to."

I looked on closely, at how he was casually leaning against the window frame. But when he looked back, I saw his eyes were more watery than usual.

He carried on coolly, "You see B, I can act like I don't care. I can play Mr. Bad-Ass, because I know that I'm still an outsider from the creature I can turn into. I was an 'honorary' member of the Lokoti Werewolf pack, being a European Werewolf. My breed is hated the whole world over and it's the reason why Grant was picked to be your mate, over me. It's also the reason why I never got to have a Joining Ceremony, or a proper Housewarming."

Declan's pain became my pain. My eyes stung as my chest hurt so I stood up and walked over to my husband to cup his face. He gratefully caught my hands and held them against his hot skin.

I said strongly, "You're MY Mr. Bad-Ass. You're MY mate who cooks for me and takes care of me. You're MY Declan Sabre, whom I had my first time with. You're MY Declan Sabre who I loved before then after Grant Elm."

He buried his nose in my right palm whilst closing his eyes and inhaling deeply. Then he emitted a small smile, "You still smell like a vase of wild flowers sitting in a kitchen while a cake is baking in the oven."

I tittered back, "And you still smell like maple syrup."

"Oh yeah?" He let out a laugh. "Well, you're the only person in this world that's allowed to say so."

I stood on tippy-toes to kiss him, as I felt his arms encircle my waist and hold me closer.

He growled out, "C'mon, let's get out of here and go home to OUR bedroom."

Just as Declan took hold of my hand to walk me out, we found Forrest and Maia watching in amusement from the bedroom doorway.

"Leaving so soon?" Forrest teased.

"We were just testing out your bedroom window." My mate joked back. "And it's a good window to kiss in front of."

"We'll take it under advisement." Maia giggled.

The two stood back to let us pass before following us downstairs to see us out.

"Thanks for your wedding presents by the way, of the microwave and the food processor." Forrest said politely.

"No problem," Declan shrugged it off and then he added on, "Just don't heat up left-over lasagne inside it..."

"...because it turns the pasta hard." Maia recited. "Yeah, I remember Uncle Dec."

"What's this?" Forrest wondered.

"I'll explain later." His new wife smiled back.

"Well bro," my mate spoke as we departed the house, "welcome to marriage. Your wife is going to drive you completely nuts where some days you'll want to bang your head against the wall; and others you'll want to kiss the life out of her. But the consolation is of course, your life will never be boring."

Maia and I shared a roll of eyes, whereas Forrest smirked.

"Since you and Aunt B have been married for the longest in the tribe, I'll take your words under advisement, Uncle."

Declan kissed her on the cheek and then so did I, before we looked on the groom once more.

"Since Maia is my little brother's Great x4 Granddaughter, so I was the one who gave permission at your Joining Ceremony..." Declan shook Forrest's hand firmly with his stronger grip, "...if you screw up and hurt her, I'll kill you."

"Uncle!" She blushed as she whacked him on the arm.

"I AM a Lokoti Werewolf, Uncle Dec." Her husband smiled wryly. "I have the same attitude about anybody who looks at Maia wrong, remember?"

"Don't worry, Declan's been saying that to every male who has ever married a female family member." I shook my head at his behaviour. "It started the day of Stuart Elm and Blanche Sabre's Housewarming."

The newlyweds walked us down the steps of the front porch when suddenly I was nearly taken out by two screaming kids!

Stioux crashed tackled Maxine to the ground, tearing her dress and getting mud all over his own clothes.

"Hey hey hey!" My mate yelled down at the two. "Watch it!"

Stioux's eyes bulged at being told off by the scariest Werewolf of the tribe. He quickly picked himself up from the ground, as he released his sister. Maxine slowly stood up and looked down at her ruined dress, before tears appeared in her eyes.

"What the hell is wrong with you?!" Declan yelled at him. "She's your little sister! You're supposed to protect her from harm, not inflict it!"

"Maxine's got my lucky quarter and she won't give it back!" The boy pointed at the little girl.

"Stioux keeps teasing me that I look like such a girl in this dress!" She pointed back.

The adults exchanged looks of amusement at the 10 year old's offence at that.

"You are a girl, that's why you're wearing a dress and your brother isn't." Declan gave her a funny look.

"I don't want to be a girl!" She cried. "I can outrun any boy my age! And I catch the most tadpoles, more than Stioux can!"

"Man, are her parent's going to have a mountain of psychiatrist bills to pay when she grows up." My mate muttered to the groom, who chuckled in agreement.

I leaned over and gently took hold of her dirty little hand, which was balled into a fist. When I gave her a frown, it prompted her to open it and an old quarter fell into my waiting one. I passed it to her brother, who immediately pocketed his good luck charm.

Forrest frowned on the boy, "You could turn into a Lokoti Werewolf one day and be one of the tribe's protectors. Now start acting like you're ready for the responsibility, by looking after your little sister!"

Maia took hold of her hand, to lead her inside and clean her up. "Come on, Maxine."

"I'll leave you to it." Declan patted Forrest on the back, before he took hold of my hand.

We left the Lokoti Werewolf to put the possible future Werewolf, in his place. Stioux's head bowed as Forrest's hands moved to his hips as he lectured the 12 year old. Declan smilingly looked back over his shoulder at the scene, whilst walking me to our parked vehicle.

"I remember giving Forrest the same speech when he was Stioux's age." My mate chuckled.

Next, he pressed his remote key for the truck's central locking then he opened my door for me. I climbed into the truck before I sighed wistfully, yet again.

"Now it's Forrest's wedding day and he's practicing for the day he has kids."

"B, don't start." He threw me a warning look as he climbed behind the wheel.

"Don't start?" I looked on, unimpressed.

"Yeah, don't start." He punched in the ignition code and the engine immediately purred to life.

"What do you mean, don't start?" I asked crankily.

"Seat belt." He prompted as he buckled his own. Then he looked both ways down the small road, before driving off.

I stared in annoyance out my window, as we drove out of the small suburb the community centre had grown into. More and more houses had sprung up with the passing of the years, thanks to the growth of the tribe.

"All I'm doing is commenting on the passing of time." I said coolly and he let out a snort of disbelief. I continued, "It's funny how life follows a certain path. Stone's eldest child who in the typical Lokoti Werewolf way, was a son. Forrest's Werewolf DNA was activated after Uncle Julian's death, prompting his change when he was 18 years old. It's good to see him practice the 'responsibility' speech on Wade's grandson for the day he'll have a son of his own. Thanks to the Lokoti Werewolf virility, it's almost a sure-thing that it will happen in about nine months. That's all I'm saying, Declan."

He glared ahead as he slowed the truck at the intersection at the bottom of the hill. I watched as he turned his head both ways to check for any traffic, before he put his foot down on the accelerator and drove onwards. The plasma-powered vehicle easily handled the steep road, which led the way home.

I sighed sadly, "It's not like we're going to have kids to give the 'responsibility speech' to, huh?"

Abruptly the truck screeched to a stop half way up the hill, when Declan slammed on the breaks!

"God give me patience...!" He muttered out with his eyes closed.

Then he started to bang his forehead on the wheel as if to compound this!

"Declan!" I stopped him by pushing him back into his seat.

"Well, I suppose you are keeping to tradition, B." He laughed bitterly. "This IS coming after a tribal function, after all."

"What?"

"THIS!" He yelled in my face. "The ole 'I can't have kids' whinge, which usually comes after a tribal function!"

I crossed my arms as I looked away from the obnoxious male.

"Every time B, every single frickin' time!" He pounded the wheel with his fist. "I've had enough! I've had to listen to it for the past 141 years! No more B, seriously! NO MORE!!"

I opened my door, climbed out of the passenger's side and slammed it behind! Then to Declan's surprise, I began to march up the hill in my high-heels.

Although my fury made my face and eyes burn, I had to pull my coat tightly, against the icy wind. Then whadyaknow, I felt a large rain drop, land on my face. Perfect! It just would have to start raining NOW, wouldn't it? I looked up at the grey sky, which looked just as dark as my mood was.

"What the hell are you doing?" He put down his window to call out. "Get back in the truck!"

However, I ignored him as I continued to walk.

"B!"

I stomped up the road as the rain began to fall harder. Next, I heard the truck drive right up behind so closely, I could feel the heat come off the bonnet. But I didn't look back, I refused to.

"Don't be stupid! Get in here out of the rain!" My husband snapped.

Screw this for a joke! I knew the domineering male would drive right on my tail, whilst shouting all the way home. So I curtailed off the road, by stumbling into the muddy woods which my heels instantly objected to.

"B...? What the hell are you doing now?!"

I hurried away from both Declan and the road, by using the trees to hide me. I paused a moment to lean against a trunk, to pull off my shoes and walk in my stocking-clad feet in the cold mud. I didn't mind getting dirty, it felt kind of liberating actually.

The rain started to pour down, drenching my black woollen overcoat as my stockings tore when I scraped past some bushes. I felt the cold, wet ferns brush against my legs. I wasn't aiming for a particular direction, but I became aware that I was walking down hill towards a familiar sound. I heard the quiet roar of the river ahead.

The river... I always seem to go there for some reason. In my defence, there's not many other places that I can go to on tribal lands, when I want to get away to think. It's either that, or sitting at the lookout on top of Sunset Point. Much further on, there's the quiet riverside glade that's inside the National Park; but it was Declan's favourite spot.

I stumbled on in the mud, whilst noticing splashes appear on my red, silk, cocktail dress. It felt therapeutic seeing my good clothes get covered in mud like this, and poetic somehow. It was like a contrast of sophisticated city apparel, in the midst of rough-n-tumble country.

Through the trees, I spotted the flowing waters of the large river which was only thirty meters away. However as I came closer, I started to pick up a familiar scent... I could smell maple syrup.

I stepped out of the woods and onto the riverbank, to see Declan standing casually with his hands in his pockets.

His suit was also wet with flecks of mud on the black material. I could tell he both heard and smelled my approach, but he stood with his back to me. He was staring out at the flowing waters, and I guessed that he not only tracked me here by my scent, but he guessed where I was heading from the direction of my trail. To show off, he thought he would beat me here; or try to make himself look good by surprising me.

"Do you mind?" I flared. "I came down here to get away from you!"

Now he thought he would ignore ME by not looking my way. So I turned around and stomped off, away from him. I walked quickly for a good five minutes by going further up the river bank. I left him standing on one part of the river, as I rounded the wide bend and through a dense plot of trees. But when I came out of the thicket...

...I found Declan standing before me, with his arms folded in front and his blue eyes icy with a cold glare, which was directed my way.

He was showing off again, by quickly and quietly slipping past with his skills as a predator.

"Stop frickin' following me!" I seethed. "I'm supposed to be storming off!"

"You can try to run, but you can't hide from me, B."

"No shit, Sherlock!" I glared back. "Or do I have to instantaneously phase to Taurus Six, instead?"

"Sounds about right." He shrugged. "It's the only way you'll escape from me, by visiting another planet. But no matter where you go on this one, I'll always track you by your scent."

"Is that supposed to impress me or just piss me off?"

"Both."

I rolled my eyes as I pulled my wet coat, tighter about me.

"This is frickin' stupid." He said in annoyance. "You're cold and wet and walking barefoot in the mud. Let's just go home."

"No." I said stubbornly. "You go home."

He fixed me with a determined look. "Not without my wife."

"Go away, Declan!" I lost the last of my patience. "Just go away so I can rant at a frickin' rock which would give me more comfort than you!"

"Fine." He said. "Pick a rock, pick it up, and then I'll carry it and your wet ass home."

"No! I'll stay out here with the frickin' rock, thank you very much!"

"Yeah right."

"I'll move out here to live with it!"

"Very funny."

"Well I think so!" I crossed my arms too.

"Go on then."

"Go on, what?"

"Pick the frickin' rock and take it home with us."

"It's not coming home with us! There is no 'us'! I'm going to live with the rock and the rock only!"

Declan smirked, "Now this I wanna see. Go on then, pick the rock."

"What?" I gave him a funny look.

"Pick the frickin' rock!"

"You want me to pick a rock, right now?!"

"Pick up the frickin' rock, B!"

"Fine then!" I growled out before I started to look around at the ground until I spotted one.

I bent over and picked up a nice, smooth, oval-shaped stone, and I held it out to show him.

"There!" I shouted at him. "There's my rock and my next husband!"

In a lightning flash move, his hand whipped out, snatched the rock from mine and he gripped it hard, in his two...

"What are you doing?!" I cried out.

...he snapped the rock in half with his supernatural strength, before he tossed the broken pieces over his shoulder!

"There." He said smugly. "My rival has been destroyed."

Out of the blue, he bent over and slung me over his right shoulder!

"Declan!" I cried out as I tried to slip from his grasp, but he was too strong.

"Now I get to claim my prize." He chuckled.

He turned away from the river and began to speedily walk though the forest, up the hill towards home.

"Declan, put me down right now!"

"Keep dreaming princess!" He laughed back as he picked up the pace.

"Declan Domitian Sabre, I'm warning you...!" I growled threateningly.

"That's what I'm hoping for baby!"

I tried to pull on his hair, but it ended up making him break into a run! He ran so fast that the trees flew by in a blur. I flinched, thinking that this would be jarring but his grip was iron-clad. It showed there was no way he would let me fall off.

The next thing I saw was my garden, as Declan sprinted out of the woods before slowing to a jog, up our porch steps. I recognized his truck, parked out on the driveway. Don't tell me he drove home and managed to reach the river first when I should have, only being halfway up the hill? Now that was really showing off!

"You cheat!" I cried out in frustration.

He laughed out loud as he unlocked the front door and carried me in. I pulled on his hair harder, as we went inside the house.

"You think you're so good, but you're not!" I yelled as I struggled so much so, he nearly lost his grip.

Reluctantly, he slid me off his shoulder but caught me just before I hit the floor. Simultaneously as he let my back gently land on the wooden floorboards, he laid on top. Our mouths instantly went for each other's, as our hands scurried to rid the other of our wet clothes.

"Get this frickin' monkey suit off me!" He growled out.

I tugged off his sodden jacket before undoing the buttons on his shirt. But I must have taken too long, as he lost his patience and tore off his shirt, over his head. My muddy dress was the next to go, and soon joined my discarded coat and shoes.

"Is this better?" I breathed as I unbuttoned his trousers.

"We're getting there." He managed back before smothering my mouth with his.

Declan didn't stop snarling bad temperedly, until we came together naked; lying on the cold, hard, polished, wooden floor.

"Now THIS is better." He muttered whilst holding my waist firmly to his as he began to push. "Oh hell yeah, this is much better!"

I didn't feel cold anymore, thanks to his hot body over mine coupled with the friction of us rubbing together oh so pleasurably.

I readjusted my hips to the angle I preferred, which he recognized from our long years of marriage. He moved himself up a little more, so our crotches were rubbing together whilst he pushed, which made my clit swell in ecstasy. Gratefully, I wrapped my legs tightly around his waist which I knew he liked, as we helped each other along.

In the midst of our love-making, he momentarily raised himself so he could look over my writhing body. But he never stopped moving, even when his eyes looked around our quiet house before they returned to mine. Eventually, he lowered himself again into my awaiting arms.

"Now THIS is why we don't want kids." He spoke plainly. "Maia and Forrest will have their new home to themselves for nine months, before it's turned into a circus of diapers, baby clothes and tripping over toys."

With that, he pressed his body against mine so my breasts were rubbing against him, as our crotches were. I knew he liked to see our flesh squashed together, as we grinded away. I held onto him tighter, as I neared my peak and my hands were practically pawing the skin on his back.

"But what about...when their kids grow up...and leave home?" I panted out.

"Nup." He moaned back. "Then they're stuck with grandkids. You heard what Wade said, once you get rid of your kids then you're stuck with theirs."

Declan held on for as long as he could, at a speed which pushed me over the precarious edge of utter delight...! I felt his body was tense and hard as his organ was. Then I felt him come seconds after I did, which made him loosen in total surrender.

"Mmm..." he closed his eyes, as if to hold onto his orgasm for as long as possible. He bumped his forehead against mine, "...I swear B, I think there's a reason why you can't conceive and I think it's related to why you were put on this planet just for me."

I looked up into his face which was so close to mine, as I waited for him to finish.

"It's like you and I have it so good that something bad has to come of it." He eventually opened his eyes to meet mine. "Sometimes I think that maybe you're being punished for ending up with a rotten apple like me; the most hated breed out there."

"Huh?" I gave him a peculiar look.

"I'm the last European Werewolf, maybe I'm not supposed to have young which can turn into monsters like me? Maybe it's nature that's designed you not to procreate, so I won't procreate. When I go, there won't be anymore of my kind to haunt humanity."

"Don't be stupid, Declan!" I retorted. "I couldn't conceive when I was with Grant either. So maybe you're being punished for being with the only Lokoti Werewolf in history who's mated a second time?"

"I had you before Grant," he declared, "and I had you after. You were always mine. Besides, I could have spoken up when the pack and the Tribal Elders first announced their idea of marrying you off... but I didn't."

"You were being considerate of Derik's feelings." I remembered.

Once upon a time, both brothers had been attracted to me, one publicly and the other in secret; and my current husband was the one in secret.

"You know what, B?" He looked down with a remorseful expression. "Sometimes I wonder if I did something wrong."

"What do you mean?"

He nervously licked his lips, "After our first time, when I went down on you because I was scared that I impregnated you. Maybe I screwed up? Maybe I did something that irreparably damaged you? Maybe I didn't just ensure that you wouldn't get pregnant by me that afternoon, but I accidentally made it so you wouldn't get pregnant, ever?"

I scanned his face, "What exactly did you do to me that afternoon, Declan?"

"I don't know exactly." He appeared perplexed. "I was guided by an instinct. The same little voice that warned me about the European Vampires or others of my kind, was the same instinct that told me what to do."

"What did it tell you to do?"

"I'm not real sure, but it said to use my saliva down there; that it could kill the egg." He guiltily confessed.

"Talk about literally being eaten out." I smirked, before I sighed out. "No Declan, what's wrong with me is nothing to do with you. You didn't harm me. It's me and my fault alone."

He instantly looked relieved, as he rolled off and onto his side to perch his head on his hand, whilst watching my face.

I added on dismally, "I think what's wrong with me is something to do with being the last Circulator."

He conceded, "Yeah, I think I smell that too."

"Huh?"

"B," he took a deep breath as if to say something important, "for the past 141 years of our marriage, your scent has never changed."

"So?" I wondered what this had to do with it.

"With humans and even some Werewolves, their smell changes with the passing of time. I think it's something to do with hormones or whatever.

They go from child to adolescent as their bodies prepare for breeding and then for females, their scent changes again when they're pregnant. Their smell alters for the last time, when they enter menopause. It's how I can tell how old a person is by their smell. But with you...? Since your body isn't changing, your scent hasn't either. You smell the same as you did when you were 18 years old."

"What...? Not even once?" I asked disappointedly.

"Nup." He shook his head. "It's why tracking you is so easy to do."

I looked away dejectedly, which made Declan continue.

"Didn't you once tell me that you can't have kids because it's like your body is in temporal flux? It's like your internal workings are frozen in time. Even if you alter your outward appearance to look older, you still smell the same because your insides haven't changed."

"How can you smell THAT?!" I asked indignantly.

"I dunno, I just can."

"Then why did you think that it had something to do with you?"

He rested his hand over my abdomen, "I guess I was worried that I may have instigated in some way, your body never changing. Perhaps stopping you from becoming pregnant, stopped you from changing in any other way."

I looked away in annoyance, "That's a stupid idea."

"I'm glad you think so, as it means that I'm off the hook."

Sulkily, I rolled onto my side so I was facing away from him. I scoffed, "As if stopping somebody from becoming pregnant would stop them from aging!"

"Like I said, I'm glad you think so."

Next, Declan began to run his hand up and down my side, following the shape of my body.

"You're my beautiful B," he spoke longingly. "My B whose body never changes. You won't grow old for a thousand years, but we'd probably evolve before then. This means you'll be my gorgeous girl forever."

I felt him sensuously kiss my shoulder blade and then down my spine, as his arm wrapped about my waist. He pushed up his crotch from behind and I felt his ardour between my legs. His physical show of love made my eyes flutter close again and a small smile escape, as I enjoyed his touch.

"Say it, B."

"Say it?"

"Say the words to me."

"Um, we're gonna evolve before I grow old, so you're stuck with me?"

He rolled me onto my back so he could lie on top again, as he snickered out, "Close enough."

~~~~~~

~ 5 ~

As Declan and I carried on with our lives, I wondered how Maia and Forrest were adjusting to their new ones, together?

Typical for newlyweds, especially where a Werewolf was involved, the two didn't socialize much during the first few months. Everyone assumed they were enjoying what each other's company had to offer. Whereas my mate and I were firmly entrenched in a routine, I guess the two were establishing theirs.

Monday to Thursday, we were woken at 7.30 AM by Declan's digital alarm clock. When the Garage was busy he worked Fridays as well, but since he owned it, he had the freedom to choose. It was handy during a full moon, and he needed the sleep in from hunting all night.

He employed three mechanics, two whom were human Lokoti and the third who was also a Werewolf. They too, usually worked four days a week. He set up the roster so he and one of his mechanics would work from Monday to Thursday, and the other two would work from Wednesday to Saturday. Then on Fridays, Declan preferred to do his 'paper work' at home.

After breakfast, I'd clean up the cooking mess from whatever he'd made, before we returned to the table. Our individual laptops would be turned on and as I did my academic work; he'd be working on rosters, calculating his worker's pay, or other book-keeping from the Garage. He'd be balancing labour with the cost of power and water, or even ordering in parts, online.

Although Declan left school at the age of thirteen to become an apprentice mechanic, he was in no way disadvantaged. His bloodlust made him a restless student, where sitting in a classroom for long periods of time, was difficult. So his mother who had run the temporary school on tribal lands after the War; reluctantly gave her permission.

Aunt Susan passed his education on to Uncle Fin, who used to run the Garage. Under the tutelage of the Lokoti Werewolf, the European one put in many a dutiful hour. Declan was taught not only how to fix engines, but he was trained to run the Garage when his supervisor was away. When Uncle Fin passed, he left the business to his loyal second-in-charge.

I found it impressive, how easily he operated the workplace. Declan was a firm but fair boss, who only employed Lokoti to spare the questions a non-Lokoti would have, about the Werewolves tardiness during a full moon. His female employee Gracie may not have been a supernatural creature, however my mate once told me she had a mental illness which could also be affected. But he jested, "With our bloodlust affecting our brain chemistry, I'm not gonna judge someone with something similar." So he simply made the decree that if you arrived late, you left late.

Just as Declan had little patience with school books, he also held instruction manuals in similar regard. But his mind was sharp as a tack and he was a fast learner. When he bought himself a new laptop or an accounting program, he would teach himself how to use it. The booklets were tossed into the recycling without being opened. Then he would sit at the table for hours, as he played with the technology and learned by trial and error.

One Friday morning, I kept hearing his computer beep out an error message.

"Damn it!" He growled under his breath.

"What are trying to do?" I looked up from my laptop.

"I'm trying to copy and paste an old spreadsheet into a new one, but the frickin' thing won't let me!"

"Well, what do the instructions say?" I queried. When he threw an unimpressed look for asking, I huffed back, "I'm not talking about the instructions you threw out, but most programs have a 'help' system. Hit the 'help' button and it will tell you how to do it."

"I don't need a frickin' computer telling me what to do!" He snarled bad-temperedly.

"You're obviously doing the wrong thing -" I began when I was interrupted.

"Got it!" He let out a cheer, before he smiled smugly. "So, you were saying?"

I rolled my eyes as I tried to stop a grin from escaping, but Declan caught it.

"Sprung!" He sung out.

Then he stood up, picked up our coffee mugs and proceeded to carry them into the kitchen to make us another. When he returned, he placed a kiss on the top of my head as he put down our beverages. He gloatingly walked around to his seat as he returned to his task.

Although we enjoyed working together on Fridays; weekends had the rule that no work was allowed.

I wasn't permitted to do anything academic and if I even looked at my laptop, it earned a growl. Occasionally on Saturdays, he'd receive a phone call from the Garage, when one of his employees had to ask for his permission on something. Last Saturday, he was on the phone for longer than five minutes and when he went outside to talk privately; I used this chance to type up my list of references on a paper I'd almost finished.

Quickly, I pulled my laptop off the shelf and turned my computer on. Whilst keeping my ears peeled to his conversation, I opened the file for my latest paper. Speedily, I typed up the references but just as I was almost finished, Declan walked in.

"Hey!" His quick-temper was ignited. "It's the weekend! No work allowed!"

"What were you doing on the phone then?" I returned.

"That's different, because the Garage is open on Saturdays." He shot back. "But I don't see you lecturing at University, on weekends!"

When he made a move to take away my computer, I squealed out, "No, wait! Just two more references and I'm finished!"

"B!"

"Declan!"

"10 – 9 – 8 – 7 – 6 – 5 – 4 – 3 – 2 – 1!" He counted down.

I just managed to hit the 'save' button, when he whipped the laptop out of my grasp. He snapped it shut as he spun on his heel. I stood there seething, as he crudely shoved it back onto the bookshelf.

"Declan, it was only five minutes of finishing up a paper, which I need to have done by the end of next week!" I snapped.

"Zip it, B!" The European Werewolf flared. "You've been away more than usual, guest lecturing on your last paper. Now with this one, it's like you're developing tunnel vision. Enough is enough! Weekends belong to me, your husband whom you're meant to fawn over and lavish attention on."

However his words had the opposite effect, when I crossed my arms and sulkily stared at the table.

"OK," he looked at his watch, "it's nearly midday, so how about we go into Alma and try that new Bakery Café for lunch? Then we'll go to the Supermarket and do the grocery shopping afterwards."

"Fine!" I stomped away, to fetch my handbag and coat.

"Gees B, don't sound so excited about it." He sung sarcastically.

"I won't." I said coldly.

*****

Thirty minutes later, our moods had improved which was greatly helped by our new surroundings.

We were seated at a table by the front window of the Café. Both of us were enjoying the warmth of the sunshine pouring in, coupled with the delicious aromas in the air. We were each holding a menu card, perusing through the selection of pastries and other bakery goods.

"Boulangerie, why does that sound familiar?" He queried as he looked on the name printed on the double-sided menu, 'Toulouse Patisserie and Boulangerie'.

"It's French." I answered. "Patisserie means pastry, and boulangerie means bakery."

"Oh, I knew that." He raised his eyebrows. "Then I guess we went to one of those, when we were in France?"

"Yep."

"You miss it, don't you?" He spoke and when I looked up questioningly, he continued. "You miss Europe. You loved travelling and living out of your suitcase for six weeks. Your aura never looked so bright, when we woke up every second or third morning, in a new country."

"Really?"

"Yup," he verified as he regarded me, "you always glow when we go on holiday."

I shrugged back, "I like seeing something new every day."

"So I gathered."

Just then, a waiter who looked like he was still in school, came over to take our orders. "Welcome to Toulouse Patisserie and Boulangerie. What can I get for you today?"

Declan ordered first, "Yeah, I'll get the croque-monsieur, the steak and onion pie, the vanilla slice, the chocolate caramel slice and a strawberry milkshake."

The teenager nodded as he jotted all of this down into his PDA, but then he turned to leave as if he thought Declan had ordered for the both of us.

"Hey hey hey!" My husband objected and the teenager quickly returned. "My wife would like to order something too."

The boy's eyes bulged at the size of Declan's appetite, before he recovered his decorum and looked my way.

"Hi." I smirked at the kid's surprise. "Can I please get a banana milkshake, the chicken and leek pie, as well as the chocolate mousse cake."

He nodded again as he put this into his PDA. But just as the teenager turned away, he paused. For some reason he passed me a second glance and we saw his eyes widen. He actually stood dead still amongst the tables, as if transfixed. When I gave him a peculiar look, he blushed and scurried away.

"What was THAT about?" I wondered aloud.

Declan gazed my way, before examining how the sunlight was coming in through the window. Then he did a scan of the other patrons, to see if they saw something too. His secretive behaviour continued, as he leaned in to whisper, "Your aura just got brighter."

"My what?"

"I was checking to see if it was the glare from the sun, or your aura became noticeable."

"Really?" I blinked in disbelief.

"What were you thinking about just then?"

"What do you mean?"

"I mean, what were you thinking about just then?" He rolled his eyes.

"Why?"

"Because your aura got so bright; that for a moment the kid who's just an ordinary human, got a glimpse of it!" He hissed.

"Yeah right!" I snorted in disbelief.

"What were you thinking about just then?" Declan pestered.

"I don't know."

"You weren't attracted to the boy, were you?" He asked jealously.

"What?" I exclaimed. "No!"

The territorial European Werewolf still looked unhappy, so I gave an innocent shrug.

"I wasn't thinking about anything much." I promised. "Maybe how nice it was sitting here; feeling the warmth of the sun coupled with the smell of bread baking."

Declan's expression changed into one of relief, as he rested his hand over mine and stroked the top of my skin with his forefinger.

"I was thinking the same thing." My husband agreed as he still regarded his wife. "You look like you're literally glowing right now."

"I do?" I asked pleasantly surprised, when he gave a nod. "Truly?" He gave another nod and I asked out of interest, "What does my aura look like?"

He dropped his voice to a decibel only I could hear. "Right now it looks a soft yellow colour, while your dark blue eyes look particularly bright, and your black hair looks extra glossy."

I smiled on his flattering description and thought I'd return the favour. "Well you look rather radiant yourself, with your hair looking extra blonde in this light."

He chuckled at my compliment, "It does?"

"Yeah." Now it was my turn to nod. "Usually your hair could be called 'dark blonde,' but right now it looks 'blonde blonde'."

"Blonde blonde?" He repeated in amusement. "It's a good thing you don't work for a cosmetics firm or a hair dye company. I can just imagine the kinda names you'd put out; 'blonde blonde', 'black black' or 'red red'."

"Oh shut up!" I snatched my hand back.

"Seriously B, and you're the one with the PhD?" He snickered. "It's a good thing that your focus is on historical data and not creative writing."

"Give it a rest, Declan." I said in annoyance, as I picked up the menu card again.

Hmm, buying a chocolate cheesecake and taking it home, sounded like a tempting idea. I made note of the price, for when the time came to pay for our orders and add on the take-away.

My mate picked up his menu card too. "Hey, we could buy our bread from here instead of the supermarket."

I nodded in agreement when we were interrupted by the waiter bringing out our orders.

The kid gave me his best grin, as he put down our drinks first and then all the plates of food. I helped out by putting the strawberry milkshake in front of Declan as I claimed the banana flavour. When I smiled at the boy to say 'thanks', the teenager gave a wink before he returned to his position behind the counter. He had to serve some other customers, but he repeatedly looked in my direction as he worked.

"Great," my mate muttered sarcastically, "should I drive home now or later, to pack up my stuff?"

"Shut up!" I blushed as I picked up my drink.

"Normally, I'd offer to fight him for you. But the kid is so scrawny, all I'd have to do is breathe on him and he'd fall over!"

"Be quiet, Declan."

"Maybe I should bite him and let him turn before I fight him. It might even be interesting that way." He went on.

When I threw him a dirty look, he chuckled at his own joke before he picked up the croque-monsieur.

"Mmm... this is good. You want?" He offered with a mouthful.

I didn't even have to answer, when he put it back onto his plate and cut off a corner to put on mine. I ate the offering with my fork before nodding in agreement. "It is good."

"How's the chicken and leek pie?" He queried, although he knew I hadn't started yet, but it was his way of asking for some.

I cut my pie into quarters and placed one on his plate, which he picked up and it was gone in sixty seconds.

"Mmm, that's good too." He gave an enthusiastic nod.

Next, he cut up his steak and onion pie as well, so I could take a piece. We ate the rest of our lunch this way and what the hell, we even sipped on each other's milkshakes. As we finished off our meal, we noticed we had attracted the attention of the other patrons.

A teenaged boy and a girl looked on askance, as if they thought what we were doing was 'sad'... A gay couple in their twenties used us as inspiration and the men began to feed each other with their forks... Then an elderly hetero couple who were doing the same thing as us, chuckled at our surprised expressions.

"You're following the French mantra, son." The man nudged Declan, when he saw him take a bite of my chocolate mouse cake. "A little bit of everything."

My husband passed a humorous look my way. We always thought it funny when elderly humans called us 'son' or 'dear', since we were older even if we didn't look it.

"The vanilla slice is delicious." He pointed at the man's dessert. "Be sure to share it with your pretty missus."

The elderly woman giggled like a school girl, before she turned to me. "And how long have you been married for, dear?"

Declan and I tried not to laugh, as I answered with, "A while and you?"

"We passed our 45th anniversary last week." The husband said proudly, as his wife looked on fondly.

"Forty-five years, huh?" My mate pretended to be impressed. "Now that IS something."

We both kept quiet on the fact that our marriage had surpassed them nearly three times.

"Kids today," the old man began, "they hardly last five years in marriage. The divorce rate is something like 83% now!"

"83%, really?" My husband echoed.

"Stan has a saying," the elderly woman spoke, "if you're not going to finish something then why the hell start?"

"Young people begin a job, but they change careers something like four times." The old man began to lecture. "I heard of one woman who started off as a Primary School Teacher and ended up doing PR! I've ALWAYS stayed in the same career, even if I've had to change jobs."

"It's because of how easy and accessible everything is nowadays." His wife agreed. "Thanks to the world wide credit system, people can apply for jobs in other countries, as easily as they apply for ones in their own."

"We come from Texas," the stranger declared, "we're just passing through Alaska on a road trip. We've always lived in that state, as it's our home, heart and kin. But last year when my grandson graduated University, he got a Stock Broker's job in Spain!"

My eyes crept towards Declan's, who was waiting to hold my gaze. If this guy thought working overseas was a big deal, I wondered what he would say about Circulators? We'd probably be lectured on how circulating through time could wreck a career or marriage...

"And what do you do, dears?" His elderly wife, enquired.

"I run a Garage on Lokoti tribal lands and B is an Ancient History Professor." My mate answered.

"Have you always been a mechanic, son?" The old man asked.

"Yup."

"At least there's some stability there." He said in satisfaction. "So, how long have you two been married for, five years?"

"Oh, you could say it's been a bit longer than that." My husband smirked, as I ducked my head to hide my laughter.

The old man went on, "And you're going to be one of those couples that disprove the divorce rate, aren't you?"

"We sure are." Declan chuckled.

"In five more years, Cindy and I are going to reach our Golden Anniversary. We're gonna get that gold, aren't we Cin?" He reached over to take his elderly wife's hand.

"Yes we will, Stan." She beamed back. "Sure as heck, we'll get there in the end."

"Well," my mate stood up first which prompted me to as well, "I wish you both the best of luck with that."

"And you too, son." The old man offered his hand to shake, which Declan took.

My mate took extra care of his supernatural strength around the elderly or children; but his strong grip still made the man gasp in surprise.

"You take care now." He wished them well. But as he gave the old man a friendly pat on the back, the force jolted him.

Flabbergasted, the elderly couple watched us walk over to the cash register to pay for our lunch.

"What kinda grits do they feed 'em up here?" The husband looked from his wife, to the food they had just consumed.

When Declan swiped his credit card and punched in his PIN, he had to have a second go because he pressed the buttons too hard. I snickered at my husband's 'Incredible Hulk' mannerisms, which earned a glare.

"Oh shut up." He said grouchily, as he returned his wallet to his pocket.

"Careful, you're making me angry." I quoted the character.

"Do you wanna walk home?" He threatened.

I was still giggling when I pulled out my own credit card. "Can I please get the chocolate cheesecake and two loaves of the sliced multigrain bread?"

"Make it four loaves." Declan ordered as he fished out his card again. "And I'll pay."

"No -" I tried to instead, when he snatched up the device to swipe his card and put in the PIN, before I could.

Since my husband was standing closely beside, as well as hitting distance of the waiter; I noticed how the boy this time, kept his eyes averted. He quickly retrieved our take-away order, as he bagged the bread and carefully boxed the cake. However when he put them on the counter, our sensitive ears caught his sharp intake of air, when he got a whiff of my pheromones.

"I'll tell you what," my mate said dryly. "If you can prove to me that you actually baked all of this yourself? I might consider sharing her with you."

"Declan!" My face burned bright red as embarrassedly, I whacked him on the arm.

"Um no, I just wait tables and serve at the register..." the teenager fumbled out.

"That's too bad because trust me, women like men who cook for them." He returned.

Then as cool as a cucumber, the European Werewolf picked up the bread and cake before escorting his mortified mate, from the café.

*****

I gave Declan the 'silent treatment,' as he parked his pick up, in the supermarket's car park. We left the cake and bread in the vehicle's cabin, before walking into the large building. As usual, he pushed the hover-trolley whilst I walked beside, holding the shopping list.

When we stopped in front of the canned tomatoes and I picked a particular brand, he objected.

"Not that one."

"Why not this one?"

"It's not 100% natural." He frowned and next he grabbed three others.

"How do you know it's not 100% natural?" I checked the label.

"I can smell it."

I looked on in disbelief, "How can you smell it? It's in a tin!"

"So? You could be inside of a tin, but I'd smell you too."

"You could not!" I argued. He took the item off me to point out the small print on the bottom. I read out, "This product contains artificial flavours and preservatives."

Just like the elderly human couple we had left, he complained as he pushed the hover-trolley down the aisle.

"It's getting harder to buy 100% natural these days. With everything being mass produced as pre-made, it's making it more difficult. People don't even cook anymore, they all buy the frozen meals or the pre-prepared crap."

I pointed out, "I buy the pre-made salads and you like those."

"I'll eat them if I'm too tired to cook, but I certainly don't enjoy. Why do you think for the past 142 years, I've preferred to make my own? It tastes better when it's home made with no artificial additives."

"Moan moan moan." I rolled my eyes.

"I don't hear you complain, when I use my culinary skills on you." He quipped before he added on, "That reminds me, more vegetables have ripened in the greenhouse. For the next two weeks, we can supplement those."

Then we stopped in front of the tinned asparagus. I picked two of the cheapest tins, when he reached past and grabbed two of the more expensive brands.

"They're more natural." He declared.

"Yeah and they're also more expensive." I said unhappily.

"We can afford it." He took hold of my hand and pulled me along.

In the following aisle, I grabbed a box of teabags and again he put another brand into the trolley instead.

"Would you stop doing that!" I snapped. "Man, this is much easier when you're not here."

"The paper used for these teabags isn't bleached." He pointed out the small print once more. "I don't know about you, but I prefer my cup of tea without toxic chemicals."

Just as we rounded the corner for a new aisle, I stopped still as my mouth fell open in horror.

I blanched upon the sight of the two, bitchy, middle-aged women, who said the mean thing about me being unable to bear young. They were standing closely together and bitching about somebody new, which I picked up with my supernatural hearing.

Damn it, I'd managed to go for a couple of years without seeing them again and I was hoping it could have continued for the rest of their human lives.

"B?" My mate turned around to give my hesitation, a funny look.

To not cause a scene, I took a deep breath before catching up. I deliberately walked closely beside, as if to use his tall, wide frame to hide behind. As we passed by, it started to work too...however their heads turned at his physique.

Their eyes scanned appreciatively his muscular build, which was evident under his jeans, t-shirt and denim jacket. Then they narrowed in jealousy, when they spotted who he was shopping with.

Frickin' hell, I could see the rabid foam building up inside their spiteful mouths! As soon as they thought we were a safe distance away, they started up.

"Typical." Bitch One hissed. "He would end up with the 'Living Barbie Doll'!"

"Just look at her, how much money does she spend on plastic surgery?" Bitch Two spat out. "We've shopped here for the past thirty years and she looks like she hasn't aged a day."

"I bet she's older than the stud beside her and in fact, he's her 'toy boy'." Bitch One cackled.

But thanks to our sensitive ears, Declan and I overheard every word they said.

My mate chuckled quietly, "You hear that, B? I'm your toy boy!"

However, I wasn't laughing when I grabbed his arm and pulled him along to hide down another corridor of produce.

"Aw, c'mon..." he poked me in the ribs, "...it's funny when you think about it."

"No it's not!" I snapped back.

I sped up to get this stupid shopping trip done. I didn't even stop to examine the items anymore, I simply grabbed them off the shelves and carelessly dropped them into the trolley. My mate frowned, as he easily kept up and periodically, he'd lean over and straighten whatever was lying on its side.

The next aisle had the feminine hygiene items, as well as the bio-degradable nappies. But when I saw what was happening here, it made me halt a second time. Because of it, Declan almost ran me over with the trolley! He opened his mouth to berate, until he saw what I was looking at and he shut it again.

Maia was sobbing as she clung to a packet of disposable diapers, and Forrest was doing his best to console her.

Oh no...we could guess what was wrong. I mean, why else would newlyweds be crying over unused nappies? Or the girl, anyway.

"C'mon, let's go before they see us." My mate whispered.

Declan grabbed my hand and started to turn the trolley around, to allow the couple their privacy, but we were spotted.

"Aunt B and Uncle Dec?" She asked plaintively.

We turned around again, to see Forrest stiffen as Maia quickly tried to dry her face. Embarrassed, she shoved the packet back onto the shelf.

"Hi..." I gave an awkward wave, "...er, how are you?"

My mate nudged me for asking such a stupid question, but I didn't mean to, I was just accustomed to greeting people as such.

"Um, I'm good thanks..." Maia tried to lie, until she dissolved into another set of tears.

"Frickin' hell, marriage isn't that bad, is it?" I joked, as I darted forward to swamp her in a hug. "At least you're not fighting with your husband over teabags and if they're bleached or not."

She let out a laugh as she clung to her great grandaunt. I held her as tightly as possible, without breaking her ribs. She emitted an appreciative sigh, when my hand sympathetically rubbed her back.

Declan asked Forrest quietly, "When did it happen?"

"Five days ago." He said flatly.

"Did Meadow say what was the reason?" My mate enquired.

"He said that sometimes there is no reason, except for the first trimester is the riskiest. All Maia did, was bend over to pick up something from the floor when the pain started." The almost-future-father, recanted sadly. "It was over within minutes, before Meadow could treat her."

Right as he said that, the almost-future-mother let out a mournful wail.

I pulled away so I could look her in the eye. "You know this isn't your fault, right?" She looked like she didn't, which made me continue, "These things happen all the time. They do, trust me. I read about this when I was researching my own condition. So it doesn't mean that you won't be able to carry to term. It just means that the next one you have, is going to be all the more special."

Because I brought up the well-known fact of my inability to conceive, Maia now looked on in hope.

"Really?" She sniffed.

"Absolutely!" I promised with another hug. "As much as you hate to hear this right now, some things happen without reason. You're not being punished, you're not being targeted and you definitely didn't do anything wrong. Sometimes bad things happen to good people, even newlyweds." This made her snicker and I went on, "Believe it or not, you're gonna feel better soon. Just as much as it's hard dealing with the tragedy; your out-of-whack hormones are making matters worse. It will get better, I promise you."

"Yeah, Meadow did say something about hormonal upheaval." Maia wiped her eyes. "I even cried during a commercial for a kid's chocolate milk drink!"

"Hey, I still can't watch the movie 'AI' without crying at least four times, just ask Declan."

My mate was smiling softly on the two of us together, before he jested, "It's true. Whenever that movie comes on, about the little robot looking for motherly love? B cries the house down."

The newlyweds laughed out their relief, before looking on their elders in appreciation.

"We were thinking of holding our first dinner party, next month. You and Uncle Declan will have to come." Maia invited.

"No excuses." Forrest agreed. "We're going to make a three-course feast, so there should be enough food to even satisfy Uncle Declan's appetite."

"I don't know about that." My mate chortled to the younger Werewolf. "You've seen the amount I can eat, during a hunt."

"The way you eat Uncle, I'm surprised the National Park has any animals left." He retorted.

"It's because of your pathetic tracking skills, that's why! Plus, it doesn't help when you keep missing everything." The European Werewolf taunted. "Sometimes I think you do it on purpose because you're secretly still a vegetarian."

"Take your husband home, Aunt B." He guffawed. "Before he attacks a frozen turkey in the freezer aisle."

"Male bonding at it's best." I nudged Maia, as we looked on in amusement.

"It's a good thing the pack has you then, to add a woman's touch." She tittered back.

"Tell me about it!" I scoffed. "If it was still a 'Boys Club,' the men would accidentally run all the way to Canada, without realizing it."

To which my husband returned, "This is coming from the woman who got lost inside the Louvre?"

"Shut up!" I kicked his leg.

Then he told the couple, "When we were trying to find the Venus De Milo, we ended up stumbling upon the Mona Lisa instead. B was reading the guide book 'B style,' which meant turning the thing upside down."

"Who was the one who finally asked for directions from the Security Guard, who then showed us the way?" I retorted.

"Who was the Lokoti growly-thing, who used her pheromones on him?" He argued back.

"You're both incorrigible!" Forrest laughed harder.

"C'mon B," my mate began to push our trolley away, "let's leave the newlyweds alone, before we frighten them off marriage, for life."

"Bye bye, you two." Maia watched us go.

"Thanks Aunt B and Uncle Dec." Her husband replaced his arm about her shoulders.

I blew a kiss their way, before we disappeared behind a row of freezers.

*****

We were both quiet as we put our purchases through the self check-out. We were even silent, when we came home and put away the groceries. The temporary 'no talking' policy continued, as I poured myself a glass of orange Fanta and then I sat on the veranda steps to drink it.

Whilst seated, I observed a wind blowing through the surrounding forest and into my garden. Our Jacaranda Tree had changed with the onset of fall, and its yellow leaves were steadily dropping onto the grass below. Our daffodils, tulips and gerberas, sitting in their garden plots, looked prepared for winter's harshness.

I really liked our garden, it's one of the best things I've done to this house. I appreciated seeing the change of seasons through my plants; blossoms in the spring, blooming in summer and then closing up in the fall. Of course we didn't see them in winter, with all the thick snow.

Next, I heard our front door open and shut as Declan came to sit beside, whilst carrying a glass of Fanta for himself.

I didn't look his way, as I was still staring at the garden. I heard him swallow a couple of mouthfuls before he sighed. Then I felt his hot hand, rest on the back of my neck and begin to massage the upper part of my spine. Eventually my eyes closed, as I enjoyed the feel of his strong fingers, kneed away my knots.

He began to speak, "As hard as it is for a woman to deal with miscarriage, I think it's harder on her Lokoti Werewolf mate. Did you see how tense Forrest's muscles were? I've never seen him look so stressed out. I bet he wishes what happened, could have been done by an external force, so he could have something to blame and tear apart. It would certainly beat the excuse, 'the first trimester is the riskiest' and he wouldn't feel so helpless."

I remained quiet with my eyes closed. To completely give over to the massage, I put down my drink and turned my back to him. He saw it was working, so he too put his drink down to use both hands. The heat of his skin on mine, also kept the chill away which was carried by the wind.

He continued to talk as he worked, "Sometimes I'm glad that I'm not a Lokoti Werewolf, so I can't feel what my mate is feeling and now is one of them. To lose a child, even if it's a month old foetus, is tough enough. But to also experience your mate's pain, on top of your own? I couldn't think of a worse agony. I know this is gonna make me sound like a total bastard when I say it, but thank providence you can't have kids. We'll never go through that and if I ever saw you in that kind of torment; I WOULD lose my hold of the bloodlust and kill somebody."

Abruptly, I spun around and hugged him with all of my might! Although the gesture surprised him, he was quick to put his arms around. I buried my face in his wide chest as I hugged him harder. Simultaneously, he gave an affectionate squeeze as I overheard him inhale my scent, when he ducked his head.

We didn't move for half an hour, we simply sat in that embrace. The wind made the woods moan and move, as more leaves fell, from the Jacaranda tree. But it truly felt like the European Werewolf was so strong, he had temporarily stopped the world, in those thirty minutes he held his mate.

*****

We had planned to catch up on some gardening in the greenhouse that afternoon, but we changed our minds.

The wind carried in a storm, over our part of the Alaska Range. This served as the perfect excuse, to snuggle indoors. Declan had started a fire, and we had pizza delivered, from a pizzeria in Alma. We worked up quite an appetite, making love on the rug by the fireplace. Then it was just enjoyable, eating our order by the fire afterwards.

Beside the empty pizza boxes, was the opened box of chocolate cheesecake. At one stage, I was instructed to lie still so he could lick the dessert off my breasts. But I couldn't, it felt too ticklish and he was knocked over when I pounced instead.

However, Declan didn't complain when he was devoured almost the same as the food was. He did groan a lot though, as I took the dominant position. His hands gripped harder onto my hips, as I pushed and pawed at him before two sets of satisfied growls, came from the living room.

Day turned into night, as our house darkened and the only source of light came from the fireplace.

Contentedly, I lay on top of my mate as we stared at the flames. This feeling was shared, as he did his customary running of his nails softly up and down my back. Our body odour was mixed in with the smell of chocolate cheesecake, from our parts which hadn't been licked clean. The sound of the rain on our roof, complimented the drumming of our heartbeats.

Out of the blue, I remarked, "It rained on Forrest and Maia's Housewarming."

"Hmm."

"I wonder what happened to the festivities, after we left?" I thought aloud.

"Hmm."

"Do you think it stopped the celebration and everyone went home?"

"Hmm."

"I suppose it would have, as I can't imagine everyone fitting inside the one house."

"Hmm."

"Remember when it rained on the day of Stone and Sharon's Housewarming?" I giggled at the memory. "The party was moved into the tribe's Meeting Hall."

"Hmm."

"But I suppose we're lucky, the Lokoti that is. It doesn't rain that often when you think about all the Housewarmings we've been to over the years."

"Hmm."

"141 years of Housewarmings; that's a lot of furniture or household goods we've given."

"Hmm."

"We've probably provided enough to fill up an entire department store."

"Hmm."

"And Declan likes to wear women's underwear and he secretly steals my lingerie to share with the rest of the males in the pack."

"Hmm... say what?" He snapped to, before he tickled me mercilessly!

I squealed with laughter, as he rolled on top and tried to pin me down to take playful bites.

"No! No! Stop it!" I giggled as I struggled against him.

"Do you really want me to?" He tested, before his head lowered to graze his teeth over my abdomen.

My eyes fluttered closed when he poked his tongue into my belly button, and then he kissed and nibbled his way back up.

"Alright, this is allowed." I tittered out my consent.

He paused at my collarbone, to caress it instead. "B?"

"Yeah?"

"I can't imagine my life any other way, but this." He said simply. "This is what life is meant to be; just you and me. I always knew it. It's the reason why I waited when you were married to another man."

"How do you mean?"

"I dunno, I can't explain it." He shrugged. "I've always known it was meant to be just you and me. I knew it, even when we grew up fighting each other."

"You did?"

"I knew what I wanted and I wanted this. I knew that you could give it to me. You and I can exist in a happy little dream world, where it's just this...you and me. The world outside of tribal lands, can blow itself up again for all I care. But just as long as our home life is untouched."

I joked back, "Yeah, but I like all the take-away shops in Alma who deliver either pizza, ribs or Chinese food, which started when the looting stopped."

He chuckled as he picked up my right hand and placed it against his larger one, to examine the difference in sizes. Then he looked into my eyes whilst wearing a serious expression.

"Hey, B?"

"Hey, Declan?"

"You've always wanted to see the UK, haven't you?"

"Do you mean we should visit Blythe Castle again?"

"No, I mean the other parts of the UK."

This made me brighten, "You mean like Stonehenge, or touring Scotland or even Ireland?"

"Let's plan our next holiday, in the UK." Declan declared.

"Really?" I sat up in excitement. "Truly?"

"You know that even though I'm not interested in time travel, I like seeing the world with you in this period, right?"

I smiled softly on my mate as I tenderly caressed the side of his face...

"Yeah Dec, I do know that."

"If you ever want to go and see somewhere in this era, just say the word and I'll take you." He promised. "But if you ever get into trouble when you're back in time, somehow I'd move heaven and earth to come and find you."

I envisioned the European Werewolf somehow sniffing out a Circulator on their own excursion through time, and threatening them to take him or else. It even made me giggle, as I pictured the scared look on the Circulator's face.

"Come here, you." I wrapped my arms about his neck to pull him back down.

~~~~~~

~ 6 ~

12th August 2236

Declan and I walked hand-in-hand through the market place of Stonehaven, a coastal town in Scotland.

The outdoor markets were an eclectic place, full of people from 'all walks of life'. Some of the humans running the stalls let alone shopping, looked like either 'hippies' or 'goths'. We even walked past some wearing olden day clothes. We exchanged a chuckle, as a couple in Victorian dress swept past in their long dress or top hat.

My mate leaned in to whisper, "That could have been us if we had moved to Canada in the 19th Century."

He was referring to when we were first 'married', some members of the tribe or even my family; didn't take to the idea. Their negativity was so bad, we even packed a suitcase to leave. Besides departing Alaska, we had also contemplated changing eras, to make a fresh start.

The stalls and their wares were just as eccentric as the people were. Anything and everything was being offered, from modern to antique art, second-hand knick-knacks, or clothes and antique music. There were food stalls, incense and oils stands and even a middle-aged lady dressed as a gypsy, sold Tarot readings. We paused to listen to her give a teenaged girl, her future fortunes.

"Ooh, the Lovers card!" The older woman said excitedly. "This means in the next six months you are going to meet a handsome young man..."

Declan snickered quietly in my ear, "Too bad if the girl is gay."

"...or it could mean that you will look on somebody you already know, in a new light." The Tarot Reader continued.

"Which means she could get drunk at a party and 'make out' with some guy." He joked. "Either way, a guy is going to get lucky but not really our girl here."

I burst out laughing which disturbed the reading. The older woman and the young girl passed us an unappreciative look. Whilst chuckling, we walked away to give the Fortune Teller some privacy.

"You should give readings." I suggested. "I think you'd be better at it, or in the very least far more funny than the Tarot lady."

"Yeah, but I don't think anybody would like my advice." He smilingly shrugged. "I'd tell that teenaged girl back there, to bitch-slap any horny male that comes near and to listen to her parents."

"I'd call that good advice." I kissed his cheek.

I could tell my husband was in a cheerful mood today. He kept cracking jokes as he pointed out different things, or he laughed loudly at mine. Sometimes he'd let go of my hand to walk with his arm about me instead, whilst planting abundant kisses on my ear or the top of my head.

"What d'ya think, B?" He held up an old record in its faded cardboard cover, of a singer called 'Nana Mouskouri'. "If we brought this home, do you think we'd be run out of the tribe?"

"Who's 'Nana Miskouri'?" I queried.

"Chinese Water Torture." He said humorously, as he put it back. "Hey B, check it out! Jimmi Hendrix!"

I watched him gleefully pick up another old record in its torn cardboard cover.

"But how are we supposed to play it? We don't have a record player at home." I pointed out.

The stall owner who overheard overhear our conversation, came over to where we were perusing. "Pete Miller's stall further down, is selling an old gramophone today."

"A gramophone?" I queried.

"Yeah B, a gramophone...and you're supposed to be the History Professor?" Declan rolled his eyes. "It's one of the first models of record players which were constructed."

"The model that Pete is selling, is dated back to the late 19th Century." The stall owner promoted.

My mate turned his way, "Is the gramophone wind-up or plasma powered?"

"It used to be wind-up, but Pete converted it to plasma powered, so it plays better." The stall owner promised.

"Right," my husband organized, "let's go and see if this gramophone is still for sale then we'll come back and buy some records."

"It's about ten stalls down." He pointed out the way. "Was there any particular records that you would like me to hold for you?"

"Definitely Hendrix." My mate handed it over.

"Amen to that!" He chuckled in agreement.

Next, the European Werewolf took charge, as he retook hold of my hand and led the way through the crowded markets. We found the stall that sold the gramophone amongst other antiques which were done-up, like an old TV set from the 1950's. There were even antique oil lamps, which had also been converted to plasma power.

I had to smile at his excitement, when he found out the gramophone was still for sale but then I gawked at the price.

"5,000 Credits?!" I cried out, incredulous. "Our surround sound music system, which came with the Internet TV as an entertainment package, altogether cost 1,000 Credits!"

"It's a valuable antique." The middle-aged Pete Miller, justified the price.

"B, how much money have you spent over the years, on your books or clothes shopping during our holidays?" My husband rebuked.

"Yeah, but my books are for work! So is most of the clothes shopping that I do." I defended. "Besides, it's only every couple of years or so that I buy new suits and then they last me for ten years."

"I'll take it." Declan handed over his credit card.

As the stall owner processed the transaction, my mate looked enraptured on his purchase.

"Would you look at this beauty!" His eyes widened. "Look at the brass speaker all polished up." Then he leaned in to sniff it. "Smell the age on this thing, it's over 300 years old and many of the parts are still the originals."

Once he got his credit card back, my mate picked up the machine and carried it to our rental four-wheel-drive, parked outside the markets. Once it was locked in the boot, we returned to the stall where the old records were sold. I waited as Declan did a search of the rest, to build up his new collection.

"The Pogues, Cindy Lauper, Pink Floyd, Siouxsie & the Banshees, Eric Clapton..." He read aloud as he passed me the records to hold. Then he paused to look my way, "...do you have any requests?"

I shrugged back, "You know more about 20th Century music than I do, and I usually like your taste."

"Is it just my taste in music you like, or my taste period?" He passed a mischievous smile.

"Both." I tittered.

As he returned his attention to the records, strangely I began to experience the peculiar sensation of the hair on the back of my neck standing on end.

I felt like I was being watched, but usually I felt these physical symptoms around other supernatural beings. My feelings of foreboding as a Circulator weren't troubling me, but my Lokoti Werewolf senses were letting me know that we weren't the only paranormal creatures here.

My eyes narrowed as I looked about the market place whilst sniffing. I was trying to ascertain what exact supernatural element was here with us. And then I saw her...

A strawberry-blonde woman, was standing thirty meters away, observing us. She was dressed eclectically, in a red velvet blouse, a long black velvet skirt and a dark green, velvet jacket. She looked like she was in her thirties and she was pretty, but her humanity smelled...odd.

Whoever she was, she was staring at Declan and I, almost transfixed. She looked half afraid and half fascinated by us. Now don't ask me how, but I could tell she knew about Declan and I somehow; that we were Werewolves. As I stared back, I started to whack my mate on his arm, to get his attention.

"What?" He asked in annoyance then he noticed the expression on my face.

When he looked over to see what I was gazing at, I heard him sniff too. I briefly glanced in his direction and saw his eyes narrow suspiciously. I think he could sense what I could; that the woman was human but there was something else about her.

So there we were, the Werewolf couple who were staring at the woman whom was staring back. She looked our way like she was hypnotized. Finally, the stalemate ended when she started to walk toward us.

As soon as she did, in one move Declan protectively came to stand in front, incase she was trouble. But I didn't want him to frighten her off – not yet anyways – so I came to stand by his side. Then he pulled back his wide shoulders as if to show off his strength, before resting a muscled arm about my shoulders.

The woman stopped short a meter away, as she looked from me to my husband and then back my way.

She began to speak in her Scottish accent, "You're both different, like I am. But you're not the same as me."

Huh...? Declan and I exchanged funny looks which we turned on her.

The woman continued, "You're both old, older than anybody here. You're both the only two of your kind. Once you leave, there won't be anyone else like you."

The European Werewolf growled under his breath, as he held his mate closer. He didn't trust the woman because she knew too much. But I thought that was what made her special and I wanted to hear more.

"Are you some kind of Tarot Reader?" He accused. "If you are, we're not interested."

Just then we were interrupted by the stall owner, coming to join us.

"So, is that your choice then?" The owner asked about the small pile of records I was still holding.

Declan nodded back whilst his eyes never the strange woman.

"I'll take those off you and tally up the price." He offered before he noticed who we were looking at. "Oh hallo there Nairn, and how are you today?"

She momentarily looked away to answer his question, "I'm well thanks, Angus. How is your back treating you?"

"All good." He chuckled. "I went to Doc Brighton just as you told me to. You were right as usual, it was a pinched nerve. But thanks to the herbal tea you gave me, I'm not getting pins and needles down my legs anymore."

As soon as he moved away to process our transaction, I asked her, "Are you a Medicine Woman?"

The stranger we now knew was named Nairn, smiled. "In a sense I am. Only I'm called a Healer or a Naturopath, around these parts."

"Or another word for you, like in the olden days would be Witch, wouldn't it?" He asked in a dangerously low voice.

Her smile dissipated as she sensed my husband's overprotective nature was in full force.

"You can relax, Declan." She said seriously. "I don't want to harm you or your mate."

Our eyes widened at how she knew his name...

"Yes, B." She looked my way again. "I know who you are. Declan is right, I can also be called a Witch. Your aura blinded me as soon as I saw you and then it showed me your lives together."

"B's not the only one with an aura here, is she?" He examined the air surrounding her.

What was that? Does this mean that Nairn has an aura too? Damn, I wish I could see these things, like other Shape Shifters can.

"Are you psychic?" I remembered the SSIT notes on such.

"Naturopath, Healer, Psychic or Seer; I've been called many things." Nairn answered patiently. "I use my abilities to help others, which in turn is my living."

"What do you want?" He asked suspiciously.

"I would like to invite you both to afternoon tea." She said simply.

My husband and I exchanged a wary look, which she caught.

"No, I will not try to serve either of you as afternoon tea, Declan." She smirked, before she frowned. "Neither of you have had a good run with other elements of the supernatural, have you?"

"That's an understatement." He said moodily.

She let out a sad sigh and then we watched her take out a business card from her handbag, which she held out.

"My name is Nairn Durrant and I live at Stonewall House. At 3.30 pm I will be serving afternoon tea and I would be delighted if you would join me."

However, the European Werewolf still held the Witch under scrutiny. After a tense moment, he snatched the card off her. I leaned in to also read her name and address, in an antique style font on the recycled cardboard.

Hang on a second...

"Durrant? Stonewall House? I know those names." I thought aloud.

The two turned quiet as they waited to hear what I had to say. They watched my eyes widen and my mouth fall open in shock. Then I surprised them both, when I gave a little jump of excitement!

I prattled off to the stranger, "You're related to Dr. Knight! Or you'd know her as Lady Vivian Dunmore. Her brother married 'dour Doreen' or Lady Durrant, I should say. My great, great grandmother Elisha, masqueraded as one of your family, when she was presented at the court of King George 2nd! It was when Elisha was in love with Sir Guy Robertson."

"Keep it down, B." My mate whispered, when he caught the curious looks of the passersby who overheard.

"Declan is descended from Guy Robertson!" I told her before I looked his way, "Remember I told you how your great, great granduncle Mike Sabre was the reincarnation of Guy Robertson? Remember I told you about Elisha saving Guy Robertson's life in India? Her charade in the 18th century was part of the Dunmore and Durrant families! Nairn is a descendant of that family!"

Right at that moment, Angus reappeared which shut me up, but he too had heard.

"Well well, it's a small world after all." He chuckled in amusement. "It sounds like you're distantly related or some such."

"Everything happens for a reason, Angus." She smiled softly. "And everything has its time and place."

This made me giggle, especially since I learned something similar when I was taught temporal causalities; A leads to B which then results in C. It felt ironic to hear a human talk about it, but in a supernatural sense.

"That's 25 records at 20 Credits each, so that's 500 Credits please sir." Angus held out his hand.

Declan passed his credit card to him, as he still looked on Nairn in distrust. It didn't stop until he glanced my way in surprise, when I had let go of his hand to shake Nairn's instead.

"I'm Bianca Grace Sabre and I'm descended from Elisha Grace Baker. My husband Declan Sabre, is descended from Sir Guy Robertson. Your ancestors knew both Elisha and Guy, from the Fox's Ball and at Court."

She shook my hand enthusiastically, "I'm pleased to make your acquaintance, B."

Next, I looked on my mate expectantly that he should do the same.

He shook her hand just the once before immediately releasing it. "Yeah, hi."

However his scepticism was disregarded, as Nairn and I smiled on each other whilst at the same time; looking on the other, fascinated.

Angus returned once more, with Declan's credit card as well as two cotton carry bags full of records, which my mate took from him.

"Here is your credit card and here are your purchases." The stall owner organized before he turned to our new friend. "Nairn, the missus wants to know if you'll be coming to the dance this Saturday night? We need to know numbers by Wednesday, so we can organize how much food and drink to order."

"I'll be coming Angus, and so will B and Declan." She answered.

"We will?" My mate raised his eyebrows. "We're only meant to be visiting Stonehaven for two nights."

"It's a rare treat for B to get Declan to dance." She passed me a knowing grin.

The European Werewolf looked on askance at the idea, whereas Angus laughed good naturedly.

"Don't worry, son." The forty-something year old stall owner, said to the male he thought was younger. "You'll be joining the many men of this town with their army of left feet. Besides, the dance is the perfect opportunity for the women to dress up and look particularly pretty on the night."

"My wife doesn't need a dance, to look pretty." He said gruffly.

This made Angus and Nairn titter at his blunt, but sweet talk.

"Aw, c'mon..." I sidled up to him and gave a beseeching look, "...what's an extra couple of nights? It won't ruin our itinerary."

Declan's mouth wavered and he clearly looked like he was trying with all of his might to say 'no'. However I knew the battle was won when he said the words which usually worked in my favour; "We'll see."

*****

It was 2 PM when we left the markets and drove back to our hotel in the CBD.

My mate carried his 'pride and joy' up to our hotel room, whilst I carried the records. However as soon as we had privacy, I instantaneously phased the two of us to Alaska. We preferred to take his purchases home immediately, rather than cart them around the UK.

In another flash of light which made the lights in our hotel room flicker, we reappeared in Stonehaven.

"It's 2.45 pm." I caught the time. "Let's go to Nairn's."

It was here that Declan faltered. "Um, B? I'm not so sure that's a good idea."

I looked on puzzled, "Why not?"

"Er, because she's a Witch...?" He looked on like I was mad. "How do you know if she's a white one? Or if she's gonna send flying monkeys after us?"

"Declan!" I snorted with laughter. "There's no such thing as 'white witches'. Wiccans worship both male and female deities whilst studying, revering and using nature's gifts."

"Then who are the weirdoes that go around sacrificing babies?"

"Satanists." I said coolly, as I walked over to open our hotel room door. "Are you coming?"

"And Werewolves are the ones that get a bad rap...?" He muttered as he reluctantly followed.

*****

The GPS feature of our rented four-wheel-drive showed us the way. We put in the address of Stonewall House and followed the directions down several streets and into the countryside. The drive took us thirty minutes, before we saw the small road we were on, was heading up a steep hill on which sat a very old house.

The building was primarily two story, with the third acting as an attic complete with gabled windows. However instead of looking cosy, the small manor looked foreboding. The grey stone looked dank and partly covered in moss, with narrow but high windows. Even the black, tiled roof looked intimidating, with formerly decorative but now broken, iron rods sitting on several crests.

"The house looks like its seen better days." He remarked, as he pulled up in front of the small garden gate.

"It does." I agreed. "I wouldn't be surprised if it's haunted. It certainly looks the like type you see in horror movies."

"Great." He rolled his eyes. "We're having afternoon tea with a Witch in a haunted house. So, whose bright idea was it that we come here?"

"Oh shut up." I opened my door first. "For a paranormal predator, you're so judgmental."

My husband snickered as he climbed out second, before turning on the central locking.

"Hey, I've an idea. How about afterwards, we instantaneously phase back to China? Another round with some Asian Werewolves only seems appropriate, after tea with a Witch in a haunted house."

"Shut up." I marched up the garden path, without waiting for him.

Declan easily caught up with his larger strides. When we reached the front door, we didn't have to knock. Perfectly timed, Nairn opened it and shone a welcoming grin our way. We were hit with a delicious aroma of something she'd prepared, which was a nice contrast to the damp air of the outside.

"Mmm, what's that smell?" The European Werewolf asked instead of simply saying 'hallo'.

Embarrassed, I whacked him on the arm before I apologized. "Sorry, he comes across as an animal but deep down inside, he's a...well um, an animal."

"Not at all," she laughingly waved it off. "Come inside, please."

We went into the huge house but once we were inside, we found it was just as cold as it was outside. We kept our coats on and observed so had Nairn, since seeing her in the market place. She led us through the foyer and into a large living room, past a grand staircase.

The house looked like it could have been fancy back in the day, but not anymore.

Dust was everywhere, the wooden staircase looked slumped in the middle and the wallpaper in the living room was peeling badly. The old carpet smelled of mould and the fabric on the couches or chairs looked tatty. There were only four signs of life that somebody lived here; open books scattered about, a fire burning in the fireplace, the delicious smell of cooking and of course, the human standing in front of us.

"Clean much?" My husband looked about, unimpressed.

I nudged him to mind his manners as I hastily added on, "What an interesting old place this is."

"No, Declan's right." She admitted. "I inherited the house in the same condition you see it now and that was ten years ago. I had grand designs to fix up the place. But a low income, major repair work and thirty rooms to clean put those plans to rest."

"Couldn't you get a loan?" He continued.

"Oh and what would you have me put down on the paperwork about my employment; Witch or Psychic?" She raised her eyebrows.

Finally that broke the ice with the European Werewolf, as he threw back his head and laughed loudly.

"Good comeback." He congratulated then he wandered over to the couch and sat down.

"Excuse me, I'll just fetch the tea." She turned to leave the room.

"Do you need a hand?" I offered.

"No thank you, B." She said appreciatively. "Please make yourself at home."

Once she had departed, I helped myself to exploring her bookshelves which ran along two of the walls.

"As usual, B hits the books." My mate remarked.

"But Declan," I said amazed, as I took down a leather volume, "some of these are hundreds of years old! They're even older than our collection at home."

"I'm not surprised." He said flatly, as he looked about the decaying decadence of the room.

Just then Nairn returned, carrying a tray which held a tea pot, sugar bowl, jug of milk and three teacups complete with saucers. She put the tray down on the coffee table in between the couches, one of which Declan was sitting on.

"Ah, you've found Chaucer." She noticed what I was holding.

Hang on, how would she know which book I had? The engraved title on the cover had faded and you had to open the book to see the title page. The leather binding also looked just like the other leather bound books. But before I could ask, she had left the room again to fetch something else.

I passed my mate an impressed look at Nairn's skills as a Seer.

"Maybe we could find a pack of cards and the two of you could have a contest of who can guess which card I'm holding up." He chuckled.

At that moment, she came back into the room with another tray. This time it held the food, which made Declan's and my mouths water. On one plate sat neatly cut, cucumber sandwiches. On another sat several scones with cream and jam. Lastly on the third dish, was chocolate slice.

"Nairn, this looks lovely. Thank you!" I gushed as I finally moved to sit beside my husband.

"It's my pleasure." She said warmly, as she sat opposite to us. "I've never entertained guests before, who are nearly two centuries old."

Declan had already begun scoffing down the sandwiches, but he almost choked when she said that!

"We use great moisturizer." I said humorously.

"You must give me the name of the brand." She giggled along.

As my husband attacked the food, Nairn and I ate more politely. However she didn't seem surprised by his appetite and even poured him a second cup of tea. But before Declan could claim the last chocolate slice, I used my light speed reflexes and snatched it up instead.

"Hey, I was reaching for that!" He objected.

"You've already eaten three." I retorted. "Didn't your mother teach you to share?"

Then I cut it in half and passed one part to Nairn, who smilingly took it.

"Oh you two!" She tittered at the fiery couple. "But rest assured Declan, I have more slice in the kitchen."

"Really?" He made a move to get it, when I pulled him back down.

"Don't even think about it!" I snapped. "You're a guest and you can't eat our host out of house and home."

Finally, he remembered his manners and sat back into the cushions instead. He even made an attempt at small talk. "So, B thinks this house is haunted."

She looked my way impressed, "Good call. When I first moved in, I did have some problems. But nothing a clearing ceremony and a cleansing spell couldn't fix."

"Sounds like something our Medicine Man occasionally does, or even our Tribal Elders." Declan looked on, impressed.

"Oh really?" Nairn listened with interest.

"Well yeah, but of course they don't do just that. Our Medicine Man delivers babies, treats the sick and sometimes does counselling." He shifted uncomfortably. "Our Tribal Elders educate the young about their culture, as well as decide on laws or preside over family disturbances. But they also lead the tribe in many spiritual areas, such as funerals or weddings."

"Is there a Medicine Woman?" She enquired.

"There are women in the tribe who practice Naturopathy and help the Medicine Man with his herbal remedies." I explained. "But the tribe's Medicine Man is usually a Werewolf, who uses his supernatural senses to help him diagnose the illness."

"There aren't any female Werewolves in your tribe?" She looked my way, puzzled.

"I'm the only one." I announced.

"Ah." She gave a nod, as if she should have known this.

My mate put a supportive hand on my lap, as he asked her, "So what are your special tricks, Nairn?"

"Well, people don't come to me for spiritual guidance, that's for sure." She giggled before she continued. "But I can 'see' what's wrong with people who come to me for help. Usually it's simple medical problems I can help with, otherwise if it's serious I refer them to a medical professional. I'm also a Midwife and occasionally I act as a fertility specialist."

Declan and I froze as soon as she said that, which she noticed.

"A fertility specialist?" My mate's eyes narrowed again.

"Why yes." She explained. "I primarily look after women who are with child, but occasionally I help those who want to be."

"You help women get pregnant?" I struggled to keep my voice neutral, although my heart began to race. "What's your success rate?"

"My success rate?" She gave a funny look.

"She's asking how many of these women have you helped become pregnant?" Declan clarified.

"All of them." Nairn shrugged.

"All of them?" I stared in surprise. "What, every single one?"

"If I know that I can't help, like they've had their reproductive organs removed from cysts or cancers then I'll tell them. However if I 'see' it's something minor obstructing pregnancy, I can help."

My eyes crept over to my mate's, who was waiting to hold my gaze.

She regarded us closely, "I didn't sense the two of you were trying to become pregnant."

"We're not." He said curtly.

"But we don't have to worry about taking preventative measures either." I sighed disappointedly.

Nairn stared in surprise, "But I thought with the pair of you being Werewolves, you would be supernaturally fertile."

"Here we go again...!" I moaned as I fell back into the sofa.

"Yeah, so did the last two Medicine Men." Declan sympathetically rubbed my leg. "But as I said to B, I'm happy that she can't conceive. I'm relieved that I'm not creating anymore European Werewolves for the world to worry about."

"But if you two had a child, it would be half Lokoti Werewolf and half European Werewolf. It would be a completely new species." Nairn said interestedly.

"B is also called the last Circulator because there hasn't been another born after her." My mate informed. "She was told that the buck stops with her."

"Oh," she turned thoughtful. "If it's been foretold, it's probably why her body is stopping conception."

"My body is stopping me from conceiving?" I almost laughed.

"You are fertile B, your Lokoti Werewolf pheromones tell me so." She declared.

"Tell me about it!" My husband groaned. "I have to stop every 'Tom, Dick and Harry' from knocking at her door, thanks to her pheromones!"

Nairn carried on bluntly, "You still have your monthly period, don't you?"

"Er, yeah?" I blushed.

"Like clockwork." He added on, as he squeezed my thigh. "I can even count down to when I'm gonna be fetching the painkillers, or ducking for cover with her PMS."

"I can 'see' you're ovulating, so we just have to find out what is preventing you from becoming pregnant." Nairn thought out loud. When Declan and I looked at each other in alarm, she queried, "Don't you want to find out?"

"Er..." he turned uneasy, "...I mean it's B's body and if she wants to find out then sure."

"I was told it was because my reproductive organs are in temporal flux." I said confused.

"But that doesn't make sense." She frowned. "If your reproductive organs were then it would stop you from having your period as well as ovulating."

"I was also told that my eggs are hard to fertilize because of it." I forced out, as I felt my face burn in embarrassment. "And the eggs can't embed themselves in my uterus, from the same thing."

"That doesn't mean you're infertile." She smiled reassuringly. "I've treated other women with similar symptoms. I can give you herbs which can change the lining of your uterus and there are different techniques I can teach you. Certain sex positions can optimize the contact of the sperm with the egg."

Although I felt a glimmer of hope at her words, I also felt disappointment. I warned, "When I was married to another Werewolf, we already tried some of these things."

"You tried the 'lotus position', or 'chakra sex' or even 'tantric sex'?" She tested. "Or any Celtic fertility spells or potions?"

"Well um, no..." I faltered.

"I could give you pair a free consultation right now." Nairn stood up from the couch to walk over to a desk. "Come and sit over here. I need to find out some more details, so I can come up with your prescribed plan."

Declan shot an unhappy look my way, as I squirmed with uncertainty.

"Um Nairn, it's very nice of you to arrange this for us. But we don't know if we want to have kids." I faltered.

"I know." She shrugged it off. "Whatever I prescribe for you today, you don't have to use immediately. You can choose to use it when you're ready."

We watched her take out a pen and paper from a draw before looking our way expectantly. I looked on my mate nervously, should we give this a go?

"Just for the sake of curiosity?" I shrugged.

He sighed loudly as if I was asking a lot and then he stood up from the couch. Whilst holding my hand, he walked me over to one of the two chairs in front of the desk. Once I was seated, he collapsed reluctantly into the other.

"Now, I need to conduct a short interview to find out more so I can prescribe the correct course of treatment." Nairn spoke in a professional manner. "Bear in mind that being a Healer, whatever you tell me will be kept in the strictest confidence."

The both of us reached for the other's hands, to seek out reassurance from each other. Today was definitely one of those days that I appreciated how large, strong and warm, his hands constantly felt.

Her pen was poised midair, to write down our answers. "To begin with, how often do the pair of you engage in sexual intercourse?"

The European Werewolf's eyes bulged in shock, so I thought I should do this one.

I tried to say casually, "Um...almost every day."

"How long have you two been married for?" She continued.

He felt comfortable enough to answer this one. "146 years."

I caught her surprised expression, but like a true professional she quickly regained her composure. I think the frequency, astounded her.

"Were the two of you sexually active prior to your marriage?"

"Yes." I said.

"And how long were the two of you sexually active, prior to your marriage?"

My husband and I looked at the other as we calculated together.

I spoke first, "Um, I think it was nearly three months before we got married."

"And that once, before you married Grant." He added on.

"Yeah, there was that too." I giggled as I felt him caress my hand. "We were each other's first time."

"During these occasions, were any preventative measures taken?" She asked as she scribbled down our responses.

"Only after our first time." I said.

She checked, "Did you take the 'morning after' pill?"

"No." I shook my head.

"Or some other medication or herb that was meant to stop pregnancy from occurring?" She wondered.

"No."

"Could you please tell me what you used then?" She looked up from her notes.

I blushed as I looked at my mate, as I didn't know how to put it.

"A Werewolf way and lets leave it at that." He said shortly.

Next, she surprised us when she wrote down; *A Werewolf method of pregnancy prevention...*

"Are you sure no one's gonna see your notes?" My husband asked worriedly.

"Oh," she saw our concerned expressions, "I'll just make notes now and once I've decided on a remedy, I'll burn them." She promised before she moved on. "When was it that B learned that she couldn't conceive?"

"When she was married to Grant." He said jealously.

"B?" She glanced my way for further information.

"My first husband and I had been married for nearly a year when I had a vision that I couldn't conceive. So I went and got myself checked out and my doctor found that my reproductive organs like many other aspects of my body, were in temporal flux. After three years of trying, nothing worked. So we gave up and Grant started talking about adoption."

Nairn passed me a sympathetic gaze, before she looked to my husband next.

"Now Declan, while B was married to Grant, did you ever have intercourse with anybody else?"

"No." He frowned. "Because I can't."

"You can't?" She raised her eyebrows, curiously.

"I can't be with a human woman without accidentally harming her or turning her." He said staunchly.

We could see this shocked her, as her mouth fell open and she dropped her pen. But she regained her professional decorum and writing instrument to continue.

"Did you engage in any activities of a sexual nature, with another Werewolf or something else supernatural?"

"No." He stated.

"How long was B was married to this Grant?" She enquired.

"Five years." He growled out his displeasure.

When she looked shocked a second time, I asked, "What's wrong?"

"Oh nothing's wrong, I'm just surprised that's all." She struggled to regain her objective façade. "It's just that Werewolves are very virile creatures. I imagine it must have been very difficult, for Declan."

"Let me put it this way," he spoke in a dangerously low voice, "if I ever found myself stuck in those five years again, I would kill Grant and kidnap B."

I hated it when he spoke like that. I pulled my hand back from his, whereas the psychic looked on my mate in understanding.

"I can see those five years were very hard on you, Declan." She said softly. "You loved her for some time, even before she was married to another, didn't you?"

The European Werewolf shifted uncomfortably in his seat, as he hated all this mushy stuff.

"As I said to B, my body sensed she was different, years before she changed." He said gruffly.

"But you couldn't act on your feelings until she did." She spoke knowingly. "When she changed, she was still kept from you, this time by Grant?"

"Sorry, what has this got to do with B not getting pregnant?" He ended the discussion.

"My apologies, I was asking these questions to find out your sexual history. I had to see if you've ever impregnated another, inadvertently or otherwise."

"Nope." He sat up straighter. "Besides the fact that B's the only partner in the bedroom I've ever wanted or had; my Catholic mother would have castrated me."

To his surprise, we watched her make note of that as well!

"Now B," she looked my way, "I understand this is still a touchy subject, but I need to learn more about what you and Grant tried, to get you to conceive."

"Um, OK...?" I said awkwardly.

Declan's shoulders stiffened as he looked downright annoyed by this questioning.

"First of all, what herbs or medication did your try?" She began.

"It was so long ago..." I tried to remember, "...my Calculator Vincent, put me on several 25th Century drugs, to either make me ovulate more or change the lining of my uterus. My Grandpa who was the tribe's Medicine Man, gave me special herbal teas but I can't remember what they did. They tasted disgusting and I nearly gagged every time I drank them."

"And Grant still tried to make you drink it?" He tried to find fault.

"Grant didn't make me do anything that I didn't want." I frowned back.

"Hmm," she frowned thoughtfully, "now were there any other measures that were taken?"

I blushed again as I didn't want to say it in front of Declan, which he picked up on.

"Should I leave the room?" He asked in annoyance.

"There's more chocolate slice in the kitchen." She offered. "If you could just give us a couple of minutes?"

I caught the growl under his breath, as he stood up in a huff and walked away. But before he left the room, he threw me a parting glare. Once he had disappeared, she looked at me expectantly.

"Um, we tried a Lokoti Werewolf way to get me to conceive." I said.

"Which was?"

"Well erm, we had sex whilst he was in his Werewolf form." I spoke quietly incase Declan was trying to listen from the other room. "When we're in our supernatural bodies, we're meant to be our most virile."

Nairn wrote this down as she asked her next question, "Have you and Declan tried this?"

"Ah no, not really." I said and when she looked up for an explanation, I added on, "Well we can't. For one, when he's in his European Werewolf shape, his strength increases dramatically and it'd harm me. The other reason is because when he's in his supernatural body, although he's naked, his er...genitalia disappears. I think it's because his body bulks up and it's protected under layers of muscle. He becomes almost indestructible with no vulnerable spots."

"I see." She scribbled all of this down.

I tried to joke, "So trying to kick a European Werewolf in the groin as a self-defence method, doesn't work if you're ever hunted by one."

"Noted." She smirked. "Now tell me B, do you orgasm during sex with Declan?"

"Yes." I said simply

"Do you orgasm every time the two of you have sex?"

"Repeatedly."

A giggle escaped from our fertility specialist, "That would explain your regularity for the activity."

"Well, he says he can tell if I don't, which makes him try harder. He's told me he can feel it, because I don't become wet enough. A couple of times, he's mentioned that he can see my aura change when I do come."

"Like a mood ring," she joked as she finished writing this up. Lastly, she called out, "Thank you Declan, it's safe to return now."

Automatically, he reappeared like he'd been waiting to be allowed back in. He walked over to his chair and sat down, whilst licking melted chocolate off his fingers.

"Declan," she turned to him, "I need to ask you a couple of questions about how you experience sexual intercourse."

The European Werewolf looked on the Witch, as if she had just slapped him in the face with a wet fish...

Nairn kept her tone professional, "Do you come every time you have sex?"

"Er yeah, that's kind of the point, isn't it?" He looked on as if she were crazy.

"Not necessarily, there are some males who don't ejaculate every time." Nairn said evenly.

He seemed offended by the idea, "Then what's the point in that?"

She moved her questioning along, "Do you masturbate?"

"No." He said adamantly. When she examined his face to see if he was being honest, he added on, "I don't need to if I'm getting some every day, now do I?"

"Some males still do, like humans for instance."

"I'm not a human male." He frowned in disapproval. "Some males can't get it up, but that's not a problem either. Most humans I've heard about, can't even go for three rounds but that's just a quiet night for us. Do you want to write that down too?"

She DID write that down, which made him look my way unimpressed.

"Maybe I should go back into the kitchen?" He tried to run away again.

But this time it wasn't Declan who left the room, it was Nairn.

"Excuse me for a moment," she suddenly stood up.

We watched her leave before we looked on the other again.

"When we visit your English relatives in Blythe Castle next week, are we going to get a 'sex quiz' too?" He seethed. "Come on B, I thought not having kids was a good idea for us."

I rubbed my face from stress, as I thought it would at least be nice to even have a choice on the matter; rather than be the 'barren chick'.

Declan exhaled noisily as he looked away. Then we sat quietly, looking in opposite directions for five minutes. His arms were crossed, as my legs were and pointing away from him; as our body language showed our unhappiness.

"OK," he eventually turned back my way, "you want to feel normal by at least being able to have kids, even if we don't end up doing that...am I right?" I gave a nod as I stared at a painting on the wall. He continued to analyze, "I always thought it was more Grant's idea to have kids, than it was yours. It was his idea in the first place to adopt, but when he died you hardly mentioned it. We've only talked about it once."

I shrugged back, whilst avoiding his gaze.

Then he said grouchily, "And how come no matter how many years go by, the subject of your dead husband still comes up? I was in love with you for four years before our first time together, but then you went and married someone else. I eventually get you back and we're together for over a century, but I'm still reminded that I'm the *second* husband."

I sighed heavily as I stared down at the desk. I could see Declan's point of view, but I still hated hearing his threats against Grant. He had been a good man and a kind husband, even if we came together in unusual circumstances.

Just then Nairn returned to the room, carrying two unopened flower buds which she handed to each of us.

"I need the two of you to take these with you, when you return to your hotel. You have to place the flowers on either side of the bed. Declan, you keep your flower on your side and B, you will do the same with yours. You'll notice that I tied a red ribbon around B's flower stalk, so you won't get them confused. When you to come back and see me tomorrow morning, bring them with you." She instructed.

Declan and I exchanged a surprised look, which we turned towards Nairn.

"What's this supposed to prove?" He asked. "If we have a green thumb?"

"I expect that tonight the two of you will be intimate, as you've told me you are almost every day." She said simply.

This time it wasn't my husband looking on the fertility specialist in disbelief, it was me.

"So we're supposed to have sex with these flower buds on our bedside tables as his and hers...?" I wanted to check if I heard this right.

"Yes."

"Just what exactly is the point of this exercise?" He asked irritated, showing he had reached the end of his patience.

"I will explain tomorrow morning." She spoke calmly.

"I don't frickin' believe this!" He growled under his breath as he rolled his eyes.

My face reddened once more, this time because of his behaviour.

"Sorry, I guess you can see that Declan's not really into this 'New Age' kind of thing." I uncomfortably tried to laugh it off.

"It's not 'New Age,' this fertility test was used by the Druids before Roman conquest." She said matter-of-factly.

"Druids?" He repeated, before we heard him grumble, "Great, now we're getting baby making tips from Stonehenge?"

I whacked him on the arm to shut up, as my cheeks were crimson in embarrassment. Why did he have to behave like this? Why does he have to make this bad situation, worse? He's 173 years old but he's behaving like an immature boy!

"Shall we call this visit to an end?" She kicked us out, politely. "Come back and see me tomorrow for morning tea and we can go over the results then."

We three stood up before she walked us out of the living room and to the front door.

But as she opened it, she gave us a parting wink. "I'll make sure there'll be a large selection of sandwiches and more chocolate slice on offer."

*****

We were both quiet during the drive back into town. It was almost dark by the time we returned to our hotel and we parked our rental before going into the elevator, up to our room. We didn't hold hands as we customarily did, and neither of us looked at the other.

"This is ridiculous!" I overheard him growl yet again.

I sensed he felt foolish carrying around a flower bud, in his large hand.

He was the first one to walk out of the elevator then down the corridor, to our door. I stood back as he swiped the security card and held the door open for me, before we both went inside. I switched on the lights then I proceeded to take off my coat and shoes, to help me unwind.

Declan took his coat off too but then he walked over to the mini bar to grab two small glasses, which he carried into the ensuite.

I sat down on the bed as I listened to him fill the glasses with water before carrying them back out. He placed one glass on my bedside table and then the other on his. Lastly, he dropped his flower bud into it so the stalk was submerged.

"Nairn didn't say put them in water." I said flatly.

"They are plants, aren't they?" He retorted. "Of course they're gonna need water."

Then he started to undress and I looked down on the flower bud in my hand.

I sighed for my millionth time that day...maybe Declan was right? Maybe we shouldn't bother with this. Maybe we shouldn't have kids at all. Maybe we shouldn't even try. It was downright humiliating discussing our sex life with a stranger today, no matter if she was a psychic healer or a fertility specialist.

Declan sat down on the bed topless, to pull off his shoes and socks.

"Well, aren't you going to get undressed?" He asked irritably. "Or is this another test of my fertility, to see if I can impregnate you while your pants are still on?"

My heart emitted a painful spasm, "I don't think you're the one under the microscope."

"It didn't feel that way this afternoon."

I sung sarcastically, "Oh I'm sorry that you got dragged into my course of treatment for a medical condition that I'm experiencing. I'll remember this the next time one of us is injured, and we have to share blood."

Although I could feel his glare at my words, I ignored him as I looked away disheartened.

"Come on, let's get this over with." He said grouchily before he stood up to take off his jeans.

I breathed out, "No."

Just as he undid his button, he paused, "Say what?"

"No."

Declan stood there with his hands on his hips as he waited for an explanation.

I ranted tearfully, "You were like this when I asked you to dance at Uncle Harry's 175th Birthday. You were like this when I asked if I could stay in Italy for two nights, to attend the academic conference in Rome. You were like this when I asked you to run to the Supermarket when I ran out of pads... have I ever kicked up a stink when you've ever asked me for something?"

"What are you talking about? You ALWAYS kick up a stink or you flat out refuse to do it!" He raised his voice. "I ask you repeatedly to heat up leftover lasagne in the oven, and you ALWAYS heat it up in the microwave! I ask you to turn down your music because the earphones would be damaging your ears and you turn it up instead! Then what about in China? When I asked you to go to Alaska, so I could take care of the Asian Werewolves and fight for my mate; you end up yelling out that you were defective, to make them turn away!"

Angrily, I stood up so I could look him in the eye. "You have NEVER asked me, you just tell me! You order me about! You don't say 'please don't heat up the lasagne in the microwave'; you bark out, 'B, what did I tell you about the frickin' lasagne!' You NEVER ask me Declan, you NEVER ask!"

"You're my mate!" He cried out in frustration. "You're supposed to sense that I'm asking these things!"

"Exactly! We're mates and we're supposed to do things for the other person and just get it done, right?" I challenged.

"Precisely!"

"Oh, you mean like right now?" I hit back, which made him pause.

"Well I DID cooperate with all of Nairn's snooping around our sex life this afternoon." He said in a surly manner.

"And you think you know when something's wrong or why I'm upset, because you can see my aura change?" I brought up.

"I've done a pretty good job so far." He said matter-of-factly.

"OK then, tell me why I stopped shopping at the supermarket in Alma for twelve months?" I demanded.

"Because you got so busy with work, you decided to shop over the internet and have it delivered instead!" He fired back.

"WRONG!" I yelled in his face. "I stopped shopping there because I overheard two middle-aged hags, bitch about me as I walked past! I heard them say, 'she may be pretty but I heard from Shana that she can't have kids. I guess looks aren't everything after all'. You're not the one seen as defective Declan, it's ME! For the last 150 years, I've had to put up with people looking at me like I'm not just a freak for being the only female Lokoti Werewolf, but I'm a reject as a barren woman!"

Declan's mouth fell open in surprise as I sat back down on the bed to fling off my socks, before I stood up again to kick off my jeans.

I vented, "So let's just do this shall we? Then we can hear the words, 'oh look at Declan's flower, it's blooming because there's nothing wrong with him. But B, sorry your flower is drooping, because your womb is. But cheer up ole girl, at least you have your period, which means you're still young even if you are a disappointment to all women kind'!"

He reached out to stop me by gently placing his hands on my shoulders. My husband looked on hurt, not because I had wounded him but because I was hurting. He turned quiet as he pulled me close, before ducking his head and kissing me softly, over and over again. But I was too angry for tenderness.

My head moved away first then my body second, as I growled under my breath. "Screw this, I'm outta here."

I turned towards the door, when my bigger mate tried to catch me.

"B...? B, wait!" He grabbed my arm but I didn't want to prolong this.

I instantaneously phased out of his stronger grip and reappeared inside of the empty elevator of the hotel.

Next, I hit the button for the ground floor and the lift began to move. I was tempted to phase back to Alaska, but Declan would smell my absence then pack up our stuff and follow me home again. Plus I would like to see Nairn again. So I decided to stay in Scotland but I'd walk off my anger instead.

Barefoot, I walked out of the hotel without my shoes, coat or purse. I guess this looked odd to the passersby, but I ignored their peculiar expressions. I already get looks of pity, or smug satisfaction over the fact that I can't have kids. So what's a couple more glances, for going for a walk on a cold night in Scotland without frickin' shoes?

I walked and I walked and I walked some more...

I headed away from our modern hotel and went into the old area of town, with the stone buildings and narrow, cobbled streets. The smell of its history, as well as looking on the antiquated architecture, momentarily cheered me. I looked on in interest, at the small doors and windows of the townhouses, as I passed under the old, iron lamp posts, which were now plasma powered.

An old horse and carriage, started to pass me down the street. I've always enjoyed the clip clop sound they made, in this instance it was by two large horses I think were called Clydesdales? However the animals caught wind of my supernatural presence, as they sensed the predator in me and became afraid.

Suddenly, the horses broke from a trot and went into a canter, as they whinnied loudly!

"Woah!" The female driver yanked on the reigns.

Oh oh, I'd better make myself scarce so not to put the humans in the carriage at risk.

Quickly, I ducked down an alleyway and walked behind a row of townhouses.

My eyes easily adjusted to the dark thanks to my Werewolf ability, since there were less street lights this way. I walked out of the alleyway and turned down another cobbled road, this time with rows of shops, cafes and restaurants. It was a tourist hub, but it looked inviting and the smell of the food made my stomach growl.

I passed an outdoor table where a young lesbian couple, were sharing a plate of fettuccine carbonara with garlic bread; making my mouth water. This made me wish I had my purse on me. But I didn't want to instantaneously phase back to the hotel get it, because I didn't want to see Declan.

In disappointment, I sighed again as I forced myself to look away from the food, when I caught a new scent...of maple syrup? Before I could wonder which café was serving pancakes with this sauce, I almost walked into my mate who was standing on the street, right in front of me!

My mouth fell open in dismay, as he was stood there casually like he'd been waiting for me. He was completely dressed and holding my coat and purse on one arm and my shoes in his other.

"Forget something, B?" He glanced down at my bare feet, before looking back up.

I harrumphed as I crossed my arms, going into my defensive posture and because I was cold.

Declan held out my coat and shoes and sulkily, I snatched them up before I walked over to a nearby fountain. I sat down on the side to pull on my shoes and then my coat. But I remained seated as he stood, looking on.

"I suppose I should be relieved that you didn't go home to Alaska and leave me alone in a foreign country again." He said dryly, as he came to sit beside.

I remained quiet, whilst staring at the other couples, enjoying their romantic dinners at the outside tables of the cafes and restaurants.

"It's a good thing you smell so good, which makes you easy to track down. But you seem to be developing this worrying habit of taking off, instead of just talking about what's bothering you. Maybe that's the Circulator in you? Your mother ran away for three months, when she was pregnant."

I bit back, "She didn't 'run away', she had to train her Circulator abilities and meet her Calculator."

"If we became pregnant, would you do that to me too?" He asked warily.

"Considering the facts that I'm the last of my kind and I'm not ever going to get pregnant, it looks like the odds are stacked in your favour." I said coolly.

My husband frowned, "Why didn't you tell me what happened in the Supermarket?" When I didn't answer, he continued. "Usually, your aura or your face helps me out, as they're pretty obvious. I suppose Grant would have sensed what happened to you in the Supermarket, as he would have experienced your pain on the day. But cut me some slack B, I've got thick skin as well as stronger physique and I try to use these, to protect you."

"I already know all of this, Declan."

"So I'm not attuned to you like another Lokoti Werewolf was, but I thought that one of the good things about us, is we're pretty vocal about what we want or don't want." Then he passed me a cheeky grin. "I enjoy our arguments and the make-up sex, which usually comes after them."

"That's not our problem." I turned away once more.

"But neither is this kids issue, B." He returned to seriousness. "Do you know what makes me angry?"

"I'm sure you're gonna tell me."

"I'm pretty good at fixing things that I see are broken, which makes me a great mechanic. But I have never seen you as broken, which is why I can't understand your pain that always brings us back to this subject. You know the saying, 'if it ain't broke, don't fix it'? That's you in spades. You ain't broken, B. You're the last Circulator and I'm the last European Werewolf. It's just the way it is and the way it's meant to be."

I looked down at the cobbled road, at the old brickwork and how all the pieces which weren't the same size; still managed to fit together.

He turned quiet as he knew me well enough by now, to know that I was listening but sometimes I just needed to let the words to soak in. Then I felt his hand settle over mine and the instant warmth which flowed through his touch. Next, his fingers intertwined with my fingers, before they massaged my palm.

A small smile escaped, as I recalled the very first time he held my hand like this, was when I was 18 years old. Declan saw this, as he had been watching my face. Lastly, he picked up my hand to deliver several soft kisses to it and I couldn't stop myself from giggling at his show of affection.

"You wanna grab something to eat?" He nodded towards the Italian Restaurant, where I had looked longingly on the pasta carbonara.

"Hell yeah!"

"OK then." He stood up first and pulled me to my feet, second. "We'll see to you getting fed and then I get to take you back to our hotel room, to feed on you."

I laughed as he growled hungrily in my ear, whilst walking with his arm about his wife.

*****

~ 7 ~

Although the 'his & hers' flower buds remained on either side of the bed, the Werewolf couple didn't.

We seemed to alternate, either I moved over him on his side of the mattress, or he rolled me over to take the dominant position on mine instead. We didn't lie the right way up either, at one stage we were lying sideways on the bed before twisting around, until our heads hung over the end. But it didn't stop there, especially when we landed on the discarded quilt on the floor.

Then we remained on it to ensure against carpet burn.

"Wait, wait, wait!" I panted out, whilst pushing his sweaty body off mine. "Shouldn't we be doing this on the bed?"

"Say what?" He gave a funny look, before flicking his wet hair off his face.

"The flower buds..." I nodded in their direction, "...don't we have to have some proximity to them?"

"Screw the flowers!" He snarled out as he tried to continue satisfying himself.

"Exactly!" I slapped him on the ass. "We're screwing because of the flowers."

In a single move, Declan heaved us both back onto the damp mattress which reminded us why we had migrated to the floor.

When he caught my face screw up in distaste, he pointed out, "We've had over ten rounds in the last hour and a half, what do you expect?"

"Fine, but I want to be on top." I tried to roll him over.

However, he stopped us halfway, so we were lying on our sides instead.

"Wait, I have another idea." He emitted a cheeky chuckle.

The pillows found themselves tossed to the floor, alongside of the quilt. I found my back against the headboard whilst he was holding my right leg up. We were still lying on our sides facing the other, whilst trying not to knock into the bedside tables.

Just then, I watched my mate pause in the middle of our love making. He momentarily looked towards the flower buds, before his eyes returned to mine. Then a silly smile broke out on his sweaty face.

"You know what? If this did work..." he referred to the fertility test, "...I'd want to have girls. I want all girls, who'd be pretty just like their mother is."

"Oh yeah?"

"Yeah, I want to be the King of the Castle, in a houseful of women."

"Why?" I looked on in amusement.

"Then I wouldn't just be the luckiest bastard in the tribe, for having the prettiest wife. Everyone would be jealous because I'd have a whole clan of beautiful Werewolves, who all the boys would be asking my permission to date."

I laughed back, "I know how overprotective you get when your female relations start dating. You'd frighten away all the boys, with your growls and glares."

"And it'll only get worse with a daughter." He smiled smugly. "I know all too well how the one-track mind works, of a man."

I tittered as he moved in closer to chew on my ear.

Then he paused to frown, "Plus if we had a daughter, I wouldn't have to be worrying about what my son is out there, doing. I'm not looking forward to producing a male that's like me. He'd have the same bloodlust let alone carnal lust, which could hurt people or even harm a human woman, if he was with her."

"But if we had a son, he'd be half Lokoti Werewolf too." I pointed out.

"Yeah, I know." He didn't look convinced. "We could be creating a whole new breed of Werewolf, half Lokoti and half European and possibly with the speed of a Circulator. I'm NOT looking forward to training something like that self-control, or trying to catch the little breed, if it should make a run at a human."

"But I'm supposed to be the last Circulator." I returned.

Declan said seriously, "What if you're only the last, because so far you can't reproduce? What if Nairn's 'hocus pocus' works then more Circulators as well as Werewolves, are created?"

"But think of my Gran for a second," I began. "She had two kids, the son was a Werewolf like his father and her daughter was a Circulator like her mother. We could have a son that's a Werewolf and then a daughter who's a Circulator."

"Or we could have a child that's like you and is both." He debated. "I remember like it was only yesterday, when you first turned. I remember the panic in the pack, when they couldn't catch you."

I still felt guilty over what I had nearly done...hunt human.

"But you caught me. You were the one who stopped me. Together we'll do the same for our children, as we teach them control." I continued.

"And the one day our child escapes?" He arched his eyebrows warily. "What if our child looses control of the bloodlust and we loose our control over the child? We could be reproducing murderers; man-eaters."

Declan's sombre words was quickly dissipating 'the mood'. I rolled onto my back, away from him to stare disheartened at the ceiling. He saw his argument was hurting his wife, and he looked on with a pained expression.

"B, can't you see that one of the reasons why I love you; is that I can enjoy the act of procreation with you without having to worry about any actual procreating goin' on?"

I asked quietly, "You really don't want to have kids, do you?"

He sighed tiredly, "If we have kids then we'll always have to watch over their bloodlust to ensure that they never lose control. When our kids have kids of their own, we'll have to watch out for them too. Then those kids will have more kids, and so on. You'd end up turning me into a Circulator, but we'd never make it to the space time continuum, because we'd be here the whole time, watching out for the homicidal tendencies in the new breed we'd created."

"So when you said you wanted to have daughters -" I began but I was interrupted.

"I'd prefer a daughter instead of a son, as a girl wouldn't be as strong as a boy which would make teaching her self-control, easier. Besides, I'd be proud to have a daughter who looked just like her mother. But she could have her father's appetite, which I'd also be wary of." Then he growled out, "not only would I be beating back human males from dating her, I'd have to fight off male Werewolves who'd want to use her to breed. Or I could be fighting off Vampires, who'd want to feed on her."

I moaned at Declan's pessimistic view and I tried to sit up, away from him. However he didn't like this and he pulled me back down into his arms. He tried to kiss me on the lips, but I turned my head away so his mouth landed on my jaw instead.

"I'm a selfish bastard, I admit it." He pressed his body up against mine. "I love your smell and how you make me feel between the sheets, but I don't want to be responsible for what comes afterwards. I don't want to be responsible for creating another monster."

Annoyed, I tried to struggle out of his stronger grip when he rolled on top instead, so his gaze could hold my own.

"Look," he said apologetically, "when we get home from this trip, we'll make formal inquiries into adoption."

"What?" I gave a start in surprise. "But you just said -"

"I don't want to pass on my European Werewolf genes but I don't want you to miss out either. I hear your biological clock, ticking. You want kids and I want you to have kids." He said firmly. "We'll adopt."

However, unbeknownst to my husband when he was working at the Garage, occasionally I perused adoption websites. I saw the Government guidelines at how they went over a perspective parent's family background, finances, employment history and ran police checks. Not to mention how long the waiting list was to adopt...years long in fact.

Advances in medicine had helped many couples to conceive the scientific way. Plus, there weren't many unplanned pregnancies thanks to the preventative injections both human males and females could take. This meant the rate of unwanted children had dropped dramatically. With the boom in the world wide economy, there weren't any 'third world' countries left, like there used to be before and shortly after, World War Three. Rich people couldn't just go and 'buy' a needy child anymore.

I growled in frustration, as I rubbed my face from the stress he had inadvertently caused.

"What?" He saw what I was doing. "What's wrong, B?"

"Do you know how hard it is to adopt?" I snapped, which surprised him. "The waiting list is years long, no matter if we go through the Government or a private adoption agency. The background checks they run are extensive and could be risky. We would have the Government poking their noses about our tribal lands. They'd become curious about the Werewolves' date of births. We'd be asked to be medically examined or forced to consent to blood tests!"

He looked on in surprise, "You've been seriously considering this, haven't you?"

I tried to shrug it off, "Maybe every six months or so, I've happened to look it up on the internet while I'm working on my papers and lectures."

We laid there quietly for a couple of minutes, until my mate turned my face his way once more.

He said gravely, "If we did have kids the natural or the supernatural way; let's just have the one and we'll ask Nairn how we can ensure it's a girl."

"No Declan," I said hurt, "you don't want to and I'm not going to force you into parenthood. I would never ever want a child to feel unwanted."

"B," he spoke firmly, "I want to father a daughter with you."

"But what if it's a boy?"

"Then we have a boy and I'm gonna watch him like a hawk." He said simply. "But I know from overhearing Meadow talk about it one day, couples can ultimately choose what sex their baby will be. It's something to do with gene therapy, which was meant to safe guard against birth defects or abnormalities. The same way medicine can now prevent Cystic Fibrosis or Down Syndrome, parents can also pick if they want a girl or boy."

His words further surprised me, as he watched my eyes grow wide and an almost hopeful expression, form.

"I want to father a daughter with you." He repeated softly, whilst holding my gaze. "I want to take care of a mini-B, who's as pretty and smart as you." He breathed out, before ducking his head to kiss me softly over and over again. "I want to teach her how to hunt responsibly. I want to cook for the both of you."

I felt him move back into position between my thighs to recommence the baby-making festivities however, I wasn't entirely convinced.

"Declan -"

But the European Werewolf used his customary method of shutting up his mate, by smothering his mouth over hers.

"Now let's give these frickin' flowers something to bloom about...!" He mumbled out.

I giggled as I wrapped my arms about his wide shoulders. Our hunger for each other quickly returned, as did our prior pleasure. We even got a little carried away when we nearly knocked his flower off the bedside table!

*****

Next morning when we awoke, I opened my weary eyes to see the time on the digital alarm clock. It was 9.16 AM, we were going to be late for morning tea. I think Nairn was expecting us at ten o'clock.

"Declan..." I moaned groggily, "...wake up."

I heard some kind of grunt, as my husband shifted his hold on his wife. He was stretched out on top of my back, whilst I'd slept on my stomach. His body heat staved off the chill since we fell asleep without the bedcovers, but he was so heavy I could barely move.

"Declan," I spoke louder, "wake up."

"Not yet B..." he grumbled back, "...just a couple more minutes."

"Declan!" I elbowed him in the ribs. "Get up!"

That got a reaction out of him for sure.

"Oow! Frickin' hell, woman! We're on holiday, we're supposed to sleep in!"

In annoyance, he rolled off my back and onto his which gave me my chance to use the bathroom first. However when he heard the shower turn on, he eventually came in to share. I washed my hair this morning, which I don't usually do, but I wanted to wash away all the sex before venturing into society.

With his shorter hair, he spent much less time under the water than I did. He got out of the shower before me and was already dressed, when I came out of the bathroom. I saw he had also stripped the bed and left the sheets and the quilt by the door, to hint to housekeeping that we needed new ones.

Once I was dressed, I sat down on the bare mattress to pull on my socks and shoes when my gaze fell upon the flower bud on my bedside table.

It looked exactly the same as it did yesterday. Curiously, I turned to look at his and saw it had opened up and was in full bloom. I emitted a sad sigh but I was hardly surprised by the results.

Declan was holding our coats, my handbag and his wallet and keys, as he stood near the door, waiting to go. But when he saw what made me pause, he didn't rush me this time. Considerately, he came over to sit beside to offer any comfort he could.

"Maybe they're not meant to bloom and maybe I'm the defective one." He tried to be kind.

"Nope," I kept my tone neutral. "You're the stud in the paddock and I'm the cow that doesn't produce any calves or milk."

He snickered at my analogy, "Yeah but you know I'm gonna charge at any other bulls that come near you."

I laughed out loud at my European Werewolf mate's typical territorial behaviour.

"Don't ever change, Dec." I planted a quick kiss on his lips.

"Likewise, B." He stood up and when I did too, he handed me my coat and bag. "Hey, what am I saying? You're in temporal flux, so you're hardly gonna change. You see? This is a good thing."

Lastly, he opened the hotel room door for us, as I grabbed the flower buds and then we left.

*****

At 10.20 am, our hostess opened the door to her guests and her infertility patients walked into her run-down house.

"Sorry we're late -" I began.

"We were up late doing 'homework'." My mate gave her a wink.

Nairn giggled at the innuendo, "Then I hope like good students, you brought it in to be marked?"

We were standing in the foyer by the sunken staircase, when I held up the two small plant clippings. I handed them over which she eagerly took, before leading us into the living room for tea. However we noticed her strides slow until she completely stopped, as she was examining the flowers.

"Extraordinary..." she breathed out.

Next, she curtailed off to stand by a window for better light to examine them. But what worried me, was although she was suitably impressed at the rate Declan's flower bloomed; she looked confounded by mine. She even held it up in the sunlight, whilst turning it about in her hand.

"Ooh yum, sandwiches and slice." My mate noticed what was on the coffee table.

Then he helped himself to walking over to the couch by the fireplace, flopping down and then picking at the plates of food on offer.

However my attention was taken away, when Nairn carefully placed the flower buds on her desk and then walked over to one of her bookshelves. I watched her pull out one of the biggest, heaviest and yet oldest looking books in her collection; before struggling to carry it over to her work area. She dropped it loudly onto the surface beside the buds and then opened it to flick through as she searched for something.

The book was so old, the paper was stained yellow with time. Also, not all of the different fonts were in the English alphabet. A couple of times, she even had to blow dust off the pages.

"What is that?" I wondered as I walked up for a closer look.

"It's very old," she said vaguely, "it's been in my family for nearly a thousand years. Each generation adds to it, as we use it to draw knowledge and remember things past."

"Yeah, but what is it?" I asked interestedly.

"It's a spell book." The European Werewolf spoke up from the couch, once he had finished his mouthful.

I turned to give him a peculiar look, "How the hell would you know what it is? You can't even see it!"

"No, but I can smell it." He said unhappily, before picking up some more food to jam inside his mouth.

But before I could argue with him, Nairn spoke, "He's right."

"Huh? This is an actual spell book?" I looked her way in surprise, before I looked back at my mate. "How would you know this?"

"There's silver, wolfs bane and garlic in the binding." He returned as he poured himself some tea. "You want a cup, B?"

"Say what?" I turned back Nairn's way, a little suspicious. "Why would those be inside the cover of the book?"

"To stop the wrong kind of people from getting their hands on it." She spoke crisply. "My kind have had to endure Witch Hunts, attacks by the odd European Vampire and even once during the 1100's, we were expected to rid the town of a European Werewolf! So this book serves somewhat as an instruction manual with a built-in security system."

"Oh, I get it." I picked it up to her surprise, for a closer look. "Silver and wolfs bane ward off Werewolves and the garlic keeps away the Vampires."

"B..." her mouth fell open in horror, "...you need to put the book down and step away from the desk."

"Why?" I gave her a puzzled look, whilst Declan watched from his seat.

"The leather covering doesn't just have silver amulets sewn into it, but there would be silver dusted over the pages." She nervously licked her lips. "There are also sprigs of wolfs bane let alone garlic, in the binding."

"Oh you mean this thing?" I held up a dry leaf I found between the pages.

"B!" Her eyes bulged. "Put it down immediately and run into the bathroom and wash your hands!"

I stood there giggling on the Witch who was having a panic attack, whereas the European Werewolf thought he should cut her some slack.

"Relax Nairn," he said calmly, "B being a Circulator as well as a Werewolf, isn't as allergic to those things as other Werewolves are. I mean, garlic doesn't do jack to us, except to add to an Italian recipe. But the rest has little effect on her."

"Really?" She tried to slow her breathing whilst resting her hand over her heart. "Truly, you're alright then?"

"Fine and dandy." I smiled, before putting the book back down to show her my uninjured hands.

"Well that's just grand, isn't it?" She laughed out her relief. "Actually this little show, would also explain a lot about the state of your flower."

"It would?" I wondered and now it was my turn to be surprised.

"Please sit down and I'll go over the results with you." She waved her hand towards one of the two chairs in front of the desk. "Declan, if you would care to join us?"

However, it was my mate that faltered. "Um, I don't think so."

"Of course! How foolish of me, please accept my apologies." She blushed before picking up the heavy book once more, to return it to the shelf. "Is that better?"

"Nope." He flinched at the sight of her desk. "I think I'll stay right here."

Now what was wrong? I leaned over to examine the surface and I even gave it a careful sniff. But as soon as I did so, I let out a gigantic sneeze!

"Aw yuck! There's silver dust that's fallen out of the book and onto the desk." I complained, before I sneezed again and again.

Declan straightened in concern, "Go and blow your nose and wash your face and hands."

I could feel the silver dust aggravate my sinuses but I managed back a nod in agreement. "I think I might...AAAaaaCHOOOooo!"

Nairn stood back helplessly, as she watched me rush from the room in a sneezing frenzy. "It's like she's got hay fever."

"She's lucky." The European Werewolf said warily. "If it had been me who took a whiff of that silver dust; I'd have blood pouring out of my eyes, nose, ears and mouth as my sinuses were burned out."

*****

Our hostess felt so bad about nearly harming her guests let alone patients, she cleaned the entire desk with multi-purpose spray. Then she threw out the sponge with the silver dust on it, before washing her hands at least five times. Hell, she even tossed her hand towel she dried her hands with, into the washing machine.

Thirty minutes later, she rejoined us in the living room and rather safe than sorry, she dealt with her clients on the couches instead of her work area.

"Right." She organized her notes and the flower buds, on the coffee table. "Let's get down to business, shall we?"

I curled up on the couch beside my mate, with the fertility specialist sitting across. Declan looked my way, before I caught him snicker.

"What?" I gave him a peculiar look.

"Your nose is so red right now, you look like 'Rudolf the Red-Nosed Reindeer'." He guffawed.

"Would you like me to grab the book again and drop it into your lap this time?" I threatened.

"Now for those results," Nairn hastily moved on. "First I'd like to say 'congratulations' to Declan. I've never seen a flower bloom as much as yours did, but I've also never had a European Werewolf for a patient before."

"Woo hoo!" He let out a cheer as his arms shot up in the air. "Did you hear that, B? Last night you probably could have left your pants on, and I'd still get the job done."

I rolled my eyes as I looked away from him and back towards the Healer.

"But as much as Declan's supernatural sex-drive is er, impressive...? I must say that B's results are the most amazing that I have ever encountered." She shook her head in bewilderment. "That's why I had to look it up in that old book which ended up causing so much bother. I've never seen anything like it before."

This made my husband put a protective arm about his wife's shoulders as he demanded, "Why? What's wrong with her?"

"Um, nothing's wrong..." she fumbled out, "...but I think I understand now, what she was trying to explain about her reproductive systems being in temporal flux."

"The flower's drooping just like my uterus is." I said sulkily.

"But it's not." She held up my flower with the red string, in the air. "It's not drooping, in fact it's far from it. It's glowing, just like you are."

I sat there looking on like she had gone mad, but it made my mate curious enough to move forwards for a closer look.

"Hey yeah," he wore a goofy smile, "its aura isn't as bright as B's, but it is glowing a little."

"No it's not." I glared at the unopened flower bud. "It's stupid and defective, just like me."

Nairn appeared confused by my cranky mood and watched as I crossed my arms, defensively.

"She can't see auras." Declan nodded his head in my direction. "She can see through time, but she must be the only Werewolf who can't see heat signatures or auras."

Our Seer's face softened as she looked my way, "Don't worry B, I can't see heat signatures either."

"Yes, but you're not a Werewolf so nobody expects it of you." I stood up to pace unhappily. "I'm not as strong as a male Lokoti Werewolf, so I'm not allowed to patrol. I can't see heat signatures like the other Werewolves can. I'm not supernaturally virile like the other Werewolves are."

"I beg to disagree." She sat back in her seat. "Everyone is different B and yet everybody contributes in their own way. Answer me this, who's faster; you or Declan?"

"She is." My mate butted in.

"Who's not as allergic to silver, like the other Werewolves are?"

"She is." He went along with her.

"Can other Werewolves travel through time, like you?" She tested.

"Nope." He proudly shook his head. "The Lokoti call Circulators, 'The Light People'."

"That's understandable, with an aura that bright." She agreed.

"OK guys," I rubbed my reddening face, "thanks for the 'pat on the back', but let's get serious now. Nairn, can you help me get pregnant?"

Pause... I looked on the psychic expectantly whom met my gaze with her steady one.

"No." She said softly.

"But yesterday you said that B was ovulating and everything was completely normal, especially with her getting her period every month." He said accusatorily.

"I know what I said, Declan." She said, before holding up my flower bud again. "But don't you two see? This is what's truly marvellous about all of this! B, your flower isn't drooping just like your uterus isn't either. If there was something wrong with you, the flower would have withered. But just look at it; it's full of life and vitality like it's still connected to the plant. It's even glowing a little!"

The European Werewolf leaned in again for another close look, before he acquiesced, "Actually that is pretty cool."

She stood up and walked over to where I was almost wearing a hole in her carpet, with my pacing.

"B, you're full of life but you're frozen in time. In fact, you're apart from time. Your Lokoti Werewolf body is ready to reproduce, but the part of you which is also a Circulator, is not letting you. But I may have an explanation for that, too."

Then she turned around to go back to her notes. We watched her sift through the pages as she searched for something. I looked puzzled towards my mate, who simply shrugged back. She found what she was looking for, roughly around the same time as I sat down beside my husband again.

"Don't get angry..." she looked nervously on the pair of predators sitting opposite, "...but after you left yesterday, I made a few phone calls."

Declan's eyes narrowed, "What kind of phone calls?"

"Well, you could say that I'm part of a psychic network. However people don't call us and pay by credit card to hear their futures. Instead, myself and other Seers and Healers, discuss case files. But of course, we never mention any names and it's all completely confidential."

However, I could tell my mate was so angered by this, his eyes began to glow green.

"Wait," I put my hand over his as I was worried about him jumping up and mauling her. "Let's just hear her out."

Nairn blanched upon the sight of his supernatural eyes, especially when his round pupils turned into narrow slits.

"I haven't betrayed the two of you in any way," she held up her hands in protest. "Nobody knows it was the two of you that I was talking about."

"Just tell us what you learned from the phone calls, Witch." He emitted a dangerously low growl.

"Alright then," she spoke quickly. "I chatted to some friends in Ireland, France, Budapest, China and the States. Actually, it was more like a conference call but it was useful because, we realized that besides me meeting 'Subject A' yesterday; no-one else has seen a female Werewolf of any breed, in years."

This made me snort in disbelief, "Well they are around, but there's just not that many of them."

"Exactly!" She pointed at me enthusiastically. "There's not many of them left and the ones that are around, it's like they're in hiding."

"For their protection," my mate sat up straighter. "The Lokoti tribe guards the secret of the existence of a female Lokoti Werewolf. Just as the Hsu Clan keep their females away from the Hsin Clan, who kidnap them to force them to breed."

"Precisely!" Nairn pointed at him next. "So what if this is simply fate's way, of protecting B from being used as a baby-making machine; in a time when female Werewolves are becoming an endangered species?"

The room turned silent for a moment or two, as Declan and I exchanged glances and the psychic watched for our reaction.

"It makes sense." I shrugged to my mate. "Didn't you say something similar when we were in China?"

In defeat, his glowing green eyes dulled to their human blue colour and he let out a weary sigh. "Yeah I did and yeah, the Witch is right."

Then I leaned against him for support and warmth and in return, he put his arm about to hold me closely.

Next, Nairn picked up all of her hand-written notes and walked them over to the fireplace. Then she tossed them into the fire, before raising her eyebrows at my overprotective mate. I think she was showing us once and for all that she wasn't a threat.

"Yeah, alright." He gave in. "Thank you for your help and thank you for calling my wife, 'Subject A'."

"You're welcome." She spoke primly, as she sat down on the couch once more.

I stared at the notepaper which was meeting its demise in the fire. It looked like the flames were literally devouring it. The sight made me shiver, when I thought about how they used to burn people accused of witchcraft.

Then I started to talk, whilst staring like I was in a daze. "You've got some good points, Nairn. A person could think it's the hand of fate. However I think it's just because my body is in temporal flux. It's not frozen in time otherwise you'd be right, I wouldn't menstruate or ovulate. But it's more like a time loop, as my hormones follow the monthly pattern. My eggs operate in a separate time differential and I guess it's just going to stay like that, until the day we evolve."

Now the Seer looked on the Circulator impressed, "Can you 'see' all of this, B?"

"Yes and no," I answered vaguely, while staring into the fireplace. "Some of it was told and some of it wasn't."

My mate planted a tender kiss on my forehead. "But we're happy, aren't we B? We've got another hundred years or so, of enjoying each other's company before we're reunited with everyone again."

"Evolve?" The psychic looked on curiously. "Do you mean passing on?"

"Long story." He warned.

"Is it the place of light that the two of you will be going to, in the end?" She queried what she had 'seen'.

I snickered at my mate's shocked expression from the Seer's accuracy.

Just then the conversation was interrupted by the sound of Declan's mobile phone ringing. The Death In Vegas song 'Aisha,' started to play and my mate and I exchanged funny looks. Then he reached into his jeans pocket and pulled out his communications device.

Who would be ringing whilst we were away on holidays? Was it a tribal emergency? Or was it somebody from the Garage, calling to ask their boss an important question? I listened to him take the call.

"Brandon?" He greeted. "What's up?"

Nairn and I remained silent as we both eavesdropped on the conversation. An incredulous expression overtook Declan's face, as he listened to our 24 year old Great x4 Grandnephew.

"Dude, you do know that I'm in Scotland on holidays right now, don't you?" Pause... "OK OK OK, calm down." He sighed as he reluctantly decided to help the younger male. "Right, so you're in the Supermarket looking at the things? Now grab anything that says 'maxi' on it, it's usually a safe bet. Uh huh. No, don't get that. Why? Because some chicks get toxic shock syndrome or whatever it's called, from using those. What? I don't know! Look, all I know is B tried those things once and she started to shiver and shake like she had a fever and never used them again."

Nairn and I shared a look of amusement, at a male's perspective of the 'female curse'.

He continued quietly, "Right, so grab the pads and then get some Ibuprofen. No, don't get Aspirin or Paracetomol. Aspirin doesn't do jack for this sort of thing. Now, before you use the self check-out, go to the breakfast foods aisle and get a jar of Nutella. Yeah, the choc-hazelnut spread. Huh? Trust me, aside from these two things, this is going to be your life saver. Well, let me put it this way; you can tame hormonal female Werewolves with this stuff."

The women in the room erupted into giggles, which made the man turn away, embarrassed.

Declan spoke with a red face, "Look, I gotta go because I'm in the middle of something. Yeah, I have my own female-related problems. Bye."

He ended the call and when he moved back around in his seat, he saw our tittering.

"Sorry, it was a newlywed crisis." He said uncomfortably as he returned the phone to his pocket. "Before we went on holiday, we went to our Great x4 Grandnephew's Housewarming. Brandon was panicking because he was sent on his first mission to the Supermarket for supplies for his wife, but he didn't know what to get."

The psychic smiled in understanding, "And because you two have been married for the longest, you're the so-called expert the younger men turn to?"

Declan rolled his eyes, "I should call myself 'Dr. D' and start charging. Sometimes it's like they come to me to fix their cars and their frickin' relationships! 'My wife isn't speaking to me after I bought her the latest exercise program'. That's because she thinks you just called her fat, you idiot. 'Declan help me, my wife is sulking for buying her a new microwave or food processor for her birthday'. That's because she thinks you're trying to make her do all the cooking, you moron! What, it would kill you to buy her something that's just for her and not related to housework?"

Nairn and I cracked up laughing! We laughed so hard, we were almost rolling around on the couches with tears coming out of our eyes. The European Werewolf's blunt mode of speech, only added to the absurdity of what he was asked.

He scoffed, "One day, this forty year old man was bitching and moaning that his wife of twenty years, was making him sleep on the couch. I was just trying to change his tyres when he wouldn't shut up. It turned out he bought her Ice Fishing equipment for Christmas, when she doesn't like fishing and going out onto frozen lakes, scares her. Conveniently, he did like Ice Fishing and offered to use it then he wondered why she got so angry?!"

"I take it these are human men, asking you for advice?" She wiped her eyes.

"You're hardly gonna see a male Werewolf, do something so stupid. Not the monogamous breeds, anyway. Since we mate for life and we need a healthy sexual relationship; we're not about to screw up our only avenue of getting laid." He gave a weary shake of his head.

Our new friend looked impressed by this. "Maybe I should start dating a Werewolf?"

"Just be careful of what breed, you do." I cautioned. "Not all of them are compassionate towards females, or any human at all."

"Yeah, it'd be a shame to find your partial remains when we've only just met you." He gave her a small smile, to show that he liked her.

~~~~~~

~ 8 ~

"Ladies, it's 7.25 PM! This 'shindig' starts at 7.30 PM! We were supposed to leave 25 minutes ago!" Declan bellowed from downstairs.

I rolled my eyes to Nairn, "He hates being late. He's such a stickler for punctuality, you can tell he was in the Military in a former life, huh?"

"I heard that!" He called back.

We erupted into giggles, as she finished off my hair in an upstairs bathroom of her house.

Declan and I had been invited to Nairn's for afternoon tea, when it was decided that we'd stay for a light dinner as well, so the girls could get ready for the dance together. For our meal, she served cold ham, potato salad and coleslaw. Whereas the women ate a small amount that could have fitted on a bread and butter plate; my husband ate a load the size of two dinner plates.

"A supper will also be served at the dance, Declan." She smirked at his large appetite.

"I know." He shrugged, before scooping the last of the potato salad out of the bowl.

Nairn was styling my straight, black hair with her hot-irons. She made it wavy whilst pulling back the front in old Edwardian style, with two tendrils on either side of my face. I was also borrowing her clothes for the evening; in the shape of a long, layered, black satin skirt, a white blouse and a purple velvet, lace-up corset over it.

She too styled her hair so it was wavy, whilst she wore a long green skirt, a black blouse and a red velvet, lace-up corset.

When I stood up, to view myself in the mirror, I remarked, "I love these corsets! Where did you get them?"

"I made them," she said simply.

"You made them?" My eyes widened, impressed.

"The purple compliments your dark blue eyes." Nairn smiled, as she came to stand beside. "You can keep it if you like."

"Really? Thanks!" I gushed appreciatively.

"B, can I ask you a question?" She stopped us, before leaving the bathroom.

"Yeah, sure."

She shut the door to prevent my mate from overhearing, indicating that this was a private discussion.

"I've noticed Declan's appetite and I'm curious." She spoke quietly. "Is he like that in the bedroom, as he is at the dinner table?"

I cracked up laughing at her question, before I replied with a, "Yep."

Her eyes widened, "I'm just asking out of professional curiosity, from the fertility test. I'd never seen a flower bloom so full, as Declan's did. Being a Werewolf, it certainly confirms his virility. But is his appetite, the reason why a human woman wouldn't survive a romantic encounter with his breed?"

"Um, it's one of the reasons I guess." I said awkwardly, wondering how much I should divulge? "If a human woman were to mate with a European Werewolf, she may not survive for several reasons. The first is because of their physical strength, besides their stamina. Or, if his breed gets too excited, they also bite and scratch. Not only do they like the taste of blood, but sharing it can be an intimate gesture."

Her mouth fell open in surprise, "Sharing blood?"

"Werewolves are flesh eaters, but we share blood to heal each other. Or, a male Lokoti Werewolf tastes the blood of his mate once, so he will always be able to track her. But with European Werewolves, they continue to crave it because during an intimate encounter, it excites them."

She turned quiet for a moment, as the information sunk in. Then she said, "No wonder he's so possessive over you. Declan craves everything about your body, as you are one of the few females on this planet who can provide what he desires."

That comment made me feel awkward, so I tried to explain. "Another reason is because we love each other. When I was married to Grant, he could have left in search for a female of his kind. But he didn't, he waited for me."

"Of course he loves you, B." She smirked. "Any stranger let alone a 'seer', can see THAT."

Then she opened the door again and I followed her out. Together we walked downstairs, to find Declan pacing impatiently whilst constantly looking at his watch. However as soon as he saw us, he stopped and a huge grin broke out, on his face.

"I get to walk into the room with the two of you on my arms? Sweet." He gloated.

"I think that's European Werewolf for, 'you look nice tonight'." I snickered to her.

"Why thank you, Declan." She smiled.

But when she started to walk over to the coat rack, he reached it first. He helped Nairn with her coat and then mine. He reached the front door before us, too.

"Ladies," he said, while gallantly holding it open...

...

... and he did the same for the front door of Stonehaven's Town Hall.

We walked in with the proud male in the middle, as our escort.

My eyes lit up, as I looked about excitedly. People were dancing to the Celtic music, which was being played by a band up on the stage. My heart leapt in time to the tunes, I love Celtic music!

The hall was decorated with long garlands of flowers and green leaves, which hung across the ceiling. There were several old portraits on the walls, of local historical figures as well as the old monarchs of the past. There was even an old shield, with a noble family's crest along with a set of swords, just above the stage.

Nairn waved at several people in the room, which they returned with a smile or a nod. I noticed Angus, who sold the records was here, along with his wife. He waved enthusiastically our way and we three waved back.

The band started a new song and I watched the people who were dancing, recognize the music.

They assembled in two lines, one for men and the other for women. They stood facing each other before they began to dance. The men skipped into the middle, bowed then skipped backwards before the women skipped into the middle, curtsied and they skipped back. Then the males danced around them before retreating, and the women copied them.

I watched in fascination, as I could tell the dance was very old. It was almost like watching a courtship ritual in itself; the men approached the women, before the women approached the men. Towards the end of the dance, a man and a woman at the end of the line, held up their hands in an arch and the rest of the couples all streamed under, to form two new lines.

"Look, the dance is like a representation of human mating." I whispered into Declan's ear. "The men bow then the women curtsey, the men dance around the women and then the women dance around the men. Lastly, they all stream under the arms of another man and woman, like it's the arches of a church or something."

My mate chuckled before he kissed my ear, "It's pretty accurate, isn't it, of human courtship?"

"What's your courtship like, then?" Nairn overheard.

"Um..." he laughed uneasily, "...I'll leave this one to you, B."

Quickly, he released our arms and practically ran away, over to the drinks table where punch was being served.

"Wuss!" I called after.

He flashed a look over his shoulder as if to say 'I heard that', but continued in his escape.

Nairn came to stand beside and linked her arm with mine, as we watched the dancing.

"Well..." I wondered how to put it, "...Lokoti you-know-what's, are similar to human courtship. But European you-know-what's, if we're to go by Declan's example? They're a little more erm, perfunctory, with taking a mate."

She started to smile, guessing my meaning. "Wham-bam-thank-you-ma'am?"

"Yeah, but without the 'thank you' at the end."

She asked unimpressed, "So there's no wooing?"

"Well..." I repeated as I frowned, "...before we were officially called mates and we saw each other in secret; there was a little bit of 'wooing'. I had orchids left on my doorstep, which was nice. He repaired things around my house, as his excuse to come and see me."

"So if a European you-know-what, ever sought to woo me; I shouldn't expect poetry readings or moonlit walks on a beach?" She sighed, disheartened.

"Definitely NO moonlit walks on a beach." I laughed ruefully. "Trust me, if you were with a European you-know-what, on a full moon that wasn't Declan? You'd be running for your life, along the said beach."

Nairn tittered, as she got my meaning whilst gazing on Declan's tall, strong build. "So your man's a one in a million then?"

I smilingly answered, "Absolutely."

We watched him engage in polite conversation, with the thirty-something woman, behind the drinks table. We saw how the lady's eyes widen, as she looked him up and down. We observed her body language, as she began to play with her hair in a flirty way.

Finally, Declan picked up on her attraction and laughed uneasily, before he shot off a 'help me' look, from across the room.

"Come on, one of the pack is sending the, 'need back up' signal." I snickered.

We walked around the dance floor to rejoin my wayward mate.

Nairn greeted the lady who was in charge of drinks, "Good evening, Brigitte."

"Hallo there, Nairn." The thirty-something woman, said back.

Then Brigitte watched him pour some punch which he handed the cup to Nairn, before he poured me one too.

But because he poured her a cup first, she thought he was Nairn's date for the evening. Her eyes narrowed as she regarded his attention to her, almost as if she was sizing up the competition. For some reason, she didn't pick up that I was his wife, even if we were the ones wearing wedding rings.

"I hear your friend comes from the States, Nairn?" She asked.

"Declan and Bianca are from Alaska, Brigitte." Our friend said perfunctory.

"Who's Bianca?" She gave her a peculiar look.

This was copied by my mate, as Declan gave her a funny look whilst he put his arm about my shoulders.

"Oh." She noticed me standing there, before glancing over my appearance in open scrutiny. "Are you a Native American?"

"Yes."

The expression on her face read, 'they look like a mismatched pair'. She stared at his thirty-something, blonde appearance then at my twenty-something, darker complexion.

Nairn must have seen this too, so she added on, "Bianca is a distant relation of mine. She's related to the Dunmore family, as well as a descendant of the Worthall's."

"The Worthall family?" Brigitte looked like the name rang a bell.

"Lord and Lady Worthall, of Blythe Castle." Our friend announced, dropping the names like anvils.

"Oh," her surprise was obvious, as was her disbelief.

"My great, great grandparents were Lord and Lady Worthall." I quipped.

"Oh," she said again, "and how is it that you live in Alaska?"

"My grandmother married a Lokoti and came to live with him on tribal lands." I said coolly.

"Well then," she sung mockingly. "Your English grandmother went from living in a castle, to living in a tee pee?"

A growl started to make its way up my throat, which Declan heard. He quickly joked, "Yeah but they're 23rd century tee pees, so they're state of the art, now. Our tee pee back home, comes complete with an indoor bathroom and a kitchen."

Brigitte let out a high-pitched laugh, thinking he was joking along with her and not at her. She even playfully slapped him on the chest! He was starting to look seriously fed up with this woman, but by now he'd have to get in line.

He said quietly in my ear, "Can I eat her? Since the pack's not here, I wouldn't be found out."

"Maybe after I clawed her face off," I hissed back.

Nairn saw the Werewolves' bloodlust boil, so she took affirmative action. "Excuse us, Brigitte."

Next, she took hold of my arm to lead me away with Declan in tow...when Brigitte grabbed his arm.

"Don't forget what we talked about, Declan." She purred. "I would be happy to take you sightseeing. I work at the Hair Salon, but on Wednesdays and Fridays I finish at midday. I could show you then you can show Bianca."

The European Werewolf's face turned to stone, as his whole demeanour went cold.

"Thanks but no thanks." He said icily. "My sights are on my wife."

Her face fell, as she watched him rest his arm on my waist, to escort his mate to the other side of the room.

When we reached it, I looked demandingly in his direction. "What was all THAT about?"

"You don't wanna know." He rolled his eyes. Then he noticed my eyes were burning in anger, so he explained, "I was making polite conversation with her. She asked about my accent so I told her we were from the States. She offered to show me a couple of old castles nearby, which was when I looked at you."

Nairn looked embarrassed by what occurred, as she threw the 'town hussy', a glare.

"Brigitte Stirling is a nasty piece of work." She did an impressive growl for a human. "She married at the age of twenty, to a boy she had chased for years. The boy was in a long term relationship with another girl, when Brigitte hit on him at a party when he was drunk. Afterwards she played the 'pregnancy card', which made the boy marry her. She had a miscarriage from crashing her car after a fight with her husband, which made him stay out of guilt. Finally, he couldn't stand it anymore and they divorced so he could go back to his true love. This angered Brigitte, who spread the rumour that the two were having an affair so the injured party, looked like the villains. Then two years ago, she broke up a couple from another town who came to me, because they were having difficulty in conceiving. While the wife was seeing me, Brigitte was seeing the husband. The wife found out about it, the same day she found out she was pregnant."

My mouth fell open in shock, as I looked over at the woman behind the drinks table, who was still staring at my husband.

Nairn seemed surprise by my reaction, "Don't things like this happen, where the two of you live?"

"Nup!" Declan said firmly. "In our tribe where everyone knows everyone; nobody wants to cause such a scandal and live with the embarrassment."

She sighed wearily, "Our town seems to live on gossip. People still invite Brigitte to dinner, hoping to get a good yarn from her. Mind you, this is while the wives are watching their husbands closely, whenever she's around."

I exchanged a long gaze with my husband, "Once upon a time, Declan and I caused a bit of a scandal. It's because I was the first and only Lokoti you-know-what, to ever mate a second time."

Our new friend asked out of interest, "How long was the first husband dead, before the two of you rekindled the flame?"

"Ten months," he answered. "Then for the two months we were together, we had to meet in secret. It was to protect not only B's, but our families' names."

"But surely ten months, is an appropriate time to mourn?" Nairn frowned in confusion.

"It is if you're *not* a Lokoti you-know-what." Declan said gruffly. "B was expected to turn into a nun at the age of 23, according to public opinion."

"What happened after the two months, you two started seeing each other?" She asked interestedly. "How was your relationship revealed?"

"B was shot in the head, with a silver bullet that was meant for me. She died but her mother and grandmother, were able to bring her back." He said stiffly.

"Hmm, sacrificing oneself does give away one's feelings." She smirked.

I interjected, "Afterwards Declan moved in and a particular member of Grant's family, didn't appreciate this. She made her opinion public, by screaming at us in the general store. But after our unofficial housewarming, nobody cared anymore, because we were backed by our families."

"You had a housewarming, but what about a wedding ceremony?" She queried. "You call each other husband and wife."

"A Housewarming is like a wedding ceremony." He shrugged. "Sometimes there's a Joining Ceremony as well as a Housewarming, but most couples prefer just the Housewarming. In our tribe, when a couple moves in together, they're considered husband and wife."

When we noticed Nairn looking at our wedding rings, he added on, "I bought the rings 135 years later. Lokoti don't wear wedding rings, but because B and I travel, I thought it would be easier if we wear them. Otherwise, we have to keep showing our drivers licenses, so strangers see that we share the same address."

"In most cases, couples decide to live together as de facto, instead of marrying. I think it's because the divorce rate is so high and if they do split up, there's less paperwork. But I guess that's not an option among the Lokoti?" She asked knowingly.

"Nope." He gave a shake of his head. "The rest of the tribe follows the example made by the pack. When a Lokoti you-know-what takes a mate, they're biologically and empathically joined. There are no separations, it's all or nothing."

Nairn frowned, "But that can't be right. What if the man and woman fall out of love? What if one of them cheats? What if the man hits the woman, can't she leave him?"

"It might happen with human couples, but definitely not with you-know-what's and their mates." He said decisively. "They feel when their female is cold or hungry or sick, which makes them overprotective. Also by the biological joining, the enjoyment in the bedroom is constant, which keeps the chemistry alive."

"And the human couples," she questioned, "what about them?"

Declan frowned, "There have been cases of human marriages dissolving, but in the tribe it's considerably lower than the outside world. Even some human couples call each other 'mates'. Human males follow the pack and the ritual of taking a mate, has been the same for thousands of years."

"And if a human male did beat his wife or children...?" Nairn pressed.

"Then the pack would have a 'conversation' with him," he said stiffly. "Plus, the Tribal Elders would end the union and send the bastard away, with just the clothes on his back."

She looked visibly relieved by this, before grinning his way. "And because you and B have been 'married' for the longest, is why you have other men coming to you for advice?"

He chuckled, "I'm no 'Yoda' on marriage, but some of the things I'm asked? My four year old great x5 grandnephew, Caesar could answer. You ask a stupid question, the four year old will give you a stupid answer. That, as well as whack you over the head with his toy hammer."

Then Nairn and I cracked up laughing, as Declan mimed hitting these men over the head with the said hammer!

"This Caesar sounds like a wise little man," she giggled.

"He's our great x4 grandniece, Maia's kid." He smiled proudly. "His father is a Lokoti you-know-what, so there's a good chance he'll become one too. He already has the gumption of one. When his Mom takes him grocery shopping, he insists on pushing the hover-trolley. One day, he saw another man try to hit on his Mom and he deliberately ran the trolley full speed, into the guy."

Nairn was laughing so hard, she had to lean on me to stand up! It was at that moment, we were joined by Pete Miller, the guy we bought the record player off. I guess he came over to see what was so funny.

"Good evening to you Nairn, you look fair this night." He smiled in approval. "You three seem to be having a good gab and giggle, I thought I might come and get a laugh as well."

Declan recanted the story, which also gave Pete a chuckle. Then he and my husband talked about what other antiques he's done up to sell, aside from the old gramophone. Pete was a man in his forties, who obviously had a thing for Nairn, as he passed her many a sideways glance. He wasn't handsome, but he did have a kindly face. I thought he seemed like a nice guy, as he behaved like the 'shy but polite type'.

At last, Pete worked up the courage to ask Nairn to dance, just as the band started to play a new song and the dancers took their places.

"Shall we risk it, Nairn?" He nodded towards the dance floor.

"I suppose we could, Pete." She smiled back.

I stood back as he took her hand and lead her out onto the floor to join the other couples.

A wistful sigh escaped, as I watched all the people dance in sync to the music.

"If that guy had waited any longer to ask her to dance, I would have asked for him." Declan chuckled, as he watched too. "It's obvious that it was the reason why he came to talk to us, in the first place."

I sighed even louder this time, as I looked disappointedly from my husband, to the festivities.

It's funny how the men in the tribe go to Declan for relationship advice, when he could behave clueless sometimes. Why doesn't he ask his own wife, if she would like to? He knows I've been looking forward to this, as we hardly ever get the opportunity to dance, back home.

Lastly, I tapped my feet along to the music and I even started to sway... but nope! He still didn't ask, he simply watched the dancing instead. I rolled my eyes as I gave up.

"Pardon my intrusion," a twenty-something man with red hair and blue eyes appeared on my other side. "But I was wondering if I could ask your husband's permission to dance with his pretty wife? It looks like she sorely wants to and I thought somebody should, before she taps a hole in the floor."

"Gladly!" I grabbed hold of the stranger's hand before he could respond.

I think I surprised the stranger with my strength when I pulled him onto the dance floor.

We joined Nairn and Pete in two lines, in some kind of Celtic jig. I poked my tongue out at a surprised Declan, before I spun around with the stranger. My husband smilingly shook his head, as he stood to the side and watched.

"The name's Don...Donald Rafferty," the red-haired man introduced.

"I'm Bianca Sabre," I smiled back, "but everybody calls me B."

"And where's your accent from, B?" He enquired.

"Alaska!" I answered, as I dosey-doed around him.

"And what's an Alaskan doing in Scotland?"

"Travelling... on holidays... meeting distant relatives." I smiled to Nairn, who returned it. "Have you always lived in Stonehaven?"

"Aye," Don answered. "I run a plumbing business, which I took over from my Dad. My family's lived in Stonehaven for several generations."

"That's like my father's family." I told him, as we skipped up and down the line of people, before retaking our positions. "The Lokoti have lived in the Lokoti National Park for eons."

"So you're a Lokoti then?" He looked on my long, dark hair.

"Yep!" I called back over the music. "So is my husband, Declan."

Don glanced over at my mate with his blonde hair, before he gave me a look of amusement. "What's his surname?"

"Sabre."

"That's a funny sort of Indian name." He chuckled.

"It's Italian."

"I see," he let out a laugh then spun me around again.

After a couple more minutes, the dance ended and the band started to play a new song.

Don looked over at Declan still standing there, before he smilingly asked. "Do you think your husband would mind if we had one more?"

"I'll tell him I kidnapped you." I giggled, as I retook hold of his hands and we moved into the new formation. Then I held up my forefinger to Declan, as I mouthed out, "One more dance?"

He held up his as he mouthed back, "One more". However, he was soon distracted by Brigitte approaching him. I almost tripped over my own feet, by the sight of her sidling up to him. Then I used my sensitive ears to eavesdrop, as I moved.

"You're kind, to let a younger man steal your younger wife from you. How about I help you steal her back, when she gets jealous by seeing you dance with me?" She teased.

"I don't dance." He said simply.

"That's a shame," she sighed, "with your big, strong arms, I can tell you would be good at sweeping a girl off her feet."

"I rarely dance and when I do, it's a slow one with my wife."

Brigitte saw how Declan was on guard, so she tried a different tact. "So what do you do, for a living?"

"I own a Garage." He said. "I'm a mechanic."

"And you cook as well?" She turned extra flirtatious. "You sound like you're very good with your hands."

His eyes narrowed, as he regarded her. "Yeah well, my wife whom I love body, heart and soul, seems to appreciate it."

By now I was dancing distractedly, which Don noticed.

"Are you alright, B?" He queried. "Or would you like to go and sit down?"

I snapped out of it, to say guiltily my dance partner, "Sorry Don. No, let's keep dancing. I was watching Brigitte, trying to hit on my husband."

He let out a loud laugh at my bluntness, before he turned his head to watch what I was.

"Do you know what we call Brigitte Stirling around these parts?" He jested. "The marriage tester."

Now it was my turn to laugh aloud!

He continued, "If there's a handsome, married man in a twenty kilometre radius, she'll set her sights and go for the kill."

I almost stopped dancing in surprise, "If she's so obvious with her behaviour, then why do people stand it?"

Don spun me around when the dance called for it, "Because it's funny to watch when she crashes and burns, which is what's about to happen right now..."

By this stage, Declan looked well and truly fed up.

I overheard him say dismissively, "Excuse me, but there's some other people that I'd prefer to be talking to right now."

Scowling, the supernatural predator walked away from the human one, towards Angus and his wife, who too had been watching.

"Ah, you've met the 'marriage tester' then." Angus laughed good naturedly, when his wife whacked him on the arm.

Don and I looked back at each other and laughed! Then the dance ended and he was polite enough to escort me back. I thought he was an agreeable, young man.

"Thank you for allowing me the honour of dancing with your wife." He smiled to Declan.

"Thank you from saving me from making an ass out of myself, by dancing." He chuckled as he replaced his arm about my waist.

"Declan, this is Don Rafferty." I introduced.

"Pleased to meet you." He shook his hand.

I noticed his strong grip surprised Don, as he had to flex his hand repeatedly when he got it back.

"I hear you're on holidays from Alaska?" Don asked.

"Alaska, eh?" Angus listened in. "That's a remote part of the world."

"Where we live is remoter still, on the tribal lands inside the Lokoti National Park which is 4.5 hours north of Anchorage and 1.5 hours south of Fairbanks." Declan educated.

"I'm Eileen, pleased to meet you." Angus' middle-aged wife, shook my hand. "Is it true that in winter, sometimes the sun doesn't rise?"

Next, we fell into a Q&A session as we answered their questions about the weather where we live and the wildlife.

Whilst we talked to our new acquaintances, I noticed my mate pass more than a few glances towards Nairn, who was still dancing with Pete.

I realized what it was he was doing, he was keeping an eye on her. Because I called Nairn family, so did he. Not only did he act zealous over my safety, but this extended to all of the females in his family. When any woman under Declan's radar, happened to skirt danger or attract any unwanted attention, he was quick to quash the unsafe element.

Maia once complained about her Uncle's overprotective behaviour, however the rest of the Lokoti Werewolves were quick to defend his actions. The mostly male pack, could certainly be called a 'boys club', as they stuck together. Sometimes, I wondered if they secretly decided on who they deemed were worthy, to date a female Lokoti? Unsurprisingly, most males who were deemed 'unworthy' came from outside of the tribe. Right now, he approved of Pete Miller, so he was allowed to dance with Nairn. But as soon as Pete did anything wrong, he'd come down on the human male like a ton of bricks.

Angus noticed what my husband was doing, "Are you right there, Declan?"

"Hmm?" He looked back.

"You've been watching Pete Miller's movements for the past half hour, like he was dating your daughter or some such!" Angus laughed. "Nairn's never mentioned that she has relatives from the States."

"That's because we'd never met until that day, in the market place." He told them.

Just then Declan's arm which remained around my waist, tightened. When I looked questioningly his way, I saw him turn his head this way and that, as he sniffed the air. He'd picked up a suspicious scent, but of what?

"Oh, so you're distant cousins then?" Eileen enquired.

"Er, yeah... or B is anyways." Declan answered distractedly, as he was still looking about the hall.

I noticed his behaviour attracted many a peculiar look, so I volunteered, "We're very distantly related. It's from ancestry relationships in the 18th Century and funnily enough, Declan and I are similarly related."

Their eyes widened at this piece of news, before they looked at him for his input. However he was sniffing loudly, whilst searching the room with narrow eyes. To draw attention away from his suspicious actions, I carried on.

"In the 18th Century, Lady Elisha who is my foremother and part of the Durrant family; was temporarily engaged to a Navy Captain, Sir Guy Robertson, who is Declan's forefather."

Angus only half heard what I said, as his attention was on my husband.

"Declan, what is it man? The look on your face right now isn't a pleasant one. Is there something troubling you?" He asked concerned.

The European Werewolf's eyes became focused on the front doors of the town hall. But what came out of his mouth surprised Angus, Eileen and Don. A low, dangerous growl, escaped through his clenched teeth.

At that moment, the doors opened and in walked a pale man and a very pale woman. They were both dressed in expensive suits, coats and shoes. But this man and woman smelled wrong. I breathed in through my nose and I sensed why...

...they were European Vampires.

They smelled like a dank room in an old, decrepit building. They tried to cover their gaunt features with make-up, but they couldn't hide their pallor. Their movements were calculated and controlled, like two snakes coiling about the floor, getting ready to strike.

The band finished their latest song and began to put down their instruments. Nairn stopped with Pete Miller and the two stood together, talking and laughing. She was completely oblivious to this new supernatural presence, I guess because Pete was a nice distraction.

"I beg your pardon," the male Vamp spoke loudly to the room, in an English accent.

Everyone quieted to hear what the strangers had to say.

He continued, "Our car has run out of power and we are parked just outside. We are sitting next to a black four-wheel drive, with the license plate UMI7834A."

"Oh that's my car," Nairn realized out loud.

"I do apologize, but could I possibly trouble you for some power until my wife and I make it to the next service station?" He asked her.

Oh oh, my feelings of foreboding hit right as my stomach shrank.

She said cheerfully, "Of course, that shouldn't be a problem. I just charged the car this afternoon, I can spare a few hundred watts."

"I have some power cables in my boot." Pete said helpfully. "I could attach them to Nairn's battery and yours."

"That's very good of you," the female Vampire commended.

Just as they started to make a move to go outside with the two strangers, Declan surprised them.

In a lightning fast move, he suddenly appeared in between the humans and the vampires.

"Well, what a stroke of luck." He forced out brightly. "I just happen to be a mechanic. Nairn and Pete, how about you give me your keys and I'll grab the power cables. I'll assist the couple in getting underway."

The European Vampires eyes widened as their nostrils flared, when they smelled the European Werewolf in him.

Declan knew that they'd read out her number plate on purpose. It was because she was a psychic, which were a favoured food source for the 'fang heads'. As well as feeding on humans, European Vampires fed off others in the supernatural world, to take on their abilities.

Being a European Werewolf, he was stronger even if the European Vampires were faster. But he was willing to go outside and risk his life, to protect Nairn. However since I was a Circulator as well as a Lokoti Werewolf, I was faster as well as stronger, than them.

"Thank you for your offer, but we already have the help of the lady and the gentleman," the male Vampire spoke crisply.

When Nairn and Pete started to make a move to go outside again, I stopped them by appearing beside my mate.

"Please, Declan and I insist." I spoke directly to them. "You won't meet a better mechanic than my husband. He wouldn't hear of Nairn going outside into the cold, dark night with strangers, when he can do it for her."

Instead of looking intimidated by two Werewolves protecting their prey, their eyes looked on hungrily. They stared at me like I was the pot of gold at the bottom of a rainbow. Declan growled quietly so only the Vampires would hear, as he moved to stand protectively in front of me too.

"Then if you *insist*, how can we say no?" The male Vamp smiled with his whiter-than-white, teeth.

"Nairn," I turned to her, "give me your keys. You too, Pete."

"We don't mind, really." She gave a funny look at how we were behaving.

I flashed a warning look as I spoke in a low voice, "We'll talk about this later but now, give me your frickin' keys."

Her eyes widened as she finally sensed that something was afoot.

Without another word, she pulled her keys out of her pocket and handed them over, before nudging Pete to do the same. I made a move to go outside with Declan and the two Euro Vamps, but my overprotective mate stopped me.

"No, stay here," he pulled the keys out of my hands. "I doubt there's only two of them and this could be a diversion."

Although my stomach knotted to let my mate go into battle without me, I nodded and reluctantly stayed put. As strong as my Lokoti Werewolf instincts were to fight alongside my mate; I also had to protect Nairn. She had less chances of fending for herself, if more Vampires should appear.

Declan planted a kiss on my lips before he followed them outside.

"What was all that about?" Angus asked as he, Eileen and Don came over.

"I think he's going overboard in the 'help' department, just because he's a mechanic." Pete said, annoyed.

"They aren't safe." I said shortly. "We've seen their kind before."

"Do you know those people?" Eileen wondered.

"In a manner of speaking." I said unhappily. "We've come across their relations in Russia."

Now Nairn's eyes bulged as she understood the danger. She asked worriedly, "Will Declan be alright?"

"He's stronger than them, but they are faster." I said warily.

"If you want to go after him, I'll be alright." She offered.

I thought on this, before I answered. "No, I have to stay with you incase the 'strangers' aren't alone."

Don laughed, I guess because he thought I was being funny. "You make it sound like you're holding down the fort, while he's away."

Nairn and I looked back with unhappy expressions, which wiped his smile off.

"Oh..." his laughter died down, "... I see."

"Who are they?" Angus demanded. "What's wrong? Should we call the police?"

"They can't be trusted." Nairn told him.

"Then he shouldn't be out there alone." Pete decided.

Then he, Angus and Don started to make a move to be Declan's back up. But they didn't get very far, when I stood in front and blocked their path. I held up my hands in a 'stop' gesture.

"No offence boys, but you would do more harm than good." I said firmly. "The less people go outside, the less problematic the situation will be. Besides, Declan knows how to fight, trust me on this."

Eileen spoke up, "If you don't want Angus, Pete and Don to go after Declan, I suppose you wouldn't want Brigitte to either?"

"Huh?" I looked from her to the doors, where I saw her trying to sneak out. She got quite the fright, as did everyone when I roared out, "BRIGITTE!! Don't even think about it!"

Suddenly the hall turned quiet, as everybody looked from me to the town's source of gossip. Everyone but Eileen, Angus, Don, Pete and Nairn; thought I was yelling at Brigitte for being 'the other woman'. They all watched me march over to her position, as if a screaming and hair-pulling match, would occur.

"I beg your pardon!" Brigitte blushed. "I can come and go as I please!"

She started to open the door when I slammed it shut! This made her take a step back at my show of strength. But I stepped up closely, so only she would see my eyes glow turquoise and hear the low growl which came out.

"When I say no, you should listen."

Brigitte's face drained as she hastily backed away. She spoke to nobody in particular, "Oh my God! Did you see that? Did you hear that?"

Next, she cowered behind a group of people, to use them as protection.

My eyes were back to their dark blue colour when I returned to Nairn.

"Remind me not to make you angry." Angus chuckled.

"I say you should have let her go." Don joked. "If those people are as dangerous as you let on, then you wouldn't have to worry about her anymore."

Speak of the devil, the front doors opened and a cranky looking Declan walked inside.

I crossed over to find out what happened, when he pulled me aside to talk quietly.

"They gave me the slip," he growled unhappily.

"What?"

"They gave me the slip!" He snapped. "As soon as we were outside, they bolted."

"Which direction did they head in?" I asked.

"I tried to follow after, but I lost their scent after two blocks." The European Werewolf said in annoyance. "They headed in a northerly direction, but I know they're gonna double back. Not only do they want to snack on a psychic, but she's just gonna be the entrée, when they try to feast on a 'Light Person' and a female Lokoti you-know-what."

Wearily, I let out a long sigh. I wasn't afraid for my life, but I was annoyed at having another vacation ruined by European Vampires. Frickin' hell! Did I have a 'fang head' magnet around my neck or something?

"OK," I tried to think, "did you see any others?"

"No, but they always exist in groups." He frowned. "These two tonight, were probably meant to bring Nairn back to the nest, where ever that is. Now they're probably telling the rest of them as we speak, that there's two females with auras and the nest will come to town, instead."

"I don't think Nairn should go home tonight," I decided.

"Agreed." He said decisively. "Her house is in the middle of nowhere and even if you and I stayed with her, we three would be sitting ducks. Unless..."

I waited to hear what he had to say, when I saw a devious grin appear.

"...unless when you phase to Alaska to get your sword, you also bring back the pack as our backup."

Instantly, I disagreed, "I don't want to give the 'fang heads' anymore supernatural things to snack on!"

"No, this is perfect." He brightened by the idea. "Me and the other Lokoti you-know-what's will wait for them in Nairn's house, while you and her phase to Alaska. When the 'fang heads' come for you two, they'll find the male you-know-what's, instead."

"No way!" I shouted in a whisper. "That plan sucks!"

"What? Why?" He looked offended.

"For one, the fangs will smell if Nairn and I aren't there, and they'll know it's a trap. Two, there's no way I'd let you fight the nest without me!" I spoke quickly.

"Fine!" He snapped. "When you go back for your sword, you bring back the pack. Then all of us will be ready and waiting, at Nairn's place. But you will be on guard duty, in a locked room with the psychic whilst the rest of us, battle it out."

I opened my mouth to argue again, but Declan interrupted. "This isn't open for debate, this is an order."

I looked on indignantly, "You can't order me!"

"Oh yes I can!" He straightened so he could loom over. "I am Second in the pack. This may be the 23rd Century, but feminism doesn't mean jack when the Lokoti you-know-what's, still operate on the natural order. You hunt what your First tells you and you have to obey your Second, as well."

My eyes narrowed as I clenched my sharpening teeth. A snarl escaped, as I felt my nails grow a centimetre longer. I wanted to jump up and down on the chauvinistic male, but he'd probably enjoy it.

"You can scratch and bite me later, but right now I'm in charge." He said coolly, as he pulled out his mobile phone. "Chiron? Yeah, we're in Stonehaven, Scotland. Ah ha. Yep, European 'fang heads'. You heard my thoughts and the pack are mobilizing? Right, in a couple of minutes, B will come and get you from our place."

Casually, he put his phone back into his pocket and took my arm, to walk over to Nairn's position.

"Declan?" She looked on, quizzically.

"It's home time," he declared.

"Oh," she now looked to Pete, "thank you for a lovely evening, but I have to be going now."

"I can come too, if another man would be helpful?" He offered.

"Thanks, but that won't be necessary." Declan dismissed the idea.

"Thank you for the dance, Don." I forced out a smile. "It's a good congregation you have here, Angus and Eileen. But we have to head off."

"Are you sure everything's alright?" Angus asked concerned. "The police station is just down the road."

"Thanks but we'll be OK." Declan said gruffly, as he began to lead Nairn away.

"Nairn?" The older woman looked on worriedly.

"It will be alright, Eileen." She smiled reassuringly. "Declan and B know what they're doing."

Then we escorted her out of the hall, whilst walking protectively on either side.

We walked down the street, which was crowded with parked cars. Declan and I kept our eyes, ears and noses peeled, as Nairn hit her remote to undo the central locking. We three climbed into the vehicle, with me sitting in the back.

"Did you want me to drop you two off at your hotel?" She offered, as she pressed in the ignition code to start her plasma-powered engine.

"We're not going to the hotel." He said. "You're driving me to your place while B goes back to Alaska, to pick up something."

She looked back in surprise, before she drove off down the road. The Werewolves kept their supernatural senses in use, as we constantly looked about. He even put his window down, so we could smell the night air.

As soon as we left the outskirts of Stonehaven, I disappeared in a bright flash of light from the back seat of Nairn's four-wheel-drive; to reappear in another, inside of my bedroom.

Quickly, I rushed over to the wardrobe where I flung open the doors. Next, I pulled out my sheathed sword, from its hiding place behind my long, black, woollen coat. Then I paused, because I heard the voices of men talking, as well as some growling in between.

I crossed over to my window and looked out, to see the fourteen male Lokoti Werewolves assembled, just in their jeans, out on my driveway. From their glowing eyes and bulked up bodies, I could tell they were reporting in for battle. I spotted in the middle of the throng Chiron, who was also changed.

In another flash of light, I instantaneously phased from my bedroom to reappear outside. As soon as they saw me, my kin growled in greeting. I growled back in acknowledgement, as I walked over to our First.

"European Vampires." I spoke to both Chiron and the pack. "So far we've seen just two, a male and a female. But Vampires live in covens, so there's a nest somewhere. The two tried to kidnap my distant relation named Nairn, for her psychic ability. Declan is now escorting her home, to a large house in the country. It's there that we'll be luring in the Vampires, so they'll come for Nairn and for me."

Chiron spoke in his thunderous, changed voice. "You'll take us to Scotland and then you'll phase yourself and your relation here, while we fight."

"No."

My male kin growled loudly at me to obey, but angrily I growled back.

"As I pointed out to Declan, the 'fang heads' may approach the house but they'll smell we're not there. They'd also smell you instead, and know it's a trap. But if Nairn and I are present, then they might risk a battle." I reasoned.

"Very well." He considered my words. "You can stay in Scotland, but you will not fight."

"No."

There was further growling and I snarled back at the sexist males.

"I am a Circulator! I was one of the three 'Light People' who were responsible for annihilating the St. Petersburg coven! European Vampires usually fight with swords and they're faster than you." I shouted over them.

OBEY OUR COMMAND – I felt their will press upon my heart and mind.

"No!" I growled back before I glared at Chiron. "I'VE killed more Vampires than Declan! I'M the one who knows how they fight, which is with swords! I'M the one who's faster than they are!"

THEY HUNT YOU BECAUSE YOU ARE A LIGHT PERSON AS WELL AS A FEMALE WEREWOLF – they thought my way.

"I know this!" I barked back. "And I'm the only one in this pack, which can fight them in the speed of light!"

YOU ARE THE WORLD'S LAST CIRCULATOR AND THE TRIBE'S FIRST AND ONLY FEMALE LOKOTI WEREWOLF – their will was iron – *YOU WILL NOT FIGHT.*

"Tough." I said stubbornly. "This is more my fight than it is yours."

I heard their dangerously low growls, but I held my head high as I stood my ground.

OBEY YOUR PACK – they demanded.

LISTEN TO ME – I thought back desperately.

Their growling died down just long enough for me to speak.

"I am Circulator and Werewolf. I am fast and I am strong. When you have Vampires waving around silver swords, in the speed of sound? You need a Circulator who can swing her silver sword in the speed of light!"

There was a moment of silence, as I felt my words had affected them. They all exchanged glances with their different coloured glowing eyes, before they looked to Chiron. Since he was First, he was the one to decide.

"You can guard Nairn," he declared. "But should the situation turn dangerous, or you see us fall, you will phase yourselves back here."

I didn't like this one little bit. Over half of the pack had mates who were still alive. There was no way in hell that I could ever face their wives to tell them that their husbands were dead, because I didn't fight.

Chiron was the first to come forward and put his hand on my shoulder, before they all stepped up. I held out my arms, which was soon covered in hands, or else on my back. Like this, the fifteen of us disappeared in an even brighter flash of light. We left the front of my house in Alaska, to reappear in another flash inside of Nairn's house, in Scotland.

I delivered us to her living room and just in time too, Nairn and Declan had arrived.

She pulled up, out the front in her four-wheel-drive. The male Lokoti Werewolves temporarily reverted back to their human appearances, so not to scare the stranger. They stood quietly, as we listened to Nairn unlock her front door before she and Declan came inside.

"Oh good, they're here." My mate said chirpily, instantly smelling our arrival.

"Who's here?" She asked before she froze.

She stopped in the doorway of her living room, to gape at the fourteen topless Native Alaskan men, who were standing around in just their jeans.

"Nairn, this is my grandnephew Chiron Riverclaw, who is First in the Lokoti Werewolf pack." I introduced.

"Your grandnephew?" She echoed in surprise, as she looked from my twenty-something façade, to the man who appeared to be in his fifties.

"Chiron," my mate nodded respectfully.

"Uncle Declan," the older man nodded back to his second-in-charge and elder.

"If B is 170 years old and Declan is 173 years old, how old are you?" She asked him.

Nairn's living room was filled with chuckling, before he answered, "I'm 109 years old."

"Then I must be the youngest one here, being 35 years old?" She looked around.

"I'm 29 years old and currently I'm the youngest in the pack." Forrest put up his hand.

"And you are?" She looked his way for an introduction.

"That's Forrest Riverclaw, my great x4 grandnephew." I told her. "Remember the story about Caesar and the shopping trolley? He's Forrest's son."

"That's my grandson." Stone said proudly, as he patted him on the back.

"And that's my great grandson." Chiron added on.

Nairn looked on the family of Lokoti Werewolves in wonder, at their twenty-something, thirty-something and fifty-something appearances.

"I see," she tried to carry on as normal.

"So we hear, which is why the Vampires want you." Meadow frowned.

Her face fell, "The Vampires want me because I'm a 'Seer'? Yes, Declan has explained that they can see my aura."

It made my mate add, "Vampires drink psychics' blood to get their ability, like they hunt Werewolves for their strength and regenerative capabilities. They've tried hunting Circulators, thinking that they might be able to get the ability to Circulate as well? However Circulators are the only beings in the supernatural world, which they can't take on their abilities."

"Why not?" She looked my way.

"We can circulate through time because of our higher bio-electromagnetic frequencies. We turn our bodies into light and pass through time and space that way. It's not biological so it can't be passed by blood." I told her.

"But I thought your ability was passed down genetically?" She frowned in confusion.

"Yes and no." I sighed. "Before my great, great grandmother Elisha Worthall, no Circulator had given birth to another Circulator. Plus, my bio-electromagnetic frequency is in temporal flux and there's no way that's genetic. Somehow the ability was passed down from Elisha, and the Circulate have never been able to figure out how."

"That would explain it then," she said mysteriously.

"Explain what?" Declan asked.

"Why time inside her, is apart from us," she thought aloud, "and how it's related to why she can't conceive. It's because the time of the Circulator has come to an end."

Meadow looked on her diagnosis impressed, whereas I shifted uncomfortably at her public declaration.

"Are you a Calculator?" He asked.

"Am I a what?" She gave a funny look.

"No, she's just a damn good Seer, which is why the Vampires have come for her." Declan grumbled, as he walked over to her living room window. "Speaking of which."

"They're here," Stone came to stand beside him.

Then they moved away from the glass, so they wouldn't be seen. As he stepped back, Stone's brown eyes began to glow bronze, as his upper body bulked up. Nairn watched the nails on his hands and feet grow longer and sharper, as did his teeth. When the other male Lokoti Werewolves followed suit, she gasped from being in a room full of flesh-eating monsters.

"Hide her in a room which is in the centre of the house!" Chiron ordered in his thunderous voice.

Declan grabbed Nairn's arm again as he led her from the room, whilst I followed closely behind.

"B, over here." He caught sight of a corridor, leading away from the entrance hallway.

"No, let's take her upstairs." I took hold of her other arm.

I pulled her up the staircase as Declan fell behind to undress, taking off his coat then his shirt. She looked over her shoulder to see what he was doing, as I hurried her along. I think this made her nervous enough to ask:

"Er, why is Declan taking off his clothes?"

"Because when he changes, he can't wear anything or they're torn apart." I answered. "Speaking of which, can I borrow some gym clothes? I can't wear these when I change, or I'll ruin them."

"Um, I suppose so... in here." She pulled me into a bedroom, which made my husband follow after.

We found ourselves in Nairn's bedroom, by her bed whilst the male continued to undress. He sat on the side to quickly pull off his shoes and socks and left them on the floor. But he held off on taking off his jeans, until she was safely sequestered away.

"Here are my gym pants and here is my elasticized singlet top." She handed me the garments from her wardrobe.

Without wasting time, I threw modesty to the wind as I hurriedly changed clothes.

"Your wardrobe is a good size." Declan commented. She gave him a peculiar look for commenting on furniture at a time like this. But she got the gist when he next said, "I think you should hide inside it."

"What?" She almost laughed. "You want me to hide in the closet?"

Just then the sound of breaking glass came from downstairs...

"Inside NOW!" Declan barked as he pushed her inside, so she was sitting on top of her shoes. Next, he started to pull all the clothes off their hangers to dump them on top of her! When she looked like she was about to object, he offered, "To cover your scent."

By the time he had shut her inside the wardrobe, I had finished changing clothes. Declan looked me over in approval, wearing her tight workout clothes with my hair done up. Lastly, he watched me pick up my sword in its sheath, and tie the belt on my back.

"Are you ready?" I looked on expectantly.

Declan dropped his pants, to expand into his huge, hulking, hairless shape of a European Werewolf. On his hind legs, the beast towered over me, as his glowing green eyes looked down. He licked his lips, which were part of his short, stubby snout.

"That's the man I married," I said warmly.

Then I too shifted shape, into my Lokoti Werewolf form as we sensed our kin downstairs had engaged the Vampires in battle.

EIGHT VAMPIRES SO FAR BUT I SMELL MORE ARE SOMEHWERE NEAR – we heard Chiron warn.

"Let's go!" I spoke in my thunderous voice.

But when I turned to run out of the room, he quickly caught me with his two front claws.

He shook his large canine head before he pointed one of his claws at the floor, in a 'stay here' gesture.

"Declan, now is NOT the time to turn domineering!" I growled in annoyance.

My mate rolled his glowing green eyes before he gestured again with his claw, to stay put.

WHO KNOWS WHERE THE OTHER VAMPIRES ARE? WE NEED YOU TO GUARD NAIRN – he thought.

Then my mate delivered a slobbery kiss to my face, in the form of a lick to the lips. Next, he bounded out of the room on all-fours, to run to the male Lokoti Werewolves aid. Bad temperedly, I kicked Nairn's tallboy which shook violently from my supernatural strength.

STAY WITH NAIRN AND GUARD HER – Chiron willed my way.

I let out a frustrated sigh as I thought back – *I ALREADY AM.*

Whilst pacing up and down, I listened to the sounds of more glass breaking downstairs, as well as lots of growling, banging, hissing, crashing and more growling. The ruckus must have been the furniture or ornaments, being knocked over. Helplessly, I listened in to the pack's short bursts of messages, to each other.

MEADOW, BEHIND YOU!

BEWARE OF THEIR SILVER SWORDS AS THEY'RE ALSO COATED WITH VAMPIRE POISON!

WADE, LOOK TO YOUR LEFT!

STONE, LOOK TO YOUR RIGHT!

THESE VAMPIRES ARE YOUNG AND INEXPERIENCED... THEIR SWINGS ARE TOO WIDE... GET UNDER THEIR DEFENSES THEN GO FOR THEIR THROATS.

DECLAN, BEHIND YOU!

When I heard this last thought, I almost ran to the aid of my mate! I recalled how badly he was injured, the last time he battled European Vampires. But then I didn't have to...

I TASTE VAMPIRE FLESH – I felt Declan gloat.

Empathically, I sensed he indulged his bloodlust tonight, by ripping his teeth into his half-dead victim.

Just as I started to relax, I was interrupted by two male European Vampires, smashing through Nairn's bedroom windows!

I'VE FOUND YOUR MISSING TWO – I mentally announced.

The Vampires landed on their hands and knees, before looking up to hiss threateningly. Their eyes were completely white, whilst two poisonous fangs jutted out from their mouths. As the enemy advanced upon my position, their decrepit stench told my sense of smell, they were two centuries old.

They're not young and inexperienced, like the ones downstairs! Then that means they set their whelps on the male Werewolves, to distract them so they could make a move on me. It was moments like these, that I could have gone without the 'personal touch', especially if it came from a cold hand holding a silver blade.

*****

~ 9 ~

I growled warningly at the older European Vampires, who hissed threateningly. They pulled their silver swords from the sheaths on their waists. In return, I unsheathed the silver Katana on my back, to meet their challenge.

They hissed further at the sight of my dangerous weapon. When I went into a defensive stance, they moved into attack postures. Each held their blades artfully, which showed both skill and decades of practice.

"If you lower your weapon, we can make your death quick as well as painless," one of the males, taunted in an English accent.

"That didn't work for Mikhail and it won't work for you either." I growled back.

I saw their white eyes widen in recognition of the Russian Vampire's name.

"So you're the creature that Mikhail and his coven were hunting?" The second Vampire spoke in a French accent, as he arched his eyebrows. "Your blood will taste sweeter still in vengeance, whilst we slowly drain you dry."

"Which we'll also do to your pet psychic!" The first hissed again.

I growled even louder at his threat, which was what his companion had wanted. He swung the first blow and I can tell I surprised them, by how quickly I parried. Then it was on! The 'fang heads' fought in the speed of sound, whilst I blocked their blows in the speed of light.

Clang clang clang clang clang cllaaaaaannggg!

The constant clash of our weapons made a loud clanging noise, almost like one long CLAAAAAANNG!

I was fighting the two together, as they swung their silver swords my way. I could smell they had also coated their blades with the same poison, excreted by their fangs. By doing so, they hoped that a tiny cut could send the Werewolf to the floor, paralyzed.

Clang clang clang clang clang cllaaaaaannggg!

The two were beginning to drive me backwards, to the wardrobe which Nairn was hiding in. I think they could smell she was in there, even under all of the clothes dumped on her. Frickin' hell, these Euro Vamps fought better than Mikhail or his coven could.

Clang clang clang clang clang cllaaaaaannggg!

Although I was fighting in the speed of light, it was me who was being driven backwards. But how is this possible? My sword was moving around so fast, it looked like a bright blur. So how are these two beating me?

I managed to look down a couple of times and I started to notice their footwork. They were slowly coming closer, by taking small but steady steps. It was how they were sneakily driving me backwards.

C'mon B! What did Gran always say, when she taught you? "Mind your footwork." OK then, two can play at this game!

Suddenly, I surprised them when I disappeared in a bright flash of light, to reappear right behind them.

I swung around my blade which injured one when it caught him unawares, however the second managed to duck in time.

Its' flesh made a burning noise, as a deep cut went straight across his back and even partly into his spine. He fell face first onto the floor, in a cry of agony. I faced off his uninjured colleague, who looked on his friend bleeding heavily, before he raised his sword again.

He hissed furiously in his English accent, "For that you will truly pay, you bitch!"

His sword swung wide and immediately I went into phase, to allow the metal to sail harmlessly through. When I reformed back into my solid shape, I lunged forward with my weapon. I started to get on top of the fight, by integrating my ability to phase with my Werewolf muscle.

Every time the 'fang head' tried to edge forwards, instead of backing off, I'd instantaneously phase to a new position.

As we fought, the injured one struggled to his feet again. Just as my heart sank at the idea I'd have to fight both at the same time again; I sensed something. I picked up the heavy footfall of something large and clawed, running on all-fours in this direction.

"You really shouldn't have called me a bitch, my mate doesn't like it when people call me that." I smiled with my elongated teeth.

The European Vampire's fanged mouths fell open in surprise, when a European Werewolf bounded into the room!

Declan's dangerous mouth was open and ready, as he leapt upon the wounded one. He devoured his entire face in one chomp! The 'fang head' flopped dead, as his kind's greatest enemy, ate his way through his head.

His colleague raised his sword to him. "Get off him, you filthy mutt!"

I swung my Katana around so hard and fast, that it didn't just rebound against his weapon; I completely hit it out of the Vampire's hands!

His sword flew through the air before it landed noisily on the wooden floor. As I swung my sword again, to lop off its' poisonous head; the Vampire ducked. He rolled away to safety and when he returned to his feet, he pulled out two long, silver knives from his belt.

Damn it, why can't he just die?!

I sniffed at the smaller blades, smelling poison on them too. Briefly, I let out a sigh before I refocused on the task at hand. I stalked towards my adversary with my weapon raised.

The European Vampire and Lokoti Werewolf circled the other, with each waiting for the other to make the next strike.

I had to admit, I was wary of seeing two poisonous blades in my opponent's hands. Momentarily, I looked over to find Declan had finished off his meal, leaving the headless corpse lying on the bloodied rug. The large monster raised himself, and turned his glowing green eyes on the new threat, to his mate.

The Vampire knew he had to move fast, if he was going to escape not one Werewolf but two... and make his move he did.

It swung one of his knives to run me through the abdomen, but I managed to leap sideways. Then he used this chance to swing around the second blade. Instead of jumping clear of the first threat, I impaled myself on the second one!

"AAAAGH!" I recoiled in agony.

The poisonous, sharp blade, cut through my strong, supernatural muscle, which was no match for the silver.

"GGGRRAAAAAAAAAWWWLLL!" My mate roared in fury!

Declan started to charge towards the 'fang head' who'd harmed his beloved B. The European Vampire turned to see an infuriated European Werewolf, run right for him. He left his second blade in my abdomen, as he took a defensive stance with his first.

Oh oh, Declan was running so fast and angry, he was about to run right onto the silver blade!

Whilst the fang head's back was turned, I used the last of my strength to swing around my sword.

The deadly blow landed right at the back of its neck! Like I was watching in slow motion, my silver blade sliced through the Vampire's weaker flesh, as it was singed by the silver. Its' decapitated head hit the floor before I did.

As the rest of his body fell like a falling tree, I was a close second. My legs gave out, but before I collapsed onto the wooden floorboards, my mate caught me in his front claws. I was shaking uncontrollably as I felt incredibly cold, but I managed to pull the blade from my body.

Bad-temperedly, Declan flicked the silver knife away and it slid across the room. I clutched my wounded stomach, as he turned me over in his huge arms to lay me on my back. His large, canine head ducked in concern, as he sniffed my wound.

"I'm - I'm - I'm cold." I managed out in my deep voice, which trembled.

I struggled to stay in my Werewolf body, because I knew my injury would be a lot worse in human form. But I wanted him to change back, so he could nurse me in his arms and warm me.

"Hold me...?" I asked plaintively.

Declan raised his head to look on with a pained expression. His green eyes glowed in concern, and I felt he wanted to. Instead, he ducked his head again, and settled his large mouth over my abdomen, to suck on my wound.

I knew what he was doing, he was trying to draw out the poison. However, this was making me bleed faster, too. I felt so cold that I started to turn numb. Then I remembered this could have been the European Vampire poison, which can paralyze Werewolves and kill humans. Frickin' hell, I'm becoming paralyzed whilst I bleed to death?

He raised his head to spit out my poisoned blood, careful not to swallow. Then his jaws sunk over my wound again, to suck harder. He did this a couple of times, as I shook from the pain as well as the cold. My body seemed to war with itself; half of me was numb and the other half was in agony, but I didn't know which side I wanted to win.

At that moment, Chiron, Stone, Forrest, Wade and Meadow; all ran into the bedroom.

They instantly froze when they saw me lying on the floor. I saw the fear in their different coloured glowing eyes. Oh great, I'm never going to hear the end of it now.

"Hi guys, I killed an old one." I tried to reassure. "And I injured the other, which made it easier for Declan to kill."

When my mate's head rose again to spit out more blood, he rolled his eyes at my pathetic excuse.

With all of this happening, nobody noticed Nairn tentatively opening her wardrobe door, to see if the danger had passed.

Her eyes widened in horror, when she saw my mate's frightening form. To her, it looked like he was drinking my blood, which was gushing out of the wound. Next, she jumped out of her wardrobe with an old tennis racquet in her hands, to beat Declan over the head with it!

"Get off her, you monster!" She screeched, as she raised the racquet in the air.

Thankfully, Chiron who was standing the closest, was able to stop her. "It's OK! He's not hurting her, he's treating her."

He shrunk back into his human form, so not to scare her any further. So did the other Lokoti Werewolves. Our First took the tennis racquet out of her hands as she looked from he to Declan, in disbelief. When my mate raised his head to spit out more poison, he growled at him to take her away.

"Do you have a First Aid kit?" He asked.

"A First Aid kit?" She looked on our First as if he were nuts. "She's going to need a bleeding hospital, not a bloody First Aid kit!"

"We can't go to hospital, incase they pick up our physiological differences." Chiron pointed out.

"Take us to the First Aid kit, Nairn." Forrest tried to soothe, as they gently pulled her away. "Come on Nairn, take us to the First Aid kit."

He and Forrest, used this request to escort her out of the room.

"Wait! Stop it! Where's Declan? He should be told about B!" She tried to object.

"That IS Declan." Stone laughed at her.

"THAT'S Declan?!" Nairn gaped at him, from the bedroom doorway.

"Yeah, and you tried to kill him with a piece of sporting equipment!" Wade guffawed, thinking it was all very funny.

Soon, their voices disappeared down the hallway, as I listened to my Lokoti kin take her downstairs.

Next, we heard her squawk, "Oh my God, would you look at my house?!"

Well, it would explain all the sounds of things breaking. I thought all of this was highly amusing, especially her reaction to my husband in his other body. I laughed weakly, as my shaking had stopped however I felt cold all over.

The agony in my abdomen, had settled into a dull but painful throb. I was feeling incredibly dizzy from the blood loss, as my mate continued to suck. I could feel my blood pool about us, on the wooden floor.

"Declan..." my eyes started to close by themselves, "...no more. Please stop, Declan. I'm weak... I'm too weak."

But he ignored my request, as he continued to suck on the wound which was by this stage, gushing blood.

Frickin' hell, I give up! I'm in no state to argue with my husband about this. I think I might fall unconscious now. So I did...

...

... I don't know how long I was out, but I started to feel warm again. More than that, I started to feel like I had some strength, too. I welcomed these sensations, as they coursed through my awakening body.

I started to feel a deliciously warm, thick and familiar tasting liquid, fill my mouth. My automatic swallowing response kicked in, which gulped it down; before more warm, thick, familiar tasting liquid, filled it again. This continued, with each time more replacing it.

My eyes slowly opened, to find myself propped up against Declan's hardened hide for a chest. His large left arm, was holding me against him, as his right wrist was pressed against my parted mouth. It was responsible for the warm, thick, familiar tasting liquid. He was sharing his blood, to heal his mate.

"She's awake." I heard Meadow announce.

When my eyes refocused, I found the Medicine Man wrapping a bandage around my abdomen.

Declan emitted a soft growl, in relief. Then his huge canine head ducked, to tenderly run his short, stubby snout across my forehead. Lastly, his hot, wet tongue darted out a couple of times, as he affectionately licked my cheek.

I looked away to see Stone and Wade, examining the two Vampire carcasses.

"These two were definitely older than the young whelps set upon us downstairs." Stone commented.

"Those younger Vampires were hardly a challenge at all." Wade agreed.

"The older ones certainly would have given Aunt B a run for her money." He stood up. "They would have been faster and more experienced."

"Did you hear the sword fighting?" Wade asked.

"Hear it?" His eyebrows rose. "That constant clanging, as Aunt B took them both on, at the same time. I thought Uncle Declan was going to have a heart attack! Did you see him charge through two the 'fang heads' at the bottom of the stairs, when they tried to stop him from coming up here?"

"We should have let him stay with the women." Wade said flatly. "We thought the fight was too easy, because it was. The older ones used the younger ones as a diversion so they could make their move."

"What kind of species is it, that instead of protecting their young, they would use them as fodder?" Stone kicked the Vampire head away, in disgust.

Wade glared down at the decapitated bodies, "Man-eaters can't be trusted."

Then Nairn returned to the room and knelt on the floor beside us. She looked on my mate's monstrous form uneasily, but forced herself to peak under my bandages to check on my wound. Then she hastily stood up and backed away.

"She's healing quickly." She announced. "The medicinal herbs I put over the wound, will prevent infection from setting into the new skin tissue."

"Are they plants that you use for antiseptic purposes?" Our Medicine Man asked with interest.

"Yes, they're part of an old Celtic poultice."

"How long have you been a healer for?" Meadow asked next.

"Fifteen years," she answered, "and you?"

"Fifty," the Lokoti Werewolf with a late thirties appearance, told her.

"Oh, I see." She tried to hide her surprise.

Chiron and Forrest came back into the room, to talk to Nairn.

"We are disposing of the Vampire bodies, so you can call the police and report this as a ransacking." Our First told her.

She gave a nod, as she stood back and watched Stone and Wade, pick up the two Vampire carcasses. They easily slung them over their shoulders like they were carrying sacks of feathers, thanks to their supernatural strength. Forrest picked up the head as well as the weapons, and followed them out.

"How are you disposing of them?" She wondered.

"We're putting them in a mass grave, on the far end of this property." Chiron advised.

"A mass grave, here?!" She blanched. "But if the police scan the perimeter, they'll be picked up."

"No they won't." He shook his head. "Vampire bodies decompose into a biological ash within seven days of their death. There won't be anything left to scan, it would be compost."

"What about the blood everywhere?" She queried. "What do I say about that?"

"You don't have to say anything." Chiron said simply. "Call the police and when they come here to assess the damage, just tell them you came home to find everything as is."

"Let the police and their forensics come up with their own conclusion." Meadow chuckled. "But I guarantee, they won't come back with a Vampire and a Werewolf battle, took place."

"And what will I tell them about you?" She looked on the tall, strong, older men with blood all over their jeans.

"We won't be here." He stated. "Aunt B should soon be well enough to instantaneously phase us back to Alaska."

I nodded in agreement with a mouth full of Declan's arm. When I tried to move my head away, he growled at me to stay still. Nairn's face twitched in fear, from how dangerous he sounded then.

I could see his European Werewolf form was making her uncomfortable, so I felt I should do something. I shook my head to say 'no more', as I pushed his arm away. However when I moved to sit up, I fell backwards against his chest from the dizziness!

"Aunt B, you need more." Meadow frowned.

Declan easily caught me, as he rolled his eyes at my stubbornness. This time I didn't object when he replaced his wrist. I clung to it, as I gulped down several more mouthfuls. His regenerative life force lessened the pain in my abdomen and soon, my dizziness was replaced with clarity.

"Is she alright?" Nairn frowned, as she looked over my pale, pasty skin.

"When we're in our Werewolf form, we're stronger." Meadow educated. "It's why Declan is remaining in his, as he shares his blood."

Her anxious expression smoothed in understanding and now she looked on Declan's beastly form with less fear in her eyes.

After another couple of minutes, I used my tongue to lick his cut and kick-start his own healing process. I heard him whine softly as he ducked his head once more, to run his nose over my skin. He could smell I was stronger and reluctantly, he released me from his claws.

When I sat upright again, this time there wasn't any dizziness. As I climbed to my feet, I shrunk back into my normal form. Nairn gaped at my healthy human appearance.

"Hi." I greeted.

"B," she looked me up and down, "how are you feeling?"

"Better," I answered before I looked at Chiron. "And if you start lecturing me how I shouldn't have fought the two older Vampires? May I point out that the two fought so fast with such skill; that if it wasn't me getting impaled, it could have been several members of the pack who lost their lives!"

His Second growled loudly at me to shut up, which unnerved the human. When Declan stood up on his hind legs, Nairn shrank back from his towering build. I think the fact that his mouth and claws were also stained with blood, didn't help. He saw her fear, so he too reverted to his normal appearance.

Nairn watched in astonishment, as this huge, hulking, hairless beast changed into the man she knew.

The European Werewolf's short, stubby snout shrank back into his head, with his sharp jaws returning to human teeth. She shuddered, as she heard the soft cracking noises his bones made, as they were contorted from a four-legged canine shape, to a bipedal human form. His height decreased into a tall human body, whilst his claws retracted into normal nails once more. His scruffy blonde hair reappeared on top of his head, as his human ears replaced his canine ones. Lastly, his glowing green eyes with narrow slits for pupils; faded into naturally bright blue ones, with circular pupils.

Within a matter of seconds, a naked, muscled man was looking on the shocked witness, but his mouth and hands were still stained with blood.

"You mind if I use your bathroom to get cleaned up?" He asked casually.

"Er..." her mouth wavered.

"Thanks."

He scooped up his clothes which were still on her bed, to take with him as he left the room.

"Excuse me," I said as I followed my mate out.

Declan picked up that I was right behind him, so he left the bathroom door ajar. I opened it and went inside, to find him washing himself down at the sink. I grabbed some extra soap for him to use, before I waited with a towel.

"What's this?" He chuckled. "To repay me for saving your life, you're my slave now?"

"Shut up." I smirked, as I waited for him to finish.

"Great, now you can do all the cooking and sit at our table for hours, to hand-make pasta, marinated olives and antipasto." He continued.

"You wish!"

"Nah, not really. I can think of a better use for you. You can start by taking off all your clothes and only wear lingerie from now on."

"You are one sick puppy, you know that?" I kicked his leg.

"You'd better believe it." He turned off the taps, before reaching for the towel I was holding.

I noticed he'd missed a couple of spots, so I wet a corner of the fabric to remove them. He smilingly stood still, watching as I cleaned him up. His large hands came to rest on my hips, as he pulled me closer.

"The police would take one look at you and arrest you for being a killer." I chastised.

"Or give me a medal for saving my wife's life tonight." He released my waist. "So, are you gonna explain yourself or what?"

"Explain myself?"

"You followed me in here to avoid a telling-off by our First." He frowned.

"Why am I going to get told off?" I asked defensively. "I fought two old ones and killed one tonight!"

"That's exactly why you're gonna get told off." He said unhappily, as he began to get dressed.

"But I followed my orders, I stayed where I was."

"You were also told that if things got dangerous, you were supposed to grab Nairn and phase yourselves back to Alaska." He paused to give a glare. I wondered how he knew this, when he rolled his eyes. "You're mated to the Second of the pack, B. When Chiron gives an order, I hear it first."

"I followed my orders and I guarded Nairn." I repeated defiantly.

"Yeah right!" Declan sneered. "You know if this was the old days, a male Lokoti Werewolf would be punished for disobeying his First."

"Oh yeah?" I crossed my arms. "By hot coals or a whip?"

"The Second would challenge the dissenter, or sometimes the whole pack could punish the one who brought chaos to order. We'd get our claws underneath their skin, and flail them." He stated.

This made me snort in disbelief, "Yeah whatever!"

Once he'd finished dressing, Declan gave a long, hard look to compound this.

"Flailed? You've got to be joking! You're just saying this crap to scare me." I shook my head.

His blue eyes turned ice cold, "And following me into the bathroom because I'm your mate, is not going to spare you for disobeying your First."

"Say what?" I blanched. "You saved my life, just so you can stand back and watch me get flailed?! I'd rather be impaled by a silver dagger again!"

Declan's face turned impassive. "In this situation, it's the Second to mete out the punishment of the dissenter, who disobeyed the First."

"You're gonna what?" I fired up, as I took a step backwards. "What the hell is all of this crap? Do you know how crazy that sounds? Nairn was right to be scared by you!"

He spoke in a detached voice, "Since this is the first time where a Second was mated to one of the pack, let alone the dissenter? New rules would apply. So along these lines, a suitable punishment has to be found."

"Declan...?" I took another step back from him. "You're not serious, right?"

My mate remained cold and aloof as his icy stare, sent shivers down my spine!

"Just because we're mates, it doesn't mean I'm going to show favouritism, B." His voice dropped warningly. "If I go soft on you, it sends out the wrong message to the rest of the pack."

"Declan, you can't be serious!" My voice turned shrill. "You're actually going to HURT me?!"

"You may as well admit your mistake and hear the verdict of your pack." He said coldly.

I shivered again and started to rub my arms. My heart hurt at how easily he could side with the pack and not his mate. Maybe this is why Dad disapproved of Declan's breed? My father never did like my husband.

His demeanour changed again, as he leaned heavily on the sink as if he was going to say something gravely serious.

"My ruling is, you have to wear only lingerie from now on, with stilettos, a matching dog's collar and you never argue with me again."

"Huh?" I looked on, blankly.

Suddenly the sound of raucous laughter, came from the other side of the bathroom door!

Even Declan's façade slipped, as he started snickering as well. I threw open the door, to find Chiron, Stone, Forrest, Wade and Meadow; all standing in the hallway, listening in! All of this had been a joke?!

"Oh Aunt B, you're face right now!" Wade laughed the hardest. "Why couldn't I have thought of this, to use on my wife when she was still alive?"

"WHAT?!" I roared in embarrassment.

My face felt scorching hot, and I imagined it was looking pretty red by this stage.

"It was this or getting flailed," Chiron simply shrugged.

Then he turned and walked off down the hallway, with the members of his pack laughingly following suit.

I stood still as a statue, mortified, as I watched them disappear downstairs. Once they were gone, I slowly turned around to face my so-called 'mate'. I saw his own face was reddening, because he was laughing so hard...

"Oh, where's a camera when you need one?" He guffawed.

Declan found himself being pelted with bottles of shampoo, conditioner and shower gel; as I threw anything I could get my hands on!

*****

When I instantaneously phased the pack back to Alaska, my husband came with us. He carried the towel he had used, as well as my sword. The pack disbanded on our driveway, so the men could go home to their wives and families. Then we went inside to shower off any last traces of blood.

The towel and gym clothes were put into the washing machine, to wash away any incriminating evidence as the Werewolf couple did the same.

Once I stepped out of the shower, I stood still to allow my mate with his better tracking skills, sniff his wife.

"You're all clear." He gave his verdict. "You did have some blood spray in your hair, but it's all gone."

Then he went under the stream of water and used the small scrubbing brush, to clean under his nails.

A quarter of an hour later, I instantaneously phased us back into Nairn's lounge room.

The decaying living area sat in further ruin, with three broken windows, smashed furniture and ornaments, and the fraying rug stained with blood. In fact, there was blood everywhere including on the walls and bookshelves. Nairn's face fell, as she surveyed the damage.

"I'm never gonna be able to afford the repair work," she tearfully shook her head. "Maybe I should just sell the place and move?"

My mate and I exchanged glances, before I put my hand on her arm.

"I'll pay," I offered.

"But this isn't your fault, B." She exhaled loudly. "The Vampires came for me first and you second. Whether you guys were here or not, the attack would have been made."

"Yeah, but I can afford the bill." I told her.

"No, I can't let you pay." Nairn rubbed her arms from the cold air coming in. "Besides, after what happened tonight, I think I'd prefer to live in town and closer to help."

Declan's eyes softened, as he looked on the shaken woman, in sympathy.

He spoke gently, "How about B and I stay with you, as the repair work gets underway? Once the house is finished, you can decide if you still want to sell up. Besides, it'll look more attractive on the market when it's fixed, than the way it is now."

"Really?" She instantly brightened by the sound of this. "You and B will put off the rest of your holiday, to stay with me?"

"Well, we won't be putting it off, just delaying it for a week or two." I counter offered.

"Why yes, that would be lovely!" The human gushed in relief, at the idea of having two Werewolves as bodyguards. "I'd feel much better if I had company, than living alone in a trashed home."

"No problem." My mate continued. "Now as B calls her PA to reschedule the rest of our travels, you call the police and report that you've been ransacked."

Then together, the women took out their mobile phones to make the calls.

*****

I instantaneously phased Declan and I to our hotel room, just before the first police car arrived. Although my mate wasn't injured in the carnage, I couldn't be around when my blood was scanned, otherwise I could be linked to the crime scene. When the police left, we'd return with our suitcases.

While my husband collected our clothes and toiletries to be repacked, I called my PA at Hodge Endeavor again.

"Don't be afraid to hire two or three teams of people, to carry out the repair work." I instructed. "Not only do I want the windows fixed and the house professionally cleaned as soon as possible, I want to repair the sunken staircase and fraying rugs. Oh, hire an antiques specialist to come too, so we can order new furniture and maybe some ornaments. Yeah, I want the house to look as good as new, just like it did in the 1700's. Uh huh. Uh huh. Oh, and maybe get some gardeners, so we can spruce up the lawns and make the outside look attractive as well. No, I don't think Nairn would mind if we put in some garden beds and added some colour to the dismal, grey building."

Declan was folding up his clothes and putting them in his suitcase, when he heard that last part.

He paused to say, "My god, I'm mated to Martha Stewart."

Then I paused in conversation, long enough to pick up my hairbrush to throw it at him too.

*****

The police investigated the ransacking of Stonewall House, right up until 6 AM. The forensics team scanned the place thoroughly, whilst samples were taken of the blood spilt. This would have included mine, which had stained Nairn's bedroom floor. I'd have to be doubly careful now, because if I was scanned, my blood work would match the evidence found.

We checked out of the hotel and drove our rental into the Scottish countryside once again.

Nairn greeted us at the front door, with a blanket draped over her shoulders. Then she led us through the damaged areas and into the kitchen. The fighting didn't reach this part of the house, so it was still in once piece. As such, she proceeded to prepare her house guests a large, hot breakfast of bacon, eggs, grilled tomato and mushrooms.

Whereas the European Werewolf ate with gusto, I noticed the human hardly touched her plate. Instead, she pulled the blanket about her more tightly. This gave her a dishevelled appearance as she looked absolutely exhausted.

"Why don't you go and lie down?" I suggested. "The repairers won't be here until midday, so you've got plenty of time to rest."

"Repairers?" She blinked in surprise.

"Yeah, I called my PA again to organize the repairs, to fix up the house and furniture." I filled her in. "They'll start today."

"My goodness, you work fast." She marvelled at the Circulator at the table.

"In light speed," Declan joked in between mouthfuls. "Once B sets her mind on something, there's no looking back."

Wearily, she rubbed her face with her hand before leaning on it, on top of the table. "I think I might lie down for a little while, after breakfast."

"Go right now, if you want." He offered. "We'll wash the dishes."

As if to illustrate, he picked up her full plate and put it on top of his empty one. In the style of 'waste not, want not', he tucked into her meal. I shook my head at his unabashed appetite, before giving our human host an apologetic look.

"Is this what you mean by 'cleaning up', Declan?" She teased.

"Mmm," his eyes momentarily closed, to show he was enjoying his meal. "The mushrooms go well with the bacon and tomato. I'm gonna have to remember that. Usually we don't use mushrooms, but hash browns instead."

Next, Nairn passed me a wide-eyed look, "I think I'm going to have to go grocery shopping again this week, to keep up with Declan's stomach."

"Nah, I'll go." He told her. "Besides, I'll know what ingredients I need when I cook up a couple of Italian dinners throughout the week."

"Ooh," she looked impressed, "a man who likes to cook as well as eat? I think I'm going to insist that the pair of you, stay longer."

"Declan's just a food-addict, period." I told her. "He delights in hunting it, killing it and eating it; or slice 'n dice it in the kitchen then consume it."

This made him turn defensive, "Yeah well, it's thanks to my hunger that my wife is still alive, as you may recall. I did eat through the head of that second 'fang head', which was attacking you."

Just then Nairn shuddered from his words, as her hands gripped tighter onto the blanket.

"C'mon you," I stood up then I helped her to her feet, "it's bedtime for all humans, who've been through bloodshed and sleep deprivation."

*****

As I put her to bed in one of the upstairs bedrooms, Declan cleaned up the kitchen. We rendezvoused at the bottom of the staircase, to talk. However, I also noticed he had his keys in his hand.

"I think she's in shock," I warned. "But I managed to get her into a warm shower before collapsing into bed. She's asleep now."

"You stay with her, while I go into town." He organized. "Do you want anything from the supermarket?"

"What are you going to make for dinner?"

"Tonight, I'll make lasagne, green salad and garlic bread. Tomorrow night, we'll eat beef cannelloni and Greek salad. The night after, tarragon chicken with roasted, herbed vegetables..." he listed off.

"Will there be any tiramisu, on any of these evenings?" I smiled cheekily. "I think it'll make Nairn feel better."

"Oh well, if it'll make Nairn feel better..." he jokingly went along, "...consider it done."

I grabbed the front of his jumper and pulled him in for a kiss, before sending him on his way.

*****

Declan was gone for a good two hours and it turned out to be a good thing I stayed, as Stonewall House was inundated with visitors.

I thought my PA told me that the cleaning and repair crews would be coming at midday, instead they turned up at 9 AM.

When I opened the front door, I found over ten people wearing work overalls, standing on the front path. Behind them were four different vans, either advertising cleaning companies or repair work, on the sides. Some of the men and women wore tool belts, as others carried cleaning equipment.

"Oh, I wasn't expecting you guys until midday." I said in surprise.

"Good day to you miss," one of the older men, tipped his cap. "We came as soon as possible, as was instructed when we accepted the job."

"Wow, talk about prompt." I held the door open. "Come on in."

I walked them through the damaged parts of the house, showing the repair crews the broken windows and the cleaning crews, the mess.

"Um, why is there so much blood, everywhere?" One of the women uneasily looked around.

"That's what the police are investigating," I half-lied. "Oh, it's safe to remove the police tape, as everything's been photographed, scanned and documented."

I tore down a couple of reams, which went across the blood-splattered bookshelves.

Then I turned back to the repair crews, "If you can first fix the front windows downstairs, later I'll show you the upstairs windows which also need replacing."

Hopefully, it would also give Nairn some uninterrupted hours of sleep.

*****

To keep out of the way, I stayed in the kitchen, sipping on a cup of tea. I sat at the kitchen table, reading a book whilst occasionally looking at my watch. As such, Pete Miller found me, when he was shown in by one of the cleaners.

"Where's Nairn?" He asked worriedly. "Is she alright?"

"She's fine, she's sleeping upstairs." I stood up to receive him. "Would you like a tea or coffee?"

"I think I should go and check on her..." he anxiously hopped from one foot to the next, "...is she injured?"

"She's fine," I repeated whilst holding up my hands in a 'calm down' gesture. "But she's in shock and she needs to rest."

"Has she been to the doctor?" He pressed.

"No, she wasn't home when the place was vandalized." I lied. "She's not hurt Pete, just in shock from what's occurred. She's been up all night, as the police didn't leave until six o'clock."

"Oh," his face flushed at the scene he was creating, "it sounds like she'll need the rest, then."

"Have a cup of tea and I think she has some scones in the fridge, we can heat up with some butter and jam." I moved away from the table to play hostess. "Nairn should be awake around midday then the repair crews can fix the upstairs windows too."

Pete stood back to let me procure the morning tea, but he was watching closely.

"So what happened last night, after you three left the dance?" He asked a little suspiciously.

"Nairn dropped us off at our hotel." I retold the story Declan and Chiron, had thought up. "We asked her if she would like to have a drink in the hotel's bar, but she said she was feeling tired. We sat in the car and talked a bit though, because Declan and I were meant to be leaving today. Then she drove home and called us after she called the police, to tell us about the state her home was in. We think it could have been the two strangers who showed up at the dance last night, along with their friends. Not sure what the deal is with all the blood though, but it's a good thing Nairn dropped Declan and I off first, so she wasn't here when it happened."

"Aye," Pete sat down heavily, at the table, "t'was a good thing, indeed."

I carried the pot of tea and his mug, over to the table before grabbing the butter and jam.

He continued, "I heard what happened from Bill Macquarie, a Detective Sergeant at the station. He interviewed me, Angus and Eileen this morning, about the strangers at the dance last night. We told him how thin and pale the two were, and he thinks they were drug addicts. He thinks some kind of drug war went on here and they picked Nairn's place, because she's a known Healer. They thought they could score some pot, or magic mushrooms, or some such nonsense."

"It would explain why they singled her out, at the dance." I went along.

"It just makes me mad," Pete seethed, "here's the softest soul in all of Stonehaven, who uses her gifts to help people. Then she has druggies trashing her house, looking for her herbal remedies."

"No, it's not right, to be hunted like that..." my voice trailed off, before I pulled myself up. "Cup of tea?"

"Please," he pushed the empty mug towards me.

As soon as I filled his cup, Declan came into the kitchen, carrying four shopping bags in each hand.

"Declan!" He shot up out of his chair, as if having tea with a married woman was cause for concern.

My mate looked on the human in amusement, as he 'dumped' the shopping bags on top of the kitchen counter.

"How's it goin', Pete?" He chuckled back. "Sit down and enjoy your tea, I've just gotta bring in more shopping from the rental."

"Let me give you a hand," Pete hurried after the bigger and stronger male. "I also wanted to say thanks for last night, how you came to Nairn's and my defence..."

I giggled into my teacup, listening to their fading voices as they went outside.

*****

At 11.43 AM, a sleepy but dressed Nairn, appeared downstairs. Now that she was awake, I gave the cleaning and repair crews the go-ahead, to work in the upper part of the house. She stared at the strangers in her home, before Declan planted her at the kitchen table, to join us for morning tea.

My mate the forever gourmet chef, had heated up the scones and even whipped some cream to have with them, instead of butter. He also followed her inspiration, by making cucumber sandwiches. We four enjoyed these delights, as the house sounded like a hive of activity, from the work crews.

"And how are you feeling today Nairn, after all that's occurred?" Pete looked on, intently.

"I'd be lying if I said I was fine." She sighed. "But I'm glad B and Declan are here."

Her suitor sat up straighter, almost a little jealously. He glanced sideways at the larger man seated on his left, who was wolfing down his scones and sandwiches. Declan's muscles were so large, they were obvious even under his clothes. Then I almost laughed, when Pete pulled back his shoulders and jutted out his chest, to show off whatever strength he had.

The European Werewolf caught on to what the human male was trying to do, and he passed his Lokoti Werewolf wife, a wink.

"Having two strong males in the house, should make you feel better." Declan turned to Nairn. "Say, how about we ask Pete, if he'd like to stay for dinner? We'll pay for his protective services, with a two-course feast."

As he spoke, the human male jutted out his chest so much so, he looked like he was about to sprain something. When he started to flex the muscles on his smaller body, it was the last straw to make Nairn and I, burst out laughing! When he saw how lightening the mood made her feel better, he even stood up to do a couple of body-builder poses.

"Would you look at that," Declan waved his way. "How can I compete with that?"

"C'mon then," he returned to his seat to taunt. "I'll give you an arm wrestle."

"Nuh uh," my mate shook his head. "You'll win and I'll look like the idiot."

"Aw, c'mon!" The smaller man jeered the bigger one. "I'll be gentle with you."

"No way, I know the better man when I see him." He shook his head. "I think I'll stick to cooking."

"You're not afraid, are you?" Pete played along.

"Please don't hurt me." Declan pretended to plead. "If you do, I won't be able to make dinner tonight."

Next, the smaller Scotsman sat back in his seat, stroking his chin as he thought about it. "Oh alright, I'll let you live so you can make Nairn her dinner."

Then the pretty Scotswoman leaned forward to say in a flirty manner, "That's very gracious of you, Pete. You truly are a kind and generous man."

*****

The work crews left at 6 PM, to return early the next morning. But with their departure, new windows were in their stead. All the broken glass and mess had been cleaned up and even half of the blood was gone.

Nairn and I walked around, surveying the work done so far, whilst Pete helped Declan in the kitchen.

I wasn't sure, but I suspected my husband had told him that she liked men who cooked. However throughout the food preparation, it became evident that he didn't do this very often. Declan even had to show him how to grate cheese, as he helped with the lasagne. Then as my mate piled the mince, pasta sheets, béchamel sauce and then the grated cheese on top of the other, he had Pete cut up the ingredients for the salad.

Before we rejoined them in the kitchen, we stood at the base of the sunken staircase. Nairn was nursing a glass of wine, from a bottle she was sharing with Pete. Declan and I didn't touch the alcohol, instead we sipped on Root Beer.

"I've hired some carpenters to fix this staircase, I hope you don't mind." I told her. "I was thinking back to that conversation we had about fixing up the place, the day we met."

"And you thought that with all the repair work, it would be the perfect excuse to fix everything else that's wrong with the house." She smiled knowingly. "No, I don't mind, B. This place is so old, it's falling apart. Maybe what happened was a good thing, to kick-start the house into regeneration."

Then I stood closer to her to say, "Curses can turn into blessings. Besides, when did you ever think that you'd see Pete Miller, cooking for you in your kitchen?"

"Actually, never!" She giggled back. "The man was so shy, it's only taken fifteen years, a battle between two supernatural creatures, now a gourmet chef for a European Werewolf, to show him how it's done."

"Let's go back," I linked my arm with hers, "the men need an audience to show off to."

"Lets," she tittered back and merrily, we returned to the hearth and heart of the house.

~~~~~~

~ 10 ~

It was a dark, rainy night and a wet gust whooshed past to rattle the windows. It whistled around the eves of the house, escalating into a scream. I could hear the branches creak in the surrounding forest, as they bent wildly in the wind. I imagined it must have been cold and dismal outside, meanwhile we were safe and snug indoors.

I found Declan standing at the kitchen sink, washing up the mess from dinner. Music played softly in the background, I think from an early 21st Century band called 'Cold Play'. I recognized their album 'Viva La Vidas', as the atmospheric tunes suited the quiet of our two-person house.

I thought I'd managed to silently sneak up behind, but he didn't act surprised when I wrapped my arms about his waist. He may not have heard me coming, but he smelled my approach instead. My hands slid down the front of his long-sleeved t-shirt, to delve into his jean pockets.

Playfully, I bit through the fabric and into his skin. "Grrrr!"

"Hello there," he smiled as he worked.

Contentedly, I hugged him from behind. "Wotcha doin'?"

"The frickin' dishwasher has 'carked it' again." He sighed. "I'll pull it apart tomorrow after work."

"Don't do the washing up tonight, I'll do it tomorrow morning." I offered.

"I don't mind," he said evenly. "I've already started."

My hands dug deeper into his front pockets, "You cook and I clean, remember?"

"Careful, you might hit somethin'," he chuckled.

"Maybe that's what I want to do?" I taunted.

"And you choose to do this NOW, when I'm up to my elbows in hot, soapy, greasy water?"

"Oh and what about the time you pounced on me in the greenhouse, when I was up to my elbows in potting mix?" I bit into his back again. "Or what about last week, when I was in the middle of my weekly beauty regime?"

"What can I say, hair removal turns me on." He laughed.

"Eeew!" I tickled him, making him laugh harder. "Anything turns YOU on!"

"So I'm a dog." He joked about his supernatural status. "When I'm living with one of the prettiest girls in the tribe, I can't help myself."

My hands returned to his front pockets. "What if I'm living with the hottest guy in the tribe?"

"Mmm." He paused in his task, as he closed his eyes to savour the moment. "A little to the left... now down a little... ah yes. That's it...!"

I left several wet, bite marks in his t-shirt, as I chewed my way down his spine. Meanwhile, my hands were shoved so far down his pockets, the front of his jeans were almost pulled down. But he wasn't exactly complaining, either.

"Mmm..." he groaned appreciatively, "...now this is the life."

"It is?" I paused to listen.

"Hey, who said you could stop?" He humorously grouched. "Return to work!"

I giggled as I obeyed his command.

"Yep this is the life, B." He closed his eyes again. "Just you and me in the warm indoors on a cold, rainy night."

Then he opened his eyes again to hurry up and finish the job. My hands left his pockets to run underneath his clothing. To further taunt, my nails extended slightly to run over his hot skin, as I bit into his right shoulder blade. Declan sped up again, with the cleaned cutlery tossed into the dish rack.

"Faster than a speeding bullet," I remarked.

"Except where it counts, of course."

"Oh so modest!"

"Oh so honest."

"Are you sure about that?"

"Does my woman have any complaints?"

I pretended to think about it before I chirped out, "Nope!" I felt him shake with inward laughter as he continued. Then I sighed loudly as I released him, to hop up onto the kitchen bench nearby. "Declan...?"

"B...?"

"Declan," I started again, "we've been married for 147 years."

"Yes we have."

"Are you happy?" I asked, as I watched his face to see his reaction.

He paused in his task, to look over his shoulder at where I was sitting. The expression on his face said, 'here we go again'. Then he returned to the dishes as he spoke.

"No B, I'm miserable." He said sarcastically. "Wow, you really are like clockwork, you know that?"

"What d'ya mean?" I gave a funny look.

"When your monthly blues comes along, it's never late and always starts on a Sunday. Around the same time, this house runs out of Nutella. You're premenstrual music like 'Hinder', 'Nickelback', 'Sarah McLachlan' or even 'Alanis Morissette', echoes throughout the house. Around this time, you ask questions like, 'are you happy?' or 'do you still desire me?'"

"Oh I'm sorry for being concerned over my husband's happiness!" I retorted.

He went on, "After a tribal shindig, you moan about your inability to have kids. After babysitting our relatives' 'small fry', I hear 'thank God we don't have kids'. My God woman, if this tribe was invaded by 'Body Snatchers', I'd immediately know it wasn't you!"

"So I'm predictable, is that it?" I asked offended.

"Yup," he stated, "even your unpredictable behaviour has predictability in it."

"Oh really?" I said, deadpan.

"If I think to myself, 'gee, what would be the most illogical thing that can be done in this situation?' I'll turn my head and see what you're doing."

"Unlike you." I glared, as I crossed my arms defensively.

He started scrubbing the casserole dish he left for last. "Oh yeah and what about me?"

"If I buy pre-made salads from the supermarket, I hear you growl about how it doesn't taste as good as when YOU make it. If I want to hire a gardener or a repairer, you growl about how YOU can do it yourself. Then you'll turn your head to see if I'm watching, like you're showing off! If I'm late home from one of my lectures, I have to put up with YOU yelling about it. If I don't devote my weekends to YOU and YOU alone, I'll hear you growl about it!"

"Damn straight!" He laughed aloud.

Then he placed the sparkling clean casserole dish with the other crockery, before he drained the water out of the sink. He dried his hands on the tea towel which hung on the oven door, before facing me directly. His expression was one of amusement, as he listened to me rant.

"If I happen to talk to a male like an academic colleague, or even like that guy in the supermarket who only wanted to ask where the condiments were; I have to keep YOU from mauling the poor bastards! You don't just exhibit territorial behaviour, but insane jealousy!"

"Sounds about right," he shrugged it off.

"And I'M the one who's so predictable?"

"Baby, I never said there was anything wrong with predictability. You're the one who's getting so defensive about it." He grinned.

"Of course I'm getting defensive about it! You're saying it in a negative tone! Your demeanour is implying that there's something wrong with my behaviour!"

"I never said it like that."

"Then what are you saying?"

"I always know where the remotes are for the stereo or Internet TV, coz you line them up in order on the coffee table. I like how you fold my clothes and arrange them by colour code, as it helps me decide what to wear. I like how you categorize and alphabetize our book shelves and music collection. I like how you rearranged the orchids by colour, in the greenhouse. I like that when I undress you, I know what colour underwear I'm gonna see, coz of what day of the week it is...shall I continue?"

I tried to hold back my smile and pretend to still be angry.

Declan turned around to look at the calendar which hung on the refrigerator.

"Tomorrow's Sunday and..." he opened the fridge door, "...the jar of 'Nutella' is missing and..." he gave a smug smile, "...I'm getting the 'are you happy' question. B, where the hell is the Alanis Morissette music?"

I was trying hard not to laugh by this stage, "The shit I put you through! Oh, poor Declan."

"I'm WAY worse than you are."

"Oh yeah?"

"Uh huh." He hopped up to sit on the bench beside. "The guys at the Garage are always telling me so."

"How so?"

"When I'm checking out women," he said casually.

My mouth fell open in surprise. "Excuse me?"

"A beautiful blonde might come to the Garage and I'll see her get out of her car but her legs might be too thin. I'll say to the guys, 'B's got better legs than that'. Or a woman with a huge rack in a tight top, might try to flirt with us to get a lower price, but it won't work on me. I tell them 'more than a handful is a waste', as I stare off into the distance and picture yours, round and firm and perfect to bite into."

Then he caught my eyes wander downwards, as I self-consciously checked myself out, which made him guffaw.

He continued, "It's the same when a woman with plastic surgery comes by. They may pay to improve their looks, but it certainly doesn't improve their scent! Man, I hate the smell of silicone or botox or whatever substances they use. It would be like eating steak with cling wrap through it! Hell, I even hate the smell of hair dye."

I gave him a peculiar look as I wondered why he was telling me all of this?

"I'm 174 years old, B." He said proudly. "I'm set in my ways, and I demand hard work from my crew. But if the guys catch me staring off into space after a woman leaves the Garage? They know I'm not thinking about her, but I'm thinking about you. They know when you're away at one of your lectures, coz I'm text messaging you every hour, asking when you'll be home."

I liked how blunt Declan could be. He called a spade a spade, no more and no less. If you tried to correct him by calling it a shovel, he'd pick up the said spade and hit you over the head with it.

Then he rolled his eyes, "And when my mate of 147 years, asks me if I still want her and why? It makes me want to bang my head against a wall at how you apply commercial ideas of romance, to our relationship. We're not in danger of separation, being biologically joined together. If I don't buy you flowers or take you out to dinner, I'm not bored in the marriage. Sure I think you look pretty when you dress up. But trust me B, you look a damn sight better when there's no fabric on your body and it's pressed up against mine."

This time he did make me giggle, as I gave him a playful shove.

"So..." he leaned in to give an evil grin.

"So what?"

"Tomorrow is Sunday."

"Yeah and?"

He moved his eyebrows up and down in a 'hey babe, how about it' intonation.

"What's this? You don't usually ask!" I cracked up laughing. "You just throw me over your shoulder and carry me back to your cave, like the Neanderthal you are!"

"Yeah I do, don't I?" He chuckled along. "That would be my 'predictable behaviour' wouldn't it?"

Happily, he hopped off the bench and then thanks to years of practice, Declan slung me over his shoulder without my feet ever touching the floor. I squealed as I pretended to struggle. With my head hanging upside down, I watched the kitchen disappear and I gathered we were heading for the stairs.

"Hang on," he stopped and turned around.

The next thing I knew, I was being carried into the lounge room.

"Declan, what are you doing?" I squirmed.

I think he came to a stop in front of the stereo system and I heard him change CD's. Just then Alanis Morissette's 'Jagged Little Pill' album, come out of the speakers.

"No way!" I laughed harder. "Turn it up! Turn it up!"

So he did, especially since we didn't have to worry about disturbing the neighbours. The closest house was a couple of minutes down the road, with woods separating us. This also meant we often left our blinds up or our curtains parted, without anybody around to see in.

The lower level of the house disappeared, as Declan jogged up the stairs and carried his mate into the bedroom before... whoomp! I was flipped onto my back, landing on top of the bed. He fell onto the covers beside, with his hands scurrying to remove the both of our clothes.

Our bedroom was cold and dark, with the sound of the wind-blown rain hitting the windows. With the chill in the air, I appreciated the feel of Declan's greater body heat. I clung to him, to keep away the chill which he seemed to like. Once he had undone my bra, he held me closer to squash my breasts against his chest.

"Your red lingerie set, yep it must be Saturday." He carelessly flung it to the floor.

"Hey, this is a new lingerie set." I pointed out.

"Your last Saturday set were red."

"Yeah but those were red satin, these are red lace."

"Yeah, they're still red!"

"But this set looks sexier!"

"B, are you seriously starting an argument about your lingerie?"

"Declan, you're a guy! You're supposed to notice these things or appreciate them or whatever." I objected.

"Damn straight I'm a guy, and I appreciate this instead!" He growled, as he moved his torso against mine.

As our skin rubbed together, he was watching how my curves were flattened against his muscle.

I grabbed his head by his hair to make him look up again, "You mean lingerie doesn't do it for you?"

"I prefer you in less clothes, sure." He shook my hand off. "But from a guy's point of view, it makes it easier when there's no fabric barring the way."

As if to illustrate, I felt him tug off my underwear and then they too were discarded.

"I won't bother about buying sexy lingerie for you anymore." I said petulantly.

"Just don't change colours on me, or I won't know what day it is. If you ever put on Monday's blue set on a Sunday morning; I'd dress for work, rock up to the Garage and wonder why I was the only one there." He smiled down.

I giggled again as he removed his boxers along with his jeans and then he laid himself over my body.

He helped himself to raising my knees on either side of his hips, as he moved into position. But instead of rushing into the main course, he rubbed his crotch against the outside of mine. His member moistened with how turned on I became, which was the effect he was aiming for.

"Mmm..." I closed my eyes, enjoying the sensations, "...you're right, this is the life."

Declan paused when I said that, which made me open my eyes again to see his expression. He looked like he was glowing at my words. Then his head dove downwards, to kiss with his usual blunt force and hunger. At least that was the good thing about our 'predictability', his constant appetite. As our mouths moved together, he slid inside my prepared body.

"Stick with me kid," he mumbled out, "I'll take care of you."

*****

On Monday morning we were woken by the internet radio coming on Declan's digital alarm clock. His arm automatically flew over, to turn it off. However, he accidentally hit it too hard when we heard CRACK!

"Huh?" Sleepily, I raised my head to check for damage. The plastic shell of the electrical device had a pronounced crack straight down the middle. "That's the tenth clock that you've killed."

"It's only cracked on the top." He said dismissively, as his arm returned to my waist. "See, you can still see the numbers."

I smiled on how he was doing his typical Monday morning routine. He'd snuggle for an extra five minutes, before he'd haul ass out of bed. Declan closed his eyes again as he buried his face in my long hair.

"We should plan our next holiday." I said, as I kept my eyes open to stop myself from falling back asleep. "It feels like you're always working at the Garage."

"Tell me about it," he grumbled.

"You've worked in the same job for 161 years." I stated.

"Not the SAME job." He frowned with his eyes shut. "I started off as an apprentice then I was a mechanic and then an assistant manager and now I run the place."

"Yeah, but you still repair vehicles."

"I don't wanna be an owner who just does paperwork, that's boring." He rolled onto his back. "Let's start planning our next holiday. Maybe somewhere with a beach, where there's nothing to do by swim and lie around, under umbrellas. What about Hawaii for a week?"

Usually, hot weather bothered him with his high body temperature. But I guess he was thinking of visiting the tropical location in its cooler months. Since it was fall and we were on our way into winter, any location that didn't have snow appealed to me.

"Let's go to Hawaii for two weeks in two months time." I haggled.

"Deal." He grinned.

Then he leaned in to playfully bite me on the nose, which I returned with a slap on the ass. He guffawed, as he rose out of bed and I remained under the covers, to let him use the bathroom first. Once I heard the toilet flush, I heaved myself to my feet and shuffled past as he was exiting.

Declan customarily dressed faster than I did, as he left the bedroom in his denim work clothes the same time as I came out of the bathroom. I put on jeans, black t-shirt, a blue zip-up sweater and sneakers, before I returned to the bathroom. There, I brushed away my bed-hair and tamed it into a ponytail. Once it was done, I paused to look on my reflection in dissatisfaction.

The bad thing about remaining youthful was that my appearance hardly changed. I've had the same hair style of long waves with a fringe, for eleven years. As I glared at the mirror over the vanity, I decided it was time for a change, to end this predictability.

I was still frowning when I came downstairs. Declan was standing in the kitchen entryway, with a coffee in one hand and a piece of toast in his other. He looked upwards as he ate and drank.

"Oh oh," he commented on my sour expression, "B's not happy about something."

I brushed past to pick up my waiting coffee, which he often made with his. I cupped the mug in the both of my hands for the warmth, as I gulped down the caffeinated, sweet, milky beverage. My eyes closed by themselves, as I savoured my first cup of the day.

Mmm... this part of our predictability wasn't annoying but appreciated.

"What's up?" He queried, whilst watching my face.

"Nothing," I sighed.

"Yeah right," he scoffed.

"It's just another Monday, where Declan goes to work at the Garage and I stay home, to work on my papers. Maybe I'll call my PA at Hodge Endeavor to discuss my schedule of picking up or dropping a lecture? Maybe I'll plan another time travel to research my next paper? Then the other academics will show their claws to shred my work. Later, sometimes years later, they'll renounce their spite and admit that I was right. 'Oh yes Dr. Bianca Riverclaw was correct in the priestesses in the Temple of Athena did burn incense during rituals'. While the bureaucracy of academia drones on, my hair will still be boring since it's been the same style for a decade now."

"Ah ha!" He put his empty mug in the sink. "Here we come to the crux of the matter, B wants a hair cut."

"I might call Maia and see what she's doing today." I thought aloud. "I'll ask if she wants to come to the hairdressers with me and maybe grab some lunch at the Bakery Café."

"If you leave tribal lands, let me know." He issued his customary command. "Send me a text message before you leave the house."

I looked on in amusement, "Why do you always say that?"

"Say what?"

"Why do you always keep tabs on my whereabouts?" I wondered. "Every time I leave the house without you, it makes you uneasy."

"Of course it makes me uneasy!" He rolled his eyes.

"But why?"

"When you think about all the problems we've had on our holidays, with other Werewolves trying to claim you, or Vampires trying to eat you; I hate not knowing where you are." He said unhappily. "I'm not worried when you go into Alma, as it's close by. But I don't like it when you go overseas for your guest lectures."

"Why, because you can't come running to the rescue?" I asked sarcastically.

He said curtly, "Because if anything did happen, I'd have to catch a flight or whatever, since I can't instantaneously phase. By the time I bound onto the scene with my teeth bared and claws ready, you could be dead or almost."

Then he slammed down his coffee mug into the sink, before he headed for the front door.

"If you leave tribal lands, you text message me!" He barked on his way out. "If you're not gonna consider your husband's feelings, consider it an order from the Second in the pack!"

And he was gone, without giving his customary kiss on the cheek. I listened to his plasma-powered pick up truck, start. Next, I overheard him reverse out and zoom off down the hill, uncharacteristically faster than usual.

"So frickin' bossy!" I muttered, as I left the kitchen.

*****

"Yeah, I'll come to the hairdressers with you." Maia said merrily over the phone. "I need a haircut and my Mom can take the kids for a couple of hours. I'd enjoy a girls' day out."

"Great," I gushed, "I'll pick you up in an hour."

I ended the call and made the next to a salon in Alma, to book us in. Once our appointment was made, I hit the 'lock keypad' function and tucked the phone into my handbag. No matter if he was husband or second-in-charge, I refused to report my comings and goings to the domineering male. I mean, it's not like I'm running away with another man, or anything.

Fifty minutes later, I departed the house and headed for the garage, where my car awaited. It was metallic lime coloured and much smaller than Declan's vehicle. But as I told him at the time we bought it, it's just to take me into Alma or Fairbanks for errands or the odd shopping. I didn't mind instantaneously phasing to different locations, but I was wary of witnesses.

I parked out the front of Maia and Forrest's place in the community centre, and beeped the horn. Not only did Maia appear from the summons, but so did Therese. The proud grandmother was carrying her second grandchild, as the first came running over to the car which I was sitting inside. I hit the window control to lower the glass.

"Hallo Caesar, how are you?" I greeted the five year old boy, with scruffy black hair.

"Aunt B, can you take me for a ride in the broom-broom car?" He asked, hopeful.

"Next time, Caesar." I promised. "This morning I'm taking your Mummy instead."

Maia came over to pick up her first born and plant a kiss on his rosy cheek.

"Go and help Grammy look after your little sister." She ordered. "If I hear you've been a good boy, I'll bring back a treat."

"Yes Mommy!" He beamed at her offer, before running back to the house.

Then she sat in the passenger's seat and did her seatbelt. However, I noticed that she took extra care to make sure the strap over her tummy wasn't tight. I also detected a peculiar smell, underneath the perfume she was wearing. She still smelled like Maia of course, but her scent was slightly off.

I started the engine whilst putting my window up, before pulling out onto the road.

"Mom can look after the kids until one," she advised, "then she and Dad are helping the Tribal Elders with something."

"Cool," I acknowledged.

We cruised out of the community centre and off tribal lands, on our way into Alma. The sight of the small wooden houses in our cosy village disappeared behind tall, thick pine trees. As we approached the larger town, bigger brick buildings appeared as well traffic lights.

"So, what have you and Uncle Dec been up to?" She asked congenially.

"Nothin' much." I shrugged as I drove. "We're talking about visiting Hawaii at the end of the year."

"That would be nice!" She said a little enviously. "I wish Forrest and I could afford something like that. But we're on a tight budget at the moment."

"Yeah, I guess so," I gave her a cheeky smile, "especially when you have two 'rug rats' and now a third on the way."

Maia's eyes widened, "You can smell it?"

"Yep."

"How do you guys do that?" She shook her head in amazement. "Werewolves, I mean."

"I don't know, we just do." I shrugged again. "Declan's better at it than I am. I think he said he can also hear the baby's heartbeat. My hearing and tracking skills aren't as good as his or the other men."

"Yeah but they can't phase or see through time, like you can Aunt." She gave a pat on the arm.

Once we found a parking spot in the busy CBD, we visited a cafe to buy take-away Lattes. Or in my case, I ordered a hazelnut mocha because I thought it tasted like liquid Nutella. Then we carried our drinks into the salon with us, to sip as we had our hair done.

The male hairdresser asked Maia, "How would you like your hair?"

"I'll get three inches cut off and layered a little on the sides, please." She eyed her reflection analytically, in the mirror.

"To frame your face?" He caught onto her thinking, whilst lifting a couple of strands to illustrate.

"Perfect." She gave a nod.

"And you, ma'am?" The female hairdresser stood behind, but caught my eye in the mirror.

My stylist looked a little punk, with bright pink hair cut in a bob and a nose ring. All the staff in the salon were wearing black, however my stylist also wore black leather arm bands with metal studs. Then I looked down and caught black biker boots on her feet.

"Cool boots," I commented, "do you ride a motorcycle?"

"Nah, I drive a jeep." She smirked.

Then my gaze returned to the mirror, "Um I don't know what I want. But I do know this; I need a change."

She started to smile with her bright purple lips, "Change, huh? I can do that. How long have you had that length for?"

"Forever."

"Have you thought about cutting it short?"

My eyes narrowed warily, "How short?"

Then she used her hands to lift up my hair past my shoulders and her silver skull ring, brushed the skin on my neck. I tensed up, before taking a deep breath and slowly letting it out. Relax B, silver only hurts you if it breaks your skin. Lucky I wasn't another Werewolf, as the contact would have burned.

"Do you mean a bob?" I wondered. "Do you think I could carry it off? I mean, my shoulders are broad so I've always had long hair to retain some femininity."

"How about we have it longer at the front and shorter at the back?" She arranged my hair a second time. "It'll look wicked."

In spite of myself, I giggled at the mischievous glint in her green eyes.

"And what about a colour, too?" I went along. "Not all one colour though, but streaks."

"What about purple streaks?" She let go of my long hair and it all came tumbling down. "It'll go with the natural black of the hair, and your dark blue eye colour."

"Cool," I gave a nod, "let's do it."

Maia who had overheard our conversation, stared in surprise. "You're cutting your hair short? Uncle Dec is gonna freak!"

"Bring it on." I sat up straighter in the chair, as if I were rising to the challenge.

"You go, girl." My stylist laughed. "Now come to the sink so I can wash your hair first."

Over the next two hours, I was shampooed, blow-dried, bleached, shampooed again, dyed, shampooed yet again and when my hair was still wet, cut.

Maia's haircut took less than an hour, but she stayed in the chair beside mine to watch. The salon wasn't busy for a Monday morning, so the staff didn't mind her taking the seat. Her eyes widened as my long wisps of hair, fell to the floor.

Over the course of the haircut, we learned my stylist's name was Casey and she was from Edmonton, Canada. She ended up in Alaska because her boyfriend worked on the pipeline, however they broke up soon after she arrived. She'd worked in a salon in Valdez and now Alma, but she wanted to make her way up to Barrow.

"Three months of non-stop sun in summer and then two months of darkness in winter, totally wicked." She ended, the same time as my final blow dry.

When she stepped back, I stared in the mirror for a good minute or so. At first I was unsure of the shortness, until she brought over a second mirror so I could see the back. Then I started to smile, as I could see what she was aiming for.

The style of the cut was a bob, but the front was longer than the back. The front went just past my shoulders but at the back, it was much shorter and exposed my neck. Then I could see what she meant with the four purple streaks, it did suit my dark blue eyes.

"This looks fantastic, Casey." I smiled before it faded. "It just looks a little out of place with my wardrobe. I think I'm going to have to go clothes shopping."

"You did say it was time for a change," her mischievous grin returned.

"I did, didn't I?" I giggled again. "Man, you're a bad influence."

"So my 'ex' kept telling me," she joked.

Afterwards, I shouted Maia lunch at the Bakery Cafe. Then at twelve-thirty, I dropped her off at home. However, instead of going home myself, I drove back into Alma. There were some new clothing boutiques inside the arcade that I wanted to look at.

The stores sold sporting goods, or shoes, or lingerie, or jeans and other casual wear. I almost lost hope, until I saw the last shop at the end of the upper level. It was more up market than the others, which also made it much more expensive. However, the kinds of clothes I saw in the holographic posters, made up for it immediately.

This store didn't cater for casual wear, but I reasoned I could wear a couple of the pieces with jeans to dress them down. But the main appeal was the way the fashion meshed classic styles with futuristic flair. I fell in love with a knee-length black dress with white pin stripes, which had a triangular neckline to accentuate the cleavage. It looked 'The Jetsons' meet Bugsy Siegel.

I bought five dresses; three were business attire which I could wear for my lectures whereas the other two could be worn as smart casual for parties or dinners. I also bought two jackets and two tops. Then I went to the shoe store next door, and bought a chunky-soled, red, 'Mary Jane' pair. Lastly, I stopped in at the lingerie shop and bought a couple of black, lacy stockings. One pair was in a stripes design, the other was a floral weave of black roses.

Finally at three o'clock I drove home, with my new haircut and my new wardrobe. But I didn't stay home, I had something else planned. I had a surprise for my husband...

After I dumped the shopping on the bed, I took out the striped, black lacy stockings and then the knee-length black dress with the white pin stripes. I put them on with my new shoes and then went into the bathroom where my make-up was kept. I applied a dark purple lipstick, before returning to the bedroom. I opened my wardrobe to use the mirror on the inside of the door, to check my appearance.

A new me looked back, complete with a modern haircut and a smart dress. I looked completely different and I also felt a little alien, especially with the short hair. Now it was time to show it off.

I grabbed my keys and left the house. Once more, I climbed into my small, metallic lime coloured car and drove back down the hill. This time I headed towards the tribe's general store, which Declan's garage sat beside.

As I approached, I saw two other vehicles using the plasma power pumps, outside. The drivers were recharging their batteries, which was what I was going to pretend to do. But I changed my mind and pulled up in front of the garage's open roller door, instead.

This made Bruce and Gracie raise their heads from the hood of the RV they were repairing. At first they gave a funny look, as if they didn't recognize me. Then Gracie started to snicker and nudged Bruce, as if she couldn't wait to see her employer's reaction.

"Hey boss, there's someone here to see you!" Bruce called out.

"Oh yeah, who?"

"You better come out and see," Gracie returned.

I saw something large moving behind the second vehicle in the repair shop. Then I saw Declan walk out, glaring at the interruption. His denim jeans and hands were smeared in grease. He looked expectantly at his employees first then recognized my car second.

Slowly, I opened the driver's door and made sure a lacy leg was shown off, before I completely climbed out.

Just as I stood up, Declan's jaw fell down. His mouth hung open as he stared in surprise. His bright blue eyes bulged, as they swung over my new look before fixating on my hair.

"So, what does a girl have to do to get a discount around here?" I jested.

Bruce and Gracie cracked up laughing whereas Declan looked dumbstruck.

I continued, "I hear brunettes with athletic legs, are given preferential treatment at your garage."

Gracie guffawed, "Only the brunette standing in front of the boss, right now."

However, the European Werewolf didn't answer, he simply stood there.

"Go on, boss." Bruce whacked him on the arm. "Why don't you give the lady's engine the once over?"

Declan's face turned pink and he cleared his throat. "Alright, that's enough. Back to work you two, the Winter's want their RV back tonight."

Smilingly, the humans obeyed but kept an eye on what next occurred.

My tall mate wandered over to where I was standing beside my car. He didn't look happy for some reason. He stood close enough that he could look down into my face, but his eyes had a cold quality about them.

"Go home, B." He said quietly. "You've made your point."

Then he turned around and walked back over to the vehicle he'd been fixing.

What, that's it? My heart hurt as my eyes stung. I blinked hard as I had to quickly look away. I felt rejected and even a little embarrassed, especially when Gracie saw this.

"Have a good afternoon guys." I forced out with a wave, before I ducked back into the car.

Disappointed, I reversed out and drove off down the road towards home again.

What the hell just happened back there? Does Declan hate my haircut THAT much? What was the point I supposedly made?

My eyes watered as I parked the car in the garage back home, before I climbed out and headed inside. Disheartened, I stomped up the veranda steps then I unlocked the front door. Lastly, I went in and shut the door behind.

I went straight into the kitchen to look for a backup jar of Nutella. However, no sooner than I did, I heard a second vehicle pull up on the driveway. It was Declan's pick up, I'd recognize the motor anywhere.

Suddenly the front door burst open and my dirty but angry mate, opened his mouth to yell.

"What the hell do you think you're doing?!" He started with. "How would you like it if I changed my appearance and rocked up to one of your lectures, to surprise you?!"

Now it was my mouth that fell open at how enraged he was.

"And - and - and your hair! Where's all your hair gone?! I loved your long hair and you cut it all off?! Why, to punish me?!" He roared.

Then he marched up with his eyes blazing and his face red, to shout some more.

"You frickin' dyed your hair after I told you I hate that smell!" He continued. "It's almost overpowered your scent! You don't smell like a vase of flowers sitting in a kitchen whilst a cake was baking in the oven; you stink like a frickin' chemical factory!"

Angrily, I started to walk past him to go upstairs when he caught my arm.

"Don't you walk off on me, I'm yelling here! You left tribal lands without telling me and you deliberately changed what I love about you! You went behind my back! Why don't I just shave off all my hair and see how you like it?!"

I was furious now, as I ripped my arm out of his grasp before I stormed towards the staircase.

"Don't you walk off on me!" He repeated, as he marched after. "Answer me B, answer the damn question! Did you cut off your hair to punish me?!"

From the bottom step, I whirled around to shout back, "No I frickin' well didn't! I wanted a change! I happen to like this haircut! Maia and Casey like it too!"

His eyes glowed green in jealousy, "Casey? Who the hell is Casey? Did you cut off your hair, for another MAN?!"

"Casey is a WOMAN!" I snapped. "She's a single girl who doesn't have to report in to a husband! She does whatever she wants, whenever she wants! Right now, that sounds VERY appealing!"

His eyes flashed as his chest swelled to bellow. "Dream on, princess! Anytime you think about getting a haircut in future, I'm coming with you! If the hairdresser even thinks about cutting your hair from the shoulders up, I'm gonna eat them!"

"I'd like to see you try!" I retorted. "I can easily instantaneously phase out of the house without you and reappear on the other side of the world! Maybe next time I'll get a cute little pixie style cut, where it's only two inches long!"

"Right, that's it," he growled out.

Declan bent over to sling me over his shoulder again, but I phased from his grasp. When I tried to go up the stairs, he grabbed me from behind. I felt my feet leave the steps as he lifted me up, so I went into phase a second time. I almost freed myself, until I realized I had no footing and fell down.

Before I went tumbling down the staircase, the European Werewolf caught hold. This time I didn't object to his strong arms enclosing about my waist. That was until I realized he'd pushed me onto my back and was now lying on top. Like that, he thought he had me pinned on top of the stairs.

"Get off!" I flared.

But his reply was a sniffing noise, as his head moved down my dress towards the skirt.

"What are you doing?!" I tried to buck him off.

His hands released my arms then they grabbed hold of the hem. He started tugging it upwards, which the slim style objected to. I was scared he'd rip it, as he forced the fabric upwards.

"Declan!" I pulled on his hair. "Stop it! If you ruin this dress -"

However, I soon saw it wasn't the dress he was targeting, as he heaved the narrow skirt up past my hips.

"Frickin' hell, that hem is tight," he complained before his eyes widened. "Thank the heavens above, you're still wearing blue panties on a Monday. Now I KNOW you're not a Body Snatcher."

Before I could stop him, his head ducked and the sniffing noise returned as he inhaled my crotch.

"What the hell...?!" I tried to push him away. "Declan, have you gone crazy?!"

He raised his face upwards to say, "Here's the woman I know and love."

His words made me pause, when he used the distraction to pull down my stockings. Once they were discarded, my legs were parted so he could press his nose against the blue cotton. He even opened his mouth to press his hot, wet tongue against the fabric. The moisture seeped through to my sensitive area on the other side and the sensuousness turned me on.

My objections were silenced, as I stopped trying to push him away.

He continued to lick the outside of my underwear, wetting both the fabric and the panty liner. Usually a drenched liner was an indication for a change, but the heat from his mouth felt intoxicating. So did the force of his tongue, as it repetitively lapped in a steady rhythm.

"Declan...!" My breath sucked in sharply, as the tingling turned into a wet, rush of warmth. I knew these sensations were about to turn into something much more pleasurable and after so long of marriage, so did he. "Oh Declan...!"

Then he slid his fingers underneath the fabric and I felt him tickle my clit as he licked. His fore and middle fingers brushed up and down, at the same pace as his tongue. Before I trembled with fury, now I shook with anticipation. The heat and wetness kept escalating, as my legs fell wider apart.

"Not yet," he pulled his head away.

"What...?" I looked down to see why he'd stopped.

Declan pushed my legs together again before his hands grabbed hold of the underwear. He removed them in a single pull and tossed them over his shoulder. As he pushed apart my thighs once more, I watched his eyes glow green as his round pupils turn into narrow slits.

"Like a cake baking in an oven," he growled out.

Then his head dove down to 'maul' between my legs.

At first he used his whole mouth to smother the small region, over and over. Then he used his hand to hold one of my legs ajar as his other, returned to my clit. Meanwhile, my back was pushed against the hard edges of the steps, but I wasn't about to complain. The discomfort was soon forgotten, or drowned under the wet heat of his mouth and tongue and the force they gouged with.

My head rolled backwards as my lips curled upwards into a silly smile. In all the years of domestic harmony or sometimes disharmony, I've never had a 'head job' on the staircase before. After today I'll have a better understanding of the expression, 'a change is as good as a holiday'. I really should have given Casey a bigger tip...

...

...afterwards, two contented Werewolves lay on the staircase, with the male's head resting on the female's abdomen.

Declan's voice broke the silence in the living room, "Can you go and have a shower?"

"Say what?" I raised my head to give a peculiar look. "After what you just did, now you're going to complain about the smell?"

"I'm not talking about down there," he indicated with his head, "but I'm talking about your hair."

"Are you saying the dye smells worse?" I asked in amusement.

"Yup." He said matter-of-factly. "I can smell the bleach they used to lighten the hair before they dyed it purple. If I hate the smell of bathroom cleaner, what makes you think I'm gonna like it on your head instead?"

I groaned as my head fell back onto the uncomfortable step.

"Instead of using chemicals and a toilet brush next time, just stick your head inside the bowl."

"Shut up!" I pulled on his hair again. "It doesn't smell that strong."

"You wanna make a bet?" He brushed my hand off with his, before he looked up. "Haven't you noticed that none of the other women who were mated to Werewolves, dye or perm or use other kinds of chemicals, on their hair?"

"Oh," I turned pensive, "I never really thought about it."

"A la naturale, thank you very much!" He rested his cheek on my tummy once more. "Or I'll never make you tiramisu again."

~~~~~~

~ 11 ~

5th May 2238

All of Friday, I excitedly prepared for Nairn's stay. I vacuumed, mopped and cleaned the bathrooms. I went grocery shopping with Declan the night before, so the kitchen was stocked. I could tell he was looking forward to her stay too, as he added extra things to the list to cook up something special. Then on the way home, we stopped in on the Shallow Water's to buy some of the smoked salmon they make.

On our way out of the supermarket, I even bought two bunches of flowers; one to sit on top of the dining table and the other to go in the guest bedroom. Upon returning home, I put the flowers in vases as my mate put away all the food. Then on Friday morning amidst all the cleaning, I made both of the single beds so Nairn had her pick of which she'd like to sleep in.

Although the house and the guest room were ready, I felt like I was forgetting something. I snapped my fingers as it came to me; towels! I always forget putting out towels for our guests.

Next, I pulled two king-sized ones out of the linen closet downstairs and placed them at the end of the beds, before I paused. I hope she likes king-size towels, they are Declan's. Personally, I didn't like towels that were too big, I preferred normal size but with his gigantic frame, he needed them.

Just to be on the safe side, I grabbed one of his towels and took it back down. Opening the linen closet again, I swapped it for one of my smaller ones to place on the end of the bed instead. There, at least this way she has a choice.

It was then that I heard Declan's truck, pull up outside. He was home earlier than usual. I left the bedroom to go downstairs, just as he walked in through the front door.

"You're home early," I greeted.

He smirked, "Why do you always say that, if I rock up before 5 PM?"

"Because it's unusual and it's an inquiry as to why you're home," I said coolly.

"Sometimes I wonder if it's because you're hiding a secret lover in the closet, who entertains you while I'm at work all day." His eyes narrowed suspiciously.

"Oh no, you can smell him, can't you?" I sung mockingly, as I stood on the bottom step.

He growled back, "I can smell another man's testosterone on you after they shake your hand. If you were hiding a human inside our house, I'd smell him even before I opened the front door."

"Thanks, I'll take that under advisement." I snickered.

I wrapped my arms about his neck as his encircled my waist and together, we pulled each other in for a kiss.

"I'd tear him to shreds and then I'd eat his mangled body to hide the evidence." He said once we separated.

"I love it when you get all obsessive/ possessive like this." I tittered, as I rubbed my nose against his.

"Baby, you're mated to a European Werewolf. We're genetically designed to be the 'jealous type' and act out." He said matter-of-factly. "Especially when we feel that somebody is encroaching on our territory."

"I like it when you call me baby." I giggled, before giving him another kiss.

As usual, Declan responded and we 'made out' in a hungry manner.

We each let our teeth sharpen and use them to chew on the other's lips, which I knew he loved. Gently, he bit into my lower lip then sucked on the tiny amount of blood which seeped out. I felt his body harden, as he gripped onto me tightly. His whole mouth completely smothered mine over and over again, as the taste of blood always excited him.

"When are you... picking up... Nairn?" He mumbled out in between kisses.

"In... about... sixty minutes?" I managed back.

He momentarily released his hold, to look up at the clock on the wall.

"Then we don't have any time to waste," he said gruffly.

*****

I ended up instantaneously phasing to Scotland a little late from showering afterwards. As soon as I appeared in her living room in a bright flash of light; Nairn stood up from the couch with her overnight bag. She looked unsurprised by the delay, perhaps because of her skills as a Seer?

"Hi!" I greeted breathlessly, as I rushed forwards to kiss her on the cheek. I began, "Sorry I'm late -"

I was going to lie with a politically correct excuse, but I stopped from the knowing look on her face.

"You're only fifteen minutes behind schedule," she smirked.

To change the subject, I took her bag to carry for her. "Are you ready?"

"Yes."

"The house is all locked up and the security system is turned on?" I looked around the place.

Although I'd seen her home a couple of times since the renovations were completed, I still got a thrill. The sunken staircase was fixed, there were new rugs which got rid of the smell of mould. Also, the antique furniture bought to replace the damaged, didn't look as tatty as its predecessors. Stonewall House today in the 23rd Century looked just as good as it did in the 18th, thanks to Hodge Endeavor picking up the tab.

"Yes." She tried not to laugh. "The house shouldn't be 'ransacked' while I'm away."

"Nothing has been left on, like any stoves or ovens or heaters?" I checked.

"No, nor are there any fires left burning in any of the fireplaces." She promised.

"Right, you are ready then." I smiled.

Then I placed my hand on her shoulder and within the blink of an eye, Nairn no longer found herself standing in her Scottish manor, but inside my smaller house, in Alaska. She blinked a couple of times from the bright flash, which momentarily blinded her. Once her sight had recovered, she looked about in disbelief.

Gone was the antique furniture, the marble fireplace and other refineries; to be replaced with country-style pine furniture, overstuffed couches and a stone fireplace. Elegance was replaced by cosiness, with the smells of cooking. But our guest smiled as if she approved of her new surroundings.

"Oh my, that WAS fast! No wonder it's your preferred mode of travel." Her eyes widened impressed. "It certainly beats changing planes and waiting in airports or feeling jet lagged."

Declan walked out of the kitchen, also showered and changed, whilst drying his hands on a tea towel. He'd just started to prepare dinner when he heard our arrival. He smiled warmly on our friend and guest.

"Nairn," he gave a nod.

"Declan!" She beamed and crossed over to place a kiss on his cheek. In amusement, she looked past into the kitchen, "You're around food as usual?"

"Of course," he chuckled.

"What's for dinner?" She asked out of interest.

"For our entree, we're having Smoked Salmon Flowers then for our main, Creamy Garlic Prawn Fettuccine." Declan spouted off. "For dessert, we're having Flourless Chocolate Cake with Thickened Cream."

"Wow..." her mouth fell open in surprise, "...you're certainly a man who knows how to cook."

"B, how long have we been married for?" He looked on his wife.

"148 years," I answered.

"And how long have I been the cook in this marriage?" He asked.

"148 years."

"What, doesn't B ever cook?" She started to laugh.

"She prefers not to." He looked my way. "Her idea of food preparation is buying pre-made meals or dialling the number for fast food delivery."

"Hey, I don't hear you complaining when you come home tired from the Garage and I have dinner waiting for you." I put my hands on my hips.

Declan conceded with a grin, "Yeah, I'll give her that. As a Lokoti Werewolf, B empathically senses when I'm too tired to cook and as a Circulator, she can 'see' when I'm going to be home. So dinner's ready by the time I walk through the door."

Nairn observed our long looks towards each other, before she cleared her throat.

"Anyway," I quickly looked away, "I'll show you to your room."

The European Werewolf returned to the kitchen as his Lokoti Werewolf wife, escorted the Psychic upstairs.

While we were gone, Declan opened a bottle of de-alcoholised wine and poured us each a glass.

When we returned, he handed out the drinks as well as offered a plate of antipasto. Nairn and I sat at the dining table so we didn't exclude him, and he could talk to us through the kitchen entryway. The females nibbled on olives, feta cheese, sun-dried tomatoes, marinated mushrooms and smoked mussels; whereas the male would come over, pick up a handful of food and down it, before returning to the stove. As he cooked, he listened to her tell us the news of Stonehaven.

"Oh, and Donald Raferty is engaged." She announced.

"Really?" I smiled at the news. "Be sure to offer my congratulations the next time you see him."

"The wedding is next month, Don said that you and Declan are invited." She advised.

"Cool!" I said excitedly, before looking over to my husband. "We hardly ever see wedding ceremonies with white dresses or tuxedos."

"Why is that?" Nairn queried. "With your long lives, I thought the two of you would have seen plenty in the younger generations."

"Not many Lokoti follow Christianity." He reminded.

"Oh that's right," she rolled her eyes at herself. "You have the Joining Ceremony and the Housewarming, or just the Housewarming."

"Besides, when a man and woman decide to live together, they become mates. The term 'husband and wife' is more of a non-Lokoti description." He said.

"Hang on, we still use those terms." I disagreed. "Mum and Dad called each other husband and wife and they had just the Housewarming. I call you my husband and I've heard you call me your wife."

Declan looked sharply my way, "When in our Werewolf form have you ever heard me think of you as my 'wife'? In the outside world, we introduce each other as husband and wife. When I fight other Werewolves or Vampires for you, they know I'm fighting for my mate. The pack calls us mates and your father called me your mate long before he called me your husband."

Nairn and I exchanged raised eyebrows at his resolution on the subject.

He continued, "The word 'mate' is more solid than the words 'husband and wife'. The latter is an uncertain human condition, which doesn't ensure permanence. But when you say somebody's your mate, it sounds more biological and brings to mind chemistry instead of legal terminology."

Nairn turned thoughtful, "I suppose mates would be a more apt description for the two of you. Human couples don't generally exchange blood during sexual intercourse, nor can they track where their other half is by smell."

"The monogamous breeds can't cheat on each other either." He added on. "As I said to B this afternoon, when she shakes hands with a man, I can smell him on her. If I was around another female, B would smell her on me."

"Then the town's 'Marriage Tester' in the shape of Brigitte, wouldn't get very far here." She giggled.

Then he walked over with the wine bottle to top up our glasses. When he did mine, I felt his free hand rest on the back of my neck to give it a caress. Lastly, he popped some more food in his mouth and gave Nairn a wink.

"Feeding and breeding, is that all you care about?" She teased.

"Some people say the meaning of life is some big, cosmic mystery." He shook his head. "But they're so busy looking at the trees, they don't see the forest. The Beatles were half right, with all you need is love. But a full fridge and a hot wife also helps."

I blushed back, "Declan!"

"What?" He shrugged it off. "Nairn, don't you think B looks better now that her hair is longer and those ridiculous purple streaks are gone?"

Embarrassed, I buried my red face in my hands. "Declan, shut up!"

Our inadvertent victim of being stuck in the middle, grinned in good humour however she kept her mouth shut.

I hoped the delicious dinner which came afterwards, made up for our behaviour.

My husband's culinary expertise really shone through tonight. The antipasto plate was delicious, the Smoked Salmon Flowers were mouth watering, whilst the Creamy Garlic Prawn Fettuccine was scrumptious. Lastly, the Flourless Chocolate Cake was divine, with the thickened cream perfectly balancing out the richness.

Three satisfied people sat back in their chairs with their hands over their full stomachs.

"Oh Declan..." she shook her head, "...I forgot how large your servings are but how good it tastes, so you can't stop eating. When you and B left after those two weeks at Stonewall, it took a month for my stomach to flatten again."

A smug grin appeared on his face as he began to round up everyone's dessert bowls.

"I've never left a woman wanting and I'm not about to start now." He jested, as he stood up to carry the cutlery and crockery over to the sink.

The European Werewolf's motto of 'killing you with kindness' via overfeeding, continued throughout her stay.

The next morning for breakfast, he cooked up pancakes with sliced banana, strawberries and maple syrup. However, Nairn drew the line at eating four, no matter how much he tried to persuade. So following his typical fashion, he ate what she didn't. The human stared, as he polished off his twelfth pancake with the last of the fruit and syrup on top.

After we ate, I stacked the dirty dishes into the dishwasher and tidied up the kitchen. Nairn stood in the kitchen entryway, sipping her coffee and chatting. She watched with interest, as Declan took down several large jars from the top shelf in the pantry.

Appreciative of having an audience, he happily showed her his marinated olives, mushrooms and sun-dried tomatoes. She also watched him take out a jar of Feta Cheese preserve, from the back of the fridge. He opened it and waved it under her nose so she could smell the aroma of the herbs he used.

"The feta we ate last night, came from this jar?" She wondered. "You marinate and preserve the cheese yourself?"

"Yup," he showed her. "I buy the ingredients from the supermarket then I put them altogether. Well, except the herbs since we grow our own, in the greenhouse. It's pretty simple to make, you just put the cheese in with some olives and specific herbs and fill it up with olive oil. I got this from a recipe book, but the ideal has been followed by Italian families for generations."

"Sometimes I think I'm married to an old Italian grandmother," I said humorously. "He's always telling me I should eat more and he sits at the dining table once a month, to hand-make his own pasta."

Nairn said enviously, "I wish there were more men like you in Scotland."

Although she meant it as a compliment, he frowned.

"Nah, you don't want that. You're still dating Pete Miller, right? At least he'll never try to eat you during a full moon. If he did then I'd eat him and go through the process all over again, of becoming the last of my kind." He spoke bitterly.

Then Declan put all the jars back into either the fridge or pantry, as Nairn looked on sympathetically.

"C'mon, I'll show you the greenhouse." He changed the subject. "It's not as big as yours back at Stonewall, but it suits us."

Like a proud father, he showed off the rows of vegetables sitting on the floor or shelves. The two of us spent many an hour, watering, weeding and tending our crops. However, when we came to the triangular shelves in the corner showing off his pride and joy, the orchids; I stepped back.

Smilingly, I turned my attention to the radishes, as I listened to him explain the different varieties. I left the greenhouse to fill a watering can from the garden hose but when I came back, I blushed again. Declan was telling Nairn about the first time he gave me flowers, as he showed her the peach coloured plant.

She giggled like a little girl when he used the gardening scissors to clip off a flower and hand it to her.

"This specimen of white orchid is the Phalaenopsis hybrid, which are also known as Moth Orchids. I gave one to B when we were secretly seeing each other before we became mates. Back in those days, the orchids I gave her came from the Huntington family, who still grow them today. Now they run a florists shop in Alma." He explained.

"It must be hard, growing a tropical flower in the harshness of an Alaskan winter." She observed. "They must need a lot of tender loving care."

"In the old days, sure." He shrugged it off. "But in the 23rd century with the advancements in plant engineering, it's much easier. In winter when there's just a few hours of sunlight, we have a timer that turns on the heat and UV lamps for twelve hours."

But before they could move on to the herb section, his mobile phone in his jeans pocket began to play 'Aisha' by Death In Vegas.

"Aisha...we've only just met...but I think you oughtta know...I'm a murderer."

"Yeah?" He answered it. "Gracie, what's up? Uh huh. Uh huh. Did you point out that those parts had to be shipped in? Right. OK, I'll be there in five minutes."

Nairn and I looked on, as we wondered what was wrong.

"I gotta go," Declan said shortly. "I'm training an employee to be an Assistant Manager. She's great with fixing engines and a whiz with the paperwork. But with her mental illness she has difficulty dealing with difficult customers."

With that, he departed the greenhouse, walked around the main house then the sound of his plasma-powered pick up truck starting, came to our ears.

We walked out into the garden, just in time to see him reverse out the driveway and drive off, down the hill.

"Is everything alright?" She checked.

"Oh yeah, everything's fine." I promised. "He's just a very hands-on boss, that's all. Just as he's overprotective of his family, it also extends to his employees."

"Whereabouts is the Garage on tribal lands?" She enquired.

"I could show you, if you like." I offered. "Do you feel up to a stroll?"

She laughed, "If I don't work off breakfast, I may not be able to fit in dinner!"

Then we headed inside to grab our coats and my keys.

*****

We walked down the steep road from our house to the community centre on tribal lands.

As we went, I pointed out the houses which used to be my parents, or my grandparents or somebody else in my family. As I did, I told her stories about Circulators, Lokoti Werewolves or ordinary humans who were extraordinary in their own way. She listened intently, occasionally interrupting to ask a question.

"And you're a hundred percent certain that you'll see everyone again, in this space time continuum?" She pondered.

"Yup."

"Oh B, if only priests or ministers could have your confidence in the after life, they'd be filling the pews for sure."

Whilst we strolled down the hill, we inhaled the cool, crisp air with its musky scent from the abundant pine in the surrounding forest.

I showed her a vantage point from a curve in the road which acted like a lookout. From the height and small clearing in the trees, we could see nearly all of the community centre. Running along the side of the village was the wide, dark blue river. She admired it and the surrounding snowy peaks of the Alaska Range, with evergreen trees on its slopes.

Once we reached the bottom of the hill, instead of going right and walking past the sports field and towards the general store; we headed left.

Next, I showed Nairn the Holy Grounds. At first she was in awe of the five Sacred Totems and she walked a little away, in deep contemplation. I watched her, as she seemed thoughtful as she perused the grassy glade. Several times she closed her eyes, put out her arms and did a couple of turns before opening them again.

Anybody who didn't know she was a Seer, would give a funny look. However, I knew better and I think she could sense something. Was it the old Lokoti Wolf, who according to tribal legend, saved our people by creating the Lokoti Werewolf pack? Or was it a collection of spirits, of the hundreds of names of the long since departed, inscribed on the back of the poles?

"B...?"

"Yeah?"

"Do the Lokoti believe in Ley Lines?"

"Um, I dunno." I crossed over to her position, as she stood by the riverbank. "I don't think they'd discount the idea, but they may not follow it either."

"It's not just a UK thing, Ley Lines run all over the planet." Nairn frowned. "Although I don't have my divining rod, I'd bet you fifty credits that the Holy Grounds are on a Ley Line junction."

"Really?" I listened with interest.

"The river runs along a Ley Line," she waved her hand. "Then another Ley Line intersects here, running off between those two mountain peaks."

"I'd believe that." I smiled. "My great, great grandmother Elisha Worthall, would love to hear this. She researched Ley Lines and Stone Circles in the UK, in the early days of SSIT."

"SSIT?"

"Supernatural Scientific Investigative Team," I brought her up to speed. "She started it at Cambridge University, with a science student called Xavier Bell. When they graduated, they made it a profession and researched a whole range of things; haunted houses, ESP, reincarnation, Werewolves, Vampires as well as Human/ Animal Shape Shifters."

"What happened to SSIT?" She wondered. "I guess with people's disbelief of those subjects, it's the reason why it's not around today."

"Yes and no." I explained. "It could have gone on with Hodge Endeavor sponsoring it. Many of the reports were made confidential, to protect the privacy of the research subjects such as the Lokoti Tribe. But World War Three was the primary reason why it stopped. Then Elisha evolved to the space time continuum and Xavier passed away from old age."

Nairn turned pensive, before she asked, "Is this Elisha your great, great, grandmother who masqueraded as one of my family, in the 18th Century?"

"One and the same," I smiled.

"And now the progeny of the Durrant family is here, on Lokoti Tribal Lands." She gave a grin. "Everything happens for a reason, and everything has its time and place."

"Or, A leads to B which then concludes in C." I laughed along.

*****

We walked into the residential area, across the sports field and towards the Garage.

As usual, loud rock music was blaring out of a portable music player. Bruce and Phil were working to the tunes on a plasma-powered engine, of a red pick up truck. They paused in their work so I could introduce them to Nairn. Then they told us that Declan was in his office, talking to Gracie.

"She's pretty upset." Bruce warned. "That man was meaner than a grizzly that'd caught its claw in a bear trap."

"I still say you shoulda let me maul 'im." Phil's brown eyes momentarily glowed a maroon colour. "The way he tried to bully her so he could pay a lower price?"

"Told ya Phil, too many witnesses," he chuckled back.

Nairn's eyes widened at Phil's supernatural state before she looked my way for guidance.

"It's cool, they know you're like family, so he doesn't have to hide it around you." I reassured.

"Oh yeah, I always make my eyes glow when I'm around outsiders." Phil said sarcastically. "I do it just for kicks."

"So this mean man was an outsider from Alma?" I guessed.

"Originally from Anchorage and just moved into town." Bruce told. "He kept yelling how cheaper it is, to get his expensive boat fixed in the big city."

"The boss told him it would cost extra to get those parts from Japan, where his motorboat was built." Phil shook his head. "But the way the man ranted and raved, it's like we were trying to con him and not the other way around."

"Why didn't he just go to a Garage in Alma, to get his motorboat fixed?" I wondered.

"That's what the boss said and told him to do in future." Bruce chuckled. "You shoulda seen him, Aunt B. This jackass was practically jumping up and down and Uncle Dec just stood there, with his arms crossed. He wouldn't budge on the bill and he called him on his bluff. The guy threatened to get the law involved and Uncle Dec said he had copies of the quote that was given, so he could sue him right back."

"And then what happened?" Nairn prompted.

"The smaller man saw he couldn't intimidate the bigger one, so he finally paid his bill." Phil told us. "But because of this asshole, Gracie's talking about quitting."

Just then the door opened to his small, corner office and two mechanics walked out. Gracie was wearing her work overalls which were smeared in oil and grease, just as her face was smeared with tears. Declan gave her a reassuring pat on the shoulder.

"C'mon Gracie, you know how blunt I can be. If I didn't think you'd make a good Assistant Manager, I would have said so. But your training and hard work shouldn't be thrown away because of one loser." He lectured.

"Yeah, I know." She sniffed, as she hugged herself. "It's just unfair that people act like that, by making everyone as miserable as they are."

At that moment, Bruce turned up the old rock song that was playing and raised his wrench in the air as a salute.

"Hey Gracie, it's your favourite; Bon Jovi!" He called out.

Then he and Phil started singing loudly the lyrics of 'Livin' On A Prayer', to cheer her up.

Declan laughingly shook his head at his workers, before giving her a gentle push in their direction.

"Don't think about that loser anymore and enjoy this Saturday afternoon," he left as his parting order. "The sun is out, summer is coming and you've got you're own personal Bon Jovi tribute band."

"Yes boss," she conceded as a small smile escaped.

Then he walked out of the Garage and over to his pick up, opening the passenger's door for Nairn and I to climb in.

*****

That afternoon, Declan cooked up and served a selection of delicacies which turned into a late lunch - slash - entree.

"What are we having for dinner?" I asked, as I watched him prepare something.

Again, Nairn and I were sitting at the dining table so he could join in on the conversation, via the kitchen entryway. He'd opened another bottle of de-alcoholised wine, which all three of us were sipping. But from seeing so many ingredients, mixing bowls and general food preparation, had me curious.

"For the main course, we're having Veal Scaloppine with white wine and parsley." He announced. "Then for dessert, I'm going to make some No-Bake Chocolate Squares."

This made me remember something, "Haven't we had those before?"

"Yeah, I took a plate along to Maia and Forrest's dinner party, a while back. You liked them, they're the ones with bits of glace cherries and nuts through it." He replied.

Next, he carried over a huge serving plate of antipasto again. Only this time, there was crostini with brie included in the mix. I ate one, before I popped a smoked mussel into my mouth then an olive.

"Mmm," Nairn relished the delights, "I think you're going to have to be careful, B."

"Hmm?" I gave a questioning look with a mouthful of food.

"I'm going to do a 'Bridget' and steal your husband and take him back to Scotland with me."

Declan, who was hovering over the table to eat what he'd just served, passed me cheeky grin.

"You hear that, B? I'm a man in demand." He gloated. "Aren't you gonna fight for me?"

I looked Nairn's way again, "Just bring him back on weekends."

"Hey!" He poked me in the side. "I'll remember you said that, the next time another Werewolf tries to claim you."

Then he returned to his domain to fix up something else. Over the course of four hours, we snacked on antipasto, before Bacon and Olive Cakes were brought out, then Cheese and Bacon Piroshki, next was Capsicum and Potato Frittata and then lastly, Persian Rolls which were made from camembert, smoked ham and asparagus. When a finished plate was taken away, another dish was presented.

"Mmm - mmm - mmm!" The women at the table salivated, as they felt spoilt rotten.

"Declan, this is delicious!" Nairn commended. "Where did you come up with these recipes?"

"This afternoon's feast comes from 'Quick 'n' Easy Finger Food', the Smoked Salmon Flowers came from 'Salads & Barbecues' and the dinner and dessert last night and tonight, comes from 'Fast Food'." He handed her the cookbooks. "They've been in mine or B's families since the early 21st Century."

Nairn examined the old paperbacks, which were creased or had water stains or the errant spot of cooking oil, from years of use.

"Hey, two of these books are Australian." She pointed out.

"Yeah, I think Elisha used to own them and they were passed down from her," I shrugged.

"We're back to causality theory again," she marvelled. "Australian cookbooks from the 21st Century turn up in Alaska in the 23rd Century."

"And they would have spent some time in England, too. They've practically circled the globe as well as through time. A leads to B which then results in C." I smilingly repeated. "But I'm still spinning that Ley Lines converge on our Holy Grounds. I can't wait to share THAT with the Tribal Elders."

The European Werewolf looked puzzled from the Circulator to the Psychic.

"How did we go from a conversation about food to trippy time travel stuff?" He wondered.

Nairn and I exchanged glances, which offended Declan.

"OK then," he stood up from the table. "At least B has somebody to talk to about this stuff now, since she's complained she only has a computer. I may not be a 'Seer', but I know what I'm good at."

Then he carried an empty plate back into the kitchen and made a start on dinner.

"Declan..." I struggled to stand up from feeling so full, "...it's not like that."

"Oh yeah?" He challenged, as he used his palms to flatten the veal. "Then what is it like?"

"While you were playing the superhero - slash - boss and leaping over assholes in a single bound; I showed Nairn the Holy Grounds. She sensed the Ley Lines and I told her about SSIT investigating them and so on." I explained.

Here he paused to look down on his wife, who was standing by his side.

"It's cool, B." He said softly. "You and Nairn can talk about time travel stuff as much as you like. Your aura always looks brighter when you can do this sort of thing. I guess I get a little jealous when you bond with someone else."

I said teasingly, "I thought you got jealous if it's with other men."

"I'll tell you what," he returned to pummelling the meat, "if we had a pyjama party where the two of you wore negligee, then I'd feel included."

"Eew!" Nairn cried out from her seat.

"Declan!" I delivered a whack to his arm. "Behave!"

"Heh heh!" He chortled at his own joke. "C'mon B, I thought you wanted to make sure my feelings weren't hurt?"

"Not those kinds of feelings!" I marched out of the kitchen.

*****

After dinner we pulled out the board game 'Monopoly' because Declan refused to play cards. When we were in Scotland and played Poker with Nairn, she kept 'seeing' our hands. Although I was able to use some of my ability back on her, my husband threw down his cards and swore never again.

"Can I be the Scottish Terrier?" She requested, as we doled out the pieces. "Since the two of you are Werewolves, you can at least let me be a Scottish Terrier."

"That's fine with me," he handed the piece to her. "Besides, I'm always the Racing Car and B likes to be the Top Hat."

Declan took over setting up the money, since he was always the 'bank'. I claimed the real estate and Nairn shuffled the 'Chance' and 'Community Chest' cards before placing them on the board. Then she picked up one of the red 'hotels' to fidget with, as she waited.

"We usually play the game where all taxes go into the middle of the board..." I started.

"... and whoever lands on 'Free Parking' wins the money?" She finished for me. "Yes, I play that way too B."

"Sweet," Declan gave her a wink, which made her giggle.

Next, I picked up the di to see who would get the highest score to go first, and rolled a seven. I handed them over to Nairn who then rolled a nine. But Declan with his greater strength, threw the di too hard and they rolled onto the floor.

She started to pick them up, when we surprised her by crying out, "Wait!"

We stood up from our seats to see Declan's score first.

"Yes, an eleven!" He cheered, before he picked up the di instead. "I go first."

The European Werewolf went again and this time they rolled all the way down to the end of the dining table.

"Six," he saw the score and moved his Racing Car, complete with sound effects, over the board. "Brrm! Brrm!"

I stood up, reached over the table and handed the di to Nairn.

She smiled in amusement, "I take it with Declan's strength that the di don't often land on the board."

"Nope," we said at the same time.

"House rules; no matter where the dice land, whatever number it shows that's it." He told her, as we exchanged a glare. "Many a battle has been fought over this issue. Once, B had a hissy-fit after I landed on 'Free Parking' and scored the cash when the di rolled under the fridge."

"You moved it before I could see if it was a six!" I retorted.

"I WAS holding up the fridge with one arm, to get the damn thing!" He snapped back.

Our guest sensed that this was still a sore spot, so she quickly moved on with the game.

"Kings Cross Station!" She cried out gleefully. "Do you two play the game that you can buy property on the first round?"

"No," we said at the same time again.

Nairn noticed from the tone of our voices as well as the icy looks, that this was another sensitive subject. But as the game progressed, she saw just how competitive a game of Monopoly could become to two Werewolves. When my Top Hat was about to land on Declan's owned Trafalgar Square, she noticed that he was counting like I was.

Before my piece even touched his property, he barked out, "That's twenty dollars."

In annoyance, I slapped down the money and she caught the growl under my breath.

"My goodness Declan!" She remarked. "You didn't even look at the card, you knew the amount off by heart."

"I'm 175 years old and even if we play this game once a year... well, you do the math."

Her eyebrows arose, "Point taken."

However, I knew the real reason why he was acting short-tempered this evening.

As we played, I noticed he'd often look up at the clock on the wall. I too glanced at the time to see it was 9.07 PM. I could feel the vibrations in the floor boards as his left leg jiggled restlessly. Then we realized so could our guest, when she looked from the clock to my husband.

"Is something the matter?" She inquired.

"No," he lied to be polite.

So she looked my way for an answer.

"It's a full moon tonight." I told her. "Usually around this time, we'd be leaving the house to meet the pack and go hunting."

"Oh," she turned sympathetic, "we can finish the game now if you like."

Just as I was about to refuse in further politeness, he looked relieved.

"Thanks." He said simply.

Within a second, Declan was out of his chair and jogging up the staircase. The next thing we heard was the bedroom door closing behind him. Nairn looked my way curiously.

"He's just gone upstairs to change." I told her, which made her eyes widen. "Oh no, not THAT kind of change! But to take his clothes off and get ready to do the other... change."

"Oh, I see." She tried to act casually.

Next, Nairn helped me pack up the game as I grabbed Declan's discarded real estate and cash. Together, we neatly put everything back into the box before I closed it. However, I sensed that my mate was waiting upstairs.

"Um, please help yourself to the kitchen, or the Internet TV, or video-phone or anything else you want. I'm sorry your visit coincided with this time of the month. The other date you were free, I had a lecture so -"

"It's quite alright." She interrupted with a smile. "Please go right ahead."

I started to make a move towards the staircase but then I looked back, as I felt bad.

"Go B," she ordered.

I went upstairs, opened the bedroom door and went inside. I saw my mate was still in human form, but his eyes were glowing green with impatience. He was pacing restlessly around the bed, in his old bathrobe he wore before or after hunting. I started to strip as I hastily put on my elasticized gym clothes. As I did, I overheard his growl of approval whilst he watched.

Once I'd finished, we came back down the stairs. Nairn, who was standing by the fireplace looking at all of our old family photos sitting on the mantle piece, turned around. Her eyes widened at the site of his glowing green ones, which looked eerie against his brown flannel robe. Then there was me, in my black three-quarter pants and singlet top.

I hesitated when Declan passed by and opened the front door to go outside.

"Um, as I said make yourself at home." I said guiltily. "If you get peckish, there's water crackers and cheese. I think we also have a packet of shortbread in the pantry, if you'd like something sweet with a coffee or a tea."

"Thank you B, I do feel at home." She said warmly. "Good hunting."

Then I too departed via the front door, shutting it behind again to keep the house warm.

Declan had taken off the bathrobe which was now hanging over the veranda railing. He stood naked on our gravel driveway before he began to expand into his European Werewolf body. His height almost doubled as his width tripled, as he morphed into his monstrous form.

He looked like a muscle-hardened, gigantic, hairless beast, when standing upright on his hind legs. Next, he fell forwards so he was on all-fours before turning his huge canine head, in my direction. Within a matter of seconds, I too expanded into my stronger body of a Lokoti Werewolf. My teeth grew elongated and sharp, although they were no match to his razor sharp jaws.

My glowing turquoise eyes met his glowing green ones, as he sniffed in my direction. Then he made the first move, by leaping into the surrounding forest in a single bound. He tore through the trees to catch up to the rest of the pack, whom we sensed were waiting for us. But before I followed after, I turned my head back towards the house.

Nairn stood by the window, holding the curtains open to watch our transformation. She looked both impressed and wary of our supernatural forms. When I raised my clawed hand in a wave of farewell, she returned it.

To her human eyes, next I seemed to vanish into thin air but in actuality, I took off into the trees after my mate. I easily caught up with my greater speed as a Circulator, as he bounded along at 300 km/h. Then I overtook him to run out in front, and he ran right on my heels. Although he was vastly stronger, he knew I liked to show off my superior velocity. The European Werewolf ran on all-fours but the Lokoti Werewolf ran on two legs.

COME TO THE NORTHWEST PLAIN, TONIGHT WE HUNT CARIBOU – we heard Chiron's mind.

WE'RE ON OUR WAY – Declan thought back.

The pack was over twenty kilometres away but within minutes, we streaked out of the tree line and into the large plain. With our supernatural sight, we saw the pack close in on several caribou. They'd been grazing in the grassy field, with the snow-tipped mountains of the Alaska Range as their majestic backdrop.

Three female caribou were trying to run away however two males decided to fight. The stronger animals made a charge towards the pack. We saw one just miss with its antlers Phil and Jake, who ducked out of the way.

GOOD – I felt my mate's satisfaction – *I LIKE IT WHEN THEY FIGHT BACK.*

Declan relished any occasion where he got to fight in his larger, stronger body. He's said his fresh kill tasted all the sweeter, when he ate his opponents in battle. Purposefully, I slowed down so he could charge past and launch himself on the second male caribou.

Phil and Jake broke off their attack when they saw my large mate bolting in their direction. Declan's fiercer bloodlust was well-known to the men under his command. When the bull caught sight of his approach, it grunted and pawed the ground. Next, it ducked its head before it too started to run forwards to ram him.

Smack BANG!

The two strong, large males hit each other in a head-on collision! With Declan's muscle bulk and hardened hide, he was barely dazed but the bull staggered almost unconsciously. Then the European Werewolf's jaws went for the creature's neck, which made it kick out. Using his greater strength, he pushed it into the grass as his teeth ruptured its' jugular.

I fleeted past as I chased after the fastest female caribou. What satisfied me was not the strength of my meal, but the speed. My bloodlust relished outrunning my kill before taking it down. My mouth was open with my elongated teeth inside, as the claws on my hands and feet were ready.

As usual during a hunt, another Lokoti Werewolf ran after me, and another then another. They were going to share my quarry and by doing so, it ensured we didn't waste any precious meat of a fresh kill. Forrest often ate with me, as did Stone and Chiron. Tonight was no different, as I ran ahead of my Riverclaw relations.

Forrest once joked, whilst licking his claws clean after a hunt, "You have the best taste when it comes to picking your prey, Aunt B."

The cow ducked left and so did we. Then she ducked right and we mirrored her movements. I roared hungrily, as I leapt on top of her first! My claws dug into her pelt, to ensure I wouldn't topple off her back. But to make it as quick and painless as possible, my sharp teeth went straight for the artery in her neck.

Forrest jumped her second then so did Chiron and Stone. Altogether, the four Lokoti Werewolves and one caribou, went crashing to the ground. The female futilely struggled as her life left her. My teeth broke through her jugular, as Forrest wrestled with her kicking hoofs. Chiron dove his clawed hand into her chest and grabbed hold of the caribou's heart. Then not just her legs, but her whole body went limp...

In the moonlight, our First in the pack raised the organ into the air as in silent thanks for what he was about to receive. Then his sharp teeth pierced the small muscle, with blood oozing between his fingers. He finished the heart then his head ducked to feast on the rest of her flesh, as we were.

The members of the pack attacked the other male and two females. The kill placated our bloodlust, but we knew this wasn't the only caribou in the National Park; our instincts wouldn't allow us to hunt an animal into annihilation. Silence settled over the plain, as the Werewolves feasted on the flesh of the fallen.

Customarily, there were four or more Lokoti Werewolves per animal but as usual the European Werewolf fed on his kill alone.

Although he was very much part of us, whereas we could hunt and feed in a pack; his bloodlust wouldn't allow him to share. A Lokoti Werewolf couldn't possibly eat a whole caribou by themselves but a European Werewolf could. We gave him a wide berth to fight the biggest or the strongest to placate his murderous needs. It was his compensation that if he couldn't hunt human, he had some other challenge instead.

Besides, I didn't mind sharing my kill with my Riverclaw relations. I appreciated how Chiron's glowing eyes were emerald green, like the evergreen trees on our land. Stone's glowing eyes were bronze coloured, and I loved Forrest's glowing yellow eyes because they'd been Uncle Julian's colour. Although I was the only female, I felt part of the pack because I had family here.

We were very much part of the natural order or food chain, with Declan's greater hunger perching him near the top. Although I was used to calming people's fears about my mate's dangerous side, I never quite mastered the knack of explaining mine. Whenever I received enquiries, I'd blush and look away. But if Declan was around, he'd make a joke that my bloodlust was no match for his. I appreciated this, as it always made me feel more ladylike when a male hungered more than me. Although we feasted on separate prey, I still felt connected to him. I tore away at the caribou's flesh as it bled profusely, and we happily gorged ourselves on the warm meat.

*****

Around four o'clock in the morning the pack ran back to tribal lands. We could tell the time by smelling the onset of dawn. Chiron ran in the lead as was typical for the First, with Declan on his left and I ran beside my mate. The Circulator and European Werewolf could run faster than a Lokoti Werewolf, but out of respect we maintained our positions.

Two kilometres away from the community centre, the pack split up. The members whom had homes in the residential area, ran in that direction. Then the Werewolves who had houses on top of the hill, bolted that way.

We ran up through the steep woods with Chiron, Stone and Jake, before they curtailed off to their own homes. Once our First was gone, I sprinted in front of Declan again. I loved running in supernaturally fast speed, as I relished the feelings of exhilaration and freedom it gave.

We were nearing the top of the hill where our property sat. But before we cleared the forest, Declan swiped out with his front left claw! This tripped me up and I landed face first, onto the dirty woodland floor.

"Oomph!" I accidentally bit my tongue on my sharp teeth, when my chin collided with the ground. Then I swung out my claw to whack him! "Oow, that HURT!"

I rolled onto my back to try to sit up, but he pinned me down. I couldn't budge with the great oaf on top, since his weight increased as did his width. His greater body heat, radiated outwards from his hardened hide. At least this staved off the chill in the permafrost earth.

A low growl rumbled out of the monster, as he leaned his huge head over mine.

His large jaws were right in my face and he could have bitten off half of my head in one chomp. Instead, his long, hot, wet tongue darted out to lick at my lips. As if he could smell the blood, his turned his canine-like head sideways so he could engulf my mouth with his. His tongue moved with mine, with his saliva effectively numbing the stinging wound.

Ah, so that's why he's stopped us instead of going straight home...

Another part of Declan's bloodlust I'd grown accustomed to, was after he'd placated part of his hunger by feasting on fresh kill, he needed to feast on his mate in a different manner. I realized he was initiating it here and now in the woods, because there was a guest in our home, who could hear us.

His tongue repetitively lapped at my bleeding one. I could taste the lingering flavour of caribou flesh on his, which made his kiss delicious. With his large head leaning sideways, he locked the bottom half of my face in his jaws, in an impassioned embrace. His razor sharp teeth dug into my cheeks whilst his tongue wrapped about mine. We kissed for some time, before he eventually released my head from his.

I kept expecting him to shrink from his hulking, hardened body into his smaller, softer human one. However tonight was different; tonight he wanted to remain in his larger form for longer. Next, I felt his sharp claws begin to tear off my tight garments, as he expertly avoided damaging the skin. Oh well, the gym clothes needed replacing anyways, being so old and stained.

The larger Werewolf moved a little away, but his jaws didn't go far. I cried out in pain when next he bit into the soft tissue of my inner thigh. I sat upright in alarm, as his teeth dug in like he was going to take his pound of flesh. My clawed hand flew around to belt him on the side of his stubby snout!

Declan released my leg to roar with his mouth dripping with my blood, and I roared right back!

He liked it when I fought back, which showed when he licked his lips whilst looking my way. Then he pounced! I landed flat on my back once more, with the larger male pinning me with his claws. I growled warningly to let go, but he snarled back as if to say, 'not likely!'

His head ducked between my legs a second time, to lick the wound he caused. His saliva closed the bloodied teeth marks, helping the skin to heal. Then he raised his head as he moved higher over his mate.

Another unusual thing happened; instead of shifting back into his human shape to have his wife, he only half changed instead. His muscle bulk began to shrink but his skin still felt like it was part hardened hide. As his four claws turned into two hands and feet again, his nails remained long. His short snout retreated back into a round face as his human features returned, but his teeth stayed sharp and jagged. His eyes also remained glowing green, which never looked away, as he lowered his hips to mine. Then he pushed with such a force, I emitted a second growl of warning!

I knew the bloodlust was still upon him. The European Werewolf was trying to dominate me, like he dominated his kill tonight. But my bloodlust refused to become subservient to no man, or Werewolf.

Briefly, I went into phase so he lost his grip then I swung out my clawed hand and knocked him off!

The larger, muscled male grabbed onto his slightly smaller, muscled female, as we proceeded to wrestle in the dirt. Each time he grabbed hold, he tried to roll on top and pin me again. But each time, I'd go into phase so my hands slipped from his grasp and knocked him off.

Finally, Declan gave up trying to pin me and he clung onto my waist instead. We continued to wrestle, which became our intercourse. We rolled around in the dirt as we fought over who would be on top, whilst we snapped with our dangerous mouths. But during all of this, our hips continued to move together.

Then in another attempt to claim the dominant position, he caught the front of my neck in his sharp teeth. Being in a position where he could rip out my throat if he had wanted, I stopped struggling. His pushing sped up and I felt the heat between my legs turn into a hot wetness, as he repeatedly came.

Meanwhile, I felt both his teeth and his nails turn into their shorter, blunter, human kind. His skin changed into his softer, more pliable epidermis. When he released my throat, his green eyes glowed appreciatively.

I remained in my supernatural body, as I climbed on top instead. His bloodlust was purged but now we had to get rid of mine. My extra muscle allowed him to push as hard as he liked in his human form, as a new rhythm was established. Now it was my turn to come, as Declan moved at the same steady pace, which he knew worked. At first I rode him, as he bucked up and down. Then I rolled us onto our sides and he held up my right leg to perfect his angle. Lastly, he pushed me onto my back for a final time and wrapped my legs around his waist.

One of his hands held onto his wife, as his other gripped onto the bark of a tree. We both panted and sweated, making the dirt stick to our wet skin. I think I also had some pine needles in my hair. My claws dug into his back, as he grunted in both ecstasy and agony that I was causing. By addressing my desires, his remaining urges were depleted. Helplessly, I clawed at his human skin as I reached my peak again and again. He held on for as long as he could, as our growls turned into groans, or the snarling turned into sighs.

Finally, I flopped backwards in satisfied exhaustion and in a similar state, Declan flopped over me.

As I tried to catch my breath, I felt my muscle bulk slip away as did any residual tension. I felt the tingling in my gums and the skin around my nails, indicating that my elongated teeth and nails were shrinking back. By the time I was breathing steadily, I lay there in my human body.

Gratefully, he nestled his sweaty face between my sweaty breasts, as he laid over his mate. My legs were still wrapped around his waist but when I started to remove them, he stubbornly put them back. He wanted to bury himself in all the glory of my female form, which meant he wanted to feel ensconced between my thighs.

I giggled as I lay on my back, staring up into the branches of the trees with my human eyes.

It was then that I noticed how bright the sky was. Oh no, we had 'purged ourselves' right through dawn! Now we had to sneak back inside in daylight, and hope Nairn doesn't see us.

Worriedly, I looked over at my torn clothes and saw that they wouldn't be much help.

"Frickin' hell, now what do we do?" I moaned.

"Huh?" He looked up.

"I have to sneak into the house with no clothes on," I grumbled.

Declan looked about in the morning light, "It's still early, maybe she's not awake yet."

Then he stood up and reached down. I thought he was about to help me to my feet, but he scooped me up into his arms. Again, I wrapped my legs about his waist and did the same with my arms about his neck. He squashed our torsos together by holding me closely, to hide my front. Like this, he carried me out of the tree line, through the garden, across the gravel driveway and up the veranda steps.

The naked couple held their breaths, as he held me in one arm and used his other to quietly open the front door.

We lingered in the doorway to listen to the sounds of the house, when silence came to our sensitive ears. Yep, Nairn's still asleep thank goodness. Next, he carried me inside, shutting the front door behind. Stealthily, he crept up our wooden stairs and ducked into the upstairs bathroom.

Then we shared a shower to wash the blood, sweat and dirt off.

I stood still as he lifted up my long, wet hair, to massage the loofah over my shoulders then down my back. He carefully cleaned the bite marks and scratches in my skin, thanks to the throws of passion, before I did the same for him. We knew they'd be healed over soon, so we didn't bother about band-aids or bandages.

Declan's digital clock read 7.03 AM by the time we climbed into bed.

We settled between the sheets, with the smell of soap lingering in our skin. As usual, we moved into our favoured position of me curling up in his arms with his leg resting over mine. I loved how high his body temperature ran, which warmed the bed within minutes. I pressed my face against his hot chest so I could enjoy his scent, as well as his hypnotizing heart beat. In return, his head ducked so his nose rested in my damp hair, to inhale me back.

Just as we were about to fall asleep, the sound of the guest bedroom door opening, startled us.

Immediately, our heads rose and we listened to Nairn's footsteps go into the bathroom then the sound of that door closing. Next, we heard her go downstairs as she began her day. We even listened to her move around the kitchen, as she made herself a cup of coffee.

We exchanged small smiles, as if we were children who'd got away with mischief. Then our heads lowered once more and our eyes drifted closed. My face buried itself in his chest, with his in my hair...

...

...the next time I looked over my slumbering husband to see his clock, I found it was 12.03 PM.

Usually after a hunt, we might sleep in until two or three in the afternoon. But because we had a guest, I was worried about being a bad host. I gently pushed his arms and legs off so I could sit up, which made him moan as he rolled onto his back. When I hauled myself out of bed, he sleepily opened his eyes to also see the time.

"Hmm..." he groaned, "...I suppose we *should* get up when we have a guest?"

I pulled on my robe which hung on the back of our bedroom door next to his; before I left to use the bathroom first. Declan was a close second, drowsily bumping into me on my way out. I was halfway through putting on my clothes when he returned to the bedroom to dress too.

When we came downstairs, we found Nairn sitting on our front veranda, sipping coffee as she checked her emails. She sat on the top step with her laptop on her legs, as she periodically looked at our garden or the surrounding forest. We gave her a pleasant surprise when we carried out our coffees to join her, with Declan carrying an extra for her.

"Why thank you," she smiled at the sight. She put down her empty mug for the full cup instead. "So, how did last night go?"

"Huh?" He gave a funny look.

"How was your hunting?" She enquired.

"Er, fine."

"Did you catch something?" She asked congenially.

The Werewolves exchanged amused looks, before he answered, "We always 'catch something'. It's not like humans fishing or hunting. We catch the scent of our prey and we track it, sometimes fight it then eat it."

"Oh," she looked abashed, "sorry."

"No problem!" I giggled. "So, what did you get up to last night?"

"I read about Celtic Mythology. You have a lot of interesting books on ancient mythology B, I'll give you that." She complimented. "I also listened to one of Declan's antique CD's. It was um, I think a band called 'U2'?"

"Reading about Celtic Mythology whilst listening to an Irish band?" Declan chuckled. "Nice."

"Were 'U2' Irish?" She asked in surprise. "Oh, Pete told me that they were Scottish."

"What?!" He roared with laughter. "No way! When did Pete say this?"

She frowned, "He came over for dinner last week and he brought with him an old record player and several old records. He said they were Scottish bands and one of them was 'U2'. But I must admit, I prefer listening to music on Internet Radio instead, as it has a clearer quality. There was a lot of background noise on those old records."

"Records were the first kind of recording device made!" My mate the music fan, objected. "You listen to them to appreciate the historical value."

"Did records just come out when the two of you were born?" She wondered.

"We're not THAT old, Nairn." He said with mild offence.

"Records were out at least a hundred years before we were born." I smirked. "Did you have a late night?"

"I stayed up until midnight," she answered.

"Did you sleep well?" I asked, as the anxious host. "Was the bed comfortable? Did you need anything?"

"I slept very well, thank you B." She smiled at my concern. "But I did wake up early though, I think it must have been the crack of dawn."

"You didn't wake up cold or anything, did you?" I worried.

"Oh no, I was as warm as toast. But I think a couple of the neighbours dogs, got into a fight. I woke up from the most hideous snarling and growling I'd ever heard! It was coming from the woods, near the house. Did the two of you hear or see anything, coming back from your hunt?"

Pause... we stared at her as our faces turned pink.

"Er, there are no dogs on tribal lands, Nairn." My mate tried to say casually. "No cats or birds either. The only pets to not get spooked, are goldfish."

"Oh, I see." She diverted her gaze towards the garden.

Then Declan passed me a wink over his mug, as we tried to carry on as normal.

~~~~~~

~ 12 ~

20th January 2239

I hated the darkness in the middle of a hard Alaskan winter... From the 18th of November to the 24th January, there was less than four hours of sunlight a day, making the freezing temperatures worse. In a surreal sunset, the tiny burning orb in the sky would stick close to the horizon, making midday a bizarre joke for the middle of the 'day'.

There was no sunlight to soften the snow or illuminate the icy roads. There was no natural light to wake up to, which was not only depressing but made me extra tired. When you wake up and see there's no sun, it makes your body think it's still night time.

I remember how Mum and Gran had a hard time during this period, too. Maybe it's because we're Circulators and as 'Light People', we hated darkness. I remembered how Dad and Grandfather worried over their mates and often they'd take time off work, to keep them company. The fiercely protective Lokoti Werewolves would have attacked melancholy, if it had a physical form to sink their teeth into.

Declan reached over and switched on his bedside lamp. He yawned out, "C'mon B, it's 7.30 in the AM."

I rolled away from the artificial light but that was the extent of my moving.

Sleepily, he rose from bed and I heard him shuffle out of the bedroom and use the bathroom first. After I heard the toilet flush, I heard the shower turn on. Whereas I always showered in the evening, Declan was a little more varied. When he came home dirty from working at the Garage, he showered before bed. But if he didn't work, like on a weekend or on holidays, he showered in the morning.

Hang on, today's Monday. Why is he showering in the morning? Today is Monday, isn't it?

Tiredly, I raised my head and looked out the window at the inky blackness outside.

I think it's Monday. Man, I hate waking up in darkness, it totally screws up my body clock, as well as my sense of days. Frickin' hell, I'm going back to sleep!

My head dropped back into the pillow and I snuggled deeper under the covers. The grogginess easily pulled me under, as I returned to unconsciousness. I wasn't sure how long I was out for, but I woke up from a dressed Declan, throwing off the covers.

"C'mon B! Move it!" He barked out. "Outta bed, now!"

"Go away!" I rolled away again.

I overheard him grumble under his breath as he left the bedroom. Whilst he went downstairs, he said gruffly, "I'm going to make breakfast and I expect you to be dressed, by the time your meal is ready."

Once he was gone I pulled up the covers again. As if he knew, he banged around the kitchen extra loudly to disturb my sleep in. The sounds of cupboard doors slamming or pots and pans clanging, came to my sensitive ears. Within minutes, the delicious aroma of bacon, eggs, sautéed mushrooms, grilled tomato, hash browns and toast wafted up.

Declan's cooking up a big breakfast on a Monday morning? He never cooks breakfast before work, just like he doesn't shower in the morning of a work day. What's going on here?

"B, your food is ready!"

Aw, why can't he just let me sleep? But I did appreciate his gesture since he was a better chef than I was. Maybe he's just trying to break the monotony of Monday mornings, especially during this depressing period? I threw off the covers and sleepily stumbled out of the bedroom and down the stairs.

Declan looked up as he carried out our plates of food and frowned at the sight of my pyjamas. He placed our meals on the dining table and I sat down in my usual spot as he did in his. In front of me sat a pile of protein, crammed onto one dinner plate, with the toast sitting on the smaller bread and butter plates. He'd even prepared freshly-squeezed orange juice which sat beside.

He chortled, "You know, kids are afraid of the dark enough as it is. I'm sure if they saw that bed-hair of yours, they'd have nightmares for weeks."

I shot off a dirty look as I picked up my cutlery and began to eat. Since I was still half-asleep, I didn't have much of an appetite although it did taste good. Declan noticed how slowly I ate as he wolfed down his.

"C'mon B, it's your favourite breakfast." He further frowned. I didn't answer, as I carefully put some tomato, egg, bacon and toast onto my fork then into my mouth. He cleared his throat, "So what paper or presentation will you be working on today?"

I swallowed before I spoke, "I'm not working on anything today."

"Why not?" He gave a funny look. "When's your next gig?"

"My guest lecture is next month." I said, as I used my fork to push around the food.

"Shouldn't you start preparing for it or something?"

"There is no preparation, coz it's on something I've already done." I sighed, as I rested my head on my hand.

"What's it on?"

"A comparative study on Ancient Gods of Love and War."

"Oh yeah and what do you talk about?"

I said flatly, "The similarities between Ancient Egyptian, Greek, Babylonian and Mesopotamian deities and how closely linked the stories are."

"Thrilling," he said sarcastically at the tone of my voice. "Hey, you wanna try eating the food instead of mutilating it?"

"You have it," I pushed away my plate. "I'm sorry but I'm just not hungry."

"Apology not accepted, now eat." He said unhappily. "C'mon B, you didn't have breakfast yesterday morning. You only ate half of your lunch and you barely ate any dinner last night."

"I told you I'm not hungry."

"I know and that's what worries me." He spoke in concern. "Last winter you lost 5 kg's and as a Circulator your weight isn't meant to change, just like your age doesn't either."

I sighed heavily as I looked away disinterested.

He went on, "How are you going to cope in outer space when we leave this planet?"

"What do you mean?"

"Well, we're not going to have the sun in this solar system anymore, to recharge your batteries. The universe is a big, cold and dark place. What's it going to be like when we're in that forever?"

"But we'll be in the space time continuum."

"Yeah and?"

"The space time continuum is a place of light. It is light. It's life. It holds up existence." I spoke hypnotically, as I recalled visiting this wonder once upon a time. "Darkness and the cold can't come near it. It's everything that's opposite to dark or cold, because it hums with life and light."

Declan watched my face closely as I talked. Then he put down his cutlery to reach out his hand and put it over mine. The heat of his skin passed through his grip and the warmth even travelled up my arm. I liked how big, strong and hot, my mate was.

"I have an idea," he began. "After breakfast we'll pack an overnight bag and go to Sydney for a couple of days."

"Sydney?" I looked up in surprise. "But what about the Garage?"

"I've closed the Garage for the week."

"Why?"

"Because."

"Because why?"

"I talked it over with my crew and we all agreed." He shrugged. "Gracie already put in for her annual leave to visit Hawaii. I think she hates this part of winter as much as you do. Bruce and Phil were all for staying home to help their wives with the kids, who play up the most around this time of year."

However, I sensed he was only half telling the truth and the whole thing was his idea.

"And?"

"And what?" He returned.

"And so you can stay with your wife who doesn't cope well with the darkness, either?"

"Ah, so you finally admit it." He smirked, before he let go of my hand to continue eating. "Hurry up and finish your breakfast then we'll pack."

"You don't have to do this." I gave an unhappy look. "I'm not some fruit cake who's about to fall apart."

"I never said you were a fruit cake." He chuckled. "I've told you to your face when I've thought you're being stupid, or when you're acting nuts."

"I'm not going nuts."

"Yes you are."

"No I'm not."

"B, you are a nut." He grinned. "You've always been nuts and you always will be nuts. It's a plain fact."

"Thanks a lot!"

"Being a Circulator, maybe you're meant to be a nut? But as female Werewolves go, you're a nice nut. I mean, the female European Werewolf Michelle; was a frickin' sociopath for a stone-cold killer, who munched on her own family."

I groaned as I leaned forwards to rest my head in my hands.

"You're a Circulator, a 'Light Person', so therefore you need light." He shrugged. "It's summer in Sydney and we haven't been there in years."

"I was there just two years ago when I did a guest lecture at the University of Western Sydney." I reminded. "Besides, it'll be hot and you hate the heat."

"The things I do for love!" He melodramatically shook his head. "Yeah, but I wouldn't mind a trip to the beach again. Plus I like the ride on the hover-ferry across the harbour, when we go to Manly or Taronga Zoo."

A smile escaped as I admitted, "So do I."

"So what's the problem?"

"I don't like it when you babysit me," I passed a glare.

"Hey, who's babysitting?" He asked innocently. "Besides, if I were 'babysitting', I'd probably be arrested for molesting my charge."

Then Declan tickled me under the table, making me squeal in laughter!

"Anyways," he went on, "I'd like the time away too. I like Sydney and I like to spend time with my wife, when she's not melancholic or sulking."

"Oh you poor thing!" I sung sarcastically. "Since I sulk a lot, it doesn't leave you room to enjoy the good bits."

"You don't sulk THAT much." He conceded before flashing an evil grin. "Anyways, I like how after 149 years of marriage, I still get my way in the bedroom."

"It's a good thing you're married to another Werewolf, so your wife has the same primal urges you have."

"Trust me B, they're NOT the same. If my bloodlust had its way, it'd prey on the humans in Alma and my mate would never be allowed to wear clothes."

My eyes widened as I cried out in indignation, "And you call ME nuts?!"

"I never said I was sane, did I?" He spoke coolly. "Which is probably why I fell in love with you in the first place, because I saw a kindred spirit."

Declan gave a wink, put aside his empty plate and reached over for my half eaten breakfast. All this time he'd been talking, he'd been eating as well. His meal had been three times the size of mine and now he was about to eat the equivalent of a fourth plate. I watched him scoff down my serving next, as I picked up the orange juice to drink instead.

After a minute or two, he noticed he had an audience. "What?"

"Nothing," I shrugged. "Sometimes I like to watch you eat."

"You do?"

"Yeah," I confessed. "Your large appetite doesn't just surprise me, but I find it reassuring."

"It is?"

"Yes, because it lets me know that you'll continue to hunger for me, like you do for food."

Immediately, his face softened and he momentarily put down his cutlery so he could pick up my hand instead.

"Always baby," he kissed it. "Always and forever."

*****

Although he cooked, after breakfast Declan helped clean up. We stowed away all the dirty dishes, glasses, cutlery and pans into the dishwasher, before turning the machine on. Then he chased me up the stairs, straight into the bedroom.

Since we weren't planning on staying long in Sydney, we shared a suitcase. We packed at the same time, the first was our underwear which was in the same drawer. Then we opened the next drawer and then the next, to pack our t-shirts, singlet tops, shorts and what else.

I must admit, I was feeling reenergized and even danced a little as I moved around the bedroom. I don't think it was from the vitamins in the juice, but it was the excitement at feeling warm sunlight again. My mate didn't mind, being in a cheeky mood himself. When I bent over to fold our clothes neatly into the suitcase, he delivered a playful smack to the arse.

"Hey!" I flared, as my left leg jutted out in a karate kick.

"Go and get dressed, woman!" He tickled next. "I'm not rocking up to a foreign country with a wife who's in pyjamas and bed-hair."

"Maybe it could be a new look for winter in Alaska." I jested.

Declan paused as he looked like he was considering the idea. "Instead of flannel pyjamas, we could make negligee the state dress."

"Eew!" I kicked out again. "I think I'd prefer red, flannel long-johns."

Then he held up his dark purple, satin, Loony Tunes 'Bugs Bunny' boxers. "How about making these into our state flag?"

"Are you kidding?" I put my hands on my hips. "Don't downgrade Bugs like that, he deserves to be on the national flag."

He snickered, as I left him to finish organizing his things and I changed into jeans and a t-shirt, before brushing my knotted hair.

*****

Before we left, I made a reservation for us at the four star hotel, Grande Rose. It was near Circular Quay and had excellent views of Sydney Harbour and the Bridge. Our stay was for four nights, so we'd be returning to Alaska before Australia Day on the 26th. That was a shame, as we'd miss the fireworks. But we couldn't afford to run away from reality forever, nor from our plants.

Although planet-wide communications were excellent, with some international calls you could still hear the occasional echo. When I booked our accommodation, the hotel staff could probably tell I was calling from overseas. I think the fact that I didn't have an Aussie accent was also a giveaway.

Once we ensured the house was locked up and everything was turned off, we instantaneously phased out of cold and dark Alaska, to bright and warm Sydney. Usually, this mode of travel momentarily blinded you however, it was the glare of the hot sunlight which made me blink repeatedly. Also going from freezing minus thirty degrees Celsius to thirty degree heat, didn't help either. Our eyes watered profusely from the sixty degree temperature change.

I'd transported us into an alleyway to ensure we weren't seen. Then holding my husband's hand as his other carried our suitcase, we walked out onto the street. We only walked for five minutes but already began to sweat.

Declan let out a sigh of relief as soon as we walked into the air conditioned lobby.

"Hi," I greeted the girl at the counter. "We have a reservation for Sabre."

The staff member typed the name into her computer before she paused.

"Um, did you just call and make this reservation?" She enquired.

"Yes, is that a problem?" I wondered.

"I was the one you talked to on the phone," she appeared puzzled. "You called from an overseas phone number."

"Yeah so?"

She gave a funny look, "How did you get here so fast?"

"Heh heh heh!" Declan forced out a laugh, as he took over. "The wonders of modern technology, don't you just love it?"

However the staff member didn't laugh, she looked on peculiarly.

"No, my cell phone has an Alaskan number." He half lied. "Instead of all this messing around with switching to an Australian number, we thought 'screw it'! Let's just keep the numbers we have."

"But there was that weird echo that you hear on international calls -"

"Flat battery," he held up his phone. "As soon as you get us checked-in, I can recharge it."

She took the hint and did her job and next he handed her his passport and credit card.

Within minutes, we were walking towards the elevator with our security card for our room. Declan carried our suitcase again, instead of extending the handle and wheeling it behind. With his muscled arms, it looked a little like he was showing off. I guess a Japanese guest thought so, as he retracted the handle on his luggage and proceeded to carry it too.

We had the lift to ourselves and as soon as the doors closed, Declan turned my way.

"Brilliant work B, call the hotel from Alaska and then be recognized minutes later, in Sydney."

"Shut up."

"You're the Circulator who pops up all over the planet. You didn't 'see' this happening? What's it like when you instantaneously phase overseas, for your lectures?"

"But I don't make hotel reservations, do I?" I gave a glare. "My bossy, domineering, control-freak for a husband, won't let me stay longer than 12 hours."

"Oh yeah, I'M the bastard for insisting my wife comes home at the end of the day and I have dinner waiting for her." He glared back.

We stood there in the confined space in a moody silence. That was until he dropped our luggage simultaneously as I leapt into his arms. Our lips mashed together as my arms flew around his neck.

Bing! The elevator doors opened and a lesbian couple with a small son, looked on in amusement. The lady on the left cleared her throat whereas her partner giggled, so did the little boy.

"Sorry," my mate cleared his throat and reclaimed our suitcase. "It's how we ride elevators where we come from."

"Declan!" I blushed, as we hastily departed.

*****

The views from our room on the twentieth floor were amazing. Large windows made up an entire wall with a long windowsill you could sit on. I basked in the sunny sights as my husband opened up our suitcase.

"I'm gonna change before we venture outside again." He grumbled. "Or, we can just stay here in our air conditioned room and admire the views."

"No, I wanna go outside." I disagreed.

"I had a feeling you were gonna say that." He shook his head, as he took off his jeans.

I moved away from the windows to change into something more summery too. Whereas Declan wore a white singlet and camel coloured cargo shorts; I put on a short, yellow, flowery dress. I'd bought it a few years ago but hardly ever wore it in Alaska, along with the sandals. Lastly, I tied my long hair into a ponytail to keep it off my neck and help me to stay cool.

"You look very nice in that dress, Mrs. Sabre." He grinned. "I see I'm gonna have to keep a close eye on you."

"Very funny," I pulled a face. "I can always tell how territorial you're going to get, when you call me 'Mrs. Sabre'."

"What do you want me to call you instead, Mr. Sabre?"

"Ha ha," I said deadpan.

Then he held open our hotel room door before we headed back towards the elevator.

However, as soon as we walked out of the hotel and were hit by the heat again, he tried to turn around and go back inside.

"No Declan, no!" I grabbed hold of his arm. "Let's do a little sightseeing today. Please? Pretty please?"

"I'll show you a sight alright; the hotel's pool." He tried to retreat.

"We'll go swimming after the sightseeing, I promise." I pulled him away from the automatic doors. "Look, there's a coffee house over there. We'll get some frappuccinos to sip on as we walk. Think of the crushed ice. C'mon Declan, please?"

Whilst grumbling under his breath again, he allowed his mate to tug him along.

Whereas I ordered a small sized caramel coffee frappuccino, the European Werewolf ordered the largest they had.

We sipped on the icy drinks as we walked around the waterside of Circular Quay, in the direction of the Opera House. In front of the famous landmark, I asked a passer-by to take a photo of Declan and I together, on the large steps. The stranger kindly obliged before returning my phone.

We continued to walk around the waterside, which led us into the nearby Botanic Gardens. Then we strayed from our course to meander along one of the many paths towards the city. We exited near the Art Gallery of New South Wales, before walking down a street past the Hyde Park Barracks. This took us to Hyde Park, where we stopped to admire the large fountain. Declan made me pose next to it so he could snap some pictures on his phone, before we moved on.

We walked through Hyde Park, under the canopy of gigantic trees which offered protection from the hot sun. At the other end of the park we came to a War Memorial. There I took a couple of snaps of Declan, reading the information about the Australians who fought in the First, Second and Third World Wars. I think he felt like a soldier himself, with his years of patrolling after World War Three.

Next, we left the park and walked over to the Queen Victoria Building. I loved the old architecture which was carefully restored, let alone the 'window shopping'. But this time I didn't go into the stores, we kept walking.

After we bought some more cold drinks, we went down George Street back towards Circular Quay. We strolled past Martin Place then Wynyard and finally turned into the street where our hotel sat. As soon as Declan recognized the building, his pace quickened. He didn't slow down again until we were inside the air conditioned foyer.

"Aw c'mon, it wasn't that bad." I taunted.

He turned to give a tired look, with sweat beaded across his brow and his body also glistening with moisture.

"Now for that swim," he took hold of my hand again, to tug me towards the lifts.

The hotel's pool was an indoor one, which I think he appreciated. We'd gone up to our room again to change into our swimmers, before making our way to the water. I put on a one-piece swim suit and Declan wore board shorts. I slowly submerged myself in the water whereas the show-off simply dove in.

"C'mon B, just jump!" He taunted. "The water's not that cold."

"Shut up."

I was holding onto the handrail as I tentatively went in, one step at a time. That was until the obnoxious male swam up, lifted me into his arms and dunked me! I resurfaced with a squeal and splashed water in his face, as he laughed at his water-logged wife.

"Come here, you..." he tried to pull me into an embrace.

"No!" I splashed water into his face again. "I'm still pissed about you trying to drown me!"

Declan guffawed, as he pretended to be a shark by circling me in the water.

"No, I don't want to play." I splashed him again and tried to swim away, but he caught my legs.

He pulled me backwards, as he taunted, "You can't get away from me that easily."

I turned around to splash him once more but Declan caught my hands. He used them to tug me closer and soon I was pressed up against his wet form. I had to admit, his hot body in the cold water did feel nice. Giggling, I stopped struggling and allowed his mouth to smother mine.

Hungrily, he made out with his wife with his hands moving down my body to grip my waist. I felt him turn us around in the water, slowly making his way towards the deep end of the pool. When I could no longer feel my feet touch the bottom, I wrapped my legs about him instead. Slowly he kicked to buoy us, whilst never letting go.

"Erm hmm," somebody cleared their throat.

Sharply, we came apart to find an elderly man with a little girl, who must have been his granddaughter. Both appeared turned off by our behaviour. They too, looked like they wanted to use the pool but our 'make out session', was putting them off.

"Sorry," I blushed as I pulled away.

"This is a public pool," the grandfather gave a pointed look.

"Yeah, we know." Declan sounded rueful.

Then the elderly man escorted his granddaughter to the other end, away from us. As the two entered the water, I saw how they stayed away by remaining in the shallow area. Feeling embarrassed, I passed my mate and awkward look.

"Let's go back to our room," he decided.

*****

We shared a shower to wash off the pool chemicals then we lounged around in the complimentary bathrobes. Declan found a bottle of de-alcoholised wine in the mini-bar and he poured us each a glass. We sipped on the sweet, fizzy drink whilst pecking at a packet of cashews, also from the mini-bar.

Whilst enjoying these delights, we sat on the large windowsill and looked out at the views. We watched hover-ferries jet across the harbour, or a couple of old yachts bob in the water. Meanwhile, the sky had turned pink and orange with sunset before slowly darkening. Then we witnessed all the lights come on and our view at night was just as spectacular.

"I'm gonna order another bottle of de-alcoholised wine with dinner, from room service." He stood up to fetch the menu. "How about we eat in our room tonight? We have the views and we have privacy, so we can eat as much as we want without people staring."

Smilingly, I watched him peruse as I thought he looked very handsome in the white robe. His scruffy blonde hair which fell past his ears, had dried wavy. This, as well as half of his chest on display from the loose garment; made my eyes follow his every move.

"Sounds good," I shrugged. "Do they have any seafood dishes?"

"Yeah, they have a lot of seafood dishes." He acknowledged, as his eyes scanned the list of meals. "What if we start with a seafood basket for two, which comes with a lobster tail each. Then we'll eat a red meat dish, like a steak with béarnaise sauce. For dessert, I'll order the crème caramel and you can order the chocolate mousse and we'll share."

"How can I say no?" I grinned.

"Do you want the steak with béarnaise sauce, or the steak with mushroom sauce?" He checked.

"With mushroom sauce, please."

"Then I'll get the béarnaise sauce and you can try some of mine as I eat some of yours." He organized, before picking up the hotel's phone. "Yeah, I'd like to order room service please."

Although the food didn't arrive until an hour later, Declan immediately began to prepare. He moved the small table and two chairs away from the wall and in front of the windows instead. Then the waitress arrived with the trolley carrying our dishes, which he wheeled over to the table.

"Mrs. Sabre," he smiled as he served me first.

"Why thank you, Mr. Sabre." I tittered.

Then I stared at the massive serving of seafood which was big enough to be a meal for four people let alone an entree for two. The steaks were thick, which was perfect when you ordered them medium rare. I didn't have any room left for dessert, but we ate them anyway.

As we savoured the sweet delights, we sat together on the windowsill again. We behaved in a mushy manner, by taking turns spooning the desserts into each other's mouths. When I'd finished my mouthful of chocolate mousse, he passed a spoonful of crème caramel.

"Mmm-mmm-mmm," I relished every bite.

"It is good, isn't it." He agreed, before spooning some more.

I swallowed, "Declan...?"

He returned, "B...?"

"Thank you."

This caught him off guard and he looked up to find my eyes waiting.

"Thanks for what? For dinner? Although I didn't make it, I'll take the compliment anyways." He jested.

"Thank you for paying for dinner, for paying for the hotel, and for taking me sightseeing. Thank you for this week away. Thank you for everything since this morning."

He turned quiet for a moment or two, as he studied my face. Then he said softly, "Don't thank me, B. It's appreciated, but not necessary. I'm never gonna stop taking care of you, like I'm never gonna stop hungering for you."

My heart pounded and although I felt like my stomach was about to burst from all the food; a new hunger coursed through my veins. It made me stand up before sitting down again, but this time in his lap. He carefully held the bowls away as I straddled him. Slowly I came closer, until my lips were moving with his and we were both breathing heavier.

"You know..." he mumbled out, "...there is something you can do for me."

"Hmm?"

"Take off your robe and let me lick chocolate mousse off your body."

"Only if I can lick crème caramel off yours," I replied.

He laughed out, "Deal!"

Then I took the dessert bowls out of his hands so he could use them to lift me up and carry me over to the bed.

*****

The following day was another hot one, 32 degrees Celsius with scorching sunlight.

We walked to Circular Quay again, this time to catch a hover-ferry to Taronga Zoo. Hover-ferries remained a popular mode of transport, especially with the tourists. Although Declan and I were no strangers to Sydney, we always enjoyed the ride for the scenic views of the harbour.

The hover-ferry pulled out of Circular Quay and slowly cruised past the Harbour Bridge, the Opera House, the Botanic Gardens and then onwards. The plasma-powered vehicle could easily speed over the water to its destination however, for the tourist's the trip could stretch to 30 minutes. This would be our third time but we didn't tire of the journey.

We stood on the front deck as we sipped on more coffee frappuccinos. They helped us keep cool, coupled with the sea breeze which fanned our hair. Declan used one hand to hold his drink and his other was tucked into the back pocket of my denim skirt. We were both wearing singlet tops and sun glasses, to keep the glare out of our Alaskan eyes.

Before the Sydney Opera House disappeared from sight, I noticed one of the large posters advertising the latest performance.

"Hey look, they're holding a production of 'Berlin'." I pointed. "Maybe we should see a show while we're here?"

"Why not?" He smilingly shrugged. "It's not like we have any opera houses in Alma, so we might as well."

Then I giggled girlishly when he planted a kiss on my bare shoulder.

The hover-ferry docked at the wharf for Taronga Zoo and we filed off the boat. We headed towards the gate to buy tickets and once inside, we went up via cable-car to the top of the hill. This way we would be walking downwards instead of up, as we viewed the animal exhibits. Also, by the time we'd finish we'd be near the jetty again for the ride back.

One of the first enclosures we saw was for the Chimpanzees.

We looked in on the members of the ape family, as they lounged around bored, either scratching themselves or grooming each other.

"Hmm," my mate frowned, as he looked on one of mankind's closest relatives. "You know what?"

"What?"

"I have to admit that as a 'growly thing', I feel closer to wolves than these animals." He said flatly.

"Oh, I don't know about that. Seeing that mother chimpanzee with the baby on her back, kinda reminds me of Maia with her young." I joked.

I was looking at the female as I spoke, when suddenly she stopped to look my way. It was as if she could sense we were different to the rest of the humans looking on. Another female did the same and a male stopped scratching himself, to stare too.

Abruptly, the mother turned around and bolted to the back of the enclosure, screeching loudly! Then the other Chimps followed after her, making the same noise. More and more joined the foray, as they turned hysterical.

We walked away quickly, so not to frighten them any further.

Whoops! Animals were the first to pick up our supernatural differences. I think we were standing too close to the fence, which made them nervous. Last time we visited the Zoo, we made sure we didn't stand near the boundaries, so the animals didn't feel threatened. As Declan held my hand, I noticed how he was steering us down the middle of the pathway. I recognized he was camouflaging us in the throng of people, to avoid attracting anymore attention.

Keeping as such, we didn't cause any further furore. We ended up having a pleasant day, although my hot-blooded mate constantly bought cold drinks to keep himself cool. For lunch, we ate hot dogs and sat on the grass to eat them. The small glade offered more views of Sydney Harbour, with the city as the backdrop.

As we continued, I noticed how Declan enjoyed viewing the predators most of all, maybe because he felt akin to them?

When we stopped at the tiger enclosure, he leant on the wall to look long and hard. Since it was the hottest part of the day, the tigers were having their afternoon snooze. But we did get a curious look by a male tiger, when he opened his eyes to examine the individual who was examining him. Then it licked its lips, closed its eyes and went back to sleep again.

"You know what B, I like that guy." He chuckled.

"The male tiger?"

"Yup."

"Why?"

"He knows exactly what we are and he doesn't feel threatened by us."

I glanced from him to the other male in question, "How do you know?"

"Look at him, he looked right at us and went back to sleep. That guy has the ego of a King. He thinks if he took us on, he'd win." He said in amusement.

"Sounds like a typical male." I rolled my eyes.

"If he took you on, he'd win."

"He would not!" I poked him in the side.

"Yeah, he would." He said smugly. "He's not as strong as you, but he's way more vicious."

"He is not!"

Declan straightened to look me in the eye, "Yes he is."

"Maybe he's more vicious than you too." I turned away, sulkily.

"No, he's not."

"What makes you so sure?" I crossed my arms.

"If you fell over this wall right now, he'd maul you. But if I landed beside you, he'd back off."

"Yeah right!"

"Let's test this theory out..." he picked me up into his arms.

"NO DECLAN!" I squealed, causing a couple of passersby to look on peculiarly.

The obnoxious male laughed as he put me back down. Once I was on firm footing, I turned around and whacked him on the arm! He laughed harder, as he moved up behind to hold me closely.

He spoke into my ear, "If I landed beside you, he wouldn't be game to touch you as he'd know what was coming to him."

"Oh yeah?"

"Just like if I went near the female tiger sleeping on the log close to him, he'd have a go at me."

"Oh really?" I arched my eyebrows at this little lesson he thought to give. "Who died and made you the David Attenborough of predator behaviour?"

Declan moved around to lean on the wall again, whilst keeping an arm about my waist. "Think about it B, maybe one day 'growly things' like us, might find ourselves in enclosures similar to this?"

I frowned at the idea, as I found the prospect disconcerting.

He continued, "The bad thing about you and me being different breeds though, they'd probably try to put us in different cages."

"Why?"

"You and the male Lokoti 'growly things', would be in a nice enclosure with lots of room. With me though, they'd put up electric fencing, titanium bars and security cameras. But you know what?"

"What?"

"They'd need a hell of a lot more than that, to keep me away from you." He tickled his wife. "I'd keep escaping my enclosure to go into yours. And if they try to mate you off to another male, I'd tear my opponent to shreds."

The picture he planted in my head made me titter. I imagined myself sleeping on the log that the female tiger was, beside a huge, hulking, hairless European Werewolf. Next, I imagined flustered Zoo Keepers trying to move the dangerous beast out of my enclosure and into his own. The territorial male would roar loudly and swing out its claws! When they were frightened away, he'd return to napping beside his female.

"You Tarzan, me Jane." I joked before I leaned in to caress his ear with my nose.

"You'd better believe it," he grinned as he gave an affectionate squeeze.

Then we continued on our way, whilst holding hands. As he walked away though, he passed a parting growl to the tiger. When I looked back, I swear I saw the tiger momentarily open his eyes and softly snarl a farewell back.

We were coming to the end of our trip to the Zoo and Declan was sipping on his fourth icy-cold drink. I thought we'd seen all the predators, until we saw a crowd around a special enclosure. We looked on the gathering in curiosity.

"What's that?" He wondered.

I shrugged back then hand-in-hand we walked over to see what all the fuss was about. With Declan's large size, he cleared the way and all I had to do was stay behind. When we reached the front of the crowd, I moved beside to read the sign.

TARONGA ZOO IS PLEASED TO PRESENT THE ARCTIC WOLF. THIS BREED IS AN ENDANGERED SPECIES AND MOSCOW ZOO IS TOURING THE ANIMAL AROUND THE WORLD TO RAISE FUNDING FOR RESEARCH. TRADITIONALLY FOUND IN THE COLDEST CLIMATES OF NORTHERN EUROPE AND RUSSIA, THIS ANIMAL APPEARS IN FOLK LORE IN SEVERAL DIFFERENT CULTURES...

It went on about how wolves are in Norse and Germanic mythology, which I already knew. Then I read how the Arctic Wolf lives in the snowy climate and copes with sleeping in the snow or on the ice, with its mate or pack. It even highlighted when a wolf takes a mate, it was for life.

We looked away from the sign and our eyes searched the enclosure. After a minute, we finally spotted the creatures. They were sleeping in the shade of a bush, beside a poorly-constructed water-hole. It was a male and female and both wolves were panting hard, showing their fatigue from the heat. With those thick, white coats, I felt sorry for them. Declan and I sensed that they were absolutely miserable in foreign territory and away from their pack.

My heart went out to them, as the Lokoti Werewolf part of me could relate to their misery, waning for one's home soil. The humans around all clicked away on their digital cameras, oblivious that they were looking on two seriously depressed animals... creatures who felt like kin.

As if they caught our supernatural scent, the male looked directly our way. This attracted the female's attention, which made her look up as well. The two Arctic Wolves then sat upright as they stared at us, almost expectantly. It was like they recognized us as relations of theirs.

"Look Daddy, puppy dogs!" A four year old girl sitting atop of her father's shoulders, pointed. "Can they play fetch like 'Digger' does?"

"I don't know sweetie, maybe if they were trained?" Her father shrugged.

Declan's head snapped around to look on incredulous. To him it was ridiculous, a wolf from the wild who was a hunter and a predator, would behave in such a way? I sensed he battled his temper as his jaw set and he moodily looked away.

My sensitive ears picked up a growl build in his throat and I think so did the wolves. Their ears picked up and the male's chest filled out, almost with pride. The two Arctic Wolves sat alert, as if waiting to see what we would do.

Call me strange, but I had the feeling that they were waiting to see if we'd show our true colours by turning right then and there. It was like they were waiting for us to scare the humans away and come to the rescue. But we didn't...

Declan and I stood there, looking back apologetically. In frustration, he was squeezing my hand so tightly, he almost crushed it! It was as if the male Arctic Wolf was saying to him:

WE'RE BOTH EUROPEAN BREEDS, WE BOTH PREFER COLD CLIMATES AND WE'RE BOTH HERE WITH OUR MATES. SO WHY IS IT YOU STANDING ON THAT SIDE OF THAT WALL AND NOT US?

Very quietly, he made a whining noise to let them know that we could feel their pain. The two wolves exchanged a sad look before lying back down near the water, to try to cool down. The female moved her head closer to the male and in return, he gave an affectionate lick to her nose.

If this was Alaska and we saw wolves mistreated in the Lokoti National Park, we could do something to stop it. But because we were on foreign soil and we were in a public place, we couldn't. We'd jeopardize the anonymity of the Lokoti Werewolf pack by being identified in the attempt to arrest us.

The sight of them made my heart hurt so much, I appreciated the fact that my hand was aching from the force Declan was squeezing it. The physical pain lessened the helpless angst.

Without saying a word, we both turned away. We headed straight for the Zoo's exit then the wharf for the hover-ferry. We both felt hot and tired and emotionally wrought.

We passed a bin when Declan dropped his half-drunk soda into it, from losing his appetite.

~~~~~~

~ 13 ~

The good thing about travelling by instantaneously phasing was I didn't have to worry about time zones.

Although Johannesburg was 12 hours ahead of Alaska, I could depart my living room at 8 AM and arrive in the ladies bathroom at Johannesburg airport at 8 AM. It was a nifty knack to have, time travelling. My passport would be stamped and I had whatever visa necessary, courtesy of Hodge Endeavor's legal department. I'd walk out of the International Arrivals and head towards whatever driver was holding up a sign which read, Dr. Bianca Carmichael. I'd hop into the hire car and be driven to my latest academic engagement at wherever the university was. This time my guest lecture was at the University of South Africa.

I wasn't a very imaginative person and I couldn't be bothered remembering elaborate lies for made-up identities. Because of this, I used family names of my ancestors for my academic personas. When I first graduated with a PhD over a hundred years ago, naturally I used my name Dr. Bianca Sabre. However, since Circulators didn't grow elderly unless they did it on purpose, let alone die of old age; I had fake Death Certificates created as well as new Birth Certificates, Passports and Drivers Licenses. This was thanks to Hodge Endeavor's legal department again, which the Circulate Mainframe controlled and monitored for me. I manipulated time inside of me to look like I was growing old whenever the aging Dr. Bianca Sabre attended academic functions. When she supposedly 'carked it', I presented new papers and lectures as Dr. Bianca Wisetail then Dr. Bianca Riverclaw.

Now I was using my grandmother's maiden name of Carmichael and I had a new paper to talk about, as a young twenty-something professor.

Inside the lecture theatre, I plugged my laptop into the electronics of the podium, so I could use the view screen behind to show my slides. I activated the 'slideshow' option on Window's picture viewer and as it showed whatever scene from the ancient world I had sneakily photographed on one of my circulations; I talked. I was wearing a dark red suit and my hair was done up in a French Roll. I looked just as formal as everyone else did, but I always felt nervous starting out in a new academic identity. The older professors sitting behind the students, always viewed new work and new adversaries, with open scrutiny.

My latest paper was titled, 'The Thrill Of The Hunt; Symbolism In the Physical and Metaphysical Ancient World'. I showed slides of temple art of the hunting rituals in the Egyptian, Greek, Babylonian and Roman cultures. I compared these to the funeral rituals and how they viewed the taking of life. I could tell the photos impressed the stuffier professors. I took them back in time when the art was still fresh whereas today they were badly faded, cracked or peeling. During the lunch break, one approached to enquire what computer program I used to recreate the damaged art with such accuracy.

I wasn't the only lecturer, for after my talk there was another hour long presentation then another. Luncheon was at 1 PM and then I did my guest lecture again to an all new audience in the same theatre. So did my fellow guest lecturers. At 5 PM, the university's Humanities Department put on an afternoon tea so we could meet the rest of the faculty.

The entertainment was attended by students and professors alike. Everyone seemed to know each other, which made me feel shy and awkward. I guess it was natural that the students and their professors knew each other, but the cliques could exclude you. So I chatted to the other two guest lecturers, Doctors Smith and Harding, who were successful archaeologists in their field. I fell into ease in their company, especially since we shared the same interests.

We started talking about how they could recreate the ancient cities as holograms from their computers. Although they could replicate the layout of the cities from the evidence found on archaeological digs, I realized they were getting the smaller details wrong. I offered to show them pictures of the colours and decorations used on the buildings, which I lied were also computer generated from archaeological evidence.

It was then that our conversation was overtaken by somebody else's. The group of people standing next to us, were listening to a particularly loud, older man. He was wearing a tweed jacket, had a bulbous red nose, thinning grey hair and a foghorn voice.

"Yes, in my latest book I reassess the findings by Dr. Sabre, Dr. Wisetail, Dr. Rouen and Dr. Mulhouse, on the importance of religion in Ancient Athens. Or should I say, I *correct* them." He sounded off then he laughed as if he just said something witty.

"Who's that guy?" I asked my colleague.

"Oh, that's Dr. Gothenburg." Dr. Smith rolled his eyes. "He's never discovered any new evidence in his career, he just tears down other people's work."

'Foghorn Leghorn' continued, "And isn't it curious how similar the work of Dr. Bianca Sabre and Dr. Bianca Wisetail, is? I read that they were related, and quite possibly were grandmother and granddaughter. Perhaps that's why Dr. Wisetail's work seems like regurgitation? Just like a mother penguin spewing into the open mouth of her young."

Then he laughed at his own remark a second time, prompting his listeners to follow.

My bloodlust began to boil, as my eyes narrowed and I examined the circle about the pompous ass. They looked like students hero-worshiping the published professor in their midst. I wondered what their reaction might be if I swiped at this loser with my claws in light speed, so fast no one would see.

Dr. Harding snickered, "Somebody should point out to him that those historians' papers, are in every respectable library around the world."

Dr. Smith agreed, "You can't say that about *his* work."

*****

At 9 PM Johannesburg time, the hire car dropped me back at the airport. Once more I headed for the ladies bathroom. As soon as the last person walked out, I used the privacy to instantaneously phase home.

I reappeared in my living area at 9 PM Alaskan time. Although my presentations could be called a success, I felt emotionally exhausted. I was relieved to come home to a quiet, cosy house in the middle of nowhere.

Curiously, all the lights downstairs were switched off. There was a small amount of illumination though, spilling down the small staircase. I knew it was from my husband's bedside lamp, indicating he was reading in bed.

I placed my briefcase with my laptop inside, on the dining table before taking off my coat. Next to go were my shoes, which had been hurting my feet all day. The heels may not have been that high, but they still made my feet and lower back ache.

In my stocking-clad feet, I trod up the staircase and into our bedroom. I found my muscled mate was indeed reading, on top of the covers in his boxers. He smelled soapy, indicating he'd showered.

Declan looked up to ask obligatory, "Hi honey, how was your day?"

"Good and bad," I said tiredly. "Why are you in bed so early?"

"I was covered in crap from work and needed a shower. I couldn't be bothered putting on clothes, just to read downstairs. So I'm reading upstairs, in my underwear which also happens to be my sleep wear."

"Oh," I saw his point and started to copy his idea.

He watched me undress by taking off my jacket and blouse first then the skirt and stockings second.

"I cooked chicken parmigiana for dinner, there's a plate in the oven for you."

"Nah," I screwed up my face. "I'm too tired to eat, I'll have it tomorrow."

"It won't taste as nice."

"Then you eat it." I said dismissively, as I took off my bra and panties.

Next, I grabbed my bathrobe which hung on the back of the bedroom door and put it on.

"Why do you always put the robe on, just to leave the bedroom and go into the bathroom? There's nobody in the house except us." He teased.

"I don't know, out of habit I guess." I shrugged. "I did it growing up when I used to live with my parents."

With this, I left the bedroom in the said bathrobe and took it off in the bathroom, once the door was closed.

The hot water was therapeutic, as it melted away the tension in my shoulders and back. I stood under the steady stream for some time before picking up the loofah and shower gel. Once the make-up was washed off and my body cleansed, I finally turned the water off.

It was nearly 10 PM when I returned to the bedroom to put on a negligee. Declan was sitting in the same spot, still reading his book. He only looked away when his naked wife took off the bathrobe to put on the sleepwear.

"I put your plate in the fridge, so you can have it tomorrow." He announced.

"OK."

"So, why was your day good and bad?" He enquired.

I finished dressing before crawling into bed and lying under the covers. He watched me roll onto my side, so I was facing in his direction. I propped up my head on my hand, with my elbow resting on the pillow.

"The lectures went OK, nothing embarrassing happened. Not like my slideshow refusing to work when I was at Harvard, or me stumbling on the stage at the University of London."

This made him guffaw as he recalled me telling him what happened years ago. Next he prompted, "Then what?"

"Oh it was some idiot advertising himself by putting down other people." I scowled. "He's just released a book or something, which is simply tearing down other historian's work, including mine."

His reaction caught me by surprise when suddenly he slammed shut his novel. "Alright, who is this idiot and where does he live?"

"Huh?"

"This idiot, what's his name and where does he live?" He demanded.

"Declan!" I laughed at his fierce temper. "Are you seriously going to go after this pompous, old git?"

"B, he's attacking you and your papers!" The European Werewolf fired up. "He's publishing words which put down your hard work!"

"He's not attacking me," I put my hand on his hot arm. "He's a coward who's attacking another historian whom he believes is dead or retired."

Angrily, he looked away as his eyes narrowed and his jaw set.

"Seriously, don't worry about it." I patted in a reassuring manner. "This stuff happens all the time in the academic world. Why do you think I prefer to stay out of it for the majority of the time?"

However, he didn't appear convinced and his blue eyes even began to look a little green...

"Declan, you're not going after this loser." My voice dropped to an authoritarian tone. "I'm not telling you who he is, so you won't get in trouble for attacking a human."

He returned, "Yeah but we're allowed to defend ourselves or our loved ones."

This made me smirk, "Going after fat, middle-aged, university professors, can't be called self-defence."

"Fine." He sat back into his pillow before he asked breezily, "Well if I can't kill him and you don't want dinner, do you wanna have sex?"

"What?" I gave a funny look.

"Food or sex always makes me feel better." He said simply.

"No thank you."

It made me giggle as I rolled over and settled down to sleep. I felt his hot hand rest on my waist, as he picked up his book once more. He only removed his hand to turn a page before returning it again.

"I'll just finish this chapter then I'll turn off my light."

I asked with my eyes closed, "What are you reading?"

"Dracula."

This piqued my curiosity and I opened my eyes to look over my shoulder. He briefly turned the cover my way for me to see. Then my head returned to its former position on the pillow.

"Haven't you read that before?" I remembered.

"Yup, twenty times before." He answered. "But the last time was like ten years ago."

"Why are you reading it again?"

"I like it."

"Why?"

"Well, besides all the repressed Victorian sexuality escaping..." he said cheekily, "...I'm fascinated by Bram Stoker describing his Vampires turning into wolves or Werewolves. I mean as a Werewolf, I'm mildly offended he'd say a 'fang head' can turn into one of our kind. But at least he got the Shape Shifter element right."

"Hmm," I thought about it. "If it makes you feel better, Dracula could also turn into mist or rats."

He sounded surprised, "You've read 'Dracula'?"

"It was years ago." I yawned. "But I liked it."

"Yeah?"

I continued, "I like examining how literature or mythology vaguely touches upon the truth about what we are, now and again."

There was a pause when I felt his moist lips plant a kiss on my bare shoulder.

"Don't ever change, B." He affectionately squeezed my waist. "Don't you dare."

~~~~~~

I found out by accident that Declan had planned a six week tour of the States to celebrate our upcoming 150th Anniversary.

Our families were in on the secret and eager to celebrate how we were nearly the tribe's longest married couple. I think my late parents were the longest so far, being married for 159 years. My husband even colluded with my PA at Hodge Endeavor about clearing my schedule.

Usually, I gave one guest lecture a month and maybe attended the odd symposium. Also programmed into my electronic schedule was the occasional Board Meeting with Hodge Endeavor. I only had to make an appearance every third month and say 'yay' or 'nay', or whatever the Circulate Mainframe suggested.

Sometimes I'd sit at the end of the very long table in the luxurious board room, with my mobile phone in my lap. The Mainframe text messaged me what to agree on, as she watched from afar. If I had any questions then I'd save them for afterwards, when I'd instantaneously phase to Circulate HQ. In the Viewing Room, the Mainframe would show me the ramifications or future fortunes of my decisions.

Yesterday, I received an email from Dr. Harding expressing his sorrow at my declining to attend the symposium at Oxford University. He was one of the speakers and he was going to talk about his holographic recreations of the cities of old. I had no idea what he was talking about and I checked my electronic schedule on my laptop. Both my PA Cassie and I had access to it, her remotely though.

Low and behold, the symposium which had been scheduled in the midst of August, was no longer showing on my upcoming events! Then as I examined my calendar, the Hodge Endeavor Board Meeting and my guest lecture had vanished too. August was completely empty, where even family gatherings were a no-show. What the hell was Cassie doing?

I frowned as I walked into the kitchen where Declan was cooking dinner. "I think my PA at Hodge Endeavor has gone nuts."

He paused in the midst of his preparation of tomato and olive bruschetta.

"What's up?" He queried.

"Cassie declined a symposium at Oxford without even consulting me! She clicked 'declined' after I had accepted. I received an unhappy email from Dr. Harding, who was expecting me."

"Who's Dr. Harding?"

"The professor I told you about, who was creating the holographs of Ancient Thebes, Babylon, Athens and Rome."

"Oh," he struggled to keep a straight face. "Um, so why is he expecting you?"

"Because he's one of the speakers! Remember I helped him with the finer details, by emailing him my photos I lied were computer generated?" I rolled my eyes at his clueless behaviour.

"When's this symposium?" He asked concerned.

"In August." I frowned. "I'm going to have a serious talk with Cassie for declining it without asking me first."

"Er, don't do that."

"What? Why?" I gave a funny look.

"Because Cassie was following my instructions," he said uncomfortably.

"Your instructions?"

"Yeah, I told her you'll be unavailable in August."

"Huh?" I looked on like he was loopy. "Why did you do that?"

"She's also rescheduled your Hodge Endeavor Board Meeting and your lecture in Melbourne. I told Forrest and Maia too that we wouldn't be able to make it to their kid's birthday party. We're not going to Stone and Sharon's anniversary dinner, either."

Just as I was about to angrily demand that he explain what was going on, I remembered... The 22nd August would be our anniversary, when we moved in together and were officially seen as mates.

"Declan," I tittered like a little girl, "have you planned a surprise holiday for our 150th Anniversary?"

He smiled secretively, "Let's just say you're busy that month."

"Ooh!" I squealed excitedly as I clapped my hands. "Where? Where?"

"Sorry, if I tell you I'd have to kill you." He joked. "And I don't wanna lose my only avenue for sex just yet."

Then he returned his attention to the bruschetta by sprinkling the chopped tomato, onion and olives on top.

"Aw c'mon, tell me!" I pleaded. "Where are we going this time?"

"Nope."

"Declan!"

"B!" He whined back.

I sidled up to him to run my hands up and down his body, "pllleeeeaaasse?"

"Hey," he growled. "No cheating."

"Not even a hint?"

"Nup."

"I could cheat you know, I'll use my ability to 'see' where I'll be in August."

"Don't you dare!" He growled even louder. "It's a surprise and that's that. You aren't finding out until the day before we leave, when I tell you what to pack."

"Oh yeah and how are you going to stop my visions?" I taunted.

"I'll blindfold you."

"I 'see' with my eyes open or closed."

"Then I'll have to keep you occupied." He gave a mischievous grin.

"What about when you go to the Garage and I'm home alone all day? How are you going to keep me busy then?" I continued.

"You'll just have to come to work with me until August." He snickered.

I hopped up onto the kitchen bench to watch him work. With the bruschetta finished, he turned his attention to preparing a salad. A raw steak was sitting beside, indicating we were having that as our main.

"Are we eating the steak plain?" I wondered.

"No, I'll whip up a creamy Diane sauce," he replied.

"Mmm yum." I licked my lips. "So, not even a hint to where we're going?"

"Nuh uh."

Declan expertly sliced the cucumber using a large, shiny blade and then I watched him scatter them over the lettuce.

Although I loved to watch him cook, I was distracted when a peculiar image flashed through my mind of a white manor on an old, southern plantation.

"The South..." I murmured, "...are we going to the South?"

"B, stop it!" He slammed down the knife. "It's meant to be a surprise!"

"I didn't mean to, it just happened." I said apologetically.

Then he saw me shut my eyes before I doubled the efforts by putting my hands over them.

He sighed in frustration, "Now what do you see?"

"Um, the Golden Gate Bridge?" I looked through my fingers to meet his angry gaze.

"Fine!" He put his hands on his hips. "Since you've spoilt it, I'll tell you. We're going on a six week tour through the States."

"Really?!" I brightened. "Yay!"

Next, I surprised HIM by hopping off the bench and onto him instead!

"We're going to visit the South and San Francisco and where else?" I laughed excitedly.

His temper faded as soon as I flung my arms about his neck.

"Chicago, New York, Miami..." he listed off. "Basically all the places you've ever wanted to go, or you've talked about in the past."

"Declan, you're the best!" I hugged him tightly.

"I know and don't you ever forget it." He smirked, before releasing me. "I'm expecting several rounds of 'thank you' sex tonight, so you'd better eat up."

As he continued with dinner, my smile faded as I looked away. It wasn't the idea of our nightly activity which deterred me, but something else. My heart even began to race with anxiety.

What the hell do I get him, to match his generosity?

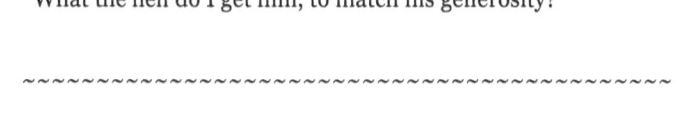

20th April, 2240

Last Thursday morning after Declan left for work, I instantaneously phased to the Viewing Room at Circulate Headquarters.

The mode of transport caused the usual electrical interference. Static momentarily appeared on the screens of the three-sided, crystal pyramid which hung upside down in the centre of the room. Then the images returned of a ceremony in the temple of Athena in Ancient Greece, life in Cuzco before the Spanish invasion and of course, my quiet, little house on tribal lands. However, all of these disappeared when I crossed over to one of the three control panels on the circular-ringed, glass-top desk. I typed in 'BRAM STOKER' to bring up his timeline.

"Welcome to Circulate Headquarters, Bianca." The computer acknowledged my presence. "I can see you are requesting to do a search. Would you like to issue voice commands or continue using the keypad?"

"Hi CM," I pulled back a chair from the desk, to sit on. "I'll use voice commands. I'd like to get an autographed copy of Dracula by its author. It's an anniversary present for Declan."

"Then I would recommend obtaining a first edition of the novel which was published in 1897." She advised. "If you asked the 19th Century author to autograph a 21st Century printed novel, it would cause suspicion."

I smiled, "As usual, you read my mind. Declan's copy is from 2020 so I was thinking of phasing to Victorian England, purchasing a first edition from a bookstore and then taking it to the writer."

"Agreed," the computer chirped. "I recommend travelling to the year 1898 where you could request the autograph when Bram Stoker was attending an afternoon tea at the Savoy. Aside from writing, Bram Stoker was also the manager for Lyceum Theatre and the personal assistant for the actor, Henry Irving. The theatre company often held entertainments for its patrons."

"Good idea," I nodded along. "It would be less creepy if a fan approached him in a public place, instead of rocking up to his home and knocking on the door."

The Mainframe continued, "There are several late Victorian era dresses in the Props Room you can choose from. I would recommend a Day Dress with a bonnet and purse. In the coins cabinet, you should find currency for that era in the form of pounds and pennies."

"Cool, I'll check it out now!" I hopped up in excitement.

I walked along the smooth, black floors of the corridors, turning down different hallways. I was accustomed to the quietness and solitude of the Headquarters, being the last member of the Circulate. I liked the soft hum of the environmental systems, which maintained the atmosphere inside the habitation dome.

When I wasn't here, the Mainframe operated the base on minimal power. However, as I walked through the several sections, wall lights came on and the many computer interfaces blinked into alert status. Although the glass dome let as much natural light in as possible and the rooms were ceiling-less to use the sunshine; Taurus Six had a multitude of tropical storms which darkened the green coloured sky.

A set of frosted-over, sliding glass doors instantly parted to allow my entrance. Beside them was the lit up panel with the words, PROPS ROOM. This space was one of the largest in the Headquarters, as it had racks of clothing from numerous cultures and eras of humanity's history.

There were kimonos from Japan, white linen skirts for Ancient Egypt, togas for Ancient Rome, empire dresses for Regency England, 1950's Chanel dresses for women, 18th Century ball gowns, 24th Century cocktail dresses and 25th Century one-piece tuxedoes. You name it, it was probably here. Every rack was labelled with the culture and era to help identifying them easier. Then in the middle of the room were display cases with accessories such as jewellery, purses, hats, footwear and money through the ages.

I spotted a rack which was labelled 1880's - 1900's UK/ EUROPEAN and headed for it. I rifled through the dresses until I saw one I liked. I took it off the rack and wandered over to one of the full-length mirrors in the room, to examine the dress against my form.

"CM?"

"Yes Bianca?" The computer's detached voice replied.

"Is this dress OK?"

"That is a Day Dress with accompanying jacket from 1893 and should be appropriate for the time frame."

"Thanks."

I hung it up on the side of the mirror and began to undress, when the computer spoke again. "You will also need to select a pair of high lace-up boots, stockings, pantaloons, a petticoat, a corset and a second petticoat with an attached rear cushion for the bustle."

This made me pause, "Say what?"

"The undergarments will be on the same rack that you found the dress and the footwear should be in Cabinet D."

I tugged off my t-shirt and went to see what she was talking about. I did find these things, however a new problem arose. I took the corset off the hanger and looked on in dissatisfaction.

"CM, there's just one slight flaw to your cunning plan... you don't have hands to tie this corset for me."

*****

Maia received a shock when her great x4 grandaunt appeared in her living area, accompanied by a bright flash of light.

She jumped whilst putting her hand on her chest, as if to slow her racing heart.

"Sorry!" I sung out apologetically. "I didn't mean to scare you."

"Aunt B...?" She gazed peculiarly at the pile of clothing and shoes in my arms. "What are you doing here? What is all of that?"

"I need your help, please." I looked on pleadingly. "It's a surprise for Declan so that's why I'm here."

"What's the surprise?"

"I need your help in doing up my corset, for a visit to Victorian England. I found out when in 1898 Bram Stoker will be at the Savoy for an afternoon tea. I'm going to buy the first edition of Dracula and ask him to sign it." I prattled off.

"Um... why?"

"Because it's one of your Uncle's favourite books," I educated. "He's read it over twenty times."

"Oh," she though on this. "Getting a favourite book signed by the author is an awesome present. I've just never heard of a person travelling two hundred years into the past, to do it."

"Yeah well, I'm weird and so is your Uncle." I shrugged it off, before looking around the house. "Where are the kids?"

"My parents have them because I worked today." She answered as she started towards her bedroom. "This way."

*****

It took me longer getting dressed than I thought it would. There were so many layers to put on! Maia kindly braided my hair so it looked similar to the way ladies had their hair then, before I put on the small hat by fastening its ribbon. In my gloved hand, I held onto a small handbag which held the currency. I also slipped in my mobile phone, incase the Circulate Mainframe had to contact me.

I was wearing a long, black velvet skirt and the jacket also had black velvet trim around bronze and silver embroidery. My gloves were grey, my hat was a bronzed colour of velvet with a few brown feathers sticking out, and my handbag was brown leather. I looked Victorian but to be honest, I felt ridiculous with the cushioned petticoat behind, for the 'bustle' of the period.

"Don't laugh," I reddened with embarrassment.

"I'm not going to laugh," she kept a straight face. "It's too bad that this is a surprise for Uncle, as I'm sure he'd love to see this."

"Thanks a lot." I pulled a face which made her giggle. "Oh well, here goes..."

Abruptly, I disappeared from her bedroom in a bright flash of light to reappear in another, in the Gate Room at Circulate HQ.

I found the computer was ready and waiting for my arrival.

"I've programmed the coordinates of the Gate for a small alleyway on a city street where a bookshop is located." She advised. "However, as soon as you arrive I would recommend leaving the alleyway as quickly as possible. In the late 1800's with the high level of poverty; theft and prostitution was rife in the back streets of London."

"Eew," my face screwed up. "So get out of the alleyway or be taken for a prostitute or robbed. OK, got it."

I lifted my skirt as I stepped up onto the circular, mirrored, elevated platform of the Gate then I looked up into the second circular mirror above. My reflection disappeared to be replaced by the smoky skyline of Victorian London. Numerous chimneys belched out smoke from coal or wood fires. I watched as the computer zoomed in, bringing the buildings into focus, as it targeted an alleyway on a specific street.

Just as I was about to put myself into phase, the computer offered helpfully, "Once purchasing the book, you may wish to catch a cab to the Savoy. There are numerous horse drawn cabs, which the middle and upper classes employ for short-range transport."

"Thanks." I said shortly.

Then I dissolved my biological body into one made of light. My solid form turned bright and see-through, which gave a rush of warmth as well as a tingling sensation. I loved phasing through time this way, because in this form I felt all floaty and free.

I concentrated hard on a date in autumn of 1898, as I stared up at my destination. Next, the floating feeling was replaced by a rushing sensation as my being of light was pushed through the mirror. Then I was no longer looking at Victorian London, I was in Victorian London.

A small, square doorway appeared before me and I felt my light particles pass through it. Then I felt my feet again and my hands and the rest of me, as my body reformed into a solid shape again. When I looked behind, the small square doorway had been a dirty shop window. However, I hadn't been seen because the shop looked dark and deserted.

The next sensation I experienced was a horrendous stench! It was coming from the narrow, cobbled alleyway I was in. It smelled like a public bathroom! Then I saw why... further down, an upstairs window opened and a woman tipped out a chamber pot!

"Eugh!" I turned away in disgust.

Hurriedly, I walked in the opposite direction. I thought there was plumbing in London by this stage? Maybe not all houses had it, but I did pass a drain which I guessed went to a sewerage tunnel somewhere. Thankfully, I came out onto the street but because I had been rushing, I nearly hit a man.

"Steady on, lass." He put his hand on my arm. He gave a curious look, before looking down the alleyway I came from. Oh oh, he doesn't think I'm a prostitute that's coming back from a 'John', does he?

"I'm - I'm lost." I spoke quickly. "I'm trying to find a bookshop."

The man straightened as his expression changed to one of sympathy. "It's not down there, I can promise you that Miss. There's a bookshop further down this street."

Then he tipped his hat and continued on his way. I watched him go, allowing a minute to pass before walking in the direction he just went in. I didn't want him to think I was following him.

True to his word, I found a small bookshop and I went inside. The storekeeper behind the counter passed a polite nod. He glanced up and down at my wardrobe and thankfully, he didn't think I was a streetwalker.

"May I help you?" He walked over.

"I need a copy of Dracula." I came straight to the point.

"Ah," he immediately curtailed off towards some shelves on the far side of the room. I watched him pull out a bright yellow, hardcover book and then head back to the counter. "That will be one shilling and thrippence."

I wasn't sure what a shilling or thrippence was, so I handed him a twenty pound note instead.

The storekeeper's eyes widened, before he managed out, "Do you have anything smaller, madam? I don't have sufficient change today."

"Do you mean three pennies for thrippence?" I wondered aloud. "Then what's a shilling?"

He passed a peculiar look which made it obvious he thought I was a loon.

"Look, here's a five pound note." I put it down on the counter. "Is that OK?"

I guess it was, as he processed the payment and handed me some smaller coins as change. Once he'd finished, I picked up the yellow book with the red writing on the hardcover. I thought it was weird that the horror novel was such a bright and cheerful colour. Declan's paperback at home was in dark tones.

"Would you like me to wrap your purchase, madam?" The storekeeper offered.

"No thanks, I'm off to get it autographed." I gave a grin then I left his shop.

It didn't take me long to catch a cab, in the original sense of the word. I told the cabby where I wanted to go, which he returned with a single nod then cracked his whip. Next, the horse trotted down the street and we passed several other 'cabs' or private carriages.

The driver didn't give me any grief when he requested payment, especially when I handed over another five pound note along with the words, "Keep the change." Then I hoisted my skirt and with the book in hand, proceeded up the stairs into the hotel. Once inside though, there was another hiccup.

Where would the afternoon tea be held, in a function room or in the restaurant? I looked around the lobby, feeling lost. I received a couple more peculiar looks, particularly from an elderly couple with the man in a top hat and tails.

"Pardon me, ma'am." A teenaged Bell Boy approached. "May I help you?"

"Yes please," I gushed in relief. "I'm looking for Bram Stoker, he might be here with the Lyceum Theatre party."

"Oh, you're here for the fundraiser." The boy thought. "This way, ma'am."

I followed the youth into the hotel's grand restaurant. It was spacious with a high, decorated ceiling, elegant table settings and several potted palms scattered around. People were either seated or standing up, whilst nursing tea cups with saucers. Everyone looked well-off and dressed in more velvets or satins or silks.

There were quite a few old ladies here and although my Day Dress looked just as fancy as everyone else's wardrobe, they passed more funny looks my way.

"Here we are, ma'am." The boy waved his arm before curtailing off.

Then I stood there like I was stuck to the spot, unsure of how to proceed...

I looked around at the men in the room, especially the ones with beards which I knew Bram Stoker had, from the Mainframe showing me his picture. The only problem was many had beards. It seemed to be the fashion, either beards or bushy moustaches.

"May I help you?" A middle-aged woman walked up, as she eyed me up and down.

"Yes please, I'm here to meet Bram Stoker."

"And you are...?" She arched an eyebrow.

"I'm a -" I almost said 'fan', but I stopped myself from the warning feeling in the pit of my stomach. "I'm Mrs. Sabre."

"Ah," she looked like she understood something now. "The name sounds continental."

"It's Italian."

"That would explain your foreign features," she smirked. "Although I've never seen dark blue eyes like yours before. I've never met an Italian woman as tall as you, either."

"I have a combination of English, Australian, Chinese and Native Alaskan, in my blood." I said coolly.

"Australian?" She looked on, confused.

"New South Wales," I remembered its old title.

"Ah, you're from the Colony?" She continued, half intrigued yet half condescending.

"I'm from what you may call 'a colony' in Alaska, but my grandmother was English and her grandmother was from New South Wales." I said shortly, disliking this cross-examination. "Can you please point out who is Bram Stoker?"

Just then a bearded man who looked to be in his fifties and standing to the side eavesdropping, turned my way.

"I am Bram Stoker."

I blinked in surprise at the man in the dark grey suit, who came to stand beside the woman in her light pink Reception Dress.

"Er, hi..." I managed out.

"You said you're part Native Alaskan, do you mean Indian?" He wondered.

"We prefer Native Alaskan, or the exact name of my tribe is Lokoti." My face flushed.

"I met some Indians when I visited the States," he went on. "I can see you have their hair but your skin, eyes and features look European."

"Erm, thanks...?" I wondered what to say to that.

"Is your husband Italian?" He continued, showing he'd heard every word we'd said.

"Yes, his name is Declan Sabre but you'd probably think that he doesn't look very Italian either; blonde hair, bright blue eyes and taller than every man in this room." I tried to joke.

"Then it's a match well-suited, as you are the tallest woman in the room." He replied humorously.

"Oh am I?" I looked from the woman standing in front of me, to a couple of other women who were also standing a little away.

Actually, he was right. I think I was taller than all the women and half of the men too. Then I remembered how people were shorter in the olden days, as I recalled visiting old houses with much smaller doorways. I wondered if this was why I got so many peculiar looks? I must stand out with my height and independent behaviour; running around without a male escort or a female chaperone.

"How may I help you, Mrs. Sabre?" He asked directly.

"Um, my husband is a big fan of yours, and our wedding anniversary is coming up. I was hoping I could convince you to autograph this first edition of Dracula that I just purchased?" I indicated the book.

The older woman rolled her eyes at my request whilst Bram Stoker cleared his throat.

"As much as I'm delighted to meet people who've enjoyed my novels, I'm here today to fundraise for my theatre." He refused diplomatically.

"For Lyceum Theatre of which you're the business manager." I nodded. "How much is it costing today, for people to drink tea in your company?"

"Tickets are ten pounds per head." The woman said snottily, as if she just announced it was a hundred dollars.

I opened my handbag and their eyes widened at the wad of white paper bills I took out. I flicked through several five, twenty and fifty pound notes, before finding the tens. I took one and held it out to the woman.

"Is this all?" Now I put on a snobby air. "Or are there raffle tickets for me to purchase, or some other competition you're holding, or maybe even an auction to raise funds?"

Out of the blue, Bram Stoker roared with laughter and clapped his hands together.

"Fetch the young lady a cup of tea and a cake, Netty." He guffawed. "Her money might be new to your old tastes, but her financial position is ample."

The middle-aged woman looked put out, as she turned around with a swish of her long skirt and walked off.

"So, do you want this ten pounds?" I handed it over. "If I give you another ten, will you sign my book?"

He smiled in amusement. "Mrs. Sabre, how about we strike a bargain? If you hand over one of those fifty pound notes, it will pay for all of the raffle tickets we're selling. It will also let you meet Mr. Irving."

"Or, how about I hand you over one of those fifty pound notes for the raffle tickets and instead of meeting Mr. Irving, you tell me about writing Dracula?"

Bram Stoker seemed surprised by my offer then his chest filled as his ego expanded.

"How can I say no to such a charming offer?" He smiled.

"Here's the fifty pounds and here's a pen to sign the book with," I took both out of my handbag.

He clasped the biro and looked on it curiously, as I held the book open for him to autograph the title page.

*****

I stayed at the afternoon tea for two hours, which I found out was to raise funds for an upcoming production. The prize I 'won' for buying all the raffle tickets was for two seats to the future play. Since I wouldn't be using them, I handed them over to this little old lady sitting by herself in the corner. She became excited and thanked me incessantly whilst shaking my hand and calling me a 'dear'.

In the meantime, I sipped on two cups of tea and snacked on some sandwiches and cakes. I ate a cucumber sandwich as well as the devilled egg. Then I nibbled on a small custard tart which was garnished with a variety of berries on top, and it was utterly delicious.

Discreetly, I checked the time on my mobile phone which was hidden in my handbag. It was still on Alaskan time and I saw after all the preparation, phasing through time, purchasing the book, the cab ride to the hotel then the afternoon tea; Declan would be home soon. I wanted to get home before he did, so I could wrap his present.

The famous actor and owner of Lyceum Theatre, Henry Irving, had moved to the centre of the room to make a speech. He started thanking everyone for coming and their generous contributions, as I was backing out of the room. I had just cleared the throng of people, when my mobile phone started ringing!

The 'ring tone' was a Lily Allen song called 'Smile'. "At first when I see you cry, yeah it makes me smile, yeah it makes me smile..."

The 21st Century music attracted everyone's attention. Even more peculiar looks were shot in my direction, as I turned around to make my apology. I wasn't sure if they were wondering where the music was coming from, or baffled by the lyrics.

"At worst, I feel bad for a while, but then I just smile, I go ahead and smile."

Hastily, I pulled the phone out of my handbag and turned it off.

"Um, sorry about that." I blushed. "But at least Lily Allen is English, which is appropriate for the location if not the era."

Before they could reply, I rushed out of the restaurant, through the lobby and out of the fancy hotel.

Instead of hailing another cab, I aimed for anything that offered privacy. I didn't have to phase to Circulate HQ via the gate, I could instantaneously phase straight home. All I had to do was find a place away from prying eyes.

I hurried down the busy street that the hotel was on. Whilst I walked, I turned my phone back on to check my messages. I had a voicemail from Declan and ignoring the further funny looks, I held the phone up to my ear as I walked.

"Hey B, it's me," his voice greeted. "I'm gonna be home soon and I'm frickin' exhausted. I know I took the mince out of the freezer to cook up spaghetti tonight, but do you mind if we get pizza delivered? We can put the mince in the fridge and I'll cook tomorrow night. Hey, where are you? You didn't say you were leaving the house today. I'll see you in fifteen minutes."

The Circulate Mainframe must have directed his voice mail through time, to warn me my surprise was about to be discovered.

Finally, I spotted another alleyway and speedily headed down it. As soon as I turned the first corner, I instantaneously phased out of Victorian London. Disappearing in one bright of flash, I reappeared in another inside my living area in 23rd Century Alaska.

It was just in time too, as Declan's plasma-powered truck parked in the garage.

Hoisting my long skirt once more, I ran up the stairs and into our bedroom. I dropped the handbag onto the bed and opened the second drawer in the tallboy. I couldn't hide the book in the underwear drawer I share with my mate, so I hid it underneath my pile of t-shirts instead.

I slammed the drawer shut, right as the front door downstairs opened.

"B? B, are you home?" He sung out. "I can smell you, are you upstairs?"

Then his eyes widened when he spotted me standing at the top of the stairs, in my Victorian garb.

"Hi honey, how was your day?" I asked obligatory.

"Where've you been?" He asked accusatorily. "I told you, when you leave the house, you text message me!"

I waltzed down the stairs as gracefully as I could muster, with one hand on the railing and the other holding up my skirt.

Declan met me at the bottom of the stairs and turned up his nose. "I can smell smoke on you and - and - and human urine?"

"Yes, I learned the hard way that not ALL houses in Victorian London use plumbing." I said coolly.

Then he passed me my tenth peculiar look today, "What the hell were you doing in Victorian London?"

"Having tea with a friend of Oscar Wilde's."

"Huh?"

"Never mind, long story." I tittered. "So, we're ordering pizza for dinner?"

"Do you mind?" He turned away to take off his denim work jacket and put his keys and wallet on the table. "I'm beat. I must have done twenty registration checks today."

"Oh, that reminds me," I swanned over to his position in my regal attire. "Can you do a registration check on my car? I'll bring it down tomorrow or the day after next."

"Yeah whatever..." he wearily rolled his eyes, "...bring it in tomorrow morning, before I check another twenty cars. Gees, it's not hard to tell when people's registrations are due; the Garage is inundated by every single vehicle on tribal lands."

Then he walked away a second time, to head for the fridge and retrieve a bottle of Dr. Pepper.

I watched him swill from the bottle before lowering it and passing an unhappy look my way.

"Can you go and get changed?" He complained. "I can still smell human urine in the fabric of your clothes."

"Charming," I rolled my eyes, too. "But what if I told you that I need help to get undressed?"

"Say what?"

"Do you know how many layers I'm wearing right now?" I arched my eyebrows. "Somebody needs to untie my corset."

Slowly, a silly smile overtook his face and he snickered like a mischievous kid.

"Sorry, did you just say the words 'corset' and 'undress me'?"

"Yes I did." I smirked.

"Heh heh!" He smugly put down his bottle of soda. "I should hide anniversary holidays from you more often."

~~~~~~

~ 14 ~

Strolling hand-in-hand, Declan and I wandered through the French Quarter of New Orleans.

Many of the buildings had balconies which were covered in iron lattice, giving them a look of elegance from long ago. This coupled with wooden shutters and French doors, made me feel like I was visiting the past instead of the 23rd Century. The feeling was accentuated when we passed a Street Musician, who was playing a jazz song on his saxophone.

It was a warm summer's day with the sun glaring down from above. It was around 28 degrees Celsius, which was considered hot to the Alaskans. So we were dressed in cargo shorts, singlets and thongs on our feet. A gentle breeze teased our hair, with icy-cold, caramel-coffee frappuccinos in each of our hands.

We meandered down the tourist-filled street, past the decorative old buildings which housed many cafes and Creole restaurants.

"What is Creole?" I wondered aloud.

"It ain't Italian that I know." He said simply.

We walked over to a menu on display by a restaurant door, to look on some examples.

"Gumbo? What's gumbo?" I gave a funny look.

"Again B, you're asking the wrong guy." He shrugged. "Maybe we should come here for dinner and try it out?"

"OK." I smiled.

We continued down the sidewalk before coming to a busy intersection. Declan pulled on my hand for us to go right, but I stopped him as I looked left. If we went right, it was just more tourist areas of shops, cafes, restaurants and etcetera. However, if we went left, there were more old buildings, which didn't look as done-up or commercial. To me, this made them more interesting.

"Hey, let's go this way." I nodded left.

Declan frowned as he looked from his mate, to the less-attractive street. "Why?"

"Because it looks less touristy and more like the 'real' New Orleans."

"We are tourists, B." He smirked. "That's what tourists do, they do touristy things."

"Screw that! I'm bored with touristy. I want to see the real city that the locals know, not what visitors see." I tugged on his hand.

He growled quietly as his protest, but he permitted me to pull him across the street when the traffic lights changed.

We headed away from the crowds and after walking down a block or two, the buildings began to look more run down. Graffiti started to pop up on some of the walls and there were some unpleasant smells coming from the gutter. Litter laid about willy-nilly, which we soon saw why.

Declan and I finished our frappuccinos and we tried to do the right thing by putting them in a bin. Unfortunately, the bin on the sidewalk was overflowing, as if the garbage collectors hadn't come in some time. We put them on top of the pile of rubbish before moving on.

"Oh yeah, this is much better than the touristy bits." He said sarcastically.

I ignored him as I became fascinated with the kind of shops we were walking past. We saw a couple of second-hand clothing or furniture stores. I stopped in front of what appeared to be an antiques dealer. There were such unusual wares sitting in the front window, it had me intrigued.

"What the...?!" He objected, as he found himself yanked inside.

Next, we perused the dusty old shop which sold antique jewellery, clothing, knick-knacks and other items of an eclectic mix. There were old Baseball Cards for sale, as well as candlesticks or even old jewellery boxes. The shop also smelled strange, like an unusual incense was burning somewhere. An African-American man came out of a backroom to serve us. He wore camel coloured slacks and crisp, white shirt.

"Welcome to my antiques store," he greeted in an unusual accent, which sounded part African and part French. "Are you looking for anything specific today?"

"No, not really." I shook my head.

"We're just looking." Declan said shortly.

My mate looked on him warily, whereas the man noticed what I was examining inside a glass cabinet.

"Do you like antique jewellery?" He queried.

"Yeah, I guess." I shrugged, although I'm not really a jewellery person.

The shopkeeper noticed the gold bracelet on my arm, which Gran bought me on my first circulation to Ancient Greece.

"That's an antique, is it not?" He pointed at it.

I held up my arm to allow him a better look. "Yes it is."

"May I?" He queried and when I nodded, he touched my arm to examine the jewellery. "Ah, it's Greek and it's old, very old in fact. The design looks to be from the Classical period."

I beamed as I said impressed, "You're right."

However, Declan was tightly holding onto my hand as he glared at the storeowner, as if he didn't trust him.

The man smiled knowingly, "You're fascinated by the ancient times, are you not?"

"Um, yeah?"

"Allow me to show you something." He gave a short bow before he disappeared into the backroom again.

I passed Declan a 'this guy is good' look, but the expression on his face read 'I don't trust him'.

"What's wrong?" I asked quietly.

"I don't know, something's not right," he replied as he sniffed the air. "Do you smell that?"

"Yeah, it's some kind of weird incense." I shrugged it off.

"I don't think its ordinary incense," he frowned.

Declan looked like he was going to say something else, but he stopped when the man returned.

The storekeeper held out a small, black velvet pouch in his right hand. We watched as he took out a beautiful gold bracelet in the shape of wound-round asp. My eyes widened as I gazed upon it.

"If you can correctly tell me about this bracelet, I'll sell it to you at a discounted price." He offered.

I released my mate's hand to pick up the snake bracelet in my two.

Unhappy that I let go, Declan put his arm about my waist instead, as he continued to scrutinize the salesman.

I held the jewellery closer to examine it. As I stared at the bracelet, I allowed my eyes to glaze over. The men quieted to allow me to think. What the storeowner didn't know but my mate did, was that I was engaging my ability to 'see'.

Numerous images flashed through my mind... I saw desert then I saw a lush green valley in the midst with a long river ... I saw men fishing on small reed boats... I saw they were topless and wearing only white a skirt around their waists... then past the river and the delta, I saw a couple of pyramids in the distance... I'd know this scenery blindfolded.

To their surprise, I announced, "It's Ancient Egyptian, from the New Kingdom between 1490 and 1436 BC."

"Then you would know how rare it is to have such a precious commodity in my shop." The African-American man smiled widely. "If you know your ancient history, than you would know that the bracelet is priceless. But I will sell it to you today for 5,000 credits."

"Gee, aren't we lucky." My mate sung sarcastically, before he asked accusatorily, "So how did you get this? If you often have these kind of antiques shipped in, how come your store is in this part of town?"

"Declan!" I whacked him on the arm for his rudeness. "Sorry."

"Your apology is accepted, Madame." The storekeeper carried on unperturbed. "Your husband is right, I do not often get antiques this valuable.

It is not stolen, as he fears. But my good fortune is today your good fortune. I know I will be selling a unique bracelet to a unique woman."

"5,000 credits?" I wanted to confirm as I handed him back the bracelet.

"B -" my mate started to object.

"This isn't just about fashion, Declan." I said in annoyance. "That bracelet is the real deal."

I thought he was complaining about my clothes shopping again. I gave him a glare, as I pulled my purse out of his backpack. Declan shut his mouth as he moodily looked away.

Then I followed the man over to the counter where he charged my credit card. He replaced the gold asp bracelet into the black, velvet pouch again. Once the transaction was approved via EFTPOS, he wrote out a receipt. Lastly, he put the receipt into the pouch and handed it over with the credit card.

"If you are interested in unusual antiquities, there is another store I can recommend." The storekeeper offered. "They have items even more rare than the bracelet."

"No thanks, that's enough shopping for us today." Declan said stroppily.

However the man continued, either ignoring or oblivious to my mate's rudeness. "It's just at the end of this street. Even if you do not buy anything, I'm sure you would be interested in seeing the kind of rarities on offer."

I put my credit card back into my purse then it and the pouch into Declan's backpack.

"Thanks, we'll check it out." I went along.

Next, the shopkeeper walked us out and politely opened the door.

"If you head in this direction, it's the store on the corner." He pointed.

"Cool," I gave a nod. "Thanks a lot for the bracelet. Bye!"

I threw him a wave as we stepped out onto the sidewalk. But my mate gave a glare as he retook hold of my hand. We started off, as I was eager to see what other bargains I could bag today.

"Let's check it out!" I said merrily. "Declan, do you know how rare it is to find a bracelet that old, in that good condition, and on sale? The last time I looked on jewellery this old, it was inside of a museum! That, or it was on the arm of an Egyptian on one of my time travels."

"I get the idea." He scowled. "But as I've learned, things that seem to be too good to be true, usually are."

"All things?" I smiled teasingly.

"OK, most things then." He chuckled.

Then he pulled me in to plant a slobbery kiss on my cheek.

"Eew!" I giggled.

He laughed when I rubbed my cheek against his arm, to put his saliva back on him.

We walked down to the end of the street and stopped on the corner of a quiet intersection. There was another store here, but it looked more rundown than the others. It also had weird and unusual things on display in the front window. There were amulets and decorated knives with ivory handles, but I wouldn't call it jewellery. I wondered if we had the right shop or not?

"This is an antiques store?" He raised his eyebrows in disbelief.

"Wait a minute," I pulled him closer to look through the grimy window.

I also saw religious figurines and icons, but I didn't think all of them were for Christianity. I looked on a couple of old medicine bottles with peculiarities inside. The labels on them read as 'Myrrh', or 'Crows Feet' or 'Crossroads Dirt'. This was enough to get my curiosity piqued.

"Come on, let's look inside." I started for the door.

Since we were holding hands, I tried to tug him along however, this time he stood firm.

"I don't know B, something's not right." His frown deepened. "I don't think we should. It's not just an antiques store, I mean look at what's in those bottles. This place smells wrong."

"Then let's check it out!" I said excitedly.

"No," he pulled me back. "I don't think we should go in there."

"But why?"

"Look at those knives, they're silver. More than that, they're ritualistic. Now what kind of store, sells silver knives for rituals? This shop is for the occult." When he saw my disbelief, he continued. "Then why would it have crow's feet and crossroads dirt? I think this is a magic shop that sells ingredients for spell work."

"Are you for real?" I looked from him, back through the shop window. "This is some kind of supernatural supermarket? Cool!"

I don't think my reaction was the one he was aiming for, so he went on.

"Look at those leather pouches next to the jars, with that painted symbol on them. I've seen it before. When Derik became a Medicine Man, he had to read up on curing supernatural ailments as well as natural ones. I think that sign is for Voodoo."

"Voodoo? Real live Voodoo?" I became fascinated. "I want to see this!"

I let go of his hand and before Declan could stop me, I went inside the shop.

"B!" He growled loudly, but it was too late.

The store was small and its walls were lined with shelves, full of jars or packets of ingredients, or some other kind of spell-casting tools.

I saw more decorative silver knives, tribal masks, crystals, ornate metal cups or painted wooden bowls. I stared at all of the items, almost transfixed. I turned around in a wide circle as I sniffed the air. This shop had the same kind of smell we picked up in the antiques store, but it was stronger and more pungent. I liked it because it made me feel very relaxed somehow, almost to the point of sleepy.

Behind the counter sat a middle-aged African American man, reading an old book. Beside him, stood an older woman of the same skin and they were both dressed in bright clothing which looked African in style. They both had faded brown eyes, which were gazing my way. They were faded in the manner you see on a decomposing body, which I found unnerving. With their mystified appearance, it was like they were staring through me, instead.

"Hi." I greeted, to be polite.

But they didn't respond, they just sat or stood there and stared.

Uneasily, I turned away as I continued to look on the wares, feeling their eyes on my back.

Just then Declan walked through the door and their faded eyes bulged upon the sight of him.

I wondered if it was his height or strong build, which made them gawk? Or, if it was because of his bright blue eyes and wavy, blonde hair, which was in direct contrast to theirs. He immediately noticed their spooky gaze, which made him walk over and take hold of my arm.

"Come on, we're outta here!" He hissed.

"No, not yet." I pulled my arm back.

I continued to examine the numerous jars on display. There truly were some strange things in this shop. I was examining what I thought were jaws which belonged to a snake. It had two long fangs on the top, with a row of human teeth at the bottom. What kind of snake had human teeth at the bottom?

"Hey Dec, what kind of snake's fangs are those?" I nodded to what I was looking at.

Sharply, he sucked in his breath which indicated his surprise. "Those AREN'T fangs from a snake, they're from a European Vampire!"

"A European Vampire?" I echoed in disbelief. "Why would a European Vampire's teeth be in a jar?"

Finally, the middle-aged man behind the counter decided to speak. "European Vampire fangs are potent ingredients in certain hexes, just like a Werewolf's canine teeth are."

Oh oh...just as I turned my head to exchange a look of dread with my mate, the man moved out from behind the counter. This didn't concern Declan, as he grabbed my arm and was about to ram him out of the way. But right as I was being pulled towards the door, the middle-aged man opened up his hand.

POOF! He blew some kind of powder into our faces! It stung my eyes, blinding me, and from the sound of my mate's growling, it did the same to him.

Suddenly, my chest constricted like I couldn't breathe! I spluttered and wheezed whilst stumbling blindly, as I heard Declan make the same noises. Oh shit, we were under attack! The powder was meant to incapacitate us!

"Declan...?" I cried out. "Declan!"

"GET OUT OF HERE B!" He blindly pushed me forwards.

I heard some kind of loud whoomp! I sensed my larger mate had knocked the human out of my way. It was then that I stumbled over, because the man who was now on the floor, grabbed my legs! Since Declan was still pushing me onwards, I fell flat on my face!

The man must have grabbed his legs too, as my cheek knocked against the floorboards a second time, when my heavy mate fell on top.

"GO B! RUN! DON'T LOOK BACK AND JUST GO!" Declan roared, as he tried to lift me up.

But then he let go, or he was made to... as I felt his hot body leave my side.

"Declan! Declan! Declan!" I reached around for him.

My eyes were burning, I couldn't see a thing and I had lost my mate!

There was some kind of struggle going on, with Declan snarling at whoever he was fighting against. The fighting died down when I heard the sound of somebody blowing something again, before I smelled the pungent incense once more. But this time it was much stronger and it... it... it... it left me feeling dazed.

"Declan! It's poison! They're drugging us!" I cried out with my eyes closed, since they stung so much.

They were hurting so badly, I had tears running down my face. My arms which were propping me up on the floor, gave way. My body completely flopped then I lay limp as a rag doll.

"Dec – Dec - Declan!" I managed out in a delirious fashion.

However, I couldn't hear him fighting or growling anymore. I strained my sensitive ears to try to locate him. I heard the sound of a heavy weight hitting the floor, which was most likely an incapacitated Declan. I tried to reach out for him, to instantaneously phase us out of danger. But my twitching hand found only empty space, as I heard somebody drag him away.

"Deeeccllann...!" I cried out afraid.

PHASE HOME!!! – He telepathically ordered.

NOT WITHOUT MY MATE! – I thought desperately.

GET OUT OF HERE B! PHASE HOME NOW! THAT'S AN ORDER! – He commanded.

NOT WITHOUT YOU! – I refused.

Silence.

DECLAN?

No response.

DECLAN? WHERE ARE YOU? SAY SOMETHING!

Nothing.

Then I felt somebody grab my legs and start to drag me along the wooden floor too.

I was dragged and dragged and dragged some more, whilst powerless to stop it. I couldn't move and I couldn't see where I was being taken to. I sensed I was being dragged into a backroom somewhere, especially when my side knocked into a doorway.

Because I wasn't unconscious, I could have instantaneously phased home. I didn't need muscles to turn myself into light and pass through time and space. But I couldn't leave my mate, it would be like leaving my heart behind. It ached in fear for his safety. I had to wait until I was beside him again, as I needed to be touching him to take him with me.

Damn it, B! Why didn't you just listen to Declan in the first place? Then none of this would have happened! His cluey European Werewolf senses were right again. If we live through this I'm going to get the loudest I TOLD YOU SO ever.

Next, I was pulled down a staircase and because I couldn't move, my head went BANG – BANG – BANG – BANG – BANG! – down every single step! From the amount of times I was knocked around, there must have been twenty stairs.

OUCH! OOW! FRICKIN' HELL MY HEAD HURTS! OOW!

The extra blows made the dizziness worse, but at least I was still conscious.

Now I felt myself being pulled across a dirt floor and whoever had my legs, dropped them to the ground. I guessed I was in some kind of basement, which was underneath the store. I smelled earth and cement, which also hinted the cellar was underground.

The middle-aged man spoke in the same unusual accent as the antiques storeowner. "He's a European Werewolf."

"She's another kind of Werewolf," the old woman said back in similar style.

"He's old but he's virile, his reproductive organs are still potent." The man continued.

"This female is clearly his mate, but she can't breed." The old woman went on. "The bitch is barren."

How the hell do they know this? Who are these people? What do they want with us?

Hold on... Voodoo. Declan said it had something to do with Voodoo. That means the man is a Voodoo Priest and maybe the old woman as well. Oh why can't they be peaceful Wiccans like Nairn? She served us afternoon tea, she didn't blow poisonous powder in our faces.

"They're still in human form, we need them to change." The Priestess said.

"If I cut the European Werewolf with a silver knife, it will make him change." The Priest returned.

No! Don't cut him! Frickin' hell, now what do I do?!

"Be careful, if you kill them they change back into human form." The Priestess warned.

"We won't kill them yet, we'll take out their minor organs before the vital ones." The Priest concurred.

"Wait, when they're in Werewolf form they not only heal faster, but they're stronger." The Priestess plotted. "The spell could wear off sooner, so tie them up."

Their footsteps momentarily faded away and I used this opportunity to sniff around for my mate. I smelled he was lying five meters to my right, so I had to somehow make myself roll over to reach him. But right now, my muscles were like jelly - wobbly and useless.

DECLAN? DECLAN CAN YOU HEAR ME? PLEASE, SAY SOMETHING! – I telepathically called.

Still no response...he must be unconscious. They called that sickly, sweet smelling powder, a spell. Was it some kind of Voodoo spell being used on us? If Declan's physically stronger than me, how come he's unconscious and I'm not? Why am I still awake?

Just then I heard a metallic rattling noise which sounded like chains. I listened to our kidnappers wrap them around Declan's huge form. Then I felt the cold, hard metal on my skin, when they did the same to me.

Ha! You think CHAINS can stop me? They might if I was just a Werewolf, but as a Circulator I could phase right through them! Maybe I should instantaneously phase out of here and then come back when I'm strong enough to fight?

No way, B! They said they were going to cut open your mate! There's no way you can leave your other half behind! I might as well cut out my heart myself, and hand it over to the Voodoo murderers.

It was then that I heard a third set of footsteps, of somebody coming down the stairs.

"Ah, so they did come to your shop." I heard the antiques dealer speak. "I thought they would."

Hang on, that's the man who told me to come here! We walked right into his trap! Frickin' hell, I really am an idiot! Declan didn't trust him and now we're tied up in chains, on a dirt floor in a basement. Can I BE anymore stupid?

The antiques guy continued, "I wouldn't cut up the female immediately, if I were you."

"Why?" The Priestess asked.

"Look at her aura," he returned.

"She's a female Werewolf," she said simply.

"Bitches don't have auras like that." He sounded annoyed. "She can see through time this one."

"I've heard female Werewolves, particularly in the European breed, are psychic." The Priest joined the conversation. "It's one of the reasons why European Vampires hunt them."

"I don't think she is simply a Seer." He speculated. "Her aura is brighter than any psychic's I've seen."

I heard him walk over to where I was lying on the floor. Next, I felt him open my eyelids to peer into my eyes, although I was still blind as a bat. Then I felt his hand run over my body and if I could have retaliated, I would have. He patted my arm and shoulder muscles and then he grabbed my breasts!

"She's firm from her Werewolf muscle but her skin, it's young, too young in fact. We should date her before we cut her up. Her mate looks at least ten years older than her, but I'd say she's the same age as him. We should find out why her aura is so bright and why she's not aging." He spoke in business-like manner.

Then he released me as he stood up and walked a little away.

I heard him kick my unconscious husband, "He's rare because there's not many of his breed left. He looks to be in his forties but he's nearly two hundred years old. Other than his fertility, strength and his regenerative capability, there's not much to harvest. But the female here, is more than meets the eye."

The Priestess said jealously, "I think the female's pheromones are working on you, Pierre."

"You didn't see her in my shop when she accurately guessed the age of the Egyptian bracelet." He said coldly. "Her aura became so bright she glowed."

"We can use every part of the male mongrel," the Priest disagreed. "Because his breed is so rare, I know many who would pay for his parts. If we skin him, there's a collector who would reward well for the hide of a European Werewolf."

SKIN Declan?! I wanted to roar in indignation! But all that came out was a pathetic whimper, as my head rolled to the side...

"She's still awake!" The Priestess hissed.

"Nonsense!" Her cohort retorted. "If he's unconscious than so is she, he's stronger than her."

"Don't underestimate her, you fool." Pierre spoke in a low voice. "Your spells may not work on her in the same way."

Wait, the dodgy antiques dealer is right. I'm not unconscious from their spell like Declan was, but why? Is it because I'm a Circulator? Is it because of my 'aura', which is a higher bio-electromagnetic frequency than theirs?

"Start stripping him for his parts." Pierre ordered. "But leave me the female, I want to examine her."

I heard the sound of Declan's chained body being dragged further away...

OK B, you've got to do something, your mate is in danger! I tried to think quickly. I could phase through these chains, but I can't move my arms or legs. I could instantaneously phase to Alaska and call on the pack, but what if they can't help my incapacitation? Either way, he's still in trouble.

Think B, think! Declan would move heaven and earth, if he heard what the Voodoo freaks were planning for you. He'd somehow regenerate, so he could change then launch himself on your attackers!

The European Werewolf would somehow regenerate? Come on B, you're not just a Lokoti Werewolf but you're also a Circulator! Gran could heal herself by going into phase, although I've never tried this before. Maybe it's related to how I can manipulate my age, from young to old and back again. OK, let's just try to think this through rationally...

However, the sound of a winch stringing up my chained mate, distracted any coherent thought. No, not my Declan! Please don't hurt him! My heart raced and all I could do was moan when I wanted to scream out!

DECLAN! DECLAN WAKE UP! DECLAN WAKE UP RIGHT NOW! – I shouted with my mind.

B...?

DECLAN, IS THAT YOU?

B...

DECLAN YOU'RE IN DANGER! WAKE UP! WAKE UP RIGHT NOW!

B... I CAN'T SEE... I CAN'T MOVE - he thought groggily.

"Look," the Priestess spoke. "His eyes are opening."

"I'll get more Sleeping Powder," the Priest said worriedly.

"Leave it," Pierre ordered. "Now that he's awake, he'll change to make himself stronger. We need him in his larger body to harvest him."

YOU'RE IN DANGER, NOW IMPRESS ME WITH YOUR STRENGTH AND BREAK FREE – I half thought and half hoped.

I CAN'T SEE, WHERE ARE YOU? – he thought weakly.

I'M A COUPLE OF METERS AWAY. WE'RE TIED UP IN CHAINS. THEY'RE ABOUT TO CUT YOU – I warned.

"He's not changing," the Priestess stated the obvious.

"Then we'll have to provoke him," the Priest said snidely.

Abruptly, I heard him punch Declan! It sounded pretty hard, too. My face hurt in sympathy, which indicated where his fist had landed.

OOW! THAT FRICKIN' HURT! – My mate thought angrily.

But it didn't stop there, the Priest punched him again and again!

NO! I felt my entire face ache, as the Voodoo freak hit my mate in the nose, the mouth and in the eye! Oh oh, I could feel the rage build up inside the European Werewolf. The Priest's punches were working...

DECLAN, DON'T CHANGE! – I thought desperately - *PLEASE DON'T! AS LONG AS YOU DON'T CHANGE, THEY CAN'T HARVEST YOU!*

But it was too late, his bloodlust was ignited! I heard him snarl at our attackers as he began to expand. At the same time I heard his clothes tear, the chains also rattled and squeaked from his larger size.

"Behold the beast." Pierre spoke in satisfaction. "Remove his reproductive organs first, since they're in his weakest area."

What the...?! And I thought I had it bad being a female Werewolf? Nooo!

I felt his frustration as he uselessly struggled against the tight chains, which squeezed his supernatural size. Then I heard the sound of a large knife being unsheathed. Petrified, mentally I cried out:

NO DECLAN! CHANGE BACK TO HUMAN! THAT OR BREAK THE CHAINS!

"Now for the female," Pierre walked over to kneel by my side again. "Let's see just how old you really are?"

GET OUT OF HERE B! NOW! JUST GO WITHOUT ME! – Declan demanded.

Instead I cringed inside whilst I heard him whine in pain, as they stuck him with the silver blade.

NOOOOOOO!!!

Then I don't know how or what happened, but I felt something occur...

Suddenly, a white, hot power surged through my body! It made my muscles contract as my eyes bulged open. Hey, I can see again! Next, I saw several ripples of light emanate from my skin, as I felt my body heat up. It made me convulse on the floor, like I was having a seizure.

Oow, that hurts! The convulsions were horrible! It was like my whole body had one agonizing cramp! I bucked and bounced on the dirty ground, as drool trickled from my mouth. My body jarred this way and that, as I twitched in pain.

But wait, I can move! It was letting me use my arms and legs again! I've healed somehow!

The bright light which had emanated from my body, momentarily distracted the Voodoo Priest. He'd started to cut into Declan with the silver knife, when he stopped to stare in surprise. So did the Priestess and Pierre. They were all shocked by the bright creature, writhing on the floor of their basement.

"See, Cecille?" Pierre sung smugly. "She's no ordinary female Werewolf."

To their astonishment, I sat upright to say, "No, I'm one pissed off Circulator and that's my mate you're cutting into."

Further to their amazement, I went into phase which made the chains slip to the floor. Moving in light speed, I stood up to grab the antiques dealer and hurl him against the wall! Then I zipped over to the Priest's position and grabbed hold of his hand, which held the knife. I snapped it backwards, breaking it, and in turn it dropped the knife. The man screeched as he recoiled in pain, which left me with the Priestess.

"You're turn." I said to her, as her eyes widened in fear.

Next, she found herself flung into a table along the wall, before she crumpled onto the floor.

I turned to Declan but because he was still blinded, he couldn't see it was me. At first, he snapped his dangerous jaws but soon he smelled who it was. I put my hand on his head and put him into phase. His large, bright, see-through form, slipped out of the chains and onto the ground. Carefully, I laid him out to examine his injured abdomen.

I STILL CAN'T SEE AND I CAN BARELY MOVE - He thought bad-temperedly.

"I'll instantaneously phase us out of here." I kissed his short, stubby snout.

Just as the words left my mouth, the Priest sprang back and so did the Priestess and Pierre. They literally leapt to their feet, which made them pretty spry for a bunch of old guys. Strangely, all three started to chant in some kind of language, as they advanced upon us.

"What's this, more Voodoo?" I raised my eyebrows. "Sorry, I don't think it works on Circulators."

Suddenly, the injured European Werewolf howled in pain! Now what? I looked down to see his tortured, glowing green eyes.

I sensed it was something to do with his stomach... but why? I placed my hand over his hardened hide when immediately, I snatched it back! Something just moved inside of him, but what?

Declan threw back his head and howled again, as his body stiffened. He couldn't move from how much pain he was in! I looked closer at his stomach and I saw something move underneath his layers of muscle. There's something alive and squirming inside of him, but how?

"What have you done to him?!" I yelled, as I held onto my mate for dear life.

However, the three Voodoo freaks continued to chant, becoming louder and louder. This also made my mate howl from whatever it was, writhing inside. OK B, first things first; shut these three up then heal your husband.

I took a deep breath as I concentrated on my abilities as a Circulator. I decided to use my bio-electromagnetic field for more than just phasing. From reading the diaries of my Circulator foremothers, I'm supposed to be able to manipulate time and other electrical fields around me. Although I've never done any of this before, today appeared to be as good a day as any.

Instead of going into phase, my body glowed brightly but it didn't turn see-through. I concentrated on heightening my frequency. As I did, I sensed the secondary electrical fields in the basement, such as the ceiling and wall light, or the one over the stairs. There wasn't much to work with, just a little wiring connecting naked light globes.

So I concentrated on the three lights and using the electrical currents. As I did, they started to flicker as the room grew colder. The air out of our mouths came out like puffs of smoke, whilst my skin steadily grew whiter and brighter.

Out of the blue, the light globe on the wall exploded, with sparks flying out from the disrupted circuit!

Our kidnappers had to duck out of the way, or be electrocuted. Just as they jumped into the centre of the room, the ceiling light exploded into sparks! When one made a move for the stairway, its light bulb also blew glass everywhere. The three cowered on the floor, as the three light fittings continued to sizzle and spit out their dangerous voltage.

I concentrated on escalating the power surge, as the walls of the room started to wobble and waver.

Of course the walls didn't actually move, but they appeared to, as the air in the room became distorted from the electrical field. The atmosphere crackled and hummed as our hair stood on end. Next, a bolt of lightning zapped out of the broken light fixture from the ceiling!

It hit the dirt floor with a humongous BOOM that sent our attackers scurrying for their lives.

The middle-aged Priest, elderly Priestess and the antiques dealer thought it would be a good time to leave. The three bolted towards the staircase and raced up, out of the basement. As if to chase them out, a second bolt of electricity hit the bottom stair with another deafening BOOM!

Then it was over...the sparks that were spitting out of the broken light fixtures faded. I stopped doing whatever it was, as I concentrated on lowering my bio-electromagnetic frequency again. As I did, my body slowly stopped glowing and the temperature of the room returned to normal.

Now we found ourselves in a blackened basement with no illumination. My dark blue eyes began to glow turquoise, to use my Werewolf sight to see in the dark. I looked down into the glowing green ones of my wounded mate.

Declan whined in agony and I saw whatever it was they'd put inside him, was still there. I felt his bio-electromagnetic field fluctuate dangerously, indicating he was dying from it. Quickly but gently, I lowered his head to the floor, leapt to my feet and ran over to get his backpack which was sitting against a wall. I couldn't risk leaving behind our wallets with our ID inside.

Once I returned to him, I instantaneously phased us out of the basement and inside of our bathroom, back at the hotel. We disappeared in a bright flash of light to reappear in another. Immediately, I dropped the backpack and sat on the tiled floor, to rest his large, canine head in my lap.

I'M SORRY B, I DON'T HAVE MUCH STRENGTH LEFT - He thought weakly.

"Shhhh," I held his huge, muscled body in my smaller arms.

His glowing green eyes were fading, which I knew was a sign that death was near. I had to get whatever it was inside of him, outside of him, before I could share my blood with my mate. I took a deep breath as I closed my eyes and concentrated again...

I've never done this before, but today seemed be the day for first times.

Yet again, I turned bright and see-through and put Declan into phase with me. I felt his biological body turn into light and I focused on his altered being. I was intent on finding the foreign energy signature which was inside, so I could remove it. However, I sensed several foreign entities.

I still wasn't sure what they were, but I concentrated on separating their energy signatures from Declan's. When I sensed they were outside of him, I had us reform into our biological bodies once more. In doing so, the foreign entities also took solid shape.

"Ssssssss," five small snakes writhed on the bathroom floor.

Snakes?! THEY were INSIDE Declan?! How the hell did they get in there? How did the Voodoo freaks do it, just by chanting?

Hastily, I expanded into my Werewolf body for the muscle bulk and then using my fist, I pounded the snakes' heads in!

BAM! BAM! BAM! BAM! BAM!

Their pointy, reptilian heads were squashed against the white, tiled floor.

With the snakes out, my mate whimpered in relief but he was still gravely ill.

Instinctively, I raised my left wrist and used my right claws, to put a gash in it. Then I lowered the injury into his awaiting mouth. He was hungry for it, as his body needed my blood to heal. I felt his jaws come down as he grabbed onto my arm with his front claws. His glowing green eyes drifted shut and I remained still to let him drink.

Declan drank for a good while. As he gulped it down, I noticed how his hold on my arm tightened as his strength returned. I watched the cut in his lower abdomen start to close as it healed over. His body as a whole regenerated as I remained in my Werewolf shape, so I wouldn't pass out from blood loss.

He drank and he drank, as I began to feel cold and dizzy. Oh oh, should I pull my arm back? But what if he needs more? As if he sensed my weakening state, he removed my arm from his mouth and panted hard. I sensed he was trying to retake control of his bloodlust and not drink his mate, dry.

At least when his concerned eyes examined mine, they were glowing brightly again. He slowly sat upright but remained in his Werewolf form to look on. The giant leaned in and sniffed me, since I was the sickly one now.

"I'm OK." I growled quietly. "Are you alright?"

I'LL LIVE – He thought back.

Then he started to shrink back into his human body. His bones made soft cracking noises as his size and shape shifted. As soon as he was kneeling on the floor as a naked man, he pulled me into his arms. I was squeezed against his bare chest, whilst he held on like he would never let go...for at least a minute anyway.

Declan held me at arms length and I sensed what was coming, the I TOLD YOU SO.

"The next time I say, 'we shouldn't go in there' would you frickin' listen to me and NOT go in there! And I gave you a direct order to instantaneously phase home! You endangered your life by staying behind! You disobeyed a direct order from your Second in the pack!"

I spoke in my deep voice, "I could no more leave you behind than you could leave me."

He started to open his mouth to refute and yell some more, but then he looked stumped.

"Fine!" He acquiesced. "But the next time I say, 'don't go into the occult shop', you say 'yes sir!' Is that understood?"

"Yes sir." I gave a salute with my clawed hand.

Then I was pulled into another embrace so fast, when my face hit his chest it felt like a slap.

"Oow." I said flatly.

I felt him chuckle back, "Sorry."

Whilst he was still holding me, Declan climbed to his feet and walked us out of the ensuite. He guided me over to our bed, where we both laid ourselves out, to rest. But it was nice lying in his arms, as we lay on our sides facing each other. Thirty minutes ago, I was scared I would never feel this again.

"Are - are you OK?" I asked in my deep, rumbling voice.

"I'll live." He sighed, as he rubbed my back.

"I'm sorry." I spoke in my Werewolf form, which sounded funny when you're trying to be apologetic. However, I had to remain as such to recoup my blood loss.

"I know B, I know."

"I was just curious, I've never seen Voodoo before."

"So I gathered," he said simply.

"Why is it with the supernatural beings we meet, there seems to be more bad than good?"

"I dunno, maybe it's just the way things are." He shrugged. "I'm the first European Werewolf not to hunt human. The Lokoti Werewolves were the first breed to successfully alter their hunting pattern towards animal. Maybe it's like the saying, power corrupts? But not ALL things that are supernatural are bad. I mean, look at Circulators. You guys were some of the most powerful in existence, but you didn't try to take over the world. Or what about Nairn, she uses her gift to help people. The three 'Seers' we have in the tribe, are on the Council of Tribal Elders and they use their visions to guide."

I pressed my face against the hot skin on his chest, as I inhaled his maple syrup scent.

He went on as he stroked my hair. "I guess it's just the Circulator inside you that makes you curious about these things. I also think it's because you're a very trusting person. You seek out the good in people. If it had been me, I would have scared off Nairn without ever getting to know her. But you sensed something and trusted her immediately."

Next, Declan gently cupped my face to look into my glowing turquoise eyes.

He said, "You do bring out the good in people, B. You sure as hell humanize me. Sometimes I wonder if I didn't have you, could I fight my bloodlust every day? Or would I give in and hunt human? That's your real light, not some scientific shit about bio-electromagnetic frequencies. It's the light inside of your heart, which comes out in your aura."

Then he placed his human lips over my parted ones to kiss tenderly, even with my elongated teeth jutting out, as I panted like a dog.

*****

Lying like that on top the bed, we fell asleep in each other's arms. Like that, in my mate's embrace, I fell into a deep slumber. Like that though, my mind fretted as my physical form regenerated.

Horrible visions invaded my thoughts and the disturbing dreams made my eyelids flicker in REM sleep; Rapid Eye Movement. To be honest, I would have been happy if my eyes didn't move at all. Then maybe I wouldn't have seen so many terrible things...

I dreamt of the dirty street we had walked down that afternoon, but at night time. Two of the street lights were broken thanks to vandalism, so the road with all its rubbish and graffiti looked even less attractive. Most of the buildings were darkened, showing the shops were closed but there were a few lights from the apartments above, indicating people lived there.

As a bodiless mass, I hovered over this small part of the large city. Like I had no control, I found myself drifting downwards, until I was floating just outside of the Occult Shop. It was dark inside, showing it was shut for the day. For some reason, I was pulled inside of the store, although I didn't want to go back. Since I didn't have a physical mass, I easily passed through the grimy front window.

The jars of peculiarities on the shelves, seemed even spookier in the dim light. I wondered what I was doing here, when I heard something. I heard chanting in the same language I'd heard this afternoon from the Voodoo Priests and Priestess. Were they casting another spell?

My question was soon answered, as I was pulled towards the door for the backroom. Through the doorway was a corridor where at the end was another door. As I passed through the wood, I saw a steep staircase leading underground. Hold on, wasn't this where I was dragged to, this afternoon?

Unwillingly, I was pulled down the stairs and as I floated into the basement, I found our attackers. The three Voodoo practitioners were busily working at the table by the wall. They operated by lamp light, since their electrical lights had short circuited.

They looked like they could have been cooking, as Pierre was grinding with a mortar and pestle, the Priestess was cutting up a dried herb and the Priest was holding a silver knife over a live chicken. If I had a body, my breath would have caught in my throat, as I watched him chop off the chicken's head! Oh that poor animal.

The Priest kept the chicken's head and tossed aside its still twitching body. With his knife, he cut off its beak and even removed its beady, little eyes... oh that poor chicken! Then he dropped the eyes and the beak inside the stone mortar that Pierre was mixing with the pestle. Next, the Priestess dropped in her cut up, dried herbs. As they mixed everything in together, all three continued to chant. Was I witnessing them perform an actual spell?

Lastly, the Priest opened up a jar and pulled out a familiar set of teeth. Two of the top teeth looked like a snake's fangs, indicating they were the European Vampire's. He dropped them into the mortar and Pierre proceeded to ground them up, along with the rest of the ingredients.

They chanted louder as the Priestess picked up something else. Instead of dropping it into the stone bowl, she held it over the mixture as a smoke started to rise. Whatever it was she was holding, she repeatedly ran it through the fumes. When I drifted closer to get a better look, I saw she was holding my gold bracelet from Ancient Greece.

Hey, when did they get hold of it? Stupidly, I tried to look at my arm to see if it was missing when I realized that d'oh you idiot! You're a bodiless mass, you don't have any arms! They could have swiped it when I was drugged and tied up. I remembered the antiques dealer feeling me up, he must have taken it then.

"Will this work?" The Priestess asked, as she waved my jewellery through the smoke.

"Whatever she is, she's still part Werewolf." Pierre said coldly. "The Hex should work on her Werewolf side."

"And what of the male?" The Priest inferred Declan.

"She's his mate and she's also his weakness. When we kill her, it will injure him. We can recapture him then." He said smoothly.

No, not my Declan! Don't you hurt my mate! I hated hearing them plot it.

I wanted to reform into my physical being and attack the psychos! However, a little voice reminded me of my training when I first turned and what differentiated me from these human monsters; that Lokoti Werewolves don't kill. I couldn't murder these sociopaths in cold blood, no matter how much I wanted to. I'd have to think of another way to stop them.

Just as these thoughts swirled inside my non-existent head, I was interrupted and so were the Voodoo practitioners.

SMASH! It sounded like the front window of the shop upstairs had been destroyed. It was pretty loud too, as if something large had crashed through the glass.

"It's the male!" Pierre barked.

The male? No, he didn't mean...? Nah, it couldn't be.

Pierre left the Priestess to continue with the spell. Next, he grabbed the silver knife from the bench as the Priest grabbed a leather pouch from nearby. He emptied out some kind of powder onto his hand. Oh oh, what was the bet that it was the same powder used this afternoon, to knock us out?

Then there was silence, not a single sound could be heard from upstairs. Pierre and the Priest exchanged wary looks, as the Priestess chanted quietly in her work.

...eeeeaaaaaarrwww....

Slowly the door to the basement opened, seemingly by its own accord. The men looked up the staircase puzzled, as there didn't seem to be anybody in the doorway. An uneasy quiet settled over the cellar, as the humans strained to see into the dark upstairs corridor.

"GRRRAAAAWWWLLL!"

The attack happened so fast! A large, male European Werewolf leapt out of the darkened corridor, sailing right over the stairs. As soon as it landed on the cellar floor, it leapt into the air a second time! It moved with lightning fast reflexes that the humans were too slow to react.

Declan's first target was taking out the lamp on the table, as he knew they would be blind in the dark without it.

As he sailed through the air past the Priest, his sharp claws swung out. The Priest blew the powder out of his hand when Declan had already passed him. With a deep claw mark in his face, the Priest fell to the ground the same time as the lamp did.

There was a second SMASH and then darkness...

"Where is it?! Where is it?!" The Priestess cried out fearfully.

"My face! My face!" The Priest cried out in agony.

"Shut up, the both of you!" Pierre hissed.

And then there was light, or barely. The antiques dealer held up an old Zippo lighter in one hand, as his other clasped the silver knife. He spun around to try to peer into the dark corners of the cellar, but he couldn't see the monster.

Like the predator he was, Declan crouched low on the ground. He knew his tanned coloured, hardened hide, would camouflage him against the dirty floor. He kept his eyes closed, but he knew exactly where everyone was by smell and hearing alone...

Then he opened his glowing green eyes, purposefully giving away his position.

"Over there! Over there!" The Priestess screeched in terror.

Before Pierre could react, Declan leapt through the air and landed right on top of him!

The human holding the silver knife was no match for the European Werewolf's size and strength. The hand that was holding the dagger, next found itself between the beast's sharp teeth. He brought down his jaws and in one tug, the man's hand was completely bitten off!

Oh no, Declan's BITTEN somebody! But that would mean the human will turn if he lives through this, or he was going to die tonight. If I had a stomach, it would have turned cold and dropped to the floor like cement.

The antiques dealer cried out in agony and horror, as he looked upon the bloodied stump at the end of his arm.

The predator tossed away the decapitated limb which was still holding onto the silver knife. The bloodied hand and weapon landed a few meters away in the dirt. Then he growled menacingly, as he lowered his dangerous face over his petrified human victim. His searing hot breath made Pierre blink and Declan's glowing green eyes burning into him, was the last thing he ever saw.

The Priestess screamed hysterically, dropping my bracelet onto the floor as she almost fell over. She ran in the direction of the stairs as the sickening, wet, crunching sound of Pierre's face being eaten through, chased her out of the room. The Priest cried out for her, as he too tried to run away.

"Cecille, wait for me!"

WHOOMP! Simultaneously as he landed face first in the dirt, he too was pulled backwards into the jaws of death. The European Werewolf's claws pierced his legs almost to the bone, as he dragged him to his demise.

"CECILLE! STOP! HELP ME!"

The old woman struggled in the dark, climbing up the stairs as quickly as she could on all fours. Her cohort's screams of agony of being eaten alive, followed her. Declan's claws tore his torso to shreds, before his large jaws snapped open the human's rib cage and he devoured the heart. My mate wasn't just murdering our attackers, he was eating them! He was tasting human flesh, which was forbidden.

Oh no... please no... please let this be a nightmare... please let all of this be a dream...please don't let any of this be real... please!

Next, I hovered upwards through the basement ceiling where I found myself in the store again. I saw broken glass all over the floor, which indicated a European Werewolf had leapt through the front window. The shop was in ruin, with many a broken bottle or jar, lying about.

The Priestess screamed, as she ran through the doorway, out of the corridor. She rounded the counter to make a run for the front door and Declan tore after her. His large build smashed through the wooden bench and he swung out his claw. He belted the back of the old woman, which made her fly sideways from the impact!

She knocked over several shelves as more broken glass appeared on the floor. The old woman landed face first with a bloodied claw mark across her back. The next thing she knew, the monster was standing over her on all-fours.

His front claw roughly rolled her over, so their eyes could meet. It was infuriated glowing green against terrified faded brown.

As she looked up at her killer, her eyes widened when she saw what was hanging loosely in his bloodied jaws...

It was my gold bracelet.

From this, the Voodoo Priestess knew why she was going to die tonight.

Declan placed his large, heavy, right claw over her face. He clutched her head in one hand and with his strength he could crush her skull if he wanted to. Instead, he broke something else. SNAP! The old woman's head now rolled on a peculiar angle, as her open eyes stared vacantly past him.

With his business finished, he casually walked over the Priestess's body, towards the door. He gave a flick of his right claw and the locked door to the shop, landed flat on the sidewalk. He slowly stalked out onto the street, where he smelled and heard the humans, before he saw them.

A small crowd had gathered and was standing across the street, pointing at the smashed shop window. When they saw his huge, hulking, hairless form, coupled with the blood around his mouth and claws, they panicked.

"Eek! It's a bear! A bear's escaped from the zoo!"

"Look at the blood all over it! It's killed somebody!"

"Someone call 911!"

The monster growled at the frightened group, who made a move to run back to their homes but then they didn't have to. He tore off down the street on all-fours, so fast he looked like a large blur. The humans hesitated outside of their apartment buildings, either trying to capture his image on their camera phones or calling emergency services.

I hovered higher and higher into the night sky, as I watched his huge but fast form, tear down the streets or alleyways of New Orleans.

When there weren't anymore narrow lanes he could hide in, he leapt up a fire escape on the side of an old, brick building. Within a flash, he scrambled up onto the rooftop and he ran like that, across the city skyline. His muscled body galloped from building to building, as it leapt over street or intersection alike. If one building was higher than another, his claws embedded themselves into the structure and he deftly scurried to the top.

His speed matched 300 km/h as he ran with a sense of purpose, back to his sleeping mate.

Then this vision, or this dream, or the nightmare, or whatever you wanted to call it, started to fade.

The last thing I saw before everything turned garbled, was my hulking mate, leaping through the air. He sailed over a busy street where below, people walked along or drove their plasma-powered vehicles, oblivious to the threat above. Skilfully, he dived through our hotel room window and landed on the carpet with a thud.

That was it, that's where the vision ended, with me staring at our hotel window. I didn't feel like I was a bodiless mass anymore. I could feel my arms and legs again, which lay weakened on the bed. My regenerative ability was working overtime, to recuperate the amount of blood I had lost.

I blinked and then I blinked again. As my eyes refocused, I realized I was still staring at our hotel room window. Instead of outside looking in, I was inside looking out. I wasn't seeing a window in a grey building, I was looking at silky white wallpaper and yellow curtains, around a large window frame.

To try to slow my racing heart, I took several deep breaths before holding the last one. When I steadily let it out, I noticed the sound of the shower running. I turned my head to find Declan wasn't lying beside me, but I could smell his wet, maple syrup scent, coming from the ensuite.

My head rose to look over at the digital clock on the bedside table. The time read as 10.08 PM. Slowly I sat upright, still in my Lokoti Werewolf form, as I looked about the room whilst sniffing repeatedly. I could smell something was afoot.

Was it...? Could it have been...? Please tell me it was all just a dream!

Slowly, I stood up and then I managed to walk over to the window. The curtains were half closed but from the sounds of the street outside, I parted them to find the window was wide open. Oh oh...

Next, I turned around to look closely on the carpeted floor. I crouched down to run my hand over the surface, when I felt the imprints of where his large claws had landed. Worse than that, I smelled first and then I saw second, a tiny droplet of blood.

It was so small, it would be missed by the human eye, but thanks to my supernatural sense of smell, I tracked it. It stained the carpet between the window and the ensuite. I lowered onto my hands and knees and bent my head to sniff it. Oh no, no, no, no way! The scent gave up who it belonged to, the Voodoo Priest.

Either from shock or disbelief, I lost my balance and fell onto my side. My body began to tremble, as my glowing turquoise eyes filled with tears. They watered as much as they did when that powder stung them.

Oh shit Declan, what have you done? They may have been psychopathic murderers, but they were still human. You killed three human beings tonight! You broke the Lokoti Werewolf code that we don't eat human!

We don't kill unless it was in war, or we were defending our family or our tribe. Could battling Voodoo crazies tonight, be grounds enough to claim it was war? Could it be seen as self defence and not vengeance?

What will we tell the pack? What will we say to the Tribal Elders? Will they try to punish you? If it was justified then why did you do this when I was asleep? Oh no Declan, what will you do? What will we do? Will we have to go on the run, from the law and the pack?

Quickly, I put my clawed hand over my mouth to smother my crying, so he wouldn't hear.

I pictured Aunt Susan's face, who'd been Declan's human mother. She raised her sons after her husband's death, who was killed by the European

Werewolf which turned Declan. She was an upstanding woman with a reputation for being strong and wise. She helped start the temporary school on Lokoti tribal lands after the War. With the occasional help from my Lokoti Werewolf grandfather, she taught her European Werewolf son to respect human life. I could see her hurt expression, as if she were here right now.

What about my grandfather, who acted as Declan's father figure? He trained the young Werewolf to hunt animal and not human. Night after night he sat with the dangerous child, teaching him the Lokoti Werewolf way. He took the tempestuous tot out hunting between full moons, and initiated him into the pack. He used kindness and wisdom let alone strength or force, to control his bloodlust.

And now Declan does this?

*****

~ 15 ~

Just then I heard the water turn off and the shower door open.

Quickly, I jumped up from the floor and sat on the end of the bed. Within a minute, my husband walked out of the bathroom with a towel wrapped around his waist. He was using a second towel to dry his hair.

"Hey, you're up." He smiled as if nothing was amiss. "How did you sleep?"

I looked on incredulous at how cheerful he was acting.

Next, he gave a funny look, "B?"

Declan was looking at me like *I* was the one behaving strangely? I stood up from the bed as I shrunk back into my smaller shape. Then I spoke to him in my human voice.

"I'm fine thank you, how are you?"

He gave a peculiar look at how formal that sounded, before he answered. "Yes I'm fine too, thanks for asking."

Then he turned around and went back into the bathroom. I heard the sound the taps turn on and off and then the noise of him brushing his teeth. He paused for a moment, when he saw me come to stand in the bathroom doorway.

"You wanna have a shower, so we can officially crash? I'm exhausted." He asked with a mouth full of toothpaste.

I didn't answer, I just stood there staring as if I could have been under a spell. Declan gave another funny look as he finished brushing his teeth. I watched him spit out the toothpaste, rinse his toothbrush then he rinsed his mouth with water.

Uncharacteristically, he opened the bottle of the hotel's complimentary mouthwash. Declan doesn't use mouthwash, he said he hates the stuff. He's joked countless times over the many years, "If I want to burn my mouth out, I'll eat some of your cooking, thanks B."

However here he was, gargling away. Tonight, he was using the mouthwash to hide the smell of human flesh on his breath. I just knew it.

"Hey, this stuff isn't so bad." He said, after he spat it out. Then he picked up the bottle to read the label. "I'll have to remember the brand and maybe we should buy some when we're home?"

Then he exited the ensuite but on his way past, his hand affectionately rubbed my waist.

Just as I turned to follow him out, something shiny caught my eye. It was sitting on the vanity and had been hidden by his large build. With his departure, it was now plain to see.

It was my gold bracelet from Ancient Greece. It gleamed, like somebody had gone to a lot of trouble to clean it. Or, to scrub off any traces of the victim's blood, perhaps? I picked up my belonging before I walked back out.

Declan was by the bed, pulling on a pair of boxer shorts. He briefly glanced my way and observed how I was holding the jewellery in both hands. Then he proceeded to pull down the covers and climb in.

"I'm going to crash." He said. "Are you going to shower now, or what?"

I looked up from the jewellery to meet his eyes with my own. "Why did you clean my bracelet?"

"Because it was dirty," he shrugged, not missing a beat. Then he stretched himself out on the mattress like he didn't have a care in the world. He comfortably closed his eyes as his head rested on the pillow.

"Where did you find it?" I continued.

"Where do you think?" He replied tiredly. "It was on the floor."

"Which floor?"

"The bathroom floor, I think you dropped it when you phased us here." Then he turned off the lamp on the bedside table, so the only light left was coming from the ensuite. "C'mon B, have your evening shower and go to bed."

Casually, he rolled over so his back was to the light and no longer in his eyes.

Mine started to water, as I wondered why was he lying to me? I opened my mouth to blurt out, "I know Declan, I know what you did!" But nothing came out.

Should I accuse him of murder? Would he see it as a betrayal? What if he doesn't want to talk about it?

After standing there and contemplating, eventually I turned around and headed inside the bathroom. I shut the door before I put the gold bracelet back on top of the vanity. As I proceeded to undress, I noticed my hands were shaking. I tried to take several deep breaths to calm myself, but it didn't work.

The hot water came out of one of those pulsating-massage shower heads. However, my shoulders felt rock hard and refused to loosen. Even under the scalding water, all I felt was cold.

*****

The next time the door of the ensuite opened, I was showered and my teeth brushed. I was wearing a negligee to sleep in and I thought he might have been asleep? However, his eyes opened and he looked on how I was silhouetted by the light.

He started to smile, but I switched off the light before coming to bed. I lay on my side and pulled the sheet up high. Although I was facing in the opposite direction, he wasn't put off by my distant behaviour.

I felt his strong arm encircle my waist and the feel of his larger body move up behind. As he spooned me, I froze like a deer in the headlights and lay there unmoving. Gradually, his breathing grew slower and deeper as he slipped into sleep.

Although I still felt weak, I was in no way tired. I ended up lying awake, staring out at the city lights via the window. My mind raced as I pondered what should we do?

What if the pack finds out what happened tonight? Will he be judged a murderer? We'd have to run away but anywhere we go in this time frame, they'd eventually sniff us out. We'd be hunted down and Declan could be destroyed.

We'd have to travel back in time and live somewhere in the past, like our old idea of moving to Canada in the 19th Century. We could live in a house somewhere in the woods, so we can change in privacy. But what if he no longer wants to hunt animal? What if tasting human flesh tonight, has ruined 174 years of abstaining?

Would I be able to stop him? I knew if I fought him as a Circulator with my silver sword, I'd stop him for good. But could I really harm my own mate?

Silently, I started to cry as I pictured me standing against him and the hurt in his eyes. His expression would say, 'I killed the crazies for you. It's your fault that it changed my hunting pattern. Now you're going to kill me for it?'

"Hmm, what?" He suddenly woke up. I froze a second time, as I realized my trembling body must have disrupted his sleep. However, he must have thought I was shivering, as he sleepily asked, "Are you cold, B?"

I found myself pushed onto my stomach, as he laid himself over me to share his body heat.

Contentedly, he rested his head on my back as he fell back asleep. I couldn't move, not without waking him. I couldn't cry anymore either. My eyes fell on the hotel's digital clock on the bedside table, whose numerals glowed back.

11.33 PM.

I watched the numbers slowly change as time progressed.

12.03 AM.

I laid there wide awake and scared stiff.

12.33 AM.

I still couldn't move with the huge male lying on top.

1.03 AM.

Just then he shifted position. Instead of rolling off, he raised himself to turn his head in the other direction. Then he gave an affectionate squeeze as he settled back down again.

1.33 AM.

My eyes were stinging by how tired I was, even with my mind racing a hundred miles an hour. But to be honest, the feel of his hot, heavy body, did bring comfort. Exhaustedly, I gave up trying to think of a solution tonight and let my eyes close...

8.03 AM.

The clock was the first thing I saw when I opened my eyes. The hotel room looked bright and cheerful in the morning light. Declan was no longer lying on top and I soon realized he wasn't even in bed.

"Can I get two of the breakfast specials?" I heard him speak.

Sleepily, I looked up to find him pacing the floor, already dressed in a t-shirt and cargo shorts and talking on the hotel's phone.

"With the breakfast specials make one with scrambled eggs and the other with fried eggs. Runny please. Oh and can I get some extra hash browns with those? Uh huh. Yeah and a short stack with maple syrup. Plus two OJ's and two Latte's. Uh huh. It'll be thirty minutes? OK, thanks."

He must be ordering Room Service. He hung up and smiled my way when he saw I was awake. But it soon disappeared and a frown took its place.

"Man, you're pale."

"Am I?" I asked in mild surprise.

"Yeah and your aura looks faded." His frown deepened.

Energetically, he leapt upon the bed to wrap his arms about my waist. Next, he ducked his head to sniff around my face and neck. Then he pulled back to look on in concern, "You're blood pressure is pretty high. If I didn't know any better, I'd say it was from stress."

He made me nervous so I tried to sit up, but he wouldn't allow it. Playfully, he growled into my ear and started to tickle me! I squealed with laughter as he engaged in a play-fight.

"Stop it!" I tittered as I pushed him off.

"There's no reason why you should be stressed, I won't allow it." He continued as he chewed on my ear. "Besides, we're on holidays. You're not allowed to be stressed when you're on vacation."

"Isn't it funny how we keep having these problems when we go away?" I said unhappily.

"You and your frickin' pheromones, I can't take you anywhere!" He repeated. Then he raised his head to mockingly glare, "If it's not your Lokoti Werewolf scent attracting them, it's your aura as a Circulator."

Feeling uncomfortable, I was about to look away but then I didn't have to. Declan bent his head to maul my neck with his open mouth. Normally I'd enjoy his ardour, but not today. I felt strung out and scared, as my mind fretted over our predicament.

"Well," he pulled back to sigh. "I was thinking today we could go and see City Park and then have dinner at that Creole restaurant we saw yesterday. But maybe we shouldn't, maybe we should take things easy."

I realized he was saying this for my benefit. We had enough on our plate without worrying about my state of health. Until I've worked out a plan, I didn't want him to fret about his mate.

"No." I said firmly. "We'll go to City Park today and Creole for dinner tonight. Besides, we're leaving New Orleans tomorrow and I don't want us to miss out."

What I almost said was, 'we might as well enjoy life as we know it, before the shit hits the fan when we go home'.

Declan didn't look convinced so I fibbed. "Seriously, I'm fine."

If he can lie then so can I. To prove I was OK, I moved to the edge of the bed but when I stood up, I got the biggest head spin! The dizziness nearly made me fall backwards. However, I took a deep breath and proceeded to put on some clothes.

He lay on his side and watched warily. I pulled on a short, denim skirt and a white singlet top before walking into the ensuite to brush my hair and pull it into a pony tail. When I returned, I found him standing by the hotel window and worriedly looking out.

"What is it?" I asked.

"What?" He quickly turned as if I startled him. "Oh, nothing." Then he looked down at my bare arms. "Why aren't you wearing your bracelet?"

"My bracelet?"

"Yeah, your bracelet."

"You mean the one I bought yesterday from one of our attackers?" I asked in a surly voice.

"No, the Greek one that your grandmother bought you," he replied in a similar manner.

"Because I don't want to," I turned away to busy myself with reorganizing my suitcase.

"Why?"

"I just don't want to!" I snapped back.

As I tied up my bag of dirty laundry, Declan passed by into the ensuite. When he came out again, he was carrying my bracelet in his hand. He stood beside, to gently take my right arm and slide the bracelet on.

"It's your favourite bracelet." He spoke soberly then he recited off by heart. "You got it on your first trip back in time when you went to Athens 449 BC with your Mom and your Gran. You wear it in memory of them."

My heart began to pound as I looked up into his waiting eyes.

Next, he reached out to touch the gold crucifix around my neck. "That was your Great, Great Gran's." Then he touched my gold earrings. "Your Dad gave you these for your hundredth birthday..." Lastly, his fingers played with my diamond engagement ring and gold wedding ring. "...and I gave you these. The jewellery you wear, were given by the people who are important to you."

Then his hand moved to pull out the small, gold crucifix he was wearing under his t-shirt, which used to be his mother's. He did it with his left hand, to show off his wedding ring. He was indicating he did the same. My chest hurt at the force my heart was beating. I looked undecided into his face, as I pondered maybe he hasn't turned into a cold blooded killer?

"Don't be unhappy, B." He whispered. "You have no reason to be."

"But yesterday -" I started when he silenced me by putting his finger over my lips.

"Don't think about yesterday. Don't think about those dangerous, crazy psychopaths again. You don't need to worry about them, you really don't."

My eyes widened and I thought I was about to hear his confession. He looked like he was about to tell me what he did. That was until he ran his thumb over my lips before pulling me in to kiss fervently. When it ended, I heard him inhale deeply.

"At least no matter how pale you are, you always smell good." He sighed.

Then he walked away to reorganize his suitcase as well.

*****

When breakfast finished, we brushed our teeth, put my purse, his wallet and our hotel security card into his backpack, then left the hotel.

We caught a tram and then wandered hand-in-hand through City Park.

It was huge, with several sections made into sporting facilities, or there was Carousel Amusement Park, New Orleans Botanical Garden or New Orleans Museum of Art. But the parts we visited were Storyland, the Sydney and Walda Besthoff Sculpture Garden or just walking around the park in general. I also enjoyed looking on the old Live Oak trees or the couple of small, stone bridges over the odd bayou.

I must admit, doing something as normal as this, helped me feel a lot better. It also felt nice how firmly he held onto my hand. The trees protected us from the majority of the sun's rays and there was a gentle breeze. However, I saw I coped better with the heat and humidity than Declan. Halfway through our sightseeing, he had to cool down by buying a gigantic cup of soda with ice.

"You want?" He angled the cup towards me, with the straw sticking through the lid.

I rewarded his sharing with an appreciative smile before I sucked some down. The cold, sweet, fizzy drink also boosted my mood. He replaced the straw in his mouth and his hand squeezed mine as we walked onwards.

At 1 PM we stopped at a cafe which was situated by a lagoon in the park. I was feeling much better, as the sunny weather cheered me and admiring the landscape got my mind off things. Even my husband's company helped, as he made me laugh at his comments about a couple of statues we looked at.

Declan led the way to a table which was in the shade. He pulled out my chair for me before he sat down. I was feeling myself again which included the return of my appetite. I picked up the menu and hungrily looked down the list of edible offers.

"You hardly touched breakfast this morning, so I don't wanna hear you're not hungry." He scolded.

"Nup, I'm STARVING!"

This made him grin. "So, what looks good?"

"It all looks good, that's the problem."

"OK, which two stand out the most?"

"Um, the nachos and the hot dogs."

"Right, you get the nachos and I'll order the hot dogs." He organized, before he held up his hand to attract the waitress.

After 150 years of marriage, we had all of our idiosyncrasies down to a tee. I knew Declan would order an extra hot dog for me and he would dip into my nachos. Sharing food had become second nature to us.

"Can I get three hot dogs, please? On two of them, I'll have mustard, ketchup and cheese and then on the third, can I just get mustard and cheese?" He ordered, as he knew I didn't like ketchup.

"The hot dogs come with fries each, do you still want fries?" She checked.

"Hell yeah!" He chuckled at her surprise.

I caught her look confused at his muscled build, as she probably wondered where he put it all?

"Can I please get the nachos?" I ordered next. "And we'll have a caramel milkshake and a banana milkshake."

The waitress put all of this in her PDA before she took our menus and then walked off to serve somebody else.

Declan reached over and put his hands over mine, as he gazed my way.

"You're looking much better," he announced.

"Yeah?"

"You've got more colour in your cheeks and your aura is almost back to normal."

I smiled back, "I'm having a nice day."

"So am I."

He gave my hands another squeeze before he let go and leaned back in his seat.

We sat in a comfortable silence as we looked out at the lagoon and gardens. I had to admit, I was really enjoying myself right now. With serene views, a comfortable breeze and anticipating a yummy lunch, I almost felt carefree. However, when I looked in his direction, I caught him watching me instead of our surroundings.

"What?" I wondered.

"Nothin'." He shrugged.

I gazed at some kids playing Frisbee in the park with their parents. I watched the happy scene for a good minute or so, as I sighed contentedly. Then my eyes moved over the outdoor cafe setting, at the other people sitting down. When I looked back at my husband, I found him watching me again.

"What?" I gave a funny look.

"Nothin'." He shrugged once more.

"Declan."

"B."

"Frickin' tell me or I'll pounce on you!"

He joked, "If that's the case, I'll keep my mouth shut."

Then he laughed when I stuck my tongue out.

"Yeah alright," he gave in. "I'm watching your aura. It's steadily getting brighter and brighter the more relaxed you become."

"It is?"

"Yup."

We both quieted when the waitress returned with our food and drinks. She lowered her tray to put down the milkshakes first and then the plate with the hot dogs, another for the fries and lastly my nachos. My eyes widened at the sight of the salsa and melted cheese over the corn chips. The sour cream and guacamole sat in small side bowls, the way I preferred.

I smiled up at her, "Thanks!"

"Enjoy," the waitress beamed back.

But as she walked away, I caught her look back in disbelief at my buff mate, as he eagerly tucked into his fries.

I swapped around our milkshakes, so the caramel was sitting beside him and I had the banana. Declan picked up the hotdog with just the mustard and the cheese and carefully put it on the side of my plate. Whilst his hand was there, he picked up a corn chip, dunked it into the sour cream and guacamole and delivered it into his waiting mouth.

"Mmm, good choice." He nodded.

Next, he picked up one of his fries, dunked it into the sour cream and guacamole then put it inside of my mouth.

"Mmm, thank you." I relished the offering.

Lastly, we picked up a hot dog each and happily chewed on these.

"Don't you just love eating?" He commented. "Food can almost cure all ills."

"Mmm," I nodded with my mouth full. After I swallowed I said, "Don't you just love being one of 'our kind', especially with our supernatural metabolism."

"Yeah," he chuckled as picked up his second hot dog already.

I snickered quietly, "The waitress is still watching us, I don't think she can believe how much food we've ordered for two people."

The European Werewolf didn't bother about being subtle. He turned his head and caught her looking as she cleared a table. Then he threw her a wave!

"Declan!" I kicked him under the table, as my face reddened.

He laughed at my embarrassment as he reached over to pick up some more nachos.

"It's hard to imagine that one day we might live without food." He speculated about evolving to the space time continuum.

"Who says there won't be food there?" I shrugged. "When they recreated the Fox's Ball for my visit, wine was being served."

He gave a funny look, "Are you telling me there'll be party food in heaven?"

"Maybe." I shrugged again. "I think the space time continuum changes. Maybe it distorts perception, or it becomes what you perceive. I think its different things to different people. To the Lokoti, it's the Holy Hunting Grounds and to my great, great grandmother, it's an 18th Century Aristocratic Ball."

"That makes sense," he gave a nod. "So to you, what will it be?"

"I don't know, I've never really thought about it." I sighed. "What about you?"

"I don't know either, I don't think I really care." He momentarily glanced away and I caught him mutter under his breath, "As long as it isn't hell."

His words hit me like a slap in the face.

Then he looked my way again to joke, "As long as it's with you for eternity, I don't care if it's frickin' 'Sesame Street'."

Suddenly I lost my appetite and I put down my half eaten hot dog. I sat back in my seat, to move away from the food as I felt nauseous. I had to look away from the table whilst taking deep breaths.

"B, what is it?" He asked concerned.

"Nothing." I lied.

"Yeah right!" He scoffed. "Your aura just faded like somebody switched off a light."

Declan's words, 'as long as it isn't hell,' echoed in my mind and sent chills down my spine.

"B -" he began and I think he was going to insist, when we were interrupted.

A young couple came and sat down at the table next to ours. They looked like they were in their twenties and the man was African-American whereas the woman was of Asian descent. They were playfully arguing, with lots of grins and giggles.

"I told you I heard something on the roof last night." The girl taunted. "And see here, my proof that I wasn't imagining it!"

She held up an iPad which showed a front page news story. She pointed at a blurry photograph on the screen, before passing it to him. He shook his head as he looked on it.

"We can't even see what it is!" He laughed at her. "The photo's so blurry, it could be my grandma and you've seen how big she is."

The girl giggled as she took her iPad back and started to read aloud the article.

"Listen to this, 'last night security cameras located on several different rooftops, filmed a large animal moving at a speed estimated at 300 km/h.' That's why the photos are blurry, because the thing was moving so fast."

I felt all the blood drain from my face as my stomach painfully knotted itself. The photo may have been blurry, but I recognized the huge, hulking shape and the colouring of its skin. It was a light tanned colour, the same as Declan's hardened hide.

"Well, what kinda animal do the police think it is?" The guy enquired.

"Witnesses said it looked like a hairless, albino, grizzly bear." She replied.

The guy scoffed, "So you're saying a hairless, albino, grizzly bear ran across the roof of our apartment building at a speed of 300km/h?"

"Then listen to this," she continued to read. "'Last night, three people died in what can only be described as a wild animal attack. Three mutilated bodies were found of two African-American males and an elderly African-American female. The police released that the bodies had teeth or claw marks, consistent with a large predator. Detectives investigating the crime are baffled by how the animal came to be in the city, as a spokesperson from the New Orleans Zoo confirmed that no animals are missing. Several eye-witnesses which saw the creature, described it as a large, hairless, albino, grizzly bear with bright green eyes. However, the Zoo Keepers which were interviewed, stated that grizzlies cannot run at speeds of 300km/h nor leap over roadways and traffic intersections in a single bound'."

My mouth turned sickeningly salty as my body became drenched in a cold sweat. However, Declan sat back in his chair, looking cool as a cucumber. The only time he looked concerned, was when he saw how I was looking.

"So where's this large, hairless, albino, grizzly bear now?" The guy asked.

"The police don't know," she frowned as her eyes skimmed over the article. "The animal disappeared from a rooftop somewhere in the CBD area."

"Oh, besides the Urban Legend of alligators in the sewers; now albino, grizzly bears are hiding on our rooftops?" He laughed out his disbelief.

She ignored her boyfriend as her eyes never left the story. Lastly, she read out, "Police have extra squad cars and sniffer dogs on patrol today and for the rest of the week. They're worried that the animal is some kind of mutant bear, like that mutant cougar that attacked those campers a couple of years ago. They're speculating it's still from the leftover radiation after the war."

"That sounds a little more believable," he mused as he picked up a menu. "Who knows what's out there from nuclear fallout? I heard of another case where a two-headed calf was born on a farm that used to be an old missile silo."

The girl agreed, "Yeah after the war there were a lot of birth defects in humans too. When I was at college, I read how in the late 21st Century, babies were born deformed or with cancer, or even both."

"Thank science for curing radiation sickness," he sighed. "So, what do you feel like for lunch?"

Suddenly, her eyes bulged as she read out something else, "One of the victims had his whole chest destroyed like something ate its way through to his heart!"

I heard my own heart pound in my ears, like the sound of the Lokoti funeral drum beat...

"Let's change the subject," the guy screwed up his face. "Read out our horoscopes for today."

Visibly relieved, she looked away from death and destruction to read something trivial instead.

Declan sat as still as a statue as he regarded me with narrow eyes. I too sat unmoving, but for my hands which were beginning to shake. Although I couldn't look at him directly, I was watching him in the corner of my eyes. Then my shocked gaze briefly met his angry one, before I jumped to my feet. He was quick to leap up too, as if he was scared I was about to run off.

"I have to go to the bathroom," I uttered out.

Speedily, I walked around the outdoor tables and into the indoor part of the café. Declan walked after, which made me barge through the door marked with a female symbol. Since I was rushing, I almost took out a mother and her young daughter, who were exiting at the same time. My eyes instantly widened in further horror, at how I had nearly harmed them.

"Oh, I'm so sorry..." I mumbled apologetically.

"No problem," the mother gave a peculiar look, as she led her daughter away.

When I turned to watch them go, I saw the two pass Declan who was standing a couple of meters away.

Like I was being chased, I disappeared inside the Ladies. I walked over to one of the sinks to lean on it, before looking up at my reflection in the mirror above. The same image I'd seen for decades, stared back albeit guiltily.

'Declan killed for you' - I thought at the person in the glass - 'You're married to a murderer'. I watched her useless tears fill her eyes. 'You're hiding his secret' – I accused – 'That makes you an accessory to murder'.

Abruptly, I bent over as if I had been winded and I gripped onto the basin hard.

What do I do? Pray? Would praying for forgiveness help?

Just then the bathroom door swung open as Declan's large frame filled the doorway. He frowned upon the sight of me leaning over. Next, he walked up and grabbed my arm to pull me away.

"Alright, that's enough." He said gruffly. "I've paid the bill now let's walk and talk."

He escorted his distraught wife through the café. However, just as we passed the counter, our ears picked up something. There was an Internet TV on a shelf above which was showing a news bulletin.

"We have more news about the shocking animal attack which occurred last night," the female newsreader announced.

As she spoke, a small window appeared in the bottom corner of the screen, showing blurry footage of a running European Werewolf. Not only did this make the Werewolves pause, but the patrons and staff as well. An elderly man whom was paying for his lunch at the register, squinted to see.

"Police are now certain that the animal which killed three people last night including a senior citizen; is the same animal filmed running across the city skyline. Forensics have confirmed the claw marks on the rooftops and on the sides of several buildings, match the claw marks on the victims. DNA analysis has also identified that the droplets of blood left behind by the animal, matched the two African-American men whose remains were found. Investigators have tracked a course mapping the animal's trajectory from the murder scene, down several alleyways and then the fire escape that the creature used to reach the rooftops. However, the animal's escape route abruptly ends in the CBD on top of the Trust Savings & Loans building. Detectives are now interviewing security guards and reviewing the building's security footage, to retrace the predator's steps."

"What, do they think I stopped off to rob a bank along the way?" He muttered under his breath. "Typical of the frickin' media to get THAT wrong!"

With that, Declan grabbed hold of my hand and yanked me out of the café.

I found myself pulled through the park as he marched us away. His hand holding mine was ironclad and he didn't come to a stop until we reached a park bench on the far side of the lagoon. There, he ceremoniously sat me down before he let go. He stood with his back to me, whilst looking out at the row boats on the water.

Neither of us said a thing for a minute or so, as I stared down at the ground and he glared at the water.

At length, he turned around to face his wife. "Have you known since last night?" He asked to which I gave a nod. "Did you smell blood on my breath?" He asked next to which I shook my head. "Did you see me come through the window, when I was covered in blood?" I shook my head again. "Did you see me change back to human and then go for my shower?" I shook my head once more. "OK then B, how do you know?"

Pause... I swallowed hard before I answered without looking up, "I saw."

"You saw?" He gave a funny look. "You saw what, B?"

"Everything."

Silence... he put his hands on his hips as he began to pace left and right.

Then he stopped to ask, "When you say you saw everything, do you mean like in a vision?" I nodded again. "So you saw everything in a vision as a Circulator?" I nodded a third time. "You saw me change and leap out of our hotel window then you saw what I did?"

"I was dreaming about the Voodoo weirdoes inside their shop, putting together a spell." I shook my head. "Then I saw you arrive."

"B," his voice dropped. "I overheard part of their conversation, it was meant for you."

"I know."

"It was some kind of hex using the fangs we saw. They were cooking up a kind of European Vampire Poison Spell against you, using your Greek bracelet. They must have taken it off your arm when they attacked us."

"I know."

"If you know all of this then you know why I stopped them."

"No, they'd already started the spell." I looked up to meet his angry gaze. "But like the snakes, it didn't work on me. Somehow as a Circulator, I'm immune to most of it. Maybe it's because my bio-electromagnetic frequency is in temporal flux? Who knows? But I saw you Declan, you were already hunting them before you found out. Whether they were performing the curse or not, you were gonna kill them."

Instead of protesting his innocence, Declan squared his shoulders as he stood straighter in defiance.

"You're right." He said coolly. "I ended the things which tried to end me and my mate."

I cried out fearfully, "But they were human, Declan! What if the pack finds out? Or what will happen if the Tribal Elders do? What if -"

"Aw, come off it B!" He snorted in disbelief. "Do you think I'd be stupid enough to get in trouble with the pack over THIS?!"

I was about to demand that he explain himself, when I was hit by a new vision. It happened literally, like a smack to the forehead. It made me flinch at first, before I leaned forward whilst closing my eyes...

... when I saw my husband standing in our ensuite, wearing one of the hotel's bathrobes. He looked on his wife's unconscious form, before closing the door for privacy. Next, he made a call on his mobile phone.

"Uncle Declan?" I heard the voice of our First. "What's wrong? We felt that you and Aunt B were in trouble."

"Voodoo." He summed up in one word, before he continued. "We were accosted by three freaks who tried to harvest us and put our parts on the black market."

"Voodoo?" Chiron echoed in surprise.

"They knocked us out with some kind of powder and then tied us up in chains. B woke me just before they stuck a silver blade into my nether regions. Then I dunno what happened, she did something trippy as a Circulator. When she was rescuing me, she made the lights in the room explode. But before we could get away, they frickin' put snakes inside me! So B put me into phase and got them out before she shared her blood."

"Good," he sounded relieved.

"But Chiron?"

"Yes?"

"It was B being a Circulator which attracted them in the first place. The Voodoo Antiques Guy tricked her into revealing her ability to see through time. It made her aura brighter which he could also see." My mate said unhappily.

"What?" He sounded taken aback. "She's not just the tribe's last Light Person, Uncle, but the world's as well. I swore to her grandfather then her father that the pack would protect her -"

"I KNOW all of this!" My husband growled. "You don't think protecting my mate is on my list of priorities, too?"

There was a moment's silence, before he said, "Gertrude sensed a disruption to the balance of light and darkness, the same time the pack felt you were in trouble." He meant one of our Tribal Elders who was also a 'Seer'. "Gertrude felt a cold darkness encroach on Aunt B's warm light. Have your Voodoo attackers been destroyed?"

"No, they ran off and I had snakes inside of me so I couldn't go after 'em."

Next, he offered, "We can call Aunt B's contact at Hodge Endeavor and arrange for a private jet to take us to New Orleans if you need back up."

"Trust me, I DON'T need back up." The European Werewolf snarled. "But I wanna know, do I have permission?"

"Do you feel that these Voodoo practitioners are that dangerous?"

"Besides nearly being skinned alive this afternoon; these freaks have a European Vampire's fangs in a jar, on sale to the public!" He rolled his eyes.

There was another pause, until our First said, "You have our permission."

Simultaneously, both men hung up the phone.

Declan walked out of the ensuite and slipped off the bathrobe. Whilst looking on his sleeping mate, his naked human body began to expand into his huge, hulking, hairless, supernatural shape. His claws pressed into the carpet as he approached the window. Minding his strength, he carefully opened it wide and without even hesitating, he leapt into the night air.

Whereas in Alaska, Chiron lowered his mobile before looking at Gertrude, Meadow, Stone and Forrest, who were sitting in his living room.

"We were right," he said unhappily to the Werewolves. "You were right," he said next to our Tribal Elder. "They were under attack, by Voodoo."

The elderly Lokoti woman's eyes widened fearfully as the Lokoti Werewolves growled threateningly.

"The darkness felt foreign just like it felt cold, it could extinguish her light." Gertrude warned.

"Her mate is ending the darkness now." Chiron proclaimed.

Then the old woman struggled to her feet, with Meadow jumping up to assist.

"Just as it should be," she straightened her back which cracked into place. "We'll use darkness against darkness. Bloodlust verses Black Magic. The green-eyed monster is released from his leash."

Then the scene of Meadow escorting our Tribal Elder disappeared as quickly as the vision had come upon me.

I became aware of my surroundings again as I came back to reality. I no longer saw the events of yesterday, instead I was back in the here and now. I was sitting on a park bench, in front of a lagoon, in a green glade.

When I looked up, I found Declan's eyes were waiting to hold mine. He stood over me with his arms folded, watching closely. When I had stopped talking and leaned forwards with my eyes closed, made him guess I was having a vision. Respectfully, he remained quiet until it was over.

"You ALL knew?!" I cried out indignantly. "Chiron knew... Gertrude knew... Stone knew... Meadow knew and even frickin' Forrest knew... you all KNEW and you DIDN'T tell me?!"

"What did you want me to say?"

"Why did you lie to me?" I asked hurt. "Why did you lie about the bracelet? Why did you sneak out when I was asleep? Why Declan, why?"

Warily, he glanced around to make sure no-one was in earshot before he answered, "Because I didn't want you to look at me like you are now, like I'm a murderer."

My mate stood there with his arms crossed and instead of appearing angry, he looked like he was hurting too.

He said unhappily, "95 years ago I destroyed the female European Werewolf Michelle, for the safety of my mate, our family and the tribe. But that day you looked at me like I was a killer, like I was a man-eater."

I shot to my feet so I could reach out and cup his face between my hands.

I bit out tearfully, "156 years ago you stopped me on the border when I first changed and I nearly ate someone. You stopped ME from becoming a murderer. For my family and my tribe, I learned self control! For 156 years I have banished my cravings for human flesh. I'm scared for you Declan, because as much as you think you're fighting for me? Really, you're losing your self control."

His eyes narrowed again as a cold quality overtook his bright blue colour. Then he surprised me when he cupped my face back, in his much larger hands.

Like this, he leaned in closely to growl out, "Of course I fight for you! You're my mate, you're my B and you're my life! I'll frickin' end anything that looks at you wrong! You're MINE! Your scent, your body and even your aura belongs to me! I will NOT tolerate any threat which could separate us."

With that, Declan took hold of my hand again and stormed out of the park.

I stopped arguing with him for the moment, as it would be as useless as arguing with a brick wall. He had a hard head just like he had a hardened hide. Once he locked onto something, like a decision, there was no letting go.

Instead of catching a tram back to our hotel, he waved down a taxi.

We sat on the back seat, as he glared out one window and I stared out of another. The taxi took us to our hotel but just as it was about to pull up out the front, we saw six police officers and three sniffer dogs. Also, two of the officers were holding forensic scanners, as they stood by the front entrance.

Frickin' hell! Now what do we do? Worriedly, I glanced at Declan who flashed a 'remain calm' look, my way.

"Can you drop us off around the corner, please?" He requested our driver.

The cabby obeyed before stopping along the side of the hotel. Declan handed over his credit card, whereupon the driver processed and returned it. We climbed out when my mate took hold of my hand again.

Warily, we peered around the corner to look at the police who were blocking our way.

I looked to my husband for ideas, as he was watching what the officers were doing.

Two policemen and one policewoman were holding the sniffer dogs, who were acting excited over the trail they'd picked up. The animals strained against their leashes, trying to go inside. The other officers' who were holding the scanners, were waving them around the hotel's doorway.

With our sensitive ears, we overheard one of them speak to somebody via walkie-talkie. "We've checked the hotel's rooftop, there are no claw marks or DNA evidence. The trail ends on top of the Trust Savings & Loans building."

The officer was looking up at the building across the street as he spoke. When we did too, we saw four more police officers standing on the rooftop of the ten story building. Oh oh, that was the roof that my mate had leapt off to land inside our hotel room!

A female voice reported back, "The bank's rooftop security camera confirms the monster was here, along with the drops of blood belonging to the victims. The footage shows the creature leaping over the side which is facing the hotel."

"Copy that," the male officer acknowledged. "But if you don't believe me, you can come and scan the hotel's rooftop yourself."

"That attitude isn't helping, Pete." His female co-worker chastised. "What are the dogs acting so excited about?"

"They've picked up a scent from inside, but the hotel employees haven't seen any large animals which match our predator. A blind guest has a guide dog and a few old ladies have the typical Chihuahua or Pomeranian, but that's it. Have you heard back from Forensics about what kind of animal we're dealing with?"

"That's a negative," the female voice replied.

"Oh come on, this is the 23rd Century!" The male officer exhorted in frustration. "We have spaceships which visit Alpha Centauri! Our scanners can tell me what my partner had for breakfast this morning! Why can't we get a definite, on the kind of animal we're supposed to be hunting?"

"Hey, don't shoot the messenger," the female voice retorted. "Whatever this monster is, it's so screwed up by radiation that it doesn't scan as 'normal' anymore. All we can get is it's some kind of mutant between the ape family and the canine family. It could be a Wes Craven version of 'Lassie', for all we know."

"Copy that," he sighed then he turned his scanner on his partner. "Hmm, waffles for breakfast, eh Tiffany?"

The female officer standing beside whacked him on the arm to 'get serious' and return to work.

I didn't like the looks of those scanners or those sniffer dogs.

"Let's instantaneously phase back to Alaska." I whispered worriedly. But he acted like he didn't hear. I tugged on his arm. "Declan, let's get out of here!"

"Wait, I have an idea." He looked back. "We're gonna walk past and see what happens when they scan us."

I looked on like he was nuts, "Are you for real?!"

"Look, if we run back to Alaska now, we'll be leaving our things inside the hotel room." He pointed out. "We have ID tags on our suitcases, which they can use to track us down."

"Then we'll find an alleyway and I'll instantaneously phase us back inside our hotel room." I thought up. "We'll grab our luggage then I'll take us back to Alaska."

"B, if we leave without paying our bill, the hotel will call the police. The hotel also has a copy of my credit card details from when we checked in!" He hissed back.

"Then we'll call the hotel when we're back in Alaska, lie and say we had to rush back because of a death in the family." I answered. "We'll pay our bill over the phone."

"What if the Police ask if any of their guests have been behaving strangely?" He frowned. "Listen, I remember something that Meadow said when he got his medical scanner last year. He scanned me and said I read as human when I'm in human form. When I'm in my other body, that's when I scan as canine. I mean, the police aren't running deep cellular scans, which is how our amorphous Shape Shifter cells would show up. They're too busy looking for claw prints and the victim's DNA. I can smell I washed off all traces of blood, last night in the shower."

His last sentence made my eyes bulge as horror grabbed hold.

"Declan, there's a tiny drop of blood on our carpet that's the Voodoo Priest's."

That got his attention and he finally looked worried.

"Right, we've got to go back to our hotel room and now." He decided. "So come on."

He tried to tug me along, but I pulled back so hard my hand was freed from his.

"They can't scan me, you idiot!" I lost my patience. "Because you're a European you-know-what, you change more than I do. But as a Lokoti growly-thing, I have a humanoid shape! I won't scan as human or canine, I'll scan as both! And don't forget the police scanned my spilt blood in Scotland, when they investigated Nairn's ransacked house."

At last he understood and he looked from his wife to the police.

"Then I'll go alone." Declan declared. "I'll let them question and scan me and you go to the alleyway behind the hotel and instantaneously phase from there. I'll meet you inside the hotel room."

"No -" I tried to refuse, but it was too late.

Like he was either overconfident or had a death wish, he rounded the corner and walked towards the officers and the dogs.

All I could do was hide behind the wall and watch what took place.

As he approached, the animals barked at him, picking up his supernatural status immediately. Damn it! No wonder pets don't last long on tribal lands and went berserk in our presence. Then I caught with my sensitive ears the European Werewolf's quiet growl. So did the police dogs, who whined and whimpered in terror.

One of the animals took off down the street, like it was running for its life! The policewoman ran after it, as the policemen had to hold onto the other two tightly. The animals crouched low on the ground in a submissive posture, as he neared their handlers.

"Excuse me," the policeman named Pete, called him to a stop.

He'd noticed the reaction and was looking on suspiciously. My husband coolly stood before the authorities, not blinking. The police man and woman carried the scanners over to his position as Declan eyed the technology.

"We're conducting a search after the death of three people last night and need to ask you some questions." Pete spoke formally, as he gazed upon the tall, broad-shouldered, muscled male. "Are you staying in this hotel?"

"I am," he answered.

"What floor are you on?"

"The eighth floor."

"Were you in your hotel room between the hours of 9-11 PM last night?"

"I was."

"Does your room face this street?"

"It does."

"Did you see anything unusual on the rooftop of the opposite building?" Pete pointed across the road.

"Nope," he said and then he snickered. "I wasn't concentrating on the view outside, if you catch my drift."

"Can you tell us what you were doing in your hotel room between 9-11 last night?"

"You mean besides getting lucky?" My mate smirked.

The policeman didn't appreciate his attitude and next he demanded, "Can we see some ID, sir?"

I rolled my eyes as I saw him reach into his backpack and pull out his wallet. I knew our drivers licenses would check out, thanks to the legal department of Hodge Endeavor updating our official documents. The policeman scanned the barcode on the back of his license and looked on the scanner to see if it checked out.

"Alaska?" The policewoman looked at his address in surprise. "You're far from home. What are you doing in New Orleans?"

"Sampling your famous 'night life', if you catch my drift." Declan smiled smugly.

"Can we please see your hands?" Pete ordered crossly.

The policewoman ran her scanner over them, as he looked over her shoulder to see the results.

"They're clean," she read off the small screen on the device. "There's no sign of blood, narcotics, gunpowder, or chemicals used in explosive devices."

However, Pete caught something else on the screen. "Hey Tiff, get a look at this."

She did, before looking on the tall blonde before her. "Do you have a medical condition, sir?"

Oh oh...my stomach wrung itself out and I had to lean on the wall I was hiding behind.

"Yeah, I'm diabetic." Declan lied smoothly. "I have to eat regularly to maintain my blood sugar levels."

"That would explain the unusual level of insulin in his system." Tiff shrugged to her partner.

"But look at his muscle density, there are several abnormally compact layers of cells. Or, what about his organic molecules, don't the atomic bonds seem peculiar to you?"

Oh no, they WERE checking at the cellular level! Worriedly, I watched incase I'd have to instantaneously phase him away if they arrested him. Whereas my cool as a cucumber husband, crossed his arms and glared at his interrogators.

"Alright, you've found me out," he said. "I'm a Werewolf who eats hot dogs, fries and nachos for lunch."

My mouth fell open but the police officers took him for being sarcastic.

"OK smartass," Pete glared back, "I'm getting tired of your attitude. Either drop it or I'll arrest your smart mouth for interfering in an investigation!"

The policewoman waved her scanner over Declan again. "At least he's telling the truth, I can see in his stomach hot dogs, fries, corn chips and other ingredients for nachos. It looks like he had a big breakfast too, there's eggs, bacon, sausage, hash brown, toast and even pancakes with maple syrup."

In surprise, she looked over his muscled build as I guess she was thinking what the waitress did, where did he put it all? Thank goodness for his supernatural metabolism. His body may have craved constant sustenance, but it was fast to use it up. The Voodoo Priest and Antiques Guy had been completely digested.

"How do you work out?" She asked impressed.

Pete rolled his eyes. "Sorry Tiff, the guy's taken. Can't you see the wedding ring on his finger?"

Her face reddened as her partner handed him back his driver's license. But the egotistical European Werewolf took it all in his stride. He even gave her a wink as he returned his wallet inside his backpack.

"Thank you Mr. Sabre for your cooperation, you may go." The policeman said dismissively.

"Thanks," he gloatingly sung. "The said wife is waiting for me upstairs. She has quite the appetite herself. She can't get enough of me, heh heh!"

Then the officers watched the cocky male disappear into the hotel via the automatic doors.

Quickly, I rushed around to the back where the staff entrance was. However, I didn't need to use it, just its privacy. In a bright flash of light, I disappeared out of the alleyway and reappeared inside our hotel room.

It was just in time too, as the door opened with Declan's arrival.

As soon as he closed it behind himself, he scanned the floor with his eyes. I watched him sniff as he moved closer to the spot on the carpet. Within seconds he found it and he dropped to his hands and knees to inhale deeply.

"Yep, it's the Voodoo Priest's blood alright." He said unhappily.

I leant against the wall with my arms folded and glared at him.

However, he ignored my accusatory gaze as he looked like he was planning something. He raised himself to his feet and passed a playful grin.

Then he offered, "How about we celebrate getting past the cops downstairs with some wine and cheese?"

What the...? I looked on like he'd gone mental! Then I watched him walk over to the hotel's phone. He winked at me as he picked it up and made the call.

"Yeah hi, I'd like to order Room Service please. Yup. I'd like to get the Fruit and Cheese Platter as well as a bottle of Cab Sav. Yep. Ten minutes? Thanks." He spoke before hanging up.

He dropped his backpack on top of the bed then he walked into the ensuite to wash his hands. I came to stand in the bathroom doorway and watch as he turned on the taps. He smiled back via the mirror as he took his sweet time. He was deliberately acting prodigious about cleanliness.

"Declan, you've officially gone insane."

After he washed them thoroughly, he dried them thoroughly. Eventually he replied, "As Baldrick said to Blackadder, 'I have a cunning plan'."

Then he brushed past as he walked back out and this time he didn't give my waist an affectionate rub.

I objected, "But we DON'T drink! Not unless you wanna get blotto, lose control of your bloodlust again and go on another killing rampage!"

He ignored me as he walked over to the window. Next, he parted the curtains and looked out at the police on the rooftop across. I stood next to him and we both frowned as we saw them collect their forensic evidence.

Lastly, he closed the curtains again to give us and our murder scene some privacy.

Just then there was a knock on the door, which made me jump!

"That was fast," he said impressed as he walked over to answer it. "Thank you, come in."

A uniformed staff member came in carrying a tray. She placed it on the small table by the wall and then smiled and departed. My husband helped himself to lifting up the lid on the Fruit and Cheese Platter. Immediately he cut into the brie, placing the parts onto two water crackers and he held one out to me.

How can he think about eating at a time like this?! I looked on incredulous as I didn't take him up on his offer. So he greedily popped his biscuit and cheese into his mouth, as well as mine. Next, he picked up the bottle of wine and opened it.

"Declan -" I stepped forward to stop him, when I didn't have to.

He tipped the open bottle upside down and poured out the entirety onto the carpet where the tiny drop of blood was!

"Whoops," he said flatly, as he dropped the now empty bottle onto the floor beside the spill.

Oh, I started to see method to his madness... The red wine will stain the carpet so when the hotel staff use their powerful cleaning equipment to remove it, they'll also remove the blood. No-one will be the wiser and the evidence will no longer exist. I looked on the murderer who was my husband, impressed.

"You see, there are good points to being married to a smartass predator." He said. "With my supernatural senses, I certainly know how to cover my tracks."

And then I saw it, his pain behind his sarcasm. It flickered across his face before being replaced with annoyance. He turned away to sit tiredly on the end of the bed and rub his forty-something face.

The scene reminded me of another moment in time, when we fought over annihilating Michelle. Only it was me who sat on the end of the bed whilst Declan knelt on the floor in front of me. This inspired me to try something.

To his surprise, I knelt on the floor before him. I rested my hands on his knees as I gazed up into his eyes. He gave a peculiar look, as I think this posture unsettled him.

"Please don't, Declan." I began. "Please don't do again what you did last night. I understand you did it because you thought you were fighting for me. But please, don't do it again."

"Don't do *it* again?" He arched his eyebrows.

"Don't kill people." I pleaded. "Not for me, not ever."

"Frickin' hell, B!" He growled as he stood up and moved away. "You really don't think about what comes out of your mouth, do you? You KNOW what I am! You KNOW what you are! You KNOW why our kind was put on this piece of rock, spinning around in space; because we ARE predators! We hunt and we feed and we copulate!"

Disheartened, I turned around and sat on the floor, resting my back against the bed. I hated it when he talked like this, because it didn't sound like it was him, but his bloodlust. Sometimes it scared me, as it made me ponder who was in control, his reasoning or his primal urges?

He ranted, "Sure there are some of our kind like the Lokoti, who can change their eating habits. Then there are others like me, who have to struggle every day! But because of my Mom and Derik and your Grandfather and for you, I beat my demons and resisted my cravings. But as soon as I feel that my mate is in danger, woe be tied and hell be damned to the threat which tips my precarious control over the edge!"

No, don't tell me this was my fault...? Does this mean Declan wouldn't have avenged himself on our attackers, if he didn't think he was doing it for me? He did say he killed Michelle for me. I buried my face in my hands, as I felt like the bloodied weapon in a murder trial.

I couldn't live with myself if that was the case. I DID NOT want to be the reason for my mate's downfall into damnation. I can't remain as his wife if I'm his bad influence. I just can't. A sickening sense of utter hopelessness settled over me and I felt weak with desolation.

"Aw, come off it B!" He rolled his eyes. "Don't look so frickin' tragic, like you're Lady Macbeth who feels guilty over helping her husband kill the King."

I raised my knees as I hugged my legs tightly. Although my heart was hurting, rationally I tried to plan what to do. I wouldn't be able to simply leave my husband, as there's the risk he'd follow. I'd have to relocate to another era to completely separate from him. Frickin' hell, I'm back to moving to Canada again...

"Fine!" He huffed. "Wrong analogy, you didn't help me and you didn't know what I was going to do. Your hands are clean!"

Screw Canada, no offence to the Canadians. If I'm going to move out of Alaska, I want to try somewhere new. Maybe I could live in Edwardian England? That might be fun, it was the richest country for that period and I could live comfortably. Maybe I'd live in a country manor, so I could hunt livestock on a full moon.

"B, stop it."

Mind you, hunting penned in sheep and cattle wouldn't pose much thrill for the bloodlust. I'd also have to be very careful about not being seen, either as a Circulator or a Werewolf. English manors were full of servants, who might pry and gossip. Meanwhile, I'd never have sex again, since I was a Lokoti Werewolf and we mate once for life. I'd be without my other half and his touch, his smell, his hard body, his hot skin...

"B, what are you worrying about now? Your aura has faded so much, it's almost non-existent!"

To his surprise, I rasped in pain as my heart emitted a painful spasm.

"B!" He knelt before me to make me meet his angry gaze. "You're fretting about something, now what is it?"

My eyebrows rose as I stared at the red wine stain. "What does my aura look like, Declan? Can you really tell my emotional states from it?"

"Pretty much," he admitted. "I may not be able to empathically feel what you're going through, but I can guess from seeing your aura change."

I remained quiet to prompt him to continue, so he did.

"Usually, your aura looks like a white line around your body, or over your uncovered skin anyways. When you get angry it turns blue and looks like you have these tiny sparks shooting outwards. I think its how you managed to affect the electromagnetic field in the basement yesterday. When you're happy, you glow a yellow colour. But when you're sad or you're weakened, it can fade."

"Are there other colours as well?"

"Most of the time it's a white line, but when you're feeling something intensely, it changes. When we make love, sometimes it turns a peach colour. It's how I know you're enjoying it."

"And when I'm sick?" I continued. "Or if I'm injured?"

"It doesn't change colour, it dims. Twice now it's completely faded."

"When was that?"

He said soberly, "When you were shot in the head and died. The other time was when you were impaled by that European Vampire. After our run in with Voodoo, I could tell it weakened you as your aura faded again."

"Oh." I said flatly. "I sound like a frickin' Christmas Tree."

Declan chuckled as he collapsed to sit beside with his back against the bed too.

"I never thought of it like that, thanks for the image." He joked. "Next Christmas I won't go into the woods and chop down a tree. Instead, I'll just put you in the corner with tinsel wrapped around."

"And - and - and when I'm scared?" I uttered out. "What about when I'm scared?"

"It dims, like it's doing right now." He frowned.

I lifted up my hand in front of my face to stare at it. It looked like a plain, old, ordinary, woman's hand to me. I didn't see any white lines, or colours, or sparks or anything. It looked pretty boring, actually.

Next, my husband sandwiched my hand in between his two. Then he parted them slightly, so there was a one centimetre gap between our skin.

"Here," his voice turned soft, "your aura is right here."

"Are your hands touching it?"

"Yep."

"Can you feel it?"

"Yes."

I removed my hand as I snorted in disbelief, "Yeah right!"

"I can see it, I can feel it and hell, I can even smell it." He said smoothly.

"You can not!"

"I've told you that you smell like a vase of wildflowers sitting in a kitchen while a cake is baking in the oven." He reminded. "Your aura is the wildflowers and your body is the cake that's baking in the oven."

"No way!"

"Yes way!" He retorted. "You're not just the only lay I've ever had, but with your aura, it's like looking at and smelling, let alone touching heaven every day. Why do you think I fight to keep not only my paradise, but my salvation? And when it curls up to me in the middle of the night, I'd push aside David and take on an army of Goliaths for you."

His magic words did the trick, my heart stopped hurting.

To his pleasant surprise, I crawled into his lap and sat there like that, facing him. He closed his eyes to savour the moment when I leaned in and slowly kissed him. His arms wrapped around my waist and soon his lips took over as he responded hungrily.

"And what about my lips... can you feel my aura... when you kiss me on the lips?" I breathed out.

"Uh huh," he kissed me again as if to demonstrate.

The tips of our tongues met before twisting around each other, as his hot, wet mouth smothered mine over and over again.

Momentarily, I pulled away to giggle girlishly, "And what about my tongue? Do I have an aura around my tongue?" Then to demonstrate, I stuck it out at him.

"Uh huh," he teasingly tried to bite it.

"Really?"

"You have an aura around every single part of you."

"And my nails and my hair?"

"They're part of you, aren't they?"

"What about when I cut them?"

"Then they're no longer part of you so no, they don't."

I gave a funny look, "I feel a little uncomfortable that you seem to know more about me than I do myself."

"I don't know more, I only know *one thing* because I see it everyday. I mean, I didn't know you could do what you did yesterday, to the lights in the basement. I didn't know you could put me into phase and remove the snakes that way." He reasoned.

"That's because I've never done it before."

"So how did you know that you could then?"

"I dunno," I shrugged. "It was part instinct and part study. I read in my great, great grandmother's diary she did the thing with the lights by accident at her engagement party, when she saw this girl she didn't like."

Declan laughed out loud, "That's better than a catfight!"

"Meeow!" I joined in.

"You do that a little too well for a Werewolf," he smirked as he held me closer. So I emitted a growl instead, which made him smile contentedly. "That's better."

He leaned in to graze my throat with his teeth and I heard as well as felt, a deep, rumbling growl, come up from his chest and out of his parted lips.

"That's *definitely* better," I tittered, as I wrapped my arms about his neck.

~~~~~~

~ 16 ~

After our latest marriage crisis was diverted, or swept under the carpet and deliberately forgotten about; we tried to make the best of what was left of our holiday.

For some reason I still felt as weak as I did after the Voodoo attack. Whenever I stood up from sitting or lying down, the head-spins almost made me fall down again. However, I tried to carry on as normal because I wanted my husband to have a good time.

On our last evening in New Orleans, we did go back to the Creole restaurant in the French Quarter.

The atmosphere was festive, with a brass band playing 'Bayou Blues' and the restaurant had a dance floor. This time I didn't ask Declan to dance, as I didn't have the energy for it. We were content to sit at our table and watch everyone else instead.

Besides, we ordered quite the feast for dinner. For our entree, we shared the Oysters Rockefeller which were baked with green herbs, butter sauce and breadcrumbs. For the soup, we each had a bowl of Shrimp Gumbo. Declan ate the Jambalaya for his main, a rice dish that had shrimp, ham, tomato and Andouille sausage in it. I ordered the Lobster Creole and in exchange for him using his strength to easily crack open the shell for me, I shared some of the succulent flesh. Lastly for dessert, he had Pecan Pie and I ate the Bread Pudding with Vanilla Whisky Sauce.

However, when it came time to leave the restaurant, Declan had to put out his arm to steady me. I think I stood up from my chair too fast, as I rose from our table and almost fell into the one beside! The couple who were having a romantic dinner of their own, passed a peculiar look my way.

"B, you look like you're drunk." He said disconcerted.

"Sorry," I blushed.

"And you didn't finish your main or your dessert." He frowned. "What's wrong, you don't like Creole food?"

"No, it was delicious," I promised. "I'm just not that hungry."

I wasn't lying either. For the rest of the holiday, I struggled to even consume half of what was put in front of me. There was nothing wrong with the food, but nausea would overtake my stomach after the first few mouthfuls.

Another unusual thing was I felt so cold I'd need to wear a sweater on a 30 degrees Celsius day. Declan would be sweating in a singlet top and gave a funny look when I pulled on the extra layer. In air conditioning I'd absolutely freeze. When we were in the rental car, I'd point all the air vents in his direction and hunker down into my seat with a sweater over me.

I didn't sleep well either as I constantly had nightmares, or that's what I hoped they were. When my eyes would begin to close, I thought I saw three dark shadows standing at the end of the bed! They looked like three people, with the third slightly shorter, as if it were a woman standing between two men.

Whenever I looked at them directly, the shadows faded from my sight. However, I swear the room dropped temperature by one or two degrees, indicating they were somewhere near. Nervously, I looked about our hotel room, trying to spot them.

The first time it happened on our last night in New Orleans, I surprised my husband by suddenly sitting upright in bed.

"Hmm...?" He stirred. "What is it?"

But by the time he'd woken, the shadows had disappeared. I knew he wouldn't see them. So like lying about my physical health, I fibbed about my sound of mind too.

"Nothing," I said vacantly. "It's nothing."

"Are you cold again?" He wondered. "I think the air conditioning must be playing up, as it's dropped a few degrees."

Then his large arm wrapped about my waist and he pulled me back down, so I was lying against his side.

"Go back to sleep, baby." He mumbled out sleepily. "We have an early start in the morning."

He was right, we checked out of our hotel at 8 AM to drive out of town.

We had morning tea in Biloxi Mississippi, lunch in Prichard Alabama then a late dinner in Tallahassee Florida, where we overnighted.

I tossed and turned so much that Declan gave up trying to spoon me, instead he slept with his arm outstretched so I could rest my cheek on it. A couple of times I snuggled into his side and used his body heat as an additional blanket. However, it didn't last long from what disturbed my slumber.

The temperature in the room began to drop, which gave me goose bumps. I half opened my eyes to take a peek then they bulged, as abruptly I sat upright. My eyes turned turquoise and my lips parted in a snarl, as my teeth and nails extended.

I saw them with my supernatural sight which made the dark as clear as day.

The three shadows stood at the end of the bed. Although they were formless, I couldn't see through them. They had mass, even if they didn't have a heartbeat or a living body.

"B, what are you growling at?" My husband stirred. "Did you have a bad dream?"

But by the time he sat up whilst rubbing sleep from his eyes, they were gone.

I sniffed the room to pick up a lingering scent but they left no evidence behind.

"C'mon," he pulled me into his arms. "It's just the air conditioning playing up again. I'll warm you."

He tried to move into our customary position where he slept over me, but I wouldn't let him. Tonight my guard was up, the shadows could come back. Although my teeth and nails had retracted, my eyes were still glowing.

"Go back to bed, babe." He yawned out. "We're driving to Orlando tomorrow, which you've been looking forward to. Soon you'll be seeing Disneyworld and Epcot."

I thought I'd check, "Declan do you smell something?"

"Nup," he closed his eyes as he spooned me from behind. "It's just the typical damp air an air conditioner pumps out."

Easily, he slipped back into sleep whereas I stayed up half the night, afraid to close my eyes.

The following morning we zoomed down the freeway towards our next stop. We were planning to stay in Orlando for two nights, before driving onwards to Miami for another two. Then we'd fly up to Washington DC and hop in another rental, to visit the top half of the country for three weeks. We'd toured the bottom half for the other three, starting in San Francisco then LA, next to Las Vegas and then the Grand Canyon and so on.

I felt exhausted with sleeplessness on top of the dizzy spells. I think Declan could tell, as he tried to make me eat all of my breakfast. I think he was following his motto that food could cure all ills.

In the car, I fidgeted with the internet radio as I tried to find a classic rock station. However, I accidentally hit the news channel and we heard part of a report. When he tried to change it, I held his hand back so I could hear what was happening.

"The New Orleans Police Department states that forensics have finally advised what kind of animal they are looking for. In spite of eye witness reports, the DNA extracted from the saliva on two of the victims did not come from a bear, but a type of wolf. Police have advised that Federal National Parks and Wildlife Services employees have joined officers to track down the unusual suspect. Working from security camera footage and genetic evidence, authorities have created a profile of the animal. The police and rangers are using the representation as well as forensic scanners, to search Louisiana and its neighbouring states Texas, Arkansas and Mississippi."

Declan's hand pushed past my own and he switched off the sound system.

"Relax B, they're not gonna find jack." He said annoyed. "I can't imagine the police searching for a Werewolf, can you?"

I turned quiet as concerned, I looked out my window.

He continued, "Humans can't comprehend us. In the Middle Ages we were called demons then science came up with the word lycanthropy, a mental illness that afflicted humans had who said they could change into wolves. Mankind has never got us right and I doubt that they'll start now."

"At least you look completely different in your other body." I sighed. "As long as you remain in your human form, you'll never be identified."

"That and I scan as mostly human in human form," he added on.

"If they had scanned me back in New Orleans, who knows what would have happened." I gazed out the windscreen.

Declan took hold of my hand and held it firmly in his, as his other was on the wheel.

"I know." He said seriously. "Why do you think you're not allowed to fight alongside the males in the pack? Not just because we're stronger than you, but you'd be recognized most of all, being the only female. We're not just protecting your safety, but your anonymity."

I joked, "And all this time, I thought it was your bloodlust refusing to share your kill. That, or your giant ego thinking you can take on the world."

"No, it was the male brain which operates on logic instead of the female brain which operates on emotions." He replied coolly.

Then he winked, showing he was joking too which made me snicker.

"You'd better hope that I operate on emotions, I mean how else do I put up with you?" I moved his hand to my mouth to playfully bite it.

"And here I thought it was because as a male, I was just using you for sex." He smirked, before moving my hand to his mouth to kiss.

A soft smile played on my lips as I looked his way. But when I turned my head towards the windscreen again, I screamed! The three dark shadows were right in front of us, on the other side of the glass.

Declan slammed on the breaks! Our rental came to a screeching halt whilst the cars behind had to swerve or hit us. They beeped in protest as they passed, with one giving us the finger.

"B, what is it?!" He cried out in alarm as he frantically looked this way and that. "Did I hit something?"

I sat as still as a rock, petrified with fear, staring out the windscreen. He looked from me to the road ahead then back to me. He clearly couldn't see the three dark shadows which were standing on the bonnet of the car.

"What is it?" He grabbed hold of my arm. "What's wrong?"

I pointed out the windscreen at them as they began to turn see-through. They were fading away again, disappearing back into the nothingness they came from. He looked out the windscreen, but still he couldn't see anything. Soon we were staring at the sunlight glinting off the silver coloured bonnet.

More cars sped past, beeping at the weirdoes who'd stopped in the middle lane. My husband put his foot down on the accelerator again and he pulled off the road, so we weren't in anyone's way. Still I didn't move, as I sat staring out the windscreen.

"B, your aura has almost vanished, now what is it?" He cupped my face to make me look at him. "Are you sick or scared?"

My eyes watered as it all came pouring out like a confession, "I think I'm both. I see them Declan, or I think it's them. Three dark shadows are following us since the death of the Voodoo Practitioners. Two of the shadows are as tall as men with the third as short as a woman."

My husband pulled back to look on his wife in a combination of shock and disbelief.

Then he asked in a low voice, "You see dead people?"

I cried out helplessly, "I know how this sounds! That's why I haven't said anything until now. I've seen dead people before, but usually they're after images when their energy leaves the timeline. I saw Derik as an 18 year old again when he passed away from old age."

This made his eyes widen as he glanced away, as the memory still affected him.

"That's how I sensed he'd died right after Rachel." I continued. "Then on our last night in New Orleans, I saw the three shadows standing at the end of our bed. Then again in Tallahassee and now they appeared on top of the bonnet of the car. And I know I'm not imagining it, because I've even seen them with my Werewolf sight."

"So that's why you were growling at something in the room last night?" He checked.

"Yes!"

He turned thoughtful as he looked from me then back out of the windscreen. "Are they here right now?"

"No, they've gone again."

"Where were they?"

"They were standing on the bonnet of the car and looking at us through the windscreen." I pointed.

"And it's definitely the Voodoo psychos?"

"I can't see them clearly, they just look like shadows." I faltered. "But their height -"

"- is the same as the two men and one woman that I killed." He finished for me.

"Yes."

Suddenly he surprised me by pounding the steering wheel with his fist! "Damn it, B! Why didn't you tell me sooner?"

"I didn't know if you'd believed me," I answered.

"Of course I believe you!" He said indignantly. "You're a Circulator, you can see the past and the future! Your warning feelings are always right! Four days ago, you saved my life by putting me into phase and getting five snakes out of my stomach! B, I'd frickin' believe you if you said that the earth wasn't round!"

Although I felt elated by his confidence in my ability, Declan was still angry.

He growled under his breath as he pulled his mobile phone out of his pocket. Then he opened his door, got out of the car and made a call. I got out of the car too, but then I had to hold onto the door as my head spun from standing up. He noticed this too, which made him roll his eyes and turn away.

"Chiron," he greeted. "You felt B's fear just then? Yeah, she's scared because she's being haunted by the Voodoo psychos. She's weak, she can't stand up without getting dizzy and she's not eating properly. To top it off, she can't sleep because dead people are standing at the end of our bed!"

Pause... then I watched his eyes widen as he looked further worried.

He echoed, "Gertrude can still see darkness surrounding her? A Voodoo spell? Yeah, but I stopped them before they could finish it! Right. OK then. We're coming home today, we'll call you back when we know flight details."

Declan hung up and headed back to the driver's side of the car.

"C'mon," he said gruffly. "We'll drop off the vehicle at the rental company at Orlando Airport then we're outta here."

I felt bad that another holiday was being ruined and maybe it was my fault. I hesitated as I tried to think of a solution. Maybe I could do something as a Circulator? Could I use my light to repel them? What if I tried to fight them in phase?

"B, can you please get in the car?" He hurried me along.

I surprised him when I said back, "No."

"No?"

"No Declan, we're not cutting short another holiday because of this." I said stubbornly.

"B, don't be stupid." He rolled his eyes. "Just get in the car, we're going home!"

"No."

He said tiredly, "Please get in the car and we'll fight about this on our way home."

"Declan," I walked around the car to stand before him. "I want us to have a nice, normal vacation of what's left of it. We can't let them ruin our 150th Wedding Anniversary. You planned this trip for months."

This made him smile as he placed his hand on my arm to give an affectionate squeeze. Then his smile faded and a glare took its place. He lectured as he walked me back to the passenger's side:

"Honey, if a Tribal Elder back in Alaska, is seeing darkness close in on you when we're all the way in Florida? It means it's time to go home so the said Tribal Elder and our Medicine Man, can undo the Voodoo curse. Now get your married ass into the car and let's get a move on."

"A Voodoo curse?" I repeated in disbelief. "But I'm a Circulator, it shouldn't work on me. The spell with the snakes didn't work, so why would this?"

"Yeah but because you're a Circulator, you can see things that I can't!"

He held open the door for me however I hesitated so I could debate this further.

"I don't understand how you can see my aura, but you can't see the three shadows following us?"

"Because I'm a frickin' European Werewolf, not a Circulator! I don't have visions like you do!" He snapped then he took a deep breath to reign in his temper. "Look baby, please just get in the car and co-operate. For me? It can even be my wedding anniversary present."

A moment passed as I looked from his bright blue eyes back to the grey leather upholstery of the car, before I reluctantly climbed in.

"Thank you!" He cried out, as he raised his eyes to the heavens above.

Then he rushed around the vehicle to his seat. He was so anxious to get underway, he slammed his door so hard that it rocked the vehicle. I passed him a tired look of my own, however he didn't see. With one hand on the wheel and the other on my leg, he rejoined the traffic on the freeway.

*****

A couple of hours later, we dropped off the hire car at one of the rental outlets at Orlando Airport.

Next, we wheeled our suitcases into the terminal as we proceeded to a counter to buy our tickets.

"We need two seats to Fairbanks, please." He told the airline staff member.

"To Fairbanks?" She echoed in surprise. "You mean in Alaska?"

"That would be it," he said coolly as he fished out his wallet.

The girl busied herself by typing into her computer. Then she read off the screen, "I can put you on the flight to Seattle that's departing in 45 minutes, but the only seats left are in First Class. Then from Seattle, there's a flight to Fairbanks."

"No problem," he tapped on the counter with his credit card. "Actually, if we can have First Class seats all the way, I don't mind paying the extra."

With his height and muscles, he needed the room. Once we flew Economy and he was squashed in so tight, he could barely move. This was especially annoying for the other guests who were seated on either side of him. We kept getting elbowed when he tried to eat and in the end he got a leg cramp.

"You have a three hour stopover in Seattle before your flight to Fairbanks." She advised as she busily tapped away on her touch screen computer.

"Fine," he said curtly. "So what's the damage?"

"That will be six thousand credits altogether," she announced. "Did you want me to check if there were Business Class seats on the other flights, so it'll be cheaper?"

"Nope," he shook his head. "We'll take what we can get."

Just as he was about to hand her his credit card, I stopped him.

"Give us a second please." I said to the girl, before I pulled my mate away from the counter. "Why are we flying? If it's so important we get back to Alaska ASAP then I'll instantaneously phase us home."

"As much as I want to rush home, we need to do this the 'normal' way," he said quietly.

"Why?"

"Because we have to leave a paper trail and be sighted on the planes," he continued.

"Why?"

"Look around us," he glanced about.

So I did, but I tried to do it subtly. I saw several security guards standing around the metal detector, as well as holding other scanning devices. There were also a couple of police officers with them and more standing around the exits of the Airport. They seemed to be looking for something or someone, and paid particular interest to anyone with pets.

"Are there more police around than usual?" I remarked.

"Uh huh."

"Because of what happened in New Orleans?"

"Yup."

"But I thought that the police were looking for a wolf." I frowned.

Declan pulled his phone out of his pocket once more, to show me a news story on the screen.

POLICE ARE INTERVIEWING DOG HANDLERS WHO MAY HAVE TRAINED THE MUTANT WOLF. AFTER FURTHER ANALYSIS OF THE FOOTAGE BY FEDERAL WILDLIFE EXPERTS, THEY BELIEVE IT HAD BEEN TRAINED TO LOOK FOR A FIRE ESCAPE TO REACH THE ROOFTOPS AND HOW TO CLIMB LADDERS. AS THE ANIMAL'S DISAPPEARANCE IN THE CBD REMAINS UNEXPLAINED, IT'S BELIEVED IT RAN TO A MEETING POINT WHERE A TRUCK MAY HAVE PICKED IT UP. POLICE ARE ALSO ANALYZING TRAFFIC CAMERAS TO LOOK FOR ANY SUSPICIOUS VEHICLES LEAVING THE CBD AREA.

"It'll look unusual if we suddenly reappear in Alaska. By travelling the ordinary way, we can show copies of tickets and boarding passes. We can't be looking suspicious at a time like this." He warned.

Then he turned back to the girl behind the counter, "I'll pay for those flights, please."

"No, wait!" I stepped up beside. "You paid for the trip, I'll pay for the early return home."

"B -"

"Here we go," I shoved my credit card into her hand before he could.

After I paid for the flights we checked-in our luggage. Then to get to our gate, we had to go through the security scanners. We've never had a problem with these scanners before, as they didn't scan the person internally but externally.

I walked through the security check first as Declan walked right behind me. The police as well as guards watched the computer screens carefully, to spot any abnormalities. My heart was pounding as I tried hard to carry on as normal.

"Excuse me," a loud voice sung out.

We froze as two security guards and policemen walked towards us. But then they kept walking, to pull up the man behind. My heart felt like it had stopped in fright, before racing onwards.

"Can you please empty your pockets, sir?" The Police Officer demanded. "Yes, we mean the one inside your jacket too."

We exchanged glances as Declan walked forwards to take hold of my hand. He gripped onto it hard as we walked to our departure gate. I don't think either of us relaxed until we were sitting on the plane.

As soon as we were in the air we emitted sighs of relief. Also, I loved takeoffs and landings as I enjoyed the rush and the inertia. I think so did Declan, as he leaned over me to look out the window. Maybe it was because we could run in supernatural speed, we enjoyed going fast period.

Once the rushing ground was replaced with sky, we both sat back in our seats.

"We're going home, Mrs. Sabre." He passed a grin.

"Thank god," I sung.

Declan patted my hand then he picked up the menu by his seat. As he scanned the list of food and drink, I read over his shoulder. When I made note of what I wanted, I glanced out the window.

Abruptly, I shoved my face into his hot chest to calm myself, as I breathed in his maple syrup scent.

"Er, did you just see them again?" He asked in surprise.

I gave a single nod and he wrapped his arms about his wife.

"Try not to look at them." He whispered in my ear. "Let's see if the ole saying 'ignore them and they'll go away', works."

I nodded again whilst keeping my face tucked into his t-shirt and he began to stroke my back.

When Declan noticed another passenger looking on peculiarly, he lied with, "Fear of flying."

"Ah," the man looked like he understood. "I used to be too, but you know what helps?"

Then the stranger toasted him with a glass of whisky.

"We can't drink," he rolled his eyes. "Times like this make me wish we could, but we can't."

"Ah," the man looked like he understood something else. "I used to be on the wagon, six months sober."

"What happened?" He gave a funny look.

"My promotion involved frequent business trips," the man gulped down the last of his beverage.

*****

The flight from Orlando to Seattle was mostly smooth sailing. My husband made sure we got our money's worth by ordering dish after dish. I snacked on a packet of mixed nuts then some biscuits and cheese, as he ate the nuts, biscuits and cheese, an entree, the main and then dessert. We were offered champagne, but we shook our heads and ordered some kind of soda instead.

To ignore the shadows outside my window, I kept occupied by watching the in-flight entertainment. Thankfully the ghosts remained outside of the plane, although I was curious why they didn't come inside. It was as if they had to keep a distance while they were following us.

We encountered turbulence between Idaho and Washington State, so bad that the Flight Attendants stopped serving food and drinks. The seat belt sign came on and the plane shook dangerously, even the Attendants had to be seated. The plane dipped then climbed before dipping again.

I could tell the turbulence made Declan uneasy, as he squeezed my hand so hard that his knuckles turned white.

"If the plane goes down, you can phase us to safety before we hit the ground, right?" He whispered worriedly.

Now it was my turn to reassure, "We're not going to die in a plane crash."

Suddenly the plane dipped again, leaving our stomachs in our mouths.

He swallowed hard, "Wouldn't it be funny if one of our kind died that way; in a plane crash." Then he lowered his voice, "Or maybe we'd live? But I suppose it'd cause suspicion if we were the only two to walk away from the wreckage."

"Declan, relax."

"Relax? Relax? Who says I'm not relaxed?" He laughed nervously. "This must be the worst turbulence ever and with our age, that's saying a lot."

I turned to look out the window to see what the weather was like outside. The clouds looked black and angry, with continuous streaks of lightning. Then I think I scared him more, by how quickly I turned again to stare at the seat in front.

"They're still there?" He guessed and when I nodded he moaned. "Man, this has to be the WORST flight ever! This even beats the time they served bad chicken which almost gave me diarrhoea."

Suddenly the plane dipped again and we heard the engines strain as the pilots fought to stabilize the aircraft.

"Y-y-yeah I'd agree to that." I stammered out.

Then he looked my way in dread. "Hey, you don't think it's the Voodoo crazies who are causing the turbulence, do you?"

I shook my head. "They're not that powerful, otherwise I'd feel them affecting the electromagnetic field around the plane."

"Well at least that's somethin'." He managed out.

However, his hand was gripping onto mine so hard that it started to hurt.

"Dec?"

"Yeah?"

"You're about to break my hand."

"Oh." He released it. "Sorry."

Then I put my hand over his instead and our fingers entwined.

*****

Forty minutes later, our plane landed safely in Seattle and we found we weren't the only terrified ones on board. The passengers erupted into applause, loud enough for the pilots to hear. We exchanged surprised glances as we too began to clap.

"I think I'm gonna need one for the road," the alcoholic/fear-of-flying/business executive told the Attendant.

Then he slipped three tiny bottles of whisky into his briefcase before disembarking.

Since our journey to Fairbanks was considered to be a connecting flight, we didn't have to worry about collecting our luggage and checking-in again. So we had three hours in Seattle Airport with nothing to do but wander around. Naturally, my husband found the food court to eat even more.

"Not again!" I whined.

"Don't you complain," he growled warningly. "You barely ate anything on the plane so I'm half doing this for you."

"What, you're stuffing your face for the sake of your wife?" I raised my eyebrows.

"Shut up." He said then looked around the court. "So what do you feel like? There's hamburgers, pasta, kebabs, Indian, Chinese and even Japanese."

"Hmmm, I haven't had sushi in a while." I shrugged back.

Declan passed a peculiar look, "They were serving smoked salmon on the plane!"

"Shut up." I repeated.

Then I headed towards the Sushi Train as he headed for the hamburgers.

We ate our take-away together in front of a wall of glass which showed the planes moving to and fro along the concourse.

There were several plasma, flat-screen televisions hanging from the ceiling. Most were showing times for arrivals and departures, but the odd one was for the Internet TV. A news channel was on, with subtitles appearing at the bottom of the screen, so we'd know what the news reader was saying.

"Hey B," he nudged my side.

I looked up from my Salmon and Avocado Nori Rolls, chopsticks and small bowl of Soy Sauce and Wasabi.

The news story was about a tornado which had touched down in Montana, which also explained the storm system we encountered over Idaho. It looked to be a bad one, too. Experts were calling it an F4 and it had annihilated two towns.

Several shots of families crying over missing loved ones, flashed across the screen.

"That's strange," I frowned. "Montana isn't in Tornado Alley."

He guiltily looked my way, "It wasn't the Voodoo ghosts, was it?"

"No," I shook my head. "If they're not strong enough to affect a plane, they can't possibly manipulate a storm system."

"Are you sure?"

"Yeah because they have to alter the cumulonimbus cloud into a Supercell, which turns rain to hail and affects the up drafts and down drafts enough to turn into a singular circulating motion."

"Gees B, I should buy you a pair of black rimmed glasses for when you go all nerdy like this." He chuckled.

However I didn't laugh and this time I nudged him, as the screen showed a bawling five year old clinging to her injured grandmother. The caption underneath read that the older woman was caring for her, as the parents were grocery shopping. The woman was wounded by debris whilst lying protectively over her granddaughter. Now the parents were missing and the grandmother's house was blown away. This made my chest hurt and eyes water, so much so I pulled out my mobile phone.

"Cassie? It's me, B." I stood up and walked a little away. "Have you seen the news about the tornado? Well, an F4 wiped out two towns in Montana. I want to use Hodge Endeavor's charity organizations to help out."

I lost my appetite again and all I wanted to do was sit out the last two hours in the departure lounge.

Our plane hadn't arrived at the gate yet, which would transport us home to 'the last frontier'. We were the only people in the lounge, as a steady stream of travellers coursed along the walkway. But I appreciated the partial isolation, as I felt emotionally wrung out.

The European Werewolf was restless though, he couldn't sit in the one place for long. Periodically, he'd stand up and walk around to stretch his legs. He'd look out the window at the empty space where the plane would dock, before walking over to another Internet TV to see what was on.

"You go," I said.

"Go where?"

"Go back to the Food Court, or go and look at the shops or something."

"I'm not interested in shopping." He returned. "That's your deal, remember?"

"You don't have to buy anything, just look around."

"Nah."

"Why not?"

"Because you're here," he said simply.

"We're not stuck together like Conjoined Twins," I tried to joke. "I don't need you to babysit me 24 hours a day, 7 days a week. You need to stretch your legs before getting on a plane again, so go."

"B, shut up."

Then he walked over to look at the technology which airline staff scanned boarding passes with.

There was nobody around to stop him, as the gate was empty. I assumed staff would appear half an hour before the flight's departure time. He even walked behind the desk they sat at, as he strolled about with his hands in his pockets.

I sunk lower into my seat as I rested my head in my hand. My eyes were stinging and I think it was because I was tired as well as upset. A couple of times when I looked at the steady flow of people going on with their lives, I'd see the shadows pass by too. It looked an eerie contrast, death strolling amongst life.

The news story of the tornado confounded these thoughts. The image of the five year old and her grandmother, haunted me as much as the actual ghosts. Every time their upset faces flashed through my mind, it made them sting even more.

Just then Declan came to sit beside and he asked knowingly, "You're still thinking about the tornado, aren't you?"

I gave a nod.

"Now it's mixed in with the ghosts and you're completely worn out," he guessed.

I nodded again.

"Your aura is looking pretty dim right now." He said. "Can you still see them?"

I nodded a third time.

"Where are they, are they here in the lounge?"

This time I shook my head then I waved my hand towards the bustling walkway. "They pass to and fro."

"What, amongst the living?"

"Yep."

"And nobody sees shadows of dead people amongst the solid shapes of the living, besides you." He mused. "Now I understand why schizophrenics lose it, when they see this sort of thing but nobody else does."

"Thanks a lot!" I rolled my eyes.

"I didn't say that you were schizophrenic," he said dryly. "I'm just speculating. I mean, in the olden days people could get lobotomized for seeing what you do."

This turned on the tears and I rasped out, "I know."

Then I felt his large arms engulf me as he pulled me in for a hug, "Shhh."

"Oh Declan..."

"Shhh," he held me tighter. "We're gonna be home soon and there'll be no more ghosts, no more tornadoes and no more Voodoo curses."

"We can't stop tornadoes from happening," I sniffed.

"Maybe one day we can."

"And what about other supernatural things attacking us?" I sighed into his chest.

"At least I can stop those," he muttered. "You may not like how I do it, but most of the time it's effective. It's not like they usually come back and cause further problems."

"Do you think Vampires have souls? I mean, we've killed a few of those over the years. What do you think happens to them?"

"I don't know and I don't care," he said unhappily. "Since they're half dead, maybe they lose their souls when they're turned?"

"Declan?"

"Yeah B?"

"We have the most interesting conversations in airport lounges."

"We do indeed."

The flight from Seattle to Fairbanks didn't take as long as the flight from Orlando to Seattle. Thankfully there wasn't any turbulence, either. However, I'd never felt so glad to be home as I did when our plane touched down.

It was around 11 PM when we walked out of Arrivals with our luggage. I thought we'd instantaneously phase home, however we spotted the tall stature of Forrest standing by an exit. I swear seeing another Lokoti never looked so good!

"Forrest!" I cried out, as I rushed forwards to swamp him in a hug.

"Hey Aunt B," he hugged me back so hard, he lifted me up. "Welcome home."

"Forrest," my mate shook his hand. "It's nice of you to come and pick us up."

"Don't mention it," he took my suitcase for me.

However, I caught him think - *MAN, HER AURA LOOKS FADED.*

To which Declan moodily thought back - *TELL ME ABOUT IT.*

"I can hear you," I sung.

"Yes dear," he replied.

I let him sit in the passenger's seat as I sat in the back. The two men talked quietly as I closed my eyes. Soon the lights of the city of Fairbanks were behind us, with nothing but dark highway ahead. The drive put me to sleep as Forrest's family car, cruised home.

Declan put down his window for a short time. Although the air was chilly, a change from Florida's heat, I appreciated the musky air. It felt good to be back in the woods, even if I couldn't see them. I felt like one of the males in the pack when they were relieved to return to home soil.

I lightly dozed, occasionally opening my eyes to see where we were. Since it was so dark, my eyes would glow turquoise to engage my night-vision. Then I'd recognize our location and it continued until I read the familiar sign; 'World Heritage Listed Lokoti National Park. Lokoti Community Centre, Population 636. To enquire about camping or hiking trails, please contact the Federal National Parks and Wildlife Services.'

"Oh, we're home." I sat upright.

"Home sweet home," my mate agreed.

Forrest drove into the small village, before turning left at the intersection to climb up the steep hill our house sat on. We cruised past the odd driveway which led to our relative's abodes before coming to our own, at the end of the cul-de-sac. The sight of our small, two-story, brown, wooden cottage with its stone chimney was a sight for sore eyes. However, our driver turned off the high beams as soon as he turned off the engine.

The three Werewolves engaged their night-vision, as we got out of the car then headed for the boot. Declan's eyes glowed green with his circular pupils turning into narrow slits, whilst Forrest's were a yellow colour and mine glowed turquoise. Once our suitcases were out, we three headed towards the veranda.

Just then a second pair of high beams shone from a car coming up the hill. Our glowing eyes faded to their natural colours, as Meadow's car parked behind Forrest's. Out climbed our Medicine Man who walked around to the passenger's side to help out our Tribal Elder. His lights remained on, so the human could see as he escorted her up the gravel drive.

"Gertrude and Meadow," I began. "What are you guys doing here? It must be the middle of the night."

"You know why we're here, Aunt B." The elderly human chastised. "Can you see them?"

This made Forrest, Declan and I pause at the bottom of the veranda stairs.

Funnily enough, I hadn't thought about the ghosts since the plane landed. It was then that I realized I hadn't seen them since Fairbanks. I looked about my dark garden, with my human sight switching to my Werewolf one to see better.

"Oh hang on," I dropped my suitcase. "They're standing at the end of the driveway."

"Yes?" The elderly Lokoti woman listened.

"They're literally standing on the edge of our property, like they can't come any closer."

"And?" She urged.

"You know what?" I realized something. "They're getting further and further away from us."

"Go on," she nodded.

"In New Orleans, they were standing at the end of our beds. When we flew, they were outside of the plane. In Seattle, they didn't come into the lounge of the boarding gate. Now, it's like they can't come onto our property." I thought aloud.

"Very good, Light Person." The Elder nodded. "They were strongest in New Orleans because you were on their territory. Now that they're on yours, they're losing power."

My mate asked in his typical blunt fashion, "So how do we rid ourselves of them, for good?"

"With a little bit of this and a little bit of that," she grinned in good humour. "Meadow, where is your Medicine Bundle?"

Our middle-aged Medicine Man gave the old woman's arm to Forrest to hold, as he quickly dashed back to his vehicle. However, when he returned it wasn't his black leather doctor's case he was carrying, it was a brown leather pouch. We watched as he opened it on the veranda and by the illumination of his headlights, he took out several feathers and crystals.

"Crystals?" I asked in disbelief.

"They're not just pretty stones you buy in a New Age store." Gertrude frowned. "They're smoky quartz which come from the caves on our land. The same caves that your ancestors took refuge in, during the winter blizzards."

Then we watched as Meadow picked up a large grey and white feather, and to our amusement he used it to 'dust off' Declan.

"What the...?" My mate took a step back. "Sorry buddy, not that you're not handsome? But I don't swing that way."

We all guffawed including Meadow however, he continued to 'cleanse' my mate with the feather.

"Humour me," he chuckled as he finished what he was doing.

Then he put the feather back and picked up two crystals which he passed to Gertrude.

Next, she sung in old Lokoti, which sounded very similar to the Lokoti Funeral Chant. I suppose it was appropriate, a song to ward off the dead sounding like the song to wish them well. She raised the crystals in the air with both hands, before passing one to Meadow. Then he joined in the chant and together they held the rocks in the air. Lastly, their singing died down and they both held out the crystals to me.

"Use your light to shine through the crystals," she instructed.

"You mean you want me to go into phase?" I wondered.

"If that's how you do it," she shrugged.

Instead of completely dissolving into light, I simply glowed. This made the light from my bio-electromagnetic frequency, briefly course through the minerals. They momentarily shone before Gertrude and Meadow took them back. As she headed up the front steps, our Medicine Man disappeared around the back of our house.

"We're putting one crystal over the front door and the other over the back, so they're protecting the entryways of the house." She explained.

Declan's lips pursed together and I sensed he felt frustrated, as he helplessly looked on. Then he asked, "Will this make them leave B alone?"

"No," the old woman shook her head. "The crystals aren't meant for her."

"What?!" My mate spluttered. "But you said if I bring her back here, you could undo the Voodoo spell!"

The same time as our Tribal Elder slowly came back down our veranda steps, our Medicine Man reappeared. She let go of the wooden handrail to take Meadow's arm once more. Then she calmly gazed up into the indignant face of my mate.

"The Voodoo Spell you stopped was for Aunt B," she acknowledged. "The darkness may surround her light, but as we've found out, they can't diminish it. Her light is timeless which thwarts the dark."

"Then what the hell was all the feathers and crystals, for?!" Declan demanded.

Oh hang on, my eyes widened as I began to understand. Meadow didn't use the feather to cleanse me, but my mate. I gawked at the big, strong male standing beside, as he seemed vulnerable now.

"The darkness couldn't pervade the light, so it tried to penetrate another darkness, which is inside you." Gertrude patted him on the chest. "We had to bring you home as soon as possible, before they could possess you."

The European Werewolf's mouth fell open in surprise, "Say what?"

Now Meadow spoke up, "If we had said that the darkness around Aunt B was trying to bypass her to get to you, you wouldn't have believed us. Or, your bloodlust would think it could fight them off, which was what caused the problem in the first place."

Declan blinked then blinked again, as he looked from them to me.

"But she's getting dizzy spells..." his voice trailed off.

"I looked that up," our Medicine Man nodded. "Circulators who use their light to excess can be drained from the experience."

"But the Voodoo freaks were after HER!" My husband refuted.

"So they didn't try to harvest you?" Meadow looked on pointedly.

This made the predator throw down his suitcase in anger, "FRICKIN' HELL!" Then he stormed off whilst muttering curses under his breath and he even kicked at the gravel.

In spite of myself, I started to giggle. "Well, I don't feel like the damsel in distress, anymore."

"Can you see the shadows?" Gertrude checked.

I looked down the darkened driveway and I couldn't see anything at the end nor on the road.

"Nope," I smiled.

"Good," she said perfunctory. "Now I'm going to bed."

Then Meadow gathered up his traditional Medicine Bundle, took the old lady's hand again and escorted her back to his car.

"I think I'll head off too," Forrest excused himself.

"No problem, thanks guys." I said as I threw them a wave.

Two plasma-powered vehicles reversed out and then disappeared down the hill.

This left me and my fuming mate in the darkness again. I picked up my suitcase and headed for the front door to unlock it. Declan had calmed down enough to reclaim his luggage and follow me inside. I turned on the living room lights and breathed in the familiar scent of home.

I watched him walk past and he looked as relieved to be back as I did. Then he put down his case again to stand before me. He looked my way long and hard.

"B, did you know?" He wondered.

"About the ghosts trying to possess you? No, I didn't." I raised my eyebrows. "It's a scary thought."

"Tell me about it," he grumbled as he momentarily looked away. Then he looked back to frown, "If you're in the all-clear then why is your aura still faded?"

"I've no idea." I yawned. "But all I can think about now, is bed."

"You got that right," he muttered.

Then he did something sweet. When I stooped to pick up my luggage one last time, he beat me to it. Then the husband followed his wife upstairs with the suitcases. However, they left all the lights on downstairs as a just-in-case, to keep the darkness outside.

~~~~~~

~ 17 ~

My weakened state continued and coincidentally, the tribe had to contend with sickness too. I found out the day after our return, when I went to Maia and Forrest's to dole out the presents I'd bought during the trip. All three of their kids were coughing and sneezing, so I kept my visit short.

Forrest walked me to my car which was parked on their driveway.

"Thanks a lot for the toys and souvenirs," he said appreciatively. "I'm just sorry the kids weren't well enough to thank you too."

"Don't worry about it," I waved it off. "Do you and Maia need anything, like medicines or whatever?"

"We're all good, thanks Aunt B." He patted my arm. "I've taken this week off work to help look after our little 'pack'."

This made me smile on the doting parent, "You're a wonderful father, Forrest."

Modestly, he ducked his head then stood back when I climbed into my vehicle.

Instead of driving straight home, I stopped off to see Therese and Julius Sabre. They were getting on in years now and it worried me to find they were sickly too. It looked like the virus which was going around, had taken hold of the young or elderly. I dropped off their gifts and didn't stay long, either.

As I drove towards the hill my house sat on, I was distracted by how I was starting to feel. My throat felt like it was swelling up and when I tried to swallow, it hurt. That's strange, a sore throat was indicative of illness and Werewolves with their regenerative ability, don't get sick.

I parked my car in the garage then went inside the main house. I could hear Declan was cooking up something in the kitchen. It smelled like he was making fettuccine carbonara for dinner.

"B?" He called out.

I couldn't reply because my throat was too sore, so I answered by coming to stand in the kitchen entryway. He glanced my way in the midst of his food preparation. But as soon as he saw me, he stopped in surprise. I don't look that bad, do I?

"B, you're as white as a sheet!" He said in concern and he crossed over to cup my face. "And your skin feels clammy. What's wrong with you?"

"I don't know..." my voice cracked, "...I don't feel well, Declan."

"If I didn't know better, I'd say you've got the flu." He frowned. "But our kind don't get sick, your regenerative ability should fight it off. I'd better call Meadow to come and take a look at you."

"I just need to lie down." I croaked out. Then I saw he'd been making garlic break to go with the pasta dish. "I'm sorry but I don't think I can eat anything."

"Go up to bed, I'll bring you a juice or something." He ordered.

Slowly, I turned away and made my way up the stairs. As soon as I entered the bedroom, I laid on top of the soft covers, shoes and coat and all. I didn't even have the strength to take them off.

"OK," he walked in soon afterwards, carrying a glass of OJ. "I've called Meadow and he's on his way."

Declan placed the glass on the bedside table then set to work by removing my shoes and coat. Once they were gone, he sat beside to feed me the juice. He looked on in concern as I managed a few sips but then I couldn't drink anymore. The acidic liquid stung my sore, swollen throat.

"C'mon B, you've gotta drink more than that." He gently chastised, pushing the glass to my mouth again. I shook my head and reluctantly he put it back down. "Maybe I should give you some of my blood instead?"

I shook my head again, as the idea turned my stomach. Right now, it objected to consuming anything. I rolled out of his arms to curl up in a ball, on my side. I even shivered as I hugged my pillow.

I feel like crap... I feel like total and utter crap...I can't remember feeling so wretched in my entire long life!

He hated seeing me shake so he curled up behind. By spooning me, he shared his body heat and mine gratefully drank it up. His overpowering warmth radiated throughout my aching being. Oh it felt like heaven!

"Hold me tighter," I pleaded.

So he did, by squeezing me against his larger and harder form, making me sigh appreciatively.

I wished we could have lain like this for eternity, but it only lasted for ten minutes. We heard a knock on the front door and sensed it was the tribe's Medicine Man, reporting in. My husband released me to go and greet him.

Next, I heard Declan say as he showed Meadow upstairs, "She's pale, she says she feels cold and she's clammy. Her throat is sore and she's even wheezing a little, like she's out of breath."

The two men walked into the bedroom and over to the invalid on the bed. Our Medicine Man put down his 'medicine bundle', which was his black leather doctor's bag. I lay still and watched as he took out his medical scanner and waved it in my direction.

Then he put the technology down to examine me the old fashioned way. He placed his hand on my forehead then he felt my glands on the sides of my neck. He checked my eyes and ears and he even put his ear against my back to listen to me breath. After he'd done all of this, he picked up the scanner to compare his diagnosis with the device's.

"Aunt B has a chest infection," he pronounced. "She's having difficulty breathing because of the mucus building up in her airways."

"A chest infection...?" My mate echoed in disbelief. "But *we* don't get viruses."

"Normally I'd agree with you. But I've seen five other patients today, all with the same symptoms. The scanner's detected a bug going around the tribe which the kids caught from playing with the children in Alma. I've heard that the doctors' surgeries in town are inundated with infected young and old." He informed.

"But how can B have caught the bug?" Declan asked unhappily.

Meadow frowned as he looked on his patient, "She's run down."

"She's run down?" He echoed again in disbelief.

"Aunt B isn't just a Lokoti Werewolf." Our physician reminded. "She's also a Circulator."

"Yeah, but even Circulators hardly ever get sick." He argued back.

"If they spent all their time in phase then a virus can't get hold of their biology. But in human form, they're just as susceptible as any other human is." Meadow pointed out.

"But her mother and grandmother hardly ever got sick."

"I'm under the impression that when they become ill, often it's after they've used their abilities to excess." Meadow mused and Declan's eyes widened. "Correct me if I'm wrong, but with your little adventure in New Orleans, Aunt B did phase more than usual, did she not?"

"Frickin' hell!" He kicked the end of the bed. "If I ever see those dead Voodoo freaks again..."

"Like a battery, she's drained." Our Medicine Man frowned. "Look at her aura, do you see how dim it is? She's completely run down."

"Yeah, I see it." He growled in annoyance and then he asked hopeful, "Will sharing my blood regenerate her?"

"If she had an injury, it would. But right now it's the Circulator side of her which needs to be tended to." He instructed. "She needs rest and plenty of it. Keep her hydrated with lots of water. If orange juice hurts her throat, give her apple and black current. And give her these three times a day"

Our Medicine Man opened up his doctor's bag again to take out a small, white, plastic jar which was label free.

"What are these?" The European Werewolf took the plastic lid off to sniff what was inside.

"A specialized blend of multivitamins and minerals combined with a unique steroid that's meant to boost a Circulator's immune system." He advised. "Vincent Moher gave them to me before he left for the space time continuum with her parents. He foresaw that as a Circulator, Aunt B may need them from time to time."

Then Meadow repacked his scanner, closed his case and prepared to leave.

"Where are you going so fast?" My mate asked in annoyance.

"I have two other patients to see, two more children with the same bug that Aunt B has. Fortunately with her immune system, her symptoms aren't as bad." He said evenly.

"What do you mean, they're not that bad?" Declan asked incredulous. "Look at her!"

"This afternoon, Moon and Ross Lightfoot had to drive their seven year old son to the hospital in Fairbanks." He said seriously. "They called me half an hour ago to say the hospital has him on a ventilator because he can't breathe. He has the same chest infection that Aunt B does. The humans in the tribe aren't as strong as Werewolves, Uncle."

Instantly, the predator looked remorseful, "Sorry."

"Drive to the drug store and pick up some Ibuprofen and 'Vicks Vaporub'." Meadow gave his last instructions. "The Ibuprofen will keep her temperature down and you rub the 'Vicks Vaporub' on her back and her chest, which will help her breathe easier. Another effective, traditional remedy is a cup of tea with lemon and honey, to help her throat."

"Copy that," he gave a nod. "Thanks Meadow."

Our physician returned it before he cast a last look my way.

As he left the room he said quietly, "When you come back, sit with her. A Lokoti Werewolf's will to live increases greatly, with their mate in close proximity. Your presence will boost her strength to fight off the infection."

Declan gave a rueful laugh, "Isn't that true of us all?"

Then the two went downstairs as he saw Meadow out.

I didn't hear much more after that. My eyes started to sting because of how dry they felt, so I closed them. I didn't mean to fall asleep, but it happened so quickly it caught me unawares...

...

... the next time I opened my eyes again, it was because of Declan removing my top, to rub in the 'Vicks Vaporub'.

"Did we have that in the house?" I wondered.

"Nope, I've been to the drug store and the supermarket while you were asleep." He answered. "Now we have enough apple and black current juice, honey and lemon tea, Ibuprofen and Vicks, to sink a ship."

"But I only closed my eyes for five minutes," I mumbled out.

He removed my jumper and my t-shirt before he reached for the jar of Vaporub.

"Now lie on your side while I smear this stuff on you." He instructed. "Or, maybe we should get you into your pyjamas first and then put on this crap?"

"Crap?" I repeated. "Great bedside manner, Declan."

"Man this stuff stinks!" He turned up his nose.

Next, he removed my jeans and socks before he helped me on with my pyjamas.

"I can't say that I've ever helped you dress before." He joked. "I've helped you *undress* plenty of times but never get dressed."

He left off my pyjama shirt so he could smear the 'Vicks Vaporub' onto my chest then my back.

"At least there's one good thing about you being sick." He said as he worked.

"Hmm?"

"This," he gave a cheeky grin.

I noticed he took his sweet time to rub the stuff on the front of my body. I rolled my eyes and turned around to make him do my back. Then he helped me put on my flannel pyjama top and did my buttons for me.

Once I was changed and stunk of eucalyptus, Declan tucked me in under the covers. But before I could go back to sleep, he insisted that I take one of the tablets with a glass of the juice he'd bought. To placate the bossy European Werewolf, I acquiesced.

At last I could finally lie down again and it didn't take long for unconsciousness to find me...

...

...I slept fitfully, tossing and turning from how much my body was aching. I must admit, the 'Vicks' did help my breathing. Whenever I started to cough, Declan would ply more to the skin on my front and back. Or he'd wake me to take my tablets with more juice.

A couple of times, I found him sitting in bed beside me, reading a book by his bedside lamp.

"What are you reading?" I asked sleepily.

He showed me the cover and I saw it was Mary Shelley's 'Frankenstein'.

"Haven't you read that before?" I queried.

"Yeah about a hundred years ago." He shrugged.

"I don't like that book." I frowned. "It's too sad."

"Yeah it is a bit." He sighed as he kept reading.

"I don't like it when the villagers blame the monster for the death of the small child." I said dismally.

"No, it's not my favourite part of the book." He frowned.

I said emotionally, "Humans can be so mean. They're afraid of us because they're scared we're more violent. But humans are way worse than we are. I mean, Werewolves aren't to blame for the extinction of entire species."

Declan held the book in his right hand as he used his left, to stroke my hair.

"Go back to sleep, B." He said gently. "It's time for all sick Circulators to get some rest."

So I did, I fell into a delirious slumber where I struggled against the covers.

I couldn't find a comfortable position to lie in because I ached so much. Even my skin was hurting! The Ibuprofen took the edge off the pain, but it didn't solve the problem. The virus was running rampant in a body which was so run down, it must have mirrored a road accident victim.

In my delirium, strange images danced inside my head. The sound of my heart beat turned into a drum beat. The eucalyptus in the 'Vicks Vaporub' turned into the musk of pine trees, in the surrounding woods. Sometimes I'd be looking over the forest as if I were floating above. Other times, I felt like I was flying through it, weaving between the trees.

"B, wake up." My mate gently shook me. "It's time to take more drugs."

"Hmm?"

"C'mon now, wakey wakey." He raised me into a sitting position.

"Come into the woods, Declan." I moaned out. "Can't you hear the drum beat? They're holding a ceremony somewhere."

"There is no drum beat, B."

"Yes there is!"

"OK, I'll break out the drum kit after you take your medication."

"We have a drum kit?"

"Sure we do, it's upstairs in the attic beside our magic carpet and our giant beanstalk."

Then I felt a tablet sit on my tongue before it was washed down my throat in a sweet, red, waterfall...

...

...into the second night of the fever, the bed was a mess as I couldn't lie still.

"I'm hot! I'm hot!" I kicked off the covers.

"No B, you need to keep the covers on." He pulled them back over.

Futilely, I struggled against him so he scooped me up, covers and all, into his arms. He sat in bed, rocking his wife however, the wife didn't want to be held. I thought he was holding on too tightly, which not only made me hotter but it affected my breathing as well.

"Shhh," he tried to soothe. "Rest now, rest."

"But I'm hot! It's hot, Declan! You're making me hot!"

"That's because your fever's finally breaking." I heard him say back. "If you kick off the covers, you could get a chill."

"I want to get a chill!"

"No you don't." He said gently. "Now rest B, rest."

I gasped as I tried to gulp down the air. I literally felt like I was suffocating! I wheezed loudly and it was like the air wasn't reaching my lungs.

"I... can't... breathe!" I struggled against him. "Get off me! I can't breathe! Don't lie on top of me, Declan!"

"I'm not lying on top of you, B!"

"I can't breathe!" I cried out frightened. "I can't breathe!"

I could feel his arms around me and I thought they were to blame. So I pushed him away and when I freed myself, I fell sideways! My face landed on top of the covers. Oh, was he holding me up to help me breathe better?

I coughed and coughed from something hard and cold in my back, which wasn't letting my lungs expand properly.

IT'S MY BACK - I thought desperately - *THERE'S SOMETHING IN MY BACK NOT LETTING ME BREATHE PROPERLY.*

Next, the European Werewolf started to thump it to loosen whatever it was. His strength might have harmed a human woman, but it was the right amount of force to shake up my chest. I spluttered but at least I could breathe again.

THANK YOU, I CAN BREATHE, BUT DON'T STOP – I pleaded.

"I won't." He said firmly.

Declan thumped for a good fifteen minutes however, he stopped when he was worried he'd bruise me. Then he sat behind, rubbing my back instead. When he stopped hitting though, my airways began to feel constricted again.

HIT ME – I requested.

"I can't hit you anymore, I could damage you."

I CAN'T BREATHE PROPERLY – I thought frightened.

So he rubbed harder. As he did, I thought on Moon and Ross Lightfoot's son on a ventilator. Right then I envied him, at least he can breathe right now.

MAYBE YOU SHOULD TAKE ME TO HOSPITAL TOO – I thought resigned.

I felt him pause as I think my words surprised him. But then he rubbed my back even harder. He moved his hand around in a circular motion, to massage my rear rib cage.

"You know I can't, B." He said in a pained voice. "The advancement in medicine will pick up your differences as a Lokoti Werewolf."

What, can't I go to hospital ever? But what if I suffocate because of this chest infection? What if I die because of this?

"We'll get through this." He promised as he worked. Then he growled under his breath, "I didn't fight off 'fang heads', other Werewolves and the Voodoo crazies, just to lose you this way."

If I could have breathed, I would have cried at how isolated, helpless and scared I was feeling.

BREATHE B, BREATHE – he willed my way – STAY WITH ME, B. STAY WITH ME...

...

...Declan didn't just rub more 'Vicks' onto my chest and back, but he tied my hair up into a pony tail so he could put it on my throat as well. He made multitudes of cups of lemon and honey tea, as the soothing, hot liquid coupled with the 'Vicks', seemed to melt the cold, hard thing in my back. Once whatever it was momentarily melted, I could breathe better.

At one stage I opened my eyes and I saw the time was 3.40 AM.

I was touched how he'd stayed up all night, tending to his sick mate. He was constantly moving around, either rubbing in the 'Vicks', or patting me hard on the back, or moving around the pillows to lie me on my side because I breathed better this way. He was in and out of the bedroom, with constant cups of tea. Our bedroom absolutely reeked of eucalyptus which his sensitive nose objected to. But he wouldn't leave my side, unless it was to make more tea.

I think Declan called Meadow again, as their thoughts intruded on mine.

B'S BREATHING IS SPORADIC - he thought to our Medicine Man - SHE NEEDS CONSTANT 'VICKS', OR TEA, OR ME TO HIT HER ON THE BACK.

DO WHAT I'M DOING WITH MAIA AND FORREST'S YOUNGEST - Meadow replied - SIT HER IN THE BATHROOM WITH THE HOT WATER TAPS ON AND CREATE A STEAM ROOM. THE VAPORS HELP THEM BREATHE. I CAN'T COME TO YOU YET, MAIA AND FORREST NEED ME HERE AS THEIR CHILD IS DANGEROUSLY ILL.

Then I felt Declan make a move off the bed, but I stopped him.

"No... I'm OK." I wheezed. "We'll... try that... as a last resort."

"Nope, we're gonna try it now." He said firmly.

He left the bedroom and from the bathroom, I heard the hot water taps for the bathroom sink, the bath tub as well as the shower come on. Then he shut the door to trap the steam inside. Next, he walked back into our bedroom and threw off the covers.

Like I weighed no more than a feather, he lifted me up into his arms and carried me into the other room.

Declan kicked shut the bathroom door behind and sat down on the side of the bath tub with his mate in his lap.

Patiently, he sweated in the steam room although he hated the heat and humidity. He returned to rubbing my back as he anxiously watched. He was waiting to see if my breathing improved...and thankfully it did.

My wheezing died down as my lungs filled easily. I even coughed less. The 'steam room' was a godsend!

As I sat there in his lap with his large hand rubbing my back, I considered how easily he could carry me around.

My weight increased when I first turned from the extra muscle. I wasn't sure of Declan's weight, especially when he turned his width tripled. Did his weight triple as well? I wonder if my weight also increased when I changed?

Out of the blue, I asked, "How much do you weigh?"

"Huh?" Declan gave a peculiar look.

I said breathlessly, "When I first turned at 18 years old... my weight went from 60 kg's to 70 kg's... in human form... Do you think that increases again.... when I change and bulk up?"

"I guess," he shrugged.

"Then how much do you weigh...?" I wondered. "Your weight must go up too... when you change?"

"As a human I weigh 120 kg's and in my Werewolf body, it goes up to 240 kg's." He said uncomfortably.

"What's wrong?" I breathed hard whilst looking on.

"Humans who are 120 kg's go on those horrible Reality TV shows like 'Diet Hell'." He scowled. "If a trainer ever tried to stop me from eating whatever I want, I'd eat him instead!"

"Yeah but... you don't look overweight... you look like a body builder." I struggled to speak and breathe at the same time. "You look like... one of the trainers on 'Diet Hell'... that boss around the fat people... and force them to eat less and work out."

Declan chuckled as he planted a kiss on my cheek, "Thanks baby."

"At least you're not a woman... it's bad for a woman... to be 170 cm's tall and weigh 70 kg's." I caught my breath before talking again. "I'm not petite or lady-like... other women ask me... to take the lids off jars for them."

"Well I'm 190 cm's tall and sometimes I have to duck or turn sideways to go through doorways." He rubbed my back. "Don't worry baby, I have it harder than you."

"I wish my shoulders weren't so broad..." I said wistfully, "... I wish I looked like my old human self."

"I don't!" He said indignant. "If you'd stayed human, I'd probably be dead now from sexual frustration! I'd die if I couldn't touch or have the woman I loved. It was my lucky day when you changed."

This made me stare into his bright blue eyes, which were wide. Sitting in his lap, our heads were around the same height so our faces were inches apart. My hand reached up to touch his lips with my fingertips.

He went on, "You're my beautiful B. You're tall and you're strong and normally you glow when you're healthy. I'm not attracted to weak women, I'm attracted to my Werewolf wife."

Ooohhh... my already pounding heart from struggling to breathe, now pounded from the force of emotion.

Then he joked, "So I'd appreciate it if you didn't die on me."

I let out a short laugh as I wrapped my arms about his neck. Declan hugged me back as he continued to rub. I was feeling much better now thanks to both the steam and his words. My cheek rested on his wide shoulder as my eyes started to close...

"B?"

"Hmm...?"

"Are you falling asleep?"

"Hmm."

"I suppose that's a good sign," he half said to himself.

"Hmm."

His hand ran up and down my back as he held his wife closely. "Sweet dreams baby and just remember to breathe for me..."

...

...the sound of my husband's heart beat turned into a drum beat once more. I could smell the pine as I floated around the woods. It was night time and I saw a distant campfire, with shadows of people dancing around it.

Why were people dancing around the campfire? It looked tribal instead of ballroom or modern. It was men with long, dark hair, dancing topless as older men, or women and children sat around, watching them. A couple of the older men played the drums and the audience sang in an old language.

I watched from above where I could feel the heat from the flames.

I feel so hot! I felt like I was being cooked like a pig on a spit. Sweat was pouring out of me, but I was too weak to do anything about it.

"Declan... take me away from the campfire... it's too hot." I whimpered. "Please Declan... take me away from the flames... I'm so hot!"

"She's been mumbling like that for three days." I heard my mate say. "If she's not dribbling about the woods, she's on about people dancing in them."

"She's been delirious that long?" Meadow sounded.

"Let's just say she's had more 'trips' in the last 72 hours than a hippy at Woodstock."

"Maybe we should turn off the heater." He suggested.

"No way!" My mate's reaction was immediate. "Heat is the only thing that helps her breathe properly. I sat her in the bathroom for an hour until the hot water ran out. As soon as it did, she started suffocating again. I found this old heater in the attic, which we used before we had central heating installed. If I take away the heater, she can't breathe."

"This summer has been warmer than usual, I'm surprised that you've needed it." Meadow mused. "The heat's been blamed for incubating the virus and helping it spread. The first case occurred in Canada during its surprise heat wave in the beginning of June."

"Trust me, the air outside is warm enough for me." Declan said unhappily. "But it's turning this room into a sauna, or a choking wife."

"Well, it looks like you've got the situation under control." Our Medicine Man commended. "I'll come and check on Aunt B tomorrow."

"Meadow," he stopped him. "If she gets worse, is there any way I can take her to a hospital? Can I just get them to help her breathe, but not run any tests?"

"I don't think so, Uncle." The physician warned. "They'd scan her to confirm what kind of virus it is, as part of her treatment."

Declan emitted a dissatisfied growl but Meadow was optimistic.

"Aunt B is doing a lot better than a quarter of the tribe who has this. So far, ten people have been rushed to Fairbanks Hospital; six elderly and four children. And these are our tribes' people, not including those in Alma. This virus has to be the worst I've seen in fifty years."

"You didn't see her last night," he warned. "She was literally suffocating at one stage."

"Keep doing what you're doing." Our Medicine Man left as his parting words. "Keep her hydrated with water and juice but try doubling the dosage of the steroid. I'll come again tomorrow to check on her."

My husband responded wearily, "If you say so."

Then their footsteps left the room as he escorted out the medical practitioner...

...

...I was feeling a little better the next time I woke up and found it was evening again. My pyjamas were damp from how much I was sweating. I reeked of eucalyptus and body odour, which made me crave a shower.

I turned my head to find Declan sitting on his side of the bed, reading another book. This time I saw it was 'Jane Eyre.' I opened my mouth to speak, when my lips hurt from how dry and cracked they were.

"Another depressing story?" I croaked out.

"My Mom recommended it." He said simply. "It was when I used to read the romantic classics before we were mates, coz I wasn't getting any."

Then he gave a wink as he continued with his book.

I recalled his mother telling me about this period in his life. It was when he read romances because he was lonely and frustrated. He'd pass them off by saying he was studying the 'classics', such as 'Lady Chatterley's Lover' etc. Personally, I thought he shouldn't have worried about it. You'd have to be pretty stupid to tease a European Werewolf about its reading material.

"When I tried reading it 150 years ago, I couldn't get into it." He continued. "It was too depressing."

"Why are you reading it now?"

"I need to keep my mind busy."

"Why don't you go to sleep?"

"Coz I can't sleep properly."

"Why?"

"Because I'm worried about you B," he turned his head to give a long look. "That's why."

"Oh."

"Being one of my kind, I feel especially angry when my mate is in danger and I can't do anything about it." He growled out. "If this virus was a person, it'd be in pieces by now. Unfortunately I can't attack sickness."

I believed him too, considering what he did to the last three people he deemed were a threat.

"Today's the first day I've heard you breathe almost normally, without the heater being on." He passed the old electrical device a glare. "You seem more lucid, too."

"How long have I been out for?" I wondered.

"Today is day four."

I blanched, "I've been asleep for that long?"

"You've been delirious for that long." He said. "Last night you asked me to take you for a ride on the magic carpet you thought we kept in the attic."

"I did?"

"You haven't eaten in four days, either." Declan declared. "Every time I tried to feed you Vegemite on toast, you'd spit it back up. Did you wanna try again?"

"What, eating?"

"No, ballet dancing." He said sarcastically. But I didn't take offence considering how tired the poor guy looked. He slowly stood up before he turned back. "I feel like some toasted cheese and tomato sandwiches. You want?"

"I'm still not hungry," I admitted.

This made him even angrier as he moved his hands to his hips to glare down.

"I'm going to make you a toasted sandwich and you're gonna eat it!" He raised his voice. "If you don't eat it, I'm going to jam my cut wrist into your mouth and force feed you that instead!"

Boy, he must be exhausted! There was no way in hell I was going to argue with an infuriated European Werewolf. I didn't have the strength for it, or to phase to safety.

"OK," I managed back.

He spun on his heel and stalked out of our bedroom with a determined look on his face.

Fifteen minutes later, a dinner plate with five toasted tomato and cheese sandwiches piled onto it, sat on my blanketed lap.

"Declan, come on!" I objected. "There's no way I can eat that much!"

"You're not expected to, four of those are mine." He said coolly.

He shoved a toasted sandwich triangle into my hand before picking up another. Then he sat beside, watching me as he munched on his. Gingerly, I took in a mouthful of cheese and tomato. He watched my jaw move up and down then my throat move when I swallowed.

"Good, that's your first bite and now for your second." He bossed about. He'd scoffed down his triangle and picked up another, as I took my second bite. He continued to watch me chew and swallow. "Go on, keep eating."

I did... and again... and then again. I managed to finish the first half of a toasted sandwich, when he handed me the second half. Oh no, I didn't think I could eat anymore, even holding the food made me feel full! I raised the triangle to my mouth, but then my hand flopped down to the bed covers.

"I can't..."

"Yes you can."

"No, I can't."

"B, please! Eat! You have to build your strength again."

"If I force this down, I'll throw it back up." I said unhappily. "But I'm feeling a bit better today, I promise."

"You still smell weak."

"That's because I'm sick."

"No shit Sherlock, now eat the frickin' sandwich!"

But I couldn't. I even tossed it away to illustrate my point that food couldn't cure my ills. The toasted sandwich triangle lay unloved on the end of the bed.

I heard a growl escape from my determined carer, as he picked up one of his triangles and moved it towards my mouth.

"No Declan," I turned my head away. "I can't, truly I can't."

He lowered the triangle as well as the plate of food, and looked away dejectedly.

"I feel disgusting..." I moaned. "...how long has it been since my last shower?"

"That's the problem," he said flatly.

"What that I stink?"

"No, that you smell a little too ripe."

"Huh?"

"Your body odour B, your pheromones are concentrated in your sweat."

"What?"

He confessed, "Half the time I'm lying here, watching you sleep and hoping that you don't stop breathing. The other half, I'm holding myself back from pouncing on you."

"Declan!"

"What?"

"I'm dying and you still wanna jump me?!" I cried out in disgust.

"Tell me about it!" He bad-temperedly slammed the plate of food on the bedside table so hard, it cracked. "Why the hell do you think I'm reading 'Jane Eyre'?!"

I rolled onto my side so my back was to him. However, he wasn't put off and he lay down behind, to spoon his mate. Next, I felt his arms wrap around as he held me close... then I overheard him inhale deeply.

"Declan," I sung warningly. "Stop it."

"You know what you remind me of? A cavewoman. With your hair all matted and your skin all sweaty, you've got the primitive look down pat. I wanna throw you over my shoulder, carry you to my cave and follow my primal urges."

"Eew!" I moaned. "I'm so *not* in the mood."

"I think my bloodlust likes your bed-hair, as you look like a feral cavewoman who could maul me in the throws of passion."

I whined out, "I want a shower! I want clean pyjamas! I want clean sheets on this bed! I want me and this room to be freshened up!"

"I don't," he retorted. "This is the fourth day that I haven't got any. The only comfort I have are your frickin' pheromones."

"Deeecccllllaaaaaan....!!"

I felt him bury his face in my messy hair, as he gave a tight squeeze before he took a deep breath then raised his head.

"Alright already," he groaned. "Shower and changed, I get it."

Reluctantly, he raised himself from the bed and left the room. But I didn't hear the shower turn on, but the bath run instead. He must have thought I hadn't the strength to stand under the water...

...

...although my husband had his faults he could also be faultlessly generous.

Not only did he carry his sick mate into the bathroom, undress her and lower her into the bathwater, but he helped wash her hair as well.

Momentarily, he left me alone to change the sheets. When he carried the dirty ones down to the laundry, he returned with a bucket. He filled it with warm water which he poured over my head. After my hair had been lathered in shampoo, he poured another over to rinse it out.

Half an hour later, I sat in a clean bed in a freshened room, feeling much more hygienic. I'd also changed pyjamas and I was in my red flannel ones with the Daffy Duck pattern. Declan who'd joined me in the bath towards the end, sat in a clean pair of boxer shorts.

"Actually, you're right." He mused. "It does feel better after that little spring clean."

I asked in surprise, "Hadn't you bathed either?"

"Babe, I haven't done jack besides play nurse to you." He said matter-of-factly. "Hell, I almost put on a little white dress and cap."

"The romantic things you say," I smirked.

"You better believe it," he gave a grin.

I snuggled down as he switched off his lamp then lay beside. I moved my head to rest on his chest and he wrapped me in his arms. I also had a leg and an arm over him, as I basked in his high body temperature. So he wouldn't overheat, he pulled up the sheet but not the quilt.

"At least you're breathing properly." He spoke in the darkness. "Your wheezing and coughing won't keep me up anymore."

"Thanks Declan," I said flatly.

"I hate it when you wheeze." He continued. "You sound like an eighty year old human in the middle of a hard winter."

"Thanks Declan."

"I married you because you WON'T age like a human does."

"Thanks Declan."

"I expect you to breathe like a twenty-something year old Werewolf, the way you look like a twenty-something year old Werewolf."

"Thanks Declan."

"And tomorrow you're gonna eat the big breakfast I'm gonna cook up and get your strength back." He ordered. "I'm so horny, I'm about to lose control!"

"Declan, shut up."

I felt him chuckle as he held me tighter. Like this, he rolled his head in my direction to sleep whilst inhaling my scent. His steady heartbeat filled my ears as his rising and falling chest, rocked me to sleep.

The pounding of his heart turned into the pounding of a drum. I was back in the woods at night time again. Through the trees, I spotted the familiar campfire that a Native Alaskan tribe of old, sat around. The younger men were dancing, as the older men played on drums made of hide. The women and children sang, as the men's dancing increased in fervour.

I noticed how their suede clothing looked like our traditional 'skins' worn for tribal celebrations such as Joining Ceremonies. But the fifteen dancers who were topless, just had suede pants on. The beadwork on the tassels looked Lokoti and some of the older men playing the music, had painted claw marks down the sides of their faces, the symbol of the Lokoti Wolf.

Suddenly the clouds parted in the sky above to reveal a full moon.

The dancing men all threw back their heads and howled! As they did, I watched their bodies expand with muscle bulk. Their eyes glowed a different colour, as their open mouths revealed their teeth turning elongated and sharp. Claws appeared on the ends of their fingers and toes, as the fifteen men turned into the fifteen members of the Lokoti Werewolf pack.

Seeing their change in the moonlight made me feel like changing to join them...

Abruptly, the pack all leapt into the woods as they raced away from the campfire. They all bolted in the same direction and I sensed they were on the hunt. They ran through the trees at speeds of up to 200 km/h as they fell into formation, flanking their First. This Werewolf had glowing purple eyes, which glinted dangerously as the bloodlust was upon him and his men.

As I watched them, my bloodlust boiled as it wanted to hunt with them. I wanted to feed with them. I wanted to taste fresh kill so badly! I needed to bask in the warm flesh and blood of my meal, right after its heart had stopped.

"B?"

I wanted to change and run beside them, on home soil under the light of the full moon.

"B, wake up!"

I want to change – no, I need to change - I have to revert! I have to make the hunger go away! I want to run with my kin and purge my bloodlust.

"B, you're glowing! Stop it! Now wake up!"

I growled at the person shouting and shaking me, as I tried to hold onto this vision...

The Lokoti Werewolves raced away and I lost them through the trees. I was just too slow in this sick, human body. But I knew how I could catch up to them...as a Circulator. I could use my ability to run in light speed and rejoin my pack.

I felt my body tingle all over as I turned into light. Going into phase freed me from my weak, mortal form. I relished these feelings as well as the rushing sensation I experienced, as my light particles passed through time.

"B, stop it! You're going into phase! You're not supposed to use your Circulator ability when you're sick!"

I think I reformed into my biological body again, but for a couple of seconds I wasn't so sure. That was until... whoomp! It felt like I'd fallen out of bed.

"B, wake up, damn it!"

My eyes popped open to find myself looking up at the leaves on a branch. Hang on, why am I gazing up at trees? Or better yet, why am I lying in the dirt? Where did the bed go?

I sat upright as my mate did too, with us both looking about the dark forest we found ourselves in.

"Um Declan, why are we in the woods, in our pyjamas?" I asked, confused.

He said indignant, "Because you just put us here!"

"Huh?" I looked on, baffled.

"You started to glow! When I tried to wake you, you frickin' went into phase! And because I was touching you, I went into phase too!" He said in annoyance.

"I brought us here?"

"Yes!"

"But – but – but where is here?" I wondered aloud.

"How the hell am I supposed to know?!" He stood up angrily. "You're the frickin' Circulator! Where the hell did you take us?!"

"I – I – I don't know." I looked about. "I had a dream I was watching the Lokoti of old and I saw the pack run into the woods -"

"Frickin' hell, you're delirious again!" He interrupted. "Oh that's just wonderful. So, can we expect either Attila the Hun, or a frickin' dinosaur come to attack us?"

"What, in Alaska?" I gave a funny look. "Look Dec, I know you only went to school until you were thirteen, but I can assure you that Attila the Hun was in another country."

He passed a dirty look before he turned and walked away to investigate our surroundings.

Slowly, I climbed to my feet from feeling incredibly weak again. I looked over to see my husband sniff as he surveyed the geography. Then he stopped in front of a certain tree.

"B, look at this," he gave a nod.

I saw it had a peculiar bend in the trunk from growing too close to another.

"That looks like the tree at home, on the edge of our property."

"Uh huh."

"What, we're home?" I examined the area.

"Look at how the ground is sloping, we're still on top of the hill that our house sits on. The only question is -"

" - when, because our house isn't here." I finished for him, as I walked over to stand beside.

"The tree looks pretty young, doesn't it?" He postured. "It's not as tall as it is in our time."

"Uh huh."

"Your grandfather told me that many of the trees on tribal lands as well as inside the National Park, are a couple of centuries old."

"So we've gone back in time by a few hundred years? At least we're still home, on Lokoti land." I sighed in relief.

"Great," he frowned about something.

"What's wrong?"

"We've gone so far back in time that this hill doesn't have any houses on it yet." He explained. "Your grandfather told me that the Lokoti didn't start to build houses like the European's, until the beginning of the 20th Century."

"So?"

"Which means that the Lokoti Werewolves in this era, will see me as a threat." He said unhappily. "I'll be a foreign foe on their territory. It'll be centuries yet until I'm adopted by the pack and they see me as one of their own."

"Oh," my face fell.

"Speaking of which," he looked in a particular direction. "They've picked up our scent and they know we're here."

"They have?" I turned my head.

I sniffed the air but I couldn't smell anything, however his hearing and sense of smell were better than mine.

"B, I think you should take us back now," he said uneasily.

"But why? They're our people." I disagreed. "When they see and smell us, they'll know we're kin."

"Yeah, when they see YOU and smell YOU, they'll tell you're Lokoti and even a Lokoti Werewolf." He argued. "But all they'll see when they look at me, is my blonde hair, blue eyes and white skin. Worse still, they'll smell I'm a European Werewolf, the most hated breed there is!"

Just then my sensitive ears picked up the sounds of heavy footfall. It was the pack running towards us, up the forest encrusted hill. Now I smelled my kin but interestingly, I caught the scent of something else. It was something different and yet something spookily familiar.

My intuition as a Circulator sensed there was something achingly familiar about this new scent. The feeling wasn't ominous, but it was telling me that there really was kin here. My heart raced in excitement to see who it was.

"C'mon, let's go." He grabbed hold of my arm.

"No, wait." I shook him off. "Declan, do you smell that?"

"Yeah, fifteen territorial Lokoti Werewolves are on their way to attack!"

"No, I mean the other smell." I spoke excitedly. "Can't you feel it?"

"B, what is WITH you tonight?!" He objected. "Take us home NOW!"

"Not yet." I shook my head.

Right as I said that, fifteen Lokoti Werewolves wearing the suede pants of old, sprang through the trees! The pack fanned about us, snarling threateningly. Their glowing eyes glinted murderously, as they faced off what they perceived as a threat.

I looked on all of their eyes and using the colours, I tried to pick out their family lineage. I saw then smelled by bloodline, who was a Riverclaw, or a Wisetail or an Elm. As I did so, I saw that the Riverclaw and Wisetail Werewolves did the same to me. They sniffed once more, to confirm it was their blood somehow inside the foreign female in their midst.

By the way the First was standing out in front with the others flanking him, I saw it was a Lightfoot with glowing purple eyes. Their Second looked to be the Riverclaw Werewolf with blue eyes, with the Wisetail standing on the side of him with his red eyes. To his side, I guessed was an Elm Werewolf with glowing silver eyes.

From their puzzled expressions, they could smell I was kin but it was my appearance which baffled them. I sensed my paler complexion from my Caucasian ancestry caused confusion. So did my pyjamas, as they looked on the unfamiliar cartoon character, printed on the fabric. The Elm Werewolf edged closer, sniffing me as he moved.

"B," my husband spoke quietly. "Slowly back up to my position."

I was about to ask why when I realized it was so we would be seen as mates.

As I took a step back, the Lokoti Werewolves jumped like they were on guard! Their eyes narrowed suspiciously, as they wondered why I was allying myself with the alien breed. Slowly, I took another step back and then another. As I came to stand beside my mate, the pack looked on in distrust.

Then something unusual happened, the Elm Werewolf slowly crept forwards as he continued to sniff.

Frickin' hell, I think he got a whiff of my pheromones and he must have been a single male.

However, I wasn't a single female. I heard a low growl emitted from my mate, which was directed at the Elm Werewolf to stop his pursuit. Oh oh, we soon found out this was the wrong thing to do, especially being strangers on their territory. We heard the escalated growls from the pack, as they rallied behind their own.

Just as I opened my mouth to try to explain that we weren't a threat, the Riverclaw and Wisetail Werewolves grabbed me! Then the rest of the pack attacked Declan! All at once, thirteen Lokoti Werewolves pounced with their mouths open and their claws ready.

"No!" I cried out, quite uselessly, as the Lokoti had no idea what the English word 'no' means.

The Riverclaw and Wisetail Werewolves tried to pull me away from what they saw as the dangerous party.

Declan with his faster reflexes even in human form, was able to toss aside four in several self defence moves. But nine more were quick to take their place. My stomach lurched, as I watched my mate battle it out.

Soon he began to falter, fighting in his human body against the thirteen Lokoti Werewolves, in their supernatural bodies.

They used their teeth and claws to inflict their harm, as he used fists and combat training. I sensed he was trying to hold off for as long as possible from changing. He knew that once the Lokoti Werewolves saw him in his other form, they'd go all out to kill him. Right now, they were trying to wound and claim dominance.

"Declan!" I flinched in sympathy.

Bloodied teeth and claw marks appeared in his human skin, as the Riverclaw and Wisetail Werewolves continued to pull me away. But I managed to dig my feet in the ground, as I refused to leave my mate! Simultaneously as I expanded into my stronger, female Lokoti Werewolf body; I heard Declan's boxer shorts tear, as he too increased into his European Werewolf shape.

The Caucasian in their midst grew in stature to almost twice their height, as his width expanded to three times as wide. The bloodied gashes in his skin regenerated as hardened hide replaced it. His face extended into a short, stubby snout over razor sharp jaws. Like this, the beast towered over the smaller predators and flexed his larger claws.

Out of the blue, the smallest Lokoti Werewolf leapt onto his huge back, like he had something to prove. He looked as young as fourteen, as he tried to dig his teeth and claws into the European Werewolf's thick neck. I almost laughed at the whole 'Scrappy Doo' mentality of, 'Let me at 'em! Let me at 'em!'

Declan who was unharmed and amused, plucked the little one from his back and held him up in the air, before his dangerous jaws. Then he shook his monstrous head at him before gently placing him on the ground. This made the pack pause, as I caught them exchange surprised glances.

They wondered why the European Werewolf didn't try to eat their kin, but put a stop to him in a way which was considerate?

Even with my extra strength, I wasn't strong enough to break free. So I surprised my captors when I used my ability to phase to slip from their grasp. It made the pack blink in disbelief, as I raced over to Declan's position in light speed. Then I stood in front of him in a protective gesture, as I growled warningly.

I don't think it was my show of muscles underneath my stretched pyjamas that made them pause, but it was the fact that I looked like a bright blur when I ran.

The Lokoti Werewolves shared their puzzled thoughts with each other.

HOLD OFF YOUR ATTACK – The Lightfoot Werewolf ordered - *THERE IS MORE THAN MEETS THE EYE WITH THIS PAIR.*

They began to back away whilst growling threateningly.

WHY IS THE FEMALE LOKOTI WEREWOLF DEFENDING THE FOREIGN BREED LIKE HE'S HER MATE? – The Wisetail Werewolf pondered.

BECAUSE HE IS MY MATE! – I thought back.

Shocked, the pack's mouths fell open as they looked on.

First, I surprised them by being a Lokoti they've never seen before. Then I surprised them by turning into a Lokoti Werewolf, since women weren't supposed to turn. Now that I could communicate with them, they didn't know what to say.

DECLAN, SAY SOMETHING – I ordered.

There was a pause, as the Lokoti looked on the European breed, sceptical that he'd be able to.

I'M TIRED AND I'M HUNGRY AND I WANT TO GO HOME TO BED – he thought grouchily.

Silence... until the Lightfoot Werewolf started to laugh, as did the Wisetail and the Riverclaw then so did the rest of the pack. Our kin now approached us in a less confrontational manner.

WHO ARE YOU? – The Riverclaw Werewolf wondered.

I AM BIANCA SABRE – I answered - *MY MOTHER IS A RIVERCLAW AND MY FATHER IS A WISETAIL.*

The Riverclaw and the Wisetail Werewolves exchanged further looks of surprise.

WHY ARE YOU HERE? – the Lightfoot Werewolf asked.

BY ACCIDENT – I admitted - *I COME FROM THE FUTURE.*

Many of the pack exchanged glances, as half believed me and the other half didn't.

I AM THE FIRST FEMALE LOKOTI WEREWOLF – I telepathically declared - *AND I AM THE LAST LIGHT PERSON.*

That got their attention, as I sensed they all understood the term 'Light Person' even in this timeframe.

SHE DID MOVE LIKE LIGHT – the Riverclaw Werewolf looked to his First.

SHE DOES HAVE AN AURA LIKE THE OTHER LIGHT PERSON – the Lightfoot Werewolf agreed.

I was quick to ask – *WHAT OTHER LIGHT PERSON?*

However, our exchange was interrupted by several human Lokoti arriving on the scene. The male Warriors moved out from the trees, armed with silver-tipped arrows on their bows. Their weapons were aimed at the gargantuan monster on their land.

Instantly, I moved in front of Declan in a protective posture. At the same time, I was hoping not to get shot with silver again. My head momentarily hurt, as it remembered the last time I was injured this way.

Since I was a much smaller than he was, I don't think I made a very good shield. Whilst he was standing upright on his hind legs, his heart and his head which needed the most protection, were above me. Then the Lightfoot Werewolf saved us the trouble, when he held up his hand to stay their weapons.

Next, he gestured for them to come to his position which they obeyed. However, they moved slowly as they kept their weapons ready, incase the giant proved dangerous. To look less intimidating, Declan shrunk back into his human shape.

The Lokoti watched fascinated by his shape shift. His bones made soft cracking noises as they contorted and his snout retreated back into his head. Then my naked mate pulled me behind him, to protect me instead.

"Purto!" The Lightfoot Werewolf waved over one of the Warriors.

A Native American man with a tattoo on the left side of his face, slowly came forwards. His bow and arrow were lowered, but he looked on my mate in mistrust. Declan and I however, gazed at him in curiosity. He seemed more South American than Native Alaskan and I could smell he wasn't Lokoti.

He openly examined my mate's blonde hair and blue eyes but when he looked at me and especially my clothes, it was in astonishment.

Then this Purto asked in English, "Is that Daffy Duck?"

*****

~ 18 ~

Declan and I shared surprised glances at how this Native dressed in the suede clothes of old, would know about Loony Tunes.

"B, this guy has the same kind of aura you do," my mate whispered in my ear.

My glowing turquoise eyes bulged at the news. Then I realized I was still in my supernatural shape. The stranger watched as I returned to human form and as such, I addressed him. "Are you a Circulator?"

Purto smiled, "I am."

My husband and I exchanged further looks of astonishment, as we'd never met a Circulator outside of my family.

He openly stared at my face as he said, "You look like a descendant of Elisha Worthall's." Then his eyes settled on the small, gold crucifix around my neck. "Your necklace, it's hers isn't it?"

Subconsciously, my hand reached for the jewellery. The Christian icon had been in my family for generations. It had belonged to Elisha, who gave it to her granddaughter Arabella Riverclaw, and she passed it on to her granddaughter, me.

"You know Elisha Worthall?" I asked excitedly.

Purto pondered, "You're not Jessica Riverclaw, are you?"

"No, Jessica Wisetail nee Riverclaw is my mother." I brought him up to speed. "I'm Bianca Sabre, Elisha's great, great granddaughter."

"Did you say your mother became Jessica Wisetail? So the argumentative girl married the quiet boy she kept running from." He smiled in amusement.

At first I wondered how he knew my parents, when I remembered that the Circulate left for the continuum when my mother was fifteen. By that age, she already had an admirer in the seventeen year old Hunter Wisetail. But it wasn't until she was eighteen that they became mates.

"Tell me, how did you come here?" Purto asked in curiosity.

"I instantaneously phased us here in my sleep." I admitted, before I waved my hand. "In the future, this is where our house stands."

"Talking about where we are," my husband interrupted, "what year is it?"

"1868 AD," the other Circulator answered then he turned my way. "You instantaneously phased here? But how is that possible? The only Circulators who can do that are Elisha, Sophie, Lucas and Kell."

"So can I." I shrugged. "But you're mistaken, there are nine Circulators within the Circulate who can instantaneously phase. They're Elisha, Sophie, Lucas, Kell, Mike, Alexandrina, Arabella, Jessica and now me, Bianca."

This made Purto's eyes widened and he even took a step back, from shock.

"Why haven't I seen you at Circulate Headquarters before?" He wondered.

"Because I was born in the year 2066 AD, four years after you guys evolved to the space time continuum." I pointed out. "Now my grandparents and parents are there as well. Where we come from, I'm called the Last Light Person."

Declan backed me up, "She's the last Circulator in the tribe and in the world."

Purto looked on the naked, muscled man standing beside me, warily. "How do you fit into all of this?"

"I'm her unpaid carer," he said sarcastically.

I whacked him on the arm to behave, before I asked Purto, "Do you know who Mike Sabre is?"

"Yes I do," he answered. "He's a Circulator and the one time amore of your great, great grandmother."

"This is Mike's great, great grandnephew, Declan Sabre." I nodded his way.

"Are you a Circulator too?" He checked.

"Not yet," my mate said coolly. "Before I die of old age, B is going to change me into one. Then I'll exist with her for all eternity inside of the space time continuum."

"Then you are..." he wondered how to put it, "...just a Werewolf?"

"I'm a European Werewolf." Declan glared. "And I'm the last of my kind."

"What year did you come from?" He turned my way but it was my husband who answered.

"We come from the year 2240."

Our new acquaintance looked me over once more, "You don't look like you're past your twenties, but I'm betting you're much older than that."

"I'm 174 years old," I smiled, "and Declan's three years older than me."

However, Purto didn't seem interested in the European Werewolf with his forty-something appearance. He stepped closer to look into my dark blue eyes. It was like he was looking for the truth, although I don't know what my eyes could tell him. Declan cleared his throat as if to remind the man to keep his distance.

"I'm sorry but seeing is believing..." he began, "...could you instantaneously phase for me now, to show me your ability?"

358

"No," my mate said curtly before frowning my way. "Your aura is faded enough as it is, I don't want you showing off."

Then I surprised everyone when I abruptly disappeared in a bright flash of light.

At the same time, I reappeared by Purto's side in a second flash. Next, I disappeared in a third flash of light, before the last when I instantaneously phased back to Declan. The little light show and disappearing act impressed Purto, the Lokoti Werewolves and Warriors, all but my husband.

"Damn it, B!" He growled. "Why is it you always do the exact opposite of what I tell you?!"

"You CAN instantaneously phase." Purto said impressed. "This means you are the ninth most powerful Circulator in the Circulate."

However, as soon as he said that, my legs gave way!

Thankfully Declan caught me, as a dizzy spell swept from head to toe. He raised me up into his arms and frowned when my head rolled backwards. Then he shot off a glare to whom he thought was to blame.

"You were saying?" He seethed.

The other Circulator took a step forwards and held his hand over my head. He closed his eyes and I think he could sense my weak bio-electromagnetic field. Meanwhile, the rest of the Werewolves and Warriors all stood around and observed. They couldn't follow our conversation because they didn't understand English, but they watched with interest.

Not only did I feel exceptionally dizzy, but sleepiness was right on its heels. I tried to raise my head, but I didn't have the energy. I looked like I had fainted, as I struggled to stay awake.

"She's drained." Purto's voice sound far away. "She's used her ability to excess which is why she's feverish."

"Gee, you don't say?" My husband sung sarcastically. "I was wondering why I was nursing her day and night, for the past week!"

"Dr. Knight should take a look at her." He said seriously. "She can be given a special medication which -"

"- will help her immune system by a special mix of vitamins, minerals and a steroid." Declan interrupted. "Yeah thanks, we already have some."

"But Dr. Knight should examine her, as she's an expert with our physiology and unique requirements." Purto continued.

"No thanks!" My mate said adamantly. "B's never sought out the Circulate of the past, as her outlook is you're before her time. She's also told me how the Circulate once drugged Elisha with DYSTAR against her will, which took her powers away. So I know some of you have your own agenda. I wouldn't trust you with my wife, if my life depended on it!"

Then I felt Declan turn around to address the Lightfoot Werewolf. The pack was still surprised how the different breed was on their wavelength to talk telepathically. So when the blonde-haired, blue-eyed foreigner also spoke fluent Lokoti, it was a double whammy.

"I am a Lokoti son. I was adopted into the pack when I was three winters old, by Emanuel Riverclaw. To my pack I am Second. I have defended this land in bloodshed and battle. My mate is a Lokoti daughter and she needs a Medicine Man."

The Elm looked on the Lightfoot Werewolf, as if asking for his permission. When he got the nod, he said back in Lokoti, "I am the Medicine Man."

Next, my mate muttered in English, "Great, it WOULD be my luck, wouldn't it? It just HAD to be the guy who was sniffing my wife."

Then the European gave the Lokoti Werewolf a nod to proceed.

Whilst warily looking on the dangerous breed, he cautiously came forwards to examine his mate. My eyelids were pried open as he checked my eyes, felt the glands on my neck, put his ear against my chest and sniffed me one last time. This time I don't think it was because of my pheromones, but he could smell the virus.

Then the Elm Werewolf said to his First, "The sickness is upon her. Her aura is faded because she is weak. She needs rest and fire and food."

The Lightfoot Werewolf spoke to Declan, "You will be granted sanctuary while we heal our Lokoti daughter."

Vaguely, I watched all of this come to pass as my head swam. My eyes were half closed as my mouth hung open, to help breathe. It felt like I was wheezing again as my chest constricted.

But amidst the illness and the arguing, I wondered two things. One was when did Declan learn to speak the old language? And two, when did I learn the old language myself, to understand what they were saying?

My mate gave another nod as his acceptance then we were led down the hill.

As the Lokoti Werewolves walked with us, they reverted to their human form. I thought this meant that they trusted Declan however, three of the Warriors still nursed arrows on their bows. Their weapons weren't pointed at him, but it showed they were still on guard.

I tried to stay awake but I kept passing out at different intervals. I guessed we'd left the hill, as the ground was no longer sloping. I was carried through more wood until we came to a small clearing by the river.

Here I saw a kind of 'village' with small huts. It was lit up by several different campfires out the front of many of the homes. Around the fires sat more Lokoti in suede clothes, or 'skins'. In fact, animal hides and pelts were everywhere. The rectangular huts with the triangular roofs were constructed of solid branches. However, the walls and rooftops were made from animal hides and smaller branches.

I didn't think they'd be very warm in winter, until I remembered that the Lokoti used to be semi-nomadic. In winter they lived in the caves further up in the range, so this was their summer home. It was by the river which offered not only clean water, but ample fish especially when the salmon swam upstream. The village wasn't that big either, with no more than twenty huts, which could house two to six family members.

The Lokoti that weren't asleep, came out of their huts to stare at the strangers. They gaped at the naked, blonde-haired, blue-eyed outsider; carrying his part Lokoti mate in the strange clothes. I think they also wondered why he was walking with the Werewolves and Warriors as a guest and not a captive?

"You will stay with my family as your mate is my kin," the Riverclaw Werewolf spoke to Declan.

Then he pulled aside an animal pelt which hung over a doorway to one of the huts.

I was carried inside with Declan ducking as he went, so he wouldn't hit his head. There, we found a woman combing her two young children's hair, when they looked up in surprise. Along three of the walls of the hut, were 'cots' to sleep on. They were constructed of branches, like the structure was, and covered in pine needles as mattresses. On top of the fauna lay two different furs. I soon found that you lay on one with another over you, as your blanket.

"Here," the Riverclaw Werewolf pointed at one of the cots.

Carefully, my mate lay me down then the Riverclaw Werewolf handed him some suede pants to put on. With blurred vision, I looked around at the dark, tiny home. The only light came from the campfire out the front. Inside, there were suede bags, an animal hide basket, more furs, spare suede clothes and a bow with arrows, all hanging from the wooden roof or wall supports.

Just then I had all of these strange faces hovering over me. It was the Elm and the Riverclaw Werewolf, as well as the Riverclaw's mate. The Elm Werewolf sniffed me again then he turned his head and spoke in Lokoti to the woman. I think he gave her instructions of some kind, as she gave a nod then disappeared from my field of vision. Within a minute she reappeared, to lift up my head and try to feed me some kind of hot liquid from a small, wooden bowl.

I felt scared as well as disorientated, being in a strange place with unfamiliar people. I didn't like the smell of that liquid either. I moved my head away as I wondered where my mate had disappeared to?

"Declan...?" I managed out.

"I'm here, B." He appeared beside the woman, now semi-dressed.

Declan took the cup from her and he tried to feed it to me too.

"What is that?" My face screwed up from the smell.

"It's a kind of tea, you need to drink it because it's medicinal." He instructed. However, I jammed my mouth shut as my refusal. "C'mon B, don't get all 'princess' on me now. It's safe, I remember Derik boiling up a batch of this a couple of times, when he was a Medicine Man."

This time when he pressed the wooden cup against my lips, I took a sip. But I soon regretted it, as it tasted just as bad as it smelled. It was like a bitter, stewed wood and I could've been drinking boiled sticks for all I knew! Blech!

"She should be taken to Circulate Headquarters for proper treatment." Purto's face reappeared.

"I said no and I mean no!" Declan declared.

"The Lokoti have treatments which work on common ailments, but none that can help a Circulator in her condition." He insisted.

"What part of 'no' don't you understand?" My mate growled. "Should I say it in English, or would you prefer it in Lokoti? Or should I explain it with my fist?"

That made Purto move away from the volatile male. Declan rolled his eyes in annoyance, before he turned back. He tried to make me take a second sip, but I rolled my head away from the cup.

I was so exhausted that the darkened hut turned completely black, as all of their faces faded into nothingness. I slipped back into the comforting oblivion of unconsciousness. Whereas to my hosts, it looked like I took a sniff of the tea then I passed out.

"She's very sick," my mate made my excuse in Lokoti.

"So we can see," the Elm Werewolf smirked.

Not to be rude, Declan raised the hot drink to his mouth and politely took a sip. Then he had to quickly turn his face away to spit it back out. However, the Riverclaw's mate saw and took the small bowl from him.

"The tea is for sickness." She said haughtily. "You are healthy."

"Thank God for that," he muttered in English.

*****

I woke up to find daylight creeping underneath the hide hanging over the doorway.

I felt so weak, I could barely move. However, I did feel undeniably warm, which I soon saw was part of the reason why I couldn't roll over. My huge husband was sleeping beside, with his arms and legs wrapped around his wife. Not only did he take up the most room in the single-sized cot, but his body temperature could put the furs to shame.

Next, I realized we both had no clothes on. His hot skin was pressed against mine, with his 'morning glory' between my legs. I blushed, especially since I realized we weren't alone. In the other two cots slept the young brother and sister in one then their parents in the other. The siblings slumbered back to back, whilst mother and father slept entwined in each other's arms.

Then I noticed everyone was sleeping naked underneath the furs. I could tell by their bare shoulders peeking out of the covers. Their 'skins' hung on pegs on the branches, which held up the walls of the hut. The air smelled a little smoky from the campfire outside, slowly going out.

The Lokoti woman slept soundly in the arms of her Lokoti Werewolf mate, who held her just like Declan was holding me. Both males appeared accustomed to sharing their body-heat with their partners. When I looked over at the children again, I pondered if this was simply the way these primitive people slept?

They didn't have much clothing to begin with, so they had to conserve what they had. The confined quarters didn't award much privacy, as the family unit must have been accustomed to undressing in the other's presence. In the winter months, the whole tribe could have slept together, in the caves. Although in that instance, I doubt they slumbered with no clothes on.

Before I slipped back into sleep, I said a silent thanks for the 23rd Century amenities of separate bedrooms and bathrooms.

*****

When I awoke again it was because of my mate shaking me.

"Man, you're out of it." He frowned. "You've slept a night and day away. You didn't even wake when I climbed into bed and out again."

He was sitting on the side of the cot topless with just suede pants on. In his hands, he nursed a small, wooden bowl of what smelled like a meat broth. I also noticed how his leg was jiggling, as he stirred the soup with a roughly carved, wooden spoon.

I raised my head to look past him out the doorway, since the hide 'door' was held open by a leather fastener. Outside, I saw it was night time but people were still going to and fro. Coupled with the golden light of the campfire, was the silver light of a full moon. The moonshine spilled onto the dirt floor and cast the hut in a pale glow.

"Is it a full moon?" I noticed.

"Uh huh," he answered as he stirred my soup.

"Was it a full moon last night?"

"Yup."

"Oh," I thought that made sense, because in my vision I saw the pack hunt on a full moon.

"In our era, it was only a half moon." He went on. "But here, it's part of the three day Luna cycle."

I confessed, "I had a dream of the pack embarking on a hunt in the days of old."

"Which made you bring us here?" He arched an eyebrow. "Next time, can you have a dream about a vault filled with treasure instead?"

Then he temporarily put the bowl down on the ground. He used both hands to sit me upright, so my back was against one of the wall supports. But when he raised me up, the blanket almost slipped off! Self-consciously, I grabbed onto the fur and held it securely over my chest.

"Declan, where are my pyjamas?" I asked awkwardly.

"Over there," he gave a careless nod as he picked up the bowl again. "Muna who's Arun's wife, thought they were your everyday clothes. When she was tending to you, she took them off as in the warmer months they're accustomed to sleeping naked."

"Who are Muna and Arun?" I wondered.

"Your Riverclaw ancestors we're staying with." He answered, as he put some soup onto the spoon.

"Declan?"

"B?"

"How come you can talk in old Lokoti to them? I only remember a few words here and there, from Grandpa teaching me when I was little. But you seem to understand it with no problem."

This made him lower the spoon in surprise. "Are you saying that you don't understand them?"

"I understand most of what they say," I frowned thoughtfully. "Otherwise I just sense what they mean."

"B, when you talk with your mind to me or the pack, it's in Lokoti."

"Say what?"

"You heard me."

Then he tried to move the spoon to my mouth but I moved my head away.

"What do you mean?" I gave a funny look. "Are you saying when we talk telepathically to each other or to the pack, it's actually in Lokoti?"

"That's what I just said," he sung. "Now shut up and eat."

"But how?" I demanded. "When Grandpa was the tribe's Medicine Man, he taught me a little here and there. He could even read the old writing on the First Sacred Totem. But I could never speak fluent Lokoti!"

"Think about it B, the Lokoti Werewolves have been around for generation upon generation. When the pack was first created they didn't speak English, did they? Therefore the first telepathy began in Lokoti and has remained ever since."

"But what about in the 23rd Century?" I quizzed. "Aren't we telepathically talking in English?"

"Some of the words are English, like when we use modern jargon or when we swear." He gave a wink. "But otherwise we talk in Lokoti, when we're talking with our minds and not our mouths. It's how the pack have always communicated with each other."

"Really?" I marvelled.

EAT THE SOUP, B – he thought to demonstrate.

I started to understand, as I 'heard' a kind of accent which I'd never noticed before.

SPEAK TO ME AGAIN – I requested.

LISTEN TO MY WORDS CAREFULLY. YOU UNDERSTAND WHAT I'M SAYING BECAUSE IT'S MY MIND SPEAKING DIRECTLY TO YOUR MIND. BUT LISTEN TO THE 'SOUND' OF THE WORDS, THE WORDS ARE LOKOTI.

Just then I opened my mouth and said, "Ana ina un te tu te che, te che ta Lokoti."

The English translation, I'd repeated what he'd said, 'but listen to the sound of the words, the words are Lokoti'.

"In unan B." He smiled softly.

Declan said, 'you're in my heart B'; which means 'I love you'.

My eyes widened in wonder as it was like learning an important clue in a mystery I'd always pondered.

Then he spoke in English, "When I was first adopted into the pack, I couldn't hear their thoughts. I don't think European Werewolves are telepaths, even if our females do develop psychic ability. But I felt the will of the pack as they took me hunting every full moon. In between, your Grandfather sat with me night after night. When I couldn't sleep because the bloodlust was eating me inside out, your Grandfather spoke softly to me in Lokoti. He'd tell me a story in your native tongue then tell me the same story again, in English. It's how I learned the language. When I started to understand, I also started to telepathically hear words in the Lokoti Werewolf will. The very first thing I ever heard with my mind was, 'hunt animal, not human'. The pack made sure I could think back to them before they allowed me to patrol. Then I could telepathically call for backup should I need it."

I turned thoughtful before I asked, "What about when you were with Leo, Michelle or Marcus, could you hear their thoughts?"

"Nope!" He said resolutely. "I wouldn't want to. I have enough trouble managing my own bloodlust, without telepathically hearing theirs."

"But you said Michelle was psychic, did you hear her?"

"Nuh uh."

"Never?"

"Nup," he tried to move the spoon to my mouth once more.

"Declan," I moved my head away again because I wanted to talk, not eat. "Were you attracted to Michelle? Did she smell tempting because she was the same breed as you?"

"No," he said whilst looking down into the bowl of broth.

"Are you sure?" I looked on closely. "Were you tempted to mate with her, to repopulate your species?"

"B, she smelled fertile." He admitted. "Because of this, the bloodlust that spurs me to eat human also tried to tempt me to copulate with her. But when I'm holding you and your aura radiates through me, she could be belly dancing and I wouldn't look twice. Michelle was vaguely tempting, but compared to you she was mutton dressed as lamb."

"Really?" I asked hopeful.

"Cross my heart and hope to die," he said dutifully. "Now will you stay still so I can get this into you?"

I felt the wooden spoon press against my mouth and if I didn't open, I would have worn it. I took several mouthfuls and it tasted like the meat was hare. My carer behaved impatiently, as he was feeding me the soup faster and faster. Another spoonful was jammed in before I'd swallowed the previous. But I saw why, by how hard his leg was jiggling. I knew that the full moon was affecting his bloodlust.

"You need to go hunting." I stated the obvious.

He looked on guiltily, "I'm sorry B, you're right. I know you're sick and we're temporarily stuck in a strange place until you get better. But I need to go out and kill something."

"That's OK."

"I'll be right back I promise."

"It's alright, Declan."

"You're here with family so I know you'll be safe."

"I know that too."

"Unless you need to come hunting too?"

"No."

"Are you going to be OK?" He gazed on in concern.

"Yes."

"At least you smell stronger," he observed. "Just save the Circulator tricks until you're all better."

"I'll be fine, really!" I giggled at the fretting male. "Now get lost, would you?"

Weakly, I tried to shove him off the bed. Declan chuckled as he leaned in to deliver a sloppy kiss to my cheek. I pushed him away again to his amusement then he returned his attention to the food.

"Alright, at least finish this bowl of soup then I'll leave you alone." He sounded relieved.

As I recommenced eating I realized we had an audience.

Outside, Arun and Muna and their two children, were sitting around the campfire in front of the hut. The squabbling strangers in their home made them pause in their eating. It looked like they were consuming the same soup I was. But instead of using wooden instruments, they were sipping straight from the bowl.

The kids were slurping down their dinner, which Arun smilingly observed. Periodically, he tipped more soup from his bowl into theirs. His eldest in following tradition was a son, and looked on his fathers bowl hungrily. He silently gave in, by tipping what was left into the boy's.

Then he handed his mate the empty dish, before standing up to begin his own preparations for the hunt.

*****

"Aaaah!"

Hmm, what was that?

"AAAAaaaaaAAagghh!"

Huh? What the hell is all that noise? It sounded like a screaming competition was going on! Was there some kind of party that I was missing?

"Aaarrgh!"

When I opened my eyes, I saw it was dawn and Declan and Arun weren't here. They were still on the hunt, no doubt, as it was only around three o'clock. But Muna and her children jumped out of their beds and acted frantic about something.

She was yelling at the two to hurry and I watched the three scramble into their clothes. Her son who looked about seven years old, didn't bother about his suede shirt. Instead, he grabbed his father's bow and arrows which were hanging on a wooden wall support.

I forced myself to sit up, to find out what was going on. As Muna frantically dressed, she grabbed my red flannel pyjamas which were hanging nearby and flung them my way. I guess she wanted me to dress, too.

"Aka! Monana! Yukilli!" She yelled in Lokoti, which translated as, "Hurry! Danger! Werewolves!"

What the...? Well of course there are Werewolves, she's married to one! What's all the fuss about?

I proceeded to put on my pyjamas under the cover. As I dressed, I saw Muna tentatively stick her head out of the pelt door. Her daughter who looked to be five years old, cried as she clung to her mother's suede skirt. Whereas her son struggled to put an arrow on his father's bow, which was so large it was the same size as him.

Are we under attack? What's going on here? I remembered the stories of battling the neighbouring Lynx Tribe, who were suspicious of the pack. Or, occasionally other tribes would ransack for food or women. Then why did she say 'werewolves'?

Over the screaming, I heard something else; a bloodcurdling howl permeated the night air.

My eyes widened in alarm. I recognized the noise came from a supernatural predator, but not by my Lokoti Werewolf kin or European Werewolf mate. It came from another breed of Werewolf, as the noise stirred something deep inside. Instinctively, my eyes started to glow as my body expanded for battle.

My muscle bulk made me feel stronger and I threw off the fur to stand up changed.

This made the mother and children stare at my glowing turquoise eyes. My elongated teeth jutted out of my parted mouth and were as sharp as the claws on the ends of my fingers and toes. The pyjamas looked tight as the flannel strained over my muscle bulk.

"Mother! Mother! Mother!" Her daughter sobbed, frightened.

"Stand back, mother!" Her son marched towards the doorway, fumbling with his father's weapons.

"Get back!" Muna waved her small son away. "Look after your sister!"

Reluctantly, he put down the weapons to pick up his younger sibling instead.

No sooner than he did, Muna was knocked backwards by something large, furry and snarling!

She landed flat on her back with the creature on top of her. For half a second, I thought it was some kind of bear, but the fur was thinner and a reddish brown colour. It had a narrow snout with sharp teeth and tall ears on the sides of its head. Its eyes were as black as night, with no pupils or whites showing. Also its' claws were longer than a bear's.

Although I'd never seen one before, I knew it was a North American Werewolf. My protective instincts were engaged, as I snarled at this foreign breed for being on MY territory! Not to mention it had its claws in an ancestor of mine.

I grabbed the attacker and yanked him off her so hard, he went flying through the hut wall!

CRASH!

Through the hole I'd inadvertently created, I saw it roll away on the ground. The North American Werewolf stopped by digging its clawed hands into the ground before leaping back onto its clawed feet. It snarled in fury and I stepped through the new opening, to meet my foe.

I took the fight outside to protect the mother and her young. Like this, the opponents circled the other, flexing their muscled arms and clawed hands. The monster was taller than me and I could smell it was stronger, but I was faster.

It made the first swing which I easily ducked. It made a second swipe and missed again. Each time the creature tried to claw me, its long nails sailed through empty air.

Momentarily, I looked away from the fight and saw Muna had deep claw marks in her shoulders. She was sitting upright with her hands on her wounds, to watch me fight. On either side of her sat her son and daughter. The little girl was still crying whereas her brother watched with interest. I think he wanted to see if a female Lokoti Werewolf could protect the tribe like the males did.

This time the North American Werewolf tried to swipe at me with both of its claws. I leapt backwards, however one of them caught on my shirt. It flew open with half of the buttons flying off.

Then something strange happened, the North American Werewolf paused when I caught it sniff... Oh oh, no, not again! Not another male Werewolf lured by my frickin' pheromones!

Embarrassed, I quickly tried to redo the remaining buttons. However my timing couldn't have been more wrong. Next, the monster leapt on top of me because I was unprepared. Good one B, how about worrying about how much skin is showing AFTER the fight?!

Instead of clawing at my skin to harm, it shredded my pyjama shirt instead! It went from hungering for flesh, to hungering for something else. I knew this behaviour well, thanks to 150 years of marriage to another Werewolf. Now I was I was trying to fight off the attacker and save my clothes at the same time.

"No, get off her!" I heard somebody yell in English.

I looked up to see Purto run behind the monster with a silver-tipped arrow on his bow. He fired it directly into the back of the North American Werewolf! Its head went up as it howled in pain.

Then it used its claw to knock it out before turning on him. When it did, I saw a small stream of red smoke rise out of the tiny, bleeding hole in its back. The second Circulator used his light speed reflexes to fire off another two silver-tipped arrows. However, they were too small to take the beast down, as they didn't penetrate past its muscle.

Uselessly, he shot a third arrow into the Werewolf's chest, but it made little impact.

"Go! Get away! Phase out of here!" I roared in my thunderous voice.

The North American Werewolf removed the arrows as if they were no more than sticks, whilst it advanced upon his position.

"I can't instantaneously phase like you can!" He shouted back.

The monster swung out its claw and he just managed to duck and roll away using his faster reflexes.

Frickin' hell, the rescuee turns into the rescuer. I staggered back to my feet, as I was feeling really weak again. Hastily, I tied my pyjama top together in a knot before engaging in a second round with my opponent.

As the monster stalked towards Purto, I stalked behind it. I swung out my clawed hand, knocking it to the ground! However, it was quick to return to its feet, snarling furiously. I don't think my blow made much of an impact.

I went into a self-defence stance as I faced off the beast. The North American Werewolf swung out its left then its right claws, which I weaved between. When it tried to leap on top of me again, I was able to catch it and flip it to the ground. However, it was always quick to return to its feet and make another attack. I ducked from another swipe and returned it with one of my own. But because there wasn't much muscle behind it, it only left a superficial scratch.

As Purto watched me fight this way, he thought he could help. He came to stand behind the monster in a self-defence stance too. However, when he tried to karate kick the beast in its ribs, he hurt his foot. Neither of our blows had any effect on the creature who had fifty times the strength of a human. Man, I wished I had my silver-coated Katana right then.

"No, just run away! Go!" I roared in desperation.

Purto limped backwards and the monster swung out its claw which sent him flying through the air! When the Circulator landed five meters away, he had a deep claw mark across his chest. The beast was about to pounce on him to finish the job, when I leapt on top of it!

Damn it, I didn't want to fight it this way! I don't have the strength for this! But it was either this, or a dead Purto.

My opponent tried to shake me off his back and I dug in my claws. The monster roared as it deliberately ran through the wall of another hut, to knock me off! I landed hard on the dirt floor. Dazed, I looked up at a grandmother, mother and small daughter, huddled together in a corner.

I opened my mouth to apologise for the intrusion, when I cried out in pain. The North American Werewolf bit down on my right leg! Like this, it dragged me back into the open. My leg was in agony as the experience taught their teeth are just as elongated and sharp as a Lokoti Werewolf's are.

However, I was soon distracted by other screams around us.

I raised my head to see the North American Werewolf wasn't alone. I saw five more, mauling several Lokoti as the humans uselessly tried to fight them off. Then another two leapt on top of four Warriors, knocking their bows and arrows to the ground. They were making mince meat of the tribe, literally.

C'mon B, do something! These are your people! They're DYING!

Enraged, I used my uninjured leg to kick my attacker in the snout! It staggered away, which enabled me to pull my leg free. Next, I leapt on top of it a second time as my dangerous mouth went for its throat! I felt its fur on my tongue as I brought down my sharp, elongated teeth. But the beast used its greater strength to claw me off, as it flung me a short distance away.

OOW that frickin' HURT! My torso felt like it was on fire, with several deep, bloodied gashes going down my abdomen. I felt like I'd been ripped open! Helplessly, I lay on my back, unable to move as the warm blood rose out of my mangled skin.

Smugly, my opponent loomed over me. It could see I was unable to get up, let alone fight. I saw the hungry look return to its blacked-over eyes, as it licked its lips. Oh well, I thought weakly, it's better that I get eaten than Muna or her children...

However, the North American Werewolf paused and I watched it turn its head. Just as I wondered why, I heard the sound of backup arrive. I swear, the howl of my kin never sounded so good!

AAAAAAARRRROOOOOOOOOOWWWWWWLLL!
The Lokoti Werewolf pack returned early from the hunt, as they ran to the aid of their mates and the tribe.

GGRRRAAAAAWWWWLLL!

Hang on, I'd know that growl anywhere. Next, a large, light-tanned blur flew past! Then I realized the North American Werewolf was no longer standing over me. Where did it go? Oh, there it is...

Like I was lying on the ground mauled, so was my opponent. I saw his reddish-brown fur become even redder with blood splatter. The European Werewolf's jaws had eaten through its supernaturally strong chest, to its heart.

At first, the North American Werewolf helplessly clawed at his larger build. Then its claws flopped to the ground, as it lay dead.

Declan raised his bloodied jaws from my attacker, as he turned his beastly head my way. Quickly, he came back to my position and I saw him lean over my mangled torso. He sniffed my wounds in concern then his large, hot, wet tongue lapped at my skin. Oh that felt good! His saliva numbed the sting as it slowed the bleeding.

However, as he was doing so, I saw another North American Werewolf run down the middle of the village. It leapt into somebody's hut and I heard the resulting screams. Helplessly, I lay on the ground and unable to assist.

"Declan, I'll be OK. Kill all the North American Werewolves! Kill them for me!" I growled out. He hesitated, as he looked from his mate to the hut the other Werewolf had run into. "Go, Declan! I'll be alright. Help the tribe!"

I think he was confused, as one minute I'm chastising him for being too extreme with the Voodoo crazies then the next I'm encouraging him. But I didn't have a choice, we were in the midst of a blood bath. After a second, he turned his glowing green eyes towards the new threat.

I heard his low growl come from his clenched jaws. Then he bounded away and his huge, hulking form, smashed through the small doorway! I almost laughed as I watched the hut shake and start to come apart. It couldn't contain a gigantic European Werewolf attacking a smaller North American Werewolf.

The small structure lurched this way and that, as the most hideous snarls, growls and whines came out of it. So did several shocked humans. Two women stumbled out of their disintegrating home, nursing bloodied claw or bite marks.

The hut collapsed into pieces and poetically timed, so did the North American Werewolf.

Next, I watched my mate rise from the remains and leap upon another who was eating two elderly men at once.

Uselessly, I lay on the ground as my male kin battled our attackers. I was starting to feel dizzy from the blood loss, as it continued to trickle out of my torn flesh. But I tried to watch for as long as possible. In the distance, I saw the fifteen members of the pack battle the other five foreign Werewolves.

I flinched when I saw that their strength was an equal match. However, my kin fought on in fury, in vengeance for their families and friends. Many an injured human lay about, in between the corpses of those who didn't make it. The Warriors left the fighting to the Werewolves, as they saw to the wounded.

My stomach shrank when I saw three of the Lokoti Werewolves fall. This included the plucky, youngest member of the pack, who tried hard to keep up. Then I saw Arun get the better of his opponent by realizing he had faster reflexes.

My Riverclaw forefather used his lightning-fast swings to shred his enemy! He swiped at his opponent so fast, his claws were like blades in a blender. The rest of the pack followed suit, as I telepathically heard:

THEY MAY BE AS STRONG AS US, BUT WE'RE FASTER. USE THEIR SLOWER REFLEXES AGAINST THEM!

I saw the Wisetail and the Lightfoot Werewolves strike their opponent down. Then using his elongated teeth, the Lightfoot Werewolf ripped out its throat! My Wisetail relative punched his clawed hand through another enemy's chest, before ripping out its heart. The Elm Werewolf used his lightning-fast reflexes to gouge his opponent's eyes, blinding him. Then he and the Shallow Water Werewolf laid it to waste.

Declan rose from his third victim – slash – meal and turned his large canine head in the direction of the fighting. He saw that the pack had the situation under control so he trotted back to my position. The human Lokoti gasped at his frightening appearance and several moved away from him.

My mate circled me the once before he sat on the ground, near my head. He raised his right claw to his mouth and used his sharp teeth to put a gash in it. Then he used his left claw to raise my head and placed his injury inside my mouth.

NEXT TIME B, LEAVE THE FIGHTING TO ME – he thought unhappily.

I THINK I WILL WHEN I'M SICK – I agreed.

The more I drank of his blood, the more the pain lessened. I felt my torn stomach muscles begin to knit together. The burning agony dulled to an ache, as my skin slowly closed up.

To help it along, Declan ducked his head to run his hot tongue over the surface wounds. His saliva to sped up my regeneration, as did his blood. I heard further gasps whilst I sucked on his wrist, which made me look around.

Several Lokoti gazed on my mate's monstrous appearance, mistaking him for eating his wife and not healing her. This included Purto, who was sitting a short distance away. He climbed back to his feet, picked up one of his silver-tipped arrows and crept up behind my husband.

I tried to move my head away but he refused to remove his wrist. Declan thought I was acting stubborn, as if I didn't want his blood. He even growled at me to stay still!

"Purto, nin!"

This caught his attention and quickly he lifted his head. He saw a wounded Muna, stagger out of her hut with her children at her side. She put out her bloodied hands in a 'stop' gesture to the second Circulator.

Declan roared in fury at the male he already disliked. His large left claw whipped out and caught Purto's throat in its supernaturally strong grip! In the meantime, he kept his right wrist in his mate's mouth, to continue healing her. I think he also did this to show off how Purto wasn't a threat, but a nuisance.

Our new acquaintance began to choke as he dropped his weapon.

DECLAN NO! – I thought in alarm, as I struggled to remove his thick wrist – *PLEASE DON'T KILL HIM! PLEASE DON'T!*

The other Lokoti Werewolves overheard my thoughts. They left the enemy's remains to come over. The Lightfoot Werewolf saw Declan strangling Purto and his command was swift.

RELEASE THE LIGHT PERSON! HE IS A GUEST! HE IS PROTECTED!

From his years of serving as Second, his clawed hand immediately opened and Purto slipped to the ground, coughing and spluttering.

OH, YOU'LL OBEY THE LIGHTFOOT WEREWOLF BUT WHEN YOUR WIFE ASKS YOU TO STOP...? – I complained.

SHUT UP AND DRINK – he inwardly grumbled.

The second Circulator sat there, gasping for breath and looking on in hatred. The European Werewolf turned his back to him and I felt his tongue return to glue my torn tissue together. The last of the pain disappeared as I felt the bleeding stop. I was almost completely healed thanks to my stronger mate.

THANK YOU – I thought gratefully.

SHUT UP AND DRINK – he repeated but warmly this time.

Over his arm, I watched Arun walk over to his injured mate. Muna collapsed in torment, into his muscled arms. Carefully, he lowered her to the ground and followed Declan's example. Using his teeth, he put a gash in his wrist, which he gently placed between his wife's lips.

DO THE SAME TO THE REST OF OUR FAMILIES AND THE TRIBE – the Lightfoot Werewolf ordered his men – *OUR BLOOD WILL HEAL OUR KIN AND STOP THEM FROM TURNING INTO WHAT ATTACKED THEM.*

The pack split up, walking away with their wrists in their mouths. They tended to the bitten ones first, as they shared their regenerative ability. The uninjured members of the tribe helped, by dressing the wounds of those who only had claw marks.

HAVE THEY GOT ENOUGH BLOOD TO GO AROUND THE WHOLE TRIBE? – I wondered as I watched.

WE HAVE NO CHOICE - the Lightfoot Werewolf answered my question - *WE MUST STOP THEM FROM TURNING INTO MAN-EATERS.*

I saw the First use his blood to heal the youngest Werewolf in his pack before attending the humans. Once the fourteen year old was back on his feet, his uninjured mother ran up to hug him. I noticed how a man didn't come forwards, which indicated his Lokoti Werewolf genes must have activated upon his father's demise.

With my wounds now taken care of, my mate affectionately licked my face in relief. Then he scooped me up in one arm and held me against his hardened hide. I wrapped my arms about his bulky neck and he carried me back inside of the Riverclaw's hut.

Since he was too big in his European Werewolf shape to use the normal doorway, he went in via the hole in the wall.

I CAN SEE YOU'VE BEEN DOING SOME REDECORATING – he thought humorously.

I HOPE THE RIVERCLAWS LIKE 'MODERN ART' – I joked along.

I felt his huge body shake with inward laughter, before he carefully lay me down on the cot.

Skilfully, he used his claws to tear off my ruined pyjamas without causing further harm. Then he pulled over the second fur, between his razor sharp teeth. After leaving another affectionate lick to my forehead, he turned away.

The sound of his bones cracking as they contorted came to my ears. Listening to them move around like that, reminded me how he said changing from man to beast and back again, caused pain. I watched as his hardened hide turned into his softer human skin, as his muscle bulk decreased along with his height.

Soon I was looking up at a naked human who grabbed a spare pair of suede pants to put on.

"B," turned back around. "I'm going outside to help them tidy up, OK?"

"I'll come with you," I tried to sit up.

"No, you need to rest." He sat on the side of the bed. "We have to kick that virus out of your system once and for all."

I said helplessly, "I don't like being sick, I feel so useless."

"I don't like you being sick either, I feel so frustrated!" He rolled his eyes. "So hurry up and get well and make your husband a happy man again."

"You are – or were – a happy man then?" I searched his bright blue eyes.

"Here we go, the ole 'are you happy' questions." He smirked. "It's a pity we're back in time, so there's no 'Nutella' or Alanis Morrisette."

"Declan -"

"B, a person wouldn't hang around for 150 years if they were unhappy. Not even a supernaturally strong creature could last in an unhappy marriage. So shut up, close your eyes and get some sleep. If you need me, just call out."

I clasped his hands and held them against my chest. "I love you Declan, you do make me happy."

"Er, thanks."

"I mean it, I love you." I rambled on. "You've always been there for me."

"B, are you delirious or something?" He laughed it off. "Now close those pretty, dark blue eyes and get some sleep!"

He ducked his head one last time to caress my forehead with his lips, before standing up.

Then he disappeared out the door. I sensed he felt bad that he couldn't share his blood with the tribe too. He couldn't risk creating anymore

European Werewolves. So instead he'd rebuild their huts and repair the other damage.

I curled up on my side as I drifted into another sickness-induced slumber.

*****

I must have slept the day away, because when I opened my eyes again, it was night and the hole in the wall had been repaired.

I heard the sound of Declan's voice, indicating he was talking to someone. When I half opened my eyes, I saw him sitting outside by the fire. Not only was he with the Riverclaws, but also Purto, an elderly Lokoti woman and the Wisetail, Elm and the Lightfoot Werewolves.

They were talking in the old language and I had to switch my brain from English to Lokoti, so I could understand them. When I did, I overheard a kind of Q&A going on. Everyone was asking my mate questions about our relationship and he was doing his best to patiently answer them.

"Your mate was the third 'Light Person' in your tribe?" Purto asked stiffly.

Declan's eyes narrowed as he regarded the Circulator with the bandages wrapped around his chest.

Eventually he answered, "Yup and now she's the one and only. Her mother and her grandmother left for the space time continuum, with their Lokoti Werewolf mates." When he saw our host's confusion, he added on, "The space time continuum is the white man's name for the Holy Hunting Grounds."

"Ah," they nodded in understanding.

"Have all the other Light People died?" The Elm Werewolf enquired.

"Er no, the Light People have a way of visiting the Holy Hunting Grounds without dying." He struggled to explain. "But once they're there, they can't come back."

"Hmm," the Lokoti nodded again, this time gravely.

"So in your era, everyone's evolved then?" Purto checked.

"Yeah, Aunt Jess, Uncle Hunter and Vincent Moher were the last to go." He answered. "B's the Last Circulator with just the Circulate Mainframe to act as her Calculator. Of course there's me, but I can't keep up with her talk about temporal causality crap."

"Of course not," the Circulator said snidely.

Declan's eyes narrowed and he was about to retort, when he thought of something else to say. He reminded, "B will turn me into a Circulator so I'll end up there too. It looks like you and I could be seeing a lot more of each other."

"What?" Purto sat up startled. "Do you really think she's going to turn YOU into a Light Person?"

"Yup," he smiled smugly. "Then you'll have to put up with me forever and ever."

The Circulator shot off a look that said, 'we'll see about that', before he rose to his feet and walked off.

The Lightfoot Werewolf asked, "Why did our cousin leave our circle angry?"

"I told him that my Light Person mate will turn me into a Light Person too and take me to the Holy Hunting Grounds with her." He said simply.

"Light People are as powerful as the sunlight and they can affect change like the moonlight." The old woman spoke. "They live lightly, like the sun's reflection dancing on the river. If you are truly to become the light Declan, you will have to release your darkness."

"Yeah I know," he sighed. "I was hoping that by evolving to the space time continuum – er – I mean by going to the Holy Hunting Grounds, that I'd be leaving my darkness behind."

"Light can illuminate the darkness, but it cannot abolish it." The old woman shook her head. "You cannot run from it, the same way a tree cannot run from its shadow. You can chop down the tree and make a hut, but then the hut will have a shadow."

"I guess so," he rubbed his face wearily. "But it feels so good touching her aura. I thought that once I was in the place of light, it would be like living in her aura all day, everyday."

"You are a hunter, Declan." The Lightfoot Werewolf observed. "You thrive on the kill because it feeds your demons. In the Holy Hunting Grounds, the prey will be different. There the predator can turn into the prey."

"You will have to shed your demons and darkness, before you cross into the light forever." The Elm Werewolf agreed. "Otherwise, you'll be taking the darkness with you and it could become your after life."

I watched Declan's face fall at their words, which made my chest tighten.

"How long have you and our Lokoti daughter been mates?" The Lightfoot Werewolf asked.

"For 150 winters," he answered.

"Was your mating approved?" The old woman asked knowingly.

"Er no, not at first." He admitted. "In the beginning, we had to hide our feelings and meet in secrecy."

"Hmm," the Werewolves frowned.

"But you proved yourself in battle?" The old woman guessed again.

"You could say that." He shrugged. "Our feelings were revealed in bloodshed. B gave up her life to save mine."

Declan looked my way and I pretended to be asleep, so I could continue to listen.

"Then her family saw yours and her hearts were one?" Arun asked.

"Yup." He straightened uncomfortably, as he hated getting 'mushy'. "Afterwards I moved in with her and from then on we were mates."

"You called her the first female Lokoti Werewolf, how many other female Lokoti Werewolves are there in your time?" The Lightfoot one queried.

"B is the one and only." He stared in my direction. "I used to think and in a way I still do, that she changed for me so I wouldn't be alone."

Then he caught the Lightfoot, Riverclaw, Wisetail and Elm Werewolves exchange glances.

"What's up?" He wondered.

"It's appropriate that the first female Lokoti Werewolf is a Riverclaw and a Wisetail." The Lightfoot Werewolf pronounced.

"It is? Why?" He gave a funny look.

"Because Aru who was the first Lokoti Werewolf, was a Riverclaw." The First declared.

Declan's eyes widened in surprise as everyone nodded in confirmation.

"You're kidding!" He exclaimed. "You know what? I've heard the story of how the first Lokoti Werewolf was created, dozens of times. But it was never told if he was a Riverclaw or a Wisetail or a whatever."

"Aru was a Riverclaw." The old woman told the story. "Aru's sister Unka was married to Yun Wisetail, who fought with him. Yun was almost dead, when Aru shoved his bleeding wrist into his brother's mouth. Wisetail became Riverclaw's Second. Together, they created the rest of the pack from the Warriors who were left alive. Then the first fifteen Lokoti Werewolves drove the raiders off their women and their land."

My mate beamed, "That makes a lot of sense actually. So many Riverclaws have been First... B's great, great grandfather Flint Riverclaw had been First. Then Harry Lightfoot was First when Flint was killed by looters, after World War Three. Flint's grandson Emanuel Riverclaw who was B's grandfather, became First when Harry died and Hunter Wisetail, who's B's father, was his Second. Now B's grandnephew Chiron Riverclaw is First, and I'm his Second."

The circle all nodded in understanding at what he just told them.

"How did you come to live on Lokoti land, Declan Sabre?" The Lightfoot Werewolf asked.

"My father was killed by the European Werewolf which turned me." He told his story. "I was meant to die that night, but Emanuel Riverclaw put his bleeding wrist in my mouth. Uncle Em inducted me into the pack and helped raise me. When I was sixteen winters old, I started to patrol the borders with the pack to keep out looters. I fell in love with B when I was seventeen winters old. But I had to keep my distance until she turned, when I was twenty-one winters old. We grew up fighting and we tried to fight our feelings for each other. It got to the stage where we realized that there was no-one else we'd rather fight with."

A couple of them laughed as they listened to his story by the fire.

"And you thought she became the first female Lokoti Werewolf, for you?" Muna smiled.

"If she hadn't turned, I'd never have been allowed to touch her." He looked downwards. "Even when she changed at the age of eighteen, I still had to be careful."

"She is attracted to your darkness which gives you your strength, the way you are attracted to her light which is her power." The old woman spoke.

He shifted uncomfortably, "If you say so."

"Declan Sabre," the Lightfoot Werewolf stood up, as did his men. "Last night you killed three of the enemy and today you helped us rebuild our camp. We are indebted to you. If you ask for something we can give, it is yours."

The European Werewolf stood up too like he had a request already.

"I would like a Joining Ceremony." Declan declared.

Say what? My eyes snapped open in surprise and I even sat up, whilst holding the fur against my form. I gave an incredulous look as the rest of our friends and family appeared baffled.

The male Lokoti Werewolves exchanged glances before they looked back at the foreigner.

"You and your mate did not have one?" The Lightfoot Werewolf wondered.

"Then how did her family allow your mating?" The Elm Werewolf queried.

"We had an unofficial Housewarming, but no Joining Ceremony." He answered. "So I'd like one."

"Then you shall have a Joining Ceremony." The Lightfoot Werewolf smirked at the odd request. Next, he looked on the old woman still sitting down. "We can arrange that for him, can't we?"

"I will speak to the rest of the Elders and see what can be done," she shrugged. "If the male European Werewolf wants to join with his female Lokoti Werewolf in a ceremony, we can provide it."

Then I watched the greying Lightfoot Werewolf reach down and help the white-haired woman to her feet.

"Thanks!" Declan grinned.

"You are a good wolf," she reached out to pat him on the chest. "You should speak to your Elders when you return home, on ways of shedding your darkness. Then you will be able to move freely into the light."

Declan stood back to watch the First of the pack escort the Tribal Elder home. However, I caught him mutter in English, "A European Werewolf taking anger management classes? Sounds like a Monty Python sketch to me."

Next, the Wisetail and the Elm Werewolves left the fire in front of the Riverclaw hut to return to their own.

"So B, did you enjoy the story time?" My mate looked my way.

"A Joining Ceremony?!" I cried indignantly to the Riverclaws' surprise. "A frickin' Joining Ceremony?!"

"Yeah so?" He shrugged it off. "What's the big deal?"

"I'm NOT going through another Joining Ceremony!" I fired his way.

"What? Why not?!" He fired back.

"Declan, do you recall what happened to the last guy I went through a Joining Ceremony with?"

"Yeah he died."

"So we are NOT having a Joining Ceremony!"

"Oh yes we are!"

"Oh no we're not!"

"Hell yeah!"

"Hell no!"

"B, we ARE having a JOINING CEREMONY!" His eyes glowed in anger.

"We don't need to when we already have these!" I waved my left hand with the wedding ring.

"A frickin' ring doesn't mean that we had a wedding!" He snapped as he came to stand in the doorway. "I want to do this properly!"

"Why?!"

"To officially make you my mate!"

"Ah ha!" I pointed at him. "You said the word 'mate'! Are we or are we not biologically bound together?"

"Yeah so?"

"If I'm already your mate, we don't need a Joining Ceremony!"

Declan leaned over my cot so our faces were level and he bared his sharpening teeth.

He roared out, "WE ARE HAVING THIS FRICKIN' JOINING CEREMONY WHETHER YOU LIKE IT OR NOT!"

I rolled over as I said coolly, "No."

The European Werewolf hated it when I turned my back to him in the middle of a fight. He gnashed his teeth and stormed out of the hut to go break or kill something. The Riverclaws saw the proverbial steam whistle out of his ears, whereas I simply went back to sleep.

~~~~~~

~ 19 ~

The next morning I was feeling much stronger with my health almost back to normal. I left the Riverclaw hut to stretch my legs in the suede clothes Muna had kindly lent. I didn't see Declan though, he must have gone somewhere with Arun.

I wandered through the camp which was busy with Lokoti going about their day-to-day tasks. I walked past a couple of people who were organizing a trade with one another, or others who were making suede clothing. I saw four women hanging up cleaned animal hides, to dry on wooden racks.

Everybody smiled warmly as I passed. I guess they'd heard they had a 'daughter from the future' visiting. Also, I think it was because I was dressed as they were, so I looked like one of them.

Altogether, I sensed warmth in the people who looked out for each other. Not only did the Lokoti have to fight off the odd warring tribe, but they had to contend with the harshness of the Alaskan weather. They were used to pooling their resources and helping out a neighbour.

I stopped to watch a barter taking place between two women. One was haggling using the salmon she was smoking, as the other had some edible plants and berries. When they noticed me standing there, the lady took out a trout from her hide basket and offered it.

"Are you hungry?" She asked.

"Oh no, but thank you!" I blushed, as I hoped they didn't think I was begging. "Thank you, I am not hungry."

The woman shrugged and returned to her business at hand, as I moved on.

It felt freaky being here and experiencing all of this. It was like being inside a living museum, or a 'This Is Your Life' episode. Instead of serenading one person, it was a testament to a people as a whole. Then I saw something standing in the middle of the village, which made me stop in surprise.

My mouth fell open as I gawked at the first Sacred Totem. It stood alone, brightly painted and carved. On the top was the tribe's most revered spirit guide, the Lokoti Wolf, with the other animals below it. Finally I realized where I was, the village was on the Holy Grounds of the future.

As I stood there staring, somebody used this as their chance to talk. I was joined by Purto, who was wearing another suede shirt which was half open. Curiously, I couldn't see any bandages underneath his clothes. In fact, his chest appeared completely healed.

"B," he greeted.

"Purto."

"You look better," he observed.

"Likewise," I inferred his previous injury.

"I went to Circulate Headquarters last night where I was treated by Dr. Knight." He advised.

"Oh, OK."

He continued, "It looks like your recuperation with the Riverclaw family, worked."

I agreed, "The Riverclaws have been so kind, Declan and I appreciate it."

"I think your family and the tribe appreciate your assistance during the attack."

"I don't know how much help I was!" I laughed it off. "Declan did most of the work."

"He's very protective of you, isn't he?" Purto remarked. "I wonder if he would've been so concerned over the tribe's safety, if you weren't Lokoti."

I turned to give an icy look. "Declan is Lokoti. My Grandfather helped his mother raise him. He's as much as a Riverclaw as he is a Sabre."

"So I've heard," he looked unconvinced. "B, I need to talk to you."

"OK."

"It's about Declan," he frowned.

"Alright," I folded my arms in front.

"When I was at Circulate Headquarters, I checked the database. I read the SSIT Report on the Different Breeds of Werewolf. The entry on European Werewolves was a cause for concern."

I rolled my eyes, "Declan is nothing like the European Werewolves in that report."

"He is EVERYTHING like what was written about his breed!" He retorted. "His short temper, his violent behaviour and his voracious appetite."

"Did you see my great, great, grandmother?"

"No, Elisha wasn't at Circulate Headquarters when I visited. She was in England, in mourning for her late human husband, Jarrod Worthall." He answered before he continued with what he wanted to say. "After I read the report, I went to the Viewing Room and I saw many a frightening image."

"What, of Declan?"

"No, of other European Werewolves." He quipped. "I'd already seen your husband in action, when he ate three of the enemy two nights ago."

"He was defending our people." I debated. "I asked him to do what he did. I doubt there'd be so many Lokoti walking around right now, if it weren't for him."

"B, the report was actually tame in comparison to what I saw in the Viewing Room." He warned. "We're concerned about you."

"Who's 'we'?"

"I discussed the situation with several members of the Circulate Council, Dr. Knight, Lucas Hodge, Rufus Kell and Sally Parson."

"You did what?" I blinked.

"When I told them that I met the world's Last Circulator, they were thrilled and asked to meet with you. However, when I told them that you were married to a European Werewolf, they shared my concerns." He went on.

"Say what?" I blinked again.

"We don't think it's safe if you remain with him." He spoke quickly. "Come with me to Circulate Headquarters and let me show you what I'm talking about."

"I beg your pardon?" I looked on incredulous, as I couldn't believe what I was hearing. "You expect me to go back in time to listen to a bunch of strangers, bad-mouth my husband? Purto, go out and buy a clue! You have no idea of the man I'm mated to."

"Your life is in danger!"

"No it's not!" I snapped. "I'm in no more danger of Declan, than of my husband suddenly turning into a vegetarian!"

"B, you're the Last Circulator and the Circulate isn't about to turn their backs when one of their member's are in trouble." He said haughtily.

"You had NO IDEA of my existence and now you're trying to separate me from my husband of 150 years?!" I flared. "I don't give a flying duck what the Circulate thinks! The only Circulate I know was my mother, grandmother and cousin Vincent Moher. My Mum and Gran approved of Declan, thank you very much!"

"Just come to Headquarters and see what I'm talking about -"

"No!" I interrupted. "I don't trust you as far as I can throw you!"

"It's not like we can kidnap you, if that's what you're worried about." He said knowingly. "We know you're stronger than us as a Lokoti Werewolf and you can instantaneously phase."

"You're damn right I can kick your ass!" I seethed.

"At least come and meet the Circulate of the past, which is your past." His voice dropped to a pleading tone. "The Circulate Council have asked to formally meet you. Wouldn't you like to learn more about your beginnings?"

I said snidely, "I already know about my beginnings. My father loved my mother and nine months later, I was born."

"B," he looked on long and hard. "Wouldn't you like to meet the Circulate that your great, great grandmother knew?"

"I don't know..." I turned away.

I had to admit, I was tempted to go with him as it had been lonely, travelling through time by myself. I missed circulating with my mother or my grandmother. I'd read about my great, great grandmother's adventures, from reading her diary. What if this was my chance to meet her, the Circulator who defied the natural order to create a lineage of Circulators? I did miss talking about history with other people who could traverse it.

"The Circulate Headquarters on Taurus Six must be a lonely place, when you're the last one left." He sung.

I thought that was rubbing salt into the wound, which made the sting worse.

"Do you know the name Sally Parson?" He continued. "Or what about Genevieve Nelson or Zachary Reece?"

I faced him again, "Didn't they go to school with Elisha?"

"They did and they're waiting for you." He answered. "Sally Parson who's your great, great grandmother's best friend, is on the Circulate Council. She's one of the people who requested to meet you."

That made me pause... but would I really meet her? Or was this a trick? I looked on in distrust.

Purto promised, "Everybody wants to meet the Last Circulator and the first female Lokoti Werewolf. There's never been a hybrid before."

I stood still as I contemplated his offer. I'd like to meet Elisha's friends. I've read so much about them, it'd be nice to put faces to names.

"What have you got to lose?" He shrugged. "Ours can be a lonely gift while we outlive our loved ones. Wouldn't you like to meet others like yourself?"

He was right, I did have the desire to meet more of my kind; other Circulators. I'd been so excited to see Purto the night Declan and I arrived. I recalled how I sensed another Circulator was present. It was the reason why I risked the confrontation between my mate and the pack.

"If we do this, I can't be gone for long." I caved-in. "I don't want to worry my husband with my absence."

He gave a nod, "Understood."

With that, he turned and walked towards the river... and I followed him.

*****

The second Circulator led us out of the village and to the riverbank a short distance away.

"What are we doing here?" I wondered.

"You're still weak so I'll take us there." Purto organized. "I can't instantaneously phase so I need a reflective surface. Since the Lokoti don't have glass or mirrors, I'll use the water."

"Oh," my eyebrows rose in surprise.

I'd read how some Circulators can do this, but I was curious to see how it was actually done.

"Can you please come and stand in front of me?" He requested, as he stood by the waters' edge.

I did but I tensed up, partly because another time I stood close to the river with a man, he pushed me in.

"Try to relax," he placed his hands on my shoulders. "Let me do the driving."

I held my breath as Purto looked over my shoulder and stared into the water. I realized he was gazing at our reflections as he concentrated. Then I felt a rush of warmth and a tingling sensation as he put us into phase. My biological body turned into one made of light, as I turned bright and see-through.

Then I felt Purto's being gently push mine forwards. If I had shoulders, I would have flinched because I thought we were about to fall in. However, I was surprised when our light waves skipped over it. The same way sunlight danced off the water as sparkles, so did we.

Next, I experienced a rushing sensation as I tried to keep track of what was happening.

Suddenly, I saw the river, the ground and then the woods, all whoosh away like I was streaming away in light speed! Next, I was seeing the black, starry, background of space, before a red planet came zooming towards us. Or maybe we were zooming towards it?

The red planet looked like it blossomed like a flower, as I saw vegetation and water such as oceans and rivers appear on the planet's surface. I realized we were phasing through time to when Mars had life. Lastly, I saw a small, shining circle on land mass and I realized that's where we were heading.

I watched it quickly grow into the large, glass, habitation dome of Circulate Headquarters. It rapidly grew a lot bigger and now it felt like were falling towards it. I wondered if I was about to bounce off the dome, when the next thing I knew, we were reforming back into our biological bodies.

As soon as we returned to solid form, I found us standing on the circular, mirrored platform of the Gate. For the first time in my life, I found people in the Gate Room who weren't related to me. A group of adults casually dressed in early 21st Century clothing, looked on expectantly.

They appeared to be different ages, with some older than others. However, I think I recognized three of the youngest from Elisha's photo albums. Purto made the introductions as they stepped forwards.

"Dr. Bianca Sabre, allow me to introduce you to Sally Parsons, Genevieve Nelson, Dr. Patrick O'Flannigan, Dr. Vivian Knight, Professor Stephen Hamilton and Dr. Rufus Kell."

Kell who had brown eyes and curly, brown hair with a thirties appearance, smiled widely. "I was impressed with the paper you wrote on 'Ancient Gods of Love and War'."

"You've read it?" I asked in surprise. "But you all evolved to the space time continuum, long before it was written."

"We *are* time travellers," the beautiful, young woman with black hair, rolled her green eyes. She looked a little Goth as she wore mostly black. "Look around you, this technology does come from the 25th Century. You don't think we can look up your academic work from the 22nd and 23rd Centuries?"

"Oh right." I saw her point.

"Ignore her, we do." The young, blonde-haired, blue-eyed man wearing glasses, smirked. He offered his hand to shake and spoke in an Irish accent. "Call me Pat and that was Nelson. This here is Sally."

"Hi B!" The young, blonde, curly-haired woman, beamed. As she shook my hand, she openly examined my overall appearance. She spoke in a Scottish accent, "I like you're dark blue eyes, they go with your dark hair. You're taller than Jessica, Arabella, Alexandrina and Elisha though, as well as stronger looking."

"Purto said that when you turn into a Lokoti Werewolf, your eyes glow turquoise." Nelson said. "Can you show us?"

"Ah Nelson," the brunette in her forties, spoke up. "Perhaps it's not a good idea to stir the natives?"

"That's Dr. Knight and this is Professor Hamilton." Pat waved their way.

"Welcome," the forty-something man with short brown hair, shook my hand.

"You were teachers at Hamilton's College," I remembered. Then I looked at Pat again, "And you're my great, great, grandmother's Calculator."

"You read all of this in Elisha's diaries, didn't you?" He asked knowingly.

"It looks like all the hours she spent typing away weren't wasted after all." Nelson said to Sally. "She can be completely clueless, but occasionally she has a bright idea."

The Scottish woman nudged her to mind her manners, especially when she was insulting their guest's great x2 grandmother.

"Purto said you don't eat human." Nelson spoke to me again. "If you don't eat human, it should be safe to see you turn, right?"

Sally nudged her friend again as she apologised, "Sorry about her! Unlike your supernatural state, she's pure bitch."

Nelson nudged her back, "What's wrong with asking to see it? When are we going to get to see something like this for real? We've only seen the Lokoti Werewolves change via the Viewing Room, since they only trust Elisha or Arabella. Plus B's a rarity being the only female."

I saw there was only one way to settle her curiosity. It was her lucky day that I didn't crave human flesh with my control over the bloodlust. In this instance, curiosity wouldn't kill the cat.

To everyone's surprise, I began to change as my dark blue eyes turned glowing turquoise. A low growl escaped out between my teeth which turned elongated and sharp. Their eyes widened, as they watched the nails on my hands turn claw-like as they extended.

However, these changes were only momentary, as I didn't want my muscle bulk to tear Muna's spare clothes. They stared as my expanding body shrunk again, whilst my nails and teeth detracted. It was just a partial change in the style of, 'now you see it and now you don't.'

"Sorry, I can't completely turn." I looked on the Goth with my glowing turquoise eyes. "Otherwise I'd ruin my clothes."

"Cool!" Nelson grinned. "I read in the SSIT report that Lokoti Werewolves become fifty times stronger, is that right?"

"But doesn't changing like that, hurt?" Sally pondered.

"It hurt in the beginning," I answered her before Nelson. "As a female, I'm not as strong as the males in the pack. My strength is forty times that of a human. But I'm stronger than Asian Werewolves or all the species of Vampire."

"But not as strong as a European Werewolf, though." Kell remarked.

"No." I said simply, as my eyes dulled back to their dark blue colour. "European Werewolves are the strongest of all the breeds. Males are a hundred times the strength of a human, with females eighty times."

"And they still eat human, don't they?" He asked warily.

"My husband is the only European Werewolf known not to hunt human." I said. "Now he's the last of his kind, you could say that European Werewolves no longer feast on human flesh."

"That is an incorrect assessment," his voice dropped to an icy tone. "Did he, or did he not, recently consume two men in New Orleans?"

What the...?! My guard went up, as I wondered how long these people had been watching. After they learned of my existence, did they do a 'crash course' of my life, in the Viewing Room?

"OK, moving right along," Pat spoke quickly. "How about a tour of the Martian Circulate Headquarters?"

"I already know the layout." I said coolly. "I walked these halls over a hundred years, before the Mainframe activated the self-destruct. I could walk to the Medical Lab, Viewing Room, Props Room, Gate Room and Mess Hall, blindfolded."

"But I thought it was destroyed by the Calculator Vincent Moher, activating the self-destruct mechanism?" Pat said in surprise.

"It was collusion between human Calculator and artificial one, as the Mainframe became B's new Calculator." Nelson said. "They both concluded it would be logical to have only the Headquarters on Taurus Six; a location which a Circulator can reach, but not mankind."

"Oh excuse me for not getting the memo!" He rolled his eyes.

"You are Elisha's Calculator, are you not, Pat?" She reminded.

"Yeah, I'm Elisha's Calculator!" He retorted. "What, now I'm in charge of her progeny too?"

"You might want to take a peek at their timeline, now and then." She gloated. "You might learn something."

Pat opened his mouth to argue when Professor Hamilton stepped in. "Thank you Calculators Nelson and Dr. O'Flannigan, that will be all."

"What of Taurus Six?" Dr. Knight enquired. "Is it operating properly?"

"Of course," I answered. "Before Vincent evolved, he made sure that the second Headquarters could function as the first one did. He had us move all the costumes to the new Props Room, bit by bit. Also, the Mainframe is an excellent Calculator. She contacts me via email or text message when she needs to warn me, or call me to the Viewing Room."

"It looks like I did a great job of programming the computer single-handedly then." Pat sneered to Nelson.

She pulled a face before turning away and pretending to be occupied by something else.

Just then it occurred to me, as I looked on the forty-something woman. "Wait, are you the Dr. Knight who's related to the Dunmore and the Durrant families?"

"Why yes I am," she answered primly in an English accent.

"I met a descendant of your family in Scotland!" I told her excitedly. "Nairn Durrant of Stonewall House."

Her eyes widened in recognition, "There are still members of the Durrant family living in Stonewall House, in the 23rd Century?"

"She's a powerful psychic." I beamed. "She uses her ability to 'see', to help people. She's a renown Healer and a Midwife. She's become a good friend to Declan and I."

Dr. Knight looked touched by the news that a relation of hers was succeeding in a similar field. But it was Kell who ruined the mood.

"I'm not sure how good of a 'Seer' she is, if she befriends European Werewolves instead of barring the door against them." He said under his breath. However, I heard every word with my acute hearing.

"Declan protects Nairn, like he looks out for all the women in his family!" I snapped at the stranger. "He's even fought off European Vampires who wanted to feed on her! Nairn is a family friend and we've been guests in her home just as she's been a guest in ours."

"How about we leave the Gate Room?" Sally changed the subject, when she saw Kell open his mouth. "We can't stand here all day, arguing."

"Agreed," Professor Hamilton said. "A presentation has been prepared in the council chambers."

"What presentation?" I queried.

"Shall we?" Pat waved towards the door.

Warily, I looked from him to Kell, whom Purto came to stand beside. Now why wasn't I surprised to see two of the anti-Declan party, standing together? One of my tell-tale feelings made my stomach tighten. I sensed I'd be hearing more anti-European Werewolf propaganda.

First I was worried I'd stand out wearing the Lokoti clothes of old. However, as we walked down the corridors, we passed two people in Roman togas then another two in Imperial Chinese silk. From the direction they were walking in, it looked like they'd left the Props Room and were heading for the Gate. It wasn't hard to guess where they were off to.

"I thought you've been here before?" Pat wondered at my wide-eyes.

"I have been here before," I returned. "But I've never seen so many people here before."

Nelson threw Pat another look as if he should have known that, when he rolled his eyes. "Oh shut up!"

I was taken to a large room I'd seen plenty of times but never used. It was the Circulate Council Chambers, which could seat every single member of the Circulate in an amphitheatre-like setting. There were rows of seats on multiple levels, which were curved around in a half circle. The seating faced a podium and a large, crystal pyramid hung upside down above. It looked like the one which was in the Viewing Room.

Inside, I found two men waiting for us. They both looked like they were in their twenties, as did Nelson, Pat and Sally. Both men also had blue eyes and brown hair, whereas one was slightly scruffy.

"You must be B," the shorter haired one shook my hand first. "I'm Zack."

"And I'm Lucas Hodge," the scruffy one shook my hand, second. "But you can call me Brett like your Great, Great Gran did. Lucas is primarily an older identity I assume as the Head Chairman of the Board. It's a pleasure to meet the Last Circulator."

I hung onto his hand a little longer, "So you're the famous Lucas Hodge who started Hodge Endeavor in the 20th Century?"

"Yeah," he grinned. "How's my company doing, in the 23rd Century?"

"Very well, thanks to the Circulate Mainframe." I commended. "It tells me which Board Meetings to attend and hasn't made a bad investment yet."

Pat leered at Nelson, "Thanks to the talented I.T. Professor who single-handedly programmed it."

To which she returned with a shove and came to stand next to Zack. I saw how he immediately put his arm about her waist. I thought they would have made an interesting couple, a Goth paired with the 'boy-next-door' type. It made me wonder if people looked on Declan and I in a similar way? I think I was about to find out.

"Let's begin." Professor Hamilton called the meeting to hand. "If everyone can take their seats?"

"Come and sit down next to me." Sally took my arm.

Everyone sat down in the front row since it was the closest, whereas Professor Hamilton stood behind the podium.

"First of all, let's begin the meeting by welcoming our special guest, the Last Circulator." He waved my way.

Everyone applauded as they smiled in my direction, which made me blush.

Purto leaned forward to catch my eye, "I told you everyone wanted to meet you."

Awkwardly, I slid lower in my seat as they clapped for longer.

"Don't be shy!" Nelson laughed. "Some Werewolf you are!"

"We're shy right up until the point you try to harm us or a loved one," I returned.

"Interesting should bring that up, B." The Professor said, as he dimmed the lights from a control on the podium. "That's what this meeting of the Circulate Council, is about."

Then an image appeared in the three-sided pyramid, which slowly turned above the speaker area. It was of Cambridge University in the beginning of the 21st Century. It showed the students walking around campus, as they went to lectures or tutorials.

"The Circulate's reports on the supernatural came from a Circulator by the name of Elisha Worthall nee Baker, your great, great, grandmother. As an investigator, she amassed scientific data and recordings of supernatural activity. She started SSIT in the year 2003 AD at Cambridge University with a science student called Xavier Bell."

"I know all of this." I interrupted. "When they first applied for funding through the Student Union, they were laughed out of the office. It was Hodge Endeavor who sponsored the student group which turned into a profession. I've read her diary entries and all of the SSIT Reports on ghosts, time warps, Ley Lines, Voodoo, ESP, the Different Breeds of Werewolf and Separate Species of Vampire."

"It was one of my best investments yet, supporting SSIT." Brett aka Lucas Hodge smirked.

"We went on a few of the investigations," Zack told me. "In fact, Pat, Nelson and I were with them for their first one, regarding ghost lights around a stone circle which was on a Ley Line junction."

"We were cold, hungry and tired." Nelson rolled her eyes. "I swore never again will I camp in the wet English countryside."

"But we did see the ghost lights caused by the electromagnetic activity." Pat conceded. "It resulted in a time warp and we discovered it's how the stories of people wandering home and glimpsing a past event, started. Or, how they mistook the strange lights for the Fae."

"Yeah, I told Nairn about that," I nodded. "When she stayed with Declan and I, she said that our Holy Grounds are on a Ley Line junction."

Just then the image in the pyramid changed to show a computer interface.

Professor Hamilton continued, "But it's the other information collected on European Werewolves that's not in the SSIT Report, we want to show you."

"Aw c'mon, guys!" I moaned tiredly. "Like I said to Purto, my mate is NOTHING like the other members of his breed."

However, everyone looked I was the one who was behind the times and not the other way around.

"So your argument is that Declan is nothing like the European Werewolves in the report?" Kell challenged.

"That's exactly what I'm saying," I said adamantly.

"Computer, highlight paragraph three in the Reproduction/Mating Habits section." Hamilton gave the voice command.

The words appeared onscreen, "'Unfortunately for humans, it would appear that the European Werewolf lust is as great as its bloodlust. With this breed's overpowering strength, it's extremely hazardous to engage in sexual relations. If a male European Werewolf does have sex with a human woman, she can die from her injuries. Also, this breed often loses control of the bloodlust in excitement, and would claw and bite the woman'."

"Yeah so?" I shrugged it off.

"Computer, display the scene chosen in conjunction with this paragraph." He ordered.

Then my face reddened as it showed the morning after Derik's death back in 2145. I had the huge bruise on my shoulder from where Declan bit too hard. We were arguing in the kitchen, when I yelled out; *"European Vampires want to drink my blood and my European Werewolf husband likes to taste my blood. Now I have to go upstairs and use a hell of a lot of stain remover to get blood off our white Egyptian Cotton sheets... NO MORE BLOOD DO YOU HEAR ME?!"*

"That's not the only time he's bitten you, is it B?" He asked softly.

"So? I bite him too! It's a Werewolf thing!" I said embarrassed.

"Your Lokoti Werewolf grandfather or father didn't continuously bite your grandmother or mother." Dr. Knight stood up to side with Professor Hamilton.

"Yeah, but Declan's a different breed than them, he has different needs!"

"We know B and this is why we're holding this meeting today, to discuss how dangerous Declan is because of his needs."

"No he's not!" I fired up. "He only becomes so when he feels that he or his mate is threatened."

"He's not just overprotective, but his possessiveness indicates obsessive behaviour to the point of endangering others." Purto agreed with them. "When I tried to bring you here so we could treat your illness, he turned threatening. He risked your life, because he refused to temporarily part with you."

"He's the one who nursed me back to health!" I refuted. "Besides, it's just his stubborn nature as he prefers to do things his own way. If I was seriously in danger, I'm sure he would've let you bring me here."

"Are you sure about that?" Kell asked knowingly.

Next, the Professor read out another section, "'This breed has the longest history, being the direct descendant of the First Werewolf. Stories of this monster stretch from early BC to the present AD and are extensive, changing with each new storyteller.' When Elisha wrote this, she'd only just started to scratch the surface. What we'll show you is how closely related the European Werewolf is to the First Werewolf which attributes to their dangerous nature."

The sides of the crystal pyramid showed a series of primitive cave paintings of stick people and monsters.

"We believe that not only was the First Werewolf responsible for creating most of the breeds, but the European Werewolf is its direct descendent. The only breed which isn't related, is the Lokoti Werewolf. Coincidentally, the Lokoti is the youngest of all the breeds, being 2,300 years old." Professor Hamilton lectured.

Then the pyramid showed a picture of Earth in the Gondwanaland stage, when all the continents were one. As we watched, it zoomed in to a particular location. I recognized we were viewing the Mesozoic era with giant reptiles roaming the earth.

"In the beginning when dinosaurs habited the world, there was the First Werewolf." He narrated.

The following scenes in the sides of the pyramid showed a familiar but frightening creature. It was larger than a Raptor but not as big as a T-Rex. It stood upright and looked like it had hardened scales which acted like armour, along with long claws on its hands and feet. Its eyes glowed green with narrow slits as pupils, which made me realize how similar European Werewolves' eyes were to a reptile's.

"The First Werewolf stood five meters high and one meter wide. It was closely related to the Raptor however, it was a hot-blooded creature. The only predator game to hunt one of these was the most famous, the T-Rex." Professor Hamilton went on. "The First Werewolf ate carnivore or herbivore alike. Those who survived an attack changed themselves. After the meteor hit, the First Werewolf and its converted went into hibernation. Just as the meteor changed the world, it also altered those who survived."

The crystal pyramid showed the First Werewolf's DNA and how similar it was to the samples taken from the Asian Werewolf or the North American Werewolf.

He continued, "The only breed which didn't mutate from the DNA template of the First Werewolf, was the European Werewolf. This breed is the strongest and the largest because it's in direct descent."

Then we saw a picture of a European Werewolf on its hind legs, standing beside the First Werewolf. He was right, besides being slightly shorter and missing the armour-like scales; the European Werewolf did look the most like the First Werewolf. Both had the same eyes and the muscle bulk and the clawed hands and feet. Whereas the First Werewolf looked reptilian, the European Werewolf had more canine aspects.

"Until 1000 BC, humans who'd been bitten always remained in their European Werewolf bodies." Hamilton went on. "It wasn't until after, this breed was able to change from human to Werewolf and back again."

My eyes widened in surprise. No, I didn't know that. I found myself leaning forward in my seat as I listened intently.

"Being the direct descendant of the First Werewolf, is the reason why a European Werewolf's behaviour is primeval. They are prehistoric. Life on earth has evolved, but they haven't. All they care about is hunting, feeding and procreating."

I pulled back in mild offence, "Alright, I'll believe that about the other European Werewolves. But Declan isn't like that! He's -"

"- a sensitive new age guy?" Nelson cut in. "Admit it, he acts just like the rest of his kind."

"He doesn't!" I argued, but I was cut off by several new images in the pyramid.

It showed a collage of Declan's and my life together. It showed all the times he lost his patience with his wife and slung her over his shoulder. It showed the evenings of a full moon and during a hunt, how he didn't share his kill. In the theme of violence, next it showed him eating through the heads of the European Vampires we'd battled. Then it showed how he exterminated the other European Werewolves Marcus and Michelle, back in St. Petersburg. Lastly, it showed him eating the two men in New Orleans before he murdered the old woman.

"I object!" I stood up. "Those humans in New Orleans attacked us first! They tried to cut us up and sell us on the black market! When Declan took them out, they were halfway through a Voodoo spell on me!"

"Do you think he was protecting you out of the goodness of his heart?" Kell raised his eyebrows. "Or perhaps as his mate, he sees you as his property? We've all seen how territorial his kind is on a hunt, by not sharing their kill."

"What the hell is YOUR problem?" I stood with my hands on my hips. "From the moment I arrived, you've been in 'attack' mode."

Kell stood up to meet my gaze, "I'm the man who had his wife ripped out of his arms, by one of the prehistoric monstrosities the meteor missed when it wiped out the dinosaurs."

My eyes widened at his words before they narrowed again, as I watched him take the podium.

"Now it's my turn as I show this foolish girl exactly what kind of killer her husband is." He said to Professor Hamilton.

The Professor looked to Purto and Dr. Knight for their opinion.

"I think we should hear what Rufus has to say," she said evenly.

"I agree," he gave a nod. "She should learn of this."

I saw Sally exchange glances with Pat, Nelson and Zack, and from their expressions, they knew it wouldn't be pretty.

"B," the Professor escorted me back to my seat before he sat down in another.

"Computer, access Viewing Room records of Circulate member Rufus Kell. In particular, locate my Roman Wedding on the Quirinus estate outside of Prato in 140 AD." Kell commanded.

"Records found when ready," the computer's female voice responded.

But before he put the images onscreen, Kell looked long and hard my way.

He spoke with feeling, "The first time I married, it was to a young woman named Diana. I'd served under her father General Quirinus in the Roman Army. We won many battles as we defended Roman territory. When I first met Diana she was fourteen. Her mother died in childbirth so Quirinus' sister Bellona raised her and ran his house. Their villa was on a country estate just outside Prato, where I was invited to stay in between campaigns. I watched Diana blossom into the most beautiful woman I'd ever seen. Originally, she was promised to an older cousin who sat in the Senate. But after saving the General's life in battle, I asked for his permission. Computer, display the image of Diana Kell on our wedding day."

An attractive girl appeared onscreen, wearing a white, silk stolae with a red veil framing her face. The stolae was long and elegant and her hair was down, showing her dark curls. She had bright hazel eyes, which were accentuated by the black eye make-up of the period called antimony.

"We married when she was sixteen." He continued. "In those days it was common for girls as young as fourteen to become brides. She was dreading her arranged marriage. I showed her I was a Circulator when I promised to take her to any time or place she chose. Then I saved General Quirinus' life in an ambush. It was one of the bloodiest battles by far against the Barbarians. I gave away my status as a Circulator again when I fought in light speed. We arose victorious from insurmountable odds and when he asked how he could reward me, I asked for the hand of his daughter. At first he was reluctant to break the promise to his powerful nephew in the Senate. But he changed his mind when he saw Diana's and my reunion."

I found myself sitting back in my seat as I became entranced by his story.

Kell went on, "Our wedding was a gala affair with many of the powerful joining the revelry. However, two days before the ceremony, government officials from several nearby towns came to the villa. They advised the General that while he'd been on campaign, there were attacks made by a gigantic, dog-like creature they were calling Cerberus. The monster had glowing green eyes, large jaws and could smash through locked doors."

Oh oh, I sensed what was coming as he struggled to speak in a detached voice.

"They asked the General to send a century of soldiers to destroy the beast. Since I was one of his best fighters and preparations for the wedding were underway, he promised he would after the celebration. The day that Diana and I were made Husband and Wife, was the first night of the full moon."

Here we go, the crux of the matter. My jaw set but I heard him out. Kell spoke with reverence for his wife, but it was blended with bitterness for the beast.

"There was feasting, dancing and music all day and night. Additional slaves were purchased and there was an abundance of food and wine. The atmosphere was joyous and merry, up until 10 PM. That's when the festivities suddenly stopped. Computer, display the wedding celebrations for that time period."

Like I was watching a movie, the image panned down from the full moon in a starry sky, to a Roman Villa in the countryside. We saw hundreds of torches were lit as we could hear music play. We watched what Kell had described, a huge party with much merrymaking. Outside, there was dancing in a courtyard and inside were several rooms of people lying on couches, eating from low lying tables covered with food. The males wore their best togas and the women wore their best stolaes. Even the slaves' tunics looked fancier than usual, as they offered trays of food or wine.

Outside, we saw Kell dancing with Diana around a fountain in the courtyard. An older man and woman were standing off to the side, smilingly watching. They must have been General Quirinus and his sister Bellona. The bride and groom looked deliriously happy. When Diana broke away to twirl around a garland of flowers, Kell clapped her on.

Abruptly, this happy scene came to an end. Sounds of shouting and screaming came from outside of the villa. The ruckus drowned out the festivities and the musicians stopped playing.

The wedding party fearfully listened to the sounds of torture and mayhem on the other side of the garden wall. However, the noise which dominated over all was a familiar GRRRRAAAAAAWWWWLLLL! The bloodcurdling roar made many a guest freeze in terror and a slave dropped a tray of food.

"Legionaries!" General Quirinus called on his guards to investigate.

But then he didn't have to when the source of the bloodshed and destruction came to him instead.

A huge, hulking, hairless, black coloured European Werewolf, leapt over the wall. It scattered the party as it sent people scurrying, screaming for their lives. Kell pulled Diana backwards, as he looked around for a weapon to use.

"Get my silver sword, the decorated one that I was awarded." General Quirinus ordered a manservant. "It's on the wall in my bedroom, now hurry!"

Next, Kell and Diana retreated to Quirinus and Bellona's positions. The four watched as twenty soldiers took on the beast with their spears or swords. However, the male European Werewolf snapped their spears like they were twigs and decimated them in a matter of minutes.

"Run and hide Diana and Bellona!" The General ordered.

However, the bride looked torn towards the groom as if she didn't want to leave him.

"Go!" Her husband urged.

Reluctantly, she turned to run with her Aunt however, Kell noticed the European Werewolf's head turn. Oh oh, I knew that lustful look in the beast's eyes. The monster made a move to follow Diana into the house, when her husband tried to stop it. He picked up a small, wooden stool and threw it at him!

"Stay away from her, you hound from hell!" He yelled, as he and the General picked up anything else they could throw.

The wooden furniture simply ricocheted off the European Werewolf's hardened hide. The black creature didn't see them as a threat, so it went after the bride. The groom and his father-in-law picked up the swords of two of the half-eaten soldiers, before they ran after it.

The house was bedlam, with wedding guest, slave or senator alike, running every which way. The huge, hulking, hairless, black beast ignored them as it jogged on all-fours after the bride. Diana went right and the beast turned right, so she ran left and the monster went left. She ran into different room after different room, as she bolted through the large villa. In a desperate attempt, she ran upstairs to hide in one of the bedrooms. The European Werewolf trotted after her, as Kell and the General ran after it.

Finally there were no more rooms to hide in and Diana stood trapped, up against a wall. The beast loomed over and lowered its dangerous head to sniff her. Petrified, she turned her head away from its scorching breath and tried not to look at it.

Kell and Quirinus skidded to a halt as they came up behind with their swords. The General attacked first when he saw its' claw reach for his only child. He struck his sword against the beast's back!

"Stay away from her!" He shouted.

But because of its muscle bulk, it barely made a mark. The General swung his weapon with all of his might, however the monster was completely unaffected. The European Werewolf roared at the interruption and swung out its claw, sending Quirinus flying! He hit the wall with a deep claw mark across his chest and blood gushing out.

"Father!" Diana cried out tearfully. "Father, no!"

In vengeance Kell launched an attack of his own. I recognized his fighting technique as I fought this way, using his light speed reflexes and his ability to instantaneously phase. Like this, he was able to duck and dodge the beast's sharp claws. The bad thing about this battle was his sword wasn't silver which meant his blows were as ineffectual as the late General's.

"Run Diana!" He grunted out, as he fought with all his strength and speed.

Unfortunately, she hesitated from shock of seeing her husband turn bright and blurry. When the monster saw she was about to get away, it decided to ignore him and go after her again. The creature swooped her up with his front claw and slung her across its back. Then it made a move for the closest window.

"Diana!" Her husband rushed after. "Diana!"

Kell caught her hands which were simultaneously reaching out for him. However, he found himself dragged along as well. The European Werewolf kept going, as it leapt out of the second floor window.

"Rufus!" She screamed when he was forced to let go. "Rufus!"

Everyone in the council chambers held their breaths, as we watched the monster land before taking off into the night. Ironically, the manservant finally arrived with Quirinus' silver sword. He ran into the room with the weapon, after searching all over for the General.

He slowed to a stop when he saw his dead master on the floor. Kell stood by the window as he memorized the direction the monster headed in. Then he whipped the silver sword out of the other man's hands.

"I'll take that!"

Then to the manservant's surprise, he zipped out of the house in light speed and zoomed over the countryside.

"Computer end playback." Kell ordered from behind the podium.

The images and sounds stopped there as the crystal pyramid continued to slowly turn.

"Did you find her?" I asked immediately.

He paused in pain before he answered, "I did."

"And was she... alive?"

"No, I found its cave in the mountains where I also found Diana..." his angry tears escaped. "...she was naked and it was evident what he'd done. She died in one of the worst ways imaginable and on her wedding night no less. There were teeth marks and scratches all over her broken body."

My eyes watered as I could understand his hatred now. It wasn't just me, but everybody was affected by the story. Purto closed his eyes as he shook his head.

Kell finished, "The European Werewolf awoke when it smelled my approach. I saw a human stand up with the beasts' glowing green eyes. Before it could attack, I instantaneously phased back in time by a few hours. Then I hid in its cave and when it approached with a still alive Diana, I used the element of surprise and killed it with the silver sword."

"So Diana lived?" I asked hopeful.

"Only because I could circulate through time," he said indignantly. "But what of her father, or the other soldiers I had served beside? They didn't survive the attack. No-one deserves to be used as food."

My eyes fell so I was staring at the floor. I felt a little guilty for having the same bloodlust the beast had. Once upon a time I hunted human, when I first changed. It was thanks to another European Werewolf who stopped me from becoming a murderer.

I stood up to say with my eyes averted, "I have to confess, I'm just as bad as the monster you just watched."

"Excuse me?" Nelson snorted. "B, compared to that thing we saw, you're the fucking St Theresa of Werewolves!"

"Computer, do you have the Viewing Room files of the night I turned in the year 2084?" I looked upwards.

"Those records are sealed and only accessible to the Circulate Council," the Mainframe reported.

I looked to Sally who ordered for me, "Access those files, authorization Circulate Member 606, password 'continuum'."

The computer chirped in compliance and the images in the crystal pyramid showed the tribal lands bathed in moonlight.

"Computer, show the events of that night," I instructed.

Kell left the podium to return to his seat and watch, as everyone did.

At first they looked on in curiosity at how I expanded into my supernatural shape. Then they saw me smash through my bedroom window, before taking off into the woods. They frowned at how I escaped the pack, who tried to take me home. Their eyes widened when they saw me run towards Alma, before Declan stopped me on the border. Purto and Kell glanced away when they witnessed the female Lokoti Werewolf and the male European Werewolf 'make out'. But they looked back to see the monster render me unconscious, by biting down on the nerve in my neck.

Everyone saw the European Werewolf sling my limp body over his muscled back. Then he carried me home back to my anxious parents. With reverence, he laid me out on the front veranda before bolting off. The room watched my Lokoti Werewolf father pick up his Lokoti Werewolf daughter, and carry her upstairs to the bathroom. There, he locked me inside and stood guard with my Lokoti Werewolf Grandpa.

I addressed the council, "I nearly became the monster which killed Kell's family and friends. But as you saw, it was a European Werewolf who stopped me. Every Werewolf has the bloodlust, being predators who crave fresh kill. But it's through hard work and guidance that we're able to prey on animal and not human."

There was silence whilst the Circulate Council members exchanged glances. I was probably making myself look as guilty as my husband, but I didn't care. I couldn't let them judge him only by the bad things he'd done.

I reasoned, "You may not like what the man is, but try to see the man himself. Every time I've needed Declan, he's been there. He's strong, he's loyal and he's generous. He may have a frightening appetite, but he also uses it for good. Computer, show us the home of Susan Sabre on the first Friday in April 2135, time index 1800 hours."

The three sides of the crystal pyramid showed the darkened community centre with the errant patch of snow lying around.

We watched an old, light blue pick up truck, turn into the driveway of a small, wooden house. Next, we saw my tall mate with his broad shoulders and blonde hair, climb out of the driver's side. He walked around to the back of the vehicle and with his strength, he easily picked up eight, cotton carry bags of groceries. The bags strained with the weight of the food, but he didn't. Casually, he walked up to the front door and went inside the house.

"Mom?" He called out as he walked into the kitchen. "I've brought some groceries."

Then we saw an old, fragile, white-haired woman, walk into the kitchen after him. "You didn't have to do that."

"It's no bother," he shrugged it off. "B and I went to the supermarket this afternoon and I thought you could use a couple of things."

He not only unloaded all of the food on the kitchen bench, but he proceeded to put it away for her.

The elderly Aunt Susan picked up a Tupperware container full of raw spaghetti and passed a knowing look. "You didn't pick this up in the supermarket."

"I made pasta last Sunday and a bit extra for you." He said. "I also brought some jars of sun-dried tomatoes, marinated olives, artichokes and eggplant. I did some preserving after the pasta-making."

"Ooh yum," his mother clapped her hands. "I'll make an antipasto plate the next time you and your brother bring over your families."

"Now we're talkin'." He chuckled in agreement. "So, what are you having for dinner tonight?"

"I don't know," she slowly sat herself down on the stool at the kitchen bench. "I've got some instant soup left in the pantry. I was thinking of having the creamy chicken with toast."

The European Werewolf stopped to look on askance, "Mom c'mon."

"What?"

"You're not having soup and toast for dinner." He frowned. "That's a snack, not a meal."

"We don't ALL have appetites of European Werewolves," she smirked. "Soup and toast will be just fine for this 'lil ole lady'."

"Right, I'm making a spaghetti bolognaise," he picked up the Tupperware container.

"Declan!" She laughed out her surprise. "Go home and make B spaghetti bolognaise!"

"We've already got some in the freezer." He replied. "Besides, the big batch I make you tonight can go in the freezer too. Then you can just heat it up in the microwave when you want it."

She smilingly shook her head as she watched him organize the ingredients next.

"Computer, end image." I ordered and the technology obeyed.

I caught a couple of surprised glances as I faced everyone again.

I explained, "What you saw then wasn't a one time thing. In the last years of Aunt Susan's life, he visited his mother twice a week. Declan would either bring her groceries, or cook for her, or do the cleaning she couldn't. He may eat a lot, but he doesn't let his loved ones go hungry either. He uses what he has to help the people he cares about, like his strength. When I was seriously ill after using my powers to excess, he tended to me day and night. He hardly had any sleep but he never faltered. I can show you that too."

"No thank you B, we believe you." Pat spoke for the room.

"Well, it looks like he has his good points too?" Sally looked towards Professor Hamilton.

"The European Werewolf called Declan Sabre seems to be a very different creature to the European Werewolf who crashed Kell's wedding." The Professor glanced at Dr. Knight.

"How long ago were you ill?" She frowned.

"Um, a couple of days ago," I answered.

Out of the blue, she stood up and walked over to my position. She used her hands to feel the glands in my neck before resting her hand on my forehead. Her frown remained as she took a step back and spoke as a medical professional.

"The virus is still in your system." Dr. Knight pronounced. "You should come to the Medical Lab and be properly seen to."

Purto agreed, "Told you so."

"But I'm feeling much better..." I faltered, "...I just need to return to tribal lands and lie down."

"Let's get you checked out." She smiled reassuringly. "It won't take long and there's a good chance I can eliminate the virus once and for all."

"I don't know." I took a step back. "How do I know you're not going to dose me with DYSTAR to stop me from returning to my mate?"

"Nearly three hundred years later THAT still comes up." Pat wearily rubbed his face.

"Told you it was a bad idea, LOSER!" Nelson punched him on the arm then stood up before he could retaliate.

However, it was Lucas Hodge himself who put my nerves to rest.

He came to stand beside the physician and say earnestly, "Look B, we understand you're a Werewolf who used to crave people. So trust me, we're not about to drug you to keep you here at Headquarters. There's too much delicate equipment that we don't want trashed by a pissed off man-eater."

In spite of myself, I laughed at his words coupled with his cheeky grin.

"Shall we?" Dr. Knight waved towards the sliding doors.

I walked out with her but before we disappeared, I looked back.

I saw Kell and Purto were talking quietly amongst themselves. I sensed that they saw me as a lost cause. Maybe I was no longer the damsel in distress in their eyes, instead I was another monster. As long as they left my marriage alone, they could see me as the Big Bad Wolf, for all I cared.

*****

I sat on the examination bench underneath the main scanner in the Medical Lab.

Since Vincent left with my parents, I've become accustomed to being scanned by the Mainframe itself. She'd log any physical changes or note if my bio-electromagnetic field altered. When I needed more painkillers for my monthly blues, she'd tell me which cabinet they were in. Occasionally, she'd tell me to go to another cabinet to take some iron tablets too.

Because I was used to just myself and the computer, it felt surreal to see two doctors and two nurses walking around the lab.

Dr. Knight looked at my results which were displayed on the large computer screen on the wall.

"You said you had a chest infection?" She checked.

"Yeah that's what Meadow our Medicine Man said. He told us it was going around the tribe. It affected both young and old." I advised.

"What started off as a chest infection turned into pneumonia." She announced. "I can see leftover residue from when your lungs filled with fluid."

"No way," I breathed out in surprise.

I hopped off the bench to stand beside and look at the results on the screen too.

"However your Werewolf immune system combated it and stopped your lungs from collapsing." She said seriously. "If you'd been human, you could have suffocated."

"No way!" I repeated in shock.

"You said your Medicine Man gave you a medication from this lab that Vincent Moher gave him?"

"Yeah, it was a steroid with a unique combination of vitamins and minerals to help Circulators when they're run down."

"I'm going to inject you with a concentration of what you described, as well as a powerful antibiotic." She walked over to one of the medicine cabinets. "Can you sit on the bench again?"

I did and from this position, I watched her ready two spray/syringes with the drugs. The fluids in the small, glass vials were green and yellow coloured. I let out a sigh of relief, as DYSTAR had been a blue liquid.

She pressed one spray/syringe on the right side of my neck and I heard it 'hiss' as it expelled the liquid through my skin. Next, she placed the second against the left side and I heard and felt the same thing. Then she walked away to discard the empty vials in the waste disposal unit.

I watched her work as well as the rest of the medical staff. They milled about, holding small, flat, portable computers as they updated medical records. Dr. Knight said something to one of the nurses which must have been about me, as he duly entered into the technology. I think she was logging what treatment she'd used.

I couldn't help but wonder if maybe these medical professionals could assist with another condition I had.

"Dr. Knight," I called on her, "can I ask you a question?"

"Yes?"

"Do you know much about infertility?"

This caught her attention and she stopped to turn my way. "What would you like to know?"

"Do you know how to treat infertility caused by a Circulator's different bio-electromagnetic frequency?"

She came back to where I was sitting. "B, a Circulator's bio-electromagnetic frequency couldn't stop conception. When we're not phasing through time, our bodies function just like any other human's. Unless of course you're a Lokoti Werewolf then your body should act like the rest of your kind."

I blurted out, "Vincent scanned me and even ran some tests on my eggs. He said that they operate on a separate time differential which was stopping conception."

This made her straighten in surprise, "This is the first time I've heard of something like this happening."

"Yeah, he said the same thing." I said tiredly. "He said I was the first Circulator to ever differ this way."

Dr. Knight frowned thoughtfully, "But B when I scanned you, I saw your ovaries were functioning normally. There weren't any infections present in your uterus, either. In fact, the scanner picked up the reason why your body's emitting a potent pheromone to attract the opposite sex, is because you're on heat."

I blinked, "Excuse me?"

"Your body is releasing the pheromone to encourage a reproductive partner." She advised. "You've heard of dogs or other animals being on heat, when they're at their most fertile. Your body as a female Lokoti Werewolf is doing exactly the same thing."

My face burned as I felt embarrassed at her news and even more confused.

"If I'm so fertile that my body as advertising this fact, then why can't I conceive?" I whined.

"Lie down again underneath the scanner." She instructed. "I'll take another look and see if I can find out about this 'time differential'."

*****

Just like the intensive scans Vincent ran, I had to lie still as the green beam of the scanner slowly moved over my abdomen.

When it was over, I could sit up again as Dr. Knight analysed the results on the computer screen.

She typed in a few commands which zoomed into the image of my reproductive organs. When she typed in more, I saw the image turn a red colour. It reminded me of what my cousin said of Red Shift and Blue Shift. Then I saw her manipulate the controls and my ovaries disappeared to show someone's sperm sample.

I didn't know who it came from, but she called over a nurse and asked him to retrieve other people's medical records.

I had to sit on my hands, literally, as I forced myself to wait to hear what she had to say.

Thirty minutes passed as I watched her work. She brought up the picture of my ovaries again and minimized it so it was a small window in the corner of the screen. Then she opened several more windows which showed different sperm samples. Some of them were a red colour like my ovaries were, whilst others were blue.

"Alright then," she took a deep breath as she returned to her patient. "I see what you mean by the time differential, but I believe it's treatable."

My heart leapt as my eyes widened in hope. "How?"

"Do you see those sperm samples on the screen and how three of them are a red colour, like your ovaries are?" She pointed out. "They're not the exact same frequency on the light spectrum as your bio-electromagnetic field. But I do believe they're a close enough match to fertilize your eggs."

My mouth fell open, "Say what?"

"As you are aware, there are nine Circulators in the Circulate who can instantaneously phase." She continued. "They're yourself, Jessica Wisetail, Arabella Riverclaw, Alexandrina Carmichael, Elisha Worthall, Sophie Wilcox, Mike Sabre, Rufus Kell and Lucas Hodge."

"Yes," I nodded as I waited for it.

"I could ask privately on your behalf if either Lucas, Mike or Rufus, would donate their sperm." She went on. "Then using IVF we could -"

"Are you frickin' nuts?!" I cut her off. "If you impregnate me with another man's sperm, my husband will go ballistic! He'd sniff that the child wasn't his then go after the real father!"

"Oh," she looked taken aback.

I buried my face in my hands, "He'd do worse to the sperm donor than what you saw happen on Kell's wedding day."

"But what if the donor was a relative of his, such as Mike Sabre?" She thought up. "Then you'd be keeping it in the family, a little like sororate marriage."

I lowered my hands to look on incredulous. "Sororate what?"

"With your doctorate in history, surely you've come across sororate marriage." Her eyebrows rose. "In the past what happened in several different cultures, was if the wife was infertile then the husband would procreate with her sister. The man would have two wives, or perhaps even three or four."

"Yeah, I read about it." I frowned. "But it's impossible in this situation. I'm a Lokoti Werewolf and I'm biologically bound to one man; my husband. Besides, I'd feel more than a little uncomfortable having the child of my mate's great, great granduncle."

Dr. Knight watched my shoulders slump as I deflated at the idea.

"Did you want to discuss this with your husband then come back with a final decision?" She offered.

"No way," I shook my head as my eyes watered. "There is no way I could ever broach this subject with him. 'Hi honey, how was your day? Oh by the way, I can get knocked up but it has to be done by another man'. It would break his heart and probably his control of the bloodlust. It would also defeat the purpose of my only desire, which is having HIS child."

The doctor looked on her patient and then delivered the only treatment she could in this situation, which was a sympathetic pat to the arm.

*****

~ 20 ~

I instantaneously phased out of the Medical Lab back to the Lokoti village of old. I reappeared behind the Riverclaw hut, so I wouldn't scare anyone by the bright flash of light. When I walked around, I found Muna talking with another woman, as their youngest chased each other around the parents' legs.

I didn't mean to be rude but I felt a sense of urgency to find my mate.

"Muna," I interrupted, "where is Declan?"

She pointed towards the river, "He is fishing in the shallows with Arun."

I nodded and turned away as the mothers watched me go.

When I arrived at the waters' edge, I walked upstream until I came to a turn in the river which had a wide, rocky bank. There I spotted Declan, Arun and a couple of other men spear fishing in the shallows. They were wading in the water with their suede shirts off, holding the wooden spears in the air.

Declan stood out with his white skin and blonde hair, amongst the Lokoti with their bronze skin and black hair. His muscle tone looked more pronounced than the Lokoti Werewolves in human form, too. You could also spot the difference between his breed and ours, by the bite mark on his left shoulder and slight claw mark. The Lokoti weren't turned by infection, we were born with the genes.

I didn't know my husband could spear fish, or perhaps he was being taught to now? Simultaneously they all stopped moving, with their eyes peeled to the water. They were standing so still, almost like statues with their spears ready. Quietly I watched, I didn't want to disturb incase I'd frighten the fish away.

Next, Arun silently pointed at a part of the water and Declan brought down his spear with his lightning fast reflexes! Then all of the men moved towards where the weapon had landed. When he raised it again, there was a 50 cm long salmon on the end of it.

"Good kill, Declan." Our host patted him on the back.

Then all of the men looked over to where I was standing on the riverbank.

"B?" My mate smiled at the sight then he joked in English, "Have you come to watch?"

I said back in the same language, "I need to talk to you."

"Oh oh," he muttered.

This made the Lokoti chuckle as they got the gist of what we said, from his reaction.

Carefully, he waded out of the water carrying his spear and his fish. When he was back on solid ground again, he planted the spear in the ground and put his catch into a suede basket sitting in the shade. He untied his suede shirt from his waist and put it on before turning my way.

"Let's go for a walk." I said shortly.

"OK," he frowned then he followed me down the riverbank. He fell into step beside, "So what's up?"

"I have to tell you something," I said distractedly.

"Where did you go with Purto?" He wondered. "Muna said she saw you walk off with him."

"To Circulate Headquarters," I answered, "but not the one on Taurus Six."

"Oh?"

"I went back in time to the one on Mars, when the Circulate were still there."

"What?" He stopped in surprise before he growled out, "That conniving little... I told him he couldn't take you there and he still did it?! I'm gonna have a long conversation with that interfering time traveller."

I stopped too so I could face him, "They didn't try to drug and kidnap me, if that's what you're worried about."

"Evidently, since you're here."

His frown deepened as he stood back to watch me pace up and down whilst wringing my hands.

"C'mon B, just spit it out." He rolled his eyes impatiently. "Something's bothering you, I haven't seen you this tetchy since New Orleans. You didn't cheat on me while you were at Circulate Headquarters, did you?"

"What...?" I blanched. "No!"

After what was discussed earlier this morning, that joke hit a little too close to home.

"Good, because I'd smell him on you if you had," he smirked. "Now just tell me what's got you so worked up."

I stopped pacing and looked at him and I opened my mouth... but nothing came out. So I went back to pacing again. He crossed his arms as he waited for it.

"Come on, you can do it. Choose your words and string them into a sentence. You're the academic with that piece of paper called a doctorate." He said sarcastically.

My face burned, "But – but – but it's embarrassing!"

He guessed, "It's not more baby nonsense, is it?"

I stopped a second time to look on in surprise. "Actually, it is related to it."

"You got yourself checked out by more Circulate doctors, didn't you?" He guessed again.

"Funny you should say that," I laughed nervously. "Dr. Knight ran some tests on me after she treated me for the virus. Did you know the chest infection had turned into pneumonia?"

"Pneumonia?!" His eyes widened. "You're kidding me! No wonder you had trouble breathing."

I rushed out, "So anyway, after Dr. Knight injected me with antibiotics to finally eliminate the virus, she scanned my ovaries."

"And what did she say?" He asked warily.

"Um, I'm..."

"Yes?"

"Um, she said that I'm on..."

"You're what?"

"She said that I'm on heat."

There, I said it! But my husband didn't look shocked by this. In fact his complete lack of reaction shocked ME.

"Yeah and?" He asked nonplussed.

"What do you mean, 'yeah and?'" I gave a funny look.

"This is the best that the Circulate doctors can come up with?"

"Declan, you don't look surprised by this."

"Of course I'm not surprised by this!" He laughed out. "Why are you acting like you didn't know?"

"But how do you know about this?!"

"I'm a male and I'm a Werewolf, of course I frickin' smell it! Your pheromones started before you turned. Remember at Ben Shallow Water's Bonfire, I had to scare off those guys who were hitting on you?"

My face burned in embarrassment, "Yes but I never thought the pheromones were a result of being on heat!"

However, when I glanced his way again, he seemed puzzled. He asked incredulous, "Are you seriously telling me that you DIDN'T know?"

I confessed, "Dr. Knight says I'm fertile and my reproductive organs are doing everything normally. But the reason why I'm not pregnant is that the sperm hasn't got the right bio-electromagnetic frequency which matches my eggs. Because I am fertile, my body is releasing the pheromones to attract a reproductive partner. Apparently, I'm on heat and I guess I'll remain this way until I'm impregnated by sperm that's in temporal flux."

"So basically she just reconfirmed what Vincent said when he scanned you, years ago." He said flatly.

I opened my mouth to refute that my Calculator didn't diagnose my treatment as accepting the sperm from another Circulator; when I shut it again.

When he saw my hurt expression, he continued. "I've always known your pheromones were a result from you being on heat. I could smell when you were ovulating, when your pheromones increased in potency. I can smell it when you have your period. The pack has always known you were on heat, B. Why do you think you were married off so young?"

I looked downwards, "I thought I was married to Grant to curb my bloodlust from human to animal."

"That was one of the reasons, sure. But your father and the pack were also worried about what kind of trouble might brew, with your pheromones. They thought that if they mated you off, your pheromones would decrease once you started to breed." Declan declared.

I said dismally, "Well I managed to screw that up."

He unfolded his arms and stepped closer to comfort his wife.

"That's not a screw up on your part, B." He rested a reassuring hand on my shoulder. "The day I found out you couldn't give Grant a child, I almost shouted for joy. It confirmed that I was right, you were meant to be mine all along. I felt like Fate was saying that the female Werewolf who couldn't breed, was meant to be with the most hated breed of Werewolf, whom people didn't want to see reproduce. Your pheromones don't just attract males, but they're also an aphrodisiac."

What the...? I looked up startled, into his awaiting his gaze. His bright blue eyes looked earnest but a mischievous grin played on his lips.

"It's true." He promised. "Did you think it's just my appetite as a European Werewolf, which makes me hungry for you, all day every day?"

I shrugged which made him laugh again.

He continued, "I thought it's why you prefer to stay home to work on your papers, because you're avoiding unwanted attention."

I looked away to stare at the river, "I just like the peace and quiet, working from home."

Declan tried to catch my gaze, "You honestly didn't know you were on heat? So you just thought I was some control freak, who panicked whenever his wife left the house without him?"

"Yes," I admitted.

"Thanks a lot!" He guffawed. "Sure, I know I can be bossy but trust me, I'm just overprotective. When you walk past and a man turns his head, I want to knock it off his shoulders!"

"I thought it was because you were the jealous type." I spoke plainly.

"Don't you notice it's only around you?" He tickled me, to make me laugh. "I mean, look at us. Look at how we've lived for the past century. We live in a cottage instead of a mansion, which we could afford thanks to your assets with Hodge Endeavour. I could buy out the Garage in Alma and be the only mechanic around, but I don't want to because I'm not ambitious."

Come to think of it, he was right. Declan hated shopping and would wear the same denim or flannel clothes for years. He didn't care about dining in fancy restaurants, as he was quite happy to cook at home. We didn't have luxury cars and the valuable ornaments we had at home, were antiques I'd picked up on my travels through time.

He went on, "I like the quiet lifestyle of the Lokoti living in harmony with nature. I look forward to hunting on a full moon and the privacy the woods afford. I can sit at the table and make pasta or pesto or preserve antipasto for hours, because I enjoy seeing your face when you eat it. When I see your aura change to a happy colour because of something I've done, it makes me feel on top of the world."

His words warmed my heart before I tested, "Maybe you're not so lucky, this 'on heat' business is just going to keep on attracting trouble."

"Turn off your 'selective hearing', B." He smilingly scolded. "Didn't I just say it keeps me hungry for you?"

My eyes skipped away, "I'd gladly give up the pheromones if it meant I could give you a child."

"Stop being such a princess." He rolled his eyes. "Nobody can have it all and neither can you. If we did have rug rats, we wouldn't be able to take those overseas vacations. They'd cut into your academic work and your circulations through time. Worst of all, I'd lose my walking, talking aphrodisiac for a wife."

"Maybe this 'on heat' business also amplifies my PMS? Maybe it's the result of my mood swings? What if it continues until the day we evolve?" I taunted.

"Yeah well, if you have to put up with my supernatural temper its only fair I put up with yours." He conceded. "Besides, we have the best sex right after a fight. Hell, the argument is usually over by the time I roll off you."

"Declan!" I whacked him on the chest.

He laughed aloud as he pulled me into his arms.

"Aren't we a pair, your paranormal PMS and my bloodlust-fuelled temper." He tickled again. "No wonder we're called 'The Tribe's Most Argumentative Couple'."

"We're pretty bad, aren't we?" I giggled in agreement.

"That's why you should marry me properly with this Joining Ceremony tomorrow." He chuckled into my ear as he held me close. "Then we'll be made legal."

"It'll legitimize our constant fighting so the tribe can say, 'oh it's OK, they're married'." I joked along.

"Exactly."

"But what if our sex dies down once we're married?"

"Not with you constantly being on heat!" He said indignantly. "See, I've thought of everything."

"What, that's your 'cunning plan'?" My eyebrows rose. "Marry the chick who's constantly on heat, so you'll never have to worry about the sex growing dull?"

"Yup," he smiled widely.

"Great plan, Dec!" I sung sarcastically as I patted him hard on the chest. "So you're taken care of for the next hundred or so years, but what about me?"

"Hey, I cook for you, don't I?" He objected. "I fix your car, I grow you orchids, I warm the bed, I take you overseas... I'm more faithful than a family dog!"

"Except when you cheat at Monopoly."

"It was a SIX!" He shouted as his temper instantly ignited. "The dice that rolled under the fridge was a six!"

"Yeah right," I turned and walked away. "Then why didn't you wait until I could see it?"

"I WAS lifting up the frickin' fridge with one arm!" He loudly followed after. "The food was about to fall out!"

"Excuses excuses," I said dismissively.

"You're the so-called 'Seer' in this relationship, if you look back in time you'll see that the dice showed a six!"

"Sure Declan, whatever you say."

"Once and for all, it was a frickin' SIX!" He ranted as we walked back into the village. "I'm serious! Instantaneously phase to that time frame and see it for yourself!"

As we headed towards the Riverclaw hut, we passed a couple of elderly women who were sitting outside of theirs, sewing some suede clothes.

They looked up from our raised voices and watched us pass before exchanging looks of amusement.

"They are the ones the Elders are holding the Joining Ceremony for, tomorrow." One woman said to the other.

"They argue like they are already mates," she said back.

"Muna said they have been mates for the last 150 winters," the first woman informed.

"Ah," she nodded like it all made sense now.

Then they returned to their sewing in a comfortable silence.

*****

That afternoon, I noticed the activity within the tribe had changed.

At first I wondered why so many people were involved in building a bonfire by the riverbank, behind the first Sacred Totem. Men constructed a square base using branches, with women and children dropping off bundles of sticks. It wasn't until sunset that I came to realize that it wasn't a bonfire, but a funeral pyre.

The council of Tribal Elders began to sing, which prompted the tribe to gather around.

Declan held my hand as we came to stand with the Riverclaws. I saw the nine Tribal Elder's faces were painted with the claw mark on the sides. I recognized the old woman from the story time by the fire, as well as the Lightfoot Werewolf and the tribe's Medicine Man, the Elm Werewolf. The third Werewolf on the council was from the Shallow Water family. They and the six human Elders, led the tribe in the funeral chant.

Another difference I noted was that the whole tribe sang. In the future that Declan and I came from, it was just the Elders. I wondered at what point in time, this changed?

Then the crowd parted and the bodies of the deceased were carried up to the large pyre. I counted eight people in total, who died in the North American Werewolf attack. The families carried their fallen, whose bodies were wrapped in funeral shrouds. Once the bodies were laid to rest, the Tribal Elders lit the pyre using the fiery torches they were holding.

The flames grew in size and gradually engulfed the human remains. Meanwhile, the women cried and the men threw back their heads and howled. They were joined by the members of the pack, who howled the loudest and the longest.

I was surprised when so did Declan, since we didn't know the deceased. But I sensed he did it as a sign of respect and in camaraderie. All I could do was stand there and hold his hand, because I couldn't.

AAAAAARRRRRROOOOOOOOOOOOOOOOOOOOOWWWWLLL!

His head was raised in the air with his eyes closed, and I could feel the force emanate out of his strong body.

AAAAAARRRRRROOOOOOOOOOOOOOOOOOOOOWWWWLLL!

Then he let go of my hand to hold me against his side. All around us was mournful singing, wailing or howling. I watched with wide eyes, as I felt a little excluded. I wish I could howl like a male Lokoti Werewolf. I wasn't sad enough to wail like the women were, either. Right then, it felt like my mate was more part of the tribe than I was.

I felt Declan give an affectionate squeeze and when I looked up, I found his blue eyes waiting. Then he took my hand and placed it on his chest, before closing his eyes and raising his head again. As he made his last howl, I sensed he was doing it for me. It was like the time after another funeral when he howled for me too.

AAAAAARRRRRROOOOOOOOOOOOOOOOOOOOOWWWWLLL!

This time I closed my eyes and raised my head, as I felt the vibrations radiate out of his wide chest.

*****

After the funeral, we ate dinner with several families. Everyone shared in roast caribou that the Wisetail Werewolf caught with his teenaged son. Firstly, the animal was skinned so its pelt could be used later. Then the meat was broken into different parts and cooked over a fire outside the Wisetail's hut. The Riverclaws including their guests from the future, were invited to partake.

We all sat together on two logs by the fire in our suede clothing of old. When Arun and Muna's children came and sat beside my mate, he looked on in pleasant surprise. Then they ate the cooked caribou with their hands, in a companionable silence. When the Wisetail Werewolf's children came to sit beside me, the parents smilingly watched us eating altogether.

"Our future," the Wisetail Werewolf whom I learned was Tenin, nodded our way.

"According to our Tribal Elder and 'Seer' Memek, she's our granddaughter in 370 winters to come." Arun nodded.

"Our families seem to mate a lot." Tenin chuckled in good humour.

"Declan says my family of Riverclaws mate with his family of Sabre's twice." Arun continued. "He was the first and his grandniece was the second."

I exchanged glances with my husband, guessing they were talking about Maia and Forrest.

"You know what, B?" The European Werewolf finished his mouthful to speak in English. "I think I have Flint Riverclaw's father sitting beside me."

My eyebrows rose, "How can you be sure?"

"Your grandfather told me that Flint was 75 years old when he finally took a mate and his father before him was nearing his fifties when he took his." Declan said.

"Really?" I smiled at the idea. "Mum would have got a kick out of this. She and Uncle Jules were quite close to their Great Grandfather Flint."

"What is the name of the tribe that Declan's family come from?" Tenin enquired, as he looked on my mate's Caucasian features in the firelight.

"He said the tribe is called Italian. His forefathers came over the sea, many winters ago." Arun answered. "Or in his time, it was many winters ago."

"Why does he and our Lokoti daughter have the same coloured eyes?" Tenin wondered. "But her eyes are darker, like her hair, which shows her Lokoti blood."

"Declan said that B has foremothers from other tribes that mated with Lokoti Werewolves." Muna answered this time.

"From the Italian tribe too?" Tenin wondered.

"No, from the tribes called China, Australia and England." Muna recited.

"England?" Tenin pondered. "Why do I know that name?"

Just then Arun stopped eating to say unhappily, "The pale-skins in the red coats we killed for taking six of our women, were called English."

All of the parents' eyes widened as their mouths fell open in shock. Declan saw their looks of astonishment, which were aimed my way. Next, he leaned over to speak quietly in our first language.

"Don't look now B, but I think your Lokoti family have a problem with your English family."

I lowered my dinner to look innocently at our hosts. "My English grandmother who was the tribe's first Light Person, married Emanuel Riverclaw."

"Did anymore 'red coats' take our Lokoti daughters?" Arun asked suspiciously.

"No, but you could say that a Lokoti Werewolf 'took' my English grandmother's heart." I smirked.

Immediately, their expressions changed to ones of relief and they recommenced eating.

"Good save," Declan gave a nudge.

The two boys on either side of us, laughed and pointed at my large mate.

"He looks big and strong when he changes, but it's his smaller female who speaks for him." Tenin's son guffawed.

"A female is never going to speak for me! If she tried, I'd drop her into the river!" Arun's son proclaimed.

Declan spoke to them in Lokoti, "You just wait until your turn comes. Then you'll be begging the woman to look at you, let alone speak for you."

"Harrumph!" Muna made an unhappy sound, as she and Tenin's wife glared at their sons.

"Besides, if you do drop a female into the river, they never let you live it down." Declan told the boys. "Women remember every wrong thing you do. If you mate with a female that lives as long as you do, you have to put up with their nagging, winter upon winter!"

The boys' eyes bulged as they actually looked intimidated by the idea.

"Declan!" I elbowed him, which earned laughter from our onlookers.

As if she were making a cry for women kind, or she'd been inspired by the funeral; Arun's small daughter threw back her head and tried to howl.

"Arrroooo0OOOooooo...!"

"Females can't howl!" Her brother scolded. "I'm the first born and a son, so I could be a Werewolf too one day. But you can't, because you're female!"

"You're sure about that, are you?" My husband challenged.

"Yes."

"Look at who I'm mated to," he nodded my way.

I made my dark blue eyes briefly flash glowing turquoise, for his benefit.

"Oh," the boy looked on askance.

Then his little sister gloatingly poked him in the ribs and ran away before he could retaliate.

It was close to midnight when Declan and I bedded down with the Riverclaw family. Arun and Muna helped their children undress for bed, before tucking them into their fur-lined, branch-constructed cot. Once the kids were taken care of, the parents stripped off before climbing into a bed of their own.

I felt awkward with our hosts undressing in the same room as me, but Declan behaved like it was commonplace. He had no problem in removing his suede pants and shirt. Before he climbed into bed, he hung his clothes on a wooden peg on a wall support. I soon found myself as the last clothed person, standing awkwardly in the hut.

"Declan," I squirmed, "don't go to bed yet. I need you to hold up the fur for me so I can undress behind it."

"What?" He looked up like I was a loon. "B, come on! You would attract more attention doing it that way than you would if you simply stripped."

I shot off a glare as my face heated up in embarrassment. Then I undressed so fast, I looked like a blur. Perfectly timed, my husband held up the fur and I leapt into bed.

"You left your clothes on the floor," he chastised.

"Shut up." I growled, which made him chuckle.

We bunked down between the furs with our fronts pressed together. Declan wrapped his arms and legs about as he held me close. I felt so snug thanks to the animal hides and my mate's hot skin, if a blizzard blew over the Alaska Range, I probably wouldn't have noticed.

Contentedly, I drifted to sleep with the sound of five other people doing the same, filling my ears.

*****

I'm not sure how long I dozed for, but it couldn't have been more than an hour. I woke up from my husband's tightening hold and even how his nails were digging in. He was clutching me so tightly, I wondered if there was another emergency?

"Hmm?" I stirred.

I opened my eyes to find it was still dark. I made out my husband's were open and looking in a particular direction. It made me want to look too, to see the cause for concern.

The children's quiet snores came to my ears, but I also heard some kind of muffled sounds. It sounded like heavy breathing, as well as bodies moving around in bed. When I turned my head in the direction of the noise, I found myself looking at Arun and Muna.

I couldn't see them but I could see the fur covering them, was moving. This, coupled with the muffled sounds should have been the give away. But because I was still half asleep, it took me a second or two to catch on.

What the...? My face burned as I felt more embarrassed than before. I turned my head around so fast, I almost head-butted my husband in the chest. I buried my face like I wanted to hide.

"I can't stand this," I heard him groan, like he was in pain.

He started to get out of bed when he pulled me up too. He lifted both his mate and the fur covering, into his arms. I found myself bundled up and carried out of the hut.

Speedily, Declan rushed us around the back of the Riverclaw hut, past another hut then into the surrounding forest.

I saw his eyes glow green so he could see better in the dark. My legs were wrapped around his waist as my arms hung about his neck. The blanket was wrapped loosely around, which hid my nakedness. The European Werewolf walked so quickly, it may have been the same speed as a human running.

Once we were well away from the Lokoti village, Declan stopped behind a cluster of trees.

He lowered his wife onto the forest floor with the fur coming undone. As he lowered himself over me, his hands spread out the animal hide. As soon as my back hit the fur, he pushed himself inside.

Declan was so hungry for it, his hot hardness delved into my unprepared body. I gasped as he pushed again and again, going further in each time. He grunted as he moved and I dug my nails into his upper arms. Usually, it was my way of telling him to slow down or ease up. But tonight his body took no heed, he was desperate and I felt his ferocity. With each heave, he pushed himself onwards and upwards.

His hands were gripping onto my waist and his speed made me wonder if we were in a race? His sexual frustration was riding him, and he and it were anxious to cross the finish line. From his ironclad grip, it was as if there was no stopping him. My crotch started to feel a little raw, from diving into the main course with no entree. My sharp nails broke his skin and I felt his warm blood under them, but still he carried on with abandon.

"Uh - uh - uh - uh...!" He grunted loudly. "I'm coming, I'm coming, I'm coming...! Oh at last I'm coming!"

Then he slumped over his wife as I felt the wet heat fill between my legs.

We lay like that for a minute, with me sprawled on the fur and my mate sprawled over me. I felt him move in and out a couple more times, as he squeezed my thighs against his waist. I could tell he liked the friction of our skin rubbing together.

At least his high body temperature staved away the chill. I lay on the fur, listening to his heavy breathing coupled with the frogs by the riverbank, or the crickets in the woods. I couldn't see the night sky, as the canopy of branches blocked out the stars.

"Mmm," he moaned appreciatively and kissed me on the lips.

His eyes were still growing green, with his pupils as narrow slits. They met his mate's human eyes as his lips moulded to hers. He kissed over and over again and I opened my mouth to let his tongue in. It twisted around mine and I felt my head pushed backwards by his fervour. He also pushed my thighs wider apart and I knew a second course was coming.

I moved my mouth away to say, "Not yet."

"Hmm?" He looked on puzzled at first, then a silly smile played on his lips. "Hmm..."

Declan left a lasting kiss on my lips then he placed another on my neck, my right shoulder, my right breast, my belly button and then all the way down to my clit. As soon as I felt him part my moist folds, my breath caught in my throat. Then his strong tongue ran circles around the sensitive protrusion, and it came out as a sigh of delight. He continued to lick hard, with the occasional chew, which made it swell in ecstasy.

When I thought he was going to move his head away, I grabbed hold of his scruffy, blonde hair.

I uttered out, "For longer...longer...I need more...more!"

My head rolled side to side, as my chest heaved and I caught him watch my breasts rise up and down. Careful of keeping away from my entrance lest he taste himself, he concentrated on the outside. His tongue teased the soft, sensitive tissue which made me writhe in rapture.

I felt like I was about to go mad from the tantalizing. Momentarily, I sat up to grab his broad shoulders and pull him back over me. This time when he pushed inside, he slid in easier than a stick of butter melting in a frying pan. I saw his eyes close as his back arched, showing his enjoyment. He moved slowly as he pushed deeper than before. I did something else I knew he liked, which was wrapping my legs about his waist.

He kept moving with his eyes closed and at the same steady rhythm. It was like he was deliberately taking his time and taking the scenic route while he was at it. I didn't mind, the speed wasn't fast enough to make me come, but it was satisfying.

After a last couple of long, hard thrusts, he raised himself off his wife then turned her around. I found myself on all-fours, with my husband pushing from behind. We picked up the pace in this position and the rocking back and forth started to work. I felt the pleasure ripple up from my crotch, indicating the intoxicating build up of an orgasm.

"I'm coming, I'm coming, I'm coming..." I breathed out.

Declan panted hard, as he tried to maintain the exact speed and angle. The consistency was working, I felt several rushes of warmth fill my groin and combine into one blissful wave. My body turned taught and I stopped moving my hips, as I tried to hold onto this wonderful, gratifying feeling. However, experience made him keep moving, or else lose it.

"Oh...! Oh...! Oh...!" I cried out to share my joy with the person who was causing it.

When for some strange reason, he returned it with a low, "Oh oh."

Suddenly, I was shoved face first into the fur, with my mate lying on top in a protective manner.

"What is it?" I whispered.

Next, I heard the footsteps of two men walking this way and I nearly panicked! However, Declan remained calm as he raised his head. His glowing green eyes narrowed, to see who it was.

"Uma Lokoti." He spoke clearly to the dark woods. "Uma tu te che unan."

The footsteps halted and it sounded like the two men hesitated. Then I heard them turn around and walk away. I laid there scared stiff, as I was petrified of being seen.

Once they were gone, Declan rolled onto his side to face me. "Relax, they were just two Warriors patrolling the outskirts of the village."

"But -" I began.

"They didn't see anything, as we were hidden behind the trees. I told them we were Lokoti and we were mates. It's no big deal." He said casually.

"But Declan - " I tried again.

I was silenced by his hungry mouth smothering mine. Whereas he had no trouble picking up where we left off, I needed convincing. Soothingly, his warm hands ran up and down my sides, following my every curve. I started to relax by their feel and his moist lips brushing the bare skin of my shoulders.

When he tried to lie on top again, I needed more coaxing. However, my husband knew his wife well. He knew exactly what to do to make her skin turn hot, her nails sharpen or the moans escape between her bared teeth...

*****

Since the river was so close, after our frolicking in the woods we took a dip to wash ourselves off.

Normally the water would be too cold to swim in, but having a European Werewolf for a mate was handy in times such as these. We waded into the water hand-in-hand, but as soon as we were neck-high, I climbed onto his back. I basked in his body heat as he slowly swam in the current.

Declan seemed fearless. The dark water frightened me because I couldn't see the bottom, but he swam to the middle of the river with ease. If I hadn't of been on his back, I wouldn't have swum out so far. However, I trusted how at home he was in this environment.

"You know what, B?" He rolled over in the water, so I wasn't clinging to his back but his front.

"What?"

"We should take holidays like this more often." He said as he looked about.

On either side of the dark water, was dark forest with the outlines of the tall evergreens between the deciduous trees. Above the tree tops, were the gigantic, mountainous peaks of the Alaska Range. Above the mountains, was a clear sky with so many stars, it looked like silver glitter had spilt over a black surface. Because there were so many, their light was almost as bright as the moon.

"Do you mean travelling through time?" I frowned. "But you don't like time travel."

"If it's anything like this trip has been, I could get used to it." He shrugged. "Hell, I could imagine us living here for good."

"You could?" I blanched. "In a hut with a dirt floor, no bathrooms, no kitchen and no refrigerator to store perishable food?"

"Yeah alright, a fridge is a necessity." He acquiesced, especially with his stomach. "But think about it, your Lokoti ancestors are happy with what they have. They don't have plasma-powered cars, so they don't have to pay to recharge them. They have campfires, instead of power bills. They don't have to worry about credit cards or credit ratings. They're used to surviving with what nature provides."

"Hmm, it is a nice change." I sighed, as I stared at the distant river bank. "Call me strange, but I think the air even smells different. It's cleaner somehow?"

"Yeah, I noticed it as soon as we arrived. Scary, huh? Where we live is considered rural, but we still get some of the smog from the big cities." He agreed.

Declan slowly kicked his legs which buoyed us, whilst holding me in his arms. Our eyes took in the sights of the dark forest, the snow-capped mountains and the thousands of stars which twinkled down. Meanwhile, our ears took in the noise of the nightlife, such as frogs, crickets and the errant hoot of an owl; rather than loud music and chatter of nightclubs or bars.

"You know what, B?" He looked back in my direction.

"What?"

"There's another thing that I like about this simple lifestyle." Declan looked directly into my eyes. "The roles of men and women are more defined."

"Huh?" I gave a funny look.

"The men go hunting and the women keep house, or hut." He continued. "Men are the providers and the protectors. When you were sick and slept all day, I liked catching those hares with Arun, which Muna made into a soup. I liked learning how to spear fish. I liked it when you told me to kill those North American Werewolves for you. B, it feels like for the first time in a long while that you've needed me."

"Yeah well, you're weird." I looked away uncomfortably.

Declan laughed loudly, which rebounded off the water before being absorbed by the surrounding woods.

"Yeah, I'm just a Neanderthal, aren't I?" He pulled me close to catch my gaze. He said lastly, "Sometimes with your lecturing or your bank balance, I wonder what I bring to this relationship?"

"Huh? Are you feeling alright, Declan?" I looked on peculiarly and I even felt his forehead. "You're not getting sick, are you?"

"Shut up and let me finish." He rolled his eyes. "I mean, I know you earn a comfortable living as a history professor that people invite everywhere. I know you've got Hodge Endeavor at your beck and call. I know that you wish you could travel more. So why the hell do you put up with a grouch, who's growing old on you?"

I looked on incredulous, "You're an idiot, do you know that too?"

"Thanks!" He grumpily glanced away, but I cupped his face to make him look back.

"I may be a Circulator, but I'm still a Lokoti Werewolf. A male Lokoti Werewolf would no sooner leave his aging mate than I would. You're MY Declan Sabre. If we were ever separated for good, I know for a cold, hard fact that I would wane." I said seriously.

"Oh yeah?" His eyes widened in hope. "Then what's with the, 'Declan are you happy' questions? Sometimes I wonder if you keep asking because you're looking for an escape."

"What? Don't be so stupid!" I fired up. "I ask because I'm scared that you'll get tired of me one day! You're not a Lokoti Werewolf, so you're not biologically bound to your mate. You can walk anytime you want to."

"What?!" He pushed me away, to hold me at arms length in the freezing water. "Now look who's being the idiot! I waited for you, B! I waited five frickin' years, when you were mated to someone else! If the pack or the tribe had kicked up a stink, or even if they tried to punish me? I still would have wanted you! Why do you think I've asked for this frickin' Joining Ceremony that YOU don't want to do?!"

"Because I don't want you to die!" I cried out in a shrill voice as I practically jumped on the guy. "I'm scared that I could be a Black Widow! The last guy I had a Joining Ceremony with, died! If you were killed, Declan..." I cupped his face again, "...I would die too! I wouldn't evolve to the space time continuum, I'd just let myself fade away. I'd slip into nothingness because I'd have lost my reason to exist."

His eyes were large and he looked like he was drinking in every word I said. "Do you mean that?"

"Of course I mean it!" I growled out as my eyes flashed turquoise in anger.

He laughed in relief as he squashed his mate against his form, and I noticed his body increased in temperature.

"Maybe we should make up our own vows?" He joked. "Declan Domitian Sabre, do you take Bianca Grace Wisetail to be your mate? Of course you idiot!"

I giggled back, "Bianca Grace Wisetail, do you take Declan Domitian Sabre to be your mate? No, I just like standing around in ceremonial dress, waiting for European Werewolves to propose."

"Well in that case, it's a good thing I'm the last one then." He kicked his strong legs to keep our heads above the water.

"The last European Werewolf marries the last Circulator," I rubbed my nose against his.

"Say the words, B." He breathed.

"Er, I'm yours and nothing but yours?" I shrugged, unsure what they were.

"Close enough," he chuckled back before his mouth engulfed mine.

I clung to his front as he held me close, whilst keeping us buoyed the whole time. As we kissed, I felt his body heat increase again. I paid little attention to the deep, dark water now, or the sparkling stars above. It's hard to think of anything else when you're ensconced in the centre of your universe.

*****

We snuck back inside the Riverclaw's hut just before dawn. Or, it was Declan carrying me against his front, wrapped in the fur again. He used his skills as a predator to soundlessly creep through the doorway, over to our cot and silently lay us down.

However, one of Arun's glowing blue eyes sleepily opened, noting our return, before he rolled over to spoon his mate.

The next time I woke up, it was from the children's chattering and laughter. I wasn't sure what time it was, but I was going to guess by the morning light, it was around eight or nine o'clock. Muna was crossly telling her young to stand still, so she could dress them up for the day's festivities. Arun was outside by the campfire, preparing breakfast.

"B, yours and Declan's clothes are over there." Muna pointed at some skins lying over her bed. They looked a little more ornate than the day-to-day suede, as it had beads around the tasselled neckline and sleeves. "You will be wearing what Arun and I wore, for our Joining Ceremony."

My mate sleepily raised his head to see what she was talking about, to find his decorated suede clothes, lying beside mine.

"Beads and tassels?" Declan muttered in English, before his head flopped back down.

"Ha ha!" I poked him. "You're going to look just as much as a showgirl as I will."

"Oh yeah?" He poked me back. "Well you've got way more beadwork on your skins than I do."

Muna couldn't understand our words because they were in English, but I think she guessed their meaning. "You two are as bad as the children!"

Her young laughed louder as her son pulled one of his sister's plaits and in return, she kicked his shin.

Then Muna took the children outside to eat and once they departed, Declan and I got out of bed. We dressed ourselves, but also helped the other. When we felt something was itching or rubbing the wrong way, the other would tug or smooth it out. I thought it was romantic, dressing your spouse for the wedding.

My suede shirt had fur on the end of the sleeves and white, red and black beads in a flowery pattern around the tasselled neckline. It was long, almost to my knees with more beadwork near the bottom. Underneath, I wore suede pants and moccasins on my feet. Declan's suede shirt also had fur trim on the sleeves and on the bottom, but it wasn't as long as mine. It had less beadwork but more tassels, especially down the arms. He also wore suede pants and moccasins.

He looked down to see a couple of leather ties attached to some feathers and beads. "What's that?"

"I think we use them in our hair."

I remembered Great Grandma plaiting my hair then tying them with those, when I first married.

"Oh," he frowned. "That rules me out, as my hair isn't long enough."

"Sit down," I pushed him onto the bed.

He sat still as I took a small tuft of his scruffy blonde hair and had him hold it while I wound round the leather tie. Then I did the same to the other side of his head. Lastly, I took a step back to smilingly look on. I thought the decorated, leather fasteners hanging loosely behind each ear, looked good on him. They certainly went with the wardrobe.

"I don't look ridiculous, do I?" He fidgeted.

"No, you look like a Lokoti Warrior of old... or for this era."

"Really?" He asked in pleasant surprise, as he stood up. "Your turn."

I sat in the spot he'd vacated. Thanks to years of babysitting, Declan was no stranger to plaiting hair. Skilfully, he separated my hair into two parts and as I held one, he plaited the other. Then I held the plait for him as he wound round a leather tie. When one side was done, he did the other.

"Bingo," he said as he stepped back to admire his work. "Am I good, or am I good?"

"Show off." I smirked as I stood up.

He took a step back to give his mate a good look up and down. "I'm finally marrying the Lokoti girl I was in love with, all along."

This made me pause, as it brought to mind what he said at Forrest and Maia's Housewarming.

"B and Declan?" Muna stuck her head in through the pelt-door. "Your food is waiting."

Typical of his nature, he was the first to leave at the mention of a meal. I think I even heard his stomach rumble. I trailed out after him, with his words in the front of my mind.

*****

Outside on another log, Declan and I ate cooked trout from wooden bowls, using our hands.

As we consumed our breakfast, the two old women I saw sewing yesterday, approached us carrying several other bowls. However, there wasn't food in them, but paint. Casually, they dipped their fingers into the colours and ran them down our faces. We stopped chewing as they painted the black, white and red claw mark. They were so experienced, they indicated we should keep eating while they worked.

Once they'd finished, Declan looked my way as I gazed in his. He had the mark of the Lokoti Wolf going down the right side of his face, whereas I had it on my left. Not only was it to symbolize the tribe's chief spirit guide; but by painting on opposites sides of our faces, represented two halves coming together to make a whole.

"It's time for the ceremony." Arun declared, standing up.

We gazed around to find the whole tribe was congregating around the Sacred Totem. Declan and I exchanged surprised glances, being the 'bridal couple' and still sitting here, eating our breakfast. It felt like the Joining Ceremony was starting without us.

Quickly, we put down our food and stood up. Then we walked through the crowd, with Arun leading the way and Muna and the children walking behind us. Then Tenin fell into step beside Arun, with his mate and young walking with Muna and the kids. Somewhere, someone started to beat a drum. Declan's large hand captured my smaller one and held onto it tightly.

The people parted at our approach to allow us through. As we passed, a couple of them reached out to touch Declan's blonde hair, or to pat him on the back. It was a contrast to the night of our arrival, where they had looked on in suspicion or fear. I recognized they were welcoming the foreigner into the tribe, for joining with their Lokoti daughter. This was accentuated by the couple of cries in their air.

"The Giant Wolf claims his mate! Our Lokoti daughter becomes the Giant Wolf's mate! The Giant Wolf becomes a Lokoti Werewolf!"

Giant Wolf? I think they were alluding to Declan's supernatural form. We exchanged smiles as we walked to the front of the crowd.

The Council of Tribal Elders sat around a campfire in front of the Sacred Totem. The right sides of their faces were also painted with the claw mark, as they had been yesterday for the funeral. To their left sat two tribesmen beating on drums made of hide. The Lightfoot Werewolf gave them a nod and instantly they stopped playing.

I was about to sit down with the Elders, when I realized Arun and Tenin were still standing in front of us. I wondered why they weren't moving away, when Declan addressed them loudly. He spoke at a volume the whole tribe could hear.

"I formally ask your permission Arun, as the head of the Riverclaw family, for the hand of your future great granddaughter, Bianca Grace Wisetail."

Oh, I'd forgotten about this part of the ceremony. The crowd hushed as everyone turned quiet to watch and listen.

"You have my permission, Declan Sabre." Arun stepped aside.

"I formally ask your permission Tenin, as the head of the Wisetail family, for the hand of your future great granddaughter, Bianca Grace Wisetail." He spoke to next.

"You have my permission, Declan Sabre." Tenin stepped aside.

Of course there were several 'greats' left out in front of the word 'granddaughter', but it'd take all morning to say them all.

With my forefathers no longer blocking the way, Declan and I sat before the Tribal Elders. Tenin and Arun stood with their families as the remainder of the tribe watched what took place. A couple of the people in the front also sat down, so the ones at the back could see.

"You have the council of the Lokoti Elders convened here for you today. What do you ask of us?" The Lightfoot Werewolf spoke.

"I have come to ask for the blessing of the Tribal Elders as the Guides of the Lokoti Wolf, to take this woman as my mate." Declan stated.

"And do you have the permission of your family for this union?" Memek asked.

I recognized her as the old woman from the story time by the fire, a few nights ago.

"He does!" A male voice called out in English, from behind.

Instantly, the crowd reacted and somebody cried out in Lokoti, "Strangers! There are strangers on our land!"

This put a stop to the ceremony and even the Tribal Elders looked up in alarm.

We turned to see Purto standing with two 'white people' whom I'd never seen before, yet were somehow familiar.

Everyone who was seated, jumped to their feet and Declan stood in front protectively, incase they were trouble.

Purto was wearing the skins of old, but the strangers were dressed in early 21st Century clothing. The young man was tall, had brown hair and eyes and looked a lot like Derik; my mate's late brother. The girl he was standing with had the same coloured hair and eyes, and looked younger than him. Her hair was long and she was carrying a gift-wrapped box in her hands.

"G'day," she smiled my way.

"Hi," the guy gave a nod to Declan.

My heart raced as I looked from the strangers to my husband, before their way again.

"Are you - you - you -" I stammered in shock.

"Yeah, I'm Elisha." She laughed at my gob smacked expression.

Suddenly, several human warriors ran onto the scene, aiming their bows and arrows at the intruders!

"Nin!" Purto yelled in Lokoti, stepping forwards. He addressed the tribe in their native language, "These are my friends! The pale-skins are Light People! The girl is related to Bianca Wisetail and the man is related to Declan Sabre!"

This made the European Werewolf blink in disbelief, as he stared at the man who looked almost identical to his human brother.

"He speaks the truth!" The Lightfoot Werewolf raised his hand to stay their weapons. "They all have auras like our Lokoti daughter!"

The members of the pack all gawked at the two people whom to them, were literally glowing.

"Light People?" The guy looked on Elisha in amusement.

"Werewolves can see our higher bio-electromagnetic fields." She explained. "To them, they look like auras."

Then the Derik look-a-like, along with Elisha and Purto, crossed over to where we were standing. I sensed my mate's heart hurt, as he looked on the relative who looked so much like his little brother. However, when the man spoke, his voice was deeper than Derik's and he was also a little taller.

"You must be Declan Sabre."

"I am," my mate answered.

"You look just like my older brother Anthony did," he smiled sadly.

"You look just like my little brother Derik did," my husband replied.

The man offered his hand, "I'm Mike Sabre, your great, great granduncle."

Declan shook it and afterwards Mike had to flex his hand, to recover from the strong grip.

"Wow," he chuckled, "I have a European Werewolf for a great, great grandnephew."

"And I have the first female Lokoti Werewolf for my great, great granddaughter." Elisha giggled back.

"You always have to be different, don't you?" Mike tickled her. "It's not enough she's the last Circulator. But YOUR great, great granddaughter has to be the first and only female Lokoti Werewolf, too."

"You're just jealous!" She tittered back.

However, we were interrupted by the Lightfoot Werewolf calling out in Lokoti, "Why have the Light People come? Why do they want to stop the ceremony?"

"Oh," Declan cleared his throat. "We just have to do this thing then we can do the family catch up."

"Go right ahead." Mike waved his arm. "It's why we're here."

"You're here for the Joining Ceremony?" My mate asked pleasantly surprised. Then his eyes narrowed suspiciously, "Hang on, you didn't come here to try to stop it?"

"No, we're not members of THAT party." Mike nodded towards Purto, who unhappily looked away. "We came to let you know that we don't agree with the rest of the Circulate. We're here to show our support."

"Say what?" Declan looked my way betrayed. "So Purto dragged you to the Circulate Headquarters of the past, to talk about me? Why, to turn you against me?!"

"Moving right along now," I laughed nervously as I grabbed hold of his arm. "We'll get hitched and talk about that later."

"B?" He wouldn't budge. "What did the Circulate say about me?"

"C'mon Declan," I yanked on his arm but he stood fast.

However, it was Elisha who intervened. "The Circulate Council put on a presentation about the dangers of European Werewolves. But B put on a little presentation of her own, showing your benefits instead."

"You heard about that?" I asked in astonishment.

"Yeah, I heard you turned the tables on them." She grinned. "You even impressed Nelson, and everyone knows she's a tough audience to win."

Declan's hard face softened at her words as he looked my way again. "So you stuck up for me?"

"Of course you idiot," I rolled my eyes.

"Then what are we doing standing around, when we could be getting married?" He retook hold of my hand.

"My sentiments exactly," Mike chuckled, as he put his arm about Elisha's waist.

Declan led me back through the crowd until we were standing before the Tribal Elders again. "Please continue with the Joining Ceremony."

Those who had been sitting returned to their previous seats, as our special guests stood back. As the ceremony proceeded in Lokoti, I overheard Purto translate it to English.

"And do you have the permission of the woman's family for this union?" Memek asked.

"He does." Arun Riverclaw answered.

"He does." Tenin Wisetail spoke.

"He does." Elisha added on, in English.

"Tu tak." Purto interpreted what she said, for the Elders.

"Declan Sabre from the Italian Tribe, we see how you care for your mate," the Lightfoot Werewolf spoke. "You fought the foreign Werewolves for her and the tribe. You helped us rebuild our huts, as you helped us rebuild our lives. We believe your visit was not by accident, but it was by the will of our father the Lokoti Wolf. It was his intention that you should be here the night of the attack. It was his will that we meet the tribe's first female Lokoti Werewolf."

The rest of the Elders nodded in agreement, as did the tribe. I glanced over my shoulder to see the people quietly whisper to each other, as they pointed at me. However, I also saw that they were looking on in approval.

Memek said, "It is through loving your mate that you are able to tame the dangerous urges inside you. By giving her your heart, you are able to channel your never ending hunger towards her and her alone. Loving a Light Person helps you to battle your darkness. It is for this reason, the Elders granted your wish for a Joining Ceremony."

In the background, I overheard Purto quietly repeat everything she just said, in English to our guests.

Then the Shallow Water Werewolf picked up the 'Sacred Cup', which was an old, painted, wooden bowl. We saw inside a sweet-smelling, maroon coloured liquid. It looked like the juice of berries, whereas at my first Joining Ceremony, it had been mead. As he passed it to my mate, he spoke.

"Declan Sabre, you and your mate may drink from the Lokoti Sacred Cup. You will be adding your blood to a vessel that generations of Lokoti Warriors and Werewolves have spilled their life force into. Therefore, you will be sealing your fates together and creating a new bloodline of Wisetail-Riverclaw-Sabre."

Tenin handed Declan the Wisetail family knife. He put down the Sacred Cup to run the sharp blade over his forefinger. I saw him dip it into the liquid which turned it redder. Next, Arun handed me the Riverclaw family blade. My mate watched as I stuck the end into my finger, then I too dipped it into the juice.

When I moved my bleeding finger to my mouth, Declan grabbed my arm.

"That's my job," he said.

Tenderly, he sucked on it and I felt the stinging cut turn numb. I picked up his injured finger and did the same. Then he gave a wink as he picked up the cup once more and we held it together.

"The Great Wolf will always have the scent of his mate, as the female Lokoti Werewolf will always have his." The Lightfoot Werewolf pronounced. "No matter where the two of you go, you will always find the other."

"Now drink," Memek instructed.

Declan angled the cup towards me to take the first sip, which I did. When I angled it his way, instead of taking a sip, he gulped the whole thing down. I snickered at his large appetite, no matter the occasion it was always there.

The Lightfoot Werewolf addressed the tribe, "During a Joining Ceremony, the Elders share the story of how the first Lokoti Werewolf was created. However, we have sat by another fire and told the story already. Our Lokoti daughter has fought as one of the pack, as has her mate. It is right and natural that the first female Lokoti Werewolf is a Riverclaw and a Wisetail, as were the pack's First and Second in the beginning. As our souls move down the river of time, everything falls into place. The river moulds the land and washes everything anew, as do the family bloodlines."

"You have sat by the fire of the Tribal Elders and you have shared your blood in the Sacred Cup." Memek said to the bridal couple. "You have the blessing of the Lokoti Wolf and you may leave us to continue your lives together."

Suddenly, the members of the pack threw back their heads and howled loudly! Next, the human Warriors all whooped and hollered. The drum beat restarted as the tribe erupted into cheers and laughter.

We stood up and I felt my mate's large arms encircle my waist.

He grinned, "I think this is the part where I can kiss the bride."

Without further ado, I grabbed hold of his suede shirt and our lips collided. The European Werewolf held on so tightly, his fingers dug into my back. But I didn't mind, not one bit. I was clinging onto his clothes like I never wanted to let go.

*****

The Wisetail family roasted what was left of the caribou, as the Riverclaw family served cooked trout. The Lightfoot family provided roasted moose and the Shallow Water family served smoked salmon. It was like the whole tribe served a banquet of Alaskan fare, including edible plant life.

Declan and I ate on a log with Mike and Elisha sitting on another. We sat opposite each other, with a campfire between us. As we ate what the different members of the tribe offered, Declan and I explained what each dish was. The Australian was more than happy to try moose or caribou, but she relished the smoked salmon.

"When Arabella started hanging out with Em; Flint would give her smoked salmon or trout, to take home." She told us, as she ate her second serving. "Man, I love eating authentic smoked salmon."

"What's that?" My ears picked up.

"Your grandmother," she swallowed, "before she mated with your grandfather, they were best friends. She did sleepovers at Em's house, all the time. When she'd phase back to London the next morning, she'd have a bag of smoked salmon or trout that Grandfather Flint gave to her. He knew we liked to eat it with our scrambled eggs."

"How very English of you," Mike smilingly shook his head. "All that's missing is the kedgeree."

"I suck at making kedgeree," she pronounced in her Australian accent. "I left that to the chef at Blythe."

Declan looked my way in amusement. He found it funny listening to my great, great grandmother with her Aussie accent, who was once known as Lady Worthall of Blythe Castle. Whenever she used words with 'er' on the end, like 'grandmother' or 'grandfather', it sounded like 'grandmatha' or 'grandfatha'.

"Oh yeah, kedgeree," my mate nodded. "I think Nairn made that for us when we stayed with her in Scotland."

"Nairn?" She straightened. "Oh, you mean that lady you met who's distantly related to Dr. Knight. Yeah, I heard about her. How freaky is that, to bump into her on your travels? It's like temporal causalities, A leads to B which results in C."

My mate laughingly shook his head, "You sound just like B."

When she looked on inquiringly, I volunteered, "Declan calls temporal mechanics, 'trippy time travel stuff'."

"It's not really." She frowned thoughtfully. "It's more like irony or karma."

"What goes around, comes around," Mike finished for her.

"Exactly," she picked up her third piece of smoked salmon to devour.

"Well on that note..." I thought aloud, "...it must be especially 'freaky' for you, sitting here with Declan and Mike."

"Huh?" She paused in her eating.

"The last time you were in the company of both, you were sixteen and they went by the names of Captain Greyson and Captain Robertson." I pointed out.

"Not this again," Declan rubbed his face.

"Not what again?" Mike looked his way.

"After B's life-after-death experience, she told me I'm some dead 18th Century, Army Captain." He shook his head.

"So, what's wrong with that?" Elisha shrugged. "I'm dating some dead 18th Century, Navy Captain."

"Would you give it a rest?" Mike moaned. "I don't remember being that guy and no, I don't want to undergo 'past life' regression!"

"Amen to that!" Declan toasted him with his roasted caribou. "Women! Or should I say, Circulators!"

Mike leaned over to tell him, "She gets obsessed with this business of the space time continuum. A leads to B which results in C, and everything must mean something!"

"Tell me about it!" My husband agreed. "It must run in the family. B's obsessed with her essays, lectures and sometimes even paperwork for Hodge Endeavor. I'll cook up a three course feast, but she refuses to clear her books or her computer off the table!"

I exchanged unhappy looks with my great x2 grandmother, who turned this expression on her date to the wedding.

"I didn't hear you complain when my visions saved your life!" She fired off.

"I've saved your life too, as you may recall." He shot back.

"You're supposed to save each other's lives," my mate said simply. "If you didn't and the other one died, then where'd you be?"

"Resting in peace," she pulled a face.

Elisha made us laugh, including Mike who gave her an affectionate nudge.

"Anyways," she sighed. We watched her put down her food and pick up the gift-wrapped box. "Here's your wedding present."

"Thanks," I took it from her. "But since we've been married for 150 years, it's more like an anniversary present."

She screwed up her face, "How can you be married to somebody for 150 years? Don't you drive each other insane? It brings to mind that song about that couple wanting to kill each other, until Tom Jones comes on the radio."

"I know that song, it's 'The Ballad of Tom Jones' by Space." Declan chortled before he sang. "You stopped us from killing each other, Tom Jones, Tom Jones. You have no idea how you saved our lives."

"Isn't that song in your music collection, back home?" I remembered.

"Yup."

I told the couple, "Declan has a huge 20th Century music collection. It's mostly old CD's but he's even got some vinyl records."

"It was a good time for music," Mike agreed. "I'm sick of 21st Century R&B songs that all sound the same."

Then Elisha insisted, "Well, hurry up and open your present."

My mate lowered his food to watch me tear off the wrapping and open the box.

"No way!" I gasped, as I gazed upon the offering. "Is this for real?!"

"What is it?" He leaned in to see. "It's a vase, which is typical for newlyweds to receive. What's the big deal, B?"

"Declan, it isn't just ANY vase!" I said with reverence, as I carefully lifted it out. "It's identical to the one we bought in Venice that Maia and Brandon broke!"

"I thought you'd like it." Elisha beamed. "I travelled through time to visit the same glassmaker you did. He made three glass-blown vases with that particular pattern. You bought one, I bought the second and I was just in time too, as more tourists bought the third."

"But - but - but how did you know...?" I stared at her.

"I saw that you and Declan bought it on your trip around Europe, when you celebrated your 55th Anniversary. I saw the kids break it, when you were babysitting. I also saw how much that vase meant to you." She spoke casually.

"You 'saw'?" My mate looked on peculiarly.

"You're both under the impression that the Circulate had no idea of B's existence, until you met Purto. However, there are members including myself, who've always known. I've often looked in on you. I was even in the after life with you." She said simply.

"Say what?" Declan's mouth hung open in shock. "B, you saw your great, great grandmother after you were shot in the head?"

I confirmed it with a nod.

Then he turned to them to say, "She said when she visited the space time continuum, it was done up as an 18th Century Aristocratic Ball."

"And who made it look like that for her?" Elisha pointed out. "I wanted to share my first circulation with the last Circulator, for her first visit to the space time continuum. I did it to show her beginnings."

My face flushed, "But I didn't recognize it was you, until I had to leave."

"I know," she smilingly shrugged it off. "But since you were dead, I didn't take it personally."

*****

When the sun set at 10.03 PM - we knew the precise time from our guest's wristwatches - they decided it would be a good time to leave. I must admit, I thought it was time for my mate and I, to depart too. It felt like we'd done everything we needed to and I was craving 23rd Century amenities.

I stood back and watched as Elisha and Mike used Purto as their interpreter, to thank our hosts for the hospitality.

Then I sidled up to my mate to whisper in his ear, "Let's go home."

He looked down into my face, in surprise. "What, now?"

I nodded, "I'm tired and I want to have a shower and crawl into our Queen-sized bed."

He wrapped his arm about my waist so I could lean against his side.

"Arun and Muna," my husband addressed them in their language. "We'd like to thank you for your kindness and let you know that we have to be going too."

"You have to leave, tonight?" Muna looked saddened by this.

"Tonight is their wedding night." Arun smilingly hinted.

She giggled at the innuendo whilst moving closer to her husband.

"I can return these clothes to you tomorrow -" I began when I was interrupted.

"No." Arun shook his head. "You keep them."

"But they're your Ceremonial clothes -" I tried.

"No," he resolutely shook his head.

Muna pointed at the decorated suede, "They're your Joining Ceremony clothes now."

I was touched by their continued generosity and so was Declan.

"Arun," he offered his hand.

"Be well, Declan Sabre," my Riverclaw forefather shook it. "I know you look after your mate first, your pack second and yourself third."

"And I always will," he released it before returning his arm.

I darted forwards to kiss Muna's cheek before doing the same to Arun.

"Look after yourself, Little Wolf." He squeezed my arm.

This made my eyes water, as it was what my father had called me. Sometimes when I thought I could hear the tribe's spirit guide, the old Lokoti Wolf speaking, he called me Little Wolf. The term was also used in the pack, when a young member joined the ranks. So I didn't think he said it in a condescending manner, but affectionately.

When I picked up the box with the vase inside, I noticed Tenin was sitting a little way away. He was helping his mate feed some caribou to their youngest. We held up our hands in farewell, which he returned.

We also waved to the Lightfoot Werewolf, to pay our last respects to the First.

As Elisha and Mike stepped away from everyone to instantaneously phase home, so did my husband and I.

"Oh, are you leaving too?" She glanced our way.

"Yup," my mate answered.

Her eyes met mine, "I almost feel like I don't have to say goodbye to you. I know we'll see each other again."

I admitted, "Yeah, I feel that way too."

"What year are you off to?" Mike asked.

"2240 and you?" Declan returned.

"2061."

"Beat you." My mate joked.

But then Mike surprised Elisha when he moved away from her side to go to Declan's.

"Hey man, there's something I've been wanting to say," he began. "I want you to know how sorry I am that you lost your father."

"Huh?" My husband blinked in surprise. "Er, he's been dead now for nearly two centuries. Thanks, but I've certainly recovered."

"No, I mean I feel like it's my fault that he died." Mike said uneasily.

"How do you figure?" Declan asked, puzzled.

"It was my letter which told your parents to go to Alaska, where it'd be safe from radiation and lawlessness. I wanted to ensure your family's survival.

I didn't mean for your father to be killed in the European Werewolf attack, which changed you." He confessed.

My husband looked from his distant relative to his wife, before he responded.

"As I once said to B, even if my family had stayed in the Lower 48, he may not have lived. He could have died from looters, instead. The way I see it, your letter did get us to safety. Me, my Mom and my little brother grew up without radiation sickness and not having to fight for food. I lost my human father, but I gained fifteen others, in the pack."

Mike gave a nod as he saw my mate meant it, then he returned to his amore.

I took hold of Declan's hand as Elisha held Mike's. They disappeared first in a bright flash of light, as the tribe stood around to see. Then the Lokoti looked at their dark-haired daughter, standing with her blonde-haired mate, in the same clothes as they. We disappeared in a second bright brilliance, which made them squint and a couple of them shiver.

Within the blink of an eye, the lit up camp of old, was replaced by our dark living room.

We looked on the pine dining table, the overstuffed couches and the stone fireplace, as we breathed in the familiar scent of home.

I put our present on the table as my husband let go of my hand, to switch on the light.

"Ah, we have plasma power again," he grinned. "It's certainly a lot easier than trying to build a campfire from scratch, if you want some light or warmth." Next, he walked into the kitchen and kissed the refrigerator. "Baby, where've you been the last week of my life?"

Just then a cramp ripped through my abdomen, which made me lean on the table for support.

"B," he looked on in concern. "Are you OK?"

"I think we came home right on time." I winced. "I certainly didn't want to experience the monthly blues without my 25th Century painkillers, or my 23rd Century sanitary pads."

Instantly, he helped by taking the cold water out of the fridge and a glass out of the cupboard. He opened another to grab the small, plastic bottle of medication. Then he crossed over to the table where I was standing, to place the tablets on my palm before handing me the glass of H2O.

Greedily, I gulped down the pain relievers then put the glass on the table when I'd finished.

"I'm gonna have a hot shower," I turned towards the stairs.

"I'll join you," he followed me up.

*****

Our 23rd Century facilities felt like luxurious niceties, after basic living. I swear a hot shower never felt so good, nor our shower gel smelled so nice, or our towels felt so soft. It was wonderful putting on modern underwear again, underneath my negligee. I tittered at my mate's Tassie Devil, satin boxers.

It felt glorious, crawling into our spacious bed and pulling up the cotton sheet. It was nice having enough room to be able to roll over in bed again. I stretched out on my back, with my legs parted and my arms above my head.

"Well, somebody looks ready for their wedding night." He joked, as he flopped onto the mattress beside.

"Oh Declan, I'm sorry but -"

"I know, you're not in the mood from the cramps." He sung knowingly. "Come on then, roll over."

I moved onto my side and immediately he spooned me, as he knew his body heat helped. He made sure his feet were touching mine, as experience taught that cold feet made the cramps worse. He also moved his hand to my swollen belly, to gently rub it.

"Declan?"

"Hmm?"

"After 150 years of marriage, aren't you sick of my PMS or cramps?"

"No..." he sounded unsure then he explained. "When it gets annoying, I realize it must be harder on you. Like you said, you can't have children but you still get the effects of being a woman? 150 years of hormonal upheaval would drive me nuts, so I don't know how you cope."

In spite of myself, I giggled at his words and then because he was softly chewing on my shoulder.

"Declan?"

"B?"

"Can you do one last thing for me, before we go to bed?"

"Hmm?"

"Open the second drawer in the tallboy."

"Why?" He wondered. "Do you have to change pads already?"

"No," I frowned, "but there's something underneath the packet of pads that I was hiding from you."

This made him sit up to look down suspiciously. "Oh yeah, like what?"

"Open the drawer and see."

Reluctantly, he climbed out of bed and crossed over to the furniture. He opened the wooden drawer and I saw him move aside my t-shirts to reach underneath the packet. When he pulled out the wrapped present, he grinned.

"Happy Anniversary," I smiled. "Go on, open it."

"Is it a book?" He wondered as he discarded the paper. Then he looked on the gift bemused. "It's a bright yellow book."

I sat up to say, "It's Dracula."

"Oh," he read the red writing on the yellow cover. "Um, I already have a copy of Dracula."

"Would you open the cover and read out the date of print then turn the pages until you read the inscription?" I rolled my eyes.

This caught his attention and so he did. "...1897? Hey, isn't that the date it was first published?"

"Yes it's a first edition, now keep going."

He turned a page or two, before he froze. His eyebrows rose as he looked stunned. After a moment, he wet his lips to read out:

"To Declan Sabre,

I understand this is a wedding anniversary present, which your wife travelled far to obtain. She appears to be a charming yet determined young lady, which should serve the marriage well. You are the first people I've met from Alaska and I thank you for your readership.

Your friend, Bram Stoker."

Then he met my waiting eyes with his wide ones. "Wait a minute, that day I came home from work and you were dressed for the Victorian era -"

"Yes, that was the day I picked up your present."

"B..." his voice trailed off, as he didn't know what to say.

"Do you like it?" I asked hopeful.

"Like it...?" He looked from the book, to his mate. "It's awesome."

"Really?" I brightened. "I truly wanted to get you something special."

Declan wandered back to the bed before sitting down with his gift. His forty-something face softened, as he gazed upon his mate with her twenty-something features. His bright blue eyes held my darker ones, before he moved in to slowly and sensuously, kiss the bride.

He pulled apart to say, "It's the perfect gift to top off the perfect day. We're married by the Lokoti Tribe in the year 1868. We meet our ancestors from both sides of the family tree. You get your favourite vase back and I get my favourite book signed by the author. How can I not like it?"

I threw my arms about his neck to kiss him again and again.

"Mmm... Declan?"

"Mmm... B?"

"Although we're back in our big bed, could you sleep over me again?"

"Hell yeah."

~~~~~~

~ 21 ~

2nd November 2263

Yesterday was Declan's 200th Birthday.

The European Werewolf looked like a tall, broad-shouldered, man in his early fifties. His hair was ash blonde these days, thanks to his numerous grey hairs. But I didn't mind, I thought they made him look debonair. He had a new haircut which was short back and sides, but longer on the top. It was swept back with his natural wave.

The night before the big day, I lay awake, watching both the time and my husband sleep.

The glowing green digits on Declan's digital alarm clock read as 12.01 AM. The numbers looked particularly bright in the dark bedroom. Outside, snow was softly falling past the window. I looked from the icy glass which separated the warm indoors from the freezing outdoors, to my slumbering mate.

I was dressed in a pair of flannel pyjamas, with cartoon characters of The Muppet Babies printed over them. However, he was wearing his typical sleepwear no matter what time of the year it was; his satin boxers. Tonight, they were his black pair with Marvin the Martian, printed all over. Although he slept on his side of the mattress as I lay on mine, he warmed the whole bed.

My head was perched on my hand, which was propped up by my elbow. I observed how peaceful the European Werewolf looked, when he was unconscious. It was in direct contrast to how loud he could be, when he was awake.

Now my loud-mouthed, bad-tempered, bossy husband, was two centuries old... Two centuries old, the thought felt more surreal than real... He was officially the oldest Werewolf in the history of the pack.

Lokoti Werewolves may live up to two hundred years, but only twice has one actually surpassed 190 years. Usually, a Lokoti Werewolf died anywhere between 120 - 180 years old. My father evolved to the space time continuum when he was 180 years old. My grandfather was 167 years old when he evolved with my grandmother.

Now my mate, who was Second in the pack, was 200 years old...

Tenderly, I reached out to touch his silvery, blonde hair. I liked his haircut, it suited his colouring. However, his skin no longer felt as smooth as it did when he was younger, and was starting to look leathery. But his muscles were still large, especially with his regular hunting.

I can't believe Declan Sabre, the boy I grew up with, was now 200 years old. The boy who quit school at the age of thirteen to become a mechanic, was now two centuries old. The bossy older brother of my late best friend, was now twenty decades old.

"B, stop it."

The suddenness of his deep voice cut through our dark bedroom and made me jump out of my skin!

"Stop what?" I asked innocently.

"Quit staring," he said grumpily. "You used to get annoyed with me, when I watched you sleep."

"It's 12.04 AM." I sung.

"Huh?"

"It's 12.04 AM, it's officially your birthday."

"Not really," he disagreed with his eyes closed. "My Mom told me I was born at 6.14 PM so officially, I've got another 18 hours left of being 199 years old."

"That's stupid," I scowled. "I don't understand why people get obsessed with what time they were born. Today's your birthday and that's that."

"Of course a Circulator who doesn't age a day, doesn't understand why people cling to a particular age." He said shortly, with his eyes still shut.

"I age!" I poked his side. "I make myself older for my academic identities!"

"Yeah and then you return to your twenty-something appearance."

"But you said you wanted me in my true form!" I argued. "I could make myself look like I'm slowly aging like you are."

"Don't you dare!" He opened his eyes and I saw they were glowing green. "You're gonna remain my 'young bit of stuff' until the day we evolve."

With that, he rolled onto his side and possessively pulled me into his arms.

I didn't mind, as I liked being pressed up against his hot body. I lowered my head to my pillow but I still watched him. He closed his eyes again and looked like he was falling back asleep.

"You're two hundred years old," I sung again, as I traced my finger down his chin to his chest. "You're officially the oldest member of the pack on record."

"Shut up," he growled.

"You're two centuries old," I continued. "I'm married to a two hundred year old man."

"I mean it, B." He frowned with his eyes closed. "I'm trying to sleep and I really don't need to be reminded."

My finger traced its way up from his chest, to his neck, over his chin and then brushed his lips.

"My husband, my mate, the man I'm biologically bonded to, is two centuries old." I mused.

"Frickin' hell!" He barked bad-temperedly, as he let go to roll over. "I'll remember this in three years time, when you turn two hundred and I wake you up!"

I moved up against his hot back and kissed his muscle-hardened shoulders. I even closed my eyes and inhaled his maple syrup scent, coming off his skin. My arms wrapped about his waist as I left several more kisses down his spine.

"Mmm," he moaned appreciatively.

"You don't look like a 200 year old."

"For...crying...out...loud," he said deadpan. "Would you give it a rest?"

"I love you."

"I know."

"But sometimes I get scared."

"Huh?" He sleepily turned his head.

"I'm scared that we could get separated by time."

"What d'you mean?"

"What if something happens and you die of old age before I turn you into a Circulator?"

"Nothing's gonna happen," he groaned tiredly. "So let your husband get some frickin' sleep!"

"Or what if something happens and we get separated on our way to the space time continuum?"

"Oh God, you're not gonna let this rest, are you...?"

"Or what if I do something wrong when I turn you into a Circulator and it sends you to the space time continuum without me?"

He buried his face into his pillow, "Kill me, kill me now."

"It scares me that you're two hundred years old." I whined. "It means you'll grow elderly now you're on the downward slope."

"Gees B, you really know how to cheer up a person!" He laughed bitterly. "Imagine what you'd be like if a depressed, elderly person called a 'help line', on their birthday. You'd have the highest mortality rate of callers, on record!"

After kissing down his spine, I proceeded to kiss my way back up and he emitted another moan of delight.

"I love you Declan Domitian Sabre," I mumbled out.

"I love you too, B." He sighed as he settled back down. "I'll pounce on you before breakfast, but let's just get some sleep."

"I'll make breakfast," I offered.

"Nah," he sounded sleepy. "I wanna have scrambled eggs and mine are creamier than yours."

"I can make you creamy scrambled eggs with crispy bacon."

"But I don't like your crispy bacon, you basically burn it." He complained. "There's an art to it, so I'll cook."

I raised my head to glare over his wide shoulder, which he noticed when he momentarily opened his eyes.

"You are the WORST person to cook for, when a wife tries to do something nice for her husband." I said unhappily. "Last year when I cooked you dinner for your birthday, you interfered. You barged into the kitchen and told me the oven was the wrong temperature and you took over the stove."

"Well, you undercooked the garlic bread, but you overcooked the pasta!" He refuted. "I had to intervene, or dinner would have been a complete write-off!"

"Declan," I sat up indignantly, "the garlic bread and the pasta were fine!"

"What are you talking about?" He rolled onto his back to look up. "They were soggy!"

"The pasta spirals were meant to be soft and garlic bread is supposed to be moist!"

"Yeah right!" He retorted. "Pasta is meant to be al dente and garlic bread is meant to be crispy on the outside but soft in the middle."

"At least the seafood marinara sauce was OK!" I raised my voice. "There was nothing wrong with that was there?"

"That's because I put some extra herbs in, when you used the bathroom!"

I was so angry, I didn't know what to say. Our eyes clashed until abruptly, I turned away and lay facing in the opposite direction. I wondered why the hell, I was worried about NOT spending eternity with THAT male!

Then I said icily, "Fine, I'll never cook for you again."

I heard him growl under his breath as he rolled over in bed, so he was spooning me.

"I'M the cook, remember?" He spoke tiredly. "I cook and you clean. I like this arrangement. It's worked well in the past."

I seethed, "You really don't get it, do you?"

"What, that it's a special treat when you cook? That you're cooking to spare me from doing it? I understand the sentimentality, but I'm the chef in this relationship. If I'm too tired to cook then we'll order take-away."

"Yeah and it has to be the take-away that YOU prefer." I said stroppily.

"That pizzeria you picked, sells cardboard for pizzas and their garlic bread was mush!" He argued again. "The other one is much nicer, even you have to agree."

I said emotionally, "Shut up, Declan."

There was a pause and I thought he realized that he'd gone too far.

"Aw, c'mon B." He wrapped his arms about my waist. "You're the one who woke ME up, so shouldn't I be the one getting angry?"

The stupid male kept digging his own grave. I shrugged off his arms and he spluttered out his objection. Then I turned my back on him once more.

"Now what, the silent treatment?" He whinged, as he rearranged his pillow. "You wake me up in the middle of the night and then you stop talking to me? Women!"

He rolled over too so we were lying in bed with our backs to each other.

I murmured, "Grumpy, old man."

"What was that?" He instantly picked up his head. "Did you just call me a grumpy, old man?"

Silence...I didn't reply which annoyed him further.

I heard a louder growl, as he punched his pillow as his way of readjusting it. Then his head flopped and I heard a couple more growls as he tried to settle. But I didn't care if he was agitated.

I was so angry, my skin burned. With the rate I was fuming, I'm surprised I didn't burn a hole in the bed like a burning ember. I even fantasized about the bed catching fire and frightening him out of the house.

*****

The next time I opened my eyes, I was woken by the smell of cooking.

Sleepily, I raised my head as I sniffed the air. The aroma of creamy, cheesy, scrambled eggs, as well as bacon cooked until it was crispy, wafted up from downstairs. I turned to see Declan's side of the bed was empty.

I knew he was up earlier, cooking, to prove a point. I rubbed my face before turning on my lamp, to illuminate the dark bedroom. It was 7.23 AM and it was black as night, with the onset of winter's shorter days.

I climbed out of bed to use the bathroom first and dress second. I pulled on a pair of jeans and my white, woollen, turtle-neck jumper. Then I returned to the bathroom to brush my long, black hair into a pony tail.

Eventually, I arrived downstairs to find the table set, complete with a small vase of orchids sitting in the middle.

"You're right on time," Declan sung from the kitchen. "I was just about to serve up."

Reluctantly, I sat in my seat which wasn't at the head of the table, because that was my domineering husband's.

Firstly, he carried out the plate with the buttered toast then secondly, our plates of food. He placed my perfectly prepared breakfast in front of me and I stared nonchalant, at my meal. Then he took his seat and instantly picked up his cutlery. He ate with robust, whereas I simply sat there.

"Aw, c'mon B," he frowned. "Why aren't you eating? Are you still pissed about the fight last night, or are you depressed that it's dark outside?"

I shrugged, as I picked up my fork to push around the food.

"I tell you what," he began. "You eat your delicious breakfast and tell me how good it was. Afterwards, you clean up the mess and I'll tell you how clean the kitchen looks."

My mouth wavered like I was about to object. Then he saw me silently laugh as I shook my head to myself. In a bizarre way, I was starting to see a method to his madness.

I said after while, "You're truly set in your ways, aren't you?"

"Damn straight," he picked up a piece of toast and crunched on it. "If it ain't broke, don't fix it."

Now he watched as I picked up my knife and using both cutlery, I began to eat.

"So," he spoke again. "What have you got planned for my birthday?"

I passed him a sly smile, "Why do you think I'm planning something?"

"Because you banned me from going to work or doing anything related to work, today." He returned.

"Well, after I clean up, we're going to take a trip into town."

"Oh yeah?" He listened. "What do we need to pick up in Alma?"

"We're not going to Alma, but Fairbanks."

He gave a funny look, "Why the city? What's there that we need, which isn't in Alma?"

"You'll find out," I sung teasingly before I was distracted. "Mmm, these scrambled eggs are good. I think they actually taste better than normal."

He grinned, "I used extra cheese today, just the way you like 'em."

I stopped chewing in surprise and he passed me a wink, before filling his mouth with more food.

*****

Once breakfast and the cleaning up was over, we departed the house wearing our thickest coats and boots.

We went into the garage and as usual, he headed for the driver's side of his truck.

"Nuh uh," I cut him off. "I'm driving."

"Say what?" He blinked. "YOU'RE driving MY truck?"

"Move it!" I stood between him and the door. "Today you're the passenger."

"Not in my truck, I'm not."

But I refused to budge, as my dark blue eyes turned turquoise and my lips parted in a snarl.

"OK, OK, OK!" He gave in.

Declan stomped around to the second door and hit his remote to unlock the vehicle. We climbed into the cabin and immediately, I adjusted the seat so my feet could comfortably reach the pedals. Ignoring the growling under his breath that I was changing around his space, I started the engine.

I reversed out and the tyres squelched through the snowy slush.

"I'm gonna have to clear the new snow off the drive, later this week." He commented.

"After today, it may not be a problem anymore." I said off-handedly.

"Huh?"

"Never mind."

"Was that a clue, to where we're going?" He wondered.

"Maybe and maybe not," I tried not to smile.

Carefully, I drove down the icy, curved road which took us off the hill and into the community centre. Next, we cruised off tribal lands then onto the road which took us into Alma. We drove through the township to reach the highway, to take us to the city of Fairbanks.

My husband turned on the Internet Radio and his favourite classic rock station came on. We bopped along to songs from bands such as Split Enz, UB40 or Bruce Springsteen. When a song from The Boss' 'Devils & Dust' album came on, he turned up the volume.

"Look at this," I tittered, "the boss is listening to 'The Boss'."

"Shut up." He chuckled before he frowned. "Hey, slow down, there's a lot of ice on the roads today."

"So orders the boss." I shook my head. "Who's so frickin' bossy, even on his birthday."

However, for safety's sake I followed his command, which meant the drive went longer than an hour and a half.

Once we passed through our part of the Alaska Range, we hit a bank of ice fog surrounding Fairbanks. Tiny crystals of ice stuck to our windscreen and I slowed down even more. Ice was everywhere, on the road, our car and there were icicles hanging from all the street lights, signs and buildings.

"Man, the ice is thick today." He glanced through the windscreen. "You want me to drive?"

"We're nearly there," I said uneasily.

I used the streetlights and the brightly lit signs to circumnavigate as I steered away from the CBD.

"Where are we headed?" He asked.

I divulged my secret just enough so he could help with the geography. That was the good thing about my mate, sometimes when he took control, he made me feel safe. Once he knew where I wanted to go, he kept an eye out for the relevant street sign. His deep voice remained calm, which also smoothed the way.

"Alright, turn left at this intersection." He directed. "Press on the break slowly, so we don't slide. OK, we have a green light so go lightly on the gas. That's it, turn the corner slowly and here we go."

"Declan?"

"Yeah?"

"Thank you."

He rested his large, hot hand on my thigh which added extra support.

We drove down the street where most of the car dealerships were situated. I'd already researched what I wanted on the internet and contacted the dealer. So when I saw the large sign for the company, I pulled into the car park.

"A car dealership?" Declan gave a peculiar look, before he climbed out. "What are we doing here?"

We hopped out of his pick up truck and walked towards the sales area. Or, it was me taking his hand and pulling him inside. There, we were met by an enthusiastic salesman.

"Mrs. Sabre?" He checked, before he shook my hand. "I'm pleased to see you after receiving your email."

"Say what?" The European Werewolf looked my way suspiciously.

"Show Declan the new hover-cars you have in stock." I pushed my mate towards the stranger.

This gave him pause and he looked from his wife to the salesman. "Did you say hover-cars?"

"Yes indeedy!" The man clapped him on the shoulder. "Hover-cars are the way of the future! You don't have to worry about flat tyres, or sliding on icy roads, or shovelling snow off the driveway. They're plasma-powered, so they're safe for the environment. And the mini models even consume less power than a standard plasma-powered vehicle, in use today."

"Hover-cars...?" Declan stared in shock.

"We're the first in Fairbanks to get them in." The salesman nodded. "But I'll tell you what, in two months you'll see these babies in every dealership. We were able to get the first models shipped in from Japan, straight from the assembly lines. Some of the models I'll show you, you've probably seen on the news. However, many Europeans as well as the Japanese are using these vehicles, today."

"Hover-cars," my mate repeated in disbelief.

"Come and take a look," the salesman waved his arm towards the showroom.

I retook my husband's hand and we trailed after our customer service representative. We walked into a massive room with bright lights and gigantic windows, which showed the ice fog outside. But inside, we found numerous luxury cars, which looked like they didn't have any wheels.

Our salesman stopped in front of a silver model and pulled a remote from his pocket. When he pointed the smaller technology at the larger one, the hover-car came to life. It powered up and floated off the floor slightly, with a soft hum. The vehicle even opened its doors to us.

"Holy crap," Declan uttered with wide eyes.

"So, would you like a test drive?" The salesman offered.

"Er, how much is it?"

The salesman tried to laugh off the vulgar subject of money.

"Oh there's no need to concern yourself about that!" He said boisterously. "Mrs. Sabre's credit check has already been approved."

But the European Werewolf repeated in a low voice, "How much is it?"

"Declan," I sidled up to him, "this is your birthday present, don't worry about the cost."

"B," he moved us away to talk privately. "I've followed the progress of hover-cars on the World Wide News. I mean, I'm a mechanic so I have to see how cars are changing. But the models I've seen in the auto shows, are the same vehicles in this showroom. Only millionaires can afford cars like these!"

"I can afford it -" I began when he cut me off.

"There is NO WAY I'd let you spend that much money on me." He shook his head. "What money are you using, Hodge Endeavor's or yours?"

"Mine -" I started when he interrupted again.

"There is NO WAY I'd let you spend your hard-earned money from your academic work, on something this expensive."

"Declan!" I grabbed hold of his arms, to enforce what I had to say. "This is your birthday present. You've achieved so much to reach your age and I know the road hasn't been easy. You deserve this!"

"B, the Pope would have to sell his own mother to afford one of these!"

However, I put my foot down as I refused to let him ruin his present.

"Declan Domitian Sabre, either you pick one of these hover-cars right now, or I'LL pick one and you know how little I care about cars."

This made him snort at his wife's lack of interest in anything mechanical.

I continued, "Like you said, you're a mechanic. So look at it this way, by buying a hover-car now, you'll not only be the first man in Alma to have one, but you'll be the first mechanic. You'll learn the ins-and-outs of the engine, before the Garage in Alma does."

He didn't appear convinced, as he looked on in uncertainty.

"They're expensive now because they're new." I tried again. "But within a decade, everyone's gonna have one. So instead of waiting for the price to go down, let's buy one now and you'll be ahead of the game."

He looked down on his smaller, but obstinate mate, in amusement.

"Nice sales pitch," he smirked.

"Thanks."

"You really want me to get a hover-car today, don't you?"

"Yes."

"What if I pay half then I can write it off as a tax deduction for work?" He counter offered. "Like you said, I'm a mechanic and I need to know how one of these works."

"No deal," I shook my head. "I'm paying because it's your birthday present."

"But if I get one, I'll be ahead of the competition when people come to me to fix their hover-cars." He haggled. "So let me pay half."

"Nope," I stood firm. "I'm paying for it and that's that."

The European Werewolf's resolve started to melt as my stubbornness gained strength. I think my feisty behaviour even turned him on. He looked from the car to his mate and then back to the car.

At last he conceded, "Actually, I do like that silver model."

"So let the man take you for a test drive."

"Take me for a test drive, or take me for a test drive in the car?" He asked wryly.

Laughingly, I whacked him on the arm to behave. "Eew!"

"Remember, I don't swing that way," he continued the joke. "I've had offers, as you may recall. But I prefer the breast brigade, or the oestrogen army."

"With those descriptions for women kind, we feel so empowered." I smilingly rolled my eyes. "Actually, I've never met a gay 'growly thing'."

"I don't think there are any," he mused. "The bloodlust which spurs us to hunt, also pushes us towards the opposite sex to ensure procreation."

"I think you might be right." I grinned in good humour. "So, getting back to the non-sexual, test drive with the salesman..."

"You mean, 'back to the test drive in the hover-car'," he smilingly corrected. "There's gonna be no test driving of your husband. Not by the salesman. Not until we get home and then baby, you can test drive me all you like."

"I've already taken you for a test drive." I poked him in the ribs. "Then I married you, which was basically buying the car."

"I must have performed well, then." He grinned mischievously.

"Let's just take a test drive in the hover-car." I pulled him back over to the salesman.

Declan ended up choosing a silver, four-door model which was less sporty than the two-door he tried. Then I surprised him when I picked a hover-car for myself. However, I chose a smaller, two-door model which was a hatch-back and metallic-orange coloured. I didn't care about size or prestige, I simply wanted something to get from A to B.

But I couldn't just choose a car for myself with my bossy husband at my side. Although I was the one who was paying, he kept telling his wife what she should be looking for. When he wasn't nagging me, he hounded the salesman about safety features and warranties.

In the sales' office, we signed the electronic paperwork on his touch-screen computer. Then he processed my credit card and the deed was done. We were the proud owners of vehicles without wheels, though we'd have to wait a fortnight until we could pick them up.

Instead of leaving Fairbanks, we lingered to have lunch at the Alaska Salmon Bake.

It was a bit touristy, but the advertisement 'All You Can Eat' was perfect for a European Werewolf's appetite. We munched on Beer-Battered Halibut, Bering Sea Cod, Fire-Grilled Salmon and Prime Rib. Whereas I tried a little of each, Declan ate them as a series of mains. I could tell the size of his stomach surprised the staff, who took away empty dish after empty dish.

"Don't get too full," I warned. "Save some room for dinner."

This made him pause in eating the ribs with his hands, as they hovered near his messy mouth.

"What else have you got planned?" He wondered.

"You'll see."

Afterwards, he went to the Men's Room to wash up and I paid the bill.

"B!" He growled, as he returned his wallet to his back pocket. "You already spent god knows what, at the car dealership. You shouldn't have paid for lunch too!"

"Declan, you know the rules," I said coolly. "Nobody pays on their birthday."

Then I grabbed his arm and pulled him out of the restaurant.

Although the ice fog had lifted, I let the domineering male drive. He was adamant that he should take the wheel. I ignored his dissatisfied snarls, as he moved the seat back into its usual position and readjusted the mirrors.

On our way home, he noticed how I looked at my watch at regular intervals.

"Are we late for something?" He queried.

"Not yet, we should be home in time." I said vaguely.

"C'mon B, what else are you planning?" He pestered.

"You'll see."

Once he parked his pick up in the garage, we went inside the house. Immediately, I headed for the kitchen and proceeded to take the clean dishes out of the dishwasher. He stood in the entryway and watched how I made sure everything was put away.

"You're not planning on cooking tonight, are you?" He tested. "Remember, that's my job."

Right on time, there was a knock on the front door which saved me from answering.

"I'll get it," I breezed past.

Declan's mouth fell open when he saw who it was. On our front veranda stood a middle-aged man and two young women, wearing black and white uniforms for a catering company. The older man was wearing chef's clothing and the younger women looked like waitresses.

"Hi, you must be Rene?" I shook his hand. "You're right on time."

"Punctuality is like preparing the perfect dish madame, one cannot falter." He replied in a thick French accent.

I stood back and let them carry in the boxes of food and catering equipment. I left the door open, as they made several trips from their van parked on the road, up and down our driveway. Then the cook left it to his assistants, as he examined our kitchen which he'd be using.

"It's a small space," the five-star chef sneered. "But I've worked in worse conditions."

"Hey!" The European Werewolf started at the stranger.

"Shhh," I placed my hand on his chest.

"But he just said -" he spluttered indignantly.

I said quietly, "Monsieur Manosque has worked in several five-star hotels. My PA at Hodge Endeavor put me in touch with him, as he's catered for some of our Board Meetings. Trust me, he's expensive but he's worth it."

My mate's face reddened in anger at how his kitchen which was his territory, was being invaded.

"Just what exactly have you got planned for tonight?!" He demanded.

"Instead of going to dinner in a fancy restaurant, we're eating in with a fancy chef coming to us." I shrugged. "This way you can eat as much as you like, without other people in a restaurant, staring."

"Say what?" He blinked. "You paid a chef and two waitresses, to come here and put on a private candlelit dinner for two?"

"Actually, it'll be a candlelit dinner for eight." I informed. "There'll be you and me, but also Chiron, Stone, Forrest, Maia, Brandon and Bec."

He stood still as he saw he had no say in this. Then he asked unhappily, "How much money did you lay down for all this?"

I said in annoyance, "Since you never let me pay our plasma power bills, let alone for groceries? It wasn't hard to save up."

Scowling, he looked away and watched the waitresses, bringing in the last of their equipment. He saw they'd also brought table decorations. They put out a long, white, crisp, cotton table cloth. Then they set the table with polished cutlery and three gold candelabras.

I took hold of his hand, "C'mon Dec, let's start getting ready. Dinner starts at six o'clock and our guests should arrive around five. When you come back down, you'll find everything prepared."

I tugged him towards the staircase and he went along unwillingly, casting a wary gaze over the preparations.

*****

In the bedroom, I opened up the wardrobe and laid out his black suit and light blue shirt. For myself, I chose a strapless, long, black, velvet dress. It was the same one I wore to the opera in Brussels, over a hundred years ago. Since it was in a classic style, it never went out of fashion.

Next, I pushed him into the bathroom to shower before I did. I hurried under the water though, because I didn't want to leave him alone for too long. I was scared he'd go back downstairs and get into a fight with the chef.

I showered as he used the basin to shave, so we ended up returning to the bedroom to dress at the same time.

He helped me with the zipper on my dress then I helped him straighten his tie. It was a silver coloured silk, which his mother had bought him on another birthday. I let him wear ties now, because of his new haircut and grey hair, they finally suited him. I thought it made him look more mature.

Declan noticed the change in my opinion. "Two centuries later, my wife finally lets me wear a tie. What are you going to let me wear on my 300th birthday?"

"I dunno," I giggled as I adjusted his apparel. "Maybe I'll let you get that nipple piercing you mentioned once."

He laughed loudly before tickling his wife then together we left the bedroom.

*****

We descended the small staircase and our eyes lit up with what we beheld.

The living room looked magnificent. Not only did the catering company bring the table setting, but flowers. There were two arrangements between the three gold candelabras, with more flowers and candles scattered around the living room. Classical music was playing softly in the background and delicious smells wafted out of the kitchen.

"No way...!" Declan's mouth hung open in shock.

One approached us carrying glasses of sparkling, white, de-alcoholised wine on a gold tray. "Mr. and Mrs. Sabre?"

"Er, thanks." He took one and stepped away.

After I claimed a glass, I chinked it with his in a silent toast and we took a sip. The non-alcoholic wine was light and refreshing. When I had chosen the menu, I specified de-alcoholised wines only and left it to the chef to choose. I have to say, he'd chosen well and I doubt the brands we'll be drinking tonight, could be found in a supermarket.

"So, what's for dinner?" My mate enquired.

"You'll find out," I took another sip.

"Would you stop saying that?" He complained. "Now tell me, what's on the menu?"

I stepped so close, our fronts were touching. "What do you smell coming from the kitchen?"

Momentarily, he closed his eyes as he sniffed several times. "I smell seafood, I smell poultry, I smell beef and I smell something chocolaty for dessert."

"So there you go," I stepped back.

Declan looked like he was about to nag however, I was saved by a second knock at the door.

"It looks like our guests are arriving," I left his side.

I opened the front door and Chiron and Stone came in. They were as formally dressed as they could, in their best pair of dark blue jeans, black or white cotton shirts and ties. It wasn't that they couldn't afford to buy a suit, but where we lived, not many situations called for one. The second waitress took their coats before the first offered them some wine.

Chiron's long hair was now completely white and his son's hair was grey. Their long hair was worn in pony tails and they accepted the refreshment on offer. The males shook hands with a friendly pat on the back or shoulder.

When our older looking First shook his younger looking Second's hand, I sensed their telepathic communication. However, they kept their thoughts private. Usually, their conversations were about pack business, so I didn't mind.

"Aunt B, you're looking as youthful as ever." Stone kissed my cheek.

I detected a little envy, but I harboured no ill-will towards the husband who recently lost his wife to old age.

"Hey, you still have some dark hair in your long mane," I jested. "So, how are you settling in, living with your Dad again?"

Stone shot a wry look to Chiron who smirked back, before he answered. "Hey we're just a couple of old bachelors now. You know how it is, keg parties and girls running all over the place."

This made me laugh, as widowed Lokoti Werewolves behaved nothing like that. The girls mentioned would have been their grandchildren or great grandchildren, they helped out by babysitting. They may have lost their human wives, but their progeny kept them alive.

There was another knock at the door and I greeted Forrest who arrived with Maia. The Lokoti Werewolf looked like he was in his early thirties whereas his human mate was in her early fifties. Maia dyed her hair to retain the dark colour and her figure remained slim, but her skin was creased with many a wrinkle. However, her husband's high regard for his wife made him oblivious to her imperfections.

"Thanks for coming," I kissed both their cheeks. "Here let us take your coats and have some wine."

Warily, Forrest sniffed the drinks to ensure they were non-alcoholic, then he picked up two glasses and handed one to his 'other half'.

"Happy Birthday, Uncle." Maia kissed his cheek.

"Thank you, Sweetie." Declan hugged her with one arm. "How are you and the kids?"

As his great x4 grandniece brought him up to speed, I watched the two together.

They looked the same age, but don't ever say that to the European Werewolf. He would huff and puff and blow your house down, with a long rant on how he was older. He showed special interest in how the next generation of Sabre-Riverclaws, were succeeding. Declan had a soft spot for their eldest, Caesar, who was just as mechanically-minded as he was. Then I listened to my mate tell our guests' about our trip to Fairbanks and his birthday present.

"Hover-cars?" Forrest looked impressed, as did Chiron and Stone. "As soon as it's delivered, you'll have Caesar crawling all over it, to investigate its' ins-and-outs."

Stone couldn't help himself, "Say Uncle, you wouldn't mind giving me a test drive, would you?"

This made the European Werewolf laugh, "As I explained to the salesman, I'm a one-woman man. I'll let you test drive the hover-car, but leave me out of it."

"Oh Uncle!" Maia blushed and whacked him on the arm.

The room was full of laughter and jokes, when there was a third knock on the door with the arrival of Brandon and his wife, Bec.

I bestowed more kisses and welcomes, before taking their coats. I had to admit, I still paused when I saw his white hair. Brandon greyed early and it felt weird seeing the formerly mischievous teen, in his early fifties too.

Bec was born and raised in Anchorage but moved to Alma to take a position as a Dental Nurse. After their first year of marriage, she was let in on the secret of the existence of the pack. Although she's never seen Declan and I in our supernatural forms, she still passed us some strange looks. This happened again tonight, as the fifty-something, overweight woman, looked upon my appearance. We first met when she was in her twenties and I think it bugged her, I still looked the same.

"Hiya Brandon," his Uncle came over to shake his hand. "How are you and Bec?"

He opened his mouth to answer when his wife spoke instead.

"Oh my arthritis is playing up again. The medication the doctors give out is slow to work, if they do anything at all. And Brandon's back is playing up again, isn't it Bran?"

He started to speak when she talked over the top of him again.

"The doctor in Alma has given him some strong painkillers, better than what that *Medicine Man*, could provide." She said snidely. "Brandon needs physiotherapy as well as more time off. But the bills are mounting that our Medical Insurance won't cover. If only we could live as comfortably as some people."

Then she cast a calculated glance over the decorated room and the champagne flutes in people's hands.

Brandon caught our unimpressed looks, so he intervened.

"But we're OK!" He tried to laugh it off. "My job's going well. I've been made Team Manager now, instead of Team Leader. There's more paperwork so the hours are longer, but it's a 5,000 increase, in salary."

"Right," I laughed uneasily. "I'll just check with Monsieur Manosque when he's ready to serve the first course."

"I'll come with you," Declan joined in my escape.

Together, we walked away from the couple whilst exchanging, 'what the hell?!' expressions.

We stood in the kitchen entryway to find the chef busily doing three things at once and we experienced his short temper, because of it.

"Madame, it's only 5.23 PM and you requested dinner to be served at 6 PM! Monsieur Manosque serves when it is time and not before then!" He raised his voice. "Monique? Monique!"

"Oui Monsieur?" The first waitress appeared beside us.

"Serve these hors d'œuvre to our impatient clientele!"

When we saw the kind of food laden on the gold tray, we let his rudeness slide. Looking oh so delicate yet delicious, were Devilled Eggs topped with Black Sturgeon Caviar. We stole one each, before she moved towards the rest of the guests with her goodies.

"Told you, he may be expensive but he's worth it." I gave a nudge.

Declan mumbled something with his mouthful, before he nodded to show he agreed.

*****

True to Monsieur Manosque's words, the feast began at six o'clock and it went for two hours, making the wait worth it.

There were six courses if you counted the cheese platter at the end. The banquet began with a soup, fish second, poultry third, red meat fourth, dessert fifth and then the fruit and cheese plate. The waitresses were efficient and never stopped moving, not for a minute. Our glasses were constantly topped up, or they were taking away one plate to replace it with another.

When I went over the menu, I told the chef that besides the soup, each course should be served in either of two sizes. For the humans, although the meals were on dinner plates, should be the size of bread and butter plates. I didn't want anyone getting too full, too fast, so they wouldn't enjoy the next course. However, with the male Werewolves, their servings could be the size of a dinner plate. Of course, I couldn't tell the chef he'd be cooking for supernatural creatures. I simply said that for four people including myself, make the servings smaller sizes.

The soup was New England Clam Chowder and it was creamy and delicious. For the fish, we ate the mouth-watering Lobster Thermidor. The poultry was Roast Brace of Pheasants and they were lovely and tender. The red meat dish was Beef Wellington, served with herbed, roast vegetables. This had everyone curious, as it was tenderloin wrapped in pâté de foie gras, duxelles and puff pastry, before cooked in an oven.

"Mmm," was the common noise around the table.

"You should have birthday parties like this, more often." Stone said in between mouthfuls.

Chiron sat at one end of the table with the 'birthday boy', on the other. I sat in my usual seat, which was to Declan's right. Maia sat on his left with Forrest next to her then Stone beside him. Brandon sat next to me, with Bec on his other side.

"I've been spoilt all day," my mate said appreciatively and momentarily squeezed my hand.

"I'll say," Brandon agreed. "A hover-car and then this five course feast?"

"By a five-star chef, no less," Bec said lightly, but I detected bitterness. "If only we could all afford pleasures like these, or spend like there's no tomorrow."

I put down my cutlery as Declan's eyes narrowed. Forrest and Stone saw I'd stopped eating, as did Chiron. But it was our First who eased the tension.

"Ah, it would be nice if luxuries such as these were commonplace." He mused. "But if you always ate like this, what would you look forward to?"

"You'd get bored of lobster and caviar, if you ate it everyday." Stone chuckled.

"I don't think I'd get bored of eating like this," Brandon munched away, not picking up the tension. Or, maybe he was just used to it, being married to the cause.

I said coolly, "I've been saving up for some time and considering my husband's age, it should give you an idea."

Declan put down his cutlery to use one hand to hold mine then in his other, he nursed his wine.

He stared into the glass, "I remember when we were growing up, how food itself was a luxury item. We either had to grow our own, or trade for it by offering a service or something else. My Mom was a teacher and that service put food on our table. B's Dad was a handyman and builder, which put food on her table. When B and I moved in together, I was a mechanic which put food on our table. But the Lokoti were lucky, having greenhouses and underground bunkers full of supplies. I was sixteen years old when I started to patrol, on the look out for looters. Or, occasionally we'd give out tinned food to people who were starving and desperate."

"I remember those days well," I gazed upon my mate. "I remember the sound of gunfire and the singing at the funerals, when an Uncle died defending his tribe. Sometimes I'd stay up all night, worrying my husband wouldn't come home alive."

He lowered his wine glass to raise my hand to his mouth instead. "But I kept my promise, didn't I? I always came back to you, safe and sound."

I appreciated the feel of his lips grazing the skin and I continued on the early days of our marriage.

"I remember how sandwich meat was often from a tin, like Spam, since we didn't have beef, or legs of ham, or chicken. The steaks or roasts we ate, was caribou, moose or duck, from the national park. Or, we ate fish from the river. Occasionally we ate bacon, because it was preserved in a bunker."

"Man, we ate a lot of caribou, moose, duck or fish." Declan shook his head at the memory. "We didn't eat steak from a cow until the supermarket in Alma reopened. It's the same with chicken or pork."

Then I smiled at my husband, "Do you remember how all the furniture and household goods which were given at Housewarmings, were secondhand? That, or somebody in the tribe made it, as a gift or their way to trade for food."

"Uh huh," he squeezed my hand again. "Our first couches were secondhand. But the pine furniture was built here, including our dining table which is still the original."

"And for years everything was recycled or reused," I sighed. "There were no music charts like there are on the Internet Radio or Internet TV. We grew up listening to the music our parents, or our grandparents, listened to."

"I did a lot trading to get my first couple of secondhand CD's." He nodded along. "I mowed lawns or fixed their lawn mowers or did other odd jobs, to get an old and sometimes scratched CD, as my reward."

"You were so protective of your music collection, growing up." I snickered. "I remember how angry you'd get, if Derik didn't return one of your CD's on time."

"Or if he took one to your house, without asking." He smilingly agreed. "He was using MY music collection to woo the girl I was in love with too. Hell, I even helped him compile that CD he gave you, with all your favourite songs."

"No way!" I squealed with laughter. "I loved that CD! I didn't know you helped him put the songs together."

Then the reverie was interrupted when Bec asked, "What's a CD?"

"Uncle Dec still has shelves of old CD's, over there." Brandon nodded in their direction. "Maia's and my lives were in jeopardy once, for almost knocking them over in a fight."

"Speaking of which," Maia wiped her mouth with her napkin. "That vase on the mantle piece looks remarkably familiar. If I didn't know any better, I'd think it's the same one we broke."

Declan and I exchanged secretive smiles, before I said vaguely, "It was a gift from a family member."

To which he added, "But you're not imagining things, it's identical to the one you and Brandon broke, because it's from the same glassmaker."

"Wow," she sat up straighter in surprise. "The same workshop in Venice you visited years ago, is still open today?"

"Not quite," her Great x4 Granduncle smirked. "A distant family member went to great pains to get its' twin, as a wedding anniversary present."

I squeezed Declan's hand, "She saw how much it was worth sentimentally rather than cost."

Stone smiled sadly, as I guess our trip down memory lane, reminded him of his years with Sharon.

When he spoke, he was looking our way but I sensed it was partly for Bec's benefit.

"With all you two have been through, it's understandable why you cling to the sentimental value, instead of the monetary one. Also, it's reasonable how Aunt B wanted to treat Uncle Dec today, after all the years they've worked hard to get where they are."

Brandon stopped eating long enough to pick up his wine glass to make a toast.

"Happy Birthday Uncle Dec, you've always been the oldest member of our family, and now you're the oldest member of the tribe."

Everyone cracked up laughing at his terrible toast and his Granduncle smilingly shook his head.

"You and B should start your own 'help line'!" He snorted. "With you two on the phone, the world wouldn't have to worry about overpopulation, anymore."

The table burst into more laughter as red-faced, I took another sip of wine.

The waitresses hovering around the table exchanged puzzled looks. They didn't understand why my husband was referred to being older than the

Native Alaskan, with the long, white hair. However, like true professionals, they carried on. One took away the empty plates, as the other topped our glasses with the wine she was holding.

*****

When Monsieur Manosque was ready to serve dessert, I stood up and turned off the lights.

A chocolate mousse cake with the words written in white chocolate, "Happy Birthday Declan", was carried out covered in candles.

I walked beside the chef as he placed the large, circular cake before my husband.

"Happy Birthday to you, Happy Birthday to you! Happy Birthday Uncle Declan, Happy Birthday to you!" Everybody sang loudly.

As soon as the 'birthday boy' blew out the candles, a waitress turned the living room lights back on.

"There's twenty candles, with each representing a decade you've been on this planet," I murmured in my husband's ear, before kissing it.

Our cook handed him the knife to cut the cake and the second waitress passed him a small plate one at a time, to put the slices on.

Soon everyone had a piece of cake, but it had to be Bec again, to spoil the mood.

"No thank you," she pushed her plate away. "I'm on a diet."

The whole table looked on the fifty-something, overweight woman, for objecting to dessert after she'd just consumed four courses; excluding the hors d'œuvre she wolfed-down.

Screw her, I thought. I slowly ate my delectable delight, relishing every bite of the rich chocolate. I paused when Declan passed a spoonful to my mouth and I closed my eyes to savour his offering. Then I passed him a spoon laden with lusciousness and he playfully bit down on the cutlery, so I couldn't pull it out.

A waitress took the leftover cake to the kitchen, so the chef could place the slices into Tupperware containers, which our guests could take home.

As the cake was being served, the catering staff also offered espresso. However I smilingly shook my head, enjoying the red, de-alcoholised wine with the chocolate instead. When the cake was over and the fruit and cheese platter was presented, I had my glass topped up.

The three humans watched the Werewolves tuck into the last offering. They were completely full, but the supernatural creatures still had room. Declan helped himself to a fig and some grapes, as well as the blue cheese. Whereas, I filled my plate with the brie, camembert and smoked cheese and the table watched, as I washed down each with the red wine.

Bec looked on enviously, as the female Lokoti Werewolf relished every bite she took. Then she saw the male Lokoti Werewolf in the shape of Forrest, offer his slim, similarly aged mate, a water cracker with the fruit cheese on top. Maia giggled girlishly, before opening her mouth and accepting the tasty morsel.

"Brandon!" His wife whacked him on the arm. "It's time to go home."

"But it's not even nine o'clock!" He objected.

"We have that thing in the morning," she stood up.

"What thing?"

Then she leaned over to growl between gritted teeth, "The thing that I'll remind you about, in the car!"

"Oh," he reluctantly put down his espresso, "THAT thing."

As the humans left the table, their Granduncle stood up to see them off, but I didn't.

"Don't forget those slices of cake to take home to the kids and grandkids," my mate reminded.

Brandon made a move to retrieve them, when he received another smack on the arm.

"We're all on a diet," she said curtly.

"We are?" Brandon sounded surprised.

"Extra weight puts extra strain on the back," she said stiffly, as she put on her coat and gloves.

"You should know," her husband muttered.

"What?!" Bec reddened with rage.

"Nothing dear," he opened the front door for her.

As soon as Declan closed it behind them, the room slipped into snickering.

"Now a marriage like that would definitely make you feel old," he shook his head, as he returned to his seat.

"Here," I passed him a piece of camembert.

"Mmm," he nodded for more.

I pushed the fruit and cheese platter towards him and smilingly watched as he filled his second plate.

~~~~~~

~ 22 ~

30th December 2269

On a cold, dark, Christmas morning, a female Lokoti Werewolf lay in bed with the covers so high, she was almost hidden. She slept soundly, with dreams of Christmas past dancing inside her head. As she snoozed, snow flakes flew past the windows in a flurry, blown on gale-force winds. They roared over the peaks of the Alaska Range and made the trees bend and groan.

The small blizzard screeched around their small, two-storey, house which had central-heating. Smells of ham and eggs being cooked for Christmas breakfast, wafted up from downstairs. The aroma was coupled with the musky fragrance of the Christmas Tree, which was in the living area. Mr. Sabre had cut it down and brought it inside then with Mrs. Sabre, decorated it. The couple hung tinsel and ornaments, which had been in the family for over two centuries. This was done whilst sipping non-alcoholic eggnog and to the tunes of John Denver and the Muppets, 'A Christmas Together'.

"I can't imagine a Christmas without listening to Kermit, Miss Piggy, Fozzy or Gonzo." The 206 year old European Werewolf, chuckled.

"The album was originally Elisha's, so it's even older than you." His wife giggled. "She listened to it when she was little, she would have played it for her children when they were little. And we listened to it when we were little."

Once the tree was finished, they placed the presents underneath including some for Nairn, who'd be spending the holiday with them.

There were more presents per person compared to the postwar years. When Alma was a ghost town and the shops in Fairbanks and Anchorage had closed due to looting, many had to make their own. I remembered making Christmas Cards growing up, or other arts and crafts. I received many a knitted jumper, scarf, socks or mittens, from family members.

The Sabre, Riverclaw and Wisetail families were some the few in the tribe who honoured the Christian holiday, so we'd celebrate altogether. The families would congregate, usually at the old Riverclaw home, for Christmas Dinner and giving of gifts. Often, it was in the style of 'Secret Santa' with one present each, as it was difficult producing presents for ten people or more. For Christmas Dinner, we didn't have turkey or ham, so we ate roast duck or goose. The fowl had been shot before flying south for winter then plucked and frozen.

I'd arrive at my Riverclaw grandparents' home with my Mum and Dad. Declan would arrive with his mother and little brother. Uncle Jules would bring his wife and children. My Wisetail grandparents would come along too. All the presents were placed under the Christmas Tree, to be doled out before eating.

In the kitchen, Aunt Susan, Aunt Danika, Mum, Gran and Nana would help Great Grandma prepare the feast. As they worked, sometimes they'd sing

Christmas Carols. Meanwhile, the Lokoti Werewolves would keep an eye on the children, or bring in wood for the fireplace, or set the table. Declan often stood with them instead of playing. At first it was because he was scared he'd hurt someone with his strength. Then he came to see himself as the 'man of the family', being the older brother, so he hung out with the other men.

Whenever I thought Phoenix was picking on Phoebe, which he did a lot, I'd punch him on the arm. He'd punch back, which made Derik punch him. I'd end up tackling my cousin on the floor, with Derik trying to help.

"OK - OK - OK!" The Werewolves would boom out. "That's enough!"

Dad would pull me up, Uncle Jules would hold back Phoenix and Declan would grab Derik by the scruff of the neck.

"Bitch-features hit me first!" My cousin pointed.

"PHOENIX!" Grandfather growled, as his eyes glowed blue in anger.

This made the boy's head duck at the chastisement over his language.

"You're such a bully to your little sister!" I retorted. "One day she's gonna be big enough to hit you herself!"

"Yeah!" Derik took my side.

Declan glared at his little brother, "You don't have to go along with EVERYTHING that B does." Then he turned his annoyance on me, "You're a GIRL for crying out loud! Why don't you start acting like one?"

I glowered at his words as the proverbial steam whistled out of my ears. Oh how I hated Declan Sabre in those days, the boy who was the first to state my shortcomings. I detested him more than Phoenix, at least with him we could punch it out.

My father didn't appreciate either, the breed he disapproved of making disparaging remarks about his beloved daughter and only child.

"B was acting like a girl, by sticking up for Phoebe like an older sister." He said staunchly.

His dark brown eyes would clash with Declan's bright blue ones, until my Grandfather changed the subject.

"I hear you're doing great work, at the Garage." He clapped the European Werewolf on the shoulder. "Finn said he's thinking of training you as an Assistant Manager, one day."

When I was fourteen, to my dismay I found out my 'Secret Santa' was Declan. I had the misfortune to pull my enemy's name from a hat then I had a month to prepare something. At home, I pleaded with my mother to swap, as her recipient that year was Derik.

"But he's my best friend," I whined. "Can't you do Declan's present and I'll do Derik's?"

"You're missing the purpose of 'Secret Santa' and even what Christmas is all about." Mum rolled her eyes. "It's the season of giving and goodwill towards all mankind."

"Yeah but Declan's not 'mankind', he's 'mean-kind'."

"B!" She laughed out her surprise. "I know that deep down, the two of you like each other. The way you constantly fight is similar to sibling rivalry."

"Maybe Derik's like my brother, but NOT Declan." I said adamantly.

That Christmas morning, I went to my Riverclaw grandparents' home as usual. Everyone arrived with a present each to put under the Tree. Then as the women went into the kitchen to help Great Grandma, the men supervised the children.

My younger cousins edged closer to the presents, to try to see which was theirs and who they were from.

"C'mon kids," Uncle Julian walked over. He picked up Phoebe and took hold of Phoenix's hand. "You know the rules, there's no peeking."

Then he led them away to help him with setting the table, instead.

"Who did you get this year?" I asked Derik, as we sat together on the couch.

"Grandpa Wisetail," he replied. "And you?"

I snuck a look towards his older brother to make sure he wouldn't hear, before I leaned in and whispered his name.

"Really?" He snickered. "That's funny because he got -"

"Derik!" The young European Werewolf boomed out. Even if he was standing on the other side of the room, he overheard. "Are you blabbing about the 'Secret Santa'? It's lucky you two aren't in National Security, with your hopelessness at keeping your mouths shut."

When Christmas Dinner was ready, everyone converged around the Tree for the gift giving first.

That year Dad played 'Santa' by handing out the presents. The kids eagerly awaited to hear their names announced, as they sat on the floor. Except me that is, I didn't want to hear Declan's name called. I was dreading him finding out that his present came from me. It was a secret until the gifts were handed out and we discovered who they were from, by the tags.

"To Declan, Merry Christmas, from B." Dad read out, before passing him the small parcel.

My worst enemy opened the newspaper-wrapped present, since gift wrapping was scarce. Newspapers were hard to come by too, but it's funny how people kept these things. If leftover Anchorage Daily News or Fairbanks Daily News-Miner weren't available, people reused any kind of paper they had.

"Socks," he said deadpan. "Thanks."

I deliberately didn't look his way, as I pretended to be interested in Derik's present. He was pleased with his books on biology, something he was fascinated with. It was years later, he became the tribe's second Medicine Man.

"To B, Merry Christmas, from Declan." Dad announced next and handed me the offering.

It's from HIM...? Frickin' hell, talk about bad luck! I expected to receive something worse than socks.

Reluctantly, I unwrapped it to find five CD's complete with hand-made covers. The boy I hated most in the world, had created compilations of my favourite music. There were Alanis Morissette songs, or Sarah McLachlan, Tori Amos, Nirvana and Live.

Startled, my eyes looked up into his waiting ones.

"But - but - but how did you know?" I wondered.

"What songs you like?" He guessed what I meant. "It wasn't hard. Every time you come over to study, Derik lets you play them over and over again. It's like Chinese Water Torture! So spare me by playing them at home, instead."

My eyes narrowed as we returned to glaring at the other.

"Oh Declan!" Aunt Susan laughed it off, as she ruffled his hair. "He spent hours picking which songs to copy and then making the covers."

At the time I was confused and even wondered what his ulterior motive was? Why did the boy who hated me, spend so much time creating a present he knew I'd love? It was four years later I learned it was because he was besotted. However, he was very good at hiding it from our parents and even from his amore.

Returning to the year 2269, I pulled up the quilt to cover my nose. It's always been sensitive to the cold, central heating or not. I could feel it seep through the glass by the wind blasting the windows with ice. I dug deeper under the covers, as if they were my protective shield.

Just then my nose itched and I wriggled it. It itched again which made me wriggle even more. The tickling continued and I raised my hand to rub it, when it collided into another one.

My eyes snapped open to find Declan's fifty-something year old face, in front of mine.

"Declan!" I complained.

"C'mon sleepy-head," he chuckled. "It's half past seven and breakfast awaits."

"Go away." I moaned, sleepily.

However, his finger kept tickling my nose, which prevented me from falling back asleep.

"Declan!" I whined and pushed his hand away.

"Nairn and I have been up for over an hour." He returned. "We're hungry and we wanna eat. So haul your ass outta bed, get dressed and come downstairs."

Then the dressed, older male rolled off the covers and left the room.

What is it with old people waking up so early? Then they go to bed early. Next morning, they wake up early and go through the whole thing again. I'd noticed it in my elderly relations and now my husband was doing it.

A loud yawn escaped as I proceeded to pull out a pair of jeans and a red, woollen jumper, from the tallboy.

After dressing, I stumbled down the stairs half asleep with un-brushed hair.

"Merry Christmas!" Nairn chimed cheerfully.

I was greeted with a kiss on the cheek as she passed a cup of coffee she'd made.

Our old friend was now a 68 year old woman with a rounded figure, although not as overweight as Bec. These days, she dyed her shorter hair to retain her strawberry blonde colour. She treasured her visits, especially when Declan spoilt her with his cooking. She never could say no to any gourmet delight he offered. I could tell our company cheered her, after her long-time boyfriend Pete Miller, passed away.

"Look at this sleepy-head," Declan taunted. "Take a seat you two and I'll serve up."

"It's the holidays," I griped, as I sat down. "People are allowed to sleep in during holiday season."

"I used to love sleeping in, when I was younger." She sighed. "But now my rheumatism and arthritis make it hard to lie still for long."

"Don't they have medication for that?" I wondered, as I sipped my beverage.

"They do and they help," she sighed. "It'd be much worse without them. But they don't get rid of it all."

Declan carried out our plates of food first before retrieving his, along with a plate of toast. I saw we had the typical Christmas Breakfast of ham and eggs, but there was a side serving of kedgeree. I knew it was a token of appreciation, from our guest.

"Kedgeree!" I cried gleefully. "Yum! Thanks Nairn!"

"It's my pleasure," she smiled as she picked up her knife and fork. "Although, Declan was telling me that the two of you didn't always have ham and eggs, on Christmas?"

I nodded as I finished my mouthful before answering properly.

"It started around 2101 AD when the supermarket in Alma reopened and we had a wider selection of food available. We got the idea from my English Gran, who missed it."

"It was also around the time we started eating turkey for Christmas Dinner. Before that, we ate duck or goose, which came from the National Park." My mate explained.

We watched him heap some kedgeree on top of some egg and ham then raised it to his mouth. Whereas he could eat the whole thing mish-mashed together, I couldn't. I ate my ham, eggs and toast separately, whilst saving the kedgeree for last.

"How Dickensian of you," she tittered. "In 'A Christmas Carol', they had goose instead of turkey."

"Great Grandma sure could cook up the perfect roast duck or goose, couldn't she?" I looked my husband's way. "The meat was never dry with the skin a golden brown."

"Hell yeah," he nodded as he ate. "That and her special gravy, was a treat alright."

I put down my cutlery to place my hand over his and look on pleadingly.

"Could you make our Christmas Dinner with the special gravy, today?"

"Sure I can." He shrugged. "I think I remember the recipe, from helping out in the kitchen."

I let him continue eating as I turned her way. "You're gonna love the gravy, it was renown in the tribe."

"Clara Riverclaw's culinary skills were famous, period." Declan said in between mouthfuls. "She was known for being a quiet woman, who expressed herself through her cooking. I don't know what happened to her cook books, I suppose Chiron has them. Or, maybe she passed on her recipes, orally."

"An oral tradition from a silent woman," I said humorously.

"I think she taught by example," he snickered in agreement.

*****

After breakfast, I stacked the dishwasher then joined Nairn and Declan in the lounge room.

Our Scottish guest was sipping on another cup of tea, as I carried out two cups of coffee. I handed one to my mate which he put on the coffee table. Then he crouched by the Christmas Tree to play 'Santa', and hand out the presents.

"To Nairn, from B." He passed her the small gift.

"Ooh," she put down her tea, to open it. When she did, her breath caught in her throat. "B, you shouldn't have!"

"You like the Grecian earrings I have, so on my last circulation, I picked up some for you too." I shrugged it off.

"Did you buy them in Athens?" She queried.

"Outside of the markets in the agora are craftsmen's shops." I explained. "One of them is a jeweller that I like. You've seen the gold bracelet my Gran gave me and they're from the same place."

"Earrings from Ancient Greece? Nice." My mate looked on, impressed. Next, he picked up another small, gift-wrapped box, "To Declan, love B."

Eagerly, I sat forward and watched as he unwrapped his present.

"It's not a pair of socks, is it?" He passed a pointed look.

However, it was enough to make me blush at the memory. "No, it's not."

Slowly, he removed the wrapping then looked up in surprise. "Tickets for a Hot Air Balloon ride?"

"Yeah," I grinned. "We've never gone Hot Air Ballooning and those tickets are for a scenic flight over Niagara Falls."

His mouth fell open, "Say what?"

"Look in the box and the pamphlet they come with," I directed. "I bought us airfare, hotel accommodation and the Hot Air Balloon ride, over the falls."

He looked through the tickets, pamphlet and itinerary containing flight and hotel information. However, I wasn't sure if he liked it or not, as he appeared gob-smacked. He read over the pamphlet before reexamining the tickets.

"What's wrong, don't you like your present?" I asked, concerned.

"Er..." he wore an uncomfortable expression, "...now that you ask, no."

"What?!" I sat upright in indignation. "We've never been Hot Air Ballooning before. With our age, it's hard buying you something you don't already have, or want."

"B, it's not that I don't appreciate the thought." He said diplomatically. "But you've seen how nervous I get on a plane if there's turbulence. So, can you imagine what I'd be like on a Hot Air Balloon?"

This made my eyes narrow, "Are you afraid of flying?"

"Yeah right!" His reaction was immediate. "I'm a European Werewolf, we're not afraid of anything."

"Then why don't you want to go up in a Hot Air Balloon?" I challenged.

"Do you know how unsafe it is?!" He flared. "And you want me to be in one, over the frickin' Niagara Falls? Are you crazy?! What if we hit turbulence? What if the Balloon breaks and we drop out of the air? What if we land in the water and get trapped underneath? What if we're forced to change to escape from certain death then people see us?"

Nairn and I exchanged looks of amusement.

"Sounds like a fear of flying, to me." I stated.

"Or perhaps a fear of Hot Air Balloons," she shrugged.

"Ladies!" He stood up to stare us down. "Didn't you hear what I said? I'm a European Werewolf! People fear us, not the other way around. We don't fear ANYTHING!"

"Then why don't you want to go for a ride in a Hot Air Balloon?" I asked coolly.

"Because it's a frickin' flying death trap!" He snapped.

Nairn turned my way to ask, "What's he like on planes?"

"He's fine, unless there's turbulence." I answered. "Then he grips the armrests so tightly, he almost rips the chair out of the floor."

We erupted into giggles to the macho male's chagrin.

"Declan," I looked his way once more. "If anything happens on the Hot Air Balloon ride, I can always instantaneously phase us to safety."

He said impatiently, "Then people will find out you're a Circulator! No, there's going to be no Hot Air Balloon rides. We're keeping our feet firmly on the ground and that's that!"

She asked out of curiosity, "If you feel that uncomfortable with flying, how do you board a plane for your overseas holidays?"

"Flying on a plane is a LOT different to floating around in a Hot Air Balloon." He said adamantly. "For one, there are seat belts and the cabin is pressurized. Secondly, there are life vests and oxygen masks available. There are also escape doors over the wings. So there's greater chance of living through a plane crash then a Hot Air Balloon just dropping out of the sky."

"It's only a four hour ride then we can return to our luxury hotel for a romantic evening." I tried to cajole.

"Nuh uh," he crossed his arms, adamantly. "I'm all for romantic evenings, but ones where our feet remain on the ground, or on a bed."

Nairn smilingly shook her head. "Oh you two!"

"I'd rather a pair of socks any day instead of 'thrills for the middle-aged'." He complained.

"Hey!" I objected. "Young people go on Hot Air Balloon rides!"

The Wiccan saw the two Werewolves were spoiling for a fight, so she interrupted.

"Moving on with the presents," she left her seat to crouch beside the tree.

Whether we had sensitive ears or not, we would have heard her knees crack. She picked up a large, fancy, embossed envelope and handed it to me. Then she slowly moved back to the couch and picked up her cup of tea again.

"To Declan and B, from Nairn." I read out the calligraphy on the thick, creamy envelop.

This attracted his attention and he came to stand on my right, to look over my shoulder.

I pulled out some official looking documents of something to do with real estate, until I recognized one with the big word, 'Will'.

"What is this?" I wondered.

"It's my last Will and Testament and those other papers are the deeds to my house." She said casually. "I'm leaving Stonewall to you and Declan, upon my demise."

Well, that acted as the proverbial cold water thrown over the room.

Puzzled, I looked from the paperwork, to our old friend then to my mate.

"Um, why?" I asked after a while.

"We already have a house." Declan said. "Here, in Alaska, where we hunt with our pack."

"I'm not expecting you to pack up and move to Scotland!" She laughed it off. "You can donate the house to National Trust, or use it as a holiday home, or do both."

I asked again, "But why us?"

"It's not like Pete and I had children to pass it on to," she pointed out. "Oh, I have some distant relations in Ireland who could inherit, but I hardly speak to them. Besides B, you spent a lot of Hodge Endeavor's money doing the place up. It's as much yours as it is mine. Plus, you have a vague family connection to the estate and the name Durrant. Although, I do feel you're more like family than my distant relatives."

"Nairn, sweetheart..." my husband began gently, "...we invite you to stay with us, because we like you. We didn't keep inviting you here, to eventually get your house."

"Thank you for explaining that, Declan." She tittered back. "Now I know your intentions are honourable."

I could understand his confusion and awkwardness, because I was feeling it too.

"Are you sure?" I gave a funny look. "Leaving us a country estate is a pretty big, 'good bye' present."

"Alright, tell me this," she sat up straighter on the couch. "What are you going to do with Stonewall?"

"Um, I don't know...." I faltered, "... I'd let the local historical society run tours through it, maybe once a week. I'd register it with the National Trust, and let them run the odd tour. I'd hire a caretaker to look after the house and grounds and maybe every now and again, I'd weekend there."

"Then how is that different to what you're doing now?" She debated. "You visit every now and again and you've already paid people, to tend to the house. I also let Stonehaven's Historical Society run tours once a fortnight. I don't mind if you list it with the National Trust, but I'd rather if the property was under yours, or Hodge Endeavor's name."

We saw Nairn's mind was made up on the matter.

"After the kind of gifts you two just handed out, my presents are going to pale in comparison." He said half jokingly.

"No, no, no, not at all!" She waved it off. "I'm sorry for being a 'wet blanket' by talking about death. I just wanted to impart this, because Pete died suddenly with his heart attack. I can't foresee when I'll kick that metaphysical bucket."

This made me thoughtful, "I wonder how that saying started, 'kick the bucket'?"

"I don't know, maybe there was a bucket somewhere that somebody kicked?" She shrugged. "Maybe it was the milkman when he was carrying buckets of milk like they did in the olden days, and it was too great a strain on his heart?"

"And as he fell dead, he kicked the bucket?" I giggled.

"OK you two, that's enough." Declan tried to bring back order. "It's Christmas, we're celebrating somebody's birth, not death."

"Yes, but isn't it strange how Easter is only a couple of months away." I continued. "It's like we celebrate Christ's birth and then a couple of months later, we celebrate his death. We even hand out chocolate to celebrate how he kicked the bucket."

"Ah well, he made a big impression in his short lifespan. After all, he has a bestselling book out there. And I can see you and Declan are wearing his merchandise." She joked about our crucifixes.

"And he has a legion of fan clubs, all with different names." I laughed. "And some of them wear strange outfits when they reach certain levels of fandom."

"And wear strange hats and use strange walking sticks," he joined in, by referring to a Bishop's costume. "Or crooks, as they called them."

"They're crooks alright, the way some of those 'fan clubs' demand, or guilt their members for money." She shook her head. "It's like they charge for membership and then charge for extras."

Then the man of the house cleared his throat for attention, before passing out the last two presents under the tree.

"To Nairn and to B, love Declan."

Together, we unwrapped our presents and emitted audible sighs.

"Oh Declan, they're beautiful..." my voice trailed off.

"Declan, you shouldn't have!" She exclaimed.

I was given a pair of pearl studded earrings and Nairn received a necklace with various crystals such as rose quartz, moonstone and amethyst.

"I use some of these crystals in spell work." She looked on admiringly. "Amethyst is often used for protection."

My mate said proudly, "Yeah, I read something about that when I bought it online from that Wiccan site."

"They're just what I wanted," I looked his way once more. "They'll go with the pearl necklace you bought me a few years ago. I can wear them with my suits, for my guest lectures."

"I thought so," he grinned.

Declan did it again, by taking the time and effort in producing gifts which showed his regard for the recipients.

"Now I feel bad," I rested my present in my lap. "I didn't give you something you wanted. I feel on par with the Christmas I gave you a pair of socks."

"You did what?" Nairn giggled.

However, it was my husband who rallied to my rescue.

"It's not her fault," he explained. "It was postwar when the shops were closed and presents were hard to come by. It also didn't help that she hated my guts."

"Yes but you still trumped me by taking the time and effort in preparing such a considerate gift." I looked downwards.

"Hey, I had to show my feelings for you somehow." He shrugged it off. "If I started leaving orchids for you when you were fourteen, your father would have had my hide."

"Alright then," I said determinedly, "what would you like for a Christmas present?"

"A romantic weekend away at Niagara Falls," he smiled softly. "Just leave out the Hot Air Ballooning."

~~~~~~

3rd March 2270

Nairn may not have been able to accurately foresee the end of her time, but the timing of her Christmas present meant she must have sensed something.

Two nights ago, I sat at the dining table typing up a paper, as Declan was cooking dinner. I typed quickly as I wanted to finish the conclusion and therefore my essay. Then all I had to do was organize the accompanying pictures for the presentation.

Periodically, the bossy European Werewolf counted down from the kitchen, "You've got fifteen minutes to get your books off the table." Then he'd follow it, "In ten minutes I want your laptop put away." His last command was, "You've got five minutes until I serve dinner."

Just then my mobile phone rang and the suddenness made me jump.

Damn it! I'm not going to finish in time. It's ruined my train of thought, too.

"Hello?" I answered crankily. "Yes, this is Bianca Sabre. Who? Sorry, who are you again? Huh? You're calling about Nairn Durrant? Yes I know her..."

This caught Declan's attention. He came to stand in the kitchen entryway, wiping his hands on a tea towel. With his sensitive ears, he could listen in even from where he was standing.

He watched my eyes bulge as I shot him a frightened look.

"Yes, we'll be there right away." I hung up before I addressed him. "It's Nairn."

His wrinkly glare turned into a wrinkly frown of concern, "Who was it who called?"

"A nurse from the Hodge Endeavor Hospital in Stonewall," I said. "We've been called as the next-in-kin."

"Nairn's had a stroke?" He checked what he overheard.

I nodded and he straightened to attention. Then his rational mind kicked-in and I watched him turn around, turn off the oven and the stove before he reappeared. Our dinner plates sat unused on the kitchen bench, with the food left to turn cold.

Next, he crossed over to the coat rack by the front door. As he was pushing his arms through the sleeves of his coat, he held out his wife's. I pulled on my thick jacket whilst he patted down his pockets, to make sure he had his wallet and his keys.

"To phase to the hospital, we have to use the Gate at Circulate Headquarters, so I can see where we're going." I told him.

He nodded his consent and I put my hand on his arm and together, we disappeared in a bright flash of light.

We reappeared in another, on the circular, mirror platform of the Gate on Taurus Six.

"Welcome to Circulate Headquarters, Bianca and Declan." The computer greeted. "I have programmed the coordinates of the Gate to put you in a supply closet on level five in the Intensive Care Unit, where Nairn is. If you concentrate on the time frame of 2115 hours, no-one will witness your arrival."

"Thanks CM," I acknowledged, whilst looking up.

Declan did too and together we saw in the second, circular mirror above, the image zoom into the modern hospital, in Stonehaven.

With my hand on his upper arm, I put us into phase and our light particles streamed through the glass surface. I concentrated hard on the time frame of 2115 hours of March 1st, 2270. I silently said the time frame over and over again, as our beings of light were channelled to the location.

We streamed through time and space and ahead of us, we saw a small square doorway. Once as we passed through it, I took us out of phase and the floating sensation was replaced with firm footing. We found ourselves standing in a small, rectangular, white room, which was lined with shelves. We were surrounded by boxes of medical supplies, indicating we were indeed in a hospital's supply closet.

My mate blinked in surprise, as he was used to instantaneously phasing with his wife, but not phasing via the Gate.

"We're here?" He wondered. "But what was that doorway we came through?"

I gave a vague nod towards a small, square mirror over a washbasin in the corner, Medical Staff used to sanitize their hands.

"We came through THAT?" He stared. "How did we fit through there?"

"We use mirrors to reflect our light particles and glass to concentrate them." I shrugged it off. "Now come on, let's find Nairn."

I grabbed hold of his hand and pulled him towards the door.

Carefully, I opened it to take a peek to see how many people were around. When I thought the coast was clear, we exited the small room. But as soon as the door shut, we walked into a male nurse!

"What are you two doin' in there?" He chastised in a Scottish accent. "Can't you read the sign which says 'Medical Personnel Only'."

"We weren't stealing any drugs, so you can see." Declan held out his arms to show they were empty.

"Sorry, we got lost." I played dumb. "Can you please tell us what room Nairn Durrant is in?"

"Go to the Nurse's Station, at the end of this corridor." He pointed. "They'll be able to tell you there."

Then he watched us walk in that direction with a peculiar look, before he went into the Supply Closet himself.

Declan looked back before he leaned in to whisper, "Nice timing by that computer of yours. If we arrived a minute later, he would have seen us."

"The Mainframe is a great Calculator," I agreed. "She's often helped me get out of a tight spot, during my Circulations."

Once we reached the desk, my husband said, "Hi, we're here to see Nairn Durrant."

An older woman in a medical uniform looked up. "I'm sorry, Miss Durrant is in Intensive Care and it's past visiting hours."

"But you called us," I told her. "We're the next-of-kin, Bianca and Declan Sabre."

This made her sit upright with a start as she looked on in astonishment.

"I'm the one who called Miss Durrant's relatives and the number I rang had a U.S. country code." She sounded surprised.

"Yeah, she had her number redirected." Declan quickly lied. "We were already in Stonehaven."

She looked on suspiciously, but eventually she typed in a couple of commands on her touch-screen computer.

"Nairn Durrant is in room 533," she reported. "Go down that hallway and the door is on your left."

Declan led the way, squeezing my hand reassuringly as we went. However, I noticed his pace was quick, showing he was just as anxious as I was. We halted in a darkened doorway, where the only visible light in the room was the lamp over her hospital bed.

An elderly Nairn was sleeping in a blue hospital gown between the white hospital sheets. We heard her breathing was shallow, which added to her frail appearance. Her aged face looked pale, especially under the small night light. As if she sensed us, she partly opened her glassy eyes.

"B and Declan, is that you?" She asked in a small voice.

For some reason she looked all around the room instead of where we were standing, in the doorway.

"We're here." I rushed over to place several kisses on her forehead. "We're here."

"I – I – I can't see you..." she began to cry, "...the stroke has taken my vision."

"You don't need to see us sweetie, you can feel us." Declan said softly, as he came over to hold her hands.

I watched his bigger, stronger ones enfold her smaller, withered ones.

"But I CAN'T see you!" She said, frightened. "When I was first brought in, I could make out shadows, but now I can't see anything at all!"

I asked in concern, "When were you brought in?"

"This afternoon," she sniffed. "The Historical Society tour found me, in the kitchen. The guide called the ambulance."

I shot an alarmed look towards my mate at the rate of her deterioration.

"When did the stroke occur?" I asked worriedly.

"This morning, just after breakfast," she puffed, as if talking was laborious. "I was cleaning up when a terrible pain started on the left side of my head. The next thing I knew, I was lying on the floor and I could hear the Tour Guide speaking to emergency services. I thought I must have hit my head or something, but the doctors are calling it a stroke."

Declan passed a guilty glance and I sensed he felt bad that we weren't there. So did I. How awful, to be found by strangers instead of family or friends.

"Nairn, how about you come back to Alaska, with us?" He offered. "You can stay as long as you like and I'll be like your live-in chef."

"Oh no, I can't put you out like that!" She laughed tearfully. "I'd never expect you and B, to wait on me hand and foot."

"If you lived in Alaska with us, you wouldn't be putting us out." He disagreed. "We need to be there, to hunt every full moon. B can arrange for Hodge Endeavor to look after your place while you're gone."

"It'd be no problem," I went along. "You can keep me company when I'm home alone all day, working on my papers. In the evening when Declan comes home from work, he'll cook dinner just like he does every night."

"And if we both have to go out, either hunting or when B has to lecture, we have grandnephews or nieces who can sit with you." He continued. "You like our Riverclaw family and they like you. It wouldn't be a hassle."

Nairn sighed sadly, "I can't come with you tonight. The doctors are talking about surgery. They say because of my unusual brain wave pattern, it's a fifty/fifty chance an operation will restore my sight."

I said unhappily, "It's because of the ESP. The electrical activity in your brain operates differently to a human without ESP. Dr. Dystar proved this with his research, back in the 21st Century. There good things and bad things about your gift. The good is you're a wicked poker player," which made her laugh, "the bad is people with ESP are in the high risk range of strokes."

"I – I – I can't move my left hand or my foot properly..." her voice trembled, "...they - they say they have to do two separate operations, one on my sight then one for my motor functions. But if the surgery doesn't succeed, I'll be a burden to society."

"Burden my ass!" Declan scolded as he squeezed her hands. "It's going to be alright, Nairn. You'll see."

"Very funny," she laughed bitterly at his accidental pun. "But I want to talk about why I called you here."

I shared a concerned gaze with my mate, who too sensed what was coming.

She took a deep breath to proclaim, "I want to know that you'll keep Stonewall when I'm gone."

"Don't talk rubbish!" He barked. "You're not going anywhere and we're not taking your house!"

"I don't want distant relatives I've only seen twice in my life, to get my home. I want to leave the house to you. I want to know you'll use it, even if it's for the odd weekend. I want YOU inside my house and if I occasionally look in, I'll see B working in the library and you Declan, in the kitchen."

"We're not taking your frickin' house!" He growled out. "It's YOUR house, where you live and where you're going to keep living."

"Oh yes you are!" She stood up to the loud European Werewolf by sitting up straighter in bed. "I may not live as long as the two of you, so I want to know I will live on through you! I want to stay with you, by you staying in my house!"

"We live in Alaska!" Declan tried to dissuade her. "What the hell are we supposed to do with a seven hundred year old house in frickin' Scotland?!"

"Remember me this way!" Nairn rebuked. "B's eternally young as a Circulator. The Circulate left behind its' Headquarters and Hodge Endeavor as its legacy, for her. This will be mine."

In frustration, Declan let go of her hands and walked away from the bed. Blindly, her right hand reached out to find where he went, so I took it instead. I sat at her side, to reassure as best as I could.

"I will age one day, Nairn." I said quietly. "If I reach 1,000 years, my biological body will begin to falter."

"Then what will happen, B?" She asked tentatively.

"It will age and if I remain in my human body, I will die." I said plainly. "The only way I can be eternal, is if I permanently go into phase and reside as such, in the space time continuum."

"And if you don't evolve?" She pressed.

"I could die a mortal death, but I'll never be returned to the timeline via reincarnation. My bio-electromagnetic field is in temporal flux, which is an energy that can't be repeated. I'd remain in the space time continuum like a dead star, whilst my loved ones travel to and fro."

Declan's eyes widened as he listened intently. He'd probably wondered this himself, over our long years together. He didn't look happy about what he was hearing, either.

I continued, "Scientifically speaking, nothing in this universe lasts forever. If I spent all my life in phase, I'd never age. When I'm in my biological body, it does deteriorate, only much more slowly. I could keep returning to a youthful form, the same way I phase through time. But time would eventually wear me down."

"Surely if you remain in a youthful form..." she wondered aloud.

"Think of rocks in a stream for a moment, sandstone is much more vulnerable to water than let's say granite. However, the granite will eventually be affected, while the sandstone has been washed away. But the sandstone could have reformed, further down the stream since it's a composite rock. Meanwhile, the granite is still in the same place in the stream, slowly but surely, being worn down." I explained.

"Why is reincarnation so important to you, B?"

"Because the Universe itself is reincarnated," I told her. "There's the Big Bang then the Big Crunch and another Big Bang. It's the cycle and recycle of existence. Energy doesn't cease to exist, it simply changes form. I don't know how long this has gone on for, or how long it will continue. But if I can't be reincarnated, I'll only have this life. My relations could return in the birth of a new universe, maybe not as humans but as something else, and I'd be left behind."

Declan's mouth fell open in shock, "Are you saying that if you don't evolve, you would die and always remain dead?"

"Yes." I stated. "I'd still end up in the space time continuum, but I'd be stuck there as if it were a graveyard."

Nairn said frantically, "Then what are you waiting around here for? Grab Declan, turn him into a Circulator and evolve while you still can!"

"He's only 206 years old, we still have time." I giggled, as I gave him a wink.

"Go B," her eyes overflowed with tears. "Why are you waiting around in these depressing circumstances, with everyone dying on you?"

"It's not depressing!" I laughed. "I have my mate, I have my pack and I have my tribe. Just like you have Declan and I here, to take care of you."

"I didn't call the two of you here to take care of me." She took an unsteady breath. "I want to know that part of me will remain with you through my house."

Declan declared, "We don't need a house to remind us of you."

"Then you'll break this old woman's heart, by discarding it?" She rasped.

The European Werewolf growled under his breath as he crossed his arms in defiance.

"We'll keep the house," I promised, "and this isn't the end, it's the beginning. Your departure is only temporary until you return for your next life."

"So I could see you again, if I'm reincarnated?" She asked, hopeful.

"Never say never, that's what I believe." I shrugged. "I don't know when or where, but one of my all-knowing feelings say we'll see each other again."

This seemed to comfort her, as she lay back into the pillows and let out a sigh of relief.

"Can I ask you both for one last thing?" She requested.

"Of course," Declan said in his deep voice.

"That you'll stay here with me, tonight?" She asked weakly. "I'm ready to go, but I don't want to die alone."

"Nobody's dying tonight." He said determinedly. "It's the 23rd Century for crying out loud! We have the miracles of modern medicine. You said yourself that the doctors are gonna operate."

However, this time she didn't debate and we watched her eyes close.

"I'm just so tired right now..." her voice trailed off, "...and Declan, this hospital does have a cafeteria."

"We're not going anywhere." I vowed. "You just rest and when you open your eyes again, we'll be here."

My heart hurt as my eyes stung, but I wouldn't let go of her hand. She slipped back into sleep and remained like this, for the last hours of her life. Periodically, I'd stroke the skin on the top of her hand, as I listened to her breathing become fainter. Once or twice she groaned and moved her head, however she remained unconscious.

*****

Around midnight, the matron whom had been sitting behind the desk, came into the room. When she suggested we should leave, Declan went out into the hallway with her, to argue we'd be staying. At least he could put his foot down on this particular matter.

Then he came back into the room and sat on the other side of her bed. His eyes wandered to and fro, from the machine which showed her vital signs, to her face. Nairn's expression was one of peace and she looked like she could have been dreaming about heaven itself.

At 3.03 AM the machine beeped out an alert and the matron and a doctor came rushing back. The physician knew there wasn't anything he could do, at the rate she deteriorated since her admittance. He pronounced her dead at 3.09 AM then he and matron left to file their paperwork.

But we didn't leave her side until dawn broke around six o'clock and finally we let them take her down to the morgue.

*****

Instead of instantaneously phasing back to Alaska, we reappeared in the lounge room at Stonewall.

Declan let go of my arm he'd hung onto, as I carried Nairn's clothes and things from the hospital. It wasn't much, just what she arrived in. However, amongst her velvet clothes and leather boots, was the necklace she got at Christmas. She must have been wearing it, the morning of the stroke.

Without saying a word, I turned and left the room. Silently, Declan followed me up the staircase and down the hallway then into her bedroom. There, I laid out her clothes and jewellery on the four-poster bed.

"What do we do?" I asked eventually. "Do we pack up her things now, or come back and do it later?"

"I'm not coming back here."

Startled, I turned in his direction however he walked away with his hands in his pockets.

"Do you mean we should start packing up her things now?" I wondered. "I'm too tired and emotional, to do it today. Let's come back and do it later in the week."

Abruptly, he bellowed out, "NO!"

Shocked, I took a step back at the brunt of his unexpected fury.

"I'm NOT packing up her stuff just like I'm NOT taking her frickin' house!" The European Werewolf roared. "It's HER house! It's HER territory! It's not yours, it's not mine, it's HERS!"

Tearfully, I shouted back, "SHE'S dead now and SHE wanted us to have it!"

"I'm NOT claiming a dead person's house like a circling vulture!"

"But she said over and over again how much she wanted us to have it!"

"I can still smell her scent inside the house!" He ranted as his eyes watered. "I can smell her in the sheets on the bed! I can smell her on the furniture she's touched! I'm not living in a dead friend's scent, it's just plain morbid!"

"I can smell it too, but it brings me comfort!" I cried. "I'm sure that's what Nairn wanted."

He stood there, looking hurt and angry then he shook his head.

"You have absolutely no problem with any of this, do you?" His voice turned cold. "You're used to just acquiring things, especially with Hodge Endeavor giving you whatever you want."

My already aching chest now felt as if it had a silver stake driven through my heart.

"Declan...that's not fair."

Then he walked up to the bed and picked up the necklace he'd given her.

"So much for amethyst bringing protection," he said snidely. "Just take me home, B. I'm never coming back to this house again."

With that, he tossed the jewellery back onto the bedcovers and walked out of the room.

~~~~~~

~ 23 ~

I felt restless. I was so tetchy, I couldn't focus on preparation for my presentation at Yale, next week. I pushed away my laptop, which knocked over a pile of books and hand-written notes. With a growl, I stood up from the dining table and began to pace.

I walked up and down in my living area until I couldn't stand the confines of indoors, anymore. Next, I grabbed my keys and left the house, slamming the front door behind. Instead of going down the veranda stairs, I jumped over the railing and landed on the gravel drive.

Bad temperedly, I stomped out of the garden then down the sealed road, towards the community centre.

I walked past Mum and Dad's old house where a new generation of Wisetails lived. I passed my old Gran and Grandfather's house where new Riverclaws resided. I passed Nana and Grandpa's old home where other Wisetails lived. Lastly, I looked on Uncle Julian and Aunt Danika's old house, in which more Riverclaws habited.

In the fifteen minutes of walking downhill, I felt like I had traversed two hundred years, as I reminisced on what once was and what had come to be.

Families change as they procreate and pass away... families except mine, that is. I still looked in my twenties and I couldn't conceive. I felt like I was stuck in a rut, as the only thing about me which changed in time, were my hairstyles.

I strolled into the community centre as I headed for the Garage where my husband was.

It was four o'clock in the afternoon, which meant school had finished for the day. As I walked around the sports field, I saw a soccer game commence. The players were primarily teenaged boys, with the odd girl volunteering. The other teenaged girls were happy to sit on the odd seat and watch, in their differing groups. Some gossiped about their boyfriends who were playing, others about hair and makeup. One group talked about their favourite band, whilst playing music on their miniature speakers.

When I was growing up, I was out on the field playing. When I hung out with other girls like my late best friends Rachel and Mandy, we didn't talk hair and makeup. Our group of four including Derik, were more interested in studies. The tribe's makeshift school after the War finished when you were fifteen, so after 'graduation', we studied together. Derik in biology to become a Medicine Man, Rachel in Naturopathy, Mandy became a teacher and eventually I got my doctorate in Ancient History and Mythology.

Suddenly, the soccer ball speedily rolled off the field and in my direction. Deftly, I stopped it with my leg then toyed with it between my feet. I heard some of the boys laugh and shout.

"You want a game, Aunt B?"

It was Tyson Riverclaw who'd called out. He was Caesar's 17 year old son. Although he wasn't a Lokoti Werewolf yet, the pack sensed he'd be the next to go through the change. He's always been tall and strong for his age, like I had been growing up. Only in my case, nobody saw my change coming since women weren't meant to.

Several teens laughed at him for inviting his Great x6 Grandaunt to play.

"Shut up!" He snapped back. "She was playing soccer when your great grandparents hadn't even been born yet!"

I smiled at his rebuttal, as well as his pride at having such a youthful looking ancestor, alive and well.

"Next time," I promised.

I kicked back the ball so hard, it looked like a blur! Several of the boys ducked out of the way, with Tyson the only one game to stop it. He teased his friends for being 'chicken' as the match continued.

Beside the sports field was the General Store and the Garage was next door.

Customary rock music blared out, which I thought was 'The Tea Party'. I found Declan and Caesar hard at work on the engine of a hover-car. The employee was underneath the propped up vehicle, with his boss leaning over the open bonnet.

Declan was wearing scuffed work boots as well as stained jeans. His grey t-shirt looked strained against his muscles, with more stains on the material. I thought it funny that although hover-cars didn't use oil, some kind of fluid could still mark his clothing.

The broad-shouldered, European Werewolf with his fifties appearance, smelled my arrival and glanced my way.

"B," he acknowledged, as he continued working.

Then Caesar rolled out from underneath the vehicle to give a grin. The Lokoti Werewolf looked like he was in his twenties, when really the father of three was 48 years old. His black hair was just as scruffy as I remembered when he was little. He'd never grown his hair long like his father or grandfather had.

"Oh hey Aunt B, this is a rare pleasure." He greeted.

"Boys," I smiled back, as I walked into the Garage.

I went into the Declan's small office to wheel out an office chair to sit on. I sat beside the hover-car and watched the men work. A couple of times, I spun around on the seat, in time to the music.

Outside, it was a grey, windy day with a chill in the air. The numerous trees on tribal lands bent in the breeze, with the deciduous dropping their leaves. I've always admired the golden colours of fall, contrasted against the bushy evergreens.

"I like 'The Tea Party'." I commented.

"It's not 'The Tea Party' playing." Declan said in a flat voice. "It's Jeff Martin."

"But he's the guy from 'The Tea Party', isn't he?" I returned.

He ignored me but our grandnephew snickered from under the car. "She's got you there, Uncle."

"Shut up, Caesar." He said grouchily. "Just tell me how the ignition's looking."

"It's definitely the starter," his employee answered. "It's fused which is why the signal's not reaching the engine."

"Do we need a S23 or an S24?" Declan checked.

"An S24...? No, hang on, an S23. I don't think it's as big as an S24." He thought aloud.

"Well, what's the model number on it?" His boss asked.

"Nope, there's no model number."

"Come on, these Chinese parts always have a model number on them!" He refuted.

"I think there used to be, but it burnt off when the starter overheated."

The European Werewolf growled under his breath. I watched him straighten to walk over to some shelves. He rifled through some small boxes which packaged the components.

"OK, I'll pass you an S23 and an S24 so you can try them both out." He instructed.

He opened two which he took the parts out of. Then he passed them down to Caesar, who rolled out to take them. Resting the computer chips on his chest, he rolled back under the hover-car.

"Well?" His boss prompted.

"I was right, it's an S23." Caesar called back. "Once I've closed the starter panel, we can try the ignition."

"OK, I'm almost finished replacing the power couplings." He responded.

The next ten minutes I watched the two work in unison, with Declan on top of the engine and Caesar under it.

Then the Lokoti Werewolf rolled out and the European one opened the driver's door to sit behind the wheel. We watched him through the windscreen as he punched in the ignition code. The engine came to life and the Lokoti raised his arms in a victory wave.

"Yes!" He cheered. "Who's your daddy? Come on, who's your daddy?!"

Declan laughingly shook his head as he climbed out. "You should know by now if it's an S23 or an S24."

"Aw c'mon Uncle, I got it in the end." Caesar laughed back, before he gave me a wink. "He's a hard task master, isn't he Aunt B?"

"Try being married to him." I joked along.

"Lucky you're the last Circulator and he's the last European Werewolf, or the world would have no hope!" He goaded.

The boss looked at the clock on the wall before eyeing his employee.

"Yeah alright, since the job's done, you can have a thirty minute early mark." Declan declared.

"Woo hoo!" He cheered and gave a nudge. "You should stop by more often, Aunt B."

I saw how my husband frowned as if he were about to disagree, then he pursed his lips together.

Caesar went over to the sink in the corner, to wash off whatever was on his hands. Declan tidied up the tools as he deliberately didn't look my way. I sensed he was annoyed about something, but what I couldn't tell.

"Marie will certainly appreciate the early mark." Our relation referred to his wife. "We need to talk to Juliette. Her teachers told us she isn't doing her homework and she's even been skipping classes. We suspect there's a boy involved, as a couple of times she's come home reeking of cologne."

I watched what my mate had to say with all of this kids talk. I couldn't imagine him dealing with a tempestuous teenaged daughter. The only picture which came to mind, was a gigantic European Werewolf chasing any and all teenaged boys off his property.

"Then you should be at home helping your wife," was all he said on the matter.

Our Great x5 Grandnephew dried his hands on an old towel before grabbing his denim coat on his way out.

"I'll send your love to Marie," he promised as he passed us by.

"Do that," I called after.

Just as he was about to cross the road, he paused when he saw a particular hover-car power down, out the front of the Garage.

A dressed up, blonde-haired woman in her late thirties, climbed out of the vehicle. I noticed she was wearing a lot of makeup, as she leaned raunchily against her hover-car. She looked on my husband in a hungry manner, like she knew him. This was confirmed when Caesar turned around and came back to greet her.

"Hi Raquel," he spoke in a polite manner. "What seems to be the problem today?"

However, she ignored the subordinate as she stared at his big, bad boss. I noticed how Declan purposefully didn't look her way, while he was tidying up. My heart skipped a beat, as I got the impression that this Raquel was a regular.

"My engine is making a peculiar noise when I change speeds." She pouted at my husband. "Could you take a look at it for me?"

Hang on, why would this non-Lokoti woman come onto tribal lands for repairs, when there's also a Garage in Alma?

The employee sighed as he looked at his watch. "I can take a quick look at it."

"It's cool Caesar, I've got it." The European Werewolf said gruffly. "You go home to Marie and the kids."

"OK," he looked from the woman, to his boss then the boss's wife. "It's good seeing you again, Aunt B. Marie said that she wanted to invite you and Uncle Dec over for dinner, next month."

I guessed he was mentioning this now, to point me out to Raquel.

Momentarily, she swung her hungry eyes away from my husband, just long enough to see me, sitting on the side.

I was wearing my baggy, about-the-house clothes, of black tracksuit pants, a blue-checkered, flannel shirt, over a white, long-sleeved t-shirt. There wasn't a trace of makeup on my face and my hair looked a little messy, from walking in the wind. Compared to her, I looked like a 'bag lady' from the days of homeless people living on the streets.

"Thanks Caesar." I replied.

He gave a wave and after casting a wary look at Raquel, he left again.

Declan remained brusque and to the point. He walked over to her hover-car and popped open the hood. I watched him glance over her engine with an analytical eye.

Next, she leaned over to flash her cleavage, as she pretended to be interested in the car.

"What kind of noise is the engine making?" He asked, as he kept his eyes on the vehicle.

"A growling noise," she replied in a sultry manner, "it goes, 'grrrr'! 'grrrr!'"

Declan ignored the intonation which came with the sound effects, as his face remained impassive.

"It sounds like your transmission, although I don't know how as the vehicle isn't two years old yet." He straightened. "I can book it in two days time, as I've got four other vehicles to fix."

"Fine with me," she said coolly. "I don't have any pressing engagements in the next few days. Perhaps I could leave the car here and you could give me a lift back into Alma?"

Startled, I sat up straighter at her subtle-as-a-sledgehammer hints, which she was dropping on my husband like anvils.

What am I, invisible or something? What is with these types of women that Declan attracts? This Raquel reminded me of a cross between Brigitte Stirling and Michelle, the last female European Werewolf. I even looked at her long, red nails, to see if they were claw-like. Seems like I'm not the only one who can attract predators...

"No can do." He said simply. "I have plans with my wife for the rest of the afternoon."

Raquel appeared crestfallen then I caught her resentful gaze in my direction.

Declan declared, "It doesn't sound like a serious problem and I can't smell any components overheating. The hover-car should be fine to drive for another two days, until you bring it in to be repaired."

"But when I drove here, I could smell something burning." She lied. "When I took it to Steve Good's Garage in Alma, he said he couldn't look at it until next week. He offered me a courtesy car to use, while I wait for the repairs. Can't you even give me a lift back into town?"

My sensitive ears picked up the growl under his breath, as he struggled not to lose his temper.

"My Garage has never had a courtesy car, as most of my clients live within walking distance, on tribal lands." He said stiffly. "If you're that adamant your vehicle is unsafe to drive, you can leave it here and I'll call you a taxi."

So she tried another tactic as she looked on him determinedly.

"I heard the Lokoti were supposed to be perfect gentlemen towards the fairer sex. Would you make your wife drive a faulty vehicle, or leave her hover-car behind and walk 10 km's back home?"

I couldn't help it, the words just slipped from my mouth. "I'd actually pay your repair bill, just to see you try to walk 10 km's in those high heels."

Her head snapped around so fast, it was almost supernatural. She reminded me of a horror movie about a woman possessed. I half expected to see her face contort in a demonic way, or vomit to come out of her mouth.

She spluttered out indignantly, "Excuse me?"

I said coolly, "My husband told you he can fix your hover-car in two days time. He also said that the vehicle is still safe to drive until that happens. Aside from being more attractive than Steve Good who runs the Garage in Alma; I'm sure my husband charges less, which is why you're here soliciting his services."

"Excuse me? How dare you...!" She fired up, before she glared his way. "Because your wife is young and doesn't know any better, I'm willing to let this transgression go! But perhaps you should explain to her the basics of commerce where the customer is always right?!"

I couldn't stop myself from laughing at how she misjudged our ages.

However, Declan retook control of the situation by remaining professional.

He said calmly, "Raquel, I can fix your hover-car in two days time. Until then you can continue to drive the vehicle. Should you return, I'll only charge 470 credits when I'm sure Steve Good's Garage would charge at least 580. As the customer, you certainly have the freedom to choose."

She cast a calculated gaze over his tall build and I could see the cogs turn inside her head.

"It's a good thing you know your competition, Declan." She sung. "You're right, Steve Good did quote 580 Credits. I'll come back in two days then."

Next, she opened the driver's side door and as she sat down, she made sure to show off her long legs. She sent a smug smile my way, as she started the ignition. Her vehicle hovered up into the air and coolly, she turned away from the Garage and cruised off tribal lands.

Once it disappeared, I sighed out, "I think the pack should start patrolling the borders again to keep out looters."

He said back, "You may be right."

Slowly, I spun around in a circle on the office chair as I regarded him.

"Is she a regular?" I queried.

"Unfortunately," he answered, whilst not looking my way.

Declan returned to tidying up his work area, to close up for the day.

"Caesar looked like you have to put up with her, a lot." I commented.

"Caesar doesn't like her."

"And you do?"

Silence... he finished packing up his moveable tool box, closed the lid and rolled it over by the wall.

"I'll take that as a yes," my eyes narrowed.

"B, she's a paying customer." He said tiredly. "If I only had business produced by the tribe, I'd be struggling."

I said quietly, "You don't need the people from Alma's money."

"No, of course not!" He scoffed. "I've only got three employees to pay as well as power bills and water rates."

"You functioned well enough during the years after the War." I said under my breath.

"Sure I did!" He said sarcastically. "That was when I was paying for just my Mom and me, until I moved in with you. Then I was paying for all three of us, until my Mom died. The next thing I knew, I was paying for our holidays."

"Our travel expenses come out of the Hodge Endeavour account," I said sulkily.

He stopped whatever it was he was doing to look on incredulous.

"For your information, the only holiday I used Hodge Endeavor's funds for, was our trip to Europe. But I paid for all the incidentals such as meals or entertainment. Basically, the PA put together the itinerary and sent me the bill for the optional extras!"

I jumped to my feet, "I paid for the clothes shopping with MY money! Don't forget I'd been lecturing and publishing papers, years before then! I didn't touch your money or the Hodge Endeavor corporate account!"

He spat out, "Who do you think has been paying for our trips, the last hundred years? I may use your PA to book the flights, car rental and hotels, but it's been MY credit card which has taken the brunt!"

Shocked, I stared at my husband and his appearance of an angry fifty year old. From the sound of things, he really did see me as a 'princess'. But every time I've opened a power or water bill, he's taken it away from me. Whenever we went grocery shopping, he'd push away my credit card and use his.

He continued, "Because our trips were spaced out every five years or so, I could save up. But a large chunk of my savings for retirement has gone into our overseas adventures. Hell, I'll be lucky if I can afford to stop working at the age of 280! Why do you think I keep nagging you, to save your money? I'm trying to prepare for the day we retire!"

Declan reached up and pulled down the large roller door. It was as wide as three hover-cars and would need either two men or a machine to raise or lower it, but he tugged it down himself. The metal infrastructure rattled loudly until it hit the cement floor with a thud. Then I watched him secure the locks and next, we were standing in a dark Garage.

"Sometimes B, you're so wrapped up in your own world, you have no idea about real life! I flinch when I see you clothes shop and how you don't even look at the price. You just hand over your credit card, automatically. Once I saw one of your credit card bills after an expedition and I almost had a heart attack! I don't think you're putting anything aside, for the day I stop working."

Why the hell is he portraying me as a spendthrift? I go clothes shopping every five years at the most, usually on our holidays. I use the money from my academic work. And what does he mean that I'm not saving up? I have a portion of my pay transferred into an investment account, which I dipped into for his 200th Birthday.

"I'm sorry, I didn't know you were so worried about our finances." I spoke crisply. "I've never been because we have Hodge Endeavor as back up."

"Exactly!" He whirled around and pointed at me. "You think because you're a Circulator, you have Hodge Endeavor at your beck and call! But you don't even pay attention to the World Wide News on Internet TV. Did you know in the last twenty years, Hodge Endeavor has undergone massive corporate restructuring and lost two Chairmen of the Board?"

"Of course it has!" I laughed in his face. "It was the Circulate Mainframe that did the firing, when it discovered embezzlement. It even sent the electronic evidence to the police, to have them arrested. Trust me, Hodge Endeavor is NOT about to go bankrupt!"

"That's it, isn't it? It's your complete faith in a machine, in this Circulate Mainframe. Don't you EVER ask questions how the money's coming in?" He demanded.

"Vincent made damn sure that the Circulate Mainframe and Hodge Endeavor would be my back up. You were there and heard him yourself! The

Mainframe practically runs the company single-handedly. Hodge Endeavor is owned by the Circulate. I am the Circulate!" I spelt it out for him.

That shut him up, as he turned around and walked into his small office.

I grabbed the office chair I was previously sitting on and wheeled it into the room behind him.

I continued, "Vincent programmed every possible contingency into the Mainframe. The computer is my Calculator now, as it keeps track of my movements. Did you know that it monitors me, whether I'm at home or travelling through time? Or, did you know that the computer can send Hodge Endeavor running to my rescue? If I'm in trouble in an era the organization exists in, they'll come to my aid."

Declan sat behind his desk with his laptop on to do the day's paperwork, but he shook his head, showing no he didn't know that.

Then I leaned over the desk to look him in the eye. "If you weren't so bent on paying for everything yourself; your anger wouldn't build up over me not pulling my weight, when I didn't know there was any weight to pull!"

Abruptly, he jumped to his feet so he could stare me down.

"Of course I'm gonna pay for our living expenses, I'm the man!" His chest filled out. "It's customary the husband provides for his family, especially if the wife is rearing children!"

As if he'd thrown icy water, I stood ill at ease at the sensitive subject he'd inadvertently brought up.

I said in a low voice, "Since there aren't any children, the wife can certainly add to the income of the household."

Now he leaned over the desk so his eyes could drill into mine.

"Since you only lecture once a month and stay home the rest of the time, it's like you're a housewife anyway." He said cruelly.

Oh no, he didn't...? Unfortunately, yes he did. Declan just put down my academic work. He intimated that it wasn't as important as working outside of the home, four or five days a week.

I spun on my heel and stormed out of his office then the Garage.

"B...!" He called after. "B, I didn't mean that."

I exited via the backdoor and slammed it shut behind. I was so hurt, I didn't know what to do. After a moment, I walked away from the building and headed home. I hoped the exercise would channel my anger and clear my head.

However, to make sure he wouldn't see me when he drove home, I walked through the woods instead of along the roadside.

*****

That evening I turned down dinner, so Declan took out leftover spaghetti bolognaise from the freezer and ate alone. Afterwards, he lay on one of the sofas in the living room, to watch a movie on Internet TV. But I was upstairs going through my financial folder, where I kept my important papers.

I sat on the bed, sifting through various bank statements Hodge Endeavor sent with annual regularity.

Declan was right about one thing, I didn't pay attention to the breakdown of my investment portfolio. I simply glanced at the total sum then filed the statements away. What he was wrong about though, it wasn't because I was avoiding the 'real world'. It was because I had faith in Vincent's work on the Mainframe and therefore Hodge Endeavor, to keep me safe.

I picked up my mobile phone and called one of my PA's at the company. I gave her instructions to sell one of my investment portfolios and to transfer the proceeds into Declan's bank account. She was so efficient, she did all of this while I was on the phone. I wrote down the date and the receipt number for the transaction and lastly, thanked her for her help.

Next, I carried these sheets of paper downstairs and over to my husband.

He was crashed out on the couch, watching 'Talladega Nights'. He was chuckling at the scene where a racing car driver was hallucinating he was on fire, with his best friend chasing after him. I remembered this bit of the movie, from seeing it before.

I stood over him and held out the statements. He sighed wearily at my interruption and paused the movie. Then he practically snatched the papers right out of my hand!

"What's this?" He grumpily asked, but I didn't answer.

I watched him frown as he glanced over the statements, which turned into a look of pure disbelief.

"Is this the balance of your Hodge Endeavor Corporate Credit Card?" He wondered.

I pointed at my name which was printed on both statements to show that no, it wasn't.

Suddenly he sat upright, as if I'd spilt scalding hot coffee in his lap.

"33 million credits?!" He referred to the statement in his right hand. "1.3 million credits?!" He referred to the statement in his left. "B, what the hell is this?!"

"This account..." I pointed at the statement on the right, "...is my family account. Elisha Worthall started it, her daughter Alexandrina Carmichael added to it, and so did my grandmother, Arabella Riverclaw. It's grown so big because it's been invested and reinvested for nearly three hundred years. The Circulate Mainframe manages the funds, as it knows which companies have the highest returns. Elisha started it as an emergency fund for her family, to help them survive the war. Then Vincent popped up as our Calculator and we never had to use it. Not only did he watch over our timelines, but our finances as well. Don't forget the many years he ran Hodge Endeavor. When Vincent evolved, he instructed the Mainframe to look after it. So you see Declan, if anything happened, we'd be taken care of."

"Then what's with the 1.3 million credits?" He waved the statement in his left hand.

"Just as the Mainframe managed Elisha's funds, it did the same for mine." I said simply. "I put aside half of every pay I received from my lectures, or royalties from my papers. After working for two centuries, I probably saved a hundred grand. But the computer turned it into 1.3 million credits by investing in successful stocks and shares."

"And what's this scribble?" He queried my writing on the second statement.

"That's the receipt number for transferring the 1.3 million credits into your bank account, to pay you back for living expenses and the vacations."

Just as I turned away, Declan leapt to his feet in indignation.

"TRANSFER IT BACK RIGHT NOW!"

"No." I said calmly, as I headed back upstairs.

"B, I'M ORDERING YOU AS YOUR HUSBAND, GET YOUR MONEY OUT OF MY ACCOUNT!"

"No." I called back from the top of the staircase.

"B, THAT'S YOUR MONEY THAT YOU EARNED! GET IT OUT OF MY ACCOUNT RIGHT NOW! I'M NEVER GONNA TOUCH IT!"

I closed the bedroom door to block out his shouting. Then I walked over to my financial folder lying open on the bed. I closed it and carried it over to the wardrobe, where I slid it back onto the top shelf. Once I shut the door, I wandered back to the bed where I collapsed on top.

I let out another sigh as my eyes fell upon a framed photo, sitting on my bedside table. It was a family picture taken at a Christmas long, long ago. It was the first Christmas Declan and I spent together, as mates.

As customary, we went to the old Riverclaw home where Gran and Grandfather lived, to spend the holiday with our families. My Mum and Dad came along, as did Nana and Grandpa. Aunt Susan was present, as was Derik, Rachel and their young son, Michael. It was also when Rachel was pregnant with Blanche, with the baby bulge evident under her clothing. Of course, Uncle Jules, Aunt Danika and my grown cousins Phoenix and Phoebe, were there too. Standing beside Phoebe in the picture, was her future husband and my Calculator, Vincent.

In the picture, Declan had one arm about his mother and another around his wife. He beamed into the camera, looking like he was on top of the world. I remember how happy he was in those days. He finally got the girl he was in love with, and his mother was still alive. Outside of holidays, nearly every Sunday evening was spent at Aunt Susan's house, along with Derik and Rachel and their two children.

In a framed photo on Declan's bedside table, was a family picture taken on one of those evenings. Aunt Susan sat on a couch, with her two grandchildren in the forms of Michael and Blanche, on either side. Sitting on the arms of the sofa were their parents, Derik and Rachel. Then standing behind the group, was Declan and I. He held me closely against his side, as he grinned like a lottery winner.

The person missing from the photo though was Mandy, who was Derik's, Rachel's and my best friend. She never married and her relationships were intermittent. Only twice did she bring a partner to a Sabre Sunday Dinner. One evening it was a boyfriend and on another it was a girlfriend. Her bisexuality was a source of curiosity to the European Werewolf. The two would playfully exchange barbs about it.

For the couple of years I taught history at the tribe's community school, Mandy and I did lesson plans together. Declan would come home from work and find the two of us, sitting at the dining table. Our books were strewn about as we colluded on ideas.

"Hey Mandy," he greeted casually, as he walked past into the kitchen. "How's your love life goin'?"

"Why are you always asking about that, Sabre?" She smilingly shook her head. "Normal people simply ask how a person is, not about their sex life."

"Are you staying for dinner?" He offered.

"I won't say no to a free feed."

"You know, if you settled down, I'm sure the guy would cook for you too."

"My last girlfriend was a superb chef," she replied as she wrote her notes. "I especially liked it when she'd use my body as the plate to eat off."

SMASH!

In shock, Declan would drop whatever it was he was holding, as we erupted into giggles.

A startled European Werewolf would come out of the kitchen. "Should I be worried about what the two of you get up to, when I'm not here?"

"Yes, these lesson plans are simply subterfuge for our secret relationship." I teased.

"Remember what I said, B." He went back into the kitchen to clean up. "Just as long as you film it, so your husband can watch later."

Declan didn't have a problem with my academic work, in those days. Aunt Susan, like my family, would encourage my studies. She looked so proud when she sat with them at my graduation, in Cambridge.

Her eldest was the boy who picked on me when I was little, who yelled at me when we were growing up, and even today he's still shouting. This is the boy who'll be coming to exist with me for all eternity, inside the space time continuum? Here's hoping that as an entity of light, he won't have a mouth anymore.

Speak of the devil... the bedroom door was suddenly thrown open and the obnoxious male stormed in. He was holding his mobile phone in one hand and my statements in his other. Ceremoniously, he dropped the pieces of paper over me, before marching out of the room and downstairs again.

I picked up the statements and noticed a new scribble beside my scribble. In Declan's hand, he wrote down a receipt number from transferring the money out of his account and back into mine. That stubborn, self-absorbed, bad-tempered ass!

Furious, I leapt off the bed to confront my husband and the current bane of my existence.

"What the hell is this?!" I objected.

He sat back down on the couch and pressed 'play' on the remote, so he wouldn't have to look at me.

Purposefully, I stood between him and the Internet TV. "Declan?"

"What does it frickin' look like?" He snapped back. "B, I'm not touching your savings! It should be your retirement fund!"

"Then why did you try to make me feel guilty, by saying that YOU were the one who paid for our holidays, the last hundred years?!" I vented.

"To try and instil some kind of sensibility into your vague head!" He retorted.

"I don't want sensibility!" I threw the crumpled statements to the floor. "I have a computer who does that for me!"

"So I found out tonight!" He glared back. "It's nice to know by the way, my wife has this financial plan which she never thought to clue me in on!"

"You've always known that I rely on the Circulate Mainframe!" I cried out, exasperated. "You've always known that Hodge Endeavor manages my finances!"

He jumped to his feet to seethe. "You NEVER told me that you've been putting aside money from your pay which a frickin' computer was investing for you!"

"You NEVER mentioned before that YOU were paying for our holidays!"

"You weren't meant to know!" He rolled his eyes.

"Then why the hell did you throw it in my face today?!"

"Because you were behaving completely clueless about my living and you were being rude to my customers!"

"I was rude to ONE customer!" I held up my finger. "And the skank totally deserved it, for hitting on my husband right in front of me!"

"You get insulted over HER?" He yelled indignantly. "Do you see me being rude to the male professors you deal with?"

"They don't even have the chance to hit on me, since my husband and my jailor, only lets me out for 12 hours at a time!" I complained.

"Oh yeah? What about that guy who used to text you once a day? What did he say, which made you stop messaging him back? Oh, that's right, 'If only we could be together in the real cities of old, instead of holographic ones!'"

"You've taken it out of context, he KNOWS I'm married!" I retorted. "Besides, I'd finished helping him with his holographic recreations of the ancient cities. There was no need to talk to him anymore."

"Yeah but he STILL text messaged you, didn't he?!" He yelled in frustration. "Fine! Go and do whatever it is you want to do! Go and spend more than 12 hours away! Go to your lectures and seminars with your stuffy academic cohorts!"

"Good! Because there's a seminar in Ephesus which goes for five days, I want to go to!" I marched towards the stairs. "I'd sent 'declined' when I received the email invitation, but I'll tell them I'm changing it to 'accepted'!"

"Whatever!" He fell back onto the couch. "At least I'll have the house to myself, for a week!"

Fuming, I stomped up the stairs and back into the bedroom. There, I knelt down to pull out a suitcase from under the bed. Then I tossed it open and began to pack.

I grabbed some casual wear from the tall boy first, like jeans and jumpers. Then I opened up the wardrobe and grabbed a couple of suits. Next, I packed a pair of black shoes to go with the formal dress. The sneakers I was already wearing would be fine for every other day.

However, when I turned to go into the bathroom to collect my toiletries, I almost walked into Declan!

He was standing in the bedroom doorway, watching with his arms crossed.

"What are you doing?" He asked unhappily.

"Packing!"

"I can see that!" He sneered. "Don't tell me this seminar starts tomorrow?"

"No, I'm going to New Haven for a couple of days."

"New Haven?" He echoed.

"Yeah, where Yale is and also where my next lecture happens to be." I said coolly. "I have to do some additional research and the books I need are in the University's library."

"Since when?" He looked on in disbelief.

"It's just ONE of the many things you don't know about me, isn't it Declan?" I rebuked. "You have no idea how much work I put off, because you don't like it when I go away!"

"I don't believe this..." He started to pace up and down in the bedroom, with his hands on his hips.

I went into the bathroom to collect my toothbrush, hairbrush and makeup kit, when I heard a strange noise coming from the bedroom.

I popped my head out of the doorway, to see Declan holding the suitcase upside down and emptying my clothes out onto the bed!

"WHAT THE HELL ARE YOU DOING?!" I roared upon my return.

"You're not going anywhere!" He put his foot down.

"Like hell I am!"

Next, he grabbed hold of my shoulders to hold my gaze.

"OK, you're angry with me and I get it." He lowered his voice. "I was out of line with what I said this afternoon -"

"Gee, you think?" I scoffed.

"But you were just as much in the wrong as I was -"

"GET BENT!" I yelled in his face.

Then I tossed my toiletries bag into the suitcase, as well as the clothes and lingerie which had been tipped out.

"What's it going to be like when we evolve to the space time continuum to live for ETERNITY?!" He spat out. "You won't be able to run away then!"

"I'm actually looking forward to the day we evolve, Declan." I paused to pass a glare. "Because you won't be a biological being anymore, means YOU WON'T HAVE A FRICKIN' MOUTH TO YELL AT ME!"

I slammed the suitcase shut and grabbed my handbag. Next, I slung it over my shoulder and picked up the case from the bed. He watched me carry both out of the bedroom and down the stairs.

"I yell at YOU?" He echoed. "Look who's talking! You yell at me too! I'm not the only one with a mouth in this marriage!"

He followed me downstairs and watched as I put my laptop into its carry bag.

"Talk about double standards!" He ranted. "You say I don't talk to YOU nicely? What about the way you treat me, sometimes? What about when you talk condescendingly, or treat me like an idiot?!"

I slung the second bag over my other shoulder and picked up the suitcase again.

"You think running away is going to solve the problem?" He stood between me and the door. "This is just so typical of you! You're always running away!"

"Oh yeah, like when?"

"In Russia, when you went off to fight the 'fang heads' without me!" He reminded. "Or, in China when you frickin' abandoned me by a broken down car. Or, how about the time you jumped out of the truck and walked in the rain, after Maia and Forrest's wedding? Or, when you go to Scotland without me!"

"I ask you all the time to come to Stonewall!" I hit back.

"AND I TOLD YOU I'D NEVER STEP FOOT IN THAT HOUSE AGAIN!"

His voice was so loud the vibration rattled the windows.

"Declan, whether you like it or not, the house is in BOTH of our names." I said coldly. "Yet I'm the only one who looks after it!"

"And I keep telling you to give the National Trust full ownership instead of partial custody!" He bickered. "We don't need a Scottish mansion! Besides, it's basically her tombstone, especially with her body rotting in the backyard."

Wearily, I looked away as I saw this was a no-win situation.

"That's why I go back, to visit her grave." I said quietly. "And because I can still picture her, inside the house."

His voice dropped too, "And that's exactly why I won't go back, so I won't see or smell her."

My eyes stung, but I took a deep breath and pulled myself together.

"Goodbye Declan."

I started for the front door but as I passed by him, he snatched the suitcase out of my hand.

"You're not going anywhere." He said adamantly.

He watched me pause and I think he thought he'd won.

"Admit it B," he said smugly. "You're being an idiot. You seriously think you can run away? We're biologically bonded together, for Pete's sake!"

Whereas the only thing I chastised myself about, was forgetting as a Circulator, I didn't need doors.

Declan's wrinkled eyes widened as I took a step towards him and my hand reached out.

"I want a divorce." I said flatly.

Then my hand touched the suitcase and together, we disappeared in a bright flash of light.

I instantaneously phased out of my living room in Alaska, to reappear in an unseen corner of a lobby in New Haven.

The suitcase Declan had been holding clattered to the floor. I picked it up and walked out unnoticed, into the main foyer. There, I crossed over to the front desk.

"Hi, I haven't made a reservation, but I'm hoping you have a room available for a couple of nights...?" I spoke in a wavering voice.

The clerk looked like she was about to ask if I was OK, but thought better of it. She checked for vacancies and then she checked me in. I gave her my credit card and ID to process and in return, she gave me an electronic key.

*****

~ 24 ~

I knew the hotel because I'd been there before. I'd lectured at Yale previously and afterwards, the University held a luncheon in the five-star function room. I enjoyed a sumptuous buffet with the other speakers who'd been invited. After the glamour of the event, I wasn't surprised by the quality of the hotel room.

A bellboy took my suitcase and showed me up. As part of the service, he opened the door for me and I followed him and hover-trolley inside. He handed back my room's electronic key and put down my luggage. Then he held out his small scanner, to receive his tip. I swiped my credit card which delivered twenty credits to his account.

"Thank you, Mrs. Sabre." He smiled and waved towards the video-phone. "If you should need anything, the number for Room Service is on speed dial."

Then he left with the hover-trolley, leaving me to my own devices. I let out a long sigh as I examined my surroundings. The first thing I noticed was the silence, which made me wonder if the walls had soundproofing between the rooms?

The colours were an earthy design, either in camel, green or brown. There was an ensuite, a Queen-sized bed, two bedside tables which on one was the phone, a big screen Internet TV and a sound system. The other furniture in the spacious room consisted of a sofa which was also facing the Internet TV, a coffee table, an armoire and of course, a mini-bar.

Wow, if this is a standard room, I wondered what the penthouse was like?

In the peace and quiet, I opened my suitcase on top of the bed. I had the whole room to myself and it was my space and mine alone. I half unpacked and half reorganized my messy things. Everything was mish-mashed together, thanks to a European Werewolf trying to tip it out.

Firstly, I hung up my suits in the armoire. Secondly, I carried my toiletries bag into the ensuite to leave on the vanity. Thirdly, I tidied up my case by refolding my lingerie and casual clothes. Lastly, I carried my case over to the luggage rack on the wall and left it there, open.

Slowly, I started to relax and even helped myself to the mini-bar. I opened a small bottle of soda which was lemon, lime and bitters flavoured. I poured it into one of the chilled glasses and sat on the couch with it. Beside, sat my handbag and laptop carry case. I eyed my computer and contemplated on doing some work.

"At first, when I see you cry, yeah it makes me smile, yeah it makes me smile."

The suddenness of my phone ringing, ending the silence, startled me. In annoyance, I pulled it out of my handbag and glared at the name which appeared on the Caller ID - Declan. Instead of answering, I put the phone down on the coffee table and watched it vibrate as it continued to ring.

"At worst, I feel bad for a while, but then I just smile, I go ahead and smile."

It stopped which meant his call was forwarded to voicemail. Next, it chimed, indicating I had a message. But I didn't need to check it, I knew it'd be more shouting.

I sat back into the sofa and nursed my drink, as I stared at the technology.

Beep beep! Beep beep!

Now my phone alerted I'd received a text message.

Frickin' hell! Can I get NO peace?! I growled under my breath, as I picked up my phone to view it.

ANSWER YOUR FRICKIN' PHONE! – Declan.

I rolled my eyes and just as I started to put my phone down again, it vibrated in my hand from another call coming in.

"At first, when I see you cry, yeah it makes me smile, yeah it makes me smile."

To shut it and him up, I put the phone on silent and carelessly dropped it onto the couch.

After a minute, the screen lit up to indicate another message had been left on my voice mail. Ten seconds later, it lit up again with the arrival of a second text message. I tapped on the touch-screen to see what he had to say now.

CALL ME! – Declan.

I let out a bitter laugh as if to say, 'no way in hell', as I got up and walked away from it and my bossy husband.

*****

The ensuite not only had a shower, but a large bath. I filled it with hot water, tipped in the complimentary jasmine-scented bubble bath and breathed in the fragrant steam. I laid in the hot water for an hour, letting the temperature and the aromatherapy evaporate the tension in my muscles.

When I climbed out, I emptied the tub and put on one of the complimentary robes. Then I noticed something else on the vanity and I picked up the complimentary moisturizer. I rubbed the luscious coconut butter into my legs then left the bathroom.

I put on my pink, flannel pyjama bottoms which had yellow stars printed over the fabric, along with a yellow singlet top. With my hair still tied up in a knot, I wandered back to the couch. There, I curled up in a corner and perused through the Room Service Menu. I didn't feel like ordering a late dinner, but I looked through the breakfast specials.

It was around 7 PM when I left Alaska and approximately 1 AM in Connecticut, when I arrived. I could have instantaneously phased to 7 PM EST and avoided the time differential, but then the lobby of the hotel wouldn't have been so quiet. I eyed the digital clock on one of the bedside tables and saw it was close to 3 AM. I thought I should go to bed soon, but I wasn't tired yet.

B...?

Huh? What was that? It almost sounds like...

B...!

...Declan, telepathically calling out to me. But could it be? Usually our mental communication occurred in close proximity to each other.

B...CAN YOU HEAR ME?

My heart pounded at the force of emotion that came with the message. It made my eyes sting but I blinked back my tears and took a deep breath. To distract myself, I read through the list of crepes.

B...!

I felt his hurt and anguish as he willed his words to me. Damn this Lokoti Werewolf mating behaviour! When babies are removed from their mothers, the umbilical cord is severed. Why couldn't we do something similar when we left our mate? Then my heart emitted a painful spasm at the idea, as it told me that the only way I could detach myself, was to cut it out.

I'm damned if I do or damned if I don't; I either stay home and be miserable with him or I leave home and be miserable without him. Gees, I'm pathetic, this mating business was like an addiction! I'm as bad as an alcoholic or a drug addict! Only in my case, the cravings would increase and if I didn't use, my health could suffer.

I stood up to clear my head and stretch my legs. I circled the couch whilst doing breathing exercises, as I tried to block his telepathy. As I paced, I noticed my phone still sitting on the sofa. The screen lit up, showing I'd received a new text message.

With a frustrated growl, I picked it up and saw I didn't have one new message waiting, but several.

WHY AREN'T U ANSWERING UR PHONE? – Declan.

R U ON EARTH OR EVEN IN THIS TIME PERIOD? – Declan.

U MUST BE STILL HERE OR I'D GET THE 'OUT OF RANGE' MSG LIKE I DO WHEN UR ON TAURUS 6 – Declan.

CALL ME BACK! - Declan.

I JUST CALLED UR P.A. & SHE SAID U CHARGED A HOTEL ROOM 2 UR CRED CARD – Declan.

WHY THE HELL R U PAYING FOR A HOTEL IN THIS COUNTRY & CENTURY WHEN U HAVE A HOUSE? – Declan.

HELL, U HAVE 2 HOUSES IF YOU INCLUDE THAT TOMB CALLED STONEWALL - Declan.

DON'T BE STUPID B, JUST COME HOME! – Declan.

R U GOING THRU A MIDLIFE CRISIS? PHYSICALLY UR STILL IN UR TWENTIES! – Declan.

STOP ACTING SO IMMATURE, UR A 214 YR OLD, NOT A 14 YR OLD! – Declan.

ANSWER UR FRICKIN' PHONE! – Declan.

WE ARE NOT GETTING A DIVORCE! – Declan.

A DIVORCE, R U FOR REAL? OUR KIND DON'T HAVE DIVORCES! – Declan.

OK, THAT'S NOT THE ONLY REASON WHY WE'RE NOT GETTING A DIVORCE. NOW GET UR ASS HOME SO WE CAN FIGHT ABOUT THIS IN PERSON! – Declan.

WUD U FRICKIN' CALL ME BACK?! – Declan.

HOW WUD U LIKE IT IF I WAS THE CIRCULATOR & I LEFT WHENEVER I FELT LIKE IT? – Declan.

Out of the blue, the hotel's phone started to ring! I knew who it was, he would have found out the name of where I'm staying, when he heard I charged it to my credit card. Determinedly, I marched over to pick up the receiver.

"Stop calling me Declan, because I'm not coming home!"

I hung up but then I left the phone off the hook. I knew he'd keep calling the hotel if he couldn't reach me via mobile phone. Wearily, I pulled down the covers on the bed as I prepared to retire from this awful day.

*****

Although my mobile was on silent and the hotel's phone was disabled, I didn't sleep well.

Maybe as a Werewolf, it made me territorial about where I rest. But I couldn't settle on the strange mattress nor adjust the pillow to my liking. I tossed and turned as I tried to find a comfortable position. Every time I rolled over, I had to pull up the quilt again, to cover my bare shoulders.

Deep down, I knew why I felt colder than usual, because I was missing a second body. If my mate were here, he'd warm the whole bed. I could spoon him from behind, like he was a giant hot water bottle.

B...?

It also didn't help that I heard Declan's thoughts in my head.

B, CAN YOU HEAR ME?

Exasperated, I climbed out of bed and went over to the couch. I picked up my handbag and pulled out my MP3 player. I put the earphones on and went back to bed.

It didn't help that the first song to come on, was Iggy Pop's 'Candy'. It was 'our' song. The image of us singing it that afternoon by the river, came with the music.

"Beautiful, beautiful girl from the north, you burned my heart with a flickering torch." Declan sung in his deep voice.

Hastily, I switched songs to stop my eyes stinging. The next was The Tea Party's 'Drawing Down The Moon'. Ah, I like The Tea Party, this should get my mind off things.

"Don't leave me now, stay with me...stay with me...stay with me...stay with me, please, please."

OK, wrong song again. I skipped to the following track on my homemade compilation of favourite music. Now, I heard Crowded House play. This should be a safe song...

"And I know I'm right, for the first time in my life... That's why I tell you, you'd better be home soon."

"Next!" I cried out as I skipped tracks once more.

Eventually, I found the Alanis Morissette songs and I listened to those, from her 'Jagged Little Pill' album.

I barely got any sleep with the earphones blasting my ears with music, but at least it drowned out his telepathy.

*****

The next time I opened my eyes, the digital clock read as 8.13 AM.

Feeling more tired than I did before I went to bed, I flung off the earphones and yawned loudly.

When I sat upright, I saw something strange; two white envelopes had been slipped underneath my door.

Frickin' hell, he's found another way to communicate. I felt sorry for the hotel staff, having to carry his messages up. Talk about being caught in the middle, especially when dealing with an angry European Werewolf over the phone.

I threw off the covers and went over to pick them up. I opened them and read the messages which were written on the hotel's stationery. Again, I felt sorry for whatever staff member who took down his correspondence.

"B, would you pick up the *bleep* phone and talk to me? Declan."

I knew what word the *bleep* replaced. It actually made me snicker at the staff's decorum. That was the first note then I read the second one.

"B, if you won't come home to me then I'm leaving home to come to you. I'm catching a midnight flight from Fairbanks. Declan."

"Oh no...!" I moaned, as I lowered the letters.

I shot off another look at the time and saw it was too late to stop him.

Sorry New Haven, you're about to be terrorized by a loud and bossy European Werewolf.

Helplessly, I dropped the messages onto the bed then went into the ensuite to start my day.

*****

Instead of ordering Room Service from the five-star hotel, I ate somewhere else.

I had a Sausage 'n Egg McMuffin with a hash brown and a latte, from McDonald's. I felt too on edge to remain in the hotel room and it was on the way to the bus stop. I was going to use public transport and catch a hover-bus to campus.

I probably looked like a student, wearing sneakers, jeans, a light blue, zip-up sweater and my hair in piggy-tails. I'd put my purse, MP3 player and the hotel's electronic key into my laptop's carry bag with the computer. Of course, I had my mobile phone on me but it was still on silent.

Mind you, the last text message he sent was a couple of hours ago and it mirrored the second note the staff relayed; he was on his way to New Haven.

Damn it, couldn't I have a couple of days Declan-free? I mean, sure I missed him but I hated how territorial he was behaving. I'm his wife he won't divorce and if she goes to the other side of the country, so will he.

I meant what I said, I did need to use Yale's library before my guest lecture. I was thinking of staying in New Haven for the next five days, leading up to the presentation. I could use the peace and quiet, to catch up on research. Also, I thought the five days apart would help by maybe making the heart grow fonder. In the very least, he might reign in his temper tantrums.

The ride on the hover-bus helped to get my mind off things. I listened to my MP3 player as I stared out at the scenery. We passed some pretty parks with the colours of fall, displayed. Giant maple trees were dropping their yellow, red and brown leaves onto the ground, leaving a crunchy, golden snow on the grass. I hopped off and walked through one of the large gardens on campus, towards the library.

I left my music on as I walked inside the building and headed for the Reference Section first. My head bopped along to Lady Gaga's album 'Fame Monster', as I used a computer to look up the books I needed. Some were in ebook format I could borrow by downloading onto my laptop, while others were in hardcopy.

After downloading, I went up a set of stairs to look for the physical books. I tried not to get lost in the row upon row of tall shelves. After perusing several aisles, I found what I was looking for. I pulled down several volumes then headed towards the study area.

I sat down at an available desk and got to work. I turned on my laptop and typed up the quotes I'd use, as well as the footnotes. I became so buried in the books, I didn't notice the hours pass.

*****

I polished off my third book and set it aside to open up the fourth. Although I used my own findings, occasionally I did comparisons to other historians' work. Then if anybody asks, "Have you read so-and-so's paper on blah blah," I could confidently answer with a, "Yes".

But as I hunkered down with the readings, I was distracted by the smell of maple syrup...

Sharply, I looked up, almost expecting to see my husband standing over. But he wasn't and I couldn't see him. I looked about the study area then at the rows of bookshelves, but I didn't spot him.

Could I be imagining this? Or, is it just some kind of crazy withdrawal symptom, for missing my mate? Maybe it's simply someone who had pancakes with maple syrup, for breakfast?

To be safe, I pulled out my mobile phone to check for any new messages. Nope, there weren't any. I checked the time and saw it was past one o'clock. If he got a midnight flight out of Fairbanks then caught several connecting ones, it's possible he could be here by now.

"Dr. Bianca Worthall?"

Huh, what was that? I looked up to find it wasn't my husband standing over, but another tall, blonde-haired man, in his early thirties. He looked lean and tanned, whereas Declan was fair skinned and muscled.

"Yes?"

"I'm Dr. Jason Garret." He smiled down. "We met last year at Columbia University. I did the lecture after yours, on my archaeological dig in Thessaly."

"Oh hi!" I suddenly remembered. "That's right, you brought those ancient pottery pieces with you."

"Guilty." He chuckled then he glanced over my pile of books. "Are you actually studying, or are you checking out the competition?"

My face heated up at how he recognized what I was doing.

"Um, both." I admitted. "I'm lecturing here in five days and I thought I'd better brush up on other people's work."

Next, he implied the books he was carrying, "If you're charged for that offence, I'd be sharing a jail cell with you."

I giggled shyly at his joke.

"Um, may I join you?" He nodded towards the spare chair opposite.

"Oh OK." I tidied up my pile to make room.

He sat down at the desk and put his own work down.

"It looks like you've got a lot done," he looked over my used books.

"Yeah, I've typed up around twelve pages of notes," I indicated my laptop.

"I'd be lost without my computer." He put his on top of the desk.

"So would I." I agreed. "If somebody swiped it, I'd consider paying a ransom to get it back."

"I think I'd do the same." He chuckled. "I've even named it."

"What did you call it?"

"Burt."

"Burt?" I tittered. "Why Burt?"

"You know, as in 'Burt & Ernie' on 'Sesame Street'? They were my favourite characters, growing up. Burt was the smart one and so is my computer. I've also put it through a lot, like Burt had to put up with Ernie's tomfoolery."

I giggled again at his analogy and self-deprecating humour.

"So I should call you Ernie?"

"Only if I can call you Bianca," he grinned.

"How about I call you Jason and you call me B?" I agreed to dropping our titles of 'Dr. This' or 'Dr. That'.

"I tell you what B," he agreed, "the world would be a better place if computers ran it. It'd be a world of logic and scientific fact and accurate mathematical equations."

"Hmm...yes and no." I thought aloud. "Computers are design specific. So if we programmed it to be good then they'll be good. But if they're programmed to be bad then they'll be bad. An evil computer could try to take over the world."

"True," he shrugged. "Then let me rephrase my previous theory; the world would be a better place with a good computer running the show. It'd be a hell of a lot more honest than most politicians who are in power, today."

I smiled back, "I can't say no to that."

"So..." he looked down on his books, "...I suppose I should breeze through these, so I can pretend to be up-to-date on other people's work. Or, do you think it's conceited that I spend the majority of my time, formulating my own theories? At least it's based on evidence I've found, instead of rehashing somebody else's ideas."

"No." I shook my head. "I rely on my own evidence instead of somebody else's."

"I know," he grinned, "which is why I like reading your papers or hearing your lectures. You don't just use somebody else's work and try to put your own spin on it. Your ideas are original and they're backed up with empirical evidence."

"Oh er, thank you." I blushed.

"That's what I love about being an Archaeologist, because I'm discovering something new, there's room for original thinking." He sighed, as he opened up one of his books to a random page. "Listen to this, 'Dr. Gothenburg speculates that the tunics worn by the Priests of Apollo were white linen. However the evidence presented by Dr. Carmichael suggests that they were in fact, blue silk. However, when the Priests ventured outside of the temple, they would have worn a white linen himation, over the blue silk tunic'."

My face turned redder when my last academic identity was read out and I ducked my head.

"See what I mean?" He rolled his eyes. "All this guy is doing is writing about other people's work then giving his own opinion!"

I snickered in agreement as I kept my head lowered.

Just then Jason paused to look on with a serious expression.

"You know what? You write a lot like Dr. Bianca Carmichael and even like Dr. Bianca Riverclaw or Dr. Bianca Wisetail. In fact, your style is the same as your first names, they're identical."

My tone of voice matched his expression, "Are you suggesting plagiarism?"

"Since some of these women died years ago, it'd be hard to prove." He smirked. "But Dr. Bianca Worthall, don't you think it funny how you write about the same topics and use the same methodology as these women...?"

My stomach knotted but I managed to sit still and keep my face expressionless, as I waited for him to continue.

"Are you related?" He wondered. "I made a bet once that you were."

"Yeah, one's my great grandmother, another my grandmother and another was an Aunt." I lied.

"Then what's the deal with the name 'Bianca'?" He queried.

"It's a family tradition." I tried to shrug it off.

"I suppose so." He rolled his eyes. "I mean, I never got why fathers called their sons after themselves, with a Junior on the end. It seems pretty egotistical, to me. I'd be pissed if I were named that way. Can you see me as a Bob Garret Jnr.?"

"Of course not," I said wryly. "You don't even like using other historians' work, so you'd hate having somebody else's name."

"Touché!" He laughed out. "And B, you just helped me win 50 credits."

"Is that for the bet?"

"Yeah and now you're going to let me use the proceeds, to take you out for coffee." He smiled mischievously.

"Um..." I looked away, unsure.

"Hey, it's coffee, not a candle-lit dinner." He held up his hands in an innocent gesture. "I see that wedding ring on your finger."

Nervously, I laughed as I fidgeted with the jewellery on my hand.

"Not many couples marry these days and certainly nobody in their twenties." He mused. "So, what did the guy do, to sweep you off your feet and get you to say yes? Or was it the girl who seduced the guy down the aisle?"

"Well, we grew up together." I began. "And where we come from, when a guy and girl move in together, they're seen as a married anyways. We just 'did the deed' to make it official."

Then he saw me frown as I looked away again, troubled.

"What's wrong?" He asked. "Are there problems in the marriage? You're making me believe the divorce statistics, are right."

"What divorce statistics?" I gave a funny look.

"The divorce rate is up to 89% and a large percentage of these couples, are those who married in their twenties."

"Oh." I straightened in surprise. "I haven't heard that before."

"You haven't? Where've you been hiding, Ancient Greece?" He jested.

"You could say that." I tittered back. "Besides, it was a lot harder for the woman to divorce a man, in those days."

"You got that right." He sat back in his chair. "Women had no independence! They were either under the control of a father or a husband."

"And if there was divorce, the husband kept the children." I shook my head.

"And he could keep the dowry, leaving the wife broke and living off a brother, if her father was dead." He continued.

"Or if she became a Hetairai - a prostitute - she still had to live off a man." I went on. "The Hetairai could attend banquets held by husbands, as the entertainment, while the wife was in another room, weaving cloth."

"And women were married off when they were as young as fifteen."

"Women from poorer families had more freedom than women in richer ones." I said emotionally. "A wealthy woman hardly ever left the house, but a poor one could fetch water from the fountain, or buy food from the markets in the agora."

To Jason's surprise, I started to cry! My eyes watered profusely and I sniffed loudly. I think the topic hit a little too close to home.

Embarrassed, I wiped my face with the sleeves of my sweater.

"So, what does Mr. Worthall do?" He changed the subject.

It took me a second to realize he meant my husband, by applying my pseudonym to him too.

"His name is Declan and he's a mechanic. He runs the Garage where we live on tribal lands. Yesterday, we had a fight about my academic work. But lately, it feels like we've been arguing about anything and everything."

"How long have you two been together?"

"Years and years," I laughed it off. "We grew up fighting and I used to think we married because there was nobody we'd rather fight with. Now, it's grown old and I long for some peace and quiet."

"Let me guess, he doesn't like it when you go away for work." He said knowingly.

"Um, yeah...?" I gave a peculiar look at how he knew that.

"I went through the same thing in my last relationship." He shared. "I lived with Claire for two years, when I was doing my PhD. She was a Mathematician who liked to experimental cook."

"Experimental cook?" I echoed.

"Yeah, she made biscuits out of breakfast cereals, or she tried making dishes using Halal or Kosher ingredients, or anything else multicultural. It was like eating in a different country each week!" He laughed at the memory.

"Really?" I listened.

"She tried to make Sushi but her Nori Rolls would fall apart." He smilingly shook his head. "Or one week, she cooked using Chinese steaming methods."

"How did the two of you meet?"

"At a Fraternity Party, at College." He stared off into the distance. "We dated for a month before we moved in together."

"That's fast," I commented.

"Yeah, I guess it was soon." He shrugged. "But we were spending nearly every night together, anyway. So when her roommate moved out, we said, 'what the hell', and I moved in to help with the rent."

"And you two lived together for two years?"

"Yeah." He sighed. "My archaeological digs hurt the relationship, especially when I'd be away for weeks at a time."

"Are you both seeing other people now?"

"I've heard she's living with a new guy," he squirmed in his seat. "But I'm keeping my options open."

"What does that mean?"

"I'm afraid to commit," he gave a goofy grin, which made me laugh. "With my work, it's hard to settle down. So I have friends with benefits instead."

"Friends with benefits...?" I shook my head. "I couldn't do something like that."

"Why not?"

"Where I come from, the values are very old fashioned." I warned. "If you're sleeping with someone, you're usually in a long term relationship."

"Is that how you and Declan got together?" He guessed again.

"You could say that."

"I could never get married." He said adamantly.

"Why?"

"To spend your life with one person and that person, alone?" He questioned. "People fall in and out of love, every day. There's no point in making an empty promise you know you can't keep."

This made me look down again and I busied myself by saving my notes.

It made me wonder what would happen if Declan and I did divorce? I was the first Lokoti Werewolf to take a second mate and now I'll be the first to leave them. Also, what would happen to our plan of turning him into a Circulator, to join me in the space time continuum? What's the etiquette, does one still exist for eternity with an ex-husband?

Our casual conversation was stirring up a big ole, emotional dust cloud.

"I don't know about you, but I know I'm not going to be able to concentrate on studying now." He grimaced at the sight of his books. "How about we go and get that cup of coffee?"

"Sure, why not."

*****

We left the library via the self-check-out so we could take the books with us. We scanned our World Wide Library Cards then the books before walking away with them. Whereas Jason could shove his into his backpack, I didn't have room in my laptop carry case. I carried my computer over the shoulder and the books in my arms.

"Can I carry that for you?" He offered as we walked out.

"No, it's cool." I smiled back. "But thanks."

I was stronger than him, which he didn't know, but I appreciated the offer.

We strolled a short distance to a nearby café and took an outdoor table in the sun.

Once we sat down, I rested my books on top of the table. We each picked up a menu and my stomach rumbled. When the waitress came to take our orders, I requested a Grilled Cheese, Tomato and Avocado Focaccia, as well as a latte.

"Actually, I'll have the same." He agreed.

The waitress input our orders in her PDA then moved on to serve someone else.

"Look, don't buy my coffee today because I'm eating as well." I said guiltily. "Shout me coffee next time."

"Hey, a bet's a bet and a deal's a deal." He smilingly shook his head. "Our lattes are 4 credits each and the focaccia is 8 credits each. Altogether, our lunch comes to 24 credits, leaving me 26 credits to spend another day."

"Then I'll pay the next time we meet up at one of these academic shindigs." I offered.

"I like the sound of that." His smile grew wider. "It means this little outing of ours, won't be a one and only event."

I looked away to stare at the surrounding parkland. The afternoon sun, shining through the fall coloured leaves, put a golden glow on things. I found myself sitting back in my seat, relaxing in the warmth of the later part of the day.

"I have a confession." Jason recalled my attention. "I've wanted to sit down and talk to you, since we met at Columbia last year. I wanted to ask about your research methods. The computer graphically enhanced photos you use, are so accurate, anyone would think that you took the pictures back in time."

I laughed loudly as if he just made a joke.

"I'm always being asked about my photos." I tittered. "And I'll tell you what I keep telling everyone else, it's all Photoshop."

"Yeah but the ruins you recreate, look brand new! When the paint's peeling or the facade is cracked, you seem to know what the artwork was like. How do you do it? How do you know a disintegrating wall was painted ochre once?"

"Easy," I shrugged. "I'm not an archaeologist so I haven't been on any digs, but I still visit the locations. If a temple wall was painted in ochre with blue and green trim in one city, I'll look at another temple in the same culture and assume it could be similar. I make a deduction and then I'll test this theory, to see if it's correct."

"Sounds a lot like what I do." He laughingly shook his head. "I have an idea of what I'm looking for then I go searching."

After a moment I said, "Look around and tell me what you see."

Jason looked about the busy café, at the waitress and waiter weaving around the tables, at the students walking past then out towards the old buildings.

"I see University life," he shrugged.

"Exactly!" I said ecstatically. "University life, a culture at this point in time and space. You're looking at a scene, or a stolen moment. We're in an era with witnesses, whose lives cross over this time and place."

He remained quiet as he listened closely.

I went on, "Have you ever walked into a building at night when it's empty, but you feel a residual energy from when it was busy? Or, have you ever been in a shopping centre after hours? The place is deserted, but you can almost hear a crowd."

He agreed, "Or, back to that building at night; like an old house for example. Everyone's gone to bed but you can hear footsteps. You get up to make sure it's not a burglar, when it's the floorboards moving back into place. But you've walked on them again, so when you go back to bed, they creak even more."

"Yeah and that's what history is to me." I told him. "You're standing in a place and recapturing moments in time and space. You're exploring people's lives, who lived long, long ago. You're becoming a witness to their era."

He smiled softly, "That's what it's like for me too, when I'm at a site and we unearth something that time has tried to hide. We bring it back to the surface after thousands of years and in a way, I feel like I'm playing a game of 'Hide & Seek' with time itself. It buries something and leaves us to find what it left behind."

"I like that," I beamed back. "'We unearth something that time has tried to hide'. It's a thrill, isn't it?"

Then the Waitress returned to our table, carrying a tray laden with our lunches.

"Ooh, yum!" My nostrils flared at the delicious smell.

"Enjoy," she smiled before she moved away.

"Oh, I think we will." Jason shared my look of anticipation.

*****

The food may have disappeared quickly, but the conversation went for longer. When the waitress came to take away our empty plates, we ordered another latte each. Then the two latte's turned into three and the three turned into four. The afternoon sun sunk lower in the sky and the air began to feel chilly.

Mainly, we talked about work. I listened to his funny stories of things that could and did go wrong on different digs. I laughed at tents collapsing in the middle of the night, or how his camping stove broke and he couldn't light a fire, so he had to eat his rations raw. I heard how he had a crash course in the language of the foreign country he was in, when his interpreters didn't turn up.

"But you know what, B?" He ended with a happy sigh. "I wouldn't trade it for the world."

"Travelling for work?"

"Yeah, it's tough on relationships but the pros outweigh the cons. I think the real reason why Claire and I split up, because she realized as much as I loved her, I probably loved my work more." He spoke honestly.

"Hmm, that would hurt." I frowned.

"Is it a source of contention for you and Declan, too?" He queried.

"He hates it when I go away." I leaned on the table. "I get in trouble if I'm gone for too long."

"But you can't quit either, can you?" He asked knowingly.

"Nope." I shook my head. "History is part of me, it makes up who I am."

"What else do you and he fight about?" He wondered. "You said that the two of you have been fighting over anything and everything."

"Long story," I said dismissively. "Besides, our relationship has its good points too. It's just worried me that it's been so bad lately."

"Maybe it means that the relationship is winding down and the two of you have come to the end of the road?" He said gently.

"Er, I don't know." I faltered. "I'd rather not talk about it, if that's OK."

"No problem," he shrugged it off. "Besides, I'm not the best relationship counsellor with my track record."

Then I noticed how low the sun was in the sky and I checked the time.

"Frickin' hell, it's past 4 PM!" I sat up straighter. "We've been talking non-stop for three hours."

"So?" He smiled. "It's been one of the best, if not the longest conversations, I've had in a while."

I had to admit, "Same here."

Next, I started to pack up my things and Jason followed suit.

"Where are you off to now?" He asked.

"I think I might head back to my hotel."

"Where are you staying?"

"In New Haven, I think it's called The Hi-Life." I answered.

"The Hi-Life?" He teased. "Now you're making me worried that you're getting paid more than me, on the lecture circuit."

I laughed uneasily at his joke then he went inside the café to settle the bill. I stood up, slung my carry bag over my shoulder and picked up my books again. I waited until he returned and he put his backpack on.

"I'm staying at the good ole Holiday Inn, which is two blocks down from your hotel. I'll see you back." He offered.

"No, it's cool." I reassured. "I know the way."

"I'm not saying you don't, but I'll split cab fare with you."

"No, I'm OK." I shook my head. "I caught a hover-bus here so I'll catch another back."

"C'mon, a cab would be easier." He needled. "Do you have a bus timetable? What if you have to wait forever?"

Oh, I didn't want to sit around waiting in the cold. After a moment, I gave a nod. He chuckled at my change of my mind then he led the way to a taxi stand.

*****

When the taxi took us to my hotel, Jason got out too. We swiped our individual credit cards then climbed out of the cab. We stood on the sidewalk and he gawked at where I was staying.

"You're living the Hi-Life and you still catch public transport?" He mocked.

"I also got McDonald's for breakfast." I giggled. "Am I a rebel or what?"

"You deviant!" He gave a playful nudge.

"So..." I wondered what to say, "...I'm sure we'll bump into each other at our lectures next week."

He took his phone out of his pocket, "What's your number? Maybe we can have dinner tomorrow night? Since we're both staying in New Haven, it makes no sense to eat alone."

I hesitated as I was unsure whether it would be proper or not. I didn't want him to get the wrong idea. But he seemed like a nice guy and I didn't want to offend. So, we exchanged phone numbers.

"OK, I'll see you tomorrow night." I put my mobile back into my pocket.

"Bye B." He said warmly then watched me go inside.

I crossed the hotel's foyer and headed straight for the elevators. I hit the button then stood back and waited. The next thing I knew, I wasn't alone.

"Jason?" I gave a peculiar look.

"I forgot my manners," he said. "We're History Professors, we should know back in the old days, it was customary for the guy to walk the girl to her door."

"Yeah, but you've already seen me back to my hotel."

The elevator doors opened and before I could stop him, he went in. I did too and I hit the button for my floor then stood back. A couple more people came inside before the doors shut again.

"Listen, did you want to go out and get a drink or something?" He offered, when the lift started to move. "You seemed upset, earlier today. Did you want to drown your sorrows while you bare your soul?"

"Er, I can't drink alcohol."

"Why?"

"I'm allergic." I lied. "Thanks for your concern, but I'll be OK."

"Or, did you want to go out to dinner, tonight?" He counter offered. "There's this Chinese restaurant near my hotel that makes a great Peking Duck."

I took a step back in the small space, as he was starting to make me feel uncomfortable.

"Um, I was planning on staying in and finishing my studies."

Then we arrived at my floor and he stepped out with me. When I started to walk down the carpeted corridor, he followed behind. I wondered how I could politely ask him to go away?

"I suppose you're right, it's not like I got any studying done today." He mused. "What if we cram together and order up some Room Service?"

I stopped in front of my door and faced him.

"Look Jason, you seem like a nice guy." I began. "But I'm a married woman."

"Not a happily married one." He returned.

"If I sent out the wrong signal then I'm sorry." I continued. "I don't think we should have dinner tonight or tomorrow night."

He shoved his hands in his pockets and his face looked a little pink.

"Wow, I'm just throwing myself at you, aren't I?" He said embarrassed.

"Yeah, you are."

"Sorry," his face reddened. "I'm probably coming across as some loser who makes passes at uninterested women. But I swear, the way we opened up to each other, today? I detected a chemistry."

Damn my pheromones, they did it again! But he was right, we did have a lot in common. I felt sorry for him and even guilty that this may have been my fault.

"Let's part as friends and catch up next week, at the lectures." I suggested, as I took out my electronic key.

Then I opened my door and we were both in for a surprise when Declan stood up from the couch.

"Who the hell are you?!" Jason demanded, as he protectively moved in front.

He thought I was being burgled, whereas my mate fixed the filthiest look I'd ever seen, on who he thought was his rival.

"No Jason, it's OK." I pulled him back. "That's Declan, my husband. Although, I don't know how he got inside my hotel room...?"

"THAT'S your husband?" He stared. "But he's so old."

I saw the veins in Declan's thick neck stand out and I sensed he was restraining himself.

To prevent a European Werewolf attack, I pushed Jason out into the hallway.

"You really need to leave now," I said gruffly.

"But B, wait a minute." He stood in the corridor. "That guy is so much older than you! No wonder your marriage isn't working out."

"Jason, please -"

"When you said you grew up with him, I thought he was your age." He carried on. "You shouldn't feel bad that you want to go out and experience the world, when he's past that. Don't be tied down to the wrong guy."

I overheard a dangerously low growl come from behind and I knew I had to act fast.

"Goodbye Jason."

I slammed the door in his face then I whirled around to confront my husband.

"I can see you got a lot of work done today." Declan said sarcastically. "You sat at that café and talked for hours."

My hands moved to my hips, "How long have you been watching me?"

"Since the idiot sat down with you in the library."

I knew it, I DID have his scent! I should have trusted my instincts. Although I couldn't see the predator, I should have known he was there.

"How did you get into my hotel room?" I demanded.

"I showed my ID at the Check-In desk to prove that I was your husband." He said coolly. "Do I need to show it to you too?"

"Ha ha, very funny," I said flatly.

"As usual, you've acted more like a 'Light Person' than a Lokoti Werewolf." He complained. "A Lokoti Werewolf would never walk out on a mate. A Lokoti Werewolf would never mention the word 'divorce'. A Lokoti Werewolf would have picked up the scent of their mate, miles away. I tracked you down by scent alone, from the hotel to that College library."

"So you're proud of your stalking? Oh yeah, there's nothing unusual or creepy in that, at all. " I rolled my eyes.

I wandered over to sit on the end of the bed as he began to pace.

"And I heard what you said to that loser, about me and about us." He said unhappily. "We DON'T argue ALL the time! Of course I don't like it when you go away for work! Wouldn't you be more worried, if I was pushing you out the door, instead?!"

"Maybe with your behaviour lately that's what you've been doing."

"With MY behaviour lately? Don't try to take the 'saintly' road with me! Our fighting has been me telling you, to clean up your act!"

What act was there for me to clean? He's accused me of being a bubble-brain when it comes to money and then got angry when I proved him wrong. I refused to let him put the guilt on me, so I stood up.

"Then I'll call my PA and she can put me in touch with a divorce lawyer so you won't have to put up with me anymore!" I announced.

I pulled out my phone when Declan moved so fast, I almost didn't see him coming.

He hit my mobile out of my hand so hard, it smashed against the wall! He hadn't hurt me, but my phone now lay in pieces on the carpet. I stood there and stared at the damage.

"I hope for your sake that the memory is still OK and I didn't just lose fifty phone numbers which aren't written down." I said coldly. "And you tell me I'm a spendthrift? Now I'm going to have to buy a new phone!"

Declan growled infuriated as he recommenced pacing up and down.

"Explain it to me B, explain the concept of divorce to the man who's been more than married, but mated to the one person all his life! Explain it to the husband who's loved his wife for nearly two centuries! Explain it to me, like you'd explain it to the pack, how you'll end the biological bond, B!"

I sat back down on the end of the bed and coolly looked away.

"Humans get divorced because they're NOT biologically bound to someone!" Declan ranted. "Humans can't hear each other's thoughts! Humans don't feel what their mate is feeling! Humans can't regenerate by feeding each other their blood! Human husbands and wives haven't fought for their lives, side-by-side, like we have!"

Then he stopped pacing to come and stand over his wife in an intimidating manner.

"Explain to me how you even came to think about THAT word?!" He bit out.

Coolly, I stood up so I could look him right in the eye, as I spoke. "The first time I thought that word in relation to us, was last night."

"Why, B?" He looked on, hurt.

"Because I won't take it anymore," I said.

"Take what anymore?"

"The way you talk to me, the way you yell at me, or the way you boss me around... and you know what, Declan?"

"No B, what?"

"It occurred to me, why would I want to spend eternity with someone like that anyway?"

Declan's face fell and he actually looked wounded by my words.

"So what, you don't want to turn me into a Circulator anymore?" He asked with wide eyes.

"You accused me last night that I don't think of the future." My eyes narrowed. "Well guess what? I think about it all the time! When I look at our past together, sometimes I wonder if we even have a future!"

His blue eyes filled with tears as it was my turn to rant and pace.

"I thought you were the rudest boy in the tribe when we were growing up! Then we fell in love and I thought you were just misunderstood. Two hundred years later, I see you really are the rudest male in the tribe. When we were little, you yelled at me, bossed me around to the point of bullying and you're STILL doing it!"

I watched his tears escape and he let them trickle down his face.

I continued, "The younger men come to YOU for advice and you call THEM morons for the mistakes they make? Well, what about us? Declan help me, my wife says I don't talk to her nicely. Then change your tone of voice, you idiot! Declan, tell me what to do, my wife says I yell at her too much. Then stop yelling at her, you fool! Declan, what do I do? My wife tells me that she's so unhappy with me that she wants to end our marriage! Then look at what's wrong with the relationship and see if your unhappiness is making her unhappy!"

His eyes dropped and he uttered out, "I am unhappy."

I stopped pacing as this revelation hit me like a bowling ball to the stomach. It didn't surprise me, but it still hurt to hear him say it. I'd suspected something was wrong but until now, he wouldn't talk about it.

"I know you are," my eyes watered. "You've been unhappy with us for the past couple of years. It's also why I came to New Haven for a week, to give you space to work things out."

"I've been unhappy for nearly a decade now," he said in a tight voice.

My chest hurt so much it physically ached and I went to sit on the couch.

I said tearfully, "It's why you're flattered by Raquel's attention. It's why you haven't told her to go and jump, like you did with Brigitte Stirling. It's why you've been yelling at me more than usual. It's why you're quick to find fault with everything I do."

Declan remained quiet as he stood by the window with his hands in his pockets. It was like all the fight had left him, which I found worrying. He was standing so still, he looked like a statue.

"But still, we've had a good run." I sighed in resignation. "We were the tribe's longest married couple, as well as the most argumentative. But I'm sure they'll understand why we've come to an end. We've not only beaten human couples, but also those involving a Werewolf. I suppose it's good that we realized this now, instead of inside the continuum when we're stuck together for eternity."

He still didn't say anything and I curled up into a ball, in a corner of the couch.

"You shouldn't feel like you're stuck with me, just because I'm your only avenue of getting laid." I spoke again. "If you wanted to turn Raquel or another woman, you could talk to the pack. They could help you train who you turn, to hunt animal instead of human."

"Shut up, B." He said in a low voice. "If you and I split, there's no way in hell I'd turn a human woman into one of my kind."

Then my Circulator mind started to plan for other contingencies to ensure that he wouldn't be alone.

I cleared my throat, "You could look for a female in another breed. Surely, there'd be female North American Werewolves out there. According to the SSIT report, they'd most likely be single too. We could use the Viewing Room to track one down and -"

"Would you STOP trying to 'pimp' me out?!" He interrupted. "If we separate, I'm NOT going to immediately screw someone else!"

"Then what do you want?!" I retorted, tired of his temper.

"You haven't even asked the important question such as WHY I'm unhappy!" He walked over to where I was sitting.

"Why are you unhappy, Declan?" I asked sarcastically.

"Well B, let's see..." he replied in a matching tone, "...I'm unhappy because I'm aging and my mate isn't! I'm unhappy at the change in people's views of us, thinking that I'm much older than you are! I'm unhappy because the old idea of you were too good for me, has come up again. I see it in people's eyes when they regard us! Your father made me feel like crap and I feel like that again!"

"Who the hell is thinking THAT?!" I demanded.

"You just saw it in that loser you had lunch with!" He flared. "I see it when I go into Alma with you."

"Yes well, they're outsiders so they don't know any better!" I sneered. "Or, have you forgotten Bitch One and Bitch Two, who used to gossip about me, in the supermarket? In fact, you used to laugh about it!"

"That was different!"

"No it wasn't!" I stood up to stare him down. "Not only did they bitch about my youthfulness, but about the fact that I couldn't have kids! They were plain spiteful and you thought it was funny!"

I walked over to the end of the bed and sat down again as Declan continued to shout.

"Why the hell did you think that running away to New Haven would help? I already hate how consumed you are with academic work, as it is! When you go away for your lectures or you become buried in your work, you don't even think about me! I cook a gourmet dinner for you, but I have to ask you over and over again to get your books off the table. Then I see you laughing over work with that academic sleaze bag, today. You and I haven't laughed like that in years!"

I couldn't take it anymore... His anger and jealousy was like a bitter bile building up, as it also weighed down my shoulders with stress. I started to cry, as I felt downtrodden by his verbal beating.

"Then what do you want...?" I cried. "For me to make myself look older? Would you stop yelling if I always looked like a fifty year old woman?"

"How many times do I have tell you?" He said tiredly. "I hate it when you make yourself older. I smell your blood pressure goes up and your bones become brittle. Everyone else loses their spouse to old age, do you think I want to see that happen to you? You're my youthful Circulator, you're my glow-in-the-dark girl."

Then Declan dropped to his knees to meet my tearful eyes with his own. His hands reached out to hold my upper arms, to help him hold my gaze. We both sniffled with our pink noses and watery eyes.

"I'm not refusing divorce because I'm scared of losing my only avenue of sex, either." He said emotionally. "B, you are my mate! Why do you have so much trouble understanding this simple concept? Why do you think that I'm unhappy because I'm tired of you? Why do you think I want to be with another woman? Why can't you see that I'm fighting for you, to keep you?"

I said sadly, "Why can't you see that your yelling and your temper tantrums are pushing me away?"

"It seems like the only time you notice me anymore, is when I yell." He rolled his eyes. "You're always making plans that don't include me. You seem happier to hang out with your work colleagues who are younger men, instead of your husband who looks like he's in his fifties."

"I used to feel proud when you corrected outsiders by telling them I was only three years younger than you." I told him. "But I haven't heard you say that in fifty years."

His fingers dug into my arms, "Of course I can't say that anymore! Certainly not off tribal lands. You're a Circulator and you're the last one at that. I could no more put you at risk, than I could point a gun at my head!"

I let out a sob and he pulled me closer to rub his wet face against mine.

His hot breath landed on my skin as he said, "You're my reason for living. I'll always watch over you. But when I watch you come and go, to and fro, as a Circulator and a History Professor? It eats me up inside, because you treat me as if you don't need me as much as I need you!"

"How can you say that when we're biologically bound together?" I asked crossly. "I heard you telepathically call me last night, all the way from Alaska!"

He kept his face squashed against mine, "You have Taurus Six and the Circulate Mainframe. You have Hodge Endeavor. You have your own money and you travel whenever and wherever you want. Sometimes I wonder, 'is today the day she doesn't come back'?"

"How can you say that?" I grabbed hold of his arms too, to give him a shake. "You're MY Declan! You're MY European Werewolf! You give me passion! You're the one who can make my aura turn a peach colour! You warm me every night and hold me like you'll never let go."

"Say that again...?" He said hoarsely.

"You're my first sex and you're my best sex. You make me laugh and you make me cry. We hunt together and we kill together. We share blood and I crave no man but you."

"Say that again...?" He breathed out.

"You're the boy who drove me home at dawn and put his hand over mine and made my heart pound. You're the one who stopped me from eating a human when I first changed. You were the boy that I liked kissing in Werewolf or human form."

His wet lips grazed mine as he murmured, "Say that again...?"

"You're the man that broke convention by seducing a Lokoti Werewolf into mating a second time."

Then Declan took over by engulfing my mouth with his. We kissed over and over, as our tongues twisted and entwined. My hands ran through his short, silvery-blonde hair, as his rested on my thighs.

"Tell me I'm the man that's going to exist with you for eternity," he briefly pulled away, "and I'll never yell at you again."

This made me pause and I looked into his wrinkled gaze and I saw truth.

"But the occasional growl is allowed," a smile escaped.

His hands ran up and down the inside of my thighs, "Baby that's a given."

My legs fell apart and he moved in closer so our crotches were touching. I clung to his old leather jacket as his lips smothered mine. He breathed hard as his hands started to unbutton my jeans.

"I like your growls," I admitted, as I tugged off his coat. Then I said, "Shoes."

His hands slid down my legs to take off my sneakers, "Oh yeah?"

"I like your sarcasm," I said, before I kissed him again.

"Good, because so do I," he chuckled, as he also removed my socks.

Hastily, he released me to whip off his jumper along with his long-sleeved t-shirt. Then he started on my zip-up sweater and my t-shirt. I helped by raising my arms so he could remove my clothes.

"I like it when you swear under your breath," I ran my hands down his muscled chest.

"You weren't supposed to hear that." He snickered.

"I like it when you sing to me," I pulled him closer.

"Candy, Candy, Candy I can't let you go," he removed my bra.

I laid back on the bed whilst pulling him over me. He came along willingly, as he kicked off his shoes then his socks. I undid his jeans and he discarded them before lying over his wife.

"Are you sure you want to be doing this, forever?" I asked liltingly.

"To eternity and back," he panted, as he rubbed his body against mine.

"Into infinity come?"

"Absolutely...!" He sighed longingly, as he removed the last bar between us, which was my underwear.

Once the cotton panties were flung away, I wrapped my legs about his hips. "Completely and utterly together?"

"For eternity, forever, absolutely, completely, utterly and times by infinity." He moaned.

I felt him rub his member around my moistening entrance and I heard him groan when we came together. At first he slowly moved in and out, with his eyes closed. But I felt his yearning, by how deeply he pushed whilst holding on tightly.

He picked up in strength before displaying it, by suddenly sitting upright and lifting me into his lap. I held onto his shoulders as I slowly started to ride him. He also had control over our speed, by pushing my hips back and forth.

"I have to admit, my sex life would have been a hell of a lot more boring, without you!" I gasped.

"Hey, once you go green, you don't go with anything else." He opened his eyes to show their supernatural colour.

My nails turned claw-like as they embedded in his skin. He continued to push slowly, as our hips came together then parted and came together again. The rhythm was hypnotic and sensuous. Then he dipped me backwards and my head rolled as my eyes closed. His hot, wet mouth engulfed my right nipple and then the left.

He heaved me up and when my eyes opened again, they were glowing turquoise. They met his glowing green ones, with the narrow slits for pupils. Our mouths were open from panting and I saw his teeth were jagged and sharp.

My mate held my moving torso tightly against his and he ducked his head. I didn't flinch or cry out when he bit into my right shoulder. Instead, my claws dug deeper into his back, drawing blood. We both groaned in pleasure and pain that the other caused.

BITE ME B, HAVE ME WHILE I HAVE YOU - He willed.

My breasts were squeezed against his wide chest, as our groins were pressed together. I closed my eyes as I inhaled his maple syrup scent coming off his sweaty skin. Then I brought my teeth down between his left shoulder and neck. His thick, salty and vaguely sweet, blood pumped into my mouth.

I felt his jaws unlock from my shoulder as his head rose in a silent roar... Then his mouth returned to the wound and I felt his tongue lap at the broken skin. I mirrored what he was doing as I felt his fluid in my mouth and between my legs. The heat of both was intoxicating and I clung to him.

Declan didn't stop moving nor did he falter, as he pushed onwards. Soon I felt my back hit the mattress, as he laid over me again. In this position, he could speed up as well as adjust the angle, as he helped his wife with her own climax.

~~~~~~

~ 25 ~

The sun set over the Andes as our hover-car zoomed around the narrow mountain road. The late afternoon light looked glorious, the sky was bright pink with the horizon a deep purple. The high, rocky peaks were contrasted against the twilight.

Either from the altitude or because it was getting dark, I felt cold. I closed my window and when Declan saw, he put up his too. His hand left the window control and so he wouldn't overheat, he turned all the air vents in his direction. Then to help warm me, he rested his hot hand on my thigh.

"Thanks," I acknowledged.

Both of us were wearing cargo shorts, t-shirts and sneakers. It had been a hot morning when we left Piura, on the north coast of Peru.   Then it steadily became cooler as we climbed and the altitude changed.

With his hand in my lap, he felt how cold I was by the goose bumps on my skin. "Gees B, why didn't you say something sooner?"

"I wasn't this cold, before." I reassured. "It came upon me, like the night."

Declan chuckled at the analogy as his hand rubbed my leg.

"That's my wife." He said fondly. "My own little 'Light Person', who needs constant warmth and sunlight. Don't worry, when we hit the jungle, you'll be feeling the heat again."

"I know," I giggled, as I momentarily captured his hand and squeezed it.

Our rental rounded a wide corner which gave way to a spectacular view. Before us was lush forest floor, with the greenish-blue hue of nature, complimenting perfectly the purple horizon. Declan was such an expert at driving, he navigated the turns with one hand while admiring the scenery at the same time.

"It's so beautiful...!" I uttered out.

"We should have done a tour of South America, sooner." He agreed.

We exchanged small smiles at the reason which brought us here; our 200th Wedding Anniversary.

Night settled over the valley first before the darkness crept up the sides of the mountains, with the last of the daylight fading over the peaks.

We cruised along the two-lane highway with the hover-car's headlights and GPS guiding the way. The road twisted and turned and my ears popped at the change in elevation. Slowly but surely, we were winding down the mountainside towards the 'selva', which was the Amazon jungle. According to the car's computer, we were in the Amazonas which was a different region, or the old name for it was the Amazonian Andes. Before the last of the light disappeared, I didn't see rainforest, but tropical forest.

As much as I was enjoying the drive, I started to feel the familiar pangs of the female curse.

"How much longer until we reach Borja?" I queried. "That's where we're staying overnight, isn't it?"

"In about two hours." He read off the GPS. "Why, do you need a bathroom break?"

I was about to tell him to keep going when the pain increased. I grunted in discomfort, before picking up my water bottle from the cup-holders. I found it was empty and when I checked Declan's, so was his.

"I think there's a small town ahead." He advised. "We can recharge the hover-car as well as get some drinks."

"Yes please." I slumped back into my seat.

He noticed how I curled up into a ball with my arms wrapped around my abdomen.

"It's not long now." He promised. "Did you remember to pack your pills?"

I bent over towards my handbag sitting on the floor. Next, I pulled out the small, white, plastic bottle and rattled the contents. He saw it as he used his hand to rub my leg again.

"That's my girl," he winked.

Then he had to take his hand back to navigate a tricky part of the road. We glided down another steep incline which was also on a sharp corner. The lights of the small town in the valley below, glimmered up like a welcome sign.

I couldn't wait to buy something sweet to drink, to wash down the painkillers. The cramps steadily grew worse, also making my hips and legs ache. Inwardly, I berated my body for its painful reminder of being a woman.

*****

We pulled into a Service Station that also had a 'cafetería', which was a combined bar and 'restaurante'.

Once Declan recharged the vehicle's power cells, he parked it on the side. Then hand-in-hand, we walked into the establishment. He pushed open the wooden door and gallantly, held it open for his wife.

"Thanks," I smiled.

After giving another wink, he led by the hand over to a table. As soon as we were seated, we picked up the laminated menus. Whereas I perused the drinks on offer, he eyed the food.

"Maybe we should have a snack, so you don't take your medication on an empty stomach." He frowned.

"You'll come up with any excuse to eat," I teased.

"Even our Medicine Man says you should take them with food," he reminded.

"If I do they don't work as fast," I scowled.

Just then, he caught me wince as another wave of agony made me double over.

"Er, waitress?" He put up his hand. "I mean, oiga por favor!"

A pretty Peruvian girl who looked just out of her teens, came over to take our order.

"Hola," he greeted. "Hay alguien aquí que hable inglés?"

"Si, I mean, yes." She nodded.

Once he established she could understand English, he went straight to business.

"Can we please get a Coca Cola, an orange Fanta and the..." his eyes skimmed over the menu, "...Anticuchos?"

She input our requests into her PDA, took our menus then walked off.

"What did you just order?" I wondered.

"I'm not sure," he said, baffled. "But it was in the starters section, so it should be snack-type food."

"As long as it isn't guinea pig or 'cuy', as they call it here." I smirked.

"Don't be so judgmental." He gave a nudge. "You eat moose, caribou, bear or dall sheep when we hunt. Some people may think that's strange, too."

Thankfully, our waitress soon returned with our drinks. Declan watched me retrieve the painkillers and put six tablets on my palm. Then he frowned when I gulped them down along with half of the Fanta.

"Six tablets?" His eyebrows rose.

"Don't start."

"When we first married you took two then around our centenary you took four. Now it's our bicentennial and you need six? You're definitely eating something." He said unhappily.

After ten minutes two things arrived, my relief from the torture and our order. She put down the plate along with our cutlery and serviettes before moving on. At the same time, Declan and I leaned over to sniff at the dish.

"They look like shish-kebabs." I observed. "But what's that dip it comes with?"

"I can smell garlic, so I think it's safe." He answered. "Look, we get some bread with it."

Now I was the one watching him, as he picked up a skewer with meat on it and took a bite.

"Mmm, it's good." He promised. "I think the meat is marinated beef heart."

That tempted me into picking up another and gingerly taking a nibble.

"Mmm, it is good." I nodded along. "We're eating a cow's heart, how apt considering what we are."

Declan chuckled in agreement as he dunked some of the bread into the dip. I followed suit then he picked up another skewer. Soon, we were scoffing down the delicious dish.

"I like sharing food." I spoke after I swallowed. "It's like we have the best of both worlds, especially when we each order something different."

"Mmm," he nodded in agreement but kept eating.

There were six Anticuchos, but I stopped at two to let him have the other four.

Smilingly, I shook my head at how fast he cleared the plate.

It was then we were interrupted and indeed, all of the 'restaurante' was. The wooden door opened so hard, it banged loudly against the wall. Six adolescent boys noisily came in, ranging between 16-18 years old. Three of them had long, dark hair as the other three had scruffy, black hair.

They seated themselves three tables away. My eyes narrowed when I saw them pull away chairs from nearby tables, without asking if they were being used. As they proceeded to sit down, they put up their feet, marking the table with their dirty shoes.

I noticed the uncomfortable looks on the other diners' faces. It appeared they recognized the rowdy boys and even the waitress and her boss looked wary. As predators, we could detect the elevated adrenaline in the humans or basically put, we could smell their fear. I wondered if we should do something? If we were on home soil then as one of our people's protectors, we'd move them on.

Declan must have sensed what I was thinking, because he said quietly, "Let's just finish our drinks and get out of here."

I nodded back and picked up my glass again.

The boys called out to the girl to come and wait on them. They also called out a couple of other things which I couldn't understand. She looked frightened and her boss glared from behind the bar. Seeing the scared look on her face made my protective instinct kick-in. My nails which were drumming on top of the table, increased in length.

"B, this isn't our territory." My mate said softly. "We can't risk a fight in such a public place and give ourselves away."

I passed him a look of disbelief that he could be so uncaring.

"Besides, can't you smell it?" He leaned in to say. "They're either drunk or on drugs, as there's something strong on their breath."

Inconspicuously, I inhaled deeply before I whispered back, "I don't think it's alcohol."

"Whatever it is, we're staying out of it." He said firmly.

Sympathetically, I looked on the harassed young woman. She tried to carry on as normal, as she ignored the shouting and went to serve some other customers. But as she passed, one of the boys smacked her on the bottom!

She squealed as she jumped in terror. Next, she scrambled away from her molesters. Meanwhile, the boys laughed loudly and congratulated their cohort.

I felt a growl build up in my throat as my sharpening teeth clenched together. I wanted to give these little hooligans a lesson in manners! Hatefully, I seethed in their direction when I noticed something about their eyes.

Typical for South Americans, they had straight, black hair and bronzed skin. But instead of having brown eyes, their eyes were yellow. In fact, the yellow irises were so large, I could barely see the whites at all. It gave them a feline-like quality, which seemed more supernatural than natural.

THEY'RE NOT HUMAN! - I sat upright, alert.

WHAT ARE YOU TALKING ABOUT? OF COURSE THEY'RE HUMAN! - he thought back.

I leaned over to whisper, "Look at their eyes, Declan."

He glanced over to see what I was talking about, when I saw him frown in concern.

"I don't know why their eyes are like that, but they're human." He spoke at a decibel only I could hear. "Maybe it has something to do with whatever's on their breath?"

"But how?" I wondered.

"Beats me!" He shrugged. "But I'm telling you, they're human."

I watched the waitress purposefully walk the long way around, to avoid the bullies. They were still calling out crass things in their native language. I wanted to smack their dirty mouths shut!

"C'mon B," he pushed away the empty plate. "Let's go before trouble starts."

Declan stood up first before pulling out my chair. Reluctantly, I followed him over to the register as he paid for our food and drinks. While I walked behind though, I heard new wolf-whistles and more shouting.

When I turned to pass them another dirty look, I found they weren't whistling at the waitress, but they were whistling at me!

As if he sensed this, Declan protectively pulled me close to his side.

"My apologies señor," the barman said awkwardly. "We have thrown them out several times in the past, but they keep coming back."

"Boys will be boys," he said unhappily, as he handed over his credit card.

The transaction was approved and he handed it back. Declan put it in his wallet then shoved them into his pocket. However, when we turned to walk out the door, we were stopped by two of the boys, blocking our path.

They spoke to us in Spanish as they looked us up and down. All I made out was, 'blah blah Gringo' or 'blah blah Señorita'. I exchanged funny looks with my husband.

"He's not thinking of starting on us, is he?" I asked, unimpressed.

"For his sake I hope not." He said gruffly as he retook hold of my hand. Next, he tried to walk us around them when they moved in our way again. The European Werewolf growled, "OK, they're seriously starting to piss me off."

"Can I hit them now?" I whined.

"Not until we know what we're dealing with, I don't want you exposing yourself." The Second in the pack, ordered.

"Oh but it's OK if you do?" I asked, irritated.

"Yeah, because if anything happens, the people in here are going to have a hard time identifying what they saw me change into." He said coolly. "You on the other hand, would easily be picked in a line-up."

The yellow-eyed youths didn't appreciate our nonplussed attitude, so one tried to take a more direct approach... He reached out to grab me, when Declan with his faster reflexes, grabbed hold of him instead. He cried out in pain, as my mate used his greater strength to crush the boy's hand!

"Weren't you taught to keep your hands to yourself?" He asked coldly.

When his friend made a move, Declan let go of my hand to catch his. My larger mate stood there, holding onto the two youths at the same time. The boys yelled for back up and their posse hastily stood up.

The barman called for the cook to come to our aid, when two of the youths cut them off. They pulled out their pocket knives and waved them threateningly. It kept the staff at bay, as the other two advanced on our position.

"You think you're strong, eh Gringo?" One of the boys sneered. "But you're not as fast as the puma!"

The boy's fist whipped around so fast, we barely saw it coming. He punched him in the jaw then stood back, expecting Declan to drop to the floor, or at least drop his friends' hands. But his head barely turned from the impact.

"Did that hurt?" I wondered.

"He does pack a good wallop for a whelp." He conceded. "Stronger than you'd expect for a kid his age."

As soon as he said that, he flung the two boys he was holding onto, into the other two! The four of them went crashing to the floor. This left the other boys, who were holding up the barman and the cook, looking on in anger.

"Paulo!" The teen guarding the chef, cried out.

Next, he rushed at Declan with his pocket knife! I had to admit, he moved a lot faster than we were used to, in a human. He swung around the blade, but thanks to experience, my mate was ready. He deflected the knife with one hand and using his other, punched him in the stomach. It sent him sprawling to the floor, too.

SMASH!

What the...? We turned around in surprise, to find the kid who'd been holding up the barman, had smashed a wooden chair over Declan's back! The kid stared in surprise at the uninjured giant, whereas my mate looked on in annoyance.

"That's gonna give me a headache later," he said unhappily.

Then the European Werewolf delivered an uppercut to the boy's chin and he and what was left of the chair, flew backwards! He landed with a heavy thud, against the bar.

"Oh come on!" I complained. "This is so easy, I could be doing this!"

"Stay out of this, B." He ordered again. "It looks less unlikely for me to win this than if it were you."

"Miguel!" One of the boys cried out in alarm, as he looked on his unconscious friend. Then he and the other four, leapt up from the floor.

The five boys with their glowing yellow eyes, proceeded to circle and snarl at us! Huh? They sounded like a cougar, or some other kind of cat-like predator.

"Did they just snarl?" I asked in curiosity.

"Yeah, they did." He smirked. "They sound like mountain lions or something."

Just then four of the teens attacked Declan at once as the fifth holding the knife, had a go at me.

Finally, somebody I can hit!

Easily, I dodged his swipes before I sent out my own. My fist landed square on the nose!   My adversary recoiled, as he cupped his face to try to stop the bleeding.

Declan was able to fend off his four even in human form. But my eyes widened when I saw the fourth ready his leg, to knee him in the groin. These kids don't fight fair!

"Oh no you don't!" I spun around.

Just as his leg was rising from the floor, I karate kicked it so hard, he lost his balance and fell over! This made my mate pause, when he realized what he was aiming for.

"Thanks," he said shortly.

Then he proceeded to toss aside one teen to the left and another to the right.

The bleeding-nose boy finally realized that this was a fight they would not win. He showed his desperation by grabbing me by the hair and raising his knife to my throat. As soon as Declan saw this, he paused a second time.

I could feel the teen was trembling as he held the blade against my skin.

"It's OK, I've got this one." I reassured.

Using my light speed reflexes, I hit the knife out of the boy's hand and elbowed him in the stomach. As he started to crumple, I turned around, grabbed HIM by the hair and banged his head against a table! He dropped to the floor like a sack of potatoes.

"Ouch!" Declan flinched. "Remind me not to make you angry."

As a last attempt, the least injured boy from this obnoxious posse, leapt up from the floor. He roared loudly, like he was a lion or something, as he rushed upon the bigger male! His hands were out in front like claws, which showed off his dirty fingernails...

Without looking his way, Declan extended his arm and caught the boy about the throat!

The kid came to a sudden stop in his iron-clad grip. Helplessly, he clawed at his larger arm and hissed like a cat, whereas my mate coolly turned his head to look on. The European Werewolf gazed at the teenager as if he were a nuisance and nothing more.

The youth frothed at the mouth and his yellow eyes burned brighter in fury. Then Declan pulled the kid in closer, as his blue eyes flashed their glowing green colour. Next, he emitted a low, dangerous growl that only the boy could hear.

"Yeah, you're not the only one with glowing eyes, bro." He rumbled out like thunder. "If I were you, I'd quit while I WASN'T ahead."

Simultaneously, Declan's eyes returned to their normal state as he released the kid. He dropped to the floor too, since his legs had stopped working from fright. Ignoring him, I walked up to examine the scratch marks in my mate's skin.

"I'll be OK." He sighed. "They'll be healed within the hour."

So I gave my big, strong, scary husband a hug instead and relished the feel of his arms wrapping about, to hold me close.

"Señor, are you alright?" The barman approached us. "I've called la policía and they're on their way."

We exchanged worried looks as we pulled away. After New Orleans, we weren't exactly eager to be questioned or scanned by the Police again.

"Yeah we're fine but we're running late though." Declan laughed nervously. "Since we've paid the bill, we'll be off now."

When I turned to pick up my handbag, I noticed it was no longer on the floor.

"Where's my bag?" I cried out.

The next thing we saw was the scared boy, who'd jumped up from the floor, running towards the back door with it!

"Hey!" I shouted. "Give me back my bag!"

Both Declan and I made a move after him but then we didn't have to.

Just as the teenager reached the back door, it was flung open by an angry looking, older, Peruvian man, also with glowing yellow eyes.

The boy halted in his steps as he looked afraid of the older man. He quickly spoke in Spanish to him, while one hand was holding onto my handbag and his other, was pointing at Declan. I couldn't be sure, but I got the impression that he was trying to blame the whole thing on us!

However, the man with the long, grey hair and wearing a colourful poncho, didn't buy it. His hand lashed out as he slapped the boy instead! It was so hard, it made him drop my bag. He backed away from his elder, before he hung his head in shame.

We watched his elder point at my handbag then point at me. The boy respectfully this time, picked up my bag and approached us. He held it out with quivering hands.

"Lo siento, señorita." He said lamely, unable to look us in the eyes.

Next, he proceeded to help his friends up from the floor. I noticed how the boys stood to attention when they saw the older man. When the unconscious youth came to, his eyes widened in fear and hastily he struggled to his feet. The six youths started to clean up the mess they made, by straightening the tables and chairs. Hell, one even picked up the cutlery which had been knocked to the floor and with a lowered head, handed them to the waitress.

I observed how it wasn't just the boys, but all of the locals seemed to recognize the older man, as they looked on with reverence.

"Machu," the barman nodded respectfully.

We watched the two fall into quiet discussion as the six teenagers looked sheepishly at the floor. I guess he was updating this Machu about the youths' behaviour. When he pointed our way, we sensed he was being told how we turned the tables back on them.

"Come on," my mate whispered.

He began to pull me backwards for us to slip silently out the front door. However, as soon as he touched the door handle, Machu's head sharply turned our way.

"I would not take your pretty wife out that way, señor." The stranger spoke in English.

"Oh yeah and why not?" He asked suspiciously.

"Because la policía are pulling up, out the front as we speak." The stranger said simply.

Damn it! We heard first and then saw second, through the front window, he was right. We exchanged unhappy looks as we wondered what to do?

"Give Julio your keys," the Elder ordered. "He will bring your vehicle to my house where you will be free to leave without further trouble."

"Say what?" He raised his eyebrows. "You expect me to just hand over our rental with our belongings inside? You've got to be kidding!"

"Explanations can come later!" Machu barked out. "I smell your strength señor, I know you are the greater predator."

What the...? We exchanged surprised glances, as it wasn't everyday we heard a human exhibit the same abilities we did. But I also sensed that this Machu could be trusted, which I confirmed with a nod.

"Quickly now," the Elder demanded. "Give Julio your keys and once la policía are gone, he'll drive your vehicle to my casa. I know you have little desire to be interrogated by the authorities, as we do."

My gut instincts were telling me not only could we trust him, but he was as supernatural as we were. I nudged Declan to do what he said before looking out the window again. The police officers, two uniformed men, had climbed out of their hover-car and were heading for the front door.

"Fine!" He said unhappily.

My husband pulled the remote for the rental out of his pocket and tossed it over to the barman.

"This way," Machu headed towards the back door, with the boys following.

Declan asked on our way past, "You know where this guy lives?"

"Of course señor," the barman reassured. "Machu is a well known Sharman in these parts. Everyone knows the way to his door."

We followed our rescuer out the back door and just in time too. As soon as we had exited, we overheard the front door open, with the entry of the police. My husband pulled me along with the sounds of the people inside, animatedly talking in Spanish.

The nine of us skulked into the tropical forest behind. Then Declan stopped and because he was holding my hand, so did I. He turned around and we saw through the trees, a second police hover-car, power down in the car park.

The European Werewolf frowned as we watched two more officers emerge carrying scanners.

"Señor, I suggest you hurry." Machu urged. "Their technology can follow us into the woods."

We nodded then proceeded to follow them again. We wove between the trees, ferns and bushes as we walked into the wilds of the Amazonas. The air was cool and humid, yet still. There was hardly a sound in the forest, except for the odd cricket, frog or mosquito. As we walked away, I noticed how Machu and the youths sped up.

"We should run," the Sharman suggested. "We can run like the puma and I know you can run like the wolf. We need to put as much distance as possible, between us and la policía's scanners."

"Agreed," my mate said shortly.

To our further surprise, as soon as we finished speaking, the old man leapt away! He bolted through the forest on two legs, like he really was a puma. So did the six youths, as they all took off in supernatural speed.

"No way...!" I looked on in shock.

"He's pretty spry for an old guy." Declan smirked. "I can keep up in my human form, can you?"

I glanced his way unimpressed for asking such a stupid question.

"I am a frickin' Circulator!" I rolled my eyes. "My mother and grandmother outran their Lokoti Werewolf husbands, even when they were pregnant."

To prove my point, I let go of his hand then seemingly disappeared from his side. In reality, I ran off in light speed and raced ahead of him, through the trees. I sped past the boys and only slowed when I was running beside the Sharman.

"That's my girl." He smirked, before he ran after.

The European Werewolf running in human form soon caught up to the group. Expertly, we streaked along the forest floor, occasionally swerving to miss a tree. All of us leapt over fern, bush or root sticking up, as well as shoving aside any branches or vines in our way.

My dark blue eyes glowed turquoise as I used my Werewolf sight to see better in the dark. When I looked behind, I saw Declan had done the same. His eyes were glowing green, as Machu's and the boys' eyes glowed yellow. As such, we easily navigated the dark forest.

Running in sub-light speed was a cinch! It felt surreal seeing everyone else look like they were running in slow motion, being in another time differential. I was running so fast, I overtook Machu in the lead, as I looked like a bright blur.

"B, not so fast!" Declan called after. "You don't know where you're going!"

Typical, one minute he's asking if I can keep up then the next he's telling me to slow down. I turned my head to scoff that he should hurry up, when I ran straight through a massive spider web! The horrible stickiness, closed around and I panicked!

"AAAEEEEEKKK!"

What if there's a massive, poisonous spider on me?! Scary scenes from the movie 'Arachnophobia' flashed through my mind. Frantically, I scrambled to rid myself of the web as I ran. Because of this, I was no longer looking where I was going.

Then my foot caught on a root and I went SMACK BANG face first, onto the damp, dirty, forest floor.

"B!"

Thankfully, my Lokoti Werewolf muscle protected me from being winded upon impact. When the males caught up, they looked down on a frantic female who was rolling around.

"Declan? Declan! Get it off me! Get it off me!" I squealed in terror.

Immediately, he crouched down beside, as Machu and the youths watched. They looked on confused as to why I was writhing on the ground. However, my husband was cool as a cucumber as he brushed me down.

"Get it off me!" I shouted.

"OK OK!" He grabbed hold of my flailing arms. "Calm down, B!"

"Get it off me, Declan!"

I HATE spiders! I didn't care if that made me any less of a predator, but I couldn't stand arachnids! Their eight long legs and horrible, bulbous behinds, made my skin crawl and hair stand on end.

My mate moved quickly and proficiently. Simultaneously, he checked to make sure there weren't any spiders whilst his hands brushed off any remaining web. After two centuries of marriage, he'd witnessed many a time, my irrational fear on the subject. My shrieks would hurt his sensitive ears and a couple of times I'd even called him home from work, to kill a creepy-crawly.

"You're clear," he promised.

However, when he helped me to my feet again, he had to catch me when my knee gave out!

"Oow!" I cried out in agony. "My knee! My knee!"

"I got you," he held me up.

"Frickin' hell, it hurts!" I whined. "I think I twisted it, my kneecap feels crooked."

Machu came forward to look on my bleeding and dirty legs.

"You've torn your ligament." He announced. "I can treat it at my house, but we cannot stop here."

"How much further is it?" Declan wondered.

"Another seven kilometres," he answered.

"Right," my mate looked my way. "It's too far for you to limp, so I'll carry you on my back."

"Then I'll instantaneously phase there," I pouted.

"How?" He gave a funny look. "You don't know where it is, so how will you 'see' where you're going?"

"I'll just slow you up." I said embarrassed at how everyone was staring. "Maybe I should instantaneously phase home and let Meadow look at it."

"Don't be stupid, B! I've carried you dozens of times." Next, he turned around so his back was facing me. "Hop up."

"Declan -"

"Just do it!" He snapped impatiently.

I let out a huff before I leapt onto his back. He didn't even strain at my weight, as he caught my legs with his hands. Carefully, he wrapped them around his waist and I grunted in pain.

"Are you ready?" He turned his head.

He caught my nod with his glowing green eyes before he looked at Machu again.

"This way," the Sharman said.

Next, he sprinted off through the trees with the youths racing after him.

Declan ran behind the boys. He could easily keep up even while carrying his wife. I clung onto his shoulders as he held my legs in his arms. Skilfully, he leapt over log, fern or bush as he kept Machu in his sights. I grunted in pain, as my injured knee jarred whenever he landed.

"Only four kilometres to go, we're nearly there," he panted.

I bit down on my lower lip as my knee was knocked about.

The ground turned steep and I got the impression we were running up a mountainside. When the group slowed to a jog, I peered over his shoulder. I saw that we were coming into a clearing.

We slowed to a walk as we came out of a borderline of trees. There, I saw a wooden house with a grass roof, sitting on a slope. The front of the structure was on wooden stilts and had a veranda out the front. I couldn't see any glass on the windows, only fly screens. But they were protected from rain by the long, grassy eaves. It was also nestled by forest, with only a tiny, dirt road trickling away from it, cut into the mountain.

Machu had a quiet word to the youths, who nodded along to whatever he said. We couldn't understand what he was saying because it was in Spanish. Then all of the boys except one, left us to walk down the driveway. I guessed they were heading home.

"What did you say to them?" Declan wondered.

"I told them to stay on the road, because the shortcut through the forest is not safe." The Sharman advised.

He looked back at the dark trees we just left, before looking at the Elder once more. "Why not?"

"There used to be eight boys who grew up together in the village, including my grandson." He indicated the one who remained. "Two have disappeared in the last six months. Paulo's parents were murdered last year and their masticated bodies were pulled from the river."

Oh oh...a warning feeling hit as dread sat in the pit of my stomach.

"And you're saying this NOW after we just came that way?" Declan demanded.

"We were a in a group so we were safe." He said simply. "Also, what is hunting us would not attack you, green-eyed wolf. It smells your strength just as we do and it is cowardly. It attacks the weak or preys on those who are alone."

"But who'd hunt YOU?" My mate asked. "You may be human, but I can see by your eyes and speed, you're not exactly helpless."

"We imbibe Yaje to become one with the Spirit of the Puma," the Sharman announced. "We may run like her, but what hunts us can run in the speed of sound."

"Shit..." I breathed, "...South American Vampires."

"Come inside my house and I will heal your mate's leg." He changed the subject. "Julio will bring your vehicle as soon as la policía are gone."

Instead of following, Declan stood still. He looked from the boy and the older man, to the forest. I sensed he was unsure if he should or not.

As if he sensed this, Machu stopped on the stairs, whereas the youth simply opened the front door and went inside.

"I mean you no harm," the Sharman promised in his thick accent. "You will be guests in my home and will be treated well."

I didn't sense any malice so I trusted what he said.

"It's OK." I said quietly. "I'm not getting any bad vibes, so it should be cool."

Reluctantly, Declan sighed before he carried his wife inside the house.

As he went up the stairs to the veranda, I looked back. I may not have had any warning feelings about the people, but I believed what they said about the woods. The silent forest didn't seem peaceful now, but more like it was hiding a secret. I even wondered if it was temporal causality again and maybe we were meant to come here. Who better to fix a Vampire problem than us, especially with our history...?

The living area wasn't fancy but it was homey. The furniture was wooden with colourful, woven rugs on the floor or as curtains over the windows. There was a separate kitchen and three doorways leading to two bedrooms and a bathroom. But what caught my eye, were all the shelves around the room, holding glass jars or wooden bowls, full of natural ingredients.

"You can rest the señora there," he pointed at a wooden-framed sofa.

Declan carried me over to the couch, where he carefully sat down on the edge. I released his shoulders the same time as he released my legs. Then he turned around to elevate them, so I was lying down. Gently, he lifted up my sore knee to put a cushion underneath.

"I don't know if you'll heal from THAT overnight," he frowned.

He was right, my right knee was so swollen, it was as almost the size of a soccer ball. Also, there were bloodied gashes in it and the left one as well. They appeared deeper than shallow grazes.

"How funny did I look, one minute running out in front and then landing face first?" I blushed.

"It was a spectacular crash." He smirked. "It was like watching a cross between 'Superman' and 'Monty Python'; faster than a speeding bullet but with slapstick thrown in."

Then he mimed with his hand, his fingers running down his arm before landing with a smack, onto his palm. As he did, he started off humming the theme to the movie 'Superman' then ended it with the tune from 'Monty Python's Flying Circus'.

I giggled at his reenactment however, we were soon distracted by raised voices, coming from the kitchen.

It sounded like Paulo was being berated over his behaviour, by his angry grandfather. But because they were bickering in Spanish, we couldn't understand what they were saying. We heard cupboard doors opening and closing as Machu worked on something in the kitchen, as he lectured.

Declan frowned, not at the chastisements, but he was sniffing the air inside the house.

"What is it?" I watched him.

"The smell that was on the youths' breath, it's coming from the kitchen." He went on guard. "I think it's some kind of plant-based drug."

"It's Yaje that you smell, señor," the Sharman reappeared carrying a large bowl and a small towel. "The Vine of the Soul."

I sat upright, "But isn't it a hallucinogen?"

Machu came to sit on the coffee table beside the couch. He placed the large bowl beside and dipped the towel into the warm water, which looked cloudy. It was mixed with something which he was going to use on my injuries. But before the towel could touch the broken skin, Declan's hand shot out as his eyes glowed green once more.

"There isn't Yaje in the water, is there?" He growled out.

"No señor, it's another plant which is used for antiseptic purposes," he said calmly.

"It won't make her hallucinate or affect her mental capacity in any way, will it?"

"No, it will ensure infection does not set in." Machu promised.

He released the Sharman's hand and looked on suspiciously, "Why are you helping us?"

"My grandson caused offence tonight." Machu said gravely, as the teenager stood nearby. "I hope he learned his lesson when he and his friends were beaten by the greater predator."

"Why are your eyes yellow?" I asked, as I looked from the Elder to the boy.

"When we partake of the 'Vine of the Soul', we become one with the Mother Puma. She guides us on our vision quest. We hunt better with the gifts she bestows, such as speed and sight." He answered.

"You mean you get high, so you can get possessed by an animal spirit?" The European Werewolf eyed him.

Machu wasn't offended by his scepticism but Paulo was.

"Don't knock it until you try it, Gringo." He said haughtily. "She gives us speed as well as heightens our senses. We can see in the dark and we track better with our ears and noses."

"Oh yeah, you're doing a great job handling that kind of responsibility!" My mate stood up.

Declan was taller than the teenager, let alone stronger, as he pulled back his wide shoulders.

He spoke in a low voice, "I've been part beast since I was three years old. I've learned the hard way that you can't lose control, not for a second, otherwise people's lives are at stake. Today, you picked on that poor waitress at that restaurant, which showed your immaturity. You're not ready for that kind of power!"

The possessed boy snarled as his yellow eyes burned brighter. My husband growled back, as his eyes glowed green and his circular pupils turned into narrow slits. It was like watching Puma Spirit verses European Werewolf. The boy looked like he was about to launch himself on his opponent again, when the Sharman intervened.

"Paulo!" He stood between them. "I should let the wolf-man take you outside and beat some sense into you!"

The youth looked on the older man in surprise, as well as betrayed how his grandfather didn't take his side.

Machu announced, "From this night on, you and your friends will not partake in Yaje again until you are 21 years old!"

"But Grandfather -" he objected.

"Today you have proven yourself unworthy of our Great Mother's gifts!" The Sharman decided.

With that, the boy spun on his heel and flounced off into his bedroom. His door slammed shut, as Declan remained on his feet, like he was standing guard. I could tell he didn't trust the strangers.

"Again, I apologise for my grandson." Machu sighed. "I realized this afternoon that some of the Yaje was missing. I'd heard reports of Paulo's behaviour and knew it had to be him. I'm thankful you behaved in moderation when Paulo did not. It's out of gratitude that I help you now."

Declan crossed his arms, "It's thanks to B's people, the Lokoti, who taught me self-control. Maybe you should be teaching your children the same thing. Teens are tempestuous enough without animal possession, thrown into the mix."

"We are trying to teach our children responsibility and how to protect themselves." He frowned. "Children today, they are arrogant and have no respect for the old ways. They don't listen and expect immediate results, having no patience for hard work."

Machu came back to sit down on the coffee table, picking up the towel once more. We watched him dip into the bowl and then use it, to clean my wounds. It stung, but I pursed my lips together as I forced myself to remain still.

He spoke as he worked, "Partaking of the Vine of the Soul is important to my people. It is meant only for ceremonies and hunting. Paulo has abused not only my trust, but his people. He and his friends will be punished by their families."

Then the Sharman paused, as he looked from me to my mate with a curious expression.

"The pretty señora, she is a different breed than you are." He noticed. "You señor are the Werewolf, your breed is the source of your kind. But the señora here, her breed is possessed by the spirit of the Wolf."

We exchanged glances at how Machu 'saw' this with his glowing yellow eyes.

He looked Declan up and down, "Your strength and your unending hunger comes from the First of your kind. All Werewolves but the señora's, come from your breed. But your bloodlust cannot be quenched, as it boils deep inside of you, waiting to take control. You use the señora's light to battle your darkness. But sometimes... sometimes you lose control when her light is threatened."

Suddenly, the Elder leapt to his feet and backed away from us.

"Leave my house!" He shouted.

"What the hell?!" My mate looked on like he was a demented old man.

But Machu wasn't as crazy as Declan would like to believe...

"Leave my house at once!" He hissed at my husband.

Next, he unsheathed a large, silver knife from his leather belt, which had been hidden under his poncho.

"Wait!" I held up my hands.

"C'mon B, let's get out of here." My mate said unhappily. "This whole frickin' country is nuts."

However, I knew what Machu was 'seeing' in his vision, as I saw it too, but on a crystal screen at Circulate Headquarters.

The European Werewolf slung my handbag over his shoulder then bent down to pick up his wife.

"No." I stopped him before looking beseechingly at the Sharman. "Wait."

My mate paused to give a peculiar look, as the Elder backed further away while waving around his silver weapon.

"You're right," I spoke quickly. "Declan as a European Werewolf, is descended from the First Werewolf."

"Say what?" This made my mate pause a second time.

"The First Werewolf existed in the dinosaur era and was the only hot-blooded predator. As a European Werewolf, Declan is in direct descent of the First Werewolf. But I'm a Lokoti Werewolf and we're the only species not in hereditary descent." I rattled off.

"Because you are possessed by the spirit of the Lokoti Wolf," Machu spoke to me before glaring Declan's way. "But you señor, you may be the last of your kind, but you have a long lineage. Your unending hunger is the result of your kind killing from the very beginning. You will continue to hunt, as it's your way and the only way you know!"

"Listen to me please!" I cried. "Use your 'sight' and you'll see that Declan is not a man-eater. He is the last of his kind and when we leave this life, there will be no other European Werewolves to haunt humanity. He's never turned a human and he even turned down a female of his kind and the chance to procreate. He's always tried to do the right thing and is a good man with a good heart."

"You are the first female of your breed..." the Sharman looked me over, "...but you can't have young?"

Declan was looking fed up, which made me talk even faster, as I tried to diffuse the situation.

"I know you can 'see' all of this, so please believe me now, Declan is in control of his bloodlust." I reassured. "You are not in danger. He's not going to eat you or your people. When he's tasted human flesh, it's been in self-defence."

The Sharman didn't appear to be convinced, as he held his silver knife even higher as his buffer.

"B, we don't need this," the European Werewolf said crankily. "I don't think a bunch of crazies who invoke animal spirits, have a right to preach."

"It was Our Mother the Puma Spirit who aided us in battling your kind before!" Machu retorted. "It was because of her we were able to drive your kind away!"

He was right, as I recalled reading something in the SSIT Report on the Different Breeds of Werewolves. In the section on North American Werewolves, in the history of the breed, it advised that they were originally South American Werewolves. But it migrated after losing several battles with a formidable foe - mankind.

"I know and you're right again," I held up my hands in a 'calm down' gesture. Then I glanced at my husband, "remember the history section on the North American Werewolf?"

"Oh yeah," he recalled reading the report once, a long time ago. He turned to Machu, "Congratulations, you got rid of them and you've gotten rid of us, too."

Then he picked me up in both arms and headed for the front door.

"Wait!" I cried out again, but he paid no heed. He kicked open the front door and tried to walk out, but I grabbed onto the wooden doorway. I rushed out, "Machu, you can see the past, but can you see the future, too? If you can, you'll know that we can help you! What if we were meant to come here, to solve your Vampire problem?"

That did the trick, the Sharman lowered his blade and looked thoughtful.

"Let go of the frickin' door!" Declan growled out as he struggled to keep going.

But I clung onto the wood as I grunted back, "We haven't got our car back! So where the hell are we going?!"

"We're NOT risking our asses to save theirs!" He tried to pull me away. "Do you remember what happened to you, the last time you battled 'fang heads'?"

But because he was stronger, I was losing my hold on the door. So I tried to solve the problem the Circulator way, by instantaneously phasing out of his arms and returning to the couch. The Sharman dropped his knife in shock, at how I disappeared in a bright flash and reappeared in another. It also made the temperature in the room drop, from the electromagnetic activity.

"B!" He growled louder.

"You are a Light Person!" Machu uttered out. His eyes bulged and he stared like I was some kind of deity. "The legends are true! I thought that you no longer existed!"

"Wait, you know about 'Light People'?" My husband's eyes widened, too. "I thought it was just a Lokoti thing."

Then it reminded me of the SSIT Report on Human/Animal Shape Shifters. In the history of the human/panther, it mentioned Purto meeting a female Shifter and a tribe who imbibed Yaje to become one with the Puma Spirit. So Machu's people had encountered Circulators before. Everything started to make sense, as all the past events leading up to this moment were like connecting dots in the timeline. A leads to B which results in C, or as Nairn said, "Everything happens for a reason and everything has its time and place."

I told the Sharman, "I'm the last Circulator. There used to be more, but they evolved to the space time continuum in the mid 21st Century. I'm all that's left of the Circulate."

"Lady of the Light!" Machu dropped to his knees, like he was half in shock and half worshipping the woman sitting on his sofa. "You are an endangered species! And you are injured, so I will help you."

Then he moved over to where I was sitting and recommenced washing down my injured legs.

"What just happened...?" Declan came back over. "I thought he was kicking us out!"

"I know that you are not a danger, señor," the Elder spoke as he worked. "You have a 'Timeless One', a 'Light Person', guiding you."

My face heated up in humility at his belief system which perched me on a pedestal. Embarrassed, I looked up at my husband who was looking down. He looked like he was trying not to laugh.

"You make her sound like a kind of goddess, or something," my husband said in amusement.

"It would explain her bright aura," Machu bristled at his disbelief. "Whereas the señora glows and her power radiates outwards, you señor are different. A dark shadow is inside you and threatens to consume you. But as long as you bask in the light, you can ward off the darkness. If she were not beside you, we would destroy you before you destroyed us."

Disgruntled, Declan looked away from the prejudice in the room.

"Not this again," he muttered out.

"As I said before, he's a good man with a good heart." I reminded.

"He is only as good as the light which is shining on the outside of him," the Sharman said stubbornly.

"Oh yeah?" My mate's eyebrows rose. "If I'm only able take but not give, would I be able to do this?"

Simultaneously, he dropped to his knees as he dropped my bag on the floor. His eyes glowed green again and when he opened his mouth, I saw his teeth turn sharp. He raised his right wrist to his mouth and bit into the flesh. He grunted in discomfort, before moving his arm to my mouth. He pressed the wound against my lips and I accepted his blood. I held onto him as I began to drink.

Seconds later, we heard a gasp from the Elder. He was looking down on my torn skin which began to knit itself together, before his very eyes. They widened, as he watched my wounds close and most of the swelling go down.

"I'll get some bandages to make sure the knee sets properly," the Healer stood up.

He went over to some shelves as I lapped at my husband's wrist to lick it shut. When we felt that it had closed, he pulled back his arm and we saw pink skin in its place. Affectionately, he smoothed back my hair then he frowned at my knee.

"It looks like it isn't completely healed," he said with dissatisfaction.

"It's mostly fixed," I caught his hand and held it close. "Thank you."

He leaned in to kiss his wife softly on the lips and when he pulled away, he looked on fondly.

The Sharman returned with some bandages which he used to wrap up my knee.

"This will help reset the kneecap as the ligaments heal." He advised. "I would like to invite you both to stay tonight. Then in the morning, I can see if our treatment worked."

"We have a hotel booked in Borja," my mate returned. "Speaking of which, where's our car?"

"Julio is driving it here, as we speak," the 'Seer' answered. "But you will not be driving to Borja tonight."

"Oh yeah and why not?" Declan's eyes narrowed.

"Ask the señora," he said simply. "Now I will go and see about some dinner for us all."

We watched him go into the kitchen once more then my husband looked my way.

"I should be healed tomorrow morning then we'll help Machu with his Vampire problem." I said chirpily.

"B."

"C'mon Declan, we were meant to come here and help them."

"B."

"It's temporal causalities again!" I explained excitedly. "We were meant to be waylaid here. We were supposed to hear about the disappearances, lately. We're going to kill the South American Vampires for them."

"B!" He lost his patience. "There's no way in hell I'm gonna let you risk your life for a bunch of crazies! If they're so sure of this Puma Spirit, let HER look after the frickin' 'fang heads'!"

"Declan," I cupped his head in my hands. "The people can run like the puma, but the Vampires can move in the speed of sound. They need somebody who can move in the speed of light."

"Nuh uh," he shook his head. "As soon as our hover-car arrives, we're outta here."

"Then I'll instantaneously phase back to Machu's and fight the Vampires alone." I said resolutely.

His mouth wavered as his eyes blazed in anger and began to look green again.

"Frickin' hell!" He stood up in a tantrum and walked away. "This is not OUR problem!"

"No, but it's the right thing to do." I said quietly. "If Machu and his people fight the 'fang heads', they've got less than a fifty percent chance of surviving. If we fight the 'fang heads', we've got a hundred percent chance of surviving."

He paced up and down the living area infuriated at how my mind was made up on the matter.

"I have one of my all-knowing feelings about this Declan, I do." I reassured. "It won't be dangerous for us but it IS dangerous for them."

"Fine then!" He snarled out as he stomped towards the front door.

"Where are you going?"

"I can hear the hover-car coming," he gnashed his teeth. "I'm gonna get our suitcases out of the boot, since we're staying the night!"

Then he flung open the fly-screen door and stormed down the veranda stairs.

*****

~ 26 ~

Although we made a new friend in Machu, I don't think Paulo liked us very much.

Firstly, we kicked his ass back at the 'restaurante' and secondly, his grandfather made him give up his room. But before Declan carried in our suitcases, the 18 year old had to tidy up and put new sheets on the bed. We heard many an obscenity uttered under the boy's breath and not all of them Spanish.

We discovered the Sharman wasn't only adept in mixing medicinal remedies using local ingredients, but his skills extended to the kitchen. For dinner he made two courses; Ceviche and Juane. Civiche was a dish made with marinated raw fish and flavoured with different herbs. The fish he used was piranha and it was tastier than I expected. Then we ate Juane that was a chicken and rice dish, wrapped in banana leaves. The rice was flavoured with turmeric and the banana leaves made it moist.

I had a bath before bed, since I couldn't stand up in the shower, and it was eleven o'clock when everyone retired.

Machu slept in his bed, Paulo slept on the sofa and Declan and I were in his double bed. Unfortunately, the mattress wasn't big enough for a European Werewolf; whose feet hung over the end and he kept knocking into his wife whenever he rolled over. I cried out in pain and punched him after he collided with my sore knee.

"I'm sorry, alright?!" He snapped. "But this bed isn't big enough for two Werewolves."

We lay on our backs and listened to the night. The soft noises of the odd frog or mosquito was carried on the air. Thankfully, the fly-screen windows kept us from being eaten alive.

"It's so quiet here that the mozzies are loud," I noticed.

"Hmm."

"I thought there'd be night birds or something else we'd hear, in the wilderness."

"Hmm."

"It kinda makes me homesick, I miss the hoot of an owl."

"Hmm."

"It's kinda surreal, being on the edge of the Amazon." I sighed. "We're finally seeing a place that I've wanted to visit, for years."

He grumbled with his eyes closed, "And we've got the heat of the jungle, to boot."

"It's not hot."

"Yes it is."

"It's so cool that I was about to ask you to pull the sheet up."

"Here," he moved closer.

Instantly, his hot skin warmed me and I snuggled against him. We were both wearing boxer shorts whereas I also wore a singlet. My bandaged right knee was elevated on a third pillow, but my feet felt cold. When I told him, he pulled the sheet over them.

"Declan...?"

"Hmm?"

"How come you're always warm?"

"You know the reason B, my body temperature sits at 43 C."

"Do you ever feel cold?"

"Sure I do, in the middle of an Alaskan winter."

"Do you ever wish you weren't hot blooded?"

"No."

"What, never?"

"If I wasn't hot blooded, I wouldn't come in handy to a mate who always feels cold." He said wryly.

I giggled then affectionately rubbed my nose against his upper arm.

"I must be one weird Werewolf," I speculated. "None of the male Lokoti Werewolves feel the cold, like I do."

"It's because you're female, it's biology." He said softly. "I notice you feel the cold more when it's that time of the month."

"Hmm," I thought on this. "I think you might be right."

"Of course I'm right," he sung mockingly. "I'm always right."

"You wish!" I punched him again, but lightly this time.

He chuckled as his put his arm about which allowed me to curl up into his side.

"Get some sleep." He said tiredly. "Hopefully in the morning, you'll be completely healed."

"Hmm," I closed my eyes. "I love you, Dec."

"Right back at ya, B."

*****

My knee was much better in the morning. Machu unwrapped the bandages to smile in approval. The swelling had gone down and there weren't any scars on the skin. The Sharman setting the knee, coupled with my mate's blood, saved the day.

Our host served breakfast which was fruit, corn bread and cheese. The fruit was a local variety which Declan and I had never tasted before. There was camu camu, mammee apple and guanabana. We four sat down at the table to discuss plans while we ate.

"The South American Vampires hunt at night, so tonight we will hunt them." Machu decided.

"How do you know they only come out at night?" Declan wondered.

"It's when the disappearances occur." Paulo said bitterly. "My parents were driving at night when they were attacked."

Sympathetically, I gazed on the teen as he moodily tore apart his bread.

"Can you tell us what happened to your parents, Paulo?" I asked gently.

"They were coming back from a dinner at an Aunt and Uncle's," he glared at his food. "They were supposed to pick me up from a friend's house on the way home, but they never came. The next morning, Grandfather and some men from the village, searched for them. They found their hover-car on a forest road with the windscreen smashed. A week later, a fishing boat discovered their chewed-on bodies, in the river."

"The authorities blamed piranhas for the multiple teeth marks," the Sharman rolled his eyes. "When another couple went missing from the same road at night, la policia closed it off. Tonight, we will start our search there."

Declan cleared his throat, "Vampires don't only come out at night, but they are photosensitive to ultraviolet rays. Wouldn't it better to search for their nest, during the day? They'd most likely be asleep, to conserve their energy."

"We've tried, señor." Machu said. "We know that they'd most likely be sleeping in a cave somewhere, but finding it is the problem."

"Well, how many caves are there in this area?" He wondered.

"Many!" Paulo scoffed. "Look around you, Gringo. We are in mountainous forest with many a waterfall. It's a cave behind one, but we've searched all those in a twenty kilometre radius."

"The water washes away their scent, which makes tracking them difficult." The Sharman agreed with his grandson.

"I can help there," the European Werewolf sat up straighter. "I'm willing to bet that a South American 'fang head' smells just as bad as a European one. They smell like a meat that's gone off, since they're part dead. I'd know that scent anywhere. Tonight, I could do a run of the woods, to pick up their trail."

This made me look his way, "Do they smell like bad meat, to you? To me, they smell dank and decrepit, like an old, decaying building."

"Either way, they don't smell edible." He said, as he picked up another piece of fruit.

"But you still eat them."

"It's the best way to kill them," he shrugged. "It's not like they taste nice, or anything."

"So why do you eat your way through their heads?" I queried.

"They can't regenerate if they're headless, can they?" He spoke with his mouthful.

"Disgusting, but effective." Machu conceded.

Then I surprised everyone when I stood up from the table, leaving my half-eaten breakfast behind.

"Where are you going?" My husband enquired. "Don't tell me the topic of conversation put you off your food?"

"Not really, I'm just not hungry." I replied. "I'm going to instantaneously phase home and get my Katana."

"Oh," he looked relieved. "If you don't want anymore..."

Then the humans watched him pick up my plate and put it on top of his, to finish off. They looked on with their dark brown eyes, as he ate his third helping. It was the first thing I noticed this morning, their eyes were back to normal. I guess this meant the Yaje and therefore the Puma Spirit, was out of their system.

To their further surprise, I disappeared in a bright flash of light. Simultaneously, I disappeared from Peru and arrived in another, in Alaska. I'd transported myself to my bedroom and walked over to the wardrobe. After opening the doors, I pulled out my sheathed sword from behind the long, black, woollen coat.

"Well Beatrix Kiddo, it looks like we've got more things to kill," I spoke to my weapon.

Next, I pulled out my gym clothes from the tall boy. I didn't pack them, because I didn't think I'd be hunting while away. In the privacy of my own bedroom, I changed into the stretchy outfit. This way, I wouldn't tear my cotton shirt and cargo shorts, when I expanded into my supernatural form.

Lastly, I tied the sheath to my back and left the same way I came; in a bright flash of light.

*****

Instead of returning to Peru immediately, I went via Circulate HQ. In another bright brilliance, I transported myself into the Viewing Room. The three sides of the crystal pyramid, showed the typical interference caused by my arrival.

"Welcome to Circulate Headquarters, Bianca."

"Hey CM, I'm guessing you know why I'm here?"

"Negative," she replied. "Please give the verbal commands."

Oh, that's weird. She's usually on-the-ball with what's happening in my life. I sat down at one of the three control panels and typed in Peru then the date I'd just left.

"I need you to run a search for a coven of South American Vampires, living in the Amazonas region." I said, as I sat back in the small chair.

"May I ask what this is regarding?"

"Yes, I'm going to kill them."

"May I ask why?"

"Er, because they're killing people...?" I gave the technology a funny look. "Haven't you been watching what's been going on?"

I heard a couple of electronic beeps as she processed my words.

After a moment, she reported, "Bianca, I cannot see the date or the location you are requesting."

Now it was my turn to say, "May I ask why?"

"Do you recall what Vincent Moher told you, the morning you and your family appeared in the Medical Lab, after your change?"

"Yes."

"You may also remember it's related to the reason why we did not foresee your head injury, when you saved Declan's life."

"Oh," my mouth fell open. "So the interference is back, blocking Circulate systems again?"

"The interference never left," she stated. "It's an ongoing problem which affects a Calculator's sight."

A feeling of dread sank in as my stomach shrank to the size of a pea.

I wet my lips to say, "Then I have another question. Could the interference also be the reason why you didn't 'see' the Voodoo attack, all those years ago?"

"Correct," she confirmed. "I can show you the interference, if you wish."

"Please."

The Circulate Mainframe narrated as she showed the images in the slowly turning, upside down, crystal pyramid.

"As you were told, pivotal points in your timeline are blanked out by an unknown interference. This prevented your Calculator Vincent Moher and Viewing Room systems, from foreseeing your future. The interruptions blanket out either hours or days of your life, effectively fragmenting our vision."

She showed the scene of Declan and I walking down the tourist-filled street in New Orleans, before a blinding white light overtook the screens. Then it jumped to the morning after, in the hotel room, when I suspected my husband of murder. Next, she showed the scene of us pulling up in the 'restaurante' car park and going inside, before the same light washed everything away. When it finally cleared, it showed something which hasn't happened yet;

a party going on in front of Machu's house. I saw we were being congratulated for killing the coven of South American Vampires.

"OK, the celebrations haven't happened yet, because I came here to find them." I stood up to pace. "You're missing the scenes of Declan and I getting into a fight with a bunch of boys and then last night, sleeping over at Machu's house."

"Have you already been involved in a violent altercation?" She sounded surprised.

"Yes and I came here to prepare for another," I moaned. "But it looks like you're not going to be much help."

The computer turned silent as I walked around the circular, glass-top desk, deep in thought.

I wondered aloud, "I told Declan I didn't have a bad feeling about fighting the South American Vampires. But now I'm worried you can't see this, or even where they are. Can you tell me what's causing the interference?"

"Negative," she reported. "Neither Vincent or I, could isolate the cause."

"But has it an energy signature?" I posed. "Can you find out where the energy might be originating from?"

"Negative," she repeated. "The interference affecting your timeline has an unknown energy signature."

"Can you see where it comes from?"

"No," she answered. "There is no origin of the interference and the type of energy it emits cannot be scientifically referenced to any known cause."

"It's not background radiation from outer space?"

"No."

"It's not from a quasar or a supernova?"

"No."

"It's not from a quantum singularity or a wormhole?"

"Negative."

"It's not from a time warp, or an after-image of somebody leaving the timeline?"

"No," the Circulate Mainframe declared. "The type of energy which is causing the interference to your timeline, does not have an astronomical or temporal reference."

"Damn," I sighed as I sat back down again. "It was worth a try."

"Vincent ran several scans of the interference and could not track its origin to anything known to 25th Century science." She continued. "However, he did have a theory."

"Which was?" I looked upwards.

"That the light interfering with your timeline, may be related to the reason why you cannot procreate."

I sat upright with a start. "How so?"

"This remains a hypothetical theory with no methodology or conclusion," she stated.

I sunk back in defeat, as I groaned out, "Typical."

*****

I returned to Machu's living room in another bright flash of light. Paulo was in the kitchen washing dishes and he noted my return with an indifferent air. He rolled his eyes as if to say, 'not you again' and returned to his task.

"You've been gone awhile." Declan walked out of our temporary bedroom. "Did you really need to take an hour to get your sword and change?"

My husband may have complained, but the Sharman looked on my gym clothes and the sword strapped to my back, in a knowing fashion.

"I will go outside and also start to prepare," he said mysteriously.

Then we watched him depart via the front door and go down the veranda stairs.

I carried my cotton shirt and cargo shorts into the bedroom. Declan stood in the doorway and watched me put my clothes back into the suitcase. While I was at it, I rearranged my messy belongings, which he noted.

"Hey, are you OK?" He watched closely. "You look distracted."

I stopped what I was doing to look his way. My mouth wavered as I wondered how to begin. But if I tell him my reservations about tonight, he'd grab our suitcases and his wife, bundle all three into the hover-car and drive off. This would leave the humans with the problem of annihilating the coven on their own.

So I pursed my lips together and refolded my underwear instead.

"C'mon B, spit it out." He walked in to sit on the end of the bed. "Every time you're worried about something, you go into a cleaning frenzy."

"No I don't!"

"Oh yeah?" His eyebrows rose. "You don't remember cleaning the house from top to bottom, before going to my Mom's for dinner, the first time as a couple?"

"No," I lied.

"Or the morning after I killed the Voodoo crazies, you reorganized your suitcase." He pointed out. "Now you're doing it again."

"I'm fine," I said falsely.

Before he could challenge this, I turned around and left the house.

I pushed open the fly-screen door and sat down on the top step. I looked down at the dirt clearing in front of Machu's house and found the Sharman building a fire. Several logs surrounded the blaze, indicating it was used as an area for people to sit. I wondered if it's where his religious rituals took place, around the campfire?

The front door opened again and I sensed without looking, it was my mate. He sat down and watched Machu, too. He didn't speak, we just sat and stared at the growing flames.

Eventually, he said softly, "B, you know I hate it when you hold back."

After another moment, I said, "But I don't want you to freak out."

"Why, has your good feeling turned into a bad one, about tonight?" He guessed.

I turned my head his way, "I know we'll win, but I don't know how the fight will go."

"You mean how bad it might be?"

I nodded.

He said again, "Tell me what you 'see'."

Irritated, I looked back at the fire. "I don't see anything and neither does the Circulate Mainframe, that's the problem."

"Huh?"

"I took so long because I came back via Headquarters." I took a deep breath. "Remember me telling you how sometimes my future is blocked out, by a white light? It's the reason why no one knew I'd get shot in the head that night."

His wrinkled blue eyes widened in recognition and horror of the memory.

"It's ongoing," I said shortly. "It's why the Circulate Mainframe didn't see our fight with the Voodoo crazies and she can't see our fight with the 'fang heads' tonight. All we could see was the celebration afterwards."

Instead of arguing, my husband's eyes remained wide but in hope.

"But that's a good thing, isn't it?" He wondered. "If we're celebrating afterwards, not only do we win, but neither of us gets hurt."

"Yeah, but I don't like the computer not being able to calculate properly, it makes me nervous." I frowned. "I'm a time traveller, I'm supposed to know what the future has in store. The computer is 25th Century technology, looking backwards in time. It's supposedly watching over us, but it can't see when danger's on the horizon."

"Hmm," he looked away. "It makes it a bit useless."

"I mean, it's great at everything else... except that."

My husband sighed loudly as he slung his arm about his wife.

"Well, you always have me," he said casually. "I can't see the future but I've kept you safe so far, haven't I?"

"You've kept ME safe or I've kept YOU safe?" I started to smile.

"Admit it, you'd be lost without me!" He melodramatically rolled his eyes.

"You wish!" I gave him a playful shove.

He returned his arm about his mate as he smiled softly, "Alright, you have your uses too."

I leaned against his large, hot body and looked up into his aged face. Then I buried my face into his chest and inhaled his maple syrup scent. I kept my eyes closed as I listened to his steady heartbeat.

"I love you, you old monster," I breathed out, when I pulled away.

For some reason he chuckled as he gazed at the fire again.

"What?" I watched him.

He looked back to give a cheeky grin, "You're more affectionate when you're hormonal."

"Oh yeah?" I straightened in annoyance. "You're more affectionate when you want sex!"

"At least it happens more than once a month!" He laughed loudly.

"Oh shut up!" I pushed him away again.

My husband guffawed in good humour, as he wrapped his arms about his wife and gave an affectionate squeeze.

*****

Preparations for the hunt began at five o'clock in the afternoon when several men from the village, turned up.

They all sat down on the logs and Machu led them in a chant. As they sung, we watched him mix together a potion using several plants, including a sample of Banisteriopsis Caapi. He had boiled it in an old pot over the fire, throughout the day. Combined with the other ingredients, he concocted the Yaje.

Declan and I watched from the top step, as Paulo hung about the veranda. When he tried to join them his grandfather sent him away. As his punishment for yesterday, he wasn't permitted to partake in the 'Vine of the Soul'. He was made to sit on the sidelines and watch from the outside.

The Sharman sipped the potion first before passing it around. Each of the eight men sipped on the strange smelling liquid, in the metallic cup. Their singing became louder, as the Sharman sat as still with his eyes closed. After a few minutes, he opened them and his dark brown irises looked large and yellow.

Three of the men threw up with one convulsing on the ground. I stood up in alarm, as it looked like he was having a seizure! Just as suddenly as he started, he stopped. When he stood up and looked about him, we saw his eyes were yellow too.

Their chanting grew louder as the last of the drugged men became possessed. As soon as their eyes turned yellow, they stopped shivering or throwing up. We saw that the transition was not an easy one, and it even reminded me of a Werewolf's change. Declan said the process caused him pain and in the first few months, it did for me too. Now I was accustomed and I even enjoyed the power it gave, feeling my muscles expand, or my nails and teeth extend. I wondered if it was the same for them, when they became possessed by the Spirit of the Puma?

The ceremony went for two hours, until the merging between human and animal spirit was complete. The sun was setting and the tropical forest darkened as it quieted. Sounds of birds faded as the buzzing of mosquitoes and singing of crickets, replaced it.

"We have changed, señor and señora." Machu turned our way. "Shouldn't you change too?"

"OK, let's get this show on the road," Declan declared, as he stood up.

The men watched him come down the veranda stairs while he undressed. He removed his t-shirt and shorts before discarding his boxers. Paulo stared at the stranger who showed no embarrassment at stripping in public. As soon as the last of the fabric was removed, he began to expand.

The villagers stared as his width tripled and his height almost doubled. His bones made soft cracking noises, as they contorted into a canine appearance. His large muscles inflated before hardening into hide, which was so tough, even the mosquitoes bounced off.

Lastly, the European Werewolf fell forwards so he was standing on all-fours. All of the men but Machu, stepped back in fright of the beast before them. Declan blinked his glowing green eyes, as his narrow slits for pupils unnerved them. They gaped at his canine jaws full of razor sharp teeth and the strong claws at the ends of his thick fingers and toes.

Coolly, I came down the stairs while undergoing my own metamorphosis. My dark blue eyes glowed turquoise, which drew their attention. Then they stared as my gym clothes expanded from my muscle bulk underneath. My hands and feet tingled as my nails grew longer, stronger and sharper. I opened my mouth and began to pant, as my teeth extended.

I came to stand beside my mate and looked enviously on his hardened hide.

"You're lucky, the mozzies are leaving you alone now." I growled out, before swatting one.

The giant panted out a laugh, before turning his beastly head and delivering an affectionate lick to my cheek.

Paulo followed us down the stairs and approached his grandfather a second time.

"You'll hunt with the Gringo-Monster, but not your own grandson?!" He raised his voice. "They were MY parents that were killed! This is MY fight! Why am I the one being left behind?"

"Paulo, you will behave!" Machu hissed.

"No!" The seventeen year old stamped his foot. "YOU behave!"

One of the villagers sided with the Sharman, "Can you not see that your friends are not here, either?"

"You must be punished for preying on the innocent and not the guilty," another agreed.

"You are not ready for the responsibility which comes with the power of the Puma." Machu denounced.

The teenager looked on betrayed at how his people remained impassive to his plea. Then he spun on his heel and stormed back upstairs. He made sure to slam the fly-screen door behind, as his protest.

Then the Sharman spoke to his men and the Werewolves, "It is time."

Several of the men snarled like large cats as the European Werewolf pawed at the ground.

The old but spry guy, leapt into the tree line and bolted through the forest! Right behind him ran the rest of the hunting party, with one on all-fours. Declan galloped past the villagers, to run alongside of Machu. I sprinted beside my husband, with my legs itching to go faster. However, this time I remained behind as if Machu was First and we were his pack.

*****

The first stop was the tiny tarred road, which wound its way along the tropical mountainside. Machu pointed out the section where Paulo's parents vehicle was found. There were still a few shards of glass lying about, as well as marks where the hover-car came to a sudden stop.

Declan ducked his head to sniff at the signs of accident, before he looked up to examine our surroundings.

"In which direction is the river?" I asked in my rumbling voice.

"That way," Machu indicated with his hand.

WE SHOULD GO THERE NEXT – My mate thought.

"Can you show us where Paulo's parents were found?" I spoke for him.

The Sharman gave a nod then indicated to the humans it was time to move on.

We ran downhill to the lush, forest floor. The trees grew closely together, forcing us to break formation and run individually. However, I always kept Declan and Machu in sight. My clawed feet pelted along the moist earth, with my arms outstretched to push aside any branch or vine in my way.

Stop

Huh, what was that? I slowed down and let Declan and Machu run off in front. The men ran past, as they bolted after their Sharman. Reluctantly, I fell into a jog as half of me want to race after, but the other half wanted to obey.

You're running in the wrong direction

Which direction were we meant to go then?

Follow your instincts, Light Person

Was I hearing the voice of my pack? Was it the bloodlust talking, like it did when I first changed? Or, could I hear our old father, the Lokoti Wolf, speaking?

You are both Circulator and Lokoti Werewolf, for a reason. Now follow the instincts both give you

I stopped still and closed my eyes. I breathed in deeply through my nose, inhaling the scent of vegetation around me. As I concentrated on the physical sensations of touch and smell, I started to feel my stomach tighten. It was the onset of an all-knowing feeling, telling me to go left.

With uncertainty, I veered off course. At first I jogged reluctantly, in case I was imagining the whole thing. Then it turned into a sprint, the stronger the sensations became. I knew I was running towards danger and I felt a little scared that I didn't have my big, strong mate at my side.

While I ran in the foreign direction, a new odour filled my nostrils. I could smell something dank and decaying, which was in contrast to the life around. My muscles hardened, as the claws on my hands and feet extended a little longer. I knew it was my Lokoti Werewolf instinct rallying for battle, as it followed my Circulator one.

At the base of a gigantic tree with numerous vines hanging down, I saw them...

Four humanoid males were crouching over somebody lying on the ground.

Instantly, they looked up upon my approach and I saw all of their eyes were red in colour. In fact, they were completely red, with no whites or pupils showing. Their mouths were bloodied, showing they were feeding and all of their teeth were pointy and sharp. Their unusual mouths reminded me of a piranha!

As I came closer, I made out who they were feeding on. When I saw the person had yellow eyes, at first I thought it was one of men in our hunting party. But he looked too young and then I realized it was Paulo. The stupid kid supped on Yaje after we left and still tried to come along. But being alone, made him a tasty target to the 'fang heads'.

"GET OFF HIM!" I roared as I ran.

My right arm reached back to pull my sword out of its sheath. By the time I'd arrived on the scene, I was armed and ready. It was just in time too, as the four 'fang heads' sprang up and I saw they too had weapons, in a sense.

Every single nail on their hands and feet were long and knife-like, as well as dirty. In fact, their whole appearance was ragged, like they were accustomed to living outdoors. Their skin, hair and clothing was caked in mud, which made them look feral.

Immediately, two tried to leap upon me but I swung around my sword. One managed to duck using his speed of sound reflexes, but my sharp weapon clipped the nails off the other. It hissed in anger as it recoiled, nursing its useless hand.

My swings kept coming as all four tried to attack. However, I kept them at bay as I swung my sword in the speed of light. I looked like a bright blur, as my blade spun faster than an electric saw. They'd leap then recoil, leap and then duck and leap again before jumping clear of my Katana.

Paulo lay helplessly, unable to assist, weakened by his multiple bite marks. I saw that his neck, wrists and right leg was injured. His arteries had been punctured and he was bleeding into the ground. His chest heaved while his yellow eyes dulled, as his life drained away. I knew I'd have to finish this fight fast, to save him.

"GRRRRAAAAAAAAAAWWWWWWLLLLL!"

My heart leapt in pride at the sound of reinforcements arriving. Declan must have noticed my absence and tracked my scent back here. I heard his heavy gallop as he ran our way. Then everyone saw him, when he pounced on one of the 'fang heads'.

The South American Vampire's back hit the ground, as he landed with a massive European Werewolf on top of him. Neither of them wasted any time in fighting. The 'fang head' drove its long nails into my mate's ribcage as simultaneously, Declan's large jaws chomped off his face!

I cringed when I saw first and felt second, its long, sharp nails, pierce his hardened hide.

OOW THAT HURTS! – Declan grimaced.

But he didn't stop, either. He crunched down on the front of the 'fang heads' skull, as he ate his way through the enemy. Brain matter, bone and hair was devoured until a headless corpse, littered the forest floor.

The third Vampire leapt on top of the European Werewolf's large back and it too, dug its nails in. Declan tried to buck it off, but it clung on by its hands and feet. This left me with the other two 'fang heads' to dispose of.

I wanted to finish this fight as soon as possible, to get the third off my husband's back.

I swung my sword around madly, as the two worked in unison to duck and send out their strikes. Its friend tried to get underneath my defences. However, when I saw what it was going to do, I disappeared in a bright flash of light.

They lowered their 'weapons' as they looked around, wondering where I went. Then I reappeared in another bright brilliance, right behind them. Before they could turn around, I swung my Katana like it was an axe and lopped off one of their heads!

It hit the ground with a soft thud, as the uninjured one let out a high-pitched scream.

Maybe it saw it wasn't going to win, so my opponent tried to make a getaway.

Using its knife-like nails which embedded into the bark of the giant tree, it scrambled up the trunk.

"Oh no you don't!" I growled in annoyance.

I guessed the direction it was heading in, before I disappeared in another bright flash of light. The 'fang head' continued to retreat, as it climbed up into the massive canopy. It released the trunk and started to scamper along a large branch, to jump to another tree. But it only got halfway across when it ran into the legs of a female Lokoti Werewolf.

Next, my foot connected with its ugly mouth, knocking his head back, which put it in the perfect position for my Katana.

Declan told me later he wondered why it began to rain blood, a decapitated head and a falling body, from the tree.

I instantaneously phased back to the ground to see the European Werewolf get the better of his foe. Since it showed no sign of letting go, he used it against him by ramming into the trunk of the tree I was just in. The whole thing trembled at the force and effectively crushed the South American Vampire.

We heard the resulting break of its bones and like a rag doll, his opponent slipped to the ground.

It lay in the dirt, wheezing in pain ironically beside his previous victim Paulo, who too lay in a weakened state.

Together, they watched a female Lokoti Werewolf with her large European Werewolf mate, loom over. The South American Vampire blinked its blood-red eyes, as the boy blinked his yellow ones. They were met by the glowing turquoise and green coloured eyes, which narrowed as they regarded them.

"One of you is going to live tonight," I rumbled out in my thunderous voice.

They saw the European Werewolf lick its lips, as it fixed a hungry look their way.

"The hunter becomes the prey," I spoke again. "The guilty fed on the innocent and now the guilty shall be fed on."

What I really wanted to do was roar in victory that we'd annihilated his coven. At the same time, there was another part of me which wanted to rage at it for doing what a Lokoti Werewolf can't; feed on human. I wanted to lecture it on empathy, to feel his victim's pain. I wanted to lean over and leer, 'how do you like dem apples?'

Then Paulo squeezed his eyes shut, as the jaws of the European Werewolf, engulfed the front of the 'fang heads' face. The human flinched at the wet crunching sound of the Vampire's head being eaten. If he had the strength to turn away, he would have.

In a matter of mouthfuls, a headless corpse soon lay beside the injured human.

It was then we realized we weren't alone. From out of the trees came Machu and his men, with their bright yellow eyes. The Sharman immediately went to his grandson, as Declan and I stood back.

"You stupid boy..." his grandfather shook his head, "...did you desire vengeance so badly, you'd die for it?"

We watched him take off his poncho and begin to tear it into strips. Then using the material, he tied them tightly over the wounds to try to stop the bleeding. But everyone knew it would be futile, as the broken arteries continued to gush. He was bleeding to death and since we were in the middle of nowhere, the Sharman was unable to stop it.

Your mate's blood may turn him into another European Werewolf, but your blood will heal him

Scenes of the Lokoti Werewolves healing their people after the North American Werewolf attack, replayed in my mind. I knew that the voice was right and what I had to do. I knelt down on the other side of the boy.

Everyone watched me raise my right wrist and using my sharp teeth, put a gash in the skin. Then I lowered the injury to the boy's mouth. Some of the men objected, so my mate tried to silence them with a growl.

One man cried out, "You're turning him into another wolf!"

Paulo rolled his head away, too scared to drink. I think he was afraid of the same thing. So I addressed the Sharman:

"My blood won't turn him into a Lokoti Werewolf, only those born with the genes can become one. But I can heal your grandson."

Machu examined me with his bright yellow eyes and I think he could 'see' I was telling the truth.

"I want you to drink her blood." He reassured. "It will save your life."

The seventeen year old looked from his grandfather to the stranger with the bleeding wrist.

I moved behind the boy so I could rest his head in my lap. This way, my supernatural body could also lend warmth to his trembling one. The next time I pressed the gash against his lips, he didn't turn away. I felt his mouth close around the wound and he began to drink.

The men gasped as they looked on. They stared at Paulo's injuries, which began to heal before their very eyes. The bleeding slowed to a stop as the arteries repaired themselves.

Slowly but surely, his bloodied bite marks began to close. However, Lokoti Werewolf blood wasn't as potent as a European Werewolf's. It would be a couple of hours until new skin replaced the broken one, but at least he was out of danger.

When I pulled back my arm, a half-healed Paulo sat up to the astonishment of the men.

Declan came forwards to lick my wound with his hot, wet tongue. His saliva sealed it shut and left new, pink skin in its place. To say 'thank you', I cupped his beastly head between my clawed hands and kissed him on the nose. Next, I held onto him as he raised himself and helped me to my feet.

"Woah...!" I stumbled sideways, as a wave of dizziness washed over.

Paulo must have drank more than I thought and I had to lean against my large mate.

HOP ONTO MY BACK, I'LL GIVE YOU BOTH A LIFT HOME – he offered.

"But you're wounded," I said in concern.

I examined the cuts in his hide however, when I ran my fingers over the marks left by the knife-like nails, I felt new skin in its place. Declan had regenerated within minutes from the superficial injuries.

I'M FINE – he promised – *BUT YOU'RE NOT, YOU'RE LEANING MORE THAN THE TOWER OF PISA.*

"Oh shut up!" I rolled my eyes.

The Sharman helped his grandson to his feet before rechecking his injuries. The bite marks on his neck, wrists and right leg were still there, but they were no longer seeping. The teen leant on the tree as he breathed hard, but my blood inside him, held him together.

Next, Machu turned to face the two Werewolves standing together, with one leaning lopsidedly on the other.

"You saved my grandson's life tonight," he spoke gravely. He looked from the male European Werewolf to the female Lokoti Werewolf. "You gave up your blood to replenish what he lost."

My right hand waved it off, as my left arm slung about my mate's neck. "Don't mention it."

However, we saw it weighed heavily on his mind, as he looked from Paulo to the men from the village.

"I lost my daughter to the Vampiros, but you have saved her son." He said as he stared off into the distance. "I swore vengeance on what you called the 'fang heads', when they took away my child. Now you have saved my grandchild."

Declan and I exchanged glances as our glowing eyes met. I sensed what we did meant a lot to the Sharman and it was hard for him to convey it. One night he was trying to banish us and the next, showering gratitude.

"If there is anything I can offer as a reward," he looked our way again, "speak it and it is yours."

The Peruvian watched the muscled female look on the larger male beside her and he sensed a silent communication took place.

SHOULD WE HIT HIM UP FOR A MILLION CREDITS? – Declan thought humorously.

WHAT THE HELL ARE WE GONNA DO WITH THAT MUCH MONEY? – his wife replied.

I DON'T KNOW, HIRE A GOURMET CHEF? – he snickered which sounded like loud panting.

YOU AND YOUR STOMACH! – she rolled her glowing turquoise eyes.

My mate delivered a slobbery lick to my face and I wiped it off before addressing the Sharman.

"Machu, don't thank us." I spoke bluntly. "Can't you sense that we were supposed to do, what we did tonight?"

The man who was now missing a poncho, blinked in surprise.

"A leads to B which then results in C," I said and ignored the whine from behind. "I heard of a tribe who imbibed Yaje to become one with the Puma Spirit, from my ancestors. You heard of a people who can travel through time by turning themselves into light, from your ancestors. We were meant to come here and help you battle a common foe."

NOT MORE TRIPPY TIME TRAVEL STUFF, PLEASE B! – my mate inwardly groaned.

Then the humans saw the European Werewolf's wife turn and shush him.

I think they were half expecting the monster to maul me. So they were in for another surprise when the four-legged giant lowered himself onto the ground instead. They stared as the muscled woman wearing the gym clothes, climbed onto its back. Then she gestured for Paulo to join them.

"Declan's gonna give us a lift back." I said.

The teen saw the look of awe on the older men's faces, which made him pull back his shoulders in pride. He would be the first and only person in his village who could claim they rode on the back of one of the world's greatest predators. Next, his grandfather helped him over to our position and he climbed on, behind me. My husband turned his beastly head in our direction and I gave a nod.

The muscled male raised himself to his four feet then trotted away.

"Machu," one of the villagers whispered to him. "You are a Seer, did you 'see' this happening?"

"Do you mean that a giant wolf would bring my grandson home?"

"Si."

"No," he smilingly shook his head. "The light temporarily blinded my vision."

Chuckling, he followed as everyone headed back to the Sharman's grass-roofed house.

*****

Upon our return, Declan and I were surprised to find that Machu's home had been invaded. Only it wasn't in the form of 'fang heads', but around ten women had taken over the campfire. They were cooking several things at once as children ran to and fro, playing. However, the men in our party recognized them.

"There's Aunt Isabelle and Aunt Maria," Paulo pointed from behind.

"Maria!" One of the men called out. "A qué hora es el la cena?"

"Pronto!" A woman answered.

"What's going on?" I wondered.

"Pablo just asked his wife when is dinner," Machu smirked. "She said soon."

Our party left the tropical forest to join in the food-making festivities. However, Declan remained, half hidden behind the trees. I think he was wary of scaring them.

As if he sensed this, the Sharman stopped and turned back around.

"It's alright wolf, you are welcome here," he promised.

Tentatively, my mate stepped out from the tree line and walked into the clearing.

Instantly, the children froze and their mothers looked up from their cooking.

Machu said something in Spanish then he pointed at Paulo sitting on Declan's back. I had no idea what he said, but it certainly made an impact. All at once, the women rushed forwards whilst cheering and waving!

Suddenly, we found ourselves in a sea of well-wishes. The women patted his hardened hide and showered the monster with kisses! A couple of the children even ran up to try to pat him, or those who were tall enough did. Two of the women helped Paulo down and then up the veranda stairs, into the house. His grandfather followed them, to tend to his injuries now that they were home.

I too, found myself 'helped down', or basically I was pulled off my mate's back and into the women's arms. So I wouldn't accidentally scratch someone with my claws, I reverted to human form. I received hug after hug, as the mothers kissed my cheek and touched my hair. I think they liked the fact that it looked similar to theirs.

Next, I heard the familiar soft cracking sounds of Declan's bones contorting, as he shrunk back into his human body.

Everyone hushed as they stood back, women, children and men alike. They watched transfixed, as his hide turned into skin, he stood on two feet and his short, stubby snout retreated into a face once more. They stared at his claws which turned into hands again. Then they were looking on a naked, silvery-blonde-haired, blue-eyed, Caucasian, with a late fifties appearance.

Pablo pointed at Declan's clothes which were still sitting on the veranda stairs, where he left them. Immediately, a little boy ran over to retrieve the garments. He boisterously made his way through the crowd, to hand them over to my husband.

"Señor," he held the clothes out.

"Gracias," Declan took them and rewarded him with a wink.

Three of the women snatched the clothes from him and proceeded to help him dress! I saw he was receiving the hero's treatment, that's for sure. Of course, the smug male was loving every minute of it! When a lady helped him on with his shirt and another did the buttons for him, he made sure I was looking.

"You see this, B? This is how a husband should be treated." He grinned. "I hope you're taking notes."

"Shut up."

Next, we were led to one of the logs by the campfire. We sat down and no sooner than we did, we had plates of food thrust our way. It looked like a selection of finger food first, with the main course still cooking. We each picked up an Empanada and took a bite. It was delicious! It was a pastry filled with spiced meat, boiled egg and olives. When we finished, more plates of food were offered.

In the background we heard music start. Three of the men retrieved instruments from the hover-cars which were parked nearby. One played a guitar and another a sort of panpipe, or a zampoña as they called it. The third man played bells which went with the lively nature of the tunes.

Declan looked my way in amusement, "This must be the festivities you saw after the fight."

"I think you might be right," I smiled back.

As the men played, some of the children started to dance. Their mothers smilingly watched, as they continued to cook and serve. One of the younger women grabbed her husband and danced with him. They received several cheers and even one or two wolf-whistles from the crowd.

We clapped our hands in time to the music as did everyone else, while the couple did a traditional dance. The only time we weren't clapping, was when we were eating. It was like we were being treated to dinner and a show.

*****

The men helped the women with the feast, as they prepared a special banquet called a Pachamanca. It was a selection of herbs, meats and vegetables, cooked underground with hot stones. The heated rocks came courtesy of the campfire and it was a slow process. However, nobody went hungry with the selection of salads and finger foods, available.

It was around midnight when dinner was served and Machu emerged from his house to eat. Paulo didn't however, as his grandfather had bandaged him up and put him to bed. We were advised that the teen was sleeping in his grandfather's bed and that Machu would sleep on the sofa tonight.

"We can just go to a hotel -" my husband began, when the Sharman shushed him.

"You are guests! You saved my grandson's life! I will not turn you out!" Machu cried.

This attracted everyone's attention and next, we found ourselves inundated with invitations!

"We have a spare bedroom."

"We can put you in the children's bedroom and the children can sleep in the living room."

"You can sleep in our bed and we'll sleep on the sofa-bed."

My hand found Declan's and he squeezed it, as we were touched by everyone's generosity.

"No," the Sharman spoke over the top of them. "They are MY guests and they have a bed tonight, or any other night they stay."

The villagers quieted at his proclamation. I looked around the circle and saw many a family unit. Sleepy children curled up on either side of their parents, with their faces peeking out from under an arm. Everyone was full and content and it showed.

"Machu, will you not tell us a story by the fire?" Pablo requested.

"Si," everyone agreed.

"We heard about the destruction of the Vampiros," his wife spoke. "But tell us about their beginning."

"Si," her friends nodded.

"Ah," Machu looked around. "I cannot tell you about the coven we fought today, but I know a little about the type of Vampiros that was eliminated."

"Was the whole species of Vampiros, destroyed?" Another wondered.

"No, there are others out there..." the Sharman looked at the dark forest with his yellow eyes, "...but they are in hiding and live in secret."

"Why?" A little boy asked.

"So they can hunt us," Machu told him. "If they lived in the open then they'd be arrested for murder. But because they live quietly, the authorities do not know about them. When they feed on us, la policia think it's a wild animal attack, or piranhas."

"Which is what they told us, when our people were fed on," the boy's father shook his head.

"Hmm," everyone frowned as they stared disgruntled, at the fire.

"The South American Vampire is an old one, as a whole." He continued. "One can live for a few hundred years, but their species has been here much longer than that. They were here before the Spanish, the Inca, the Chimu and even before the Aguarunas. They adjust to each new dynasty like it's the latest fashion. They use what is useful and disregard the rest."

"That's true," I recalled the SSIT Report on the subject. "A couple of Aztec Priests were even South American Vampires. They left after the Spanish invasion, to find new hunting grounds. When the human sacrificial ceremonies stopped, it drove away the Vampires. They travelled so far north, they crossed into Alaska. There, in the Alaska Range they battled my kin, the Lokoti Werewolves."

Everyone listened as they looked expectantly my way, waiting to hear more.

"Then what happened?" The little boy urged. "Did you destroy them then, as you did today?"

"My forefathers fought them and it was said to have been a bloodied battle." I told him. "Ultimately, the Werewolves won but they lost many lives."

Declan chimed in, "Werewolves have always been the enemy of Vampires."

The boy cocked his head to the side. "Why?"

"The 'fang heads' hunt us for our regenerative capabilities." He advised. "Vampires can survive on animal blood, but human blood is tastier and if they want to increase their strength, Werewolf blood is the best."

This made the children's mouths fall open as they stared in surprise.

"In the beginning, European Vampires fought European Werewolves over territory. Neither of us liked to share our kill. Sure, a coven will feed altogether, but they don't want to share with a Werewolf who eats ten times more than they do. So in the beginning, they killed us so we wouldn't kill their humans. Then they discovered the healing properties in our blood. Now I'm the last of my kind, since the rest of my breed was too stupid and violent to survive." He said bitterly.

"But you're not," a little girl spoke up.

"That's because I was raised by B's people, the Lokoti, who taught me there's a better way." Declan said.

I squeezed his hand as I smiled softly on him, in the firelight.

"Vampiros and Werewolves are not the only Shape Shifters we have encountered," Machu announced.

"Oh yeah?" My husband listened. "Who or should I say, *what* else have you met?"

"A long time ago, around the time when Light People freely travelled the Earth, there were Human/Animal Shape Shifters." The Sharman advised. "In the Andes, there were humans who could transform into panthers. But I have not seen one in a long, long time."

"No way...!" Declan breathed. "Are you serious, actual humans turning into animals?"

"So do you señor, so I do not understand your surprise." Machu smirked.

"Yeah, but I'm a Werewolf." He sat up straighter. "Even in my other shape, I still have some kind of human semblance."

"Just as you turn into the wolf and back again, these humans could turn into panthers." The Sharman continued. "The full moon affected them too and they were as strong as the señora."

Machu meant me, which meant their strength was possibly the equivalent of a Lokoti Werewolf.

"What happened to them?" My mate wondered. "Don't tell me they're now extinct?"

"The first and last time I saw one, I was thirteen." He answered. "I was hunting in the forest with my father when we became separated. I wandered alone, trying to make my way home until I realized I was being watched. It was then I looked up and saw IT, sitting on a branch above. At first I thought it was an ordinary panther and it was about to ambush me! Then I saw its eyes and they were completely black."

The children and their parents sucked in their breath as they hung on his every word. Even my husband was listening closely with an incredulous expression. He looked like he half believed him and half didn't.

"Then what happened?" The little boy urged again.

"I was so scared, my legs stopped working!" He spoke animatedly. "Then the panther gave me a nod. At first, I thought I was imagining things, how can a panther know body language? So I asked it if it understood me and it nodded again! Then I asked if it had seen my father and it pointed its paw in a particular direction."

"And then what happened?" The little girl pressed.

"I thanked it for its help and went the way it had shown." Machu chuckled. "As I walked, I could hear the rustling of the leaves in the trees above. I knew it was following me but I didn't feel afraid anymore. I knew it was protecting me and it stayed until I found my father."

The parents and children sat back in awe, whereas Declan leaned forward.

"How do you know it wasn't hunting you?" He disagreed. "Was it a full moon?"

"Human/Animal Shape Shifters don't hunt human," I put my hand on his leg.

This made him look on peculiarly, "How would you know?"

I opened my mouth and was about to blab about the SSIT Report on the subject, when I remembered something.

Most of the SSIT Reports were made confidential and for good reason. Only the Circulate and the Lokoti Tribe saw the one made on the Different Breeds of Werewolves, to protect the anonymity of the pack. My great, great grandmother also shared with the Lokoti the SSIT Report on the Separate Species of Vampires. However, there was one report which the Circulate never shared and it was the one on Human/Animal Shape Shifters.

"Woman's instinct," I lied as I looked away.

"The señora's right," Machu agreed. "Human/Animal Shape Shifters do not hunger for human like Werewolves or Vampires do."

"But you said the full moon affects them -" Declan debated.

"Si señor, I did." He said evenly. "Because the moon affects someone, it does not necessarily turn them into killers. It might do that to you, but it does not do that to all your kind. The moonlight made them shift, it didn't make them murderers."

"How do you know for sure?" My husband tested. "You met ONE and that could have been a fluke. If there were more of my kind out there, I tell you now you WOULDN'T want to meet them. You certainly wouldn't walk away, afterwards."

"I know because my people have always known," Machu spoke patiently. "Our history and legends are passed down orally. My father taught me, his father taught him and so on. There was a time when my people who are blessed with gifts from Our Mother Puma, hunted on a full moon with people who could turn into panthers. We lived together peacefully, until the Inca came and the Spanish after them. That Human/Animal Shape Shifter I saw when I was thirteen, may have been the last of its kind."

A quiet settled over the group as everyone's eyes dropped guiltily that another creature had met its extinction.

That was until like a tiny flame of hope, I experienced another one of my all-knowing feelings, a second time that day.

"No, it wasn't the last of its kind." I said softly. "But I think they've relocated to new hunting grounds, though."

~~~~~~

~ 27 ~

15th February 2291

I sat on the side of the 164 year old Chiron's bed, holding his frail hand between my stronger ones. It was like I was holding on for dear life, afraid to let go because I didn't want to let go of him. My grandnephew who was born 61 years after me, was dying of old age.

Behind me stood my husband and Second in the pack. His hands rested supportively on my shoulders, as he sadly looked on. Surrounding the bed were Chiron's children, grandchildren, great grandchildren and great, great grandchildren. At the end of the bed stood his elderly son Stone, his middle-aged grandson Forrest, his great grandson Caesar and great, great grandson Tyson. All of whom were Lokoti Werewolves, thanks to the Riverclaw genes.

The pack has always had a Riverclaw and a Wisetail, although some families weren't always activated. Thanks to our trip back in time, now Declan and I knew why; Aru who was the very first Lokoti Werewolf, had been a Riverclaw and he made a Wisetail his Second. However, this was the first time the pack had five Riverclaws as members. If one thought of a set of scales, I guess Chiron's departure was meant to bring back some balance.

With my grandnephew dying, I felt like I was losing another tie to my past. Chiron was my cousin Phoenix's son and the grandson of Uncle Julian, who was my mother's brother. My grandparents Arabella and Emanuel Riverclaw had twins, a boy and girl. The daughter became a Circulator like her mother and the son a Lokoti Werewolf, like his father. When another Lokoti Werewolf in the shape of Hunter Wisetail, mated with my mother, bingo! I was born, the Last Circulator and the first female Lokoti Werewolf.

I squeezed Chiron's hand as I wished I could will my long life onto him. His eyes remained closed, as his breathing grew slower and more labored. I trembled as tears left my eyes, from sensing his body's energy field, grow weaker. He was so frail, he no longer had the strength to keep his eyes open.

After a long exhale, his lungs didn't expand with a new inhale. Chiron didn't take another breath again. Everybody in the room froze, as they stared at the unmoving figure in the bed. With our acute hearing, we all heard his heart had stopped.

Silence...nobody moved nor said a thing. Everyone wanted to hold onto their memories of the elder who'd departed this life for the next. All the men stood still like statues, allowing their watery eyes to overflow.

After a minute, Stone eventually said, "He's with Mom now."

Everyone let go of their long-held breaths, with Forrest moving to give his father a supportive pat on the back.

Declan squeezed my shoulders, "C'mon B, he's with Rain, like he's with all who've left."

But I didn't move because I couldn't. I sat there, uselessly clinging to his hand as I mourned. The only part of me which moved were the hot tears, streaming down my face.

The image of a teenage Chiron flashed through my mind, as I remembered dancing with him at Uncle Harry's 175th Birthday Party. I recalled encouraging him to go and talk to his crush, Rain Lightfoot. I recalled how proudly he showed off his firstborn, the day of Stone's birth. It was identical to the day his first grandchild, Forrest was born. I closed my eyes as I pictured how he looked, tenderly rocking the tiny babe in his large arms.

Like all Lokoti Werewolves, Chiron was a devoted husband and father. He had Phoenix's cheeky sense of humour, but also Emanuel's patience. Grandfather would often talk over family problems with the younger Werewolf, who had the same disposition as him. They'd discuss my mother's infamous temper and ideas to modernize the family, which her Calculator would encourage. Upon occasion, they'd even discuss Vincent and his mistrust of our kind. If the pack were headed towards a violent altercation with outsiders, Chiron would be included in Grandfather and Dad's discussions, when they were First and Second. Because of this, it was no surprise the afternoon they announced Chiron would become First. He kept the peace in the family, the pack and even the tribe, in his position as an Elder.

The same day Chiron became First, he asked Declan to be his Second. I remember how proud my husband felt when he was asked in front of the pack. Over the many years, he proved his loyalty and valour a hundred times. He's not only fought for his wife, but his family and his pack. They made an unbeatable team, with Chiron's patience and Declan's bluntness. The pack greatly respected their First and Second, which made his absence harder.

Finally, I released his hand and gently placed it over his chest. Then I slowly rose to my unsteady feet. I noticed how my husband remained near his wife, lest she fall over. He could tell I was stiff from sitting for so long.

"C'mon," he cajoled, "let's get a cup of coffee downstairs."

His hand reached for mine but I pulled away. I didn't want a drink and I certainly didn't want to eat, either. I left the bedroom and then the house. I had to get out and get some air...

Downstairs, I found the rest of the pack quietly wandering around the living room.

They looked up upon my approach almost expectantly. They sensed the death of their First, so I don't know why they were looking at me like that. Were they waiting for me to announce that Chiron was alive and well, and it all had been a mistake?

I went straight for the front door, which I accidentally opened too hard. It banged loudly against the wall before I could stop it. Accidentally again, I slammed it behind, as I hurried down the veranda stairs.

The gravel drive was caked in snow, with mounds of it along the sides. I stomped through the slush as I headed for the tree line. I went for a spontaneous walk down to the river, no never mind I didn't have my coat or snow boots to prevent frostbite. I was going to gamble that my supernatural muscle would protect from serious harm.

But I had to walk, to get some air, to get away from it all... Life... Death... Afterlife... Reincarnation... The cycle and recycle of existence.

Chiron was surrounded by family when he left, his legacy was his progeny. When I evolve, what will I leave behind? The Circulate Mainframe inside an empty headquarters and the multinational corporation, Hodge Endeavor? Since the Circulate was kept a secret as was its control of the company, nobody would know. Who would know about my instructions to finance the world's charities? Who would hear how I supported the terra forming projects, as I funded the off-world colonies? Nobody knew Circulators existed, except a select few in the supernatural world, which was a minority compared to the natural one.

I'd leave no genetic legacy, because I couldn't procreate. I was the Last Circulator and because my bio-electromagnetic field was in temporal flux, I wouldn't be reincarnated. Sometimes, my situation made me feel like I wasn't even alive. Everyone else reproduces, ages then dies. Meanwhile, I'm stagnant, unchanging and I stuck out like a scarecrow. Life was passing me by, with crops being sewn and grown then harvested, while I looked on.

I stomped down the snowy slope, sometimes slipping knee-deep into sink holes. My sneakers and jeans turned wet but I trudged onwards. I liked the quiet of the woods in winter, although they looked a little desolate. The only greenery was the boughs of the evergreen trees and with the snow smothering everything else, it was like an icy, white desert.

As I marched onwards, I became aware of the sound of running water and I realized I was approaching the riverbank.

It's funny how often I turn to this piece of geography, for meditation. I'm sure others have come here before and probably will after I'm gone. This land is legacy and its' life was its progeny. It was a mother who provided for us, with the land her womb and nature the nourishing umbilical chord.

I stopped at the waters edge and sighed heavily. My dark blue eyes were the same colour as the river, except for the errant block of ice floating on top. Like a traffic jam, I watched the pieces follow the current and occasionally collide. Imagining how cold the water must be, made me shiver and I hugged myself.

In three days time, Chiron's ashes would be sprinkled into these waters. But sometime today, another Tribal Elder with a helper, will come to wrap his body in a woven funeral shroud. Then as the funeral pyre is readied, his body will lie in the 'Holy Room', which was the spiritual equivalent of a waiting room and physically part of the tribe's Meeting Hall. I heard a voice speak from memory:

"It's a special room where the deceased are kept before the funeral."
Grandpa explained. "Two Lokoti painted as the Lokoti Wolf who is the
protector of our tribe, stand guard to watch over them. Then the deceased are
taken to the Holy Grounds on the third night after their passing. They are
sent into the next life by family and the tribe as the Tribal Elders lead the
funeral chant. The flames of the funeral pyre and our singing, releases their
spirit and enables them to leave behind their earthly concerns. Then in the
Holy Hunting Grounds, the departed will be reunited with loved ones who
died before them. There they are altogether for a little while, before they come

back to be reborn. This is why the deceased's ashes are sprinkled into the river, to symbolize the ongoing nature of life."

I stood still on the snowy riverbank and stared as if hypnotized, out at icy waters.

"Welcome Chiron to the afterlife, won't you Grandpa? Help him find Rain again. Let him be reunited with his lost loved ones. Let him leave this life peacefully, so he'll return refreshed." I murmured.

Only the quiet roar of the river was my response, as I shivered in the frozen forest.

*****

When it turned dark, I left the river and began the hike up the hill, back to my house.

The closer I came, I could smell dinner cooking. By the aroma, I guessed Declan was making fettuccine carbonara. It was one of my favourites and I smiled, sensing he did it to cheer his wife. Although I appreciated the gesture, I didn't have an appetite.

I walked out of the woods and crossed my snowy garden. I had to take particular care when I stomped up the slippery, icy veranda steps. However, once I was inside I paused, for the table was set which showed dinner was ready. Oh oh...

When I stopped in the kitchen entryway, I saw Declan was serving up.

"Um hi, I'm not hungry." I warned.

He paused in his food preparation, long enough to glance my way. My aging mate looked on in concern. His hair was more silver than blonde these days, and his wrinkled brow furrowed.

"B, you haven't eaten since breakfast this morning."

"I know, but I don't feel like anything."

He frowned as he returned to pouring the creamy carbonara sauce, over the pasta. "I think you should at least try."

I looked away and my eyes wandered towards the staircase. "I think I might have a hot bath. Maybe I'll be hungry afterwards?"

"Good idea."

Then I turned around and headed upstairs. I undressed in our bedroom and tugged off my wet shoes, socks then jeans. Not only were they soaked through, but they were partly frozen. I wiggled my toes which confirmed I hadn't suffered from frostbite. If I'd been human, I could have been in danger of losing them.

Fifteen minutes later, I lay in a steaming-hot, bubble bath, with my long, dark hair tied up in a bun.

My previously blue skin now looked red with a layer of sweat on my face. But it was the perfect temperature to evaporate any residual tension. The aromatherapy of the scented bubble bath also helped.

I sighed, as I lay my head back on the edge of the tub. I stared at the white tiled wall then at the tiny spots of mould on the bathroom ceiling. Next, I picked up my yellow, duck-shaped sponge. I squeezed all the soapy water out of it then I dunked it in the water before squeezing it again.

As I watched the sponge behave as it should, I contemplated further on the afterlife.

I wondered if they have baths in the space time continuum? Not that they'd need them, if one existed as a being of light and energy. But if an 18th Century Aristocratic Ball could be reproduced, I'm sure the powers-that-be could replicate bathwater. Hell, science is always reporting on water being found on planets or other celestial objects. Surely they wouldn't deny a girl her favourite form of stress relief?

*****

Fifty minutes later, I returned wearing 'Ugg Boots' and my tartan, flannel pyjamas. As soon as I arrived downstairs, Declan paused whatever he was watching on the Internet TV.

He stood up from the couch to order, "Take a seat, I'll get dinner."

Silently, I sat down in the spot he'd just vacated. I heard him move around the kitchen, opening the oven before shutting it again. Then he carried out two dinner plates of fettuccine carbonara, complete with garlic bread.

"Oh yum!" My eyes widened as soon as I saw.

Declan smiled smugly at my reaction as he sat down beside. I thought it was sweet he'd waited to eat with me. Casually, he picked up the remote again and pressed 'play'. An early 21st Century program called 'That 70's Show', appeared on the Internet TV.

The sitcom was just what the doctor ordered. We guffawed at the hints of what the teens got up to, in the smoke-filled basement. When one of the kids was called upstairs by his parents, I giggled at how they made it look like the walls were moving. Declan periodically looked my way, to watch me devour my delicious dinner in between laughter.

"We'd never had gotten away with doing something like that, at that age." He commented.

"I couldn't because my Lokoti Werewolf father would smell it a mile away." I agreed. "You couldn't, as the pack would lecture you on how it could affect your European Werewolf bloodlust."

"You got that right," he muttered in between mouthfuls.

I lowered my plate as I speculated, "Actually, I don't think there was any 'pot' on tribal lands, when we were growing up."

"I don't think so either, I never heard of anyone getting stoned." He agreed. "I didn't find out what marijuana smelled like, until we visited Amsterdam."

The memory made me laugh, "The look on your face when that Waiter in the café, offered you a hash brownie."

"You almost took him up on his offer!" He retorted.

"Maybe eating it wouldn't have the same effects as smoking it...?"

"There was no way in hell, I was gonna let you find out," he said firmly.

"Bossy-boots," I smiled softly.

"Stick with me kid, I'll take care of you." He patted my thigh before recommencing his meal.

When his head turned to continue watching the show, I studied his profile. I thought he was still handsome, no matter how old he looked. In my opinion, the lines around his eyes or on his forehead, made him more look mature. His aged face suited his domineering nature.

Then I said, "You do take care of me."

His response was to lift up my legs and rest them on top of his. Periodically, he rubbed them affectionately as he watched the sitcom. This was of course, in between him shovelling food into his mouth.

I managed to eat half of my serving. Once he depleted his meal, I passed him mine to finish. However, I did remove the garlic bread from the plate and ate that instead.

Is this what life is? Or, is this what OUR life is? We have each other and I think it's enough for him. He seemed content, how he curled up with his mate on the couch, or in bed each night. Occasionally, I'd still hear him inhale my scent when he held me in his arms. Now and then his eyes would glaze over and I'd guess he was staring at my aura.

Sometimes I wondered if we hadn't ended up together, what would he being doing instead? Would his bloodlust win and he'd collapse underneath the overpowering hunger? With his mother and brother deceased, who were part of his reasons for abstaining; would he give in and hunt human?

Declan's legacy he'd be leaving was the end of the European Werewolf. He'd been so careful not to create anymore of his kind, either by procreation or contamination. The humans he'd bitten, he ensured they wouldn't survive. The wet-crunching sound of him devouring flesh and bone inside his massive, canine jaws, still rang in my ears.

So we wouldn't be leaving behind any children, maybe that's a good thing? That was his other quality, how he made the fact that his wife was barren, a blessing instead of a curse. Whereas Chiron was a tender father, Declan could be a tender husband. Chiron looked on his children and grandchildren as tiny miracles. Declan looked on the tribe's female Lokoti Werewolf as his personal miracle. In spite of my tall stature, broad shoulders and athletic build, he could make me feel sexy or girlish. Hell, his favourite chastisement was calling me 'princess'.

This was our legacy – our relationship.

We were renown as the tribe's 'Most Argumentative Couple' as well as the longest married pair. Our romance was created from adversity and our mating was born in bloodshed. In the beginning, his love was shown in the form of loathing, as he feared rejection and ridicule. He knew my father didn't approve of him and their enmity continued, throughout our marriage.

Declan and I fought each other and fought for the other. We grew up together, moved in together and cared for one another. I'd turn him into a Circulator then together, we'd evolve to the space time continuum. Then our names will be carved together, on the back of one of the Sacred Totem Poles. This way, we'll be remembered together; the Last Circulator and the last European Werewolf; light and darkness; Yin and Yang.

With a legacy such as this, I really shouldn't complain.

~~~~~~

19th February 2291

Going to Chiron's funeral was hard. Although Declan and I had attended many thanks to our long lives, they didn't get any easier. They only served as a reminder of how unusual we were, which could be isolating.

We stood with my Riverclaw family up the front of the crowd, as the whole tribe came to farewell their Tribal Elder. Standing in the freezing night air on the snowy Holy Grounds, we watched the flames of the funeral pyre engulf the wrapped-up body. The other Tribal Elders sang the funeral chant to the drum beat, as everyone looked on in respectful silence.

No matter how many times I go to one of these things, I always found it hard to watch the body to burn. It hurt especially because they made me relive Grant's funeral. I remember how difficult it had been to send off my first mate into the afterlife, so much so I didn't want to believe he was gone. I remember how afraid I was of the flames extinguishing his body, which I wanted to save. I didn't have a problem with scattering the ashes into the river, but it was how the body became ashes, which bothered me.

So, I did what I always did at funerals; I fixed my gaze at the tips of the flames which reached high into the starry sky. I envisioned his spirit using them to ride the heat upwards, like a metaphysical rocket. Then I imagined his spirit leaving this planet's atmosphere and floating into outer space. I pictured him travelling towards the space time continuum, which looked like a borderline of white light, on the edge of the existence.

As customary, Declan and I stood together, holding hands. My left hand was gloved but my right one wasn't. His hot hand certainly kept it warm as his fingers entwined with mine. Then I felt his fingertips massage my palm and I knew it was his way of comforting me. Appreciatively, I squeezed his larger hand back as our eyes remained fixed ahead.

*****

The funeral pyre would burn all night to reduce the body to cinders, but the ceremony went for an hour.

The tribe began to dissipate and the parents with young children were the first to leave. They led away their rugged-up 'rug rats' and bundled them into their warm hover-cars. In a steady stream, the vehicles floated away towards the community centre and therefore home, in a soft hum.

Forrest turned our way to say, "We're serving refreshments at our house, in a small family gathering."

Immediately, Declan looked my way to show he'd go along with whatever I decided.

"Thank you Forrest," I said in a tight voice. "But I think we'll head home."

He sensed as my husband did, that I couldn't cope being social now, even if it was just family. He gave a nod before he turned to leave with Caesar, his wife Maria and their children. I remained there for a moment, as I watched the large family walk away.

My husband put his arm about my waist and as such, he guided me to our hover-car parked on the side of the road.

I'd forced myself to not to cry, so I could look as strong as a male Lokoti Werewolf. I managed to hold it in during the funeral, not break down when we walked back to our hover-car, or even inside the vehicle for the ride home. Declan opened the car door for me and once I was inside, he closed it behind. It felt like I was holding my breath, by how tight my chest felt or my eyes stung.

When we arrived home, he unlocked the front door and escorted me inside. I gripped onto the banister hard, as I pulled myself up the staircase. Then as soon as I walked through my bedroom doorway, I howled in grief! I sobbed loudly as I collapsed face-first, on top of the bed.

Chiron... Chiron's gone... my grandnephew whom I loved... my First whom I respected and obeyed...is gone.

I heard Declan sigh loudly as he came into the bedroom. Then I felt the bed rock as he collapsed beside his wife. I felt his large hand rub my back, as he tried to be there for his mate.

Momentarily, I stopped crying to manage out, "I'm OK, you don't have to babysit me."

"Yeah well, what if I'm not OK and I need someone to comfort me too?"

In surprise, I turned my head and saw his blue eyes were full of tears...

As quick as lightning, I grabbed hold of him, the same time as he grabbed hold of me.

We clung to each other in a tight embrace. As he rolled onto his back, he pulled me on top and held me against his heaving chest. With his strength, if I'd been human, my rib cage could have been crushed! But I appreciated the force right then. It let me know he needed me just as much as I needed him.

After ten minutes, Declan loosened his hold to cup my face. He angled it upwards to examine my youthful features and I felt his relief. I sensed he relished the fact that it was unchanging.

"Thank God I've got you, B..." he uttered out, "...thank God I've got you."

My husband wasn't an overly a religious man, although he wore the small, gold crucifix which had been his mother's. I saw his watery blue eyes look down and next, one of his hands tugged out the small, gold crucifix I was wearing underneath my clothes. He knew it had been my great, great grandmother's.

"I remember reading in Elisha's diary of when her Cambridge friends found out she was a Circulator." I sniffed. "You wanna know one of the first questions they asked?"

"What?"

"Have you ever met Jesus Christ?" I giggled and it made Declan laugh too. I continued, "But if you did travel back in time to see him, what would you say to the guy? I mean, if he really was the son of God, he'd know you were from the future. Would you walk up and shake his hand and say 'thanks for being tortured to death, for me'?"

"Maybe he'd appreciate the gratitude." He smilingly shrugged. "Or you could warn that every time he sees a Roman, he should duck and hide."

We both laughed again and the humour felt good at that moment.

I thought aloud, "Isn't it funny how many aspects of Christianity or Buddhism, or our Lokoti beliefs in the afterlife, are so similar? In Christianity, Jesus arose from the dead to live again. He was resurrected, so in a sense that's like reincarnation. Buddhists believe in reincarnation. The Lokoti believe in reincarnation. With the Circulate believing there's the Big Bang, the Big Crunch and another Big Bang, that's like reincarnation."

Declan's face softened as he looked on his mate with love. His hands tenderly dried my face, before he pulled it in for a kiss. His lips smothered mine and I closed my eyes to enjoy the sensuousness.

Then he pulled away to say, "Well you're not boring, I'll give you that much."

He rolled over on the bed again and I found myself lying underneath him. He turned amorous as he kissed his wife over and over. He pushed apart my lips with his and I felt his tongue touch mine. His kisses grew in fervour as they lasted for longer. I felt his hands remove my coat and then his, before he temporarily raised himself to take off our snow boots and thick socks.

"Declan," I began.

"Hmm...?" He sounded to show he was listening, while he was undressing us.

"Do you think there is a God?" I wondered.

"Do you mean a Christian God?" He asked back, as he removed his black jacket.

"A Christian God, or a Jewish God, or an Islamic God, or a Buddha, or a Wicca Goddess, or whatever humans call 'He', 'She' or 'It'. Do you believe in a divine and powerful entity? Do you think we might meet them, in the space time continuum?"

He gave a funny look which momentarily disappeared when he pulled off his black shirt over his head.

"You're the one who's been there, so you tell me." He shrugged.

I frowned as I started to unbutton my black business suit.

"Yeah but I saw somebody else's version of the space time continuum. Remember, Elisha made it look like an 18th Century Ball. Also, I was under the impression where I was, was like a 'waiting room', just outside the continuum. It was where those who were inside, could come outside and visit. When Great Grandma and Great Grandfather walked in to tell me I had to go back, they'd come from the Holy Hunting Grounds."

This made him pause in the midst of our undressing, "You saw David and Clara Riverclaw there, too?"

"Yeah, didn't I tell you?"

"No."

Then he unbuttoned his black jeans and pushed them down, as I removed my suit jacket and trousers. I raised my arms so he could pull off my white blouse over my head, then it was only our underwear which remained.

"That makes sense." He conceded after a moment. "Maybe what you saw, was a preview of what's to come?"

My eyes widened at his words, "That's what you said to me, as Greyson!"

His hands slipped into my panties and he caressed the sensitive skin, before removing them. My bra was the next to go and his boxers were the last. Then he laid himself over his wife and made himself comfortable, by adjusting her body to fit his. He parted my legs and raised my knees so he could lie between my thighs.

He smiled mischievously, "I hope as Greyson, I was well-behaved towards you?"

"Definitely not!" I giggled. "You were a cheeky bastard."

"Good." He snickered back. "If you told me I'd behaved like the perfect gentleman, I wouldn't have believed you."

He growled as he used his teeth to graze my jaw line. Declan chewed on my ear before reclaiming my mouth with his. I felt his teeth pierce my bottom lip, making me whimper. No sooner than I did, he sucked on the wound to taste my blood whilst simultaneously healing it. I felt him harden in arousal by his member now pressing into my moist folds.

I clung to my large husband as I basked in his body heat. His muscle tone may not be the same as it was, but it was still there. The bedcovers felt cold against my bare skin, so his high temperature staved off the chill. I held onto him as he moved up and down, rubbing his crotch against the outside of mine. When we felt I'd become wet in excitement, he slowly eased himself inside and emitted a low growl of contentment.

"Hey B...?" He uttered out, as I began to move my hips back and forth.

"Uh huh...?" I managed back, as he pushed deeper.

"You...wanna know...why I don't want...to evolve... yet?"

"Why?"

Declan stopped and raised himself above me and questioningly, I gazed up at him.

"So I can do this with you for the rest of my life, before we turn into beings of light and no longer have bodies." He said seriously. "I don't know how I'm gonna handle eternity without your touch or smell. Living forever in the continuum, sounds like a frickin' long time without sex to me!"

I cracked up laughing at his point of view, although his expression was earnest.

He went on, "We're physical beings, Werewolves. We rely on touch and taste and smell. You as my mate, keep my bloodlust boiling. You keep me hungry. B, you keep me alive."

My eyes widened at his words, before I reached up to pull him back down.

His mouth mashed against mine and we breathed through our noses. He recommenced moving over his mate, as I moved my hips in sync with his. As he increased in strength and speed, my nails dug into the skin on his back. After a while, I had to move my mouth away to let out a gasp, as his pushing turned into pounding. But still I clung onto him, while I closed my eyes and concentrated on the sensations he brought out.

Several times, Declan adjusted position as he tried to find that perfect angle which would tip his wife's control over the edge. When he found it, he heard her growl and saw her dark blue eyes burn turquoise. My mouth which was parted to let out gasps, now emitted growls between sharpening teeth. I was squashed against the mattress, still clinging to the cause, as I felt the hypnotising waves of heat, move up through my torso. The heat brought with it a tingling sensation, which felt like my body was opening itself up.

My face was crushed against his chest with his head above mine, as he strained to maintain the speed and angle which was working. His shaft rubbed against my clit as he pushed in and out at the velocity of a race horse. We held onto each other as he pushed so hard and fast, we were making the bed vibrate. My thighs squeezed his hips as my nails broke through his skin.

Suddenly, my legs and even my whole body went stiff and he knew what this meant.

The vibrations of the rocking bed, the clitoral contact and his huge member delving into my nether regions, worked. The waves of heat and the tingling and opening sensation, combined into the euphoria of an orgasm. It radiated outwards, down my legs and arms in waves of ecstasy. I held my breath as I tried to hold onto the bliss.

"Oh shit – oh shit – oh shit – that was good!" He panted out with a red face. Temporarily, he stopped to look down and ask, "Are you ready to go again?"

Instead of saying so, I pulled him over me once more. My face returned to his chest, as the rest of me was squashed between him and the bed. But did I mind? Hell no! Especially when the recommencement of activities so soon after the other pleasurable activity; was like riding on the coattails of utter delight. The second orgasm didn't take long to arrive and the third was right behind it.

This is how Declan and I coped by outliving everyone, with each other. Our want, our need and our obsession for the other brought comfort and sexual satisfaction. As Werewolves, we had the bloodlust which pulled on our self control. We had the murderous inclinations, which if they were in a human, society would declare them unsafe and put them away. However, it was the same bloodlust that made us hunger after the one person whose scent, whose body and whose touch, dominated every fibre of our being.

Mating...the biological bond of Werewolf husband and Werewolf wife.

~~~~~~

25th February, 2291

Declan took the week off work of Chiron's funeral and closed the Garage. The Lokoti didn't mind, as it wasn't just our First's family who were in mourning, but the whole tribe was. I didn't do any academic work that week either, although I'd been booked to do a guest lecture. Instead, I called my PA at Hodge Endeavor and she rescheduled, due to a 'death in the family'.

My Personal Assistant not only served as my academic contact, but she was also my liaison with the company. She kept my appointments for Board Meetings and any invitations to lecture or attend a seminar, went through her. She'd forward on important correspondence and we both had access to my electronic schedule. If the Board Members wanted to contact me, I'd hear about it from her or the Circulate Mainframe. Both she and the computer kept my anonymity from the public and maintained a safe distance from the media.

The Mainframe also oversaw Declan's and my birth certificates, driver's licenses, passports, marriage certificates and death certificates. It would send instructions to the Hodge Endeavour office in Washington D.C. and its Legal Department would liaise with the appropriate sectors of government. The birth certificates would be issued by the Hodge Endeavour Hospital in Anchorage.

The multinational corporation had its metaphorical fingers in many pies, as it sponsored hospitals, owned pharmaceutical companies, funded educational facilities such as the former Hamilton's College, or renown Universities. It was part of the World Stock Exchange in New York and in London. Also, it held controlling shares in several high tech corporations, which were responsible for many new inventions.

After my first academic persona Dr. Bianca Sabre 'died', I received my death certificate in the mail. In amusement, I carried it out to show Declan, who was working on his orchids in the greenhouse.

"Hey look, I'm dead!" I laughed, as I held up the document.

He glared at the piece of paper before he continued working. I sensed he didn't think it was funny, as death to old age had become his worst enemy. Especially since our human family members, continued to be swept away with the tide of time.

When my identity as Dr. Bianca Wisetail came to an end, I received another death certificate along with a new birth certificate and other forms of I.D. to become Dr. Bianca Riverclaw. I carried it over to our garage, where Declan was working on his car.

"Check it out, your 'second wife' just 'carked it'!" I joked.

Again he glared at the piece of paper and with a dissatisfied snarl, he returned to his engine.

Since it was a bone of contention, when my alias as Dr. Bianca Carmichael came to a close, complete with a new death certificate; I didn't show him. Without thinking, I left it lying on top of the table, along with our other mail. It was a winter's evening and I went upstairs to have a hot shower and change into my flannel pyjamas.

I heard Declan come home from work, by the front door opening and closing. When I came back downstairs, I found him standing by our fireplace, ripping up the certificate and feeding it to the flames! He must have seen it when he was checking the mail.

"What are you doing?!" I cried out in alarm.

"What does it frickin' look like?!" He snapped. "I'm sick and tired of these things!"

"That's not going to solve anything!" I rebuked. "Now I have to get my PA to send me another one!"

I saw how much Chiron's passing affected Declan. During the week he was home, he couldn't sit still. He invited old Heath Huntington over, to talk about their orchids and what fertilizer worked the best. He spent a whole day in the greenhouse, planting new radishes, lettuce, cucumber, celery, tomatoes, eggplant and artichokes. He reorganized the pantry and the pots and pans cupboard. He even went on a cooking frenzy, preparing six new jars of antipasto mix or his feta cheese preserve. In the evenings, he made three course dinners complete with exotic desserts such as tiramisu, chocolate mousse, Crème Brule or profiteroles.

On Friday afternoon, the European Werewolf thought of a way of combining his two favourite things; food and sex. He created an 'indoor picnic' for us, on the rug by the fireplace. He pushed aside the coffee table and one of the couches, to make room. When I was allowed to come downstairs and see, I found him with a picnic hamper, in front of a roaring fire.

"What's this?" I enquired, as I descended the stairs.

"What does it look like?" He smirked. "But you are aware this function has a dress code?"

I looked him up and down as he stood in our living room, wearing a pair of jeans and an undone, chequered, flannel shirt.

"Oh yeah and what does this 'dress code' require?" I arched an eyebrow.

"That you get undressed," he gave a mischievous grin.

He walked over to where I was standing on the bottom step and whether I was ready or not, he made it clear my clothes were coming off...

...

...afterwards, we lay back in the cushions which he set up on the rug. I had on his large, flannel shirt but left it half unbuttoned. Declan pulled his boxers back on, but left off his jeans.

As such, he opened up the hamper and took out a bottle of de-alcoholised wine, two wine glasses and the food. I watched as he poured the drinks first then opened the Tupperware containers full of food, second. The delectable delights he concocted were Capsicum and Potato Frittata, Persian Rolls - the ones with camembert, smoked ham and asparagus spears wrapped in Persian bread – which he knew I loved. There were also Stuffed Button Bouches, which were baked mushrooms with a delicious bacon, onion and herb filling. And of course, he served one of his antipasto platters with feta preserve.

We ate in a comfortable silence and from looking at the size of our feast, we had enough for six people. But with Declan's appetite, the food was gone in fifteen minutes. I had to be quick to eat what I could, as he 'vacuumed' it up. I snickered as I watched him chase the last few olives around the plate, before they too disappeared into the 'black hole' which was his stomach.

Then we sipped on the de-alcoholised wine and stared into the fire. I think the both of us were feeling full and satisfied. I felt his right hand rest over my left one and his fingers fidgeted with my wedding ring. He kept fidgeting with the jewellery, even as he began to talk.

"Ah B, this is the life, I should close the Garage more often." He sighed contentedly then he frowned. "It's too bad somebody has to die, to make it happen."

I looked on his aged features in the firelight. "You could always retire."

He straightened as he looked uncomfortable at the idea. "Not yet."

"Why not?" I wondered. "Declan, you're 228 years old and you've worked at that Garage for the last 215 years."

"Thanks a lot!" He snorted. "You really know how to make it sound like a negative, you know that?"

"Well, when were you thinking of retiring?"

"I dunno..." he stared off into the distance, "...maybe after my 250th Birthday?"

"You can afford to retire now," I said gently.

"And what, live off my rich, younger wife?" He raised his eyebrows. "That'll REALLY give people something to talk about."

I rolled my eyes, "Don't give me that crap, I'm only three years younger than you."

"I'm not ready to retire and mooch around the house, for the next seventy years." He said stubbornly.

"You don't 'mooch'!" I laughed aloud. "I think this is the first time you've sat still, all week!"

"More importantly B, would YOU retire to keep me company?" He looked me right in the eye. "Could YOU stop writing your academic papers and give up your research?"

My stomach shrank at the idea and I think he saw me flinch.

"I thought so..." he moodily gazed back at the fire, "...you couldn't stop researching, because it'd mean you'd have to stop circulating through time."

I wet my lips to say, "I'm always circulating through time, like when I instantaneously phase to Taurus Six or to Stonewall House."

"You know what I mean," he frowned. "You couldn't circulate to Egypt or Greece or Rome or wherever you go, to collect your evidence."

I said awkwardly, "But what if I worked part time -"

"You already work part time," he interrupted, "by not accepting any permanent places at those Universities you teach at."

"No, I mean I'd only work on my papers two or three days a week and instead of lecturing once a month, it'd be once every two months." I offered.

Declan leaned back into the cushions once more as he fixed me with a long, hard look.

"You can't quit, can you?" He said knowingly. "It'd be like asking you to cut off an arm, or something."

"I'm a Circulator," I shrugged helplessly. "That's what I do, I circulate."

"I know that," he smiled softly. "And I'm a European Werewolf, I'm not designed to be housebound. I'm meant to keep on the move."

My head ducked at the point he made, which he saw. So he reached out to pull me down to rest against his chest. I laid on top of him, with my head over his heart.

I closed my eyes and concentrated on the steady beat of his strong organ. Next, I pressed my nose against his skin, to inhale his maple syrup scent. Spending a winter without him, would be a daunting prospect to this female Lokoti Werewolf. I wondered how the male Lokoti Werewolves coped when they lost their spouse? The cold and dark could really make a person feel isolated and cut-off from the rest of the world.

"I wonder how the pack copes without their mates? I think winter is the loneliest time in Alaska. Sometimes I hate being home alone during the day, when you're at the Garage." I confessed.

"So I've noticed," he chuckled as he rubbed my back. "You visit me at work the most, when there's less daylight than darkness."

"Do you mind?"

"Nope," he gave an affectionate squeeze. "I hate coming home to an empty house when you're away at one of your lectures or seminars."

"So I've noticed, you always have dinner waiting even if I come home late." I giggled then kissed his chest.

He admitted, "I like the idea of you working from home. I like that the first thing I see when I open the front door, is you sitting at the table with your computer. So when you're away, I wonder what exactly am I coming home to?"

I felt his fingertips trace my spine as he thought about what I'd brought up.

Declan continued, "I suppose the Lokoti Werewolves continue on, because they have their children and their children's children to look after. But there have been cases in the past, where a Lokoti Werewolf has waned after losing their mate. Remember when Jake Wisetail passed away at the age of eighty, right after his wife? We all sensed he'd lost his will to live. If I ever lost you, I know I would too."

I recalled what he was talking about, as we all felt our pack member's pain. His death was unusual because Jake had looked like a man in his forties. When he passed away the same winter his mate did, he looked like a zombie, wondering the earth with an empty look on his face. Not even his children or grandchildren, could cheer him.

I raised my head so I could meet his gaze, "Don't talk that way."

"Don't talk what way?"

"Don't talk about your demise." I said. "I don't like it when you talk like that."

He gave a funny look, "Why, because it's true? Sorry babe, but as the saying goes, truth hurts! You are my life and if you were taken away from me, there'd be nothing left to keep me here. I may not be a Lokoti Werewolf, but I waned when you were married to Grant. However, I had to be strong for my Mom and Derik. Now that they're gone and if I lost you too, it'd be 'so long and sayonara' for this grumpy old wolf. Why do you think I'm so overprotective of you? If anything did happen to you then something would definitely happen to me."

I lowered my head and rested it over his heart again, so the sound of the beat could reverberate through me. I still didn't like hearing his resolution that his life would end. Instead, I gave him a tight squeeze as I closed my eyes and took comfort in the here and now. At this moment, my mate was safe and well and in my arms.

*****

On Sunday afternoon, the last day of Declan's week off, he practiced his monthly ritual which was hand-making his own pasta.

The sound system boomed out his customary rock music to work to and today it was Bruce Springsteen's Greatest Hits. He was seated at the dining table with the tools he'd need, as well as the ingredients. A large mixing bowl full of raw pasta mix, sat in the middle of the table, with a large chopping board before him, to knead the dough then carve out whatever shape or form he wanted it in. He knew off-by-heart the skills that had been taught to him as a boy, by his mother.

When Declan's family arrived on tribal lands, Aunt Susan found that our General Store stocked little in the way of pasta, or particular ingredients for her recipes. Her grandparents had migrated from Italy and she'd married a man also from an Italian background. It was her knowledge of their culture that she shared with her sons. In true Italian tradition, the family's recipes and culinary skills were handed down and the European Werewolf's love of eating, complimented his passion for preparing delicious dishes.

Thus, 'pasta day' was a monthly ritual in the Sabre household and this tradition continued, even after Aunt Susan passed away.

My fussiness over cleanliness fitted in perfectly with my husband's fussiness in the kitchen. Occasionally, I'd bite his head off, over leaving something in his pockets when I did the laundry. More than occasionally, he'd bite my head off over cooking something the wrong way. So we stopped intruding on the other's territory and let each other get on with it.

But today I felt differently...today, as I looked on my husband work...I wanted to join him.

I'd finished the housework and our wooden floors and bathroom shined. There was not a spec of dust to be seen and a week's worth of laundry was done. So I walked over to our dining table and looked down on my mate. He was off in his own world, mouthing the words to the song 'Hungry Heart', as he kneaded the dough.

"What can I do to help?" I offered.

Declan looked up with a start and blinked in surprise.

"Huh?" He managed out, as if he'd misheard.

I sat down at the table across from him and looked on the dough.

"What can I do to help?" I asked again.

"To make pasta...?" He stared in disbelief.

"No, to learn the Highland Fling!" I laughed at his astonishment. "Yes of course I mean the pasta."

"But you don't like cooking." He said warily.

"I don't hate it either!" I snapped. "Now frickin' tell me how I can help, or I'll never ask again!"

Declan smirked, "With your expertise which equals zero, I'll give you an easy task. You can flatten the dough and I'll shape it."

Then he stood up and walked into the kitchen and returned with another large chopping board. He put it before me then dipped his hand into a second bowl which was full of flour. He sprinkled it over the wooden board, grabbed a handful of dough and slapped it down, into the white powder. Then he passed me a rolling pin.

"Right," he said gruffly as he reclaimed his seat. "I'll start you on a simple task, which is flattening the mix to make lasagne sheets."

To his further surprise, I used my strength to pulverize the glob of dough! I picked it up, slapped it down again and used the palm of my hand, to flatten it once more. Then I attacked it with the rolling pin.

Declan watched with wide eyes before giving a funny look.

"What?" I caught his expression. "I've seen you do this to the dough first, before you do the rolling pin thing."

"I know and that's what surprises me." He remarked. "I never knew you were paying attention."

"Surprise surprise," I smirked.

"Will wonders ever cease?" He teased.

No sooner than those words left his mouth, we were interrupted by the sound of three hover-cars landing on our gravel driveway.

We exchanged surprised glances, wondering what the occasion was which warranted so many guests at once.

Together, we stood up from the table and went into the kitchen to wash our hands at the sink. By the time we'd wiped them dry, we heard a knock on the front door.

"Come in!" He called out.

Meadow, Stone, Forrest and Caesar came in, as well as Nancy and Bob, who were on the council of Tribal Elders. Immediately, I sensed the seriousness of the situation by the fact that they came altogether. I think Declan did too, as he frowned while resting his hand on my waist.

"Uncle Declan and Aunt B." Bob gave a respectful nod.

"Bob and Nancy," my husband nodded back at the elderly humans, before acknowledging the Werewolves. "Meadow, Stone, Forrest and Caesar."

Everyone stood awkwardly in the living room until I politely offered, "Would you like to sit down?"

"Thanks Aunt B." Forrest nodded.

Then the six of them split up to sit down on two of our couches.

"Can I get anyone a drink?" I offered next.

"No thank you, Aunt B." Nancy shook her head. "I expect you can sense this isn't a social call."

Furtively, my eyes flitted to Declan's and he gave my waist a supportive squeeze.

"Could the two of you take a seat?" Meadow requested. "There's something we need to talk over with Uncle Declan."

Since there was only one seat left, Declan sat down in the easy chair and I sat beside him, on the armrest. His arm remained about my waist as I rested my hands in my lap. Already, my hands started to sweat with anticipation at what they had to say.

Stone began, "Uncle Dec, we've come to discuss pack business."

"Uh huh," the European Werewolf's eyes narrowed.

Meadow spoke again, "As you both know, when a First dies, usually the Second takes his place."

"Uh huh," I shrugged, "so what's the big deal?"

Then we saw the four male Lokoti Werewolves exchange glances before Caesar spoke.

"Uncle Dec, you are our Second."

"Uh huh," my husband watched the four together.

Forrest finished for his son, "We have come here today to ask that you remain as Second as a new First is elected."

"Say what?" I blinked in astonishment.

Knowingly, Declan turned his glare in Caesar's direction.

"I take it that *you* have been elected?" He asked the younger male in a flat tone.

"Who, Caesar?" My face screwed up in confusion. "But why Caesar?"

As if he were rising to the responsibility, Caesar moved forward on the couch to meet the European Werewolf's gaze.

"Last night, Grandfather, Dad and Meadow, came over to discuss it with me." He advised.

"But – but – but it's Declan's turn to be First," I stuttered out from shock. "He's been Second for years!"

"And the pack has never had such a loyal and strong Second." Stone said in a deep voice, before he added on, "Except your father of course, Aunt B."

"It's for this reason, we have come today to ask Uncle Declan to remain as Second and accept Caesar as First." Forrest said gravely.

"Uncle Declan and Uncle Chiron made an amazing team, a Lokoti Werewolf and a European Werewolf, working together." Nancy tried to put it in another light. "We would like to pass on this workmanship with Uncle Declan remaining as Second, and helping a new Lokoti Werewolf as First."

What the hell...?! That's racist! I can't believe what I'm hearing right now! They don't want a European Werewolf as First! The fact that they discussed this last night, was like going behind our backs!

Bob said next, "Caesar is 59 years old and he's old enough to have some experience, yet young enough to lead the pack for many years. He's the right age to become First."

"I can't believe what I'm hearing right now!" I stood up to stare them down. "When Declan killed Michelle, the last female European Werewolf, my Grandpa told me that day that he was now a Lokoti Werewolf! He was no longer seen as an 'honorary member' of the pack!"

"Aunt B -" Nancy began, but I cut her off.

"Since the age of sixteen, Declan has fought for this tribe and land!" I lectured. "He has risked his life over and over again, for the safety of our people!"

"Aunt B -" Bob began, but I cut him off too.

"Declan is more Lokoti than any of you, because he's lived here longer than anyone!" I pointed at them. "He's even more Lokoti than I am, since he arrived on these lands before I was born!"

"Aunt B -" Stone tried, but I interrupted him.

"Declan has risked his life more times than I can count, protecting his mate, his family, his pack and the tribe!" I ranted. "Hell, one night he nearly did die while protecting his loved ones. It was the same night I took a silver bullet to the brain, to protect him!"

Then I choked up on tears at the memory of nearly losing him and how I would have been lost without my mate.

Caesar stood up too, to take hold of my hands in a comforting gesture.

He said gently, "We know this Aunt B, that's why we're asking Uncle Dec to remain as Second."

"Huh?" I looked on puzzled, with my watery eyes.

"You're right, Uncle Dec is the strongest and the most loyal and whether he's Lokoti or not, is not in question. It's not because of his breed that we've decided this. There are other factors at stake here." He continued.

Troubled, I glanced down at Declan but he didn't look surprised by this. He did not look surprised at all. His expression was one of resignation, like he wasn't going to dispute the decision.

"But why...?" I asked in a hurt manner.

"B," my husband spoke up, "I don't want to be First."

"But – but - but why?" I asked incredulous.

Caesar opened his mouth to answer, but Declan spoke for him.

"B, just drop it." He said softly. "Let sleeping dogs lie."

I whipped my hands out of Caesar's and turned around to face him.

"No!" I raised my voice. "Just tell me why! Why aren't you fighting this injustice and not taking your place as First?!"

My husband stood up to look down into my face, "Because of you, B."

"What?" I blinked in disbelief. "Me?"

Stone stood up and came to stand beside Caesar, as did Forrest.

"You are the first and only female Lokoti Werewolf," Stone began. "Before you, the pack has never had to worry about a First being romantically attached to another member."

Forrest continued, "In the heat of battle, the First has to concentrate on the positioning of the pack. He cannot be distracted by focussing only on one Werewolf."

"He'd be hindered because of his personal bias towards one member." Caesar summed up. "Or if an occasion called for everyone to fight, he'd have to knowingly put his mate in danger."

"What?!" I blanched. "This is the stupidest thing I've ever heard!"

"If Marie was a female Lokoti Werewolf, I couldn't be First and knowingly put her in jeopardy." He said calmly.

I ranted, "This pack's sexism is getting beyond a joke! My Mum and Gran helped me take down a coven of European Vampires! It was my Gran who took down the European Werewolf, which changed Declan! I've fought European Vampires, South American Vampires, North American Werewolves, European Werewolves and Voodoo! Now you want to penalize my husband for being married to a female Lokoti Werewolf? GET BENT!"

Suddenly, Declan covered my mouth with his hand and proceeded to pull me towards the backdoor. As we went, he said to our guests, "Would you please excuse us? I need a moment to privately confer with my wife."

I was practically carried out of the living room then out of the house via the rear entrance. As soon as he went down the back steps, he released me. I was deposited on the icy, stone pathway, leading to the greenhouse.

Then we yelled at each other at the same time, "What the hell are you doing?!"

"I'm standing up for my mate!" I said vehemently.

"That's the problem!" He pointed in my direction.

"What's the problem?!"

"You talking for me! If I were First, I'd look biased or weak, letting someone else give orders! If I were First, I couldn't have anyone making decisions for me, or contradicting me, in front of the pack!"

"But I'm your wife!"

"EXACTLY!" He roared. "You're my wife and because I love you so god damn much, I let you have your way! But if I were First, I couldn't do this! It would make me look weak and indecisive!"

I crossed my arms in the cold and tearfully glared away.

Declan continued, "What if it did come down to fighting? What if the occasion did call for a Circulator to fence in the speed of light, with her silver sword? If we were in that situation, there's no way in hell I could put you at risk!"

"What the hell are you talking about? I hardly get to fight as it is!" I retorted.

"If I had it my way, you would NEVER fight at all!" Declan declared.

"What?!"

"If I had it my way, I'd use the pack as your personal bodyguards! If I had it my way, no 'fang heads' would ever come close to you! If I had it my way, I'd use the pack to take out anything that looked at you wrong! If I had it my way, you'd be encased in cotton wool and tucked away nice and safe!"

His rant stunned me into silence and I stood there, gaping at him.

"That's why I can't be First, B!" He fumed. "There is no way I can function objectively, when I'm worrying about you!"

I looked away, crestfallen. He made it seem such a hindrance, being with me. I wasn't as helpless as he made me sound, either.

Declan grabbed hold of my arms to make me face him, "Don't you get it? If anything threatens you, my bloodlust goes nuts! My European Werewolf instincts want to tear apart anything which could hurt my mate, because you're MY territory! If you're in danger, there's no way I can rationally and logically, lead the pack. I can't function as First, when I'm constantly looking sideways to see what you're doing or what's coming at you."

But his words couldn't penetrate my angry resolve. My watery eyes were the first to wander away and the rest of me second. However, he wasn't about to let go of his wife or his argument. He cupped my cold, wet face between his large, hot hands.

"It's you and me B, now and forever. I don't want the responsibility of being First. I don't want to lead the Lokoti Werewolves. To be honest, when I started patrolling the borders at sixteen, I didn't do it for the tribe. Really, I was doing it for my Mom, Derik, Uncle Em and for you."

This gave me a start as I couldn't believe what I just heard.

I recalled, "But I thought you didn't develop feelings for me until you were seventeen?"

"Yeah well, I may not have been sexually attracted to you, but I always had a soft spot for the glow-in-the-dark girl." He confessed as he let go. "When I was sixteen and you were thirteen, you still looked like a kid. Then you started developing at fourteen and as soon as that body of yours changed from flat surfaces to curves? My body said, 'oh baby!'"

"Declan!" I whacked him to behave, scared those inside would hear.

He laughingly pulled me into his arms, "There are so many things you don't remember about me, when we were growing up."

"Oh yeah, like what?" I challenged.

"On your first birthday, I got into trouble for punching an eleven year old Grant, when he tried to pull you away." He said.

"No way...!" My mouth fell open.

"I used to hold you for hours, but you were too young to remember. When Grant walked up and lifted you away, I punched him and got in trouble for it. Your Dad took me outside to lecture me and I remember feeling so angry, I shook with rage. He said I could have hurt you as well as Grant. I told him I'd never do that, but your Dad said I was being irresponsible. No matter how hard I tried to be responsible, it was never good enough for Hunter Wisetail. I looked after my mother and little brother, I provided for them and I patrolled for them. But if I'd known Grant would have done the same thing seventeen years later, like taking you away from me? I would have killed him instead."

Still, I hated hearing him threaten my first mate. My head lowered so he used his right hand to gently raise my chin. His wrinkled blue eyes tried to hold onto my darker ones.

"Do you remember when you were seven and you were having a sleepover at our house? There was a massive storm which scared you and Derik. Mom lost her patience and yelled because you two wouldn't stay in bed. So you both snuck into my bedroom and slept with me that night. I couldn't move because I had Derik on one side and you on the other. But that's how you finally fell asleep, curled up against me." He said fondly.

Instantly, I remembered the night he was talking about and slowly, a smile appeared on my chilled face.

"It was one of the few times you were nice to me, growing up." I recalled. "You didn't kick us out and you even put your arms about us. You did call us wimps though, for being afraid of the thunder and lightning. I thought you were the strongest and bravest boy I knew, because you were a Werewolf like my father and grandfather were."

"You see, B?" He grinned at my compliment. "Just because you can swing swords around in the speed of light, it doesn't mean I'm going to stop protecting you. It's always gonna be like that night when you were afraid of the storm. Hell, I would have crash-tackled Zeus for throwing his bolts of lightning, to make your aura brighter with happiness."

Next, he felt me shake with inward laughter, before I rested my forehead on his chest. When I looked upwards again, I found his eyes waiting. I examined his older face which was inches away from mine.

"Is there anything that you wouldn't do for me, Declan Sabre?"

"Nope and the pack knows it too. How can I be First, when I'm too busy obsessing about you?" He spoke bluntly. "So let's go inside and politely tell the Tribal Elders and our new First, that there's nothing to worry about. The sooner we do this, the sooner they'll leave and we'll have our house to ourselves again."

Then he gave a mischievous wink. I laughed at his one-track mind as I pulled away. He reached for the backdoor and held it open for his wife, before following her inside.

~~~~~~

~ 28 ~

Although I couldn't convince the European Werewolf to retire just yet, I did talk him into reducing his hours. Instead of working full time at the Garage, he went part time. Three days a week he left the house at 8 AM and returned at 5 PM, but at least he wasn't as sore or tired.

Old age was catching up to my supernatural husband, so much so, leaning over the engine of a hover-car would aggravate his back. In winter, his joints began to crack when he stood up after sitting down. At first when I heard the noise, I thought he was expanding into his other body.

Eventually, he had to accept the arthritis medication our Medicine Man prescribed. The medicine cabinet above our fridge used to house only my pain relief, coupled with iron tablets I needed during the 'female curse'. Now, Declan had more meds than I did, which he had to take everyday. Aside from his painkillers, he had Fish Oil tablets with Omega-3 in them, as well as his Glucosamine with Chondroitin capsules, to help his joints.

The aging Meadow would call once a month to check on my aging husband. Sometimes I felt sorry for him, having a European Werewolf for a patient. The Medicine Man would suggest herbal teas or particular foods which could help, but my mate refused. Declan's stubbornness made him more rigid than a block of cement. He growled at the idea of altering his diet or eating less of certain dishes.

My mate didn't even like to admit he suffered pains in his creaking joints. So the cunning Lokoti Werewolf would make his check-ups look like a social visit. He'd accept a cup of coffee and some biscotti, my husband had baked. Then he'd complain about his own sore back or stiff shoulders. This induced the European Werewolf to sympathise and share stories of his own troubles. Then the Medicine Man would open his 'medicine bundle' and give him a prescription-only medicine, he 'conveniently' just happened to have on him.

Declan's pride was just as bad, as he objected to the very notion of 'slowing down'. In the warmer months, he still insisted on mowing our lawn himself. Last summer, I was scared the hot-blooded male would keel over, as he mowed in the scorching sun. Sweat seemed to be dripping off every part of his body.

I carried out a glass of chilled water to him, which he turned off the mower to accept.

"It's thirty degrees Celsius today, or so says the Weather Channel." I remarked. "Do you wanna call it quits and finish the mowing tomorrow? There's supposed to be a cool change, coming in tonight."

"B, stop fussing!" He snarled, as he shoved the empty glass my way.

So I tried a different tact as I took it from him.

"Do you know Ki Lightfoot, Bertha's sixteen year old boy? He's trying to save up to buy a second-hand hover-car, so the tribe has been giving him odd-jobs to do. He'll mow our lawn for fifty credits a month."

To which he replied with the same response I'd heard for the last two hundred years:

"I'm not gonna pay someone to do something which I can do myself!"

Then he turned his back on his wife as he restarted the mower and pushed onwards.

Before the end of summer, I left a print out of an advertisement for a ride-on hover-mower, on the kitchen bench. Instead of taking the hint, the hard-headed male snatched up the piece of paper and threw it into the recycling bin.

"Our yard isn't big enough for one of those sit-down things," he growled.

"But it'd make the job easier!"

"If you're that concerned, why don't you frickin' mow the lawn yourself?" He snapped.

"Fine then!" I accepted his challenge. "I'll do it next month!"

Then the smug bastard said under his breath, "Have fun with all the spiders and other creepy-crawlies."

Damn it, he knew that was why I didn't do much gardening. Don't get me wrong, I liked spending time in the cultivated area around our house. We'd bought lawn furniture, which we placed under the canopy of our huge Jacaranda Tree. We've eaten lunch or dinner in the outdoor setting, numerous times. But I hated mowing or weeding, because inevitably one of my eight-legged enemies, would show up.

"I'm calling Ki Lightfoot," I picked up the phone.

"B!" He snatched it off me. "I'm NOT paying somebody to mow our lawn!"

"You won't have to pay, I'LL pay!" I tried to take it back. "I'll use MY money from my lecturing!"

"Oh, here we go..." he said unhappily, "...the 'I'll pay' attitude I was worried about, if I retired."

"Declan -"

But it was too late, he'd stormed out of the kitchen then out of the house, to do something else outside.

With all the domestic drama, I actually welcomed the onset of fall then winter after it. At least the grass didn't grow when it was smothered under snow. It also meant there was no gardening to take care of, so my proud mate had less to do.

When Declan was home, I wouldn't do any academic work. He'd be baking in the kitchen, or maybe some preserving. I'd do a little housework then join him.

"Wotcha doin'?" I asked, as I hopped up onto the kitchen bench.

The tall man with the silver hair, looked in my direction. He smiled at how his wife would sit and watch. He's always liked having an audience to show off to.

"Well my dear Watson, I'm preserving some bocconcini." He put on a Sherlock Holmes voice.

"Did you make the bocconcini yourself?"

"Hell no!" He emitted a short laugh. "Do you see any water buffaloes in our backyard?"

"Er, no."

"Bocconcini is made from water, cow's milk and water buffalo's milk," he educated. "This bocconcini here, came courtesy of the supermarket in Alma. I'm preserving it with some herbs, like I do with my feta preserve."

"Is bocconcini the cheese you used on those yummy bread rolls yesterday, with tomato and basil pesto?" I remembered.

"You *were* paying attention," he sung sarcastically.

Playfully, I swung out my leg to gently kick the male with the fifty-something appearance.

He chuckled as he used his supernatural strength to put the lids on the jars so tightly, a human had no hope of opening.

"They have to be airtight, to prevent bacteria from getting in." He advised.

Then I watched him put the three jars of bocconcini preserve, in the back of the refrigerator. They joined his last jar of feta preserve as well as an opened jar of antipasto mix. His other jars of unopened antipasto, sun-dried tomatoes, olives or marinated mushrooms, were in the pantry.

"What's for dinner?" I asked next.

"I dunno, what do you feel like?"

"Did you wanna order pizza delivery?"

He lowered his head to fix his wife with a knowing look. "B, don't."

"Don't what?"

"Don't order delivery just so your husband won't have to cook."

Now I emitted a short laugh, "That's not what I was doing!"

However, he stood in the kitchen with his hands on his hips, in a demanding fashion.

"Well..." I conceded, "...I would offer to cook myself, but my husband's always telling me how he's the greater chef."

"He does cook better than you."

"He does not!"

"Hell yeah, he does!"

"I used to be a good cook, at one stage." I looked away. "My first husband thought so."

"He was a Lokoti Werewolf who was empathically attuned to you, of course he didn't want to hurt your feelings!"

"Unlike my second husband, who's a European Werewolf and doesn't give a damn?" I arched my eyebrows.

Just then he let out a loud growl, as he turned away. Next, he slunk back to where I was sitting, in a guilty manner. He rubbed his face, showing his frustration before meeting my gaze.

"I'm sorry B," he said helplessly. "I think I'm getting 'cabin fever', for being home so often. Maybe I should return to full time work, at the Garage?"

"And make your sore back, worse?" I pointed out. "Look, let's go outside. We'll go for a walk or something and clear our heads."

He glanced out the kitchen window that was over the sink. Outside, the skies looked dark and foreboding. A few snowflakes flew past, carried on the wind.

"They've forecasted a blizzard moving in, I don't think we have time." He frowned.

I hopped off the kitchen bench, "A short walk then, halfway down the hill and back."

He stood back and watched as I approached the coat rack, by the front door. I pulled on my thick coat first then picked up my snow boots, second. I carried them over to the couch and proceeded to change shoes.

I looked up, "Are you coming?"

"Yeah, alright." He gave in with a groan.

He did the same and once we'd finished, two rugged-up Werewolves stood up from the couch. We each pulled out our gloves and beanies from our coat pockets and put them on. Then we left the warm indoors for the freezing outdoors.

Once we were outside, the dark skies looked even worse than they did, when we were inside. The wind picked up in strength, as we crunched down our icy gravel drive. We walked down the frozen, concealed road, past the snowy forest, the icicles hanging on plasma power lines, and our neighbours' houses which were smothered in more snow.

The icy wind stung my face and I fell behind my mate, to use his larger size to block the blasts. As if he sensed this, he deliberately walked in front. When a twist in the road made the wind hit me from side on, he gallantly walked beside, to block it again.

We stopped at the sharp turn which was also a makeshift lookout. From this vantage point, we looked down on the frozen tribal lands which were lit up by people's homes. The warm light from people's windows looked yellow against the bluish, winter's twilight. The river running alongside was partially frozen over, with the tall mountain peaks a stark white.

The European Werewolf tapped me on the shoulder then pointed at something. I looked in the direction he indicated and saw. It looked both haunting and intimidating...

Together, we watched a wall of whiteness, move across the mountain range and bombard the community centre. When it approached us, the winds hit us like a hurricane before the flurry of snowflakes, blinded us. The snow was the white colour carried on the wind, which was the blizzard we were expecting.

I felt my husband take hold of my arm and lead us back. One of his hands tried to protect his eyes, as my other hand did the same. We could barely see anything as they badly stung. Within minutes, the blizzard made the temperature drop at least another ten degrees. As our eyes watered, we felt tiny icicles form on our eyelashes.

This was ridiculous, I couldn't see anything even if I did trust my mate's tracking skills, in these conditions. I didn't want to trudge home, up the hill, blind as a bat. My face had turned completely numb and I couldn't feel my lips anymore.

I stopped still, which pulled back on his arm that was tugging me along. I think he turned around to see why, but I couldn't see him properly. While one set of our arms were hanging onto each other, I reached out my free hand and placed it on his chest.

Then we no longer felt the icy winds lashing us, or the flurry of snowflakes, hitting our faces. Momentarily, we felt light and floating and free. Another second later, we felt the warmth of central heating and we could see again.

We both gasped, him in surprise and me in relief, as we looked around our living area.

"Home again, home again, jiggety-jig." I mumbled out of my unfeeling lips.

I let go of him and proceeded to remove my gloves, beanie, thick coat and snow shoes, which were caked in snowflakes.

"Never let it be forgotten, that this ability of yours to instantaneously phase, is a godsend!" Declan declared. "I'll go and get some wood to start a fire."

"No -" I tried to stop him, but it was too late.

He went out the backdoor in a hurried manner. I thought it was sweet he was going to brave the blizzard again, to fetch wood for a fire. I just didn't want him going out into the cold, for my sake.

Within a minute he returned, carrying a heap of chopped wood in his arms. Although we primarily used central heating, we still enjoyed the odd fire. Every fall, my husband would make sure we had a stockpile of chopped wood, stacked along one of the greenhouse walls.

I watched him kneel down by the fireplace, place the wooden pieces in the grate, grab the 'firestarter' and set it alight. The small, hand-held laser, burned the wood and the bark caught fire. As the flames engulfed the rest of the fuel, he stood up to take off his winter coverings, too.

Soon, his coat, gloves, beanie and snow boots joined mine, either on or by the coat rack.

I crouched down on the rug before the fireplace to 'defrost'. My face stung again as it thawed, as did my hands. Feeling returned to my extremities and I felt my cheeks turn wet. It was from the icicles on my eyelashes and eyebrows, melting.

When Declan returned from the coat rack, he came to sit on the rug too. We sat side by side, holding up our hands in front of the flames. As the fire increased in size and strength, so did the warmth.

Our silence ended when I said out of the blue, "Sorry."

"Huh?" He gave a funny look. "Sorry for what?"

"For dragging you out, into a blizzard," I apologised.

"Shut up, B." He growled quietly. "You haven't done anything you should apologise for."

We sat together, staring into the flames and feeding off the heat.

"I liked the walk," he spoke again. "I needed to clear my head and stretch my legs. Besides, it was pretty spectacular, watching the blizzard come towards us."

"It was," I relived the moment in my mind. "It looked like a wall of whiteness, moving our way."

"It did," he nodded along. "You know what, now I don't feel like cooking anymore. But in this weather, I doubt we can get pizza delivered. You mind if I take the spaghetti bolognaise out of the freezer and defrost that instead?"

To his surprise, suddenly I burst out laughing!

"What?" He looked on peculiarly.

"Just sit the spaghetti bolognaise on the rug and it can defrost along with us." I giggled.

He laughed with his wife, as he put his arm about her and held her close.

*****

Hunting on a full moon never loses its charm, even in the midst of an Alaskan winter. Although the temperature could drop to -52 C, our supernatural body heat fought off the chill, as we fought our prey. The animals that didn't migrate south for winter, nor go into hibernation, satiated our burning bloodlust.

Last Tuesday was such a night, it was – 44 C and a full moon and what made it remarkable was the fact it was also Valentines Day.

For humans, this day may be spent canoodling in front of a fire with an alcoholic drink, such as champagne. Or the guy would buy his girl chocolates in a red, heart shaped box, like I'd seen in the movies. But being mated to a European Werewolf, I'd learned centuries ago not to expect cards or chocolates. I never received anything which was, 'a commercialistic ideal designed to make us spend more money', quote unquote.

Declan's idea of romance occasionally included flowers, but the kind he grew himself. If chocolate came into it, it'd be in a tiramisu he made. We've never gone out to dinner in a restaurant on Valentines Day. He'd rather stuff his face at home then work off the calories in the bedroom. During a hard Alaskan winter, I wasn't about to complain. Besides, I think this suited me as a female Lokoti Werewolf. With our animal instincts, we could be consumed by food or sex, or both. If we got to kill the source of the meat ourselves, or 'claim' our mate, it brought bliss to our existence.

At four o'clock in the afternoon, I was summoned by my husband's call. "Come and get it!"

A minute later, I descended the stairs to find a feast waiting on the dining table. It wasn't unusual he served dinner early before a hunt, but the gourmet delights on offer, were. He'd prepared an entrée of smoked salmon, cream cheese and onion bruschetta, followed by Angel Hair Pasta with Scallops and Rocket for our main and lastly, chocolate mousse for dessert.

"What's the special occasion?" I queried, as I crossed over to my chair.

"It's Valentines Day!" He chirpily replied.

My 248 year old husband went so far as pulling out my chair for me, which earned a funny look.

"But you don't celebrate Valentines Day." I returned.

"There's always a first." He winked, before tucking in my seat.

"Are you feeling alright?"

"I'm very alright, thanks for asking," he chuckled in good humour.

Then he disappeared into the kitchen and I looked at the scrumptious food, laid out on the table.

"OK Declan, what's wrong?" My eyes narrowed suspiciously. "You NEVER celebrate Valentine's Day."

"That's not true," he replied in an even voice. "I've given you flowers or made you something special for dinner, a couple of times now."

"Yeah, orchids from the greenhouse, or whatever's in our pantry," I muttered.

"Then I'm keeping to tradition, as tonight's feast comes from our refrigerator, pantry or greenhouse."

"So you didn't go out and buy all of this?"

"You mean the ingredients? We bought them last month when we went grocery shopping."

I'd wondered why our shopping list looked longer than usual. I recognized the main course came from one of our recipe books. Has Declan been planning this for a month?

He returned to the table carrying a bottle of de-alcoholised wine and two wine glasses. I watched him carefully open the bottle, minding his supernatural strength, before pouring the sparkling beverage into the glasses. Surely, we didn't have a bottle of de-alcoholised wine, just lying around?

"No seriously, what's the special occasion?" I wondered.

My eyes left the food to peer up into his face. His features have looked the same for over thirty years, but his hair was different. There was hardly any blonde left and it had thinned somewhat. He wasn't balding, but he returned to his crew-cut, to try to hide it.

In return, he gazed longingly at his wife, as he looked from her long, dark hair, to her dark blue eyes and the skin in between.

"Do you know that you only look a few years older than you did, the first time we had sex?" He announced.

"Oh, really?" I frowned. "I thought I looked ten years older."

"At least you don't look thirty years older," he grumbled, as he took his seat.

Declan sat at the head of the table and I sat on his immediate right. For over two centuries of marriage, we've sat in the same places. If there was a dining table in the space time continuum, we'd probably sit as such for all eternity.

"Yes, but I like your face." I reassured. "It's more rounded than it was when you were younger, which suits your 'laugh lines'."

He was about to pick up his bruschetta, when he paused. "Are you saying my face is fat?"

"What? No!" I cracked up laughing.

"Then what are you saying?"

"Well, you've always had a square jaw, but with age, your face looks rounder now."

"Great," he sat back in his seat as he looked away. "I compliment my wife and get insulted in return."

"Say what?!" I guffawed. "Declan, stop it. You're starting to sound like a 'girl', worrying about your looks."

"Oh yeah?" He started to smile. "Well, if this isn't the stove calling the kettle black! Who's the 'princess' in this house, who frets when she has to dress up to go out?"

"Yes, you're being called a 'girl' by a 'princess', now how do you feel?" I teased.

Instead of answering, he showed me. He picked up his wine glass in a toast, which prompted me to pick up mine. We clinked glasses as he smiled softly on his wife.

"Happy Valentines Day, B."

After taking a sip, my eyes narrowed and returned to regarding him suspiciously.

I brought up again, "You said you hated Valentines Day, because it's cheesy, cliché, commercial crap."

"Can't a guy change his mind?" He snickered, as he put down his wine then picked up the bruschetta.

"No."

"And why not?" He listened, as he put a piece on my plate and another on his.

"You're not a guy, you're a European Werewolf." I debated. "Once you latch onto something, like an idea or even prey, you never let go."

"Damn straight!" He straightened proudly. "I've still got you in that chair two centuries later, don't I?"

This made me giggle, "You're celebrating the fact that you've managed to keep me for this long?"

"We should be submitted to the Guinness World Records." He raised his bruschetta to his mouth. Before he crunched down on it, he said lastly, "The Most Argumentative Couple who is coincidentally, the longest married one."

Tentatively, I took a bite of my entrée, as I tried to keep the topping from falling off. However, Declan dropped crumbs and bits of onion all over his plate. He ate with his typical gusto, never minding the mess he made.

After I finished my mouthful, I pondered, "I wonder if there's a European Vampire couple who've been married longer than us? I mean, they can live for 500 years."

"B, please." He frowned. "Don't talk of 'fang heads' or anything else disgusting, at the dinner table."

"Yes, oh lord and master." I smirked.

"Thank you, oh humble wife." He joked then pretended to flinch, when I kicked him.

We finished off the bruschetta which left behind two messy bread and butter plates. Next, Declan served the pasta dish on dinner plates. He heaped on the angel hair pasta and the scallops on top of it. I waited until he finished serving his mate then himself, before I picked up my cutlery.

He stabbed his fork into the stringy pasta. Just before he shovelled it into his mouth, he muttered, "I can't imagine a 'fang head' being married for 500 years. They'd sooner kill or betray each other, before that happened."

Then he munched on his mouthful while spinning his fork in his food, already preparing for the next bite. I sighed, as I gently pushed my fork through a scallop and raised it to my mouth. I wished we could engage in a philosophical discussion on the subject, but I didn't want to trigger a temper tantrum.

Slowly, I chewed on the delicious seafood which had been cooked in garlic butter. Then I tried the pasta and it was delicious. The semi-dried tomatoes, rocket leaves and parmesan had fused it with flavour.

"Anyways, it's Valentines Day which so happens to fall on a full moon." He changed the subject. "How often after a romantic meal, do we get to go out and kill something?"

"Not a lot," I smiled at his enthusiasm.

"Precisely!" He cried boisterously. "Now hurry up and eat, so we can get in a couple of rounds in the bedroom, before hunting."

"Oh, be still my beating heart." I said dead-pan. "When you say it like that, I go into a swoon."

"That'll come after the chocolate mousse," he gave another wink.

*****

After we'd eaten, Declan helped me clean up by stacking the dishes into the dishwasher.

Whereas I was pedantic about what goes where, he shoved them in haphazardly. He was in a hurry to move onto the second part of his plans for this evening. I noticed his glances towards the antique clock which hung on the wall and the way his leg jiggled. It was after 5 PM and the moonlight sparkled on the snow outside.

I placed a detergent pellet into the slot before I shut the machine door. As soon as I hit the 'start' button, I felt my mate's arms encircle my waist. He held me against him as his lips enveloped my right ear. Playfully, he chewed on it before murmuring under his hot breath:

"C'mon Mrs. Sabre, I've fed you and now it's time for you to feed me."

I giggled, as my mate pulled me from the kitchen and towards the staircase.

In our darkened bedroom, the queen sized bed squeaked as we steadily moved. I was sitting on top, gyrating my hips with his. I used my thighs to push myself up, before coming back down. He held onto my waist, squeezing my crotch against his then loosening his hold, allowing me to rise again.

The moonlight poured through our bedroom windows and onto the floorboards. We had curtains, but hardly ever closed them since there was no need to worry about privacy, being surrounded by forest. I think it also had something to do being part animal, we liked to see the sun or the moon.

Declan met my gaze and tried to hold it as he pushed. With the rhythmic movements of his body coupled with the light of la luna, I felt my animal instincts ignite. The dim bedroom lit up as clear as day, thanks to my glowing turquoise eyes, while my nails turned long and sharp. My clawed hands rested on his hot chest and he looked up in admiration.

"Yes, yes, yes, yes...!" He momentarily closed his eyes, as he pushed extra hard.

I felt a wave of heat wash upwards from my crotch, which I recognized was his come. However, I wasn't there yet. Like salmon swimming upstream to reproduce then die; we were slaves to similar programming. We'd pant, claw, bite, push and pull on each other, until we achieved the gratification which was connected to the act of procreation.

Before his body could turn limp in satisfied exhaustion, I growled out, "Not yet, I need more!"

"Well, you're with the right breed for that." He gave an evil grin.

His blue eyes turned glowing green and I sensed he was using his supernatural strength to keep up. My strong, athletic body pushed against his, over and over again. To help me along, he lowered his right hand to my moist folds and began to massage. I liked it, it felt delicious which my low, rumbling growl affirmed. The feel of his fingers rubbing my swollen clit, doubled the delight.

As his right hand massaged, his left hand moved up from my waist. It cupped my right breast and squeezed it. Then his thumb teased the nipple, tripling my pleasure. He made me gasp in between my panting, as my hair flicked side to side. My husband liked watching my loss of control, as his eyes never left my face.

With his assistance, I was able to come and a few minutes later, a second orgasm followed it. The hypnotising ripples of ecstasy rose up from the muscles in my groin, through my abdomen and outwards from my chest. He came too, which I felt by his pleasurable release. Our combined fluids wetted the sheets which were already damp with his sweat.

Satiated, I slumped over his torso and nestled my face in his neck. My nose was pressed against his skin and I could feel his pulse, as I inhaled his maple syrup scent. Contentedly, we lay there and felt each other's pounding hearts slow and our panting subside.

"Mmm...that was good." I sighed out. "Don't you think it's funny? No matter how long we've been doing it, it never loses its appeal."

"You got that right." I felt him chuckle in agreement. "Although sometimes you have me worried."

"Huh?" I raised my head to look on. "What do you mean?"

Gently, he rolled me off so he could lie on his side, to meet my gaze.

"Sometimes you look like you're thinking, 'here we go again'." He spoke frankly.

"Do I?" I asked in surprise. Then I wondered, "Well, with all the years we've been married and with our regularity, don't you ever get bored?"

His face hardened and I realized I'd accidentally hurt his feelings.

He said unhappily, "Obviously not, if I'm the one starting it all the time."

Then he rolled away to face the other direction, as his form of protest.

"Not ALL of the time," I giggled, "I've pounced on you more than once."

I tried to lie on top of him again but he refused to lie on his back.

"Oh yeah, like once a month which isn't much, considering it's me every other night of the frickin' year." He said crankily.

Then he sat upright and swung his legs over the side of the bed.

"Where are you going?" I complained. "I thought we were cuddling."

"You can cuddle all you want, but I'm going hunting." He stood up.

Quickly, I grabbed hold of his spiky hair and pulled him backwards, so he landed on the mattress.

"Oow!" He bad-temperedly swatted away my hand. "Would you stop pulling my hair?!"

While he was down, I sat on top of him again and even tried to pin him.

"Since you're bigger and stronger than me, it's the only thing that works on you." I smirked.

I ducked my head to bite him on his left nipple and he lay still, enjoying the sensation of my teeth chewing on his tough exterior.

Then he said, "You're right, I am bigger and stronger than you."

Easily, he lifted up his wife and put her aside before getting up again.

However, he didn't get very far when my fingers locked onto his hair and I pulled him back into my clutches once more.

"Sorry Sabre, but you're never gonna get away from me." I growled into his ear before chewing on it.

"You wanna make a bet?"

Out of the blue, he spun around to pin me to the mattress instead! Then he remained like that, chuckling, as he watched me struggle. He raised himself over his wife and I sensed he liked this vantage point. A couple of times, I caught his eyes move up and down my naked body.

"Man, you like to play the dominant!" I snarled.

"Maybe I just like it when you fight back?" He grinned.

I put my right arm into phase which made him lose his grip. Then my free hand reached up and grabbed hold of his short hair. I tugged hard and his head leaned sideways, but he wouldn't let go.

"Careful B, you're getting me excited again." He snickered, liking our 'play fight'. Next, he looked over to see the time on his digital alarm clock. "OK, we have time for one more round, if we're fast."

"I thought you hated missing the beginning of a hunt?" I returned.

"I'm not missing out, because I'm feasting on my prey right now."

As soon as he said that, he bared his sharpening teeth as his eyes glowed green, with his round pupils turning into narrow slits.

If a man let alone a predator smiled at a woman like that, it would send her running, screaming into the night. However, I giggled like a school girl, especially when Declan bent his head to 'maul' me. I stretched out on top of the bed and closed my eyes, enjoying the effects of our marriage.

My back buckled at the feel of his sharp teeth, biting through the soft tissue of my left breast. I wasn't scared of the harm he could cause, because I knew he would remedy it afterwards. I was right too, no sooner did blood appear on the broken skin, his mouth covered the wound. He sucked on it, enjoying the flavour of my life-giving liquid, before licking it shut. The pain was short lived and in fact, it was fused with pleasure. His right hand had returned to between my legs, as his sharp teeth turned to my right breast.

I continued to writhe with my eyes squeezed shut, as he rubbed and bit and rubbed some more.

All of a sudden, maybe he saw what the time was; he pushed himself inside with a loud heave. I clung to his back as he clung to the side of the mattress, pushing at a breakneck speed. The bed shuddered and squealed in protest, as our panting filled the moonlit room.

"Higher, higher!" I grunted.

Immediately, Declan repositioned his body and therefore his crotch. We recommenced our physical activity and our groins rubbed together, so the outside was getting the same stimulation as the inside. This, as well as the rocking bed and our bodies slamming together, was just the trick. However, he came first and I was scared he'd stop. I was uphill skiing the slippery slope of the sought after orgasm and I didn't want to lose my momentum.

"Just two more minutes!" I cried out, as I rocked my hips back and forth. "Just two more minutes and then you can go out and kill something!"

*****

Fifteen minutes later, a freshly showered couple left the house. The wife was wearing stretchy, black, gym pants and singlet top, whereas the husband wore only an old, stained, bathrobe. He removed the garment and rested it over the icy veranda railing. Then in all his natural glory, he went down the steps and stood in the snow.

I followed him down the veranda stairs and instantly my bare feet stung, as soon as they touched the frozen driveway.

Without wasting any time, I watched my middle-aged mate expand into a European Werewolf. His leathery skin hardened into a light tanned hide, as his muscles expanded to triple their size. His bones cracked as his height increased and his human face turned into a wolf's, complete with a short, stubby snout. His glowing green eyes returned, as his teeth turned razor sharp inside his canine jaws. He fell forwards, so he was standing on all-fours, with his thick claws embedding themselves in the snow.

I shivered as I watched him turn, but as soon as I underwent my own change, I barely felt the cold.

My broad shoulders grew wider as my upper body increased with muscle. The nails on my hands and feet extended and hardened, as my teeth turned elongated and sharp. My glowing turquoise eyes returned, with my black pupils disappearing. Although my legs didn't expand as much as my arms did, the soles of my feet hardened. The ice no longer stung the exposed skin and I was ready to run in supernatural speed.

He sniffed the icy air then indicated with his head the direction we'd run in. He took off first, leaping into the tree line of the frozen forest. It didn't take me long to catch up and I slowed, to make sure I wouldn't overtake him. As we ran, our claws gave us extra grip in the icy patches and ensured we didn't slip over. However, with Declan's extra weight in his other body, he'd sink in the thick patches of snow, which slowed us up.

We joined the pack in the north east passage, which was a narrow valley in the huge mountain range.

We saw they were chasing down some stray moose along the valley floor. Declan overtook them on all-fours, in his huge, hulking, hairless body. I sensed he was targeting a young bull, who was bolting away with two cows, an older and younger female.

Usually, the pack could run in speeds of 200 km/h, but the thick snow was a hindrance to all. I saw the animals had the same problem, as they struggled through a deep patch. A couple of times I saw the older female fall, but she toiled onwards, running for her life.

Although the bloodlust boiled the blood in my very veins, the plight of the older, female moose, tugged on my heart. I slowed down, letting the rest of the pack overtake me. My mate's greater hunger showed no mercy at all, I sensed the only regret he felt, was that the young bull may not put up much of a fight.

I slowed to a stop, standing knee-deep in snow, as I watched the males take down their quarry. The European Werewolf leapt upon the bull, which tried to buck him off, as the Lokoti Werewolves attacked the two cows. The animals thrashed against their attackers, but it was no use, as their lives came to a violent end.

With my night-vision, I made out the red blood spill upon the sparkling ice. With my sensitive ears, I heard the sounds of the male Werewolves, tearing through flesh and crunching on bone. Well, that's the males bloodlust placated, but what about me? I've missed out on the kill, so now I needed something else to hunt.

Just then, I smelled first and spotted second, something standing high up, on an overlook. It had large antlers, dark eyes and was watching the moose's demise. I think it was a kind of reindeer, as it was smaller than a caribou and from its hormones, it smelled male.

Yes, a challenge to kill! A strong bull, which could run faster than that poor, old cow. Although I didn't recognize its species, which meant it possibly wasn't native to Alaska; I saw it as a belated Christmas Dinner.

The reindeer caught sight of me and bolted away. I started to scramble up the slope after it and I ran as fast as I could, but the snow made racing in light speed impossible. I sunk in several sink holes, right up to my waist, which drenched my gym clothes. But with my bloodlust burning inside, all I felt was driven to catch my prey.

Out of the blue, I felt the snow tremble. What was that...? I stopped to look around and I literally saw the surrounding snow ripple, like the surface of the river. Next, I felt the ground shudder underneath, which made me realize we were experiencing an earthquake.

It only lasted a minute and to double check I wasn't imagining it, I looked down at the pack. Declan had already devoured over half his prey and the rest of the men weren't far behind with their fresh kill. But I saw they'd stopped eating when they too, felt the earth quake and quiver.

"AUNT B!" Caesar called in his thunderous voice.

All of the males glowing eyes were turned my way, including my mate's. I felt their concern, like they were worried about me for some reason. I don't know why, the earthquake was over as quickly as it begun. I didn't think I was in any danger, so I threw them a wave and turned to continue the chase...

...but as soon as I did, I paused again...

...the tremor was so mild, it would hardly have caused damage to a house. But a steep slope covered in snow, was a different matter. The rumbling was quiet at first, but as the avalanche grew in size and strength, it became louder.

I was faced with a tonne of snow, tumbling and toppling towards me!

I froze, if you'll excuse the pun, as I stood waist high in icy slush, hypnotized by the spectacle.

In all my years I've lived in Alaska, I'd never actually seen an avalanche. Occasionally, when they occurred I'd view the after effects. Right now, it looked a wide, white wave, rolling towards me, with the sound of thunder.

B! – My husband thought desperately – *GET OUT OF THERE, NOW!*

Oh oh, I could instantaneously phase out of danger, but what about my mate and pack? They were on the valley floor, also in the path of the avalanche. They were scattered about and I wasn't sure if I'd be able to get them all to safety.

DECLAN! – My heart and mind cried out.

Just as the tidal wave of ice came crashing down on my position, I disappeared in a bright flash of light. In another, I reappeared at Declan's side. I placed my hand on his huge frame and I stretched out to touch Stone too, who was standing the closest, when I ran out of time.

Stone crouched down, as did Forrest, Caesar and the rest of the pack. Next, I found myself knocked to the ground so hard, it winded me. It was by Declan, who leapt on top of his wife and inadvertently squashed her, as he used himself as a shield.

EVERYBODY TAKE A DEEP BREATH AND HOLD IT – Caesar sent his last command before everything went dark.

Before I could recover my breath, the European Werewolf's heavy body felt a hell of a lot heavier, as the tumbling ice hit and the moonlight disappeared.

I felt a cold, crushing force on my right as the avalanche hit us side on. Declan's hold on me tightened, increasing the pressure and not letting my lungs expand. I felt a combination of hot and cold, by the heat of my mate's body and the ice smothering us. The noise was deafening, being buried under the cause. I felt my mate's supernaturally strong muscles strain, as he tried to protect the both of us, using his hardened hide and muscle bulk.

The remaining gaps created by his large body, disappeared fast under the compressed ice. Snow got into my ears, nose and mouth, extinguishing the last of my oxygen. My heart raced as my mind whirled in panic that I was suffocating!

Dizziness was quick to follow the fear and I wasn't thinking rationally enough to instantaneously phase us out from under. I felt claustrophobic in the darkness, with Declan's heavy body crushing me and the gargantuan amount of ice, crushing him. Futilely, I tried to struggle but the deafening noise was ongoing, which meant the avalanche wasn't over yet. If I tried to dig my way out now, more snow could land on top.

DECLAN, I CAN'T BREATHE! – I thought dizzily.

HOLD YOUR BREATH – He thought back.

WHAT BREATH?! – I retorted – *YOU'RE TOO HEAVY, GET OFF ME!*

I CAN'T MOVE – He replied – *TRY TO REMAIN CALM AND I'LL DIG US OUT WHEN IT'S OVER.*

BUT I CAN'T BREATHE!!! - I telepathically screamed.

I think he 'said' something else with his mind, but it didn't register. By now it was too late, the cold darkness which was smothering us, overtook my brain. I'd stop thinking to him or myself, as all I registered was blackness. My life was slipping away, like a person slipping over on ice, only in our case we were trapped underneath it.

The last thought to float through the ether of unconsciousness was; 'this is Santa's punishment for hunting one of his reindeer...'

...

...unlike my last near-death experience, I didn't find myself flying through outer space. I didn't see the white borderline of the space time continuum, on the edge of existence. There was no comforting light nor did any dearly departed, come to welcome me. I didn't even feel an out-of-body sensation, which made me wonder if I was dead or merely unconscious?

Somehow, I don't know if was from basic instinct or I was becoming aware, I experienced pain and a tugging motion.

Then this means I'm not dead. But where am I? I still felt like I was encased in cold darkness and I couldn't move. Instead, it was like somebody else was moving me. The pain was coming from my left shoulder, like something strong and sharp had latched onto it.

The pain turned into agony, as if my shoulder bone was under duress. Something had clamped down on it, like the inescapable jaws of a bear trap. But how did my shoulder get caught in a bear trap?

HOLD ON B, WE'RE NEARLY THERE – Declan's thoughts breezed through my mind, like a wind blowing through a ghost town.

I felt a pressure against my head, as if I were being shoved head-first through a wall of snow. It put a strain on my neck and my already sore shoulder. I didn't like this torture and I found myself longing for an out-of-body experience, instead.

Finally, the floating sensation I was waiting for! All of a sudden, the pressure against my head and body vanished and even the bear trap was removed from my shoulder. However, along with the absence of pressure, came the absence of heat. A bitterly cold wind stung my skin and it felt like I'd been put inside a freezer.

BREATHE B, BREATHE! – Declan willed – *YOU'RE OUT OF THE ICE, SO FRICKIN' BREATHE!*

I felt another strange sensation of something moving inside my mouth. Call me crazy, but it felt like fingers and I realized they were removing the snow. Then I felt a rush of air, blown down my throat then another and another. It continued, as I felt oxygen reanimate my lungs.

WILL MY BLOOD REGENERATE HER? – Declan fretted.

WE HAVE TO GET HER BREATHING FIRST – Meadow replied.

DAD, DIG YOUR FATHER OUT – I felt Caesar's concern – *WE'RE STILL MISSING FOUR MEMBERS.*

I CAN SMELL WHERE HE IS – Forrest promised.

After several more puffs, I felt my lungs start to expand and contract then expand again, on their own. I'm breathing again! I had been alive this whole time, after all. I must have only passed out from lack of oxygen.

FINALLY! – Declan thought in relief – *NOW CAN I FEED HER MY BLOOD TO FIX HER SHOULDER?*

"Give her a minute or two, until her breathing becomes steady." Meadow said verbally this time. "Keep her warm while I see to the rest of the pack."

Although it felt good to breathe again, an icy wind had struck up which aggravated my raw throat and lungs. I started to cough then cough some more. Weakly, I rolled onto my side to try to clear my airways.

To help his wife, Declan lay closely beside on the uneven snow. I felt his hardened hide against my heaving back as he used his huge, hot body as both a wind barrier and a warmer. I started to shiver, lying on the ice in my wet gym clothes, so he moved closer. Next, I felt his hot, wet tongue lap at my injured shoulder, to use his saliva to help it heal. It eased the stinging as well as made me feel warmer.

When I opened my eyes again, I saw mounds of broken ice, glitter under the moonlight. The sky was so full of stars, they twinkled down like diamonds against black velvet. Everything looked serene compared to what just happened, although on the slopes I did make out a couple of broken trees.

I stopped coughing long enough to hear several others in the pack, were spluttering too.

"I'm getting too old, to hold my breath for that long." Stone wheezed in protest.

"Is that all of the pack?" Caesar checked, as he looked around.

"We're all here." Forrest reassured. "Dad was the last one out."

"Stone's always last." The elderly Phil taunted, which made the men chuckle.

"Gimme a break, I'm 135 years old!" Stone retorted.

"Our Second has another hundred years on top of that and he was able to dig himself and his unconscious mate, out." Phil teased.

"Speaking of which, how is she Meadow?" Our First enquired.

The Medicine Man returned to my side, to check my pupils then my pulse and lastly, my sore shoulder.

"Declan's saliva has slowed the bleeding, but it's not healing properly." He frowned. "She needs to get out of the cold to stop frost bite from setting in."

Immediately, my mate raised himself to his four claws, which also meant my source of warmth was taken away. I shivered uncontrollably as my body couldn't warm itself. My shaking didn't subside until the European Werewolf leaned over and slung me across his hard, hot back.

"Take her home and I'll come to you shortly," Meadow organized, "I have to see to Stone and Phil."

My mate turned his monstrous head towards our First, who gave the nod. Usually, the Second would remain to help the First tend to the men. Instead, the First gave his Second permission to leave, so he could tend to his mate.

Next, the ground whooshed past and I was knocked around, as Declan bolted home.

He ran as fast as he could at speeds of 300 km/h, when the snow would let him. I sensed his urgency to get his injured mate home as soon as possible. The north east valley was 50 km's away from Lokoti settlement, which spurred him to gallop faster.

I watched the terrain change from snowy plains to snowy woodland and all the while, the majestic peaks of the Alaska Range was our backdrop. But it was hard to sightsee when you were bouncing against a rock-hard hide. I almost complained, but it was that same rock-hard hide, which saved us from being crushed to death.

Then I realized he was running up the forest-encrusted hill our house sat on. By the time we reached our frozen gravel driveway, he'd slowed to a trot. As he approached the veranda, I felt him shrink into his bipedal body whilst he was still carrying me. His bones made the familiar soft cracking noises, as his height shrunk and his muscle bulk reduced. His hardened hide turned into leathery skin once more, which felt softer to knock into.

Declan never stopped moving; from running to trotting to walking. His wife who was slung across his back, found herself slung over his shoulder. He raised himself to walk on his hind legs, which turned into human legs.

A fifty-something year old, muscled man, carried his wife into the house via the front door.

"Here we go," he knelt down on the rug by the fireplace to gently 'unload' his mate.

Thankfully, there was still a small fire burning which Declan created as part of our romantic evening. My naked husband removed the safety grill to feed it more pieces of wood, before stoking it. Then he returned the poker to the rack and turned his attention my way. I watched his wrinkled eyes widen, as he gazed down in concern.

"Frickin' hell, it's not just your lips that are blue, but you're blue all over." He said unhappily. "And it looks like you've got frost bite in your wound."

Without further ado, his eyes glowed green, his teeth turned sharp and he used them to put a deep gash in his right wrist. Carefully, he used his left hand to raise my head before pressing his injury against my lips. Tenderly, as if he were feeding a newborn, he fed his wife his blood, to aid her regeneration.

At first, my lips were so numb, I couldn't suck properly. When he saw this, he used his left hand to tilt my head back and he used gravity to drip his blood inside my mouth. I let it pool before swallowing and after the first mouthful, feeling returned to my face. After several more, I regained feeling in my hands, arms, feet and legs. My hands reached up to grab hold of his arm and I sucked on his cut. He pressed his injury against my mouth even harder, to encourage me to drink more.

"Have as much as you want, we have to get that wound closed." He instructed. "I'm sorry I bit you like that, but I was using all of my claws to dig the both of us out and I had to drag you with me."

My glowing turquoise eyes bulged and in surprise, I almost stopped drinking.

So HE was the 'bear trap' I thought was latched onto my shoulder? Talk about the 'jaws of life'! But what really impressed me, was how he protected the two of us from an avalanche and afterwards, dug the both of us out. And, all of this was done, in a single breath! Man, he really is the strongest breed in all the world...

When I thought I'd drunk enough, I moved my mouth away to say, "Ferris Bueller you're my hero."

Declan's blue eyes widened a second time then he chuckled at the humorous movie quote.

"You'd better believe it, baby." He boasted, as he sat me upright. "Meadow may have resuscitated you, but it was ME who protected your ass from being pelted with large chunks of ice. It was ME who saved you from being buried alive, underneath an avalanche. So the next time you think I can't mow a lawn because of old age, remember tonight!"

To show off his indestructibility, he put his right wrist back into his mouth and when he took it out again, the gash was healed over.

He added, "Besides which, I'm not about to let a natural disaster or even a supernatural one, take away my favourite avenue of getting laid."

I tittered, as I cupped his face between my hands and drew him in for a kiss. Afterwards, he rubbed his nose against mine in an affectionate manner. Then he held me at arms length to examine the effects his blood had, on my wound.

The broken skin had new pink tissue in its place. Next, he moved my arm around to make sure my muscles had knitted together and there wasn't permanent damage to my shoulder blade. When he was happy with my healing, he sat back on the rug and relaxed.

"Declan, are you and the rest of the pack OK?" I wondered. "Can't avalanches kill people, by crushing them?"

He smiled softly at my concern before he answered the question.

"It can crush humans and a couple of times, I thought my back was about break, under the pressure. However, I didn't panic until I saw your aura fading. I don't think the avalanche was over yet, but I started to claw us out of the ice anyway. As I dug us out, I think our life together, flashed before my eyes. It wasn't from holding my breath for so long, but it was the thought of losing my reason for living."

I sat up straighter as I stared at him then I took hold of his hands in mine.

"That's what it was like for me too! When I saw you on the valley floor, in the path of the avalanche, it was like my heart and my mind cried out for you."

"B, how could you have been so stupid?" He suddenly snapped. "You should have instantaneously phased out of the valley, instead of to my side!"

Then I repeated what I said once before, in New Orleans, "I could no more leave you behind than you could leave me."

"So what, you thought it'd be better to die together?" He arched his eyebrows. Then he let go of my hands to cup my face and drill his eyes into mine. "B, remember what you said to Nairn, in the hospital? You're a Circulator and I'm not yet. If I die, I'll be reincarnated and I'll find you again. But if you die, you'll never be reborn and I'd be separated from you."

This time it was my eyes which went wide, "You remember all of that? I thought you didn't like 'trippy time travel stuff'."

"Of course I was listening, my pretty little princess!" He rolled his eyes as he let go of his wife. "You were only discussing the small but important matter of remaining together for eternity, or what could jeopardize it."

In spite of his insult, I couldn't help but to laugh at his sarcasm.

I was still giggling, as I climbed into his lap and straddled him, so we were face-to-face.

"Look, I phased to your position because I wanted to get you and Stone out first, before trying to save the rest of the pack." I told him then my eyes looked downwards in a guilty manner. "But I wasn't fast enough."

"You're a 'Light Person' B, you're not God." My husband spoke in his typical, blunt fashion. "I know it was a boost to your ego when Machu worshipped the very ground you walked on; but you're mortal, just as the rest of us are."

"Yeah but -"

"But what?"

"But sometimes I feel like I should do more, or be able to." I confessed. "When I read my grandmother's diary of how she could phase at the age of thirteen and I couldn't until I was eighteen -"

"B, shut up." He smilingly shook his head. "You're not a religious deity so nobody expects you to be perfect."

Then Declan started to rub my arms as he examined my damp clothing.

"C'mon," he lifted me off his lap to stand up and I heard his arthritic joints crack. He pulled me to my feet as he said, "Let's get you out of those wet things and into a hot bath. In fact, I'll even join you. My back is aching something fierce and I'll try one of those 'bath bombs' you bought, which dissolves tension."

I held his hand but before he could lead us upstairs, I tugged him towards the kitchen.

"Before we do, you should take some more of your tablets." I ordered. "No arguments, as I'm sure Meadow would agree. You have problems with your back as it is, without a tonne of ice landing on top of it."

"Yes ma'am!" He gave a mock salute with his free arm.

Dutifully, he stood by the kitchen bench as I readied a glass of water then took his medication out of the medicine cabinet.

Just as I removed the lid off the jar, I froze... I stood completely still and Declan stopped moving, too. The only indicator which showed we hadn't turned to stone, was the both of our eyes filling with tears.

STONE HAS PASSED AWAY – Our First sent out to his pack.

MY FATHER HAS DIED – Forrest's sorrow hit us next.

IF AUNT B IS DOING MUCH BETTER, I'LL COME BY TOMORROW TO CHECK ON HER – Meadow thought lastly – *RIGHT NOW I'M HELPING THE RIVERCLAW'S*.

Accidentally, I dropped the medication on the bench top and the tablets scattered everywhere...

With a haunted look, I turned to my husband, "But – but – but he was alive when we left!"

Declan didn't reply, he just looked on sadly.

"I tried to save him!" I sobbed loudly. "I tried to reach out and touch him while I was touching you!"

Without saying a word, my husband reached out and grabbed me. He pulled me into his arms so fast, our chests collided. He squeezed me against his muscled frame with one arm, as his other hand stroked my damp hair.

"I have to be touching somebody to phase them to safety!" I cried into his bare shoulder. "He was standing too far away!"

"Shhh," he murmured. "You haven't done anything wrong."

"But -"

"He said so himself, he's 135 years old." He said emotionally. "It's simply his time, B. He's with Sharon now."

After another minute or two, eventually he let go. Next, I watched him pick up one of the spilt tablets as well as the glass of water. He downed the medication, put down the glass and retook my hand.

"C'mon, let's go have that bath then it's off to bed." He spoke in resignation. "We're gonna need to get up early, buy breakfast of croissants or something, take it to the Riverclaw's and help with funeral arrangements or final instructions."

With hanging heads, we left the kitchen, turned off the downstairs lights then climbed the staircase.

~~~~~~

~ 29 ~

20th August 2350

I stood at the sink, holding an empty glass and staring out the kitchen window. I'd been standing like that for five minutes. Initially, I poured myself a glass of water, drank it then went to put it in the dishwasher. However, when I saw my husband outside, he caught my attention.

The 287 year old European Werewolf with the appearance of a man in his sixties, was wandering around the garden.

He seemed to be surveying the scene, deep in thought. He wandered over to our lawn furniture and rearranged the chairs around the table. Next, he brushed off the fallen leaves from our Jacaranda Tree. Then he wandered over to one of our flower patches and pulled out an errant weed.

Since Declan had handed over ownership of the Garage, he didn't know what to do with himself. My elderly husband was restless with all the free time on his hands. He'd been doing extra tasks in the garden as well as in the greenhouse, which I'm sure wasn't good for his back. But he couldn't sit still, he was always tidying something or cooking something, in the kitchen.

Although his strength wasn't what it used to be, he was in no way frail. However, his skin was sprinkled with 'liver spots' and it looked loose on his face, hands and feet. But his torso, arms and legs were still muscled, albeit they had 'deflated' somewhat compared to his younger days. In human form, he no longer looked like a bodybuilder, but more like an aging gridiron player.

Next, I watched him walk down the driveway to check the mailbox. Although most of our correspondence came via email, occasionally we'd receive official documents from Hodge Endeavor, or paper invitations from family members, to attend someone's birthday, dinner party or housewarming. He cherished the children's drawings his great grandnephews and nieces drew and 'posted' to him, complete with our address scribbled in crayon.

Disheartened, he lowered the lid and ambled up the drive, empty handed. That was until he spotted another weed growing in the gravel, which he stooped to pick. He tossed it away and frowned, as he gazed around the garden again. Then I watched him meander over to another flower plot and pull out several more.

My eyes stung as my chest ached, but I took a deep breath and blinked. It hurt seeing him like this, he seemed lost somehow. I wondered if the male Lokoti Werewolves felt like this, watching their mates age before they did. Time was a fickle friend, you either had too much or too little of it.

Finally, I looked away from the window and put the glass in the dishwasher. Watching Declan think to himself got me thinking too. So did pondering how the male members of the pack, coped.

I stopped in the kitchen entryway as I was struck by an idea...

Grandfather was 167 years old and Dad was 180 years old, when their wives turned them into Circulators. Gran and Mum didn't wait until their husbands were 'knocking on heaven's door', they changed them before their lives ended. What's stopping me from turning Declan into a Circulator, now? Why don't we make plans to depart for the space time continuum? We've lived our life and surely it was time to move on.

"Hey B, I'm gonna wash my hands then I'll get started on lunch."

"Huh?" I gave a start. "What?"

Declan had come in through the front door and paused on his way into the downstairs bathroom – combined – laundry.

He smiled, "You looked a million miles away, then."

"Oh, I was." I smiled back.

I watched him go into the other room and turn on the tap, to wash the dirt off his hands.

"I was thinking of making some toasted ham and cheese sandwiches," he called out.

"OK."

He turned off the tap and dried his hands on a towel. "I'm not sure what to make for dinner, though. What do you feel like?"

"I dunno."

"Chicken, steak or fish?" He offered, as he walked past into the kitchen. "I wanna take it out of the freezer now, so it'll start defrosting."

"I dunno," I repeated with a shrug.

"We haven't had fish in a while..." he drawled, as he opened up the refrigerator. "How about I make Salmon and Dill Potato Patties with Lime Mayonnaise?"

"Great," I smilingly nodded. "Will we eat it with a salad or something?"

"Yeah, I'll whip up a Caesar salad."

"Yum," I salivated at the sound of it.

I leant against the kitchen entryway, as I watched him take out the frozen salmon and rest it on the sink. Next, I watched him take out the smoked ham and Swiss cheese from the fridge, as well as the bread and butter. Then he opened up a cupboard and pulled out the toasted sandwich maker.

Just like the very first time he made sandwiches for us, I admired his skill.

Breezily, he buttered the slices of bread and I counted he was making his wife two and himself four. Expertly, he sliced the cheese and the ham thinly. Next, he placed the cheese on top of the ham, on top of the bread. By the time the sandwiches were constructed, the toasted sandwich maker was hot and ready to go.

"You make it look so easy," I sighed.

Declan gave a wink as his response then he toasted our lunch.

When the food was ready, he suggested we eat on the veranda. I didn't mind since it was a sunny day outside. I followed him out the front door and we sat down on the wooden seat.

I ate slowly, savouring the texture of the melted Swiss cheese with the smoked ham. Also, I was preoccupied by my previous thoughts on our departure. I wondered how to suggest it to the European Werewolf, who was still attached to earthly pleasures, such as food.

"B?"

"Hmm?" I wondered why he was looking at my empty plate.

"Man, you're out of it today." He chuckled as he took the crockery, rested it on his and carried both inside.

I stood up and went into the house and found him stacking our lunch mess into the dishwasher.

"Hey, cleaning is my department." I scolded.

"Too late, I beat you to it," he sung. "Besides, weren't you going to do some academic work this afternoon?"

I put our used coffee mugs into the machine before he could.

"So?" I gave a funny look. "I can do housework AND academic work, just as I've done so for the last two and a half centuries."

"Yeah well, it's not like I have anything better to do." He frowned. "Since you're the 'breadwinner' now, I want to make myself useful somehow."

Before I could stop him, he picked up the sponge and the multipurpose spray and wiped down the benches.

"Declan, you're retired," I reminded. "You're supposed to be taking things easy."

"How easy do you want me to take it?" He arched his eyebrows. "Comatose or corpse-like?"

My heart hurt at his frustration and I wished I could do something to help.

"Look, I won't do any work today." I offered. "Why don't we go for a walk?"

"Nah, I don't feel like it." He said flatly. "Besides, I'm tired of always walking to the river, or to the Holy Grounds, or to Sunset Point."

"It's a lovely day, why don't we read in the garden?"

"No," he turned me down again. "The temperature's supposed to reach 25 C and I'll overheat if I'm out there for too long."

"Then what do you want to do?" I asked.

"I want to tend to my orchids and I want you to work on your papers."

"How about I give you a hand in the greenhouse?" I counter offered.

"No," his frown deepened. "You've cut back on your academic work as it is. You do less than half of what you used to. I know you only lecture a couple of times a year now, so you can stay home and babysit your husband."

"I'm not babysitting you." I reassured. "We're supposed to slow down and enjoy these last years before -"

I stopped short but he guessed what I tried not to say.

"- before I keel over and die of old age?" He asked knowingly. "Or before you turn me into a Circulator and we depart for the afterlife together?"

"It's not just the 'afterlife', it's the space time continuum -"

"Yeah, but it's still the place dead people end up, isn't it?" He bitterly cut in.

I had to turn away as my eyes watered and I tried to cover it, by staring out the kitchen window.

Declan said it so negatively, it was like he wasn't looking forward to it. Well, that throws a spanner into the works. How could I broach the subject of making final plans, now?

He stopped what he was doing to look on, "B, are you crying?"

"No..." I managed out.

Next, he put the sponge and the spray on the sink then pulled me into his arms.

"Come here," he sounded remorseful. "I didn't mean to snap at you, I know you're just trying to help."

He ran his hands up and down my back in a soothing manner.

"It's not just that," I sniffed.

"What else is wrong?" He asked softly.

"It's – it's – it's the fact that you're old!"

The words came tumbling out of my mouth in a tearful confession.

"You're crying because I'm old?" He laughed out his surprise.

I ranted, "I don't like it when your back aches! I don't like hearing your joints crack, unless you're changing! I don't like using the word 'elderly' in reference to you! I don't like how you tire easily! I don't like how you go to bed early and rise even earlier! I don't like how you fall asleep when we're watching movies! I don't like how unhappy you feel because you're aging!"

"I'm only unhappy when young men hit on you in the supermarket, by telling you how nice you are, for taking your grandfather shopping!" He retorted.

Declan was alluding to what happened last month when we went into Alma. We'd momentarily split up after we realized we forgot a few items. He stayed by the hover-trolley as I dashed down another aisle. When he saw the man hitting on his mate, he almost rammed him over with the trolley!

"Then I'll make myself look your age!" I cried out. "This way we'll look like an old married couple."

"Don't you dare!" He waved his finger in my face. "I love you B and that means I love you how you REALLY are! Don't even think about making yourself decrepit like me! Do you think I want you to go through the aches and pains too, when you don't have to?"

"I love you too Dec and I don't want to lose you!"

"You're not going to lose me!" He laughed again. "I'm not going anywhere, where am I gonna go?"

"I want to change you into a Circulator right now!" I cried out. "Sometimes, I watch you when you sleep, because I'm scared you'll die the way Derik and Rachel did! I'm scared you might slip over in the shower! I'm scared you'll slip over some ice! I'm scared the next time you hunt grizzly, the grizzly will be stronger than you! Instead of you mauling the bear, the bear will maul you! I'm scared you'll suddenly keel over in the garden, from pushing yourself too hard! When I watch you sleep, I'm tempted to turn you into a Circulator and when you wake up, you'll be strong again."

Silence... he stared in surprise and I looked back in the same way, at how all my secrets came out like that.

For a second time I turned away, only this time I opened the refrigerator door and stared blankly at the stocked shelves.

"What are you doing?" He gave a funny look.

"Looking."

"Looking for what?"

"Um, I don't know..."

He rolled his eyes, "And I'M the one who's supposed to being growing old and senile?"

Tenderly, the husband turned his wife around and pulled her into his arms.

"Oh that's what I was looking for," I nestled my face into his wrinkly neck. "This."

Declan ducked his head to rub his nose against mine, before planting a soft kiss on my lips.

He said, "I like hearing how you're restraining yourself around me, because for years I was one who restrained himself around you."

Our eyes met and held, which made me notice something else time had taken away; his blue eyes weren't as bright as they used to be. They'd faded and weren't as wide, as I remembered. To fight off my fears, I returned my face to his neck and held onto him tighter.

"Mmm...this is nice," I sighed.

"Mmm...I'd have to agree." He rubbed my back once more.

However, my contentment was short-lived as I contemplated how to ask. I looked up anxiously, feeling nervous about how to broach the subject. Then again, subtlety has never been a strong suit, nor was it Declan's. We could be as blunt as two bricks crashing together.

"Let me turn you into a Circulator now?" I blurted out. I saw his hesitation, so hastily I continued, "We don't have to evolve immediately, we can stay here for a couple more years, if you like. But if you let me change you, you won't grow any older."

Declan looked dumbfounded by the idea and not entirely convinced of this course of action.

He recovered enough to ask in a serious tone, "How is this done?"

"Well..." I began, "...I go into phase and put you into phase. I'll raise your bio-electromagnetic frequency, so it registers at a Circulator's level."

"So you'll be putting me into temporal flux?" He recalled the procedure, after seeing it happen to my Grandfather.

"Yes, that's part of it."

"What does it feel like?"

"I think it feels the same as it does when I phase you somewhere, you feel all light and tingly. Maybe you're even recharged with new energy?" I guessed.

"That's not what I mean." He rolled his eyes. "What I'm asking is, what will it feel like once you've changed me?"

"You should feel the same." I shrugged it off.

"I should?"

"Remember when my Gran changed my Grandfather?" I reminded. "He didn't look like he was in pain, did he?"

"No, you don't get it." He frowned before taking hold of my shoulders. "If you turn me into a Circulator, will I still feel things the same way?"

I gave a funny look, "You're right, I don't get it."

"I mean, I'm used to being a European Werewolf." He spoke honestly. "I love food, especially the smell of it when it's cooking. I love eating a delicious dish and the satisfaction afterwards, from a full stomach. It's the same with hunting, I love the thrill of the chase then the battle and the feasting. It's the same when you and I fight then make love afterwards..."

"And?" I listened.

"...will all of this change, when I become a Circulator?" He looked on warily.

"You don't feel anything less." I squeezed his hands. "Look at me, I love making love, don't I? I love eating, don't I? I love hunting, don't I? You'll still be you, Declan. You'll still be a European Werewolf while we're on Earth, but in the space time continuum, you'll be something else."

He quieted as he looked away, looking more lost than ever. This worried me and I tried to catch his gaze, but his eyes skipped away. He wandered over to the kitchen sink and stared out the window at the garden again.

"OK," he swallowed hard. "I'll get started on dinner and I'll even make tiramisu, for dessert. Then I'll make love to my wife for the last time as a

European Werewolf. Afterwards, my Circulator wife will make me into a Circulator too."

Then he opened up the pantry and proceeded to take out the ingredients for the sweet treat.

"Declan," I stood to the side, worrying about how he was treating this. "You make it sound like you're on death row! Tonight isn't your last meal, you don't die when you become a Circulator. You become ongoing and eternal, by evolving to the space time continuum."

"I know." He paused long enough to look back. "But I do change, don't I?"

I sensed he wasn't looking forward to this and I wondered why? We'd been planning this for centuries. Why did he see this as the end and not the beginning?

"Don't you want to be a Circulator?" I asked in a small voice.

Next, he bent over to take out a mixing bowl as well as the beaters, from a lower cupboard.

"I want to be with you forever and to do that, I have to become one." He said perfunctory.

My eyes watered as I said emotionally, "It's just that if I don't turn you into a Circulator and you die of old age; I could follow you to the space time continuum, but we'd be separated when you're reincarnated."

"I know all of this, B." He threw a sharp look.

He continued in his food preparation, making the cake part of the dessert, first. He seemed to be deliberately not looking my way, as he measured the ingredients he'd need. Then he tipped them into the mixing bowl and turned on the beaters.

I started to leave the kitchen and my husband to his task, when I turned around to offer, "Did you want to ask me any questions?"

"If I do, I will." He said gruffly, as he turned up the speed.

I sensed he did this, to increase the volume and end our conversation.

I walked past the dining table before I spun around and returned to the kitchen entryway once more.

"Why are you angry?" I asked loudly, over the noise.

"I'm not angry." He said coolly.

You didn't have to be a Lokoti Werewolf to sense that he was lying. I noticed how tense his shoulders looked and how he frowned. I sensed another emotion under his moodiness, which he was trying to hide.

"Why are you dreading this?" I asked bluntly.

He turned off the beaters to pass a look of annoyance, "Why do you think?"

"It doesn't hurt, you're still Declan Sabre and you're still a European Werewolf." I summed up. "You still feel things the same as you do now. All that changes, is you'll be able to phase through time and you won't be reincarnated, because you'll live for eternity in the continuum."

Declan rested the beaters on the side of the bowl so he could face his wife.

"B, I said I'd do it, so I'll do it!" He snapped. "Would you let me make dinner in peace?!"

"But I don't understand what's bothering you?" I cried out helplessly. "Please Declan, just tell me so we can talk about this!"

"Because you'll be changing me forever!" He raised his voice. "Once I'm a Circulator, there's no going back, is there? It can't be undone, can it? There's no cancellations, no refunds and there's no trial period! I become a Circulator, I evolve to this continuum thing and I'm no longer a European Werewolf, am I? I'm a cloud of light, frickin' floating around in outer space!"

Another silence fell over the kitchen... or rather, it was like a distant quietness between a bickering married couple.

So this is what it comes down to? My mate can freely admit that I'm the only woman for him. My mate can talk on and on about the crush he had, when we were growing up. My mate can be overprotective or just plain territorial, as he fought off anything natural or supernatural, which might take me away. But the crux of the matter was, Declan doesn't want to be a Circulator, like his mate is.

And that was that.

My breath caught in my throat as I stared, crestfallen, at the male who broke his promise.

"Look," he sighed wearily, "don't turn me into a Circulator tonight. I'm not about to die on you B, not yet. When I'm on my death bed then turn me. We'll leave together for the continuum, like I'd be going there anyway, if I did die."

I found myself leaning on the entryway for support and I leaned on it heavily. If the wooden, rectangular archway wasn't there, I'd probably have fallen to the floor. I felt like my body was going into shock, as my skin turned cold and I found it hard to breathe. The room didn't spin, but everything started to darken like a light had gone out.

Anxiety gripped my heart and it felt like it pulled the organ out, along with the rest of my insides. It turned me into a hollow shell. The emptiness I felt was almost identical to the loss I experienced the day that Grant died. The day I became a widowed Lokoti Werewolf without their mate...

"You don't want to go at all," I said distantly.

"Well that would be pretty stupid, wouldn't it? I can't avoid dying."

"But you can avoid being like me..." I uttered out, before I looked him in the eye, "...I'll never turn you into a Circulator."

"Say what?"

Before my eyes overflowed with tears and my chest heaved with sobs, I let go of the entryway and stumbled towards the staircase.

"B...?"

I ignored his calls, as I gripped onto the banister and pulled myself up the stairs.

Everything felt surreal, like life had turned as empty as I had. I made my way into the bedroom which looked bright in the afternoon sun. Instead of feeling any warmth from the light, I felt chilled to the bone.

Just in time, I made it to the bed the moment my legs gave out. I collapsed on top of the covers and buried my face in the quilt, to smother my crying. Quietly, I sobbed face-first into the fabric, which took the brunt of my sorrow. Hot tears or the errant drool escaped from my open mouth, soaking the material.

I'm losing him... Declan's gonna die, just like Grant did... I begged and pleaded with Grant to heed my vision as a Circulator... I begged and pleaded with Declan to turn him into a Circulator... Why do I pick men who don't listen...? Or maybe, I pick men who don't really want to be with me...?

Next, the scene of attending Gran and Grandfather's Memorial Service, replayed inside my mind.

I remember looking on the Sacred Totem Poles and wondering if it would say, Declan Sabre Born 2063 and Departed 2363? Or, would it say, Declan Sabre Born 2063 and Died 2363. It was the day he promised to be turned into a Circulator and evolve with his mate. I'd always pictured we'd have a joint Memorial with the word, 'Departed', next to our names. Now, it looks like it's gonna say 'Died' beside his.

The very idea of attending his funeral put my heart in agony. I couldn't see another body burn on top of the funeral pyre and especially not HIS. There was no way in hell, I could survive mourning Declan. There was no way I could watch the flames consume him. No way in hell!

I sat upright in determination, as my emptiness was overcome with anger.

There's no reason for me to continue in this mortal existence, knowing I'll eventually evolve alone. I may as well leave for the space time continuum now, before he passes away. There is no way in hell, I'm just going to sit around and watch him die! NO WAY IN HELL!

Then I stood up from the bed, feeling enraged at the male who broke his promise!

Next, I knelt down to pull the two suitcases out from underneath the bed. Once they lay open on top of the covers, I started to pull out all of my clothes from the tallboy. I dumped them carelessly inside the cases, never mind packing neatly.

Out of the blue, I heard Declan swear, "Frickin' hell, not again!"

I turned to see him standing in the bedroom doorway, with his hands on his hips.

"You're running away because I don't want to be turned into a Circulator, today?" He asked incredulous.

"I'm NOT going to hang around and see them put your body on top of the funeral pyre!" I growled as my watery eyes flashed turquoise. "I'm NOT going to mourn a second husband!"

"I'm not dying today, B! Stop overreacting!" He flared.

I continued packing and he watched me grab the photos on my bedside table and toss them in with the clothes.

"Why are you packing every single item of your clothing, from the tallboy?" He asked suspiciously. "And why are you taking the photos with you?"

However, I ignored him as I opened up the wardrobe and began to pull all my clothes off the hangers.

"Why do you need all your clothes and photos, for a business trip?" He asked next.

I remained silent as I reached for my file of important documents, sitting on the top shelf.

"Why do you need your financial papers, birth certificates and death certificates, to take with you?" He wondered aloud. "You're not packing a few things for an academic conference, are you? You're packing like you're moving out!"

I continued to ignore him as I dumped my business suits and the file, into the overflowing suitcases.

"B!" He marched up to spin me around. "Stop this!"

Determinedly, I pulled free and returned to the wardrobe to grab my family's photo albums.

"Oh no you don't!" He snatched them up. "They're staying right here, like you are!"

So, I dropped to my knees and started throwing all of my shoes at the suitcases. Some of them landed on top of the clothing, most didn't.

"Put those back!" He dropped the albums.

Declan tried to catch my shoes, but since there was so many, he gave up. He dropped the ones he had caught and grabbed my arms instead. He pulled me to my feet and tried to hold my gaze.

"Stop this, B!" He squeezed my shoulders. "Would you just get a grip?!"

"If I can't live without you, what makes you think that I can die the same way? Of course I'll frickin' come with you as a Circulator." I quoted.

Declan froze as he remembered when he said that; at my grandparents' memorial.

"I'M NOT WATCHING ANOTHER HUSBAND BURN ON TOP OF THE FUNERAL PYRE!" I screeched hysterically.

"FOR ONCE AND FOR ALL, I'M NOT FRICKIN' DYING!" He roared back.

"YES YOU ARE, RIGHT NOW YOU'RE DYING OF OLD AGE!"

"Fine!" He squared off against his wife. "Change me! Change me right now! Change me and get it over and done with!"

I cried louder at his words, 'get it over and done with', as it compounded that he didn't want this. I stumbled away from him and out of our bedroom. I had to get away and I almost fell down the stairs, because of my wobbly legs.

Once I reached the bottom, I released the banister and hovered in front of my bookshelves.

Next, I started to rip the books off the shelves. I enjoyed the crashing sound they made, as they hit the wooden floor. It mirrored how the world was crashing down around me.

"Now what are you doing...?" He moaned, as he came downstairs. "I'm not cleaning that up!"

I moved along the shelves, knocking over book after book. Text books, notebooks, picture books, scattered across our living room. Some of them fell open, with one spookily displaying a photo of the Valley of the Kings, in Egypt. A picture of people's tombs, how appropriate.

"B, you've gone loopy!"

Declan rushed forwards, almost tripping over some of the books on the floor, to grab my arms again.

"Would you frickin' wake up to yourself?!" He tried to shake some sense into his wife. "Nobody's going anywhere!"

"There's too many books..." I mumbled incoherently. "...I'll have to hire removalists to bring boxes and help me pack."

I tore myself away from him, to pick up my mobile phone which was sitting on top of the dining table.

"Who are you calling?" He demanded. "Removalists, are you for real?! Oh no you don't!"

He snatched the phone right out of my hand and put it in his jeans pocket.

Then he glared tearfully, "You're not going anywhere and neither are your things!"

I refused to meet his hurt eyes and as mine moved away, they landed on the photos on the mantelpiece.

Declan watched me amble towards the fireplace then he marched after. "Don't even think about it! They're not just YOUR photos, they're MINE too!"

I tried to reach for them, but he grabbed hold of my waist and spun me around. When I tried to push him away, he pushed me onto the floor! The next thing I knew, I was lying on the rug with my husband sitting on top, restraining me!

"GET OFF!" I growled warningly.

"Not likely!" He growled back, as his eyes flashed green. "You've gone berserk!"

To show off his greater strength even in his elderly body, the European Werewolf pinned his mate to the rug.

"You think this is gonna stop me?" I leered. "I'm a Circulator you moron, I can phase!"

However, he refused to release his hold as he tearfully glared down.

B, STOP THIS! – He thought and I felt his fear – *YOU'RE SERIOUSLY FREAKING ME OUT!*

But I ignored him by closing my eyes and making my skin glow...

STOP RUNNING AWAY FROM ME! – He willed on his wife.

My legs and arms went into phase first and the bright light made him squint. He lost his grip, so in a last ditch attempt, he grabbed hold of my glowing torso. He laid over his mate as he wrapped his arms about and held on tightly.

STAY WITH ME! – Declan thought over and over again – *STAY WITH ME STAY WITH ME STAY WITH ME STAY WITH ME STAY WITH ME!*

For some reason, I couldn't put the rest of me into phase. Then I realized what Declan was doing, he was using our telepathy to disrupt my concentration. Once upon a time, Grant did this too, to stop his mate from escaping him and hunting human.

LET ME GO! – I used my will to deflect his.

This started to work, as I felt my bio-electromagnetic field increase in output and my torso started to dissolve into sparkling light.

"B, please don't!" He sobbed out when he felt his wife disappear. "Please B, please!"

Just as I was about to instantaneously phase out the room and therefore the house, I faltered.

"Stay with me B, please!" He openly cried. "I'm not going anywhere and neither are you. Together forever, remember? Together forever!"

Declan's pain became my pain as his anguish washed over me. Damn this biological bonding to one's mate! It made my body return to a solid shape and I felt his heavy form, lying over mine again.

"I'm not gonna die on you! I would NEVER leave you! So would you please stop trying to leave me?" He rasped out.

I opened my eyes and saw his face was bright red, with the veins in his neck standing out. They gave away that he was either really angry or really upset. The sixty year old bawled like a baby, as he clung to his wife. His cheeks were soaked with tears, which landed on my already sodden face.

"Calm down B, just frickin' calm down!" He rubbed his wet face against mine. "Always and forever, remember? Always and forever."

Just then, in the worst possible timing, we were interrupted by new telepathy:

I NEED BACK UP. HUMANS ARE IN THE NATIONAL PARK HUNTING WOLVES AND OTHER PROTECTED ANIMALS. COME AT ONCE!

We recognized it was Walt Wisetail who sent the message. He was a new member of the pack and also a Park Ranger. He wasn't prone to exaggeration, so we sensed the seriousness of the situation. This was confirmed by the next message we received from our First:

WALT SAYS THE DRUNK HUMANS ARE RIDING IN THE BACK OF A HOVER-TRUCK, HEADING TOWARDS THE SOUTHEAST VALLEY. WE'LL CONFRONT THEM THERE. BE WARY, THEY'RE ARMED WITH LASER RIFLES.

My husband partially rose as he looked towards the front door. Usually when he heard the battle cry, he'd be racing out while hurriedly undressing. But to my surprise, today he didn't.

Declan didn't spring to his feet and run off to help. He remained on the rug, holding his wife in his arms. He did look torn though, as he glanced anxiously at the door then back to his mate.

"Change me," he said.

Huh?

"Change me," he said again.

"What?"

"Change me!" He barked out. "C'mon B, change me!"

I said quietly, "No."

"We don't have time for this, now hurry up and change me!"

"No!"

"CHANGE ME!" He roared.

"NO!" I roared right back at him.

"I'm not leaving this house until you change me!" Declan declared. "Then YOU can explain to our First why his Second ignored the call for back up!"

Coolly, I turned my head away to show that laying on the guilt, wouldn't work.

"Please B, just frickin' change me!" His eyes renewed with tears. "I'm scared if I run out of this house, when I come back, I won't have a wife to return to."

I looked up at his red, wet, wrinkled face and said flatly, "You don't want to be a Circulator."

"Right now, I'm more worried about losing you than what I would lose, if I became one!" He retorted. "So hurry up and change me! We're wasting time!"

"No."

"Change me, B! Change me! Change your husband!"

"NO!"

BAM!

Declan punched the nearby couch and it banged loudly against the wall! His eyes glowed green as his round pupils turned into narrow slits. He growled threateningly between his sharpening teeth.

"CHANGE ME!" He raged. "CHANGE ME B!"

"No," I turned my head away again.

Next, he punched the floorboards so hard, the vibrations made the furniture jump! Our other couch and coffee table bounced into the air and landed with a thud and a squeak.

"Don't look away from me, damn you!" He shouted. "CHANGE ME! Change your mate!"

He pounded his fist again and I heard a splitting sound come from the wooden floor.

I lay perfectly still, not even blinking at his show of force, as I stared in the opposite direction. I knew I wasn't in any danger. I also knew that my silence worked better than one of his tantrums.

"You're MY mate!" He huffed and he puffed, with his hot breath. "You always were mine and you always will be mine! MINE!"

Then he ducked his head to sniff around my face, before lowering his mouth to my throat. I felt his wet mouth 'maul' the tender tissue before grazing the skin with his sharp teeth. I knew what was happening, his bloodlust was ignited and it wanted to reclaim his territory.

YOU ARE MY MATE NOW AND FOREVER, BIANCA SABRE – his will beat down – *YOU BELONG TO ME JUST AS I BELONG TO YOU!*

Then he spoke soberly, "So change me already."

However, before I could answer, we were interrupted by somebody else's thoughts.

UNCLE DECLAN, WHERE ARE YOU? – Our First called on his Second – *THERE ARE DRUNK HUMANS HUNTING IN THE NATIONAL PARK, SHOOTING WOLVES AND OTHER PROTECTED ANIMALS! COME AT ONCE!*

My mate looked pained towards the door and he appeared truly torn in two. Half of him wanted to answer the call to arms, as the other half wanted to guard me, to prevent my escape.

"Go." I said curtly. "If you leave, I will be here when you return."

I heard him whine from his conflicting emotions. We both knew the pack needed their second-in-command, who was also their strongest and fiercest fighter. But he was right, I didn't want to tell the pack that I was the reason why he didn't come.

"Go!" I barked out. "Go, Declan! Go!"

In a lightning fast move, he leapt up from the floor and raced out the door.

As he ran, I heard the sounds of his body contorting and the fabric of his clothes, tearing. He didn't bother undressing first, he simply turned as he ran. He bolted out of the house as a human, then from our property as a

European Werewolf. He also left our front door open with his speedy departure.

With a sigh, I sat up then stood up. I meandered over to the door and looked out at the sunny woods. I too felt the urge to protect these lands, but as a female, I wasn't permitted. Oh well, perhaps this is the last sexism I'll ever encounter, before existing inside the space time continuum? I shook my head as I shut the door.

*****

While the males in the pack prepared for battle, the female prepared for her departure. However, as she worked, she eavesdropped on their thoughts. Scenes of bloodshed filled her mind, as she tried to bring order to chaos in her home.

She opened the attic hatch and pulled down the fold-out ladder. She climbed up into the small, dusty space, where she found some old, cardboard boxes. They were dropped through the hatch then carried downstairs.

In the woods, Walt Wisetail saw a wounded and pregnant Lokoti Wolf. Carefully, he picked her up and carried her over to his U.S. Forest Service vehicle. Softly, he whined to the animal, to convey he felt its pain and he could help. He took off his jacket and rested it over her, to keep her warm and from going in shock. Next, he took off his uniformed shirt, boots and socks, to expand into his Lokoti Werewolf shape.

She carried two of the boxes into her bedroom. What clothes and shoes wouldn't fit into a suitcase, she dumped into a box. She didn't bother about folding them neatly, as she didn't expect to wear them again.

The fourteen Lokoti Werewolves and one European Werewolf, convened in the south east valley. On their way, they ran past more wounded, littering the forest floor. The poor creatures had gaping holes surrounded by burn marks. There was even a charred Bald Eagle lying at the base of a tree, with all of its feathers singed off.

When she'd finished in the bedroom, she went downstairs. One at a time, she picked up each book, adjusted any bent or broken pages and carefully packed them. However, she wasn't even halfway through her task when she realized she didn't have enough boxes to put them in.

The male Werewolves hid behind some trees. Using the path of destruction the humans left behind, they judged the direction they were heading in. They didn't have to wait long, soon the humans' hovercraft was careening towards them. Along with it came loud music, beers being tossed aside and random laserfire; as the four teenaged boys shot at anything that moved.

She stopped packing and sat still on the floor, as she knew this would soon include her mate and pack.

Then the onslaught of thoughts hit her, as the male Werewolves put a stop to it.

FORREST, STAY BACK! THE HUMANS' GUNS ARE TRAINED ON YOUR POSITION!

THE HUMANS ARE SO DRUNK, THEIR REFLEXES ARE SLOW. GET UNDER THEIR WEAPONS' FIRE!

TYSON, YOU NEED TO MOVE FASTER!

THE BOY ON THE LEFT IS DRUNKER THAN THE OTHERS, TAKE HIM OUT FIRST!

MAN, I CAN SMELL THE ALCOHOL ON THEIR BREATH FROM HERE – My mate thought – *I'LL DRAW THEIR FIRE, CAESAR AND TYSON, GET READY.*

BE CAREFUL DECLAN, THE BOY IN THE MIDDLE HAS BETTER AIM THAN THE REST – Caesar warned.

I pictured the European Werewolf leaping through the air, amongst the laser fire, as he distracted the teens with his frightening form.

GOT YOU! – Tyson mentally cried out.

THERE! – Caesar thought too, leaping upon his target.

WHO DO YOU GUYS THINK YOU ARE, ACTION MOVIE HEROES?! – Declan grumbled about the boys who were still shooting.

Using my sight as a Circulator, I 'saw' he ran in a wide circle, galloping from tree to tree, in a supernaturally fast speed. He used the trunks as his cover, before leaping on the last two. He ran so fast, he managed to pounce on them from behind. As they were knocked to the ground, they were also knocked unconscious.

STUPID KIDS – He complained – *WHERE THE HELL ARE THEIR PARENTS? WHY AREN'T THEY STOPPING THEIR SIXTEEN YEAR OLDS FROM DRINKING? HOW THE HELL DID THEY GET THEIR 'TRIGGER HAPPY' HANDS ON THESE KINDS OF WEAPONS?*

I THINK THEIR PARENTS OWN THEM – Tyson pointed out – *LOOK AT THE LICENSE NUMBER ON THE GUNS.*

STUPID HUMANS – He thought in annoyance – *REMIND ME AGAIN WHY IT'S WRONG TO HUNT THEM?*

With the skirmish now over, the flurry of thoughts began to die down.

I knew Walt would put his uniform back on and call the Sheriff's Station in Alma, the other Park Rangers he worked with, as well as the Paramedics. By the time they arrived, the pack would have left. He would claim he found the boys' crashed vehicle after following the trail of dead animals. Their accident will be blamed on drunk driving, which will also be suggested what rendered them unconscious. The paramedics will take them to hospital and once they're released, the police would arrest them. If the boys tried to tell of topless, muscled men, with glowing eyes, elongated teeth and claws; their consumption of alcohol would be blamed. And while all of this was happening, Walt and the other rangers, would tend to the real victims of this mess; the wounded wildlife.

I returned to packing when I almost dropped a pile of books I was holding, by the next thought to enter my mind.

I'M COMING FOR YOU – Declan willed my way.

Wearily, I let out a sigh as he let me know in no uncertain terms, this particular fight wasn't over.

*****

Ten minutes later, my naked husband in human form, opened the front door. He came inside and carried with him his torn clothes, ruined shoes and my mobile phone, which had fallen out. However, I wouldn't look his way, as I continued stacking the books which needed to be boxed.

"I put some new clothes over there," I nodded towards the easy chair.

In the corner of my eye, I watched him walk over to the seat. He put down his ripped garments to pull on the whole ones. He remained quiet as he put on the apparel and I didn't say anything else.

Once he was dressed, he walked barefoot over to my position. He came to stand beside as he examined the empty shelves. He saw that I'd packed up half of my collection, with two bookshelves to go.

"Look at how much dust there is," he commented.

Finally, I looked his way with an incredulous expression. His wife is leaving him and he's passing judgement on her housekeeping? I rolled my eyes as I returned to my work.

"Well, once I'm gone and my things are too, I'm sure you'll find many a dusty spot I missed." I said in a surly manner.

"You're probably right." He said. "I didn't see a lot of things, when I was only looking at you."

I pulled some more books off a shelf and stacked them into another pile. As I worked, I tried to keep the stacks in relevant order, by not mixing up the books on Ancient Greece with the ones on Ancient Egypt. Also, I made sure to keep my work separate from the other historians.

"Where did you get the boxes?" He wondered.

"I found them in the attic," I answered. "We put them up there after the Internet TV and Sound System were delivered, as well as a couple of other things over the years."

"I thought we'd have more, if you compared it to how many years we've been together."

"It's not like we went on many shopping sprees and regularly bought large electronics or appliances…" I looked up at him when I froze, "…Declan?"

"Yeah, I know, B." He said softly. "I've been shot, but I'll heal."

My eyes widened as my breath was sucked in, as I stared at the red stain. It was steadily growing bigger, on the bottom of his blue, chequered, flannel shirt. He must have been shot just above his right hip, as his blood stained the top of his jeans, too.

"But you're not healing from it, you're bleeding heavily!" I cried out.

Quickly, I stood up from the floor, grabbed his arm and pulled him over to the dining table. I made him sit on top of it, before I rushed into the kitchen to grab a clean tea towel. I ran it under the tap before rushing back to him.

"Hold your shirt up." I ordered. Then I used the wet tea towel, to wipe away the excess of blood and get a better look at it. "Why didn't you say something sooner?"

"And say what? Don't leave me B, I've been shot?" He asked dryly, but his voice wavered which gave away his pain.

"How come I didn't sense your injury, when you were fighting?" I wondered.

"I don't know."

"I was listening in to the fight and I heard your thoughts." I frowned. "I felt it when the Voodoo crazies stabbed you, so how come I didn't feel this?"

"I don't know..." he repeated, "...I vaguely felt it when the kid shot me, but my mind was on other matters. I didn't even realize I was bleeding until Ki pointed it out. He wanted to treat me but I said I had somewhere else to be."

My heart raced as I examined the burn mark with the bleeding hole in the middle. His injury looked exactly the same as the poor animals' wounds. I pressed the damp tea towel against it to try to stop the bleeding, but the material became soaked with his blood.

"You're bleeding too quickly, you're not regenerating fast enough." I spoke in a trembling voice. "Keep your hand on the tea towel and I'll get another one."

I took his hand and tried to make it hold onto his makeshift dressing, but he latched onto my hand instead.

"Aren't you gonna ask what I was thinking about?" His eyes met mine.

"Not now Declan, we have to get you healed first!" I tried to pull away.

"I was wondering what eternity would be like without you..." he refused to let go, "...I was imagining all my reincarnations without you in them."

"Declan, I have to get some more towels!" I struggled.

"And you know what I came up with, B?" He went on.

"Declan please, we have to stop the bleeding!"

"Pain..." he said flatly, "...an unending pain that's worse than getting shot with a laser rifle or a silver bullet. Is that what you felt, B? Is that why you went nuts? The idea of being born over and over again without a reason to live, brought me to the brink of madness."

I paused long enough to look into his face and not only did I see a tortured expression, but his lips were turning white.

"Declan, you're bleeding to death!" I cried out tearfully.

"But I don't feel it B, I don't." He spoke in a delirious fashion. "I don't feel anything, when I don't have you."

I closed my eyes and concentrated with all my might to our Medicine Man – *KI, COME QUICK! DECLAN IS INJURED! I THINK HE'S BLEEDING TO DEATH!*

Finally, I pulled myself out of his grasp and raced back into the kitchen. I opened the bottom drawer and grabbed the pile of tea towels. Then I rushed back to my mate and I laid him out, on top of the table. I held the stack of tea towels over his injury and pushed down, to try to slow the bleeding. I felt his body begin to shake as he went into shock.

"We're gonna have to warn the rest of the pack about laser rifles..." he uttered out, "...they're just as bad as silver bullets."

"I think you might be right." I blinked back my tears as I tried to remain calm.

"I don't think our regenerative ability knows what to do against modern warfare."

"Shhh..." I said gently, "...try to remain still."

"I guess it doesn't help when the Werewolf is 287 years old, either."

"Shhh Declan, conserve your strength." I tried to soothe.

He put his hands over mine and it worried me how cold they felt.

"Man, you're nice and warm," he said longingly.

I switched around so his hands were on the tea towels and my hands were over his, to warm them.

Just then, deep inside my heart, I felt the familiar rumbling, ***Your mate needs you, Little Wolf.***

The voice was right and I knew what to do.

"Declan, I want you to keep your hands on the tea towels," I instructed.

Then I walked around the table so I was standing by his head. As I moved into position, I morphed into my Lokoti Werewolf shape. My stretchy t-shirt strained at the seams from the extra muscle. Then I raised my right wrist to my mouth and using my sharper teeth, I put a gash in the skin.

I lowered it to his mouth, but he moved his head away. "No."

"Don't be stupid, Declan." I spoke in my deep voice.

"I'm not drinking my ex-wife's blood," he said stubbornly.

"And I'm not going to be widowed today!" I growled fiercely.

Then I jammed my bleeding wrist into his mouth, whether he wanted it or not.

I closed my eyes and breathed deeply, to regulate my blood flow. I felt him begin to drink, as his hands remained over his wound. His shaking started to subside the more he drank. His faded blue eyes looked up and locked onto my glowing turquoise ones.

I sensed he was becoming stronger and in relief, I placed a kiss on his forehead. I held my muscled arm steady for him as he consumed my life force.

Then he kept one hand over the tea towels, as his other held onto my arm. He gripped onto it tightly as he supped from his wife.

Suddenly, our front door was thrown open with Ki's entrance. The topless, muscled, Lokoti Werewolf stood there, with his 'Medicine Bundle' in his clawed hand. We guessed he'd run home in supernatural speed to retrieve it, before coming here. His glowing pink eyes surveyed scene, before he helped himself into our home.

When Meadow Shallow Water passed away, his apprentice Ki Lightfoot became the next Medicine Man. The 55 year old Lokoti Werewolf who looked to be in his thirties, took his job seriously. He was often seen with a frown and his medical advice could come with a lecture. If he thought his patient was behaving foolishly, he'd tell them so.

With that kind of attitude, I thought he was the perfect practitioner for a European Werewolf. Once he found out Declan hadn't taken his back medication and he threatened to hold him down and ram the tablets into him. Of course it was all talk, but it won the predator's respect and he never missed a dose again.

Ki rushed over to the table and shoved the tea towels aside to examine the wound.

"I told the old fool I needed to check him out, but he didn't hear me." Ki growled in annoyance. "He ran straight home to you."

He opened up his 'Medicine Bundle' which was the familiar, old, black leather, doctor's bag. I watched him take out some kind of new medicine I'd never seen before. It looked like an aerosol can, which he pressed into Declan's wound. When he pressed on the nozzle, a strong smelling foam, frothed out.

"Aaarrrgghh!" My mate moved his mouth away, to cry in pain.

"What is that?" I asked in my thunderous Werewolf voice.

"It's a new antiseptic on the market." Ki answered in a similar manner. "It sterilizes the wound, as it clots the blood, effectively stopping the bleeding."

Declan writhed in agony with two Lokoti Werewolves holding him down.

He continued, "It stings for the first couple of minutes then it turns the wound numb, as the healing takes effect."

"Do humans go through this?" I wondered, as I sensed the extent of pain the European Werewolf was in.

"Usually when this is applied, the human patient is sedated in a hospital." The Medicine Man said gruffly. "Unfortunately, I don't have a travelling operating theatre, for emergencies such as these."

Eventually, Declan stopped writhing before collapsing back into my strong arms. He lay weakened and looked as white as a ghost. I replaced my wrist in his mouth and after a moment, I felt him start to drink again.

"He's going to need my blood too." Ki frowned. "Give him as much as you can without harming yourself, while I close his wound."

I nodded as I held my arm firmly against Declan's mouth. I felt him suck as he looked up appreciatively. I smiled as warmly as I could, to try to take his mind off the pain. But it was probably negated by my watery eyes and elongated teeth. Ki prepared some kind medical tape and I saw my mate flinch, as the Medicine Man stuck together the scorched skin.

"Drink Declan, it will lessen the pain, as well as aid in your regeneration." I growled softly.

His eyes were squeezed shut from the agony he was in and my free hand rubbed his arm in a supportive manner.

"So, what's with the boxes?" Ki talked as he worked. "Are you retiring from academic life, Aunt B? Or are the two of you making final plans for your evolution?"

My husband's eyes snapped open and met mine in a silent challenge.

"Long story." I said sharply, which made it clear I didn't want to discuss it.

Ki didn't say anything else as he worked quickly and efficiently to close the wound.

"Leave the bandage tape on for at least six hours." He instructed. "Even if it itches or it looks like the skin has closed up, don't take it off."

I nodded to show I understood and our Medicine Man packed up his old fashioned doctor's case.

"I'll give Uncle Declan my blood now." He said next. "Have you got some juice or a soda in the fridge? Pour me a glass and one for yourself while you're at it, so we don't get dizzy from the transfusion."

When I tried to pull my arm back, my husband wouldn't let it go. Next, I felt his tongue lick the gash to kick start my own regeneration. When I did take my wrist back, I saw his saliva had worked and there was new pink skin in its place. Then he looked on helplessly as I left his side, to go into the kitchen and procure the drinks.

Ki used the claws on his left hand to cut his right wrist too. He lowered the gash to his mouth and my mate screwed up his face in distaste. He even turned his head away.

"Dude, my wife tastes so much better than you." He complained.

"I should hope so!" Ki chuckled. "Now hold still, you stubborn old wolf."

I couldn't help but to smirk as I reverted to my human appearance. As such, I opened the fridge, picked up the orange juice and retrieved two glasses from the cupboard. I carried our drinks over to the table and placed the second glass in front of Ki.

"Thanks," he acknowledged.

I sat down in one of the chairs and sipped on my beverage. But as soon as I had the first taste, my body craved more. I gulped it down in a matter of seconds, which made me realize how much it needed the sugar.

Declan turned his head away to say, "Aw, where's mine?"

"You've already got a drink." I said coolly.

"Stay still, Uncle Declan!" Our Healer snapped impatiently. "Sharing blood with you is like trying to feed a one year old. Only, there's no high chair large enough, to sit your big ass down."

My husband chuckled, "Great bedside manner you've got there."

"Have you ever considered my tone matches the person I'm dealing with?" He asked wryly.

Their banter relieved me as it made me think that the danger had passed.

"So Declan's going to be OK?" I checked.

"He'll live, unfortunately." Ki jested, as he removed his wrist.

"Remind me NOT to save your ass again from a drunk, sixteen year old with a laser rifle." Declan groaned, as he sat upright.

"You didn't save me, you were merely showing off." He chuckled.

Next, the Medicine Man tended to himself by running an alcohol wipe over his wound which was already half healed. Then he picked up his drink and gulped it all down. Lastly, he rested the glass on the table and picked up his doctor's case.

"Right, now that the emergency is over, I'm going to hold an urgent meeting with the Council of Tribal Elders. I'll let them know what happened and about the new threat to the pack." He organized.

"Yeah, thanks Ki." My mate said gruffly.

"I'll come by tomorrow morning for a check up and make sure that you've healed properly." He said as his farewell.

"Thank you Ki." I stood up to see him off.

He walked past the boxes and stacks of books on the floor while passing another look their way. Then he gave a nod in our direction before he disappeared through the front door. I sighed as I turned around to look on my husband, the same time he turned his gaze on his wife.

"Do I get pardoned for bad behaviour, because I got shot?" Declan asked hopeful. Then he saw how I crossed my arms defensively and he gloomily looked away. "I thought not."

I picked up the glasses from the table and carried them into the kitchen. Then I opened up the dishwasher and added them to the rest of the dirty dishes. However, I paused when I looked on the ingredients for the dessert he started to make.

"Do you want me to clean that up?" I pointed at it.

"Gimme a moment and I'll finish making it." He answered, before he grumbled under his breath, "Unlike some people, I finish what I start."

Right, that's it!

I marched towards him with a pointed finger, "YOU'RE the one who doesn't want to spend eternity with me!"

"I NEVER said that!"

"How else were you going to remain with me, if not as a Circulator?"

"I told you not to change me YET!"

"You bit my head off this afternoon and you made it loud and clear that you don't want to be like me!"

"I did NOT bite your head off!"

"You yelled at me today and you promised you would stop!"

"B, I haven't yelled at you in a VERY long time!"

"What makes you think that you can start yelling now?" I stood there with my hands on my hips. "Unless of course that's your 'cunning plan', by treating me like crap so I won't want to spend eternity with you!"

"You're an idiot." He wearily shook his head. "Don't you get it, or do I have to spell it out for you?"

My eyes narrowed as I stood there, glowering at the obnoxious male.

"I'm scared of losing our chemistry. I like making you angry and seeing the sparks come flying off your aura. I love making love to you and seeing your aura change again. I love it when you're on heat and your pheromones get stronger. I love the fact that I can tell by smell alone, what stage of your reproductive cycle you're in. But I'm scared that if you turn me into a Circulator like you, then I won't have these things anymore."

I gave a funny look, "I already told you, you don't lose these things when you change -"

He interrupted, "You can't see auras can you? You don't see your aura, you don't see other Circulator's auras and you can't see a psychic's aura. You don't see heat signatures, either. The male Lokoti Werewolves and I, always thought that because you're a Circulator, your sight is different from ours."

My eyes turned downcast as his point hurt and so did the truth.

Carefully, Declan slid off the table to stand before his mate. We stood maybe thirty centimetres apart, but it was close enough to feel his body heat radiate outwards. At least that was reassuring, his normally high temperature had returned.

He continued, "Your sense of smell isn't as keen as a male Lokoti Werewolf. Your hearing isn't as acute and your tracking skills are sketchy at best. We don't blame it on the fact that you're female, we take it as part of being a Circulator. You're the fastest in the pack, you can see and travel in time and you're not as allergic to silver, like the rest of us are."

Abruptly, he cupped my face and leaned in to inhale deeply. He closed his eyes to savour the scent, like he was sniffing a fine wine or flowers in bloom. When he opened them again, he gazed into my face and kept his hands pressed against my cheeks.

"Your aura was what attracted me to you first, your figure second and your scent third." He explained. "When I first set eyes on you, I was in awe of the glowing girl. Eventually, I realized my Mom and Derik couldn't see it, because they were human and I wasn't. Your Grandfather explained he could see it too, as could all the Lokoti Werewolves. Those nights the bloodlust ate me inside out and I hated myself because of it, one of the things that kept me going was I could see auras. I had a special power most of the tribe didn't. I could spot you, your mother and your grandmother a mile away, because of your auras. I can tell if somebody's psychic, whether or not they have an aura. Hell, I had a special power that not even some of the Lokoti Werewolves had, which was I could feel your aura when I touched you."

I pondered, "You don't want to become a Circulator yet, because you don't want to stop seeing auras, or lose your keen sense of smell?"

Declan's faded blue eyes held my darker ones as he spoke honestly.

"I'm caught between a rock and a hard place, because as much as I want to be with you forever? I'm scared that if you change me into a Circulator, I'll lose the only things I like about myself. I know I'm gaining a lot in becoming like you, but you need to understand I'm also losing a lot too."

Disheartened, I turned away when Declan pulled me back to him.

"So, do we have a deal?"

This made me look up in surprise, "Huh?"

"We will be together forever, B." He said seriously. "But respect my wishes and wait until the last possible minute, to turn me into a Circulator."

I ducked my head as my silent consent.

Then the elderly husband wrapped his arms about his younger wife and held her tightly. He squeezed her so hard out of relief, he almost lifted her off the floor. Slowly, her arms wrapped around his waist and eventually she hugged him back.

To his surprise, I pulled away with a moan. "Ooh!"

"What?"

"Now I have to go and unpack everything."

"Told you, I'm not cleaning that up." He smirked.

"Shut up."

He smilingly walked into the kitchen, "Well the good news is, by the time you've finished, dinner will be ready."

"Declan, you can't cook within an hour of being shot!"

"Oh no?" He picked up the beaters once more. "Watch me."

~ ~

~ **30** ~

3rd November, 2363

"B...? B! C'mon, it's 6.55 PM! We're supposed to be there in five minutes!"

Declan bellowed from the bottom of the stairs, as I was hopping around the bedroom, from one foot to the other. I was pulling on my high heels whilst hunting around for my small, black evening bag. I'd taken it out of the wardrobe this afternoon when I planned my outfit, now it had disappeared.

"You've got ten seconds to get your ass downstairs, or I'll come and get it!" He threatened.

I rolled my eyes at his typical temper which never changed, even after 300 years.

"I'm coming!" I called back.

I finished dressing the same time as I found my evening bag. No wonder I couldn't see it, it had fallen on the floor between the bed and bedside table. I snatched it up and opened it, to make sure my keys, driver's license and credit card were still inside.

After checking my appearance one last time in the mirror, I felt ready. I left the bedroom and my black, strappy, high heels made 'clip clop' sounds as I went down the stairs. I was wearing a long, black, lacy, evening gown which was scattered with sequins. My dark hair was done up in a French roll, with various wisps hanging around my ears and neck. For jewellery, I was wearing the pearl earrings and necklace my husband had bought, years ago.

The tall man, who appeared to be in his seventies, with his white hair in a crew cut; glanced up and grinned.

"Not bad," he said, as he looked his wife up and down.

He was wearing a black suit, a crisp white shirt and a light blue, silk tie, which matched his faded blue eyes. I looked him over, just as impressed, as I arrived at his side. My elderly husband filled out his suit nicely, thanks to his supernatural muscle.

"Very suave, Mr. Bond," I jested. "I see I'm going to have to keep a short leash on you tonight."

He growled playfully, as he pulled me closer to hold my body against his.

"And you look just as a femme fatale in a 'Bond' film should," he raised my hand to his wrinkled lips. "Come on, my beautiful B."

Next, he rested my hand on his arm and escorted me out of the house.

Declan locked the front door behind then in the icy air, he draped my long, black, woolen overcoat about my shoulders. As we walked over to the garage, I noticed he snuck several glances at my cleavage through the black lace. When he thought I wasn't looking he'd often stare, or even if I did notice, he didn't look away.

He hit his remote key and the automatic garage door opened. When he pressed the remote a second time, his silver coloured, hover-car, unlocked itself. He started to escort me to the passenger's door, but I surprised him when I walked around to the driver's side instead.

"Not again," he rolled his eyes.

"I'm driving," I said coolly.

"What, you don't think I can drive down to the Elm's dinner party and back?" He arched his eyebrows. "I mention ONCE that I'm having trouble with my eyesight and my wife automatically thinks that I'm going blind."

"Keys," I held out my hand.

"B, I can frickin' drive and if you're worried about me driving in the dark, I'll use my night-vision."

To prove it, his blue eyes started to glow green.

I was probably jeopardizing the surprise by doing this, but I was unsure of how else to get him there.

"You heard me," I said coolly. "Besides, your eyesight isn't in question. I just feel like driving tonight."

"OK then, Miss Random." He gave a peculiar look.

He tossed the remote over and I caught it with one hand.

We sat down in the vehicle with his wife behind the wheel. To his chagrin, I changed around the driver's seat then I punched in the ignition code. As the hover-car rose into the air, he regarded me suspiciously. Speedily, I reversed out of the garage and down the driveway, when I turned sharply midair then gunned down the hill.

"Um B, I think you left the transmission on the road back there." He joked. "You want to stop now, or shall we pick it up on the way home?"

"Shut up." I giggled.

He chuckled too, as he placed his hand behind my neck and caressed the skin.

I surprised him a second time once we were in the community centre. Instead of turning right into the street for Derik and Uma Elm's, I went left. We cruised past the sports field, the General Store and the Garage, before pulling up out the front of the Meeting Hall.

The large, wooden building, brightly decorated in tribal colours, had all the lights on. He knew something was afoot by the activity and especially how every single hover-car in the tribe, was parked around.

"Gee, what are we doing here?" He feigned surprise.

"Um, I have to pick up something." I lied lamely. "Feather said she'd lend me some of the records kept by the Council of Tribal Elders."

"Right," he rolled his eyes.

"It'll only take a second then we'll go on to the Elm's," I continued. "Can you give me a hand?"

We climbed out of the vehicle and I hit the remote to lock the doors behind. Together, we walked along the stone path towards the main door. However, it didn't help matters when we heard with our sensitive ears:

"Ssshh, they're here!"

He snickered, "Smooth, real smooth."

I tittered, as I took his arm and walked him to the doors, which opened upon our approach.

"SURPRISE!"

Declan's eyes still widened, even if he knew what was coming, as he walked into the Hall.

I think he was touched to see the whole tribe had convened to celebrate his 300th Birthday.

Of course, the pack was here, as were their families, their parents, brothers-in-law and sisters-in-law, aunts, uncles, nephews and nieces. We spotted the pack standing up the front, along with their mates, or those that were still alive. The recently widowed Caesar stood with his long ago widowed father Forrest, with Tyson and his wife Tania and their two children, on the other side.

"Happy Birthday Uncle Declan!"

"Happy Birthday Uncle Dec!"

"Happy Birthday Uncle!"

"Happy Birthday!"

As everyone cheered, I pointed out the hand-made, paper banner, hanging from the wooden ceiling which read; HAPPY BIRTHDAY UNCLE DECLAN.

My mate looked up and saw and his eyes turned misty. I sensed he really appreciated his not so surprising, 'surprise party'. I guess he never knew how much the tribe let alone the pack, appreciated him.

Next, the twelve year old Holly Sabre ran up. She was our great x7 grandniece and a favourite of his, particularly because she wasn't afraid of him. When we visited Holly's family, she always crawled into his lap for a cuddle, or asked for a piggy-back ride. She wasn't even afraid of her Granduncle's other form, which she'd seen once.

Three years ago, Holly and her family were involved in an accident. They were driving back to tribal lands when another hover-car hit them, in a head-on collision. Since it happened on the night of a full moon, the pack who were already out in the woods, heard the noise. We ran to help, with Declan using his superior strength and claws, to rip open the buckled doors.

"Uncle Dec, is that you...?" The nine year old with the deep cut in her forehead, gazed up at her rescuer.

The huge, hairless, monster, carefully lifted her out and held her close, using his body heat to stave off shock. He stayed with her, softly growling in a tender manner, until the police and paramedics arrived. When the outsiders took over the scene, he hid in the woods, but remained nearby to watch.

Now, the little girl beamed up at my husband like he was the best thing since sliced bread, as she held out her hand-made birthday card.

"Happy Birthday, Great, Great, Great, Great, Great, Great, Great, Granduncle Declan." She recited, taking care to get in the right number of 'greats'.

"You made this for me?" Declan smiled tearfully, touched by her gesture.

He took the card from her and together we looked on. On the cover, was a childish drawing of a European Werewolf that looked more like an albino, grizzly bear, with bright green eyes. My husband and I exchanged small smiles, at the twelve year old's interpretation.

MAN, SHE MUST HAVE BEEN OUT OF IT THAT NIGHT – Declan thought humorously.

Then he handed me the card before he picked her up and held her securely in his strong arms.

"Thank you, sweetie," he kissed her on the cheek.

"Do you like it?" She asked anxiously.

"I love it." He reassured.

Next, we were pleasantly surprised when somebody else stepped out from the crowd to greet us.

The middle-aged Jarrod Worthall, wearing his blue and grey ISF uniform, came forward.

"Jarrod!" I cried out in delight, as I swamped him in a hug. "What are you doing here? Last I heard, International Space Fleet sent your ship beyond Alpha Centauri."

He was our distant relation from the Worthall family who still resided at Blythe Castle. After graduating from ISF Academy, he came to Alaska to meet us. I still remember the young man, who couldn't believe his eyes that close relations of his ancestry, were still alive and well. That day back in 2340, he was so nervous, he couldn't even talk properly.

"We got back last night." He answered in his English accent. "We found a new planet which we can put forward to ISF as another terra forming project."

"Thanks for sending me those amazing pictures of the astronomical phenomena you've seen." I gushed. "I love getting your emails with the photos attached."

"She does," my husband told him, as he gently put Holly down. "I always know when she receives one of your communiqués, as she screams out, 'Declan, come and look at this!' She's so loud, the whole tribe can hear her."

Laughingly, I whacked him on the arm. "Shut up!"

"I can hear her," the little girl went along with whatever her granduncle said.

"No you can't!" I tweaked her nose, which made her giggle.

"Anyway, thanks for coming." Declan shook Jarrod's hand. "I think it's been ten years since we last saw you."

"The repercussions of deep space exploration," the Englishman sighed. "But I couldn't miss your 300th Birthday."

I looked fondly on the middle-aged officer with grey hair, whereas he examined my features in curiosity.

"I say B, you don't look a day older than when we first met." He remarked.

"Tell me about it!" My husband rolled his eyes. "Sometimes I think she's growing younger, while the rest of us 'mere mortals' stumble over with time."

"You can't talk," the human smirked, "I'll be lucky if I reach my hundredth birthday, let alone three-hundredth."

Just then music started to play, as the MC in the corner of the hall, turned on the tunes. I'd discussed with him what to play, after sifting through Declan's favourites in his gigantic music collection. The first song to come on was Vast's 'Free'.

We saw the Meeting Hall was decked out for a typical tribal celebration. Three quarters of the room had tables and chairs set up, where families could sit down and eat, with the last quarter made into a dance area. Along the far side of the wall, several tables were put together to form one long one, where food and non-alcoholic drinks were offered. I guessed everyone had brought a dish and drink to share, as usual for a gathering.

Caesar came over to say, "We're all sitting at that table over there, if you'd like to join us."

We looked over and saw that Forrest, Tyson, Tania and their children, were already sitting down with plates of food.

Then he said to the human, "There's a seat for you too."

"Why thank you," Jarrod acknowledged.

"How appropriate," I giggled, "the First of the Lokoti Werewolf pack and the Captain of the USS Darwin, sitting together. So, does this mean we're eating at the Captain's table?"

The Lokoti and the Englishman exchanged amused glances.

"Yeah yeah," Declan smilingly rolled his eyes, "A leads to B which then results in C. Even at a birthday party, B will still relate it to 'trippy time travel stuff'."

Then my husband turned his grandniece in the direction of her parents and sent her off to sit with them.

*****

The birthday party was a success with festivities lasting until 12 AM.

Of course the families with young children left before the clock struck midnight. However, when anybody departed, they swung by our table first to bestow their well wishes. I felt my mate's mild embarrassment and humility, at being treated like a celebrity.

Declan received more hand-made birthday cards by the children in the tribe. However, he didn't receive any presents nor did he expect them. After all, what do you buy someone who's been around for three centuries? We had everything we needed and had even given away some of our things, we no longer used.

The whole tribe had chipped in to buy a large, three tiered, birthday cake. It was Neapolitan flavour, which meant there were layers of chocolate, vanilla and strawberry, separated by cream filling. Then the whole thing was smothered in white frosting and decorated with bright green ivy, made of more icing. Everyone knew that the green represented the colour of his European Werewolf eyes.

"It looks like a frickin' wedding cake," my mate muttered.

"Well, we never had a wedding cake at our Housewarming or our Joining Ceremony, so you can think of it that way, if you like." I giggled.

"In that case, you'd better help me cut it then." He pulled me along.

Together, we held the large knife and sliced into the bottom layer, to much cheering and clapping. We were momentarily blinded by the flashes from every one's digital cameras or camera phones, going off. Then the cake was wheeled away by several members of the tribe, who looked after dispensing it.

Afterwards, as we were eating the delicious dessert, Holly ran up to us with her mother's camera.

"Look at the photos Mommy and I took," she thrust the view screen into her Granduncle's face.

"OK, what have we got here?" He pulled her onto his lap.

The twelve year old used the controls for the display and I looked over his shoulder to see.

There was a photo of Declan and I, chatting with Derik and Uma Elm. Then I smiled on the picture of my mate dancing with his grandniece, as she stood on his feet and he slowly waltzed. But I stared at the one of us, dancing together, with the elderly man holding closely his youthful wife. The last shot was of us cutting the cake, with our white and dark hair, contrasted against the other.

Like I'd lost control of myself, I had to turn away and blink back unexpected tears.

"Which were the photos that you took?" Declan asked.

"I took the ones of you and Aunt B dancing and cutting the cake," she pointed.

"Gee, I really like these pictures." He said sweetly. "Do you think that you could email me the photos?"

"I'll do it tonight!" She beamed proudly then hopped off his lap and ran away.

"I don't mean right at this moment," he chuckled, as he watched her go. Then I sensed he looked my way. "B, are you OK?"

"Yeah, I'm fine." I sniffed. "Just some mascara in my eyes."

"Again?" He chuckled. "Either your make-up application skills are slipping, or you're getting emotional in your old age."

A loud laugh escaped then I turned around to look on the man whom I've been married to, through good times and bad.

"I think you might be right," I tittered tearfully. "You can't take me anywhere, can you?"

Next, he looked down at his watch to see the time.

"It's 11.10 PM, do you think anybody would mind if we slipped out?" He wondered.

"Do you wanna leave?"

He straightened as his face contorted in pain. "I don't think my back likes these fold-up chairs."

Instantly, I stood up and reached for my coat which was draped over the back of my seat.

"C'mon on, let's get you home." I said firmly. "I've got a new 'bath bomb' we can try out. It's got ginger in it as well as some other herbs which will help."

"I'm gonna pass on the bath, but I'll take some more tablets." He sighed. "That and bed, sounds like a godsend to this old man."

Slowly, he stood up and I heard his joints crack. He gave a small stretch before he took my arm and we headed out. On our way, we walked past Caesar, Jarrod and Ki talking together.

Our First noticed, "Are you two heading off?"

His Second grinned in good humour, "I'm not a 'spring chicken' anymore, tonight's party is proof of that."

The Medicine Man's eyes narrowed, as he regarded the way the husband was leaning on his wife.

"Back pain?" He guessed. "I'll come with you, to make sure you're alright."

"Aw, come off it Ki!" My mate said, embarrassed. "I'm old, but I'm not an invalid. Besides, my wife hasn't given me her birthday present yet."

Then he moved his eyebrows up and down in a cheeky fashion.

"Declan!" I elbowed him in the ribs, while blushing.

"Take the stubborn, old wolf home, Aunt B." Our Healer laughed it off. "But if his back doesn't improve, call me."

"Will do," I nodded then looked towards Jarrod. "Do you need a place to crash tonight?"

"Unfortunately, I can't stay." He sighed. "I have a meeting with ISF Command at 0800 hours. I'll be shuttling to London, tonight."

"Well thanks for coming," Declan shook his hand again.

"G'night, it was great catching up with you again." I gave a small wave.

"I'll keep in touch," the ISF Captain, promised.

Then the three men watched us depart via the main entrance as we headed for our hover-car.

*****

Uncharacteristically, I was in bed before my husband that night.

Usually, I was the one who took the longest to retire. Perfunctorily, Declan would clean his teeth and use the toilet then go to bed. When he was finished with the bathroom, it was my turn. I'd clean my teeth, brush my long hair and put moisturizer on, especially in winter as the cold could dry out my skin.

But tonight, when I came into the bedroom, I didn't find him waiting in bed.

I pulled down the covers and climbed in. Then I lay on my side in my new negligee and waited. I looked over at his digital alarm clock and saw the time was 11.43 PM. I hope he's not going to be too tired, to enjoy his 'birthday present'.

After five minutes, Declan wandered into the bedroom wearing flannel pyjama bottoms. That was another thing time had changed, he no longer slept in boxers twelve months of the year. The last couple of years, he's started to feel the cold.

I watched him place Holly's birthday card on top of the tallboy and he stepped back to look on it.

"You know what, B?"

"What?"

"When Holly saw me that night, sure she was woosy thanks to her head being cracked open like a coconut; but she recognized me." He sounded impressed. "She didn't even get scared when she saw me in my other form."

"Well, you're actually not that scary." I smirked.

"I'm not?" He looked my way.

"Nope."

"Maybe you're only saying that, because we've been married for 273 years."

I pretended to think about it before I said again, "Nope!"

"Maybe I'm scary now, for being a dirty, old man beside a beautiful, young woman." His voice dropped soberly.

Again, I pretended to contemplate until I said, "Nup!"

"Are you still attracted to me, B?" He looked on, longingly.

"Always," I smiled softly. "You still smell like maple syrup."

Declan chuckled as he took a step closer to the bed, "And you still smell like a vase of wildflowers sitting in a kitchen, while a cake is baking in the oven."

"Really?"

"Truly."

"You're not tired of this body yet?" I enquired, as I showed it off in my new sleepwear. "A body that never changes, except when I turn, of course."

"B, it's a bit hard to tire of perfection."

I held up the covers for him, "Then get in here and stop making me wait."

"Yes ma'am!"

The old man leapt between the sheets like he was still a young Werewolf. Bad back or not, sex still invigorated him. He settled over my body as I parted my legs, to welcome him. They wrapped around his waist, which made him smile down.

"We've had some good times, haven't we, B?"

"We've had some VERY good times, Dec." I ran my hands up and down his leathery chest.

"We've fought each other and we've fought for the other." He reminisced. "We've come up against every conceivable problem a couple could have."

"Hating each other in the beginning and nuclear fall out..." I began.

"...getting shot by looters," he added on. "Facing disapproval from our family and tribe."

"European Vampires, European Werewolves, Asian Werewolves, North American Werewolves, Voodoo Priests, South American Vampires..." I listed off.

"...your insecurities about being unable to conceive, or even your insecurities about other women..." he chuckled.

"...your jealousy of other men, your temper tantrums and your stubbornness."

Declan rolled his eyes, "It's a hard task being married to you B, but somebody had to do it."

I was about to retort when I didn't get a chance to.

His mouth smothered mine as his hardening body rubbed against his mate's. My hands tugged down his pyjama bottoms as his tugged upwards the negligee. Our mouths moved together, as we kissed non-stop, initiating a tantalizing, tender, hour of sex.

We may not have the same 'marathons in the bedroom' as we used to, but it effectively stopped any further taunts that evening.

*****

Next morning when I awoke, the first thing I saw were our pyjamas lying on the floor.

Sleepily, I smiled to myself, as it reminded me of all the other mornings I'd woken up to a similar sight.

I was 'snug as a bug in a rug' under the covers, lying on my side, with my mate tucked against my back. My half-opened eyes wandered around the dim bedroom, before glancing at the clock. The time was 8.23 AM and although it wasn't as bright as it was in summer, I thought it was better than waking up to darkness, mid-winter.

A loud but contented sigh escaped as I rolled onto my back. As I did, I accidentally knocked into my mate. I thought he would have growled in complaint, but I didn't hear a thing.

"Sorry," I said obligatory.

There was no response which I thought was unusual. I thought he'd be awake, since he's been rising earlier in his old age. When I turned my head to look, I saw he was completely out to the world.

"Somebody's a sleepy-head this morning." I giggled. "Don't tell me, I wore you out last night?"

The loudness of my voice should have roused him and I was expecting him to rise to my tease... but nothing.

I rolled onto my other side so I was facing him. I rested my hand on his chest and noticed how cool his skin felt. That's weird, it's not as hot as it usually is. In fact, as I felt his torso, shoulders and arms, I noticed he felt cool all over. He was barely even warm!

"Declan?" I raised myself to look down in concern. "Declan."

I gave him a gentle shake but still he didn't stir.

In alarm, I put my right ear over his heart. Instead of pounding away with its usual strength, it sounded slower and softer. Then I put my fingers against his wrinkled neck, to search for his pulse and I barely felt it!

By this stage, I was trying not to panic as I wondered what to do?

"Declan?" I shook him harder. "Declan!"

Nothing. He didn't wake up and I noticed something else that was wrong, his pallor. Even his lips looked drained of colour! Ice-cold panic gripped my heart so hard, it almost stopped.

"Declan, please!"

Then I heard him moan quietly as he rolled his head in my direction...

"Declan?"

"B..." he uttered without opening his eyes, "...I feel so weak...so tired."

My stomach felt like it abruptly shrunk to the size of a pea.

KI, COME HERE RIGHT NOW! – I thought fearfully.

After a moment, he replied – *I'M ON MY WAY.*

My eyes watered as my face hovered over my husband's. After a moment, he opened his eyes and tried to focus on his wife, but I could see it was a struggle. His faded blue eyes looked glassy and I couldn't hold his gaze.

"Declan, stay with me please!" I gripped his arms. "Just hold on, Ki's on his way now."

"...I think it's time, B..." He managed out.

Then he closed his eyes again and his head rolled to the side, as he fell back unconscious.

I started to expand into my Lokoti Werewolf body, as I raised my wrist to my sharpening teeth. I was about to injure myself then bleed into his mouth, but I stopped. A new thought occurred which made me return to human form.

No, my blood isn't going to regenerate him. If a Lokoti Werewolf could stop people dying of old age, the pack would never lose their mates or each other. There was nothing I could do as a Lokoti Werewolf, but there was something I could do, as a Circulator.

I'd have to irreparably change Declan into a 'Light Person', after all.

*****

I knew Ki would arrive at any moment, so I got out of bed and put on my negligee and robe. Hurriedly, I picked up Declan's pyjama bottoms and dressed him too. No sooner than I did, I heard the front door downstairs, open.

"Aunt B?" He called.

"I'm up here...!" I replied in a wavering voice.

I listened to him jog up the stairs and I looked up to see him stop in our bedroom doorway.

The Medicine Man surveyed the scene, of a wife holding her unconscious husband's hand like she was clinging on for dear life.

Next, he rushed over while opening up his 'Medicine Bundle' as he went. He rested the old, black leather, doctor's bag on top of the bed and took out a medical scanner. He waved the portable, hand-held device over my mate, before checking the readouts.

"His heart rate is only 40 beats per minute, his blood pressure is barely registering and his temperature is 20 degrees Celsius, which is 23 degrees below normal." Ki said seriously. "He's fading fast."

"Will my blood regenerate him?" I double-checked.

"I'm afraid not." He said gently. "There are few things in this world that our regenerative ability can't cure and unfortunately one of them is old age."

Ki put away the technology to examine him the old fashioned way, by touching his skin then putting his head over my husband's chest.

"Frankly, I'm amazed he lasted this long." He sighed as he rose. "It's said European Werewolves can live for three centuries, but Uncle Dec is the only member of his species ever documented to hit the big 300. Before the others reached his age, they were killed by their own kind, or by European Vampires."

My body started to shake as I held Declan's limp hand between my two. My chest hurt so much, I struggled to breathe. My eyes overflowed with tears as I helplessly looked on.

"But – but – but why is he fading so fast?" I asked in a tight voice. "Yesterday he was fine, you saw him last night at his birthday party."

"It must be the way of his species." Ki speculated. "They're built to be fighters until the very end. They're genetically designed to be strong, but when they go, they go fast. It's all or nothing."

Then the Medicine Man placed a supportive hand on my shoulder.

"You gave him a lot to live for." He said softly. "Everybody saw it, the pack included. You were his life, which is probably why he hung in there, to spend every possible moment with you."

As soon as those words left his mouth, loud sobs came out of mine...

Then he took back his hand to say, "Aunt B, I understand that you and Uncle Declan had an arrangement. I heard that the two of you had agreed to turn him into a Circulator before he dies of old age? I think that the moment has come."

I said sadly, "But he said he wasn't ready for it. He said he was scared that if I turn him into a Circulator, it would make him less of a European Werewolf."

"How so?"

"He's worried that he'll no longer see auras." I said dismally.

"Why would he think that?" Ki wondered.

"Because I can't see auras," I reminded. "He's always telling me that I'm more 'Light Person' than Lokoti Werewolf."

He chuckled, "Yeah, the pack has noticed this too."

"Remember the day Declan was shot with a laser rifle and you noticed that I was packing?" I brought up. "We had a fight about it. He admitted he didn't want to become a Circulator and lose what he loved about being a European Werewolf. I nearly went nuts, thinking I'd spend eternity without him."

"That explains a lot," Ki thought aloud. "So your arrangement no longer exists then?"

"He told me not to change him until he was on death's door." I sniffed. "He said he'd become a Circulator and travel to the space time continuum, the same way he'd go there if he died anyway."

The Healer opened his mouth to say something else, when we were interrupted by the sound of the front door, opening again. We both knew it was Caesar arriving. Our First sensed his Second was dying.

"You have some thinking to do," the Medicine Man said understandingly. "I'll be downstairs if you need me."

I watched Ki leave the bedroom to report on Declan's status. I heard their hushed voices as they talked privately. I guess he was telling Caesar what I just told him.

Distraught, I gazed down at my frail husband. His skin was almost as white as his hair. His breathing became shallower every minute that passed. I felt him slipping further and further away...

No matter if it was the right or wrong choice, each had final consequences. Either I turn my mate into a Circulator and we exist together for eternity inside the continuum; or I let him die as a European Werewolf and risk being separated by reincarnation.

My stomach knotted as I felt torn in two. I knew what *I* wanted to do, I wanted to be with the stubborn, bad-tempered male, forever! Declan said he wanted this too, but he just didn't like the idea of how it was achieved.

I needed to hear his consent, I wanted him to formally give his permission before I did this.

"Declan...?" I called softly, but there was no response. "Declan, can you hear me?"

Nope, still nothing.

I sensed he wasn't going to open his eyes again, not in the state that he was in. Fresh tears coursed down my cheeks as I bent over and rested my wet face on his cool chest.

Pathetically, I tried to wrap his arms about but they kept sliding off. I wanted to snuggle just one more time, to help me think. Things never seemed so bad, when he held me in his strong arms and I basked in his body heat. I wanted to feel ensconced in his embrace, just one more time. But his arms kept slipping off his wife and landed on uselessly on the bed.

As I lay beside him on the mattress, new sounds came to my ears.

I heard the front door downstairs open several more times, with the footfall of more people coming in. I sensed it was the rest of the pack, reporting in, just as they did whenever a member was lost or created. Out of respect, they kept their voices hushed, as the Medicine Man filled them in.

"Aunt B is upstairs with Uncle Declan." He advised. "Today, our Second is going to die, or he'll live for all time."

"He's not gonna die!" Forrest scoffed. "Aunt B is going to change him."

"That's what they planned, wasn't it?" Tyson queried.

Caesar must have held up his hands for quiet because they returned to whispering.

And there you go, there was my answer...

If the rest of the pack was sure of this, why wasn't I? Besides, what did Declan say, when he was conscious for those few moments? *"...I think it's time, B..."* Call me crazy, but it sounded like his consent.

Slowly, I raised my head to look on the grey face of my dying husband. A new strength filled me, washing away all my previous doubts. It wasn't from my supernatural muscle either, but it was hardened resolve.

"In unan, Declan." I wiped my face. "You are my mate, now and forever."

I picked up his left hand again and held it over my heart, while I rested my left hand over his.

Then I closed my eyes and concentrated, putting the both of us into phase. Our biological bodies dissolved into beings of light and if a stranger walked into the room, they'd think they were looking at two ghosts. In phase, we looked bright and see-through, while retaining our human shape.

I've never done something like this before, but I was following one of my all-knowing feelings.

Like the time I removed live snakes from his stomach, I concentrated on his being at the molecular level. Instead of differentiating his phased particles, I focused on strengthening them. As I did, I felt his bio-electromagnetic field rise in output. I continued to raise it, heightening the wavelength and frequency so it matched mine. But I knew this wasn't the only thing I had to do, I had to impart my temporal signature onto him, to put him into temporal flux.

While I was concentrating on raising his bio-electromagnetic field, I started to reverse time inside him. It wasn't hard to do all three at once, in fact, they seemed to blend into what I was already doing. His bio-electromagnetic field kept climbing, his energy signature went into temporal flux and his cellular degradation went into reversal. I felt his old strength return and it renewed itself with abundance!

By this stage, our bright forms on top of the bed turned blinding, as the air in the bedroom hummed with electrostatic charge.

I stopped raising his bio-electromagnetic field as I felt his supernatural strength take over. It was like his whole body roared back to life! It felt like a power surge and we were both the conduits. It ran from him to me and our human shapes started to blur, like we were turning into orbs of pure light.

The pack looked up dumbstruck, at the series of blinding flashes coming from upstairs.

Oh oh, Declan's bio-electromagnetic field was rising too high and too fast. We were about to evolve right then and there! We were on the verge of changing permanently into non-biological entities that looked like shimmering clouds of energy and light. It was what my parents and my grandparents looked like, when they evolved.

Quickly, I tried to regain control of the situation. Now I focused with all my might on stabilizing our energy signatures. I concentrated as hard as I could, to bring us out of phase. By reforming into our biological bodies, it would force our bio-electromagnetic fields to lower to a natural level.

After a minute, I felt it begin to work...I went out of phase first then Declan second.

Frickin' hell, my head and heart were hurting! It felt like I was having a stroke and a heart attack, at the same time! No wonder it nearly killed Elisha, when her bio-electromagnetic field rose against her control. It made me so dizzy, I fell off the bed...

Whoomp!

I landed on the hard, wooden floor in my corporeal body, which hurt even more. I rolled onto my back, gasping for breath, with my hands over my chest. Just breathe B, catch your breath and let your Werewolf regenerative ability do the rest. At least I have this to fall back on, whereas Elisha was only human.

I had to close my eyes from the blinding headache, but once I was breathing normally, the pain began to subside. My heart stopped having agonising spasms and the sharp pain inside my head dissolved away. Thank goodness our kind don't have heart attacks or strokes, otherwise I could have 'carked it'.

"B?"

Huh, what was that?

My eyes snapped open in surprise and I found myself looking up into Declan's. They were bright blue and wide, which I hadn't seen in a long time. Around them was smooth skin which was wrinkle free and he had a square jaw again.

"B, are you alright?" He gazed down in concern, from the bed.

"I – I – I'm fine...!" I rasped in shock.

"Then what are you doing on the floor?" He looked on peculiarly.

But I couldn't answer, I was too busy staring. When Declan moved to sit on the side, I saw his torso. His skin no longer looked like old leather instead it was smooth and tight. His 'liver spots' were gone and his muscles were so huge, you'd swear you were looking at a weightlifter. Coupled with his handsome face, blonde hair and blue eyes, he looked identical to how he did when he was 21 years old.

"Earth to B, come in B." He recalled my attention. "C'mon, up you get."

He reached down a muscled arm and easily lifted me up with one hand. Then he planted me on the bed, beside him. I caught him examining me, as I was gaping at him.

Declan raised his right hand to cup my face as he looked on closely. When he did, I noticed his hands didn't feel so worn now. I also saw that the sunspots as well as the 'liver spots', had disappeared too.

"B, have you been crying?" He frowned. "What's wrong?"

"Um..." I didn't know what to say.

"Stop crying, would you?" He sounded annoyed. "It makes me want to go out and break something."

Abruptly, I burst into laughter at how normal he was acting.

"I'm OK." I giggled. "Are you OK?"

He gave a funny look, "Yeah, I'm just peachy."

With that, he let go of his wife, swung his legs over and stood up. I watched him as he proceeded to yawn and stretch. I was surprised that he wasn't talking about his change, or maybe he hasn't noticed yet?

"I'm starved! I'll use the bathroom first then how about I fry us up some bacon, eggs, tomato, mushrooms and hash browns? Eating always makes me feel better." He offered.

Then he gave a wink before he turned and left.

Through the bedroom doorway, I saw him pause when he smelled that we had company. He looked down the stairs in surprise, at the assembled pack in our living room. I bet he was wondering what they were all doing here?

"Er, guys?" He greeted, puzzled. "Did we have a meeting today that I forgot about?"

"Uncle Declan?" I heard Caesar say in astonishment.

"You're looking much better," Ki sounded impressed.

"Er, thanks, you look well too." My mate returned awkwardly. "Um, just give me a minute to use the bathroom then dress and I'll be right down."

"Take all the time you need, Uncle." Forrest said good humouredly. "It looks like time isn't going to be a problem for you anymore."

This earned a few chuckles which I heard from upstairs.

He still hadn't figured out what was happening and I watched him shake his head. He didn't get the joke and he continued on to the bathroom. We heard him shut the door then a minute or two later, not only did we hear, but possibly the whole tribe as well:

"OH MY GOD, B! WHAT THE HELL HAVE YOU DONE?!"

Declan must have caught sight of his reflection in the bathroom mirror. The pack roared with laughter and even I couldn't help but to giggle. Finally, he's realized what's happened.

Suddenly, the bathroom door was thrown open as my husband burst out. He rushed back into the bedroom to stare with his big blue eyes.

"B, have you - did you – turn me?"

"Yes."

"I'm - I'm a Circulator?" He checked.

"Yes."

Next, he marched over to our wardrobe and opened the door, so he could use the full-length mirror on the inside.

"B..." he stared, gob smacked, "...I'm glowing!"

My eyes widened in surprise. "You can see your aura?"

"See it?!" He snorted. "I have a glowing outline around my body! Yes, I can frickin' see it!"

I stood up from the bed and went over to his position. He was looking from himself to the mirror then to me. Next, he moved his arm beside mine, as if he were comparing our auras.

"Yours is a tiny bit brighter than mine," he thought aloud.

His fascination with auras was momentarily put aside as he noticed something else. He leaned in, to look closely into the reflective glass. His hands touched his youthful face then ran down his smooth, rippled body.

"...and I'm young again...!" He breathed in astonishment.

"I know," I smiled. "When I raised your bio-electromagnetic frequency and put it into temporal flux, I put your cellular degradation into reversal."

Declan's mouth fell open in shock, as he stared transfixed at his reflection in the mirror.

"I forgot how big my muscles were, when I was younger..." he gaped, "...it looks like somebody's pumped air into them!"

Then he flexed them while watching in the mirror.

"Yeah and your eyes are wider now, like they were when you were younger." I pointed out.

"I'm wide-eyed and bushy tailed again!" He chuckled. "Speaking of which, my hair feels thicker too."

He ran his hand through his blonde hair which was still in a crew-cut.

I came to stand beside him so I could look on us standing together.

At first I smiled at the sight, of a young, dark-haired wife with her young, blonde-haired husband. My athletic form complimented his muscled build. My dark blue eyes matched his bright blue ones. But then I noticed a couple of little things, which made this picture look uneven...

"Um, Dec? I think I made you look too young." I frowned.

"Huh?" He gave an incredulous look. "Why? We both look like we're in our twenties."

"I look like I'm 29 years old and you look like you're 21!" I complained.

He cracked up laughing as he poked me in the side.

"Now who's the dirty old person shagging the young bit of stuff?"

"I don't like this..." I felt my face flush, "...I think I'm going to make you look a little older."

"Don't you dare!" He immediately moved away. "Besides, I've seen you make yourself look older, dozens of times! Can't you just make yourself look younger, too?"

"I don't know..." I faltered, "...I suppose I can, but not today."

"Why not today?" He wondered. "B, are you alright? Your aura is fluctuating in a weird way."

"I'm a little drained, that's all." I sighed, as I turned away.

Declan frowned in concern, as he watched me wander back to the bed and sit down.

He followed after and sat down beside. "B, is this because of what you did to me?"

"I don't know..." I said tiredly, "...I've never turned a person into a Circulator before, so I don't know what to expect."

"So that's why everyone's downstairs, huh? Because today nearly became the day I died...?" He glanced towards the bedroom doorway.

"You could say that," I waved it off. "But I'm glad you've lost nothing that you cherished, being a European Werewolf."

He pulled back to look on, bewildered.

"How weird is that, I'm a Circulator and a European Werewolf and I can still see auras and..." he leaned in to inhale deeply, "...my sense of smell is the same. In fact, I can even smell your scent has changed."

"My scent has changed?" I asked, in alarm. "Does that mean that I don't smell attractive anymore?"

"What?" Declan looked on like I was nuts. "Of course you still smell attractive!"

"Then how has it changed?"

"Instead of smelling like a vase of wildflowers sitting in a kitchen, while a cake is baking in the oven? You smell like a freshly baked cake, sitting in a field of wildflowers."

"I do?" I gave a funny look. "It sounds like the same as before."

"Hell no, you smell even better...!" He growled hungrily, as he pulled me into his large arms.

I laughed loudly, in relief to have my husband back and in delight at his young, strong appearance.

"I love you, Dec!" I threw my arms about his neck.

"In unan, B." He held me back tightly.

He placed a sloppy kiss on my cheek then while he was at it, he helped himself to kissing his way down my neck. Just as he started to undo my robe, so his lips could reach my shoulders, we were interrupted.

"Erm hmm."

We pulled away with a start, to find Ki standing in our bedroom doorway.

"Sorry to spoil your reunion, guys." The Medicine Man smirked. "I thought I should do a 'check up' on the patient first, before he undertakes any 'strenuous activities'."

Declan scowled, "Can you make it quick?"

Ki headed for his 'Medicine Bundle', still sitting on the bed. Swiftly, he picked up the medical scanner and switched it on. We watched him wave it over my husband, before his eyes bulged when he looked on the readouts.

"Woah...!" His surprise slipped out. "Er, officially you have a clean bill of heath."

"So what's wrong?" I watched his reaction.

Ki said in a startled voice, "The scanner thinks I just scanned a healthy, twenty-one year old! His bone density no longer resembles an elderly person and even the arthritis in his joints, has disappeared!"

"Really?" My eyebrows arose, in pleasant surprise.

"Great," Declan said flippantly. "Now can you get the hell out of my bedroom? And while you're at it, take that bunch of Lokoti Werewolves in my living room, with you."

We heard raucous laughter from downstairs, as the rest of the pack overheard.

"Right," Ki tried to maintain his medical professionalism, as he packed up his things. "Well, I'll just um, leave then. But Uncle Dec, I'll come by tomorrow for a follow up. I've never examined a person who's had their age reversed. We wouldn't want any nasty side effects, would we?"

Then we watched our Medicine Man hastily back out of the bedroom, bumping into the doorway on his way out, before we heard him go downstairs.

"He's fine," he said to our First.

"Alright men, crisis has been averted," we overheard Caesar announce. "We can all get back to our families and our plans for today."

All of their voices faded away, as we heard the front door open then after a few moments close again, with their departure.

Once they were gone, I whacked my husband on the arm. "Don't be so rude!"

"Oh excuse me for wanting to be alone with my wife, after my brush with death!" He retorted.

Then he paused for some reason, as a curious expression overtook his face.

"Hit me again," he said.

"Say what?"

"Hit my arm again."

"Why?"

"Just hit my frickin' arm, would you?!"

My right hand delivered another slap to his upper arm.

His eyes widened and for some reason, he looked on in amazement.

"B, did you feel that?"

"Feel what?" I scoffed. "Your wife bitch-slapping you?"

"Not that, but our auras touching."

"Huh?"

Declan grabbed hold of my right hand then placed it on his left arm and he shuddered.

"Oh my God B, do you feel that?" He asked excitedly. "It's our auras interacting! I can feel your bio-electromagnetic field mixing with my bio-electromagnetic field!"

Warily, I pulled back my hand and looked at my husband as if he'd lost his marbles.

"Do it again!" He insisted.

"No."

"OK I'll touch you then."

He opened my robe and made it slip from my shoulders, so I was sitting there in my negligee.

Declan's eyes widened as he took in the sight of my skin, along with the black lace and purple satin.

"I didn't appreciate properly your 'birthday present' last night," he gave a mischievous grin.

Then he placed both of his hands on my shoulders and slowly ran them down my arms, as he closed his eyes.

I watched a blissful expression take over his youthful features and he exhaled loudly.

"What?" I wondered.

"I can feel our auras connecting," he spoke with his eyes closed.

Then he moved his hands back up and over to my breasts, which stuck out underneath the satin.

He opened his eyes again as he cupped my clothed cleavage, "I can't feel your aura when there are clothes in the way."

"Well, that makes sense." I mused. "In New Orleans when you were telling me about my aura, you said you could see it above my uncovered skin."

"So I did," he gave an evil grin. "I guess we'll just have to remove any coverings that are in the way, won't we?"

"Declan!" I giggled out.

His fingers slid underneath the straps of the negligee and he removed them from my shoulders. Then the rest of the negligee slipped down my body and I stood up, so it could slide to the floor. My mate stood too, as he dropped his pyjama pants and we stood there, naked.

He took a step closer so our fronts were touching and I enjoyed the feel of the heat coming off his skin, as he enjoyed the sensation of our auras touching. I could tell because he closed his eyes again. I moved closer so our bare skin was pressed together, which made him sharply inhale.

"What does it feel like?" I whispered.

"Like heaven..." he uttered out before opening his eyes once more, "...you honestly don't feel it?"

"I can feel your body heat passing from your skin into mine."

"You can't see my aura and you can't feel my aura?" He wanted to clarify.

With a frown, I looked away as I thought about it. I mean, I can sense people's bio-electromagnetic fields. I can feel it if it's weak because they're dying, or I can feel it if it's strong because they're healthy. But I don't think it's the same.

"Wait, I have an idea," he said.

Then Declan gently pushed me backwards onto the bed. No sooner did my back hit the covers, he climbed on top and lay over his mate. I parted my thighs to accommodate him and he started to rub his body against mine. Now it was my breath which sucked inwards, feeling his solid body press against my softer curves.

"Do you feel it now?" He watched my reaction.

"I can feel our flesh pressed together...?"

"Can you feel anything else?"

He continued to move slowly, up and down, in the same movement of intercourse, but it was the outside of our bodies he was concentrating on.

Actually, I did feel a little more tingly than usual...

"Is it a tingling sensation?" I checked.

A grin stretched out across his face, "Uh huh."

"I do feel tingly over the areas your body is touching mine."

"That's the friction of our auras rubbing together," he said.

I felt his member harden with arousal by the way our skin and auras interacted. When he pressed it into my moist folds, we both gasped from the exquisite delight. As he started to move it up and down the sides of my clit, we both groaned.

"Can you feel that, B?"

"It's like there's an extra attraction between us, pulling us together." I managed out. "Kinda like an electromagnetic charge."

He chuckled back, "Trust my wife the Professor, to get all scientific during sex."

"Oh shut up and have me already!"

My hands slid down his smooth back and grabbed hold of his waist. The same time as I pulled him closer, he pushed himself inside with an audible heave. Then I definitely felt what he was talking about, the magnetic force between us turned into a steady current of ecstasy.

"Oh my gosh! Oh my gosh! Oh my gosh!" I practically squealed, as he started to push. "Declan, I can frickin' feel THAT!"

I clung to his wide body as it grinded against mine and we both breathed hard.

"Holy crap, I feel like there's a current of electricity passing from me to you...!" He managed out.

Then he looked down to see if I agreed, but I couldn't talk from the 'feeling overload' I was experiencing, so I gave a nod instead.

His pushing increased as I ran my hands up and down his back. I enjoyed the suppleness of his skin and the hardness of his muscle underneath. I haven't felt him this hard in a hundred years.

A couple of times our eyes met and held and I relished his bright blue colour. They were brighter than a summer's sky and coupled with his body heat, it put you in a warm hue. I also loved how big they were, like they were taking you in, drawing you into him.

When he came, it actually made me jump. I swear I felt something like an electric shock. It was bizarre, it's not every day a person experiences a zap on the inside. In fact, it was kind of kinky and I liked it...

"Frickin' hell!" I cried out. "Do that again!"

"As if I could stop now," he moaned helplessly.

He raised himself before lifting me up, too. I found myself on my knees, hanging onto the bed head for support, with my husband pushing from behind. As he moved in and out, I felt the friction on the inside of my body as well as the outside.

The rhythm was bringing on the hypnotising and oh so divine muscle spasm, which brought extra sparks to our sex.

"Oh shit, oh shit, oh shit, I can feel you coming!" He struggled to stay on his knees.

It literally felt like the orgasm travelled from my body to his, making us both collapse sideways upon impact.

As we lay together on the mattress, I noticed that we were gasping instead of panting. There was no regularity to our breathing and our hearts were pounding so loudly, the noise filled the bedroom. They sounded like two sets of drums, following the same beat.

Better yet, I could feel my heart pound in my groin, which was the blood flow increasing, when I was hyper aroused.

"I should have turned you into a Circulator, years ago!" I said in amazement.

"I shouldn't have kicked up a fuss, years ago." He agreed. "If I knew it was going to be like this, I would have signed up when we were in our twenties!"

Giggling, I rolled in his direction, "Admit it, you're a moron!"

Chuckling, he rolled onto his side so he was facing his mate. "You're right, I am an idiot!"

Declan wrapped his arms about to hold me close and I placed a soft kiss on his lips, which made me notice something else.

"Gees, even your lips are full again," I tittered, as I brushed them with my fingertips. "I can't believe how much a person changes with time."

"I can't believe we'll have to give up these earthly pleasures, when we leave for the space time continuum." He said disappointedly.

I rubbed my nose against his, "We don't have to leave immediately."

"We don't?"

"I mean, we've still got a couple of days at least, as we pack up the house and give away our possessions." I smiled devilishly.

He caught onto my thinking and another grin broke out on his smooth face.

"Of course we're going to have to pack up properly and not do a 'rush job'." He went along. "It could even take a couple of weeks."

"Of course," I giggled again.

Then he pushed me onto my back so he could lie on top of his wife again.

"You know what, B?"

"What, Declan?"

"This is going to be an interesting eternity together."

I beamed back, as I remembered he said something similar, when we first moved in together.

He lowered his head to give a long, sensuous kiss. His lips parted mine and the tips of our tongues touched. Then my arms wrapped around his torso as the rest of my body, accepted his. Slowly, we started to move again, with our kisses increasing in fervour as our rocking waists increased in speed.

It was like we couldn't get enough of each other and now we were both Circulators, we wouldn't have to worry about running out of time, ever again.

*****

The next morning I awoke, I was hit by the strongest sense of déjà vu.

I saw our pyjamas were lying on the floor, which made me sleepily smile to myself. I felt warm and snug, tucked in my mate's embrace. This time though, his arm was draped over my waist and it moved upwards. Gently, he used his hand to angle my face towards him.

"Good morning," he smiled down.

"Morning," I turned my sleepy smile on him. "What's the time?"

"It's nearly 9 AM." He answered. "I thought you needed a sleep-in after yesterday and last night. I was worried I wore you out."

"Dream on, Sabre." I retaliated to his taunt.

"I'm starved!" Declan declared. "How about I make that big breakfast, I didn't get around to making yesterday?"

"How can I say no?" I tittered. "Great sex and breakfast afterwards?"

"You're a lucky woman Bianca Sabre, don't you ever forget it!" He boasted.

Then he made a move out of bed. I watched him swing his legs over the side and he sat there a moment, as if getting his bearings. Then he paused and I heard him sniff a couple of times. He turned his head this way and that, while sniffing, as if he was trying to track the smell.

"What?" I watched him out of curiosity. "What's up?"

Declan kept sniffing loudly as he looked around, puzzled. Hell, he even leaned over and sniffed me! I watched him inhale deeply then I saw his face fall in shock.

"Maybe I should shower before breakfast." My own face burned in embarrassment. "It's been two days since I had one."

"B, you smell different."

"I know, you said that yesterday." I gave a funny look.

"That's not it."

"Look, I already said I'll have a shower."

"B..." his astonished eyes met mine, "...you're pregnant."

*****

650

SSIT Report On
The Different Breeds Of Werewolf

By Elisha Worthall and Dr. Xavier Bell

INTRODUCTION

The following report by the Supernatural Scientific Investigative Team is an analysis of the different breeds of Werewolves in the world.

Unlike Vampires, whose species can be found in most countries, Werewolves are localized to certain continents. No breeds were found in Africa, Australia or South America because other Shape Shifters or paranormal predators claim the African and South American region. Whereas with Australia, it is believed but not yet verified that before the continents divided after the Gondwanaland period, Werewolf migration had not spread that far.

From Elisha Worthall utilizing the Circulate's 25th Century technology, she was able to see back into the Mesozoic era. The Circulator worked in conjunction with her Calculator Patrick O'Flannigan, to track the history of the 'First Werewolf' by homing in on the Werewolf's DNA.

It is now documented that the First Werewolf was a hot-blooded creature, with teeth and claws similar to the Raptor. In fact, the Raptor was the most closely related to this creature in physical characteristics, but it fell short in height and surprisingly, in temperament. Indeed, the only predator that was game to hunt the First Werewolf was the largest of all carnivores, the T-Rex.

If the First Werewolf's prey survived an attack, they would begin to develop many of the First Werewolf's physical characteristics. This was from the dominant Shape Shifter DNA present in the First Werewolf's saliva. The prey in turn, would spread these characteristics when they hunted. Even previous herbivores would turn into carnivores from their mutation. Thus, the Werewolf DNA was spread with each new breed of Werewolf developing.

When the meteor impacted and dust blanketed Earth in an icy darkness, the First Werewolf's 'followers' managed to survive by going into hibernation. Then, as life on the surface of the planet changed, so did its mutated followers. To prevent itself from becoming extinct, the changed prey bred with another species that was the closest that came to a genetic cousin; an early form of the Canidae family. From this coupling, its offspring came to feature more canine aspects.

The First Werewolf's offspring lost it's hard, protective, reptilian-like scales that covered its skin, but its superior strength remained. It also began to decrease in size, with each new mutation through the eons. Today, the breed that most resembles the First Werewolf is the European Werewolf. The size, strength and temperament of this monster today, is in direct hereditary descent from its prehistoric forefather.

Werewolves are man-eaters, attributing their longevity from the bloodlust demanding fresh kill. The only exception to this rule is the Lokoti Werewolf, who started out hunting human, but for the safety of the humans in the Lokoti Tribe, they were able to curb their bloodlust towards animal. Interestingly, the Lokoti Werewolf is the only breed that is not directly descended from the First Werewolf. Similar to animal-spirit possession in other Shape Shifters in Africa; the Lokoti Tribe's history indicates that they were created from both the sharing of blood and spirit between a Lokoti Wolf - a rare subspecies of Grey Wolf in Alaska - and a human tribal member.

With all breeds of Werewolf, four commonalities can be found:
- Allergy to silver; all species of Werewolves like Vampires and other Shape Shifters, are allergic to this metal. They can be killed by either a silver bullet to the heart and brain, or a silver sword through the heart.
- The change when a Werewolf shifts its shape from human to beast.
- The bloodlust which is the controlling urge to feast on fresh flesh.
- The impact of the full moon on the bloodlust, which can trigger a Werewolf to shape shift.

Scanning the cellular structure of several species of Vampire and breeds of Werewolf, it became apparent that both are Shape Shifters. They are able to alter their physical form to hunt or when engaged in combat. The basic 'fight or flight' instinct appears to be the trigger, which engages a Shape Shifter's change. However, a Werewolf shifts their shape the most, particularly the Asian Werewolf.

After further years of extensive study and travelling, we came to realize that similar to human beings, Werewolves also had different physical characteristics. Just as with natural species, supernatural creatures also adapt differently depending on their environment. Some Werewolves were susceptive to meeting us under the strictest understanding that their names would be excluded and the reports would be made confidential. Others, particularly the more dangerous of the breeds, were studied under subterfuge.

Due to the predatory nature of the European Werewolf, when we filmed this breed changing, this was done covertly by Elisha Worthall acting alone. Since European Werewolves are man-eaters, Elisha Worthall was able to use her Circulator ability to instantaneously phase out of danger as soon as the Werewolf picked up her scent. Those who were open to our research were the Lokoti Werewolf pack and one of the Asian Werewolves, from the Hsu Clan.

For a tentative first meeting, Elisha Worthall met three members of the Lokoti Werewolf pack, who were on the Council of Lokoti Tribal Elders. An exchange of information was initiated; in return for SSIT investigating the Lokoti Werewolf, the tribe was permitted to learn about Elisha Worthall's ability as a Circulator. She was instantly recognized as such, whom the Lokoti call 'The Light People'.

A productive union was formed between SSIT and the tribe, as we shared our notes on the four breeds; Lokoti, Asian, European and North American Werewolves. It was from the Lokoti that my associate learned something new about herself; she was informed that Circulators have auras, which can be seen by Werewolves. In fact, we learned that Werewolves could also see a psychic's aura, as can other Shape Shifters such as Vampires.

The Lokoti Werewolves are highly respected by the human members of the tribe, and the secrecy of who was a Werewolf is closely guarded. Indeed, secrecy as Werewolves was a common theme in all of the breeds that were investigated. Just as human murderers must hide their crimes from society to avoid punishment; the Werewolves must hide their supernatural identities to ensure their feeding and therefore survival. This became apparent in every breed but the Lokoti Werewolves, who continue to hunt and feed on human.

LOKOTI WEREWOLF

~Physical Characteristics~

This breed appears the most 'human' in supernatural form, because they maintain their humanoid shape.

When a Lokoti Werewolf shape shifts from human to other, their muscles expand in size as their strength increases by fifty fold. Their eyes glow a different colour, e.g. brown eyes turn blue or yellow. No member of the pack has the same coloured glowing eyes and indeed, a colour can be passed down to the next in genealogy. In their supernatural state, their sight can take on infrared qualities to assist in hunting. Their hand and toenails increase in size and thickness, to become claw-like, as their teeth become elongated and sharper; in particular their canine teeth.

This breed of Werewolf is always male, with fifteen in the pack - no more and no less. When a pack member dies, a human male from the tribe is 'activated', going through the change on the next full moon. It has become evident that the Lokoti Werewolf gene is inherited in all males of the tribe. The age a new Lokoti Werewolf is activated, is typically between 10 - 25 years old.

They have lightening fast reflexes, and can run up to speeds of 200 km/h. Lokoti Werewolves have a keen sense of smell and can track quarry up to 100 km's away. After tasting the blood of their mate, they can track their female's scent over large distances, sometimes up to thousands of kilometres.

The Lokoti Werewolf pack is empathic and can communicate with its members by ESP. Although this breed isn't as skilled as telepaths, they can send out short commands to one another. They empathically sense when another of the pack is in trouble and the same when they take a human female for a mate. They become attuned to the other members and their mate, by feeling their emotions.

This breed no longer hunts human. They successfully placate their bloodlust with animal flesh. Every full moon, the pack hunts together to chase down their quarry on foot, and attack using their claws and elongated teeth. Lokoti Werewolves hunt large game in Alaska, such as caribou, moose, grizzly, black bear, Dall sheep etc. However, they are so attuned to their environment, they can sense when numbers are low and move on to hunt other quarry.

On this note, they are tied to their hunting grounds, so much so they can wane if they are away for long periods of time. They will also wane if they're separated from their pack or mate. When this occurs, the first sign is they can lose control of the bloodlust, although never turning on family or a human in the tribe. Their protective instinct even dominates their murderous inclinations. The second sign is severe depression where the Lokoti Werewolf may lose their will to live and die in their sleep, even if they're not elderly.

However, they have an unusually long lifespan, which can reach up to 200 years. They do not become elderly until surpassing their hundredth birthday. But even in old age, they retain their supernatural strength when they shape shift from human to other. This is due to the bloodlust, as they continue to hunt every full moon, until death.

This breed is supernaturally fast healers; however, like all Werewolves, they are severely allergic to silver. When a Lokoti Werewolf is wounded, another member of the pack will share their blood to aid in their regeneration. This breed can recover from most injuries, although not all. In supernatural form, if one is shot in the head and heart by a normal bullet, there is a fifty percent chance that they will recover. However, if one was riddled with a multitude of bullets, they can die.

~History~

The Lokoti Werewolf has always lived in a particular geographic location, the Lokoti National Park in the Alaska Range. It's situated 4.5 hours north of Anchorage and 1.5 hours south of Fairbanks. The Lokoti is the only breed of Werewolf that is genetically tied to land. The story of how the first Lokoti Werewolf was created is part of the history of the tribe as a whole.

According to the Tribal Elders, the Lokoti Wolf shared his blood with Aru as the warrior lay dying. The human was grievously wounded after trying to defend his people from an invading tribe that came to take their land and women. It's said to have been a great battle where only fifteen of the warriors survived.

In the legend, the Lokoti Wolf smelled that Aru had a noble spirit and saw he was dying because of defending his mate, young and territory. Since the Lokoti Wolf mates for life, it recognized similar behaviour in the dying human. The old wolf gave his blood, as he gave up his life, so the wounded warrior could live. His spirit also merged with the human, and as the light faded from the wolf's blue eyes, Aru's brown eyes began to glow blue. From this merging, Aru arose as the first Lokoti Werewolf and shared his blood with the fourteen other injured tribesmen. Henceforth, it created the fifteen members of the pack and altogether they drove out the invaders and rescued their families.

According to three members of the pack who sit on the council of Tribal Elders, no Lokoti Werewolf has partaken in human flesh for two centuries. The story of the last time this breed ate human happened in July 1777 AD, during the U.S. War of Independence. What is known of the event, the Lokoti Werewolves attacked a party of English Soldiers, in retribution for the kidnapping and rape of six of their women. The Werewolves killed between 60 - 70 English Soldiers in a brutal attack which did not spare a single soldier's life. Then the Werewolves returned the women to their tribe.

When another party of English Soldiers found the massacre days later, wild animals were blamed for the attack. Due to the fact that none survived, with the appearance of the unused muskets and rifles, it was viewed that the attack had been so sudden that the soldiers were unable to get a shot off in defence. It was because of the magnitude of the violence, the Lokoti Tribal Lands were deemed unsafe for European Settlement for many years.

Then the tribe had little contact with the English, French, Russian or Colonial Americans for another hundred years. That was until Russian Trappers and Colonial Americans, settled in the region next to tribal lands, which eventually became the small township of Alma.

~Reproduction/Mating Habits~

As previously mentioned, the Lokoti Werewolves have, at any one time, fifteen in the pack. The gene is passed along the bloodline from father to son. In cases where there is more than one male child, the gene is activated in the eldest. However, there have been instances in the advent of death of the eldest, can trigger a change in the next male child. This signals that the Lokoti Werewolf gene is present but dormant in the entire male lineage.

When a Lokoti Werewolf reproduces, the tribe call it 'mating'. This process has been described when the Werewolf procreates with a woman, he claims her as his 'mate'. The sexual act has not only the reproductive fluids passing from the male to the female, but the Werewolf also ingests some of the blood of the woman. By doing so, he gains her scent, enabling him to track her up to distances as great as thousands of kilometres away.

The process also hints at some level of empathic as well as biological bonding, as there have been incidents reported where the Werewolf is able to sense if his mate is in trouble and runs to her location, by tracking her scent. Other cases show the biological asymmetry of his genetic qualities, such as strength and regeneration, also developing in the woman.

The reproductive fluids and even the pheromones to lure a mate are potent, with a high fertility rate. There has never been a case where a mating has not produced at least one child, and a male child at that. However, it has also been proven that they are able to control how many children it produces. If the Werewolf senses pregnancy may harm their mate, their bodies decrease sperm production. It's said that the first years of the mating process are the most fertile for the Werewolf, and afterwards it can choose to stop reproducing.

The mating process is for life with the partnership only severed by death. However, with the longevity of a Lokoti Werewolf, when his mate dies he does not take another. This behaviour is similar to other canines such as the fox, which mate only the once. There have also been cases where a mate has died, and sometimes the Lokoti Werewolf wanes to such an extent that they too, lose their will to live.

NORTH AMERICAN WEREWOLF

~Physical Characteristics~

The North American Werewolf has the physical appearance of an upright wolf, which walks and runs on its hind legs.

The hands and feet are changed from a human's five fingers and toes to four, with the small finger and toe conjoining. The North American Werewolf is completely covered in a reddish-brown fur, with a narrow snout and tall ears. Their eyes are completely black and although they cannot see infrared, they have night-vision. Their teeth as well as their nails, become elongated and sharp.

This breed doesn't have supernatural speed like the other breeds of Werewolves. However, they have exceptional hearing, detecting the slightest of noise. They are excellent trackers and can smell their quarry up to distances of a hundred kilometres away. Their physical strength increases by fifty fold when they change, like the Lokoti Werewolf. But unlike their supernatural 'brothers', both men and women can change if they are bitten and the female is just as strong as her male counterpart.

The North American Werewolf has the same lifespan as a human. Like other breeds, the full moon triggers their bloodlust and forces them to change. Even if they are elderly, they are still covered in a reddish-brown fur and are supernaturally strong. They are also allergic to silver, but this breed doesn't have the regenerative capabilities like the others do. This means they can be killed by normal bullets, if they were shot through the heart or head.

This species changes involuntarily every full moon and 'black out' during the process. In some cases, humans who change into this breed are not even aware that they are a North American Werewolf. As they have only been sighted during a full moon, it's conjectured they may transform only during this period.

When the moon is full, this breed will hunt human. It's because of this, they are often found living in the country. When they become aware of their supernatural state, they attempt to isolate themselves for the safety of others. However, due to the 'black outs', this attempt turns futile when the bloodlust takes control.

~History~

The North American Werewolf is often a nomad, and prefers to stay away from large towns or cities. They roam all over the United States and Canada and as such, tracking the source of their origin was difficult. It's believed that this breed wandered the American continent up to a thousand years before European settlement. From the oral histories of several Native American tribes, the creature's migration had been noted by their dealings with it.

It's been recently proven using the Circulate's Viewing Room systems that the North American Werewolf originally came from South America. The former 'South' American Werewolf, migrated to new hunting grounds when it encountered a greater predator than itself; mankind. Certain South American tribes induce animal spirits to encourage possession of a human host, temporarily giving the human extra sensory perception or increasing physical prowess. Before European weapons such as muskets were introduced, many South American tribes ritualized war and hunting. Using animal spirit possession, it enabled the humans to battle the 'South' American Werewolf as well as the South American Vampire. As such, it caused a territorial dispute and thus this breed travelled north.

Over the centuries this man-eater attacked many, with some killing the creatures or survivors who found out about their change, the following full moon. Those who were lucky enough to live through an attack were changed by bite, to turn into the monster they thought they destroyed. Upon learning of the blood on their hands after their first change, the new Werewolf went on the run. According to the oral history of one tribe, one group of North American Werewolves 'ran' so far up north, they entered Alaska.

The Lokoti Tribal Elders told SSIT of the time the Lokoti Werewolves battled a band of eight North American Werewolves, in the mid 19th Century. This is the only case that SSIT came upon, of the North American Werewolf existing in a pack. The Elders told that upon their change, the North American Werewolves who were made up of both Colonial Americans and members of differing Native American tribes; had to leave their homes when they became wanted for murder.

It was a night of the full moon when the eight North American Werewolves, stumbled into Lokoti Werewolf territory. The man-eating breed was hunting and attacked the tribe when the pack was away, on its own hunt. However, the Lokoti Werewolves empathically sensed their human mates' distress and returned early. It's said to be a bloody battle, with the North American Werewolf strength an equal match to the Lokoti Werewolf. However, the Lokoti gained the upper hand with their faster reflexes.

The fifteen Lokoti Werewolves decimated the eight North American Werewolves. Then they shared their blood with the injured humans of the tribe. Their blood's regenerative properties helped to heal, as the anti-bodies destroyed the North American Werewolf DNA in the bite marks. This prevented the humans from turning into new North American Werewolves on the next full moon.

This instance also implicates that cross-contamination would not work, if a human was bitten by two separate breeds. The human would either turn into one breed or another, but not have elements of both. This feature sets Werewolf genetics apart from its other Shape Shifter 'cousin', the Vampire. When investigating the separate species of Vampires, SSIT found that the North American Vampire was a hybrid of the South American and the European. However, this is also remarkable of Lokoti Werewolf DNA; that it will not turn humans into their kind, but it can be used to stop a transformation into another breed.

Although the eight North American Werewolves didn't survive to tell the tale, it's interesting to note that this breed never crossed into Alaska again. This hints that their survival instinct navigates them away from another's territory, once an enemy becomes known. The fact that this breed has never returned to the continent of South America, supports this theory. But how this information is relayed, either genetically or by means of ESP, is unknown.

~Reproduction/Mating Habits~

North American Werewolf genes cannot be carried on via means of sexual reproduction. Therefore, a child born to a parent who is a North American Werewolf does not have the genes to turn into this breed. Instead, they multiply by infecting humans with the saliva in their bite. However, due to the dangerous nature of the bloodlust, not many survive an attack and therefore, the numbers created are few.

This breed has never been sighted with a long term mate. It's believed because of their nomadic nature, they are often on the run. The second reason is due to their inability to control the bloodlust during their change. There have been tragic incidents where a person who was a North American Werewolf and not know it, discovered their dangerous nature the morning after. When this occurs, the Werewolf awakens to find their spouse or family's partial remains, with their hands and mouths covered in the victim's blood.

As such, they normally live alone in remote areas as they attempt to avert disaster by isolating themselves.

ASIAN WEREWOLF

~Physical Characteristics~

This breed appears the most like a wolf when it shifts shape.

The body completely changes from an upright, bipedal human appearance, to a four-legged form of a large wolf, with a silvery-grey coat. The fur springs forth from the pores in the skin then retreats back into the body, when they revert. They have white eyes with small black dots, as pupils. In the dark, their eyes appear to be glowing white, by reflecting the light. In their Werewolf form, this breed does have night-vision.

Asian Werewolves walk and run on all fours, with their shoulder and hip bones contorting to adjust to the front and back legs. Indeed in their supernatural form, it's hard to distinguish an Asian Werewolf from a Grey Wolf, except for the white eyes, larger size and their front legs being slightly shorter than their back legs. With such a dramatic shape shift, the Asian Werewolf is the only breed which remains in their supernatural form if they should die as such, whereas the others return to human.

Their strength increases by twenty fold and both males and females, can change into this breed; with females just as strong and as fast as their male counterparts. Although Asian Werewolves are not as strong as the other kinds, they are the fastest, running up to speeds of 400 km/h. They are also the best trackers as their sense of smell is legendary. There are stories of victims being unable to escape a vendetta placed on them, even if they moved to the other side of the world.

The life span of this breed is up to 150 years and even if the Asian Werewolf is elderly, it's still strong and fast in its supernatural form. Like all breeds, the full moon triggers its bloodlust and causes it to shape shift. However, it can also turn without this influence, when it's tracking a target or to engage in combat.

~History~

The Asian Werewolf has been sighted all throughout Asia, predominantly in Mongolia, China, Korea and Japan. However, there are reports of clans so far as Hong Kong, Taiwan, Malaysia and the Philippines. This breed is both nomadic just as it is territorial. Some Asian Werewolves travel extensively, due to the bloodlust making it difficult for them to hunt in one location. With others, and particularly in the case of clans, live in rural areas and have claimed the region for centuries.

Like the European Werewolf, this breed has the most sightings and coincidentally, an extensive history recorded by humanity. The sightings of this species go back to BC – Before Christ. The Asian Werewolf has appeared in literature, as well as artwork in temples and lastly, in ceremonies similar to the Dragon Dance, which is usually performed on Chinese New Year.

In Buddhist temples in China, Korea and Thailand, as well as a Shinto temple in northern Japan; artwork has been sighted depicting enlarged wolves, with silvery-grey coats and glowing white eyes. In one of the ancient ruins inside the jungles of Cambodia, there is a carving on a wall of a past King fighting an enlarged dog-like creature, with claws and teeth like a tiger.

Similar to 'hell money' used for the deceased, there are customs for protection against Asian Werewolves. One such custom in China is to bang cooking utensils during a lunar eclipse, to scare 'the dog of heaven' (1). Small, silver charms tied together with red wool, are strewn over doorways; however, this tradition is not only to protect the inhabitants from Asian Werewolves, but also Asian Vampires. Silver charms also decorate some cribs, due to the fact that pregnant women and infants are said to be an Asian Vampire's source of nourishment. In India, small silver bells on bracelets and anklets are commonplace with a sari, whereas with Feng Shui, silver bells are also used to dispel negative energy in clearing ceremonies. This was also a tactic used to ascertain if a Shape Shifter was darkening your home.

Although the majority are man-eaters, some clans are highly respected in protector-like roles. In rural areas where they have lived for centuries, humans pay them homage. Arrangements exist where humans will not be preyed upon if they keep to an agreement or, a clan will protect a town from stray Werewolves or even from Asian Vampires. An intricate honour system prevails, similar to a social class system, where giving offence could be treated as a death sentence.

On this note, Asian Werewolves are extremely territorial, and wars among the clans are typical. There is one example of where the Hsu and the Hsin Clans, in two neighbouring provinces by the Great Wall of China, have been battling for centuries. The war started when a male Asian Werewolf from the Hsin family, eloped with a female Asian Werewolf from the Hsu Clan. Since the Hsu family didn't bestow their permission on the courtship, the marriage was called a kidnapping; although the bride willingly went to live with her husband and his kin. Ironically, over time with the reduction in female Werewolves in the world, kidnappings have become a reoccurring theme. Sadly though, in these instances, the 'brides' aren't whisked away in romantic circumstances.

Once a vendetta is placed on you and the Asian Werewolf never gives in, it would appear that these two sides will continue to fight until the other is eradicated. When Dr. Xavier Bell asked a member of the Hsu Clan why peace-talks have never been initiated, he inadvertently almost placed a vendetta on himself. Apparently, any talks of ending the dispute would be seen as 'losing face', a high dishonour in this culture. After the doctor apologized profusely for his gross offence, the vendetta was never placed upon him.

~Reproduction/Mating Habits~

When the Asian Werewolf reproduces, its progeny also turns when the child reaches puberty.

This breed can also turn humans into their kind by bite, or sharing blood with the chosen. However, they are cautious over whom they turn, and there is never an accidental turning of a stranger. If an Asian Werewolf bites a human, it is either to kill them, eat them or to change them, in a carefully planned manoeuvre.

Since Asian Werewolves are territorial, this in turn makes them overprotective of their mates and young. This breed is monogamous whilst their mate is alive; however, if they die then they may take another. Those who live in clans can communicate with its members via ESP, which also results in couples becoming empathically attuned to one another. If they sense their mate is in trouble, they run to their aid using their keen sense of smell.

Due to their dangerous natures, if an Asian Werewolf takes a human for a mate, they will attempt to turn them. This is to ensure their survival, so they will not be accidentally eaten in the bloodlust-induced craze. In turn, couples and family units can be seen hunting together, under a full moon.

EUROPEAN WEREWOLF

WARNING: this breed is both the largest and the strongest and coincidentally, the most dangerous.

~Physical Characteristics~

The appearance of a European Werewolf is a giant, hairless beast, part man and part wolf.

When they change from human to other, their height almost doubles and their width triples. Their weight is attributed to their strength, which is increased by a hundred fold and even in human form, its overpowering. Both men and women can turn into this breed; however, females are not as strong or as large as their male counterparts.

They have glowing green eyes, with their circular pupils changing into narrow slits. In Werewolf form, they can see infrared which aids in their hunting. Their hands and feet become claw-like, which are sharp and strong and can cut through metal. Their heads take on canine features with a short, stubby snout over jaws of razor sharp teeth. The colouring of the European Werewolf changes, depending on the hair colour in human form. For a person with blonde hair, their hairless skin becomes a light tanned colour; for a person with brown hair, they become brown all over; for a person with black hair, their hairless skin turns a black colour.

The European Werewolf's sense of smell is almost a match to the Asian Werewolf and they are the second fastest of the species. Although this breed can walk upright, it runs on all-fours and can reach speeds up to 300 km/h. They have the highest body temperature of all the Werewolves, consistently sitting at 43 degrees Celsius, which in a human being would be fatal.

This breed is a man-eater and is capable of changing in between full moon cycles, to hunt human. Because of their large appetites, the bloodlust is the strongest in their kind, which causes them to constantly crave human flesh. Coincidentally, many turn into sociopaths since their dangerous cravings conflict with society's morals.

European Werewolves live the longest, up to 300 years old. With such a longevity they do not become elderly until they reach 250 years. However, since they are extensively hunted by European Vampires, it's seldom they reach old age. European Werewolves are superior healers of all the breeds and are able to regenerate from almost all kinds of injuries. It is for this reason that European Vampires hunt them, to drink their blood and temporarily take on their regenerative capabilities. However, like all Shape Shifters, this breed is severely allergic to silver. The few ways to kill a European Werewolf is decapitation, or to run a silver sword through its heart, or silver bullets through both its heart and its head.

It's postured that one of the reasons why European Werewolves have such a powerful regenerative ability, is because their enemy the European Vampire has poisonous fangs. Their poison will not kill the Werewolf, but it can paralyse the monster for up to seven days. However, European Werewolves can heal each other from poisoning by sharing blood. The ingestion of another's life force strengthens their body's immune system and adds to their own.

~History~

European Werewolves have always been at war with European Vampires. What started as a territorial dispute between the predators, turned into Werewolves becoming the Vampires' prey. Since European Vampires cannot heal without imbibing blood from a living being, what better nourishment than a creature which can heal from almost anything.

European Vampires have the longest lives in the supernatural world, reaching 500 years old. They are also the fastest species of Vampire, as they can move at the speed of sound. However, they are not that strong nor can they heal easily, like other Shape Shifters can. Because of this fact, they turned hunting European Werewolves into somewhat of a 'blood sport'; as animals to feed upon for their strength and regenerative capabilities. But just as hunting can be a dangerous sport in the human world, many a European Vampire has been killed by the monsters it was preying upon.

In the medieval times, a high concentration of European Werewolf numbers were found in mountainous parts of Eastern Europe. This is where recorded battles took place between European Werewolves and European Vampires - as the Vampires fought for dominance and the Werewolves fought for survival. Even today these battles continue, although not in as great as numbers as they occurred then.

Now in the 21st Century, European Werewolves in dwindling numbers are scattered all over the continent, particularly in the northerly regions. With their high body temperatures, they only venture southwards to the Mediterranean in the cooler months of the year. They are nomadic, constantly moving around because of the bloodlust forcing them to continually hunt. With such a dangerous appetite, this man-eater is always running from the law.

This breed has the longest history, being the direct descendant of the First Werewolf. Stories of this monster stretch from early BC to the present AD and are extensive, changing with each new storyteller. There is the legend of 'Cerberus' in Ancient Greek mythology, to Skoll and Hati in Germanic mythology. The large wolves, Skoll or Hati, both born by a giantess, are said to chase the sun or the moon across the sky (2); which resembles European Werewolves in their huge, hulking bodies and of course, their never ending hunger. Or, there are horror stories such as 'Hell Hounds'. Canines with scorching breath and described to come from the depths of hell, could be relegated to a European Werewolf's abnormally high body temperature and glowing eyes.

There are records in several Roman Catholic and Orthodox Church documents, from the European Witch Hunts and onwards, which give examples how this breed may only be killed by silver weapons. The documents disclose cases where humans have made unsuccessful attempts to either burn, drown or decapitate, captured European Werewolves.

In 16th Century Budapest, the Church Inquisitors tried to burn a male European Werewolf by tying it to a stake. However, when it changed, its hardened skin and muscle bulk, coupled with its speedy-regeneration, was able to withstand serious damage from the flames. Once the thick rope which held it captive was burned through, the European Werewolf leapt upon the Church Inquisitors and ate them before the horrified crowd.

In 17th Century Prague, an angry mob tried to drown a female European Werewolf for eating several young children. They chained it to a log and then held it under water. But the female European Werewolf changed into it's stronger and larger shape, breaking the thin chains. Next, it leapt out of the water and ate several more humans, sending the rest running for their lives.

In 18th Century Lyon, a male European Werewolf was arrested after fighting in a tavern, where it ate several people including a barmaid. When it had passed out from excessive drinking, it was dragged to a jail cell to wait execution, which was to take place the next morning. However, just before the law-keepers were able to behead the creature in the guillotine, it woke up. It expanded into its Werewolf shape and the guillotine which was not made of silver, actually bounced off its hardened hide and went flying into the executioner, cutting him in half instead. The European Werewolf ate the leftovers and then bounded off, through the screaming audience.

~Reproduction/Mating Habits~

This breed has never been sighted with a long-term mate, as they prefer to live alone. This is attributed to being extremely territorial during a hunt, as they do not like to share their kill. This puts them in direct contrast to Asian or Lokoti Werewolves, who hunt in packs and share their prey.

With their volatile temperaments, after the medieval wars, they have not been sighted in packs again. This is especially since small arguments can erupt into a fight to the death among their kind. On this note, it's very rare a male or female European Werewolf will mate with each other. If this does occur, the union is short lived when a physical fight ensues and they cease their association.

Unfortunately for humans, it would appear that the European Werewolf lust is as great as its bloodlust. With this breed's overpowering strength, it's extremely hazardous to engage in sexual relations. Also, this breed often loses control of the bloodlust in excitement, and would claw and bite the woman. If a male European Werewolf does have sex with a human woman, she can die from her injuries.

With this said of the male, it could be different in the case of the female. Since female European Werewolves are not as strong or as large as their male counterparts, a human male has a greater chance of surviving a sexual encounter. This is of course providing the female does not lose control of her bloodlust, and claw and bite the man.

If a female European Werewolf is impregnated by a human, the foetus develops as a full Werewolf, proving that even the DNA of this monster is overpowering. As such, European Werewolf children are born immediately as Werewolves. However, throughout the long history of this breed, European Werewolf young are rarely sighted. It's believed because their Werewolf parent loses their temper if the child misbehaves, and destroys their offspring.

With such a dangerous nature, sexual reproduction of this species is limited. Therefore, in the majority of cases, European Werewolves are created by being bitten by another. Humans will also turn if they become infected with this breed's blood. The supernatural DNA changes the human on the next full moon, when the lunar cycle impacts the bloodlust. But because of the size, strength and temperament of this predator, hardly any humans survive an attack. This, as well as being hunted by European Vampires, fortunately keeps numbers low.

CONCLUSION

When SSIT investigated Vampire legends in Eastern Europe, we stumbled across the existence of Werewolves. By studying numerous historical documents and talking to members of the community; our investigators came across stories which linked European Vampires to European Werewolves. After we filmed, scanned and unsuccessfully tried to interview a European Werewolf subject, this led to researching the other breeds.

As previously noted, if a human is cross-contaminated with the DNA of two separate breeds of Werewolf, they will turn into one or the other but not both. On this note, there has never been a case of the differing breeds mating with each other to create a cross-breed. Due to this, there is no scientific evidence to back up or dispute that this would even be possible. Instead, it would appear that whenever they do cross paths, they attempt to destroy each other in violent territorial displays.

However, another commonality the differing breeds have is how their flesh reacts to silver. Although all Shape Shifters are severely allergic to this alloy, Werewolves have the greatest reaction. Not only do they bleed heavily, but a red smoke will appear where their flesh came into contact with it. This indicates a chemical reaction between the flesh and the metal.

It was many years later that SSIT came across another branch in this supernatural family - Human/Animal Shape Shifters. All across the globe in various cultures, there are human beings who are able to morph into an animal of similar size. The histories of how this anomaly has occurred are bountiful; from spirit possession to genetic mutation and even through cross-species reproduction. Although the kinds of animals the humans can turn into is varied, there is a commonality in every single one - the eyes. Whenever a Human/Animal Shape Shifter changes into their supernatural form, their eyes appear completely black.

In India whilst in the jungle, SSIT caught on camera, an adult tiger minding a small human child. Upon zooming in, the investigators noted that the tiger's eyes were unusual by the fact that they were 'blacked out'. Further to the investigator's surprise, the tiger changed the child's diaper and then slung it onto its back, to take it into town. My partner in SSIT Elisha Worthall, was able to follow unnoticed by engaging her ability to instantaneously phase. She later reported how the tiger went through a backdoor of a house, which was on the outskirts of town and then minutes later, a woman walked out the front door carrying the same child. When the woman recognized Elisha Worthall from the jungle, her brown eyes blacked over, as a warning.

Indeed, SSIT discovered the indicator linking Human/Animal Shape Shifters to Werewolves and even to Vampires - is the eyes. The eyes of the North American Werewolf are also completely black, when they shift into their supernatural shape. An Asian Werewolf's white eyes with only the black pupils, is identical to a West African Vampire or similar to a European Vampire's completely white eyes. A member of the Lokoti Werewolf pack has glowing red eyes, whereas the South American Vampire has red eyes. Both Lokoti and European Werewolves eyes glow, and both can see infrared.

What is interesting, as much as the members of the Shape Shifter family are similar; each will refute it vehemently. All three have fought over territory, when protecting their own, or to feed off the other. Cannibalism is rife, particularly in the Vampire species whose parasitic natures rely on absorbing another creature's life force. But instead of making allowances, they try to cancel the other out and claim dominance. Although Human/Animal Shape Shifters do not lust after flesh or blood of the living, the bloodlust is inherent in their absolute abhorrence for their supernatural cousins. This is a shame, considering how similar Werewolves and Human/Animal Shape Shifters really are.

*****

(1) Cotterell, Arthur. <u>The Encyclopedia of Mythology; Classical, Celtic, Norse</u>. Annes Publishing Limited. London. 1996. p. 226

(2) *ibid*, p. 226

~ The Circulate Series ~

By K.R. Smith

~ Book One: Circulate ~

Elisha Baker learns something new about herself when she attends the haunted international boarding school, Hamilton's College.

~ Book Two: Circulating ~

Elisha and her friends graduate from Hamilton's and the Circulate; to begin University and SSIT – Supernatural Scientific Investigative Team.

~ Book Three: Circulation ~

Armed with degrees, Elisha and her friends continue with SSIT. However adult life isn't as straightforward as they imagined, especially when an investigation into past lives interferes with a present romance.

~ Book Four: Progeny ~

Alexandrina and twin brother Bastian, grew up without a mother and a distant father. But it's to Jarrod's chagrin that his daughter mirrors his late wife, with the fact that she too is a Circulator.

~ Book Five: Ardor & Redolence ~

Arabella joins her grandmother on a SSIT case and meets Emanuel Riverclaw. Eventually they marry and create twins Julian and Jessica; a son who will become a Lokoti Werewolf like his father and a daughter who is a Circulator like her mother.

~ Book Six: Scent ~

At first the Last Circulator can't stand the tribe's most dangerous Werewolf, then Bianca and Declan's fiery arguments turn into something else.

~ Book Seven: Sororate ~

Claws come out in the marriage of the tribe's first female Lokoti Werewolf and the world's last European Werewolf; who spend their tumultuous years together traveling the world and through time.

~ Book Eight: Small Fry ~

Declan swore he wouldn't create anymore European Werewolves like himself, so his wife's new condition has his already hot blood boiling.

~ Book Nine: Alma ~

The new girl in Alma High School called Mali Roanne, suspects there's more than meets the eye with her Lokoti friends. However Mali is hiding a supernatural secret of her own.

~ Book Ten: Heterogeneous ~

In a space age, the different breeds of Werewolves are confined to Earth because of the influence of its one moon. But there's no such holds on the separate species of Vampires or even Human/ Animal Shape Shifters.

~ Book Eleven: Cohesion ~

Parents become grandparents when their children marry and procreate; with all of the different elements of the supernatural combining into one unusual family.

~ Book Twelve: Full Circle ~

The end is nigh, with answers as to why the futuristic Circulate technology never advanced past the 25th Century; because humankind doesn't.

To find out more on the series or the author please visit:

http://onaya3.blogspot.com/

http://www.facebook.com/Circulate.Series.KRSmith

~ References ~

Cover photo of Matanuska Glacier taken by Nina Ackerman © 2007

http://en.wikipedia.org/wiki/Fairbanks,_Alaska

http://www.absak.com/library/average-annual-insolation-alaska

http://www.chugachschools.com/community_information/community_pages/fairbanks.html

Chisolm, Jane. Millard, Anne. The Usborne Book of the Ancient Worlds. Usborne. London. 1991

Goldman, Jane. The X-Files Book of Unexplained, Book 1. Simon & Schuster. London. 1995

Goldman, Jane. The X-Files Book of Unexplained, Book 2. Simon & Schuster. London. 1996

Pennick, Nigel. Mysteries of the Ancient World: Leylines. Weidenfeld & Nicolson. London. 1997

Smith, K.R. SSIT Reports on the Different Breeds of Werewolf, Separate Species of Vampire and Human/Animal Shape Shifters By Elisha Worthall and Dr. Xavier Bell. K.R. Smith. Sydney. 2011

http://en.wikipedia.org/wiki/New_Orleans

http://en.wikipedia.org/wiki/Louisiana_Creole_cuisine

http://en.wikipedia.org/wiki/Beef_Wellington

http://www.asliceofcherrypie.com/archives/a-brace-of-pheasants-and-a-chocolate-and-chestnut-truffle-cake/

http://en.wikipedia.org/wiki/New_England_clam_chowder

http://cookit.e2bn.org/historycookbook/921-kedgeree.html

http://en.wikipedia.org/wiki/Peru

http://en.wikipedia.org/wiki/Amazonas_region

http://en.wikipedia.org/wiki/Peruvian_cuisine

http://mypage.direct.ca/k/kenbinns/index.html

http://en.wikipedia.org/wiki/Bram_Stoker

Martin, Robyn. Quick 'n' Easy Finger Food. Concept Publishing. Auckland. 1999

Sutherland Smith, Beverley. Salads & Barbecues. The Five Mile Press Pty Ltd. Noble Park. 1998

Lewis, Lyn (Ed.) Fast Food: Quick and Easy Everyday Ideas For Cooks in a Hurry. Murdoch Books Pty Ltd. Millers Point. 2009

www.ingramcontent.com/pod-product-compliance
Lightning Source LLC
Chambersburg PA
CBHW032250020726
47495CB00001B/37